EMPIRE OF STORMS

Books by Sarah J. Maas

The Throne of Glass series

Throne of Glass
Crown of Midnight
Heir of Fire
Queen of Shadows
Empire of Storms

•

The Assassin's Blade

•

The Throne of Glass Coloring Book

A Court of Thorns and Roses
A Court of Mist and Fury

EMPIRE OF STORMS

A *Throne of Glass* NOVEL

SARAH J. MAAS

BLOOMSBURY
NEW YORK LONDON OXFORD NEW DELHI SYDNEY

First published in the United States of America in September 2016
by Bloomsbury Children's Books
www.bloomsbury.com

Library of Congress Cataloging-in-Publication Data
Names: Maas, Sarah J., author.
Title: Empire of storms / by Sarah J. Maas.
Description: New York : Bloomsbury Children's Books, 2016. | Sequel to: Queen of shadows.
Summary: The long path to the throne has only just begun for Aelin Galathynius. Loyalties have been broken and bought, friends have been lost and gained, and those who possess magic find themselves at odds with those who don't. As the kingdoms of Erilea fracture around her, enemies must become allies if Aelin is to keep those she loves from falling to the dark forces poised to claim her world.
Identifiers: LCCN 2016014512 (print) | LCCN 2016034618 (e-book)
ISBN 978-1-61963-607-1 (hardcover) • ISBN 978-1-61963-608-8 (e-book)
Subjects: | CYAC: Fantasy. | Kings, queens, rulers, etc.—Fiction. | Love—Fiction. |
BISAC: JUVENILE FICTION / Fantasy & Magic. | JUVENILE FICTION /
Love & Romance. | JUVENILE FICTION / Action & Adventure / General.
Classification: LCC PZ7.M111575 Em 2016 (print) | LCC PZ7.M111575 (ebook) |
DDC [Fic]—dc23
LC record available at https://lccn.loc.gov/2016014512

ISBN 978-1-68119-428-8 (signed edition) • ISBN 978-1-68119-427-1 (special edition)
ISBN 978-1-68119-357-1 (exclusive edition) • ISBN 978-1-68119-515-5 (signed exclusive edition)

Series design by Regina Flath
Typeset by RefineCatch Limited, Bungay, Suffolk
Printed and bound in the U.S.A. by Berryville Graphics Inc., Berryville, Virginia
2 4 6 8 10 9 7 5 3 1

All papers used by Bloomsbury Publishing, Inc., are natural, recyclable products made from wood grown in well-managed forests. The manufacturing processes conform to the environmental regulations of the country of origin.

For Tamar,
my champion, fairy godmother, and knight in shining armor.
Thank you for believing in this series from page one.

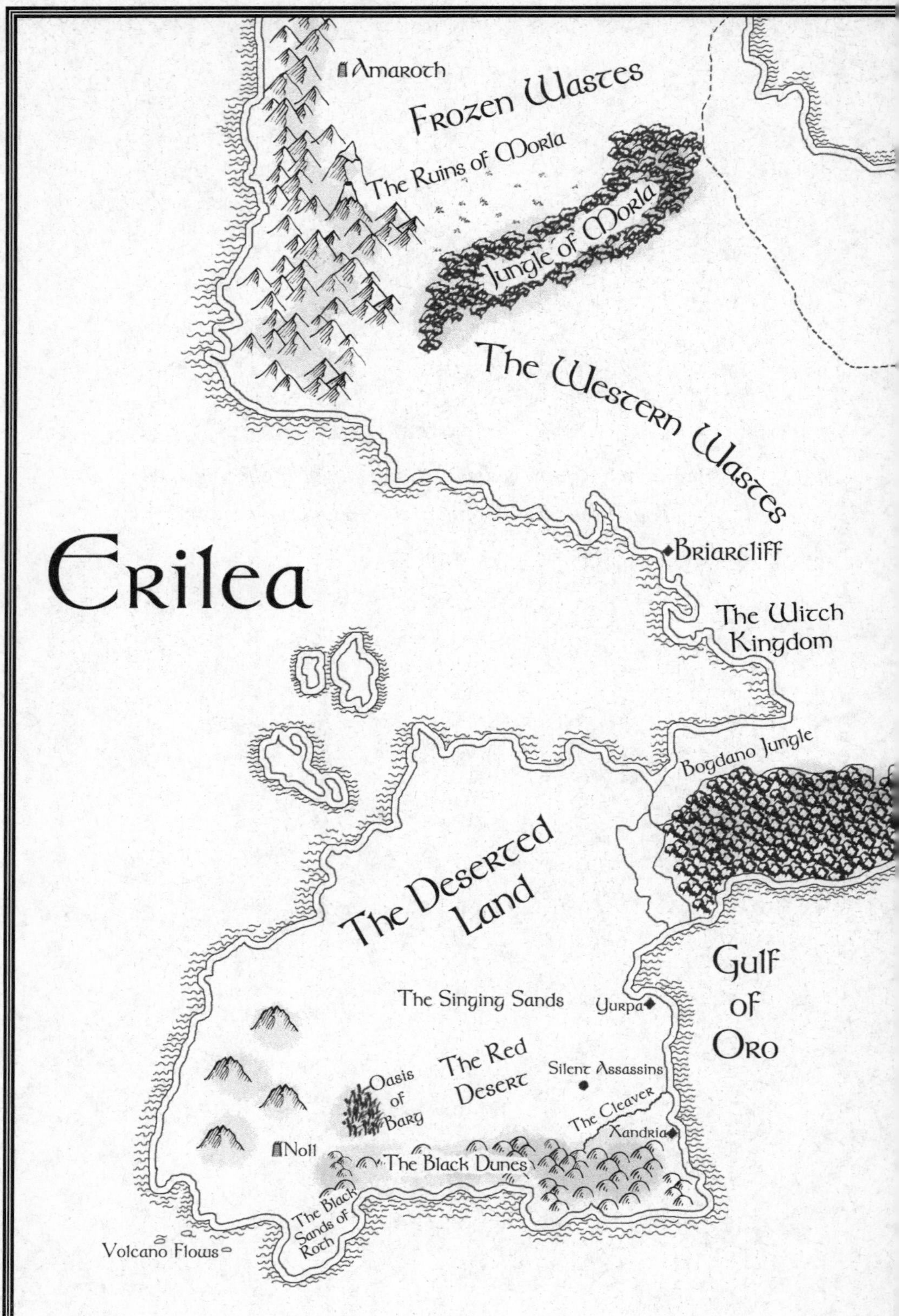
Amaroth
Frozen Wastes
The Ruins of Morla
Jungle of Morla
The Western Wastes
Erilea
Briarcliff
The Witch Kingdom
Bogdano Jungle
The Deserted Land
Gulf of Oro
The Singing Sands
Yurpa
The Red Desert
Silent Assassins
Oasis of Barg
The Cleaver
Xandria
Noll
The Black Dunes
The Black Sands of Roth
Volcano Flows

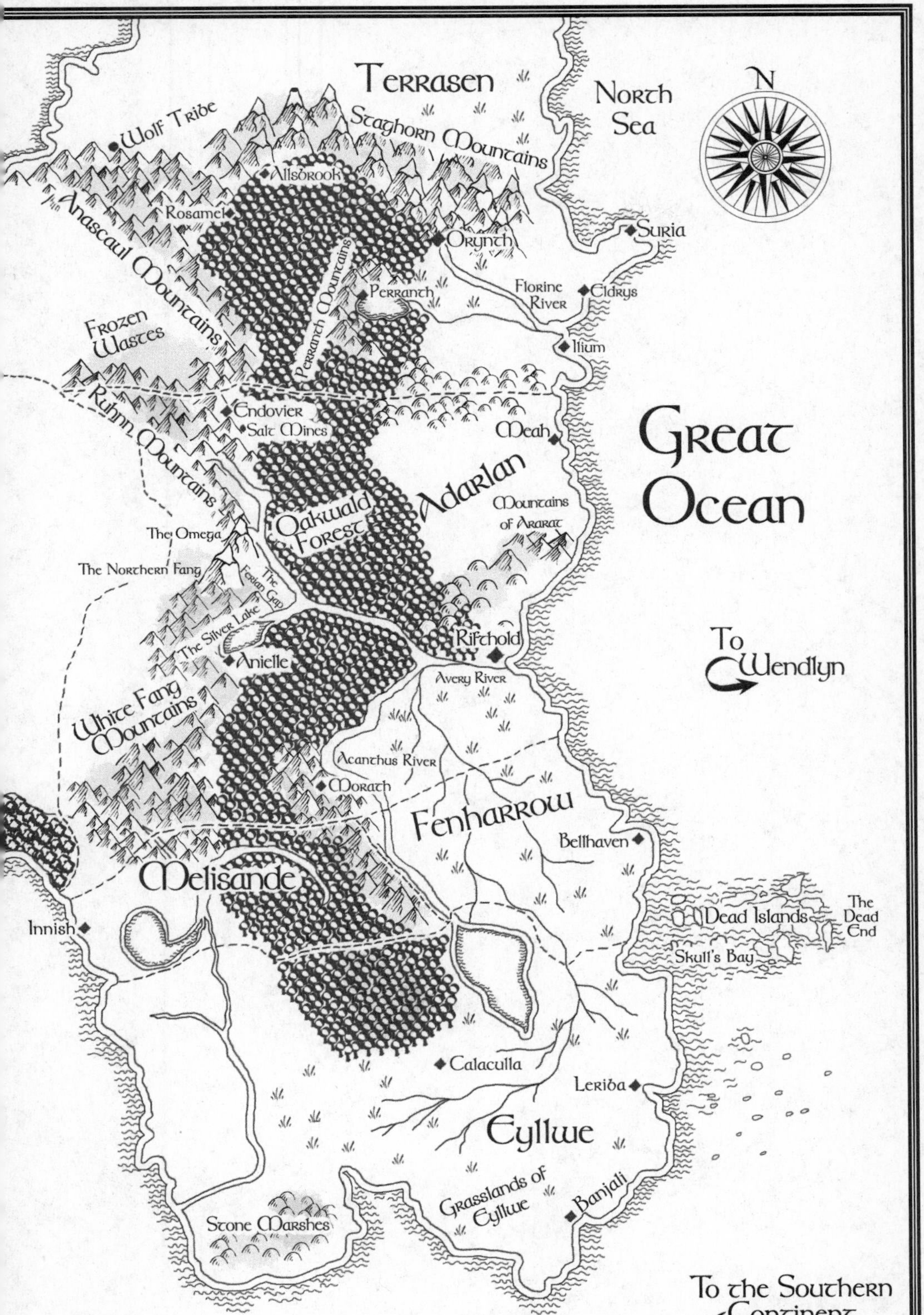

Terrasen
North Sea
N
Wolf Tribe
Staghorn Mountains
Allsbrook
Rosamel
Anascaul Mountains
Orynth
Suria
Perranth Mountains
Perranth
Florine River
Eldrys
Frozen Wastes
Ilium
Endovier
Salt Mines
Ruhnn Mountains
Meah
Great Ocean
Adarlan
Oakwald Forest
Mountains of Ararat
The Omega
The Northern Fang
The Ferian Gap
The Silver Lake
Rifthold
Anielle
To Wendlyn
Avery River
White Fang Mountains
Acanthus River
Morath
Fenharrow
Bellhaven
Melisande
Innish
Dead Islands
The Dead End
Skull's Bay
Calaculla
Leriba
Eyllwe
Grasslands of Eyllwe
Banjali
Stone Marshes
To the Southern Continent
The Narrow Sea

Empire of Storms

NIGHTFALL

The bone drums had been pounding across the jagged slopes of the Black Mountains since sundown.

From the rocky outcropping on which her war tent groaned against the dry wind, Princess Elena Galathynius had monitored the dread-lord's army all afternoon as it washed across those mountains in ebony waves. And now that the sun had long since vanished, the enemy camp-fires flickered across the mountains and valley below like a blanket of stars.

So many fires—so many, compared to those burning on her side of the valley.

She did not need the gift of her Fae ears to hear the prayers of her human army, both spoken and silent. She'd offered up several herself in the past few hours, though she knew they would go unanswered.

Elena had never considered where she might die—never considered that it might be so far from the rocky green of Terrasen. That her body might not be burned, but devoured by the dread-lord's beasts.

There would be no marker to tell the world where a Princess of Terrasen had fallen. There would be no marker for any of them.

"You need rest," a rough male voice said from the tent entrance behind her.

Elena looked over her shoulder, her unbound silver hair snagging on the intricate leather scales of her armor. But Gavin's dark gaze was already on the two armies stretching below them. On that narrow black band of demarcation, too soon to be breached.

For all his talk of rest, Gavin hadn't removed his own armor upon entering their tent hours before. Only minutes ago had his war leaders finally shoved out of the tent, bearing maps in their hands and not a shred of hope in their hearts. She could scent it on them—the fear. The despair.

Gavin's steps hardly crunched on the dry, rocky earth as he approached her lonely vigil, near-silent thanks to his years roaming the wilds of the South. Elena again faced those countless enemy fires.

He said hoarsely, "Your father's forces could still make it."

A fool's hope. Her immortal hearing had picked up every word of the hours of debate raging inside the tent behind them. "This valley is now a death trap," Elena said.

And she had led them all here.

Gavin did not answer.

"Come dawn," Elena went on, "it will be bathed in blood."

The war leader at her side remained silent. So rare for Gavin, that silence. Not a flicker of that untamed fierceness shone in his uptilted eyes, and his shaggy brown hair hung limp. She couldn't remember the last time either of them had bathed.

Gavin turned to her with that frank assessment that had stripped her bare from the moment she'd first met him in her father's hall nearly a year ago. Lifetimes ago.

Such a different time, a different world—when the lands had still been full of singing and light, when magic hadn't begun to flicker in the growing shadow of Erawan and his demon soldiers. She wondered how long Orynth would hold out once the slaughter here in the South had ended. Wondered if Erawan would first destroy her father's shining palace atop the mountain, or if he would burn the royal library—burn the heart and knowledge of an age. And then burn its people.

"Dawn is yet hours away," said Gavin, his throat bobbing. "Time enough for you to make a run for it."

"They'd tear us to shreds before we could clear the passes—"

"Not us. You." The firelight cast his tan face in flickering relief. "You alone."

"I will not abandon these people." Her fingers grazed his. "Or you."

Gavin's face didn't stir. "There is no avoiding tomorrow. Or the bloodshed. You overheard what the messenger said—I know you did. Anielle is a slaughterhouse. Our allies from the North are gone. Your father's army is too far behind. We will all die before the sun is fully risen."

"We'll all die one day anyway."

"No." Gavin squeezed her hand. "I will die. Those people down there—they will die. Either by sword or time. But you . . ." His gaze flicked to her delicately pointed ears, the heritage of her father. "You could live for centuries. Millennia. Do not throw it away for a doomed battle."

"I would sooner die tomorrow than live for a thousand years with a coward's shame."

But Gavin stared across the valley again. At his people, the last line of defense against Erawan's horde.

"Get behind your father's lines," he said roughly, "and continue the fight from there."

She swallowed hard. "It would be no use."

Slowly, Gavin looked at her. And after all these months, all this time, she confessed, "My father's power is failing. He is close—decades now—from the fading. Mala's light dims inside him with every passing day. He cannot stand against Erawan and win." Her father's last words before she'd set out on this doomed quest months ago: *My sun is setting, Elena. You must find a way to ensure yours still rises.*

Gavin's face leeched of color. "You choose now to tell me this?"

"I choose now, Gavin, because there is no hope for me, either—whether I flee tonight or fight tomorrow. The continent will fall."

Gavin shifted toward the dozen tents on the outcropping. His friends.

Her friends.

"None of us are walking away tomorrow," he said.

And it was the way his words broke, the way his eyes shone, that had her reaching for his hand once more. Never—not once in all their adventures, in all the horrors that they had endured together—had she seen him cry.

"Erawan will win and rule this land, and all others, for eternity," Gavin whispered.

Soldiers stirred in their camp below. Men and women, murmuring, swearing, weeping. Elena tracked the source of their terror—all the way across the valley.

One by one, as if a great hand of darkness wiped them away, the fires of the dread-lord's camp went out. The bone drums beat louder.

He had arrived at last.

Erawan himself had come to oversee the final stand of Gavin's army.

"They are not going to wait until dawn," Gavin said, a hand lurching to where Damaris was sheathed at his side.

But Elena gripped his arm, the hard muscle like granite beneath his leather armor.

Erawan had come.

Perhaps the gods were still listening. Perhaps her mother's fiery soul had convinced them.

She took in Gavin's harsh, wild face—the face that she had come to cherish above all others. And she said, "We are not going to win this battle. And we are not going to win this war."

His body quivered with the restraint to keep from going to his war leaders, but he gave her the respect of listening. They'd both given each other that, had learned it the hard way.

With her free hand, Elena lifted her fingers in the air between them. The raw magic in her veins now danced, from flame to water to curling vine to cracking ice. Not an endless abyss like her father's, but a versatile, nimble gift of magic. Granted by her mother. "We are not going to win this war," Elena repeated, Gavin's face aglow in the light of her uncut power. "But we can delay it a little while. I can get across that valley in an hour or two." She curled her fingers into a fist, and snuffed out her magic.

Gavin's brows furrowed. "What you speak of is madness, Elena. Suicide. His lieutenants will catch you before you can even slip through the lines."

"Exactly. They'll bring me right to him, now that he has come. They'll consider me his prized prisoner—not his assassin."

"No." An order and a plea.

"Kill Erawan, and his beasts will panic. Long enough for my father's forces to arrive, unite with whatever remains of ours, and crush the enemy legions."

"You say 'kill Erawan' as if that is some easy task. He is a Valg *king*, Elena. Even if they bring you to him, he will leash you to his will before you can make a move."

Her heart strained, but she forced the words out. "That is why . . ." She couldn't stop her wobbling lips. "That is why I need you to come with me instead of fight with your men."

Gavin only stared at her.

"Because I need . . ." Tears slid down her cheeks. "I need you as a distraction. I need you to buy me time to get past his inner defenses." Just as the battle tomorrow would buy them time.

Because Erawan would go for Gavin first. The human warrior who had been a bastion against the Dark Lord's forces for so long, who had fought him when no other would . . . Erawan's hatred for the human prince was rivaled only by his hatred for her father.

Gavin studied her for a long moment, then reached to brush her tears away. "He cannot be killed, Elena. You heard what your father's oracle whispered."

She nodded. "I know."

"And even if we manage to contain him—trap him . . ." Gavin considered her words. "You know that we are only pushing the war onto someone else—to whoever one day rules these lands."

"This war," she said quietly, "is but the second movement in a game that has been played since those ancient days across the sea."

"We put it off for someone else to inherit if he's freed. And it will not save those soldiers down there from slaughter tomorrow."

"If we do not act, there won't be anyone to inherit this war," Elena said. Doubt danced in Gavin's eyes. "Even now," she pushed, "our magic is failing, our gods abandoning us. Running from us. We have no Fae allies beyond those in my father's army. And their power, like his, is fading. But perhaps, when that third movement comes . . . perhaps the players in our unfinished game will be different. Perhaps it will be a future in which Fae and humans fight side by side, ripe with power. Maybe they will find a way to end this. So we will lose this battle, Gavin," she said. "Our friends will die on that killing field come dawn, and we will use it as our distraction to contain Erawan so that Erilea might have a future."

His lips tightened, his sapphire eyes wide.

"No one must know," she said, her voice breaking. "Even if we succeed, no one must know what we do."

Doubt etched deep lines into his face. She gripped his hand harder. "*No one*, Gavin."

Agony rippled across his features. But he nodded.

Hand in hand, they stared toward the darkness coating the mountains, the dread-lord's bone drums pounding like hammers on iron. Too soon, those drums would be drowned out by the screams of dying soldiers. Too soon, the valley fields would be carved with streams of blood.

Gavin said, "If we are to do this, we need to leave now." His attention again snagged on the nearby tents. No good-byes. No last words. "I'll give Holdren the order to lead tomorrow. He'll know what to tell the others."

She nodded, and it was confirmation enough. Gavin released her hand, striding for the tent closest to their own, to where his dearest friend and most loyal war leader was likely making the best of his final hours with his new wife.

Elena drew her eyes away before Gavin's broad shoulders pushed through the heavy flaps.

She gazed over the fires, across the valley, to the darkness perched on the other side. She could have sworn it stared back, sworn she heard the thousand whetstones as the dread-lord's beasts sharpened their poison-slick claws.

She lifted her eyes toward the smoke-stained sky, the plumes parting for a heartbeat to reveal a star-flecked night.

The Lord of the North flickered down at her. Perhaps the final gift of Mala to these lands—in this age, at least. Perhaps a thank-you to Elena herself, and a farewell.

Because for Terrasen, for Erilea, Elena would walk into the eternal darkness lurking across the valley to buy them all a chance.

Elena sent up a final prayer on a pillar of smoke rising from the valley floor that the unborn, faraway scions of this night, heirs to a burden that would doom or save Erilea, would forgive her for what she was about to do.

PART ONE

The Fire-Bringer

CHAPTER 1

Elide Lochan's breath scorched her throat with every gasping inhale as she limped up the steep forest hill.

Beneath the soggy leaves coating Oakwald's floor, loose gray stones made the slope treacherous, the towering oaks stretching too high above for her to grip any branches should she tumble down. Braving the potential fall in favor of speed, Elide scrambled over the lip of the craggy summit, her leg twanging with pain as she slumped to her knees.

Forested hills rolled away in every direction, the trees like the bars of a never-ending cage.

Weeks. It had been weeks since Manon Blackbeak and the Thirteen had left her in this forest, the Wing Leader ordering her to head north. To find her lost queen, now grown and mighty—and to also find Celaena Sardothien, whoever she was, so that Elide might repay the life debt she owed to Kaltain Rompier.

Even weeks later, her dreams were plagued by those final moments in Morath: the guards who had tried to drag her to be implanted with Valg offspring, the Wing Leader's complete massacre of them, and Kaltain Rompier's final act—carving the strange, dark stone from where it had been sewn into her arm and ordering Elide to take it to Celaena Sardothien.

Right before Kaltain turned Morath into a smoldering ruin.

Elide put a dirty, near-trembling hand to the hard lump tucked in the breast pocket of the flying leathers she still wore. She could have sworn a faint throbbing echoed into her skin, a counterbeat to her own racing heart.

Elide shuddered in the watery sunlight trickling through the green canopy. Summer lay heavy over the world, the heat now oppressive enough that water had become her most precious commodity.

It had been from the start—but now her entire day, her *life*, revolved around it.

Fortunately, Oakwald was rife with streams after the last of the melted mountain snows had snaked from their peaks. Unfortunately, Elide had learned the hard way about what water to drink.

Three days, she'd been near death with vomiting and fever after gulping down that stagnant pond water. Three days, she'd shivered so badly she thought her bones would crack apart. Three days, quietly weeping in pitiful despair that she'd die here, alone in this endless forest, and no one would ever know.

And through it all, that stone in her breast pocket thrummed and throbbed. In her fevered dreams, she could have sworn it whispered to her, sang lullabies in languages that she did not think human tongues could utter.

She hadn't heard it since, but she still wondered. Wondered if most humans would have died.

Wondered whether she carried a gift or a curse northward. And if this Celaena Sardothien would know what to do with it.

Tell her that you can open any door, if you have the key, Kaltain had said. Elide often studied the iridescent black stone whenever she halted for a needed break. It certainly didn't look like a key: rough-hewn, as if it had been cleaved from a larger chunk of stone. Perhaps Kaltain's words were a riddle meant only for its recipient.

Elide unslung her too-light pack from her shoulders and yanked open the canvas flap. She'd run out of food a week ago and had taken to scavenging for berries. They were all foreign, but a whisper of a memory from her years with her nursemaid, Finnula, had warned her to rub them on her wrist first—to see if they raised any reaction.

Most of the time, too much of the time, they did.

But every now and then she'd stumble across a bush sagging with the right ones, and she'd gorge herself before filling her pack. Fishing inside the pink-and-blue-stained canvas interior, Elide dug out the last handful, wrapped in her spare shirt, the white fabric now a splotchy red and purple.

One handful—to last until she found her next meal.

Hunger gnawed at her, but Elide ate only half. Maybe she'd find more before she stopped for the night.

She didn't know how to hunt—and the thought of catching another living thing, of snapping its neck or bashing in its skull with a rock . . . She was not yet that desperate.

Perhaps it made her not a Blackbeak after all, despite her mother's hidden bloodline.

Elide licked her fingers clean of the berry juice, dirt and all, and hissed as she stood on stiff, sore legs. She wouldn't last long without food but couldn't risk venturing into a village with the money Manon had given her, or toward any of the hunters' fires she'd spotted these past few weeks.

No—she had seen enough of the kindness and mercy of men. She would never forget how those guards had leered at her naked body, why her uncle had sold her to Duke Perrington.

Wincing, Elide swung her pack over her shoulders and carefully set off down the hill's far slope, picking her way among the rocks and roots.

Maybe she'd made a wrong turn. How would she know when she'd crossed Terrasen's border, anyway?

And how would she ever find her queen—her court?

Elide shoved the thoughts away, keeping to the murky shadows and avoiding the splotches of sunlight. It'd only make her thirstier, hotter.

Find water, perhaps more important than finding berries, before darkness set in.

She reached the foot of the hill, suppressing a groan at the labyrinth of wood and stone.

It seemed she now stood in a dried streambed wending between the hills. It curved sharply ahead—northward. A sigh rattled out of her. Thank Anneith. At least the Lady of Wise Things had not abandoned her yet.

She'd follow the streambed for as long as possible, staying northward, and then—

Elide didn't know what sense, exactly, picked up on it. Not smell or sight or sound, for nothing beyond the rot of the loam and the sunlight and stones and the whispering of the high-above leaves was out of the ordinary.

But—there. Like some thread in a great tapestry had snagged, her body locked up.

The humming and rustling of the forest went quiet a heartbeat later.

Elide scanned the hills, the streambed. The roots of an oak atop the nearest hill jutted from the slope's grassy side, providing a thatch of wood and moss over the dead stream. Perfect.

She limped for it, ruined leg barking, stones clattering and wrenching at her ankles. She could nearly touch the tips of the roots when the first hollowed-out *boom* echoed.

Not thunder. No, she would never forget this one particular sound—for it, too, haunted her dreams both awake and asleep.

The beating of mighty, leathery wings. Wyverns.

And perhaps more deadly: the Ironteeth witches who rode them, senses as sharp and fine-tuned as their mounts'.

Elide lunged for the overhang of thick roots as the wing beats neared, the forest silent as a graveyard. Stones and sticks ripped at her bare hands, her knees banging on the rocky dirt as she pressed herself into the hillside and peered at the canopy through the latticework of roots.

One beat—then another not even a heartbeat after. Synced enough that anyone in the forest might think it was only an echo, but Elide knew: two witches.

She'd picked up enough in her time in Morath to know the Ironteeth were under orders to keep their numbers hidden. They'd fly in perfect, mirrored formation, so listening ears might only report one wyvern.

But these two, whoever they were, were sloppy. Or as sloppy as one of the immortal, lethal witches could be. Lower-level coven members, perhaps. Out on a scouting mission.

Or hunting for someone, a small, petrified voice whispered in her head.

Elide pressed harder into the soil, roots digging into her back as she monitored the canopy.

And *there*. The blur of a swift-moving, massive shape gliding right above the canopy, rattling the leaves. A leathery, membranous wing, its edge tipped in a curved, poison-slick talon, flashed in the sunlight.

Rarely—so rarely—were they ever out in daylight. Whatever they hunted—it had to be important.

Elide didn't dare breathe too loudly until those wing beats faded, sailing due north.

Toward the Ferian Gap—where Manon had mentioned the second half of the host was camped.

Elide only moved when the forest's buzzing and chittering resumed. Staying still for so long had caused her muscles to cramp, and she groaned as she stretched out her legs, then her arms, then rolled her shoulders.

Endless—this journey was endless. She'd give anything for a safe roof over her head. And a hot meal. Maybe seeking them out, if only for a night, was worth the risk.

Picking her way along the bone-dry streambed, Elide made it two steps before that sense-that-was-not-a-sense twanged again, as if a warm, female hand had gripped her shoulder to stop.

The tangled wood murmured with life. But she could feel it—feel something out there.

Not witches or wyverns or beasts. But someone—someone was watching her.

Someone was following her.

Elide casually unsheathed the fighting knife Manon had given her upon leaving this miserable forest.

She wished the witch had taught her how to kill.

Lorcan Salvaterre had been running from those gods-damned beasts for two days now.

He didn't blame them. The witches had been pissed when he'd snuck into their forest camp in the dead of night, slaughtered three of their sentinels without them or their mounts noticing, and dragged a fourth into the trees for questioning.

It had taken him two hours to get the Yellowlegs witch to break, hidden so deep down the throat of a cave that even her screams had been contained. Two hours, and then she was singing for him.

Twin witch armies now stood poised to take the continent: one in Morath, one in the Ferian Gap. The Yellowlegs knew nothing of what power Duke Perrington wielded—knew nothing of what Lorcan hunted: the other two Wyrdkeys, the siblings to the one he wore on a long chain around his neck. Three slivers of stone cleaved from an unholy Wyrdgate, each key capable of tremendous and terrible power. And when all three

Wyrdkeys were united . . . they could open that gate between worlds. Destroy those worlds—or summon their armies. And far, far worse.

Lorcan had granted the witch the gift of a swift death.

Her sisters had been hunting him since.

Crouched in a thicket tucked into the side of a steep slope, Lorcan watched the girl ease from the roots. He'd been hiding here first, listening to the clamor of her clumsy approach, and had watched her stumble and limp when she finally heard what swept toward them.

She was delicately built, small enough that he might have thought her barely past her first bleed were it not for the full breasts beneath her close-fitting leathers.

Those clothes had snared his interest immediately. The Yellowlegs had been wearing similar ones—all the witches had. Yet this girl was human.

And when she turned in his direction, those dark eyes scanned the forest with an assessment that was too old, too practiced, to belong to a child. At least eighteen—maybe older. Her pale face was dirty, gaunt. She'd likely been out here for a while, struggling to find food. And the knife she palmed shook enough to suggest she likely had no idea what to do with it.

Lorcan remained hidden, watching her scan the hills, the stream, the canopy.

She knew he was out there, somehow.

Interesting. When he wanted to stay hidden, few could find him.

Every muscle in her body was tense—but she finished scanning the gully, forcing a soft breath through her pursed lips, and continued on. Away from him.

Each step was limping; she'd likely hurt herself crashing through the trees.

The length of her braid snapped against her pack, her silky hair dark like his own. Darker. Black as a starless night.

The wind shifted, blowing her scent toward him, and Lorcan breathed it in, allowing his Fae senses—the senses he'd inherited from his prick of a father—to assess, analyze, as they had done for over five centuries.

Human. Definitely human, but—

He knew that scent.

During the past few months, he'd slaughtered many, many creatures who bore its reek.

Well, wasn't this convenient. Perhaps a gift from the gods: someone useful to interrogate. But later—once he had a chance to study her. Learn her weaknesses.

Lorcan eased from the thicket, not even a twig rustling at his passing.

The demon-possessed girl limped up the streambed, that useless knife still out, her grip on its hilt wholly ineffective. Good.

And so Lorcan began his hunt.

CHAPTER 2

The patter of rain trickling through the leaves and low-lying mists of Oakwald Forest nearly drowned out the gurgle of the swollen stream cutting between the bumps and hollows.

Crouched beside the brook, empty skins forgotten on the mossy bank, Aelin Ashryver Galathynius extended a scarred hand over the rushing water and let the song of the early-morning storm wash over her.

The groaning of breaking thunderheads and the sear of answering lightning had been a violent, frenzied beat since the hour before dawn—now spreading farther apart, calming their fury, as Aelin soothed her own burning core of magic.

She breathed in the chill mists and fresh rain, dragging them deep into her lungs. Her magic guttered in answer, as if yawning good morning and tumbling back to sleep.

Indeed, around the camp just within view, her companions still slept, protected from the storm by an invisible shield of Rowan's making, and warmed from the northern chill that persisted even in the height of summer by a merry ruby flame that she'd kept burning all night. It was the flame that had been the difficult thing to work around—how to keep it crackling while also summoning the small gift of water her mother had given her.

Aelin flexed her fingers over the stream.

Across the brook, atop a mossy boulder tucked into the arms of a gnarled oak, a pair of tiny bone-white fingers flexed and cracked, a mirror to her own movements.

Aelin smiled and said so quietly it was barely audible over the stream and rain, "If you have any pointers, friend, I'd love to hear them."

The spindly fingers darted back over the crest of the rock—which, like so many in these woods, had been carved with symbols and whorls.

The Little Folk had been tracking them since they crossed the border into Terrasen. *Escorting*, Aedion had insisted whenever they spotted large, depthless eyes blinking from a tangle of brambles or peering through a cluster of leaves atop one of Oakwald's famed trees. They hadn't come close enough for Aelin to even get a solid look at them.

But they'd left small gifts just outside the border of Rowan's nightly shields, somehow deposited without alerting whichever of them was on watch.

One morning, it had been a crown of forest violets. Aelin had given it to Evangeline, who had worn the crown on her red-gold head until it fell apart. The next morning, two crowns waited: one for Aelin, and a smaller one for the scarred girl. Another day, the Little Folk left a replica of Rowan's hawk form, crafted from gathered sparrow feathers, acorns, and beetle husks. Her Fae Prince had smiled a bit when he'd found it—and carried it in his saddlebag since.

Aelin herself smiled at the memory. Though knowing the Little Folk were following their every step, listening and watching, had made things . . . difficult. Not in any real way that mattered, but slipping off into the trees with Rowan was certainly less romantic knowing they had an audience. Especially whenever Aedion and Lysandra got so sick of their silent, heated glances that the two made up flimsy excuses to get Aelin and Rowan out of sight and scent for a while: the lady had dropped her nonexistent handkerchief on the nonexistent path far behind; they needed more logs for a fire that did not require wood to burn.

And as for her current audience . . .

Aelin splayed her fingers over the stream, letting her heart become as still as a sun-warmed forest pool, letting her mind shake free of its normal boundaries.

A ribbon of water fluttered up from the stream, gray and clear, and she wended it through her spread fingers as if she were threading a loom.

She tilted her wrist, admiring the way she could see her skin through the water, letting it slip down her hand and curl about her wrist. She said to the faerie watching from the other side of the boulder, "Not much to report to your companions, is it?"

Soggy leaves crunched behind her, and Aelin knew it was only because Rowan wanted her to hear his approach. "Careful, or they'll leave something wet and cold in your bedroll next time."

Aelin made herself release the water into the stream before she looked over a shoulder. "Do you think they take requests? Because I'd hand over my kingdom for a hot bath right about now."

Rowan's eyes danced as she eased to her feet. She lowered the shield she'd put around herself to keep dry—the steam off the invisible flame blending with the mist around them. The Fae Prince lifted a brow. "Should I be concerned that you're so chatty this early in the morning?"

She rolled her eyes and turned toward the rock where the faerie had been monitoring her shoddy attempts to master water. But only rain-slick leaves and snaking mist remained.

Strong hands slid over her waist, tugging her into his warmth, as Rowan's lips grazed her neck, right under her ear.

Aelin arched back into him while his mouth roved across her throat, heating mist-chilled skin. "Good morning to you," she breathed.

Rowan's responding grumble set her toes curling.

They hadn't dared stop at an inn, even after crossing into Terrasen three days ago, not when there were still so many enemy eyes fixed on the roads and taprooms. Not when there were still streaming lines of Adarlanian soldiers finally marching out of her gods-damned territory—thanks to Dorian's decrees.

Especially when those soldiers might very well march right back here, might choose to ally themselves with the monster squatting down in Morath rather than their true king.

"If you want to take a bath so badly," Rowan murmured against her neck, "I spotted a pool about a quarter mile back. You could heat it—for both of us."

She ran her nails down the back of his hands, up his forearms. "I'd boil all the fish and frogs inside it. I doubt it'd be very pleasant then."

"At least we'd have breakfast prepared."

She laughed under her breath, and Rowan's canines scratched the sensitive spot where her neck met her shoulder. Aelin dug her fingers into the powerful muscles of his forearms, savoring the strength there. "The lords won't be here until sundown. We've got time." Her words were breathless, barely more than a whisper.

Upon crossing the border, Aedion had sent messages to the few lords he trusted, coordinating the meeting that was to happen today—in this clearing, which Aedion himself had used for covert rebel meetings these long years.

They'd arrived early to scope out the land, the pitfalls and advantages. Not a trace of any humans lingered: Aedion and the Bane had always ensured any evidence was wiped away from unfriendly eyes. Her cousin and his legendary legion had already done so much to ensure the safety of

Terrasen this past decade. But they were still taking no risks, even with lords who had once been her uncle's banner men.

"Tempting as it might be," Rowan said, nipping her ear in a way that made it hard to think, "I need to be on my way in an hour." To scout the land ahead for any threats. Featherlight kisses brushed over her jaw, her cheek. "And what I said still holds. I'm not taking you against a tree the first time."

"It wouldn't be against a tree—it'd be in a pool." A dark laugh against her now-burning skin. It was an effort to keep from taking one of his hands and guiding it up to her breasts, to beg him to touch, take, taste. "You know, I'm starting to think you're a sadist."

"Trust me, I don't find it easy, either." He tugged her a bit harder against him, letting her feel the evidence pushing with impressive demand against her backside. She nearly groaned at that, too.

Then Rowan pulled away, and she frowned at the loss of his warmth, at the loss of those hands and that body and that mouth. She turned, finding his pine-green eyes pinned on her, and a thrill sparked through her blood brighter than any magic.

But he said, "Why *are* you so coherent this early?"

She stuck out her tongue. "I took over the watch for Aedion, since Lysandra and Fleetfoot were snoring loud enough to wake the dead." Rowan's mouth twitched upward, but Aelin shrugged. "I couldn't sleep anyway."

His jaw tightened as he glanced to where the amulet was hidden beneath her shirt and the dark leather jacket atop it. "Is the Wyrdkey bothering you?"

"No, it's not that." She'd taken to wearing the amulet after Evangeline had looted through her saddlebags and donned the necklace. They'd only discovered it because the child had returned from washing herself with the Amulet of Orynth proudly displayed over her traveling clothes. Thank the gods they'd been deep in Oakwald at the time, but—Aelin wasn't taking any other chances.

Especially since Lorcan still believed he had the real thing.

They hadn't heard from the immortal warrior since he'd left Rifthold, and Aelin often wondered how far south he'd gotten—if he'd yet realized he bore a fake Wyrdkey within an equally fake Amulet of Orynth. If he'd discovered where the other two had been hidden by the King of Adarlan and Duke Perrington.

Not Perrington—Erawan.

A chill snaked down her back, as if the shadow of Morath had taken form behind her and run a clawed finger along her spine.

"It's just . . . this meeting," Aelin said, waving a hand. "Should we have done it in Orynth? Out in the woods like this just seems so . . . cloak-and-dagger."

Rowan's eyes again drifted toward the northern horizon. At least another week lay between them and the city—the once-glorious heart of her kingdom. Of this continent. And when they got there, it would be an endless stream of councils and preparations and decisions that only she could make. This meeting Aedion had arranged would just be the start of it.

"Better to go into the city with established allies than to enter not knowing what you might find," Rowan said at last. He gave her a wry smile and aimed a pointed look at Goldryn, sheathed across her back, and the various knives strapped to her. "And besides: I thought 'cloak-and-dagger' was your middle name."

She offered him a vulgar gesture in return.

Aedion had been so careful with his messages while setting up the meeting—had selected this spot far from any possible casualties or spying eyes. And even though he trusted the lords, whom he'd familiarized her with these past weeks, Aedion still hadn't informed them how many traveled in their party—what their talents were. Just in case.

No matter that Aelin was the bearer of a weapon capable of wiping out this entire valley, along with the gray Staghorn Mountains watching over it. And that was just her magic.

Rowan played with a strand of her hair—grown almost to her breasts again. "You're worried because Erawan hasn't made a move yet."

She sucked on a tooth. "What is he waiting for? Are we fools for expecting an invitation to march on him? Or is he letting us gather our strength, letting *me* return with Aedion to get the Bane and raise a larger army around it, only so he can savor our utter despair when we fail?"

Rowan's fingers stilled in her hair. "You heard Aedion's messenger. That blast took out a good chunk of Morath. He might be rebuilding himself."

"No one has claimed that blast as their doing. I don't trust it."

"You trust nothing."

She met his eyes. "I trust you."

Rowan brushed a finger along her cheek. The rain turned heavy again, its soft patter the only sound for miles.

Aelin lifted onto her toes. She felt Rowan's eyes on her the whole time, felt his body go still with predatory focus, as she kissed the corner of his mouth, the bow of his lips, the other corner.

Soft, taunting kisses. Designed to see which one of them yielded first.

Rowan did.

With a sharp intake of breath, he gripped her hips, tugging her against him as he slanted his mouth over hers, deepening the kiss until her knees threatened to buckle. His tongue brushed hers—lazy, deft strokes that told her precisely what he was capable of doing elsewhere.

Embers sparked in her blood, and the moss beneath them hissed as rain turned to steam.

Aelin broke the kiss, breathing ragged, satisfied to find Rowan's own chest rising and falling in an uneven rhythm. So new—this thing between them was still so new, so . . . raw. Utterly consuming. The desire was only the start of it.

Rowan made her magic sing. And maybe that was the *carranam* bond between them, but . . . her magic wanted to dance with his. And from the frost sparkling in his eyes, she knew his own demanded the same.

Rowan leaned forward until they were brow-to-brow. "Soon," he promised, his voice rough and low. "Let's get somewhere safe—somewhere defensible."

Because her safety always would come first. For him, keeping her protected, keeping her alive, would always come first. He'd learned it the hard way.

Her heart strained, and she pulled back to lift a hand to his face. Rowan read the softness in her eyes, her body, and his own inherent fierceness slipped into a gentleness that so few would ever see. Her throat ached with the effort of keeping the words in.

She'd been in love with him for a while now. Longer than she wanted to admit.

She tried not to think about it, whether he felt the same. Those things—those wishes—were at the bottom of a very, very long and bloody priority list.

So Aelin kissed Rowan gently, his hands again locking around her hips.

"Fireheart," he said onto her mouth.

"Buzzard," she murmured onto his.

Rowan laughed, the rumble echoing in her chest.

From the camp, Evangeline's sweet voice chirped through the rain, "Is it time for breakfast?"

Aelin snorted. Sure enough, Fleetfoot and Evangeline were now nudging at poor Lysandra, sprawled out as a ghost leopard by the immortal-burning fire. Aedion, across the fire, lay as unmoving as a boulder. Fleetfoot would likely leap on him next.

"This cannot end well," Rowan muttered.

Evangeline howled, "*Fooooood!*" Fleetfoot's answering howl followed a heartbeat later.

Then Lysandra's snarl rippled toward them, silencing girl and hound.

Rowan laughed again—and Aelin thought she might never get sick of it, that laugh. That smile.

"We should make breakfast," he said, turning toward the camp, "before Evangeline and Fleetfoot ransack the whole site."

Aelin chuckled but glanced over her shoulder to the forest stretching toward the Staghorns. Toward the lords who were hopefully making their way southward—to decide how they would proceed with war . . . and rebuilding their broken kingdom.

When she looked back, Rowan was halfway to the camp, Evangeline's red-gold hair flashing as she bounded through the dripping trees, begging the prince for toast and eggs.

Her family—and her kingdom.

Two dreams long believed lost, she realized as the northern wind ruffled her hair. That she would do anything—ruin herself, sell herself—to protect.

Aelin was about to head for the camp to spare Evangeline from Rowan's cooking when she noticed the object atop the boulder across the stream.

She cleared the stream in one bound and carefully studied what the faerie had left.

Fashioned with twigs, cobwebs, and fish scales, the tiny wyvern was unnervingly accurate, its wings spread wide and thorn-fanged mouth roaring.

Aelin left the wyvern where it was, but her eyes shifted southward, toward the ancient flow of Oakwald, and Morath looming far beyond it. To Erawan reborn, waiting for her with his host of Ironteeth witches and Valg foot soldiers.

And Aelin Galathynius, Queen of Terrasen, knew the time would soon come to prove just how much she'd bleed for Erilea.

It was useful, Aedion Ashryver thought, to travel with two gifted magic-wielders. Especially during piss-poor weather.

The rains lingered throughout the day as they prepared for the meeting. Rowan had flown northward twice now to track the progress of the lords, but he hadn't seen or scented them.

No one braved the notoriously muddy Terrasen roads in this weather. But with Ren Allsbrook in their company, Aedion had little doubt they'd stay hidden until sunset anyway. Unless the weather had delayed them. Which was a good possibility.

Thunder boomed, so close that the trees shuddered. Lightning flashed with little pause for breath, limning the soaked leaves with silver, illuminating the world so brightly that his Fae senses were blinded. But at least he was dry. And warm.

They'd avoided civilization so much that Aedion had hardly witnessed or been able to track how many magic-wielders had crept out of hiding—or who was now enjoying the return of their gifts. He'd only seen one girl, no older than nine, weaving tendrils of water above her village's lone fountain for the entertainment and delight of a gaggle of children.

Stone-faced, scarred adults had looked on from the shadows, but none had interfered for better or worse. Aedion's messengers had already confirmed that most people now knew the King of Adarlan had wielded his dark powers to repress magic these last ten years. But even so, he doubted those who had suffered its loss, then the extermination of their kind, would comfortably reveal their powers anytime soon.

At least until people like his companions, and that girl in the square, showed the world it was safe to do so. That a girl with a gift of water could ensure her village and its farmlands thrived.

Aedion frowned at the darkening sky, idly twirling the Sword of Orynth between his palms. Even before magic had vanished, there had been one kind feared above all others, its bearers pariahs at best, dead at worst. Courts in every land had sought them as spies and assassins for centuries. But *his* court—

A delighted, throaty purr rumbled through their little camp, and Aedion shifted his stare to the subject of his thoughts. Evangeline was kneeling on her sleeping mat, humming to herself as she gently ran the horse's brush through Lysandra's fur.

It had taken him days to get used to the ghost leopard form. Years in the Staghorns had drilled the gut-level terror into him. But there was Lysandra, claws retracted, sprawled on her belly as her ward groomed her.

Spy and assassin indeed. A smile tugged on his lips at the pale green eyes heavy-lidded with pleasure. That'd be a fine sight for the lords to see when they arrived.

The shape-shifter had used these weeks of travel to try out new forms: birds, beasts, insects that had a tendency to buzz in his ear or bite him. Rarely—so rarely—had Lysandra taken the human form he'd met her in. Given all that had been done to her and all she'd been forced to do in that human body, Aedion didn't blame her.

Though she'd have to take human form soon, when she was introduced as a lady in Aelin's court. He wondered if she'd wear that exquisite face, or find another human skin that suited her.

More than that, he often wondered what it felt like to be able to change bone and skin and color—though he hadn't asked. Mostly because Lysandra hadn't been in human form long enough to do so.

Aedion looked to Aelin, seated across the fire with Fleetfoot sprawled in her lap, playing with the hound's long ears—waiting, as they all were. His cousin, however, was studying the ancient blade—her father's blade—that Aedion so unceremoniously twirled and tossed from hand to hand, every inch of the metal hilt and cracked bone pommel as familiar to him as his own face. Sorrow flickered in her eyes, as fast as the lightning above, and then vanished.

She'd returned the sword to him upon their departure from Rifthold, choosing to bear Goldryn instead. He'd tried to convince her to keep

Terrasen's sacred blade, but she'd insisted it was better off in his hands, that he deserved the honor more than anyone else, including her.

She'd grown quieter the farther north they'd traveled. Perhaps weeks on the road had sapped her.

After tonight, depending on what the lords reported, he'd try to find her a quiet place to rest for a day or two before they made the last leg of the trek to Orynth.

Aedion uncoiled to his feet, sheathing the sword beside the knife Rowan had gifted him, and stalked to her. Fleetfoot's feathery tail thumped in greeting as he sat beside his queen.

"You could use a haircut," she said. Indeed, his hair had grown longer than he usually kept it. "It's almost the same length as mine." She frowned. "It makes us look like we coordinated it."

Aedion snorted, stroking the dog's head. "So what if we did?"

Aelin shrugged. "If you want to start wearing matching outfits as well, I'm in."

He grinned. "The Bane would never let me live it down."

His legion now camped just outside of Orynth, where he'd ordered them to shore up the city's defenses and wait. Wait to kill and die for her.

And with the money Aelin had schemed and butchered to claim from her former master this spring, they could buy themselves an army to follow behind the Bane. Perhaps mercenaries, too.

The spark in Aelin's eyes died a bit as if she, too, considered all that commanding his legion implied. The risks and costs—not of gold, but lives. Aedion could have sworn the campfire guttered as well.

She had slaughtered and fought and nearly died again and again for the past ten years. Yet he knew she would balk at sending soldiers—at sending *him*—to fight.

That, above all else, would be her first test as queen.

But before that . . . this meeting. "You remember everything I told you about them?"

Aelin gave him a flat look. "Yes, I remember everything, cousin." She poked him hard in the ribs, right where the still-healing tattoo Rowan had inked on him three days ago now lay. All their names, entwined in a complex Terrasen knot right near his heart. Aedion winced as she jabbed the sore flesh, and he batted away her hand as she recited, "Murtaugh was a farmer's son, but married Ren's grandmother. Though he wasn't born into the Allsbrook line, he still commands the seat, despite his insistence that Ren take up the title." She looked skyward. "Darrow is the wealthiest landowner after yours truly, and more than that, he holds sway over the few surviving lords, mostly through his years of carefully handling Adarlan during the occupation." She gave him a glare sharp enough to slice skin.

Aedion lifted his hands. "Can you blame me for wanting to make sure this goes smoothly?"

She shrugged but didn't bite his head off.

"Darrow was your uncle's lover," he added, stretching his legs out before him. "For decades. He's never spoken once to me about your uncle, but . . . they were very close, Aelin. Darrow didn't publicly mourn Orlon beyond what was required after the passing of a king, but he became a different man afterward. He's a hard bastard now, but still a fair one. Much of what he's done has been out of his unfading love for Orlon—and for Terrasen. His own maneuvering kept us from becoming completely starved and destitute. Remember that." Indeed, Darrow had long straddled a line between serving the King of Adarlan and undermining him.

"I. Know," she said tightly. Pushing too far—that tone was likely her first and last warning that he was starting to piss her off. He'd spent many of the miles they'd traveled these past few days telling her about Ren, and Murtaugh, and Darrow. Aedion knew she could likely now recite their land holdings, what crops and livestock and goods they yielded, their ancestors, and dead and surviving family members from this past decade. But pushing her about it one last time, making sure she knew . . . He couldn't shut the instincts down to ensure it all went well. Not when so much was at stake.

From where he'd been perched on a high branch to monitor the forest, Rowan clicked his beak and flapped into the rain, sailing through his shield as if it parted for him.

Aedion eased to his feet, scanning the forest, listening. Only the trickle of rain on leaves filled his ears. Lysandra stretched, baring her long teeth as she did so, her needlelike claws slipping free and glinting in the firelight.

Until Rowan gave the all clear—until it was just those lords and no one else—the safety protocols they'd established would hold.

Evangeline, as they had taught her, crept to the fire. The flames pulled apart like drawn curtains to allow her and Fleetfoot, sensing the child's fear and pressing close, passage to an inner ring that would not burn her. But would melt the bones of their enemies.

Aelin merely glanced at Aedion in silent order, and he stepped toward the western side of the fire, Lysandra taking up a spot at the southern point. Aelin took the northern but gazed west—toward where Rowan had flapped away.

A dry, hot breeze flowed through their little bubble, and sparks danced like fireflies at Aelin's fingers, her hand hanging casually at her side. The other gripped Goldryn, the ruby in its hilt bright as an ember.

Leaves rustled and branches snapped, and the Sword of Orynth gleamed gold and red in the light of Aelin's flames as he drew it free. He angled the ancient dagger Rowan had gifted him in his other hand. Rowan had been teaching Aedion—teaching all of them, really—about the Old Ways these weeks. About the long-forgotten traditions and codes of the Fae, mostly abandoned even in Maeve's court. But reborn here, and enacted now, as they fell into the roles and duties that they had sorted out and decided for themselves.

Rowan emerged from the rain in his Fae form, his silver hair plastered to his head, his tattoo stark on his tan face. No sign of the lords.

But Rowan held his hunting knife against the bared throat of a young, slender-nosed man and escorted him toward the fire—the stranger's travel-stained, soaked clothes bearing Darrow's crest of a striking badger.

"A messenger," Rowan ground out.

Aelin decided right then and there she didn't particularly enjoy surprises.

The messenger's blue eyes were wide, but his rain-slick, freckled face was calm. Steady. Even as he took in Lysandra, her fangs gilded with firelight. Even as Rowan nudged him forward, that cruel knife still angled at his throat.

Aedion jerked his chin at Rowan. "He can't very well deliver the message with a blade at his windpipe."

Rowan lowered his weapon, but the Fae Prince didn't sheathe his knife. Didn't move more than a foot from the man.

Aedion demanded, "Where are they?"

The man bowed swiftly to her cousin. "At a tavern, four miles from here, General—"

The words died as Aelin at last stepped around the curve of the fire. She kept it burning high, kept Evangeline and Fleetfoot ensconced within. The messenger let out a small noise.

He knew. With the way he kept glancing between her and Aedion, seeing the same eyes, the same hair color . . . he knew. And as if the thought had hit him, the messenger bowed.

Aelin watched the way the man lowered his eyes, watched the exposed back of his neck, his skin shining with rain. Her magic simmered in response. And that thing—that hideous power hanging between her breasts—seemed to open an ancient eye at all the commotion.

The messenger stiffened, wide-eyed at Lysandra's silent approach, her whiskers twitching as she sniffed at his wet clothes. He was smart enough to remain still.

"Is the meeting canceled?" Aedion said tightly, scanning the woods again.

The man winced. "No, General—but they want you to come to the tavern where they're staying. Because of the rain."

Aedion rolled his eyes. "Go tell Darrow to drag his carcass out here. Water won't kill him."

"It's not Lord Darrow," the man said quickly. "With all due respect, Lord Murtaugh's slowed down this summer. Lord Ren didn't want him out in the dark and rain."

The old man had ridden across the kingdoms like a demon from hell this spring, Aelin remembered. Perhaps it had taken its toll. Aedion sighed. "You know we'll need to scout the tavern first. The meeting will be later than they want."

"Of course, General. They'll expect that." The messenger cringed as he at last spotted Evangeline and Fleetfoot within the flame's ring of safety. And despite the Fae Prince armed beside him, despite the ghost leopard with unsheathed claws sniffing at him, the sight of Aelin's fire made his face go deathly pale. "But they are waiting—and Lord Darrow is impatient. Being outside Orynth's walls makes him anxious. Makes us all anxious, these days."

Aelin snorted softly. *Indeed.*

CHAPTER 3

Manon Blackbeak stood at attention by one end of the long, dark bridge into Morath and watched her grandmother's coven descend from the gray clouds.

Even with the plumes and pillars of smoke from the countless forges, the High Witch of the Blackbeak Witch-Clan's voluminous obsidian robes were unmistakable. No other dressed as the Matron did. Her coven swept from the heavy cloud cover, keeping a respectful distance from the Matron and the extra rider flanking her massive bull.

Manon, her Thirteen in rank behind her, made no movement as the wyverns and their riders landed on the dark stones of the courtyard across the bridge. Far below, the rushing of a filthy, ruined river roared, vying with the scrape of talons on stone and the rustle of settling wings.

Her grandmother had come to Morath.

Or what was left of it, when one-third was nothing more than rubble.

Asterin hissed in a breath as Manon's grandmother dismounted in a smooth movement, scowling at the black fortress looming above Manon and her Thirteen. Duke Perrington was already waiting in his council chamber, and Manon had no doubt his pet, Lord Vernon, would do his best to undermine and shake her at every turn. If Vernon were to make a move to be rid of Manon, it would be now—when her grandmother was seeing for herself what Manon had accomplished.

And failed to do.

Manon kept her back straight as her grandmother strode across the broad stone bridge, her steps drowned out by the rush of the river, the beat of distant wings, and those forges working day and night to equip their army. When she could see the white in her grandmother's eyes, Manon bowed.

The creak of flying leathers told her the Thirteen had followed suit.

When Manon lifted her head, her grandmother was before her.

Death, cruel and cunning, waited in that gold-flecked onyx stare.

"Take me to the duke," the Matron said by way of greeting.

Manon felt her Thirteen stiffen. Not at the words, but at the High Witch's coven now following on her heels. Rare—so rare for them to track her, guard her.

But this was a citadel of men—and demons. And this would be an extended stay, if not permanent, judging by the fact that her grandmother had brought along the beautiful, dark-haired young witch currently warming her bed. The Matron would be a fool not to take extra protection. Even if the Thirteen had always been enough. Should have been enough.

It was an effort not to flick out her iron nails at the imagined threat.

Manon bowed again and turned in to the towering, open doors to Morath. The Thirteen parted for Manon and the Matron as they passed, then closed ranks like a lethal veil. No chances—not when the heir and the Matron were concerned.

Manon's steps were near-silent as she led her grandmother through the dark halls, the Thirteen and the Matron's coven trailing close. The servants, through either spying or some human instinct, were nowhere to be found.

The Matron spoke as they ascended the first of many spiral stairwells toward the duke's new council chamber. "Anything to report?"

"No, Grandmother." Manon avoided the urge to glance sidelong at the witch—at the silver-streaked dark hair, the pale features carved with ancient hate, the rusted teeth on permanent display.

The face of the High Witch who had branded Manon's Second. Who had cast Asterin's stillborn witchling into the fire, denying her the right to hold her once. Who had then beaten and broken her Second, thrown her into the snow to die, and lied to Manon about it for nearly a century.

Manon wondered what thoughts now churned through Asterin's head as they walked. Wondered what went through the heads of Sorrel and Vesta, who had found Asterin in the snow. Then healed her.

And never told Manon about it, either.

Her grandmother's creature—that's what Manon was. It had never seemed like a hateful thing.

"Did you discover who caused the explosion?" The Matron's robes swirled behind her as they entered the long, narrow hallway toward the duke's council chamber.

"No, Grandmother."

Those gold-flecked black eyes snapped to her. "How convenient, Wing Leader, that you complain about the duke's breeding experiments—only for the Yellowlegs to be incinerated days later."

Good riddance, Manon almost said. Despite the covens lost in the blast, good rutting riddance that the breeding of those Yellowlegs-Valg witchlings had stopped. But Manon felt, rather than saw or heard, her Thirteen's attention fix on her grandmother's back.

And perhaps something like fear went through Manon.

At the Matron's accusation—and the line her Thirteen were drawing. Had drawn for some time now.

Defiance. That's what it had been these past months. If the High Witch learned of it, she'd tie Manon to a post and whip her back until her skin was hanging in strips. She'd make the Thirteen watch, to prove their powerlessness to defend their heir, and then give them the same treatment. Perhaps chucking salted water on them when she was done. Then do it again, day after day.

Manon said coolly, "I heard a rumor it was the duke's pet—that human woman. But as she was incinerated in the blaze, no one can confirm. I didn't want to waste your time with gossip and theories."

"She was leashed to him."

"It would seem her shadowfire was not." Shadowfire—the mighty power that would have melted their enemies within heartbeats when combined with the mirror-lined witch towers the three Matrons had been building in the Ferian Gap. But with Kaltain gone . . . so was the threat of pure annihilation.

Even if the duke would suffer no other master now that his king was dead. He'd rejected the Crown Prince's claim to the throne.

Her grandmother said nothing as they continued onward.

The other piece on the board—the sapphire-eyed prince who had once been in thrall to a Valg prince himself. Now free. And allied with that golden-haired young queen.

They reached the council room doors, and Manon wiped all thoughts from her head as the blank-faced guards opened the black rock for them.

Manon's senses honed to a killing calm the moment she laid eyes on the ebony glass table and who stood at it.

Vernon: tall, lanky, ever-smirking, clad in Terrasen green.

And a golden-haired man, his skin pale as ivory.

No sign of the duke. The stranger twisted toward them. Even her grandmother gave pause.

Not at the man's beauty, not at the strength in his sculpted body or the fine black clothes he wore. But at those gold eyes. Twin to Manon's.

The eyes of the Valg kings.

Manon assessed the exits, the windows, the weapons she would use when they fought their way out. Instinct had her stepping in front of her grandmother; training had her palming two knives before the golden-eyed man could blink.

But the man fixed those Valg eyes on her. He smiled.

"Wing Leader." He looked to her grandmother and inclined his head. "Matron."

The voice was carnal and lovely and cruel. But the tone, the demand in it . . .

Something in Vernon's smirk now seemed too strained, his tan skin too pale.

"Who are you," Manon said to the stranger, more an order than a question.

The man jerked his chin toward the unclaimed seats at the table. "You know perfectly well who I am, Manon Blackbeak."

Perrington. In another body, somehow. Because . . .

Because that otherworldly, foul thing she had sometimes glimpsed staring out through his eyes . . . Here it was, given flesh.

The Matron's tight face told her she'd already guessed.

"I grew tired of wearing that sagging meat," he said, sliding with feline grace into the chair beside Vernon. A wave of long, powerful fingers. "My enemies know who I am. My allies might as well, too."

Vernon bowed his head and murmured, "My Lord Erawan, if it would please you, allow me to fetch the Matron refreshments. Her journey has been long."

Manon assessed the tall, reedy man. Two gifts he had offered them: respect to her grandmother, and the knowledge of the duke's true name. Erawan.

She wondered what Ghislaine, on guard in the hall beyond, knew of him.

The Valg king nodded his approval. The Lord of Perranth hustled to the small buffet table against the wall, grabbing a ewer as Manon and the Matron slid into the seats across from the demon king.

Respect—something Vernon had not once offered without a mocking grin. But now . . .

Perhaps now that the Lord of Perranth realized what manner of monster held his leash, he was desperate for allies. Knew, perhaps, that Manon . . . that Manon might have indeed been part of that explosion.

Manon accepted the carved-horn cups of water Vernon set before them but did not drink. Neither did her grandmother.

Across the table, Erawan smiled faintly. No darkness, no corruption leaked from him—as if he were powerful enough to keep it contained, unnoticed, save for those eyes. Her eyes.

Behind them, the rest of the Thirteen and her grandmother's coven remained in the hall, only their Seconds lingering in the room as the doors were sealed again.

Trapping them all with the Valg king.

"So," Erawan said, looking them over in a way that had Manon clamping her lips to keep from baring her teeth, "are the forces at the Ferian Gap prepared?"

Her grandmother yielded a short dip of her chin. "They move at sundown. They'll be in Rifthold two days after that."

Manon didn't dare shift in her seat. "You're sending the host to Rifthold?"

The demon king flashed her a narrowed glance. "I am sending *you* to Rifthold, to take back my city. When you have finished your task, the Ferian legion will be stationed there under the command of Iskra Yellowlegs."

To Rifthold. To finally, *finally* fight, to see what their wyverns could do in battle— "Do they suspect the attack?"

A lifeless smile. "Our forces will move too swiftly for word to reach them." No doubt why this information had been contained until now.

Manon tapped a foot on the slate floor, already itching to move, to command the others in preparations. "How many of the Morath covens do I bring northward?"

"Iskra flies with the second half of our aerial legion. I would think that only a few covens from Morath would be necessary." A challenge—and a test.

Manon considered. "I fly with my Thirteen and two escort covens." No need for their enemies to get a good count on how many covens flew in the aerial legion—or for the entirety to go when she'd bet good money that even the Thirteen would be enough to sack the capital.

Erawan just inclined his head in agreement. Her grandmother gave her a barely perceptible nod—as close to approval as she'd ever get.

But Manon asked, "What of the prince?" King. King Dorian.

Her grandmother shot her a look, but the demon said, "I want you to personally bring him to me. If he survives the attack."

And with the fiery queen now gone, Dorian Havilliard and his city were defenseless.

It mattered little to her. It was war.

Fight this war, and go home to the Wastes at the end of it. Even if this man, this demon king, might very well renege on his word.

She'd deal with that later. But first . . . open battle. She could already hear its wild song in her blood.

The demon king and her grandmother were speaking again, and Manon cleared away the melody of clashing shields and sparking swords long enough to process their words.

"Once the capital is secured, I want those boats on the Avery."

"The men of the Silver Lake have agreed?" Her grandmother studied the map weighted to the glass table by smooth stones. Manon followed the

Matron's stare to the Silver Lake, at the other end of the Avery, and to its city, nestled against the White Fangs: Anielle.

Perrington—Erawan—shrugged his broad shoulders. "Its lord has not yet declared allegiance to me or the boy-king. I suspect when word reaches him of Rifthold's demise, we will find his messengers groveling on our doorstep." A flicker of a smile. "Their Keep along the Western Falls of the lake still bears scars from the last time my armies marched. I have seen the countless monuments in Anielle to that war—its lord will know how easily I can again turn his city into a charnel house."

Manon studied the map again, shutting out the questions.

Old. The Valg king was so old as to make her feel young. To make her grandmother look like a child, too.

Fool—perhaps her grandmother had been a fool to sell them into an unwitting alliance with this creature. She made herself meet Erawan's stare. "With strongholds in Morath, Rifthold, and Anielle, that only covers the southern half of Adarlan. What of north of the Ferian Gap? Or south of Adarlan?"

"Bellhaven remains under my control—its lords and merchants love their gold too much. Melisande . . ." The demon king's golden eyes fixed on the western country across the mountains. "Eyllwe lies shattered beneath her, Fenharrow in barren shambles to the east. It remains in Melisande's best interest to continue allying her forces with my own, especially when Terrasen hasn't a copper to its name." The king's stare roamed northward. "Aelin Galathynius will have reached her seat by now. And when Rifthold is gone, she will also find how very alone she is in the North. Brannon's heir has no allies on this continent. Not anymore."

But Manon noted the way the demon king's eyes darted to Eyllwe—just for a flicker.

She looked to her grandmother, silent yet watching Manon with an expression that promised death if she pushed too far. But Manon said to

Erawan, "Your capital is the heart of your commerce. If I unleash my legion upon it, you will have few human allies—"

"Last I looked, Manon Blackbeak, it was *my* legion."

Manon held Erawan's burning gaze, even as it stripped her bare. "Turn Rifthold into a complete ruin," she said flatly, "and rulers like the Lord of Anielle or the Queen of Melisande or the Lords of Fenharrow might very well find it worth the risk to rally against you. If you wreck your own capital, why should they believe your claims of alliance? Send a decree ahead of us that the king, the queen are enemies to the continent. Establish us as liberators of Rifthold, not conquerors, and you will have the other rulers thinking twice before allying with Terrasen. I will sack the city for you enough to display our might—but keep the Ironteeth host from leaving it in rubble."

Those gold eyes narrowed with consideration.

She knew her grandmother was one more word away from gouging her nails down Manon's cheek, but she kept her shoulders back. She didn't care about the city, its people. But this war could indeed turn against them if the annihilation of Rifthold united their scattered enemies. And delay the Blackbeaks that much more from returning to the Wastes.

Vernon's eyes flicked to meet hers. Fear—and calculation. He murmured to Erawan, "The Wing Leader has a point, milord." What did Vernon know that she didn't?

But Erawan angled his head, his golden hair sliding across his brow. "That is why you are my Wing Leader, Manon Blackbeak, and why Iskra Yellowlegs did not win the position."

Disgust and pride warred in her, but she nodded.

"One more thing."

She remained still, waiting.

The demon king lounged in his seat. "There is a glass wall in Rifthold. Impossible to miss." She knew it—had perched atop it. "Damage the city enough to instill fear, show our power. But that wall . . . Bring it down."

She only said, "Why?"

Those golden eyes simmered like hot coals. "Because destroying a symbol can break the spirits of men as much as bloodshed."

That glass wall—Aelin Galathynius's power. And mercy. Manon held that gaze long enough to nod. The king jerked his chin toward the shut doors in silent dismissal.

Manon was out of the room before he'd turned back to Vernon. It did not occur to her until she was long gone that she should have remained to protect the Matron.

The Thirteen did not speak until they had landed at their personal armory in the army camp below, had not even risked it while saddling their wyverns in the new aerie.

Sweeping through the smoke and gloom that always wreathed Morath, the two escort covens Manon had selected—both Blackbeaks—steered for their own armories. Good.

Now standing in the mud of the valley floor outside the cobbled-together labyrinth of forges and tents, Manon said to her assembled Thirteen, "We fly in thirty minutes." Behind them, blacksmiths and handlers were already rushing to haul armor onto the chained-down wyverns.

If they were smart, or fast, they wouldn't wind up between those jaws. Already, Asterin's sky-blue mare was sizing up the man closest to her.

Manon was half tempted to see if she'd take a bite out of him, but she said to her coven, "If we are lucky, we will arrive before Iskra and set the tone for how the sacking unfolds. If we are not, we seek out Iskra and her coven upon arriving and staunch the slaughter. Leave the prince to me." She didn't dare look at Asterin as she said it. "I have no doubt the Yellowlegs will try to claim his head. Stop any one of them who dares take it."

And perhaps put an end to Iskra as well. Accidents happened all the time in battle.

The Thirteen bowed their heads in acquiescence. Manon jerked her head over a shoulder, to the armory under the shoddy canvas tents. "Full armor." She gave them a slashing grin. "We don't want to make our grand appearance looking anything but our best."

Twelve matching grins met hers, and they peeled away, heading toward the tables and dummies where their armor had been carefully and meticulously built these past months.

Only Asterin remained at her side as Manon grabbed Ghislaine by an arm when the curly-haired sentinel strode past.

She murmured over the clank of forges and roar of wyverns, "Tell us what you know of Erawan." Ghislaine opened her mouth, dark skin wan, and Manon snapped, "*Concisely*."

Ghislaine swallowed hard, nodding as the rest of the Thirteen readied beyond them. The warrior-scholar whispered so only Manon and Asterin could hear. "He was one of the three Valg kings who invaded this world at the dawn of time. The other two were either killed or sent back to their dark world. He was stranded here, with a small army. He fled to this continent after Maeve and Brannon squashed his forces, and spent a thousand years rebuilding his numbers in secret, deep beyond the White Fangs. When he was ready, when he noticed that King Brannon's flame was dimming, Erawan launched his attack to claim this continent. Legend has it that he was defeated by Brannon's own daughter and her human mate."

Asterin snorted. "It would seem that legend is wrong."

Manon released Ghislaine's arm. "Get ready. Tell the others when you can."

Ghislaine bowed her head and stalked into the arsenal.

Manon ignored Asterin's narrow stare. Now was not the time for this conversation.

She found the mute blacksmith by his usual forge, sweat streaming down his soot-stained brow. But his eyes were solid, calm, as he pulled back the canvas tarp on his worktable to reveal her armor. Polished, ready.

The suit of dark metal had been fashioned like intricate wyvern scales. Manon ran a finger along the overlapping plates and lifted a gauntlet, perfectly formed to her own hand. "It's beautiful."

Horrible, yet beautiful. She wondered what he made of the fact that he'd forged this armor for her to wear while ending the lives of his countrymen. His ruddy face revealed nothing.

She stripped off her red cloak and began donning the armor bit by bit. It slid over her like a second skin, flexible and pliant where she needed it to be, unyielding where her life depended on it.

When she was done, the blacksmith looked her over and nodded, then reached below his table to place another object on its surface. For a heartbeat, Manon only stared at the crowned helmet.

It had been forged of the same dark metal, the nose and brow guards fashioned so that most of her face would be in shadow—save for her mouth. And her iron teeth. The six lances of the crown jutted upward like small swords.

A conqueror's helm. A demon's helm.

Manon felt the eyes of her Thirteen, now armed, upon her as she tucked her braid into the neck of her armor and lifted the helmet over her head.

It fitted easily, its interior cool against her hot skin. Even with the shadows that hid most of her face, she could see the blacksmith with perfect clarity as his chin dipped in approval.

She had no idea why she bothered, but Manon found herself saying, "Thank you."

Another shallow nod was his only reply before she swept from his table.

Soldiers cowered from her storming path as she signaled to the Thirteen and mounted Abraxos, her wyvern preening in his new armor.

She didn't look back at Morath as they took to the gray skies.

CHAPTER 4

Aedion and Rowan did not let Darrow's messenger go ahead to warn the lords of their arrival. If this was some maneuver to get them on uneven footing, despite all that Murtaugh and Ren had done for them this spring, then they'd gain the advantage whatever way they could.

Aelin supposed that she should have taken the stormy weather as an omen. Or perhaps Murtaugh's age provided a convenient excuse for Darrow to test her. She leashed her temper at the thought.

The tavern was erected at a crossroads just inside the tangle of Oakwald. With the rain and night settling in, it was packed, and they had to pay double to stable their horses. Aelin was fairly certain that one word from her, one flicker of that telltale fire, would have cleared out not only the stables, but also the tavern itself.

Lysandra had padded off half a mile away, and when they arrived, she slunk from the bushes and nodded her fuzzy, drenched head at Aelin. All clear.

Inside the inn, there were no rooms to be found for rent, and the taproom itself was crammed full of travelers, hunters, and whoever else was escaping the downpour. Some even sat against the walls—and Aelin supposed that it was how she and her friends might very well spend their evening once this meeting concluded.

A few heads twisted their way as they entered, but dripping hoods and cloaks concealed their faces and weapons, and those heads quickly returned to their drinks or cards or drunken songs.

Lysandra had finally shifted back into her human form—and true to her oath months ago, her once-full breasts were now smaller. Despite what awaited them in the private dining room at the back of the inn, Aelin caught the shape-shifter's eye and smirked.

"Better?" she murmured over Evangeline's head as Darrow's messenger, Aedion at his side, strolled through the crowd.

Lysandra's grin was half feral. "Oh, you have no idea."

Behind them, Aelin could have sworn Rowan chuckled.

The messenger and Aedion turned down a hallway, the dim candlelight flickering amongst the raindrops still sliding off the round, scarred shield strapped across her cousin's back. The Wolf of the North, who, even though he had won battles with his Fae speed and strength, had earned the respect and loyalty of his legion as a man—as a human. Aelin, still in her Fae form, wondered if she should have shifted herself.

Ren Allsbrook waited in there. Ren, another childhood friend, whom she had almost killed, *tried* to kill this past winter, and who had no idea who she really was. Who had stayed at her apartment without realizing it belonged to his lost queen. And Murtaugh . . . She had vague memories of the man, mostly involving him sitting at her uncle's table, slipping her extra blackberry tarts.

Any good that remained, any shred of safety, it was thanks to Aedion, the dents and scratches marring his shield utter proof of it, and to the three men who awaited her.

Aelin's shoulders began to curve inward, but Aedion and the messenger paused before a wooden door, knocking once. Fleetfoot brushed against her calf, tail wagging, and Aelin smiled down at the hound, who shook herself again, flinging droplets of water. Lysandra snorted. Bringing a wet dog into a covert meeting—very queenly.

But Aelin had promised herself, months and months ago, that she would not pretend to be anything but what she was. She had crawled through darkness and blood and despair—she had survived. And even if Lord Darrow could offer men and funding for a war . . . she had both, too. More would be better, but—she was not empty-handed. She had done that for herself. For them all.

Aelin squared her shoulders as Aedion stepped into the room, already speaking to those inside: "Just like you bastards to make us trudge through the rain because you don't want to get wet. Ren, looking put-out, as usual. Murtaugh, always a pleasure. Darrow—your hair looks as bad as mine."

Someone said from within in a dry, cold voice, "Given the secrecy with which you arranged this meeting, one would think you were sneaking through your own kingdom, Aedion."

Aelin reached the ajar door, debating whether it was worth it to open the conversation by telling the fools inside to keep their voices down, but—

They were. With her Fae ears, she picked up more sounds than the average human. She stepped ahead of Lysandra and Evangeline, letting them enter behind her as she paused in the doorway to survey the private dining room.

One window, cracked to soothe the stifling heat of the inn. A large rectangular table before a roaring hearth, littered with empty plates, crumbs, and worn serving platters. Two old men sat at it, one with the messenger whispering something in his ear too softly for her Fae hearing before he bowed to all of them and saw himself out. Both old men straightened as they looked past where Aedion stood before the table—to her.

But Aelin focused upon the dark-haired young man by the hearth, an arm braced against the mantel, his scarred, tan face slack.

She remembered those twin swords at his back. Those dark, burning eyes.

Her mouth had gone slightly dry by the time she tugged back her hood. Ren Allsbrook started.

But the old men had risen to their feet. She knew one of them.

Aelin didn't know how she hadn't recognized Murtaugh that night she'd gone to the warehouse to end so many of them. Especially when he'd been the one who halted her slaughtering.

The other old man, though . . . while wrinkled, his face was strong—hard. Without amusement or joy or warmth. A man used to getting his way, to being obeyed without question. His body was thin and wiry, but his spine was still straight. Not a warrior of the sword, but of the mind.

Her great-uncle, Orlon, had been both. And kind—she'd never heard a stern or raging word from Orlon. This man, though . . . Aelin held Darrow's gray-eyed gaze, predator recognizing predator.

"Lord Darrow," she said, inclining her head. She couldn't help the crooked grin. "You look toasty."

Darrow's plain face remained unmoved. Unimpressed.

Well, then.

Aelin watched Darrow, waiting—refusing to break his stare until he bowed.

A dip of his head was all he offered.

"A bit lower," she purred.

Aedion's gaze snapped to her, full of warning.

Darrow did no such thing.

It was Murtaugh who bowed deeply at the waist and said, "Majesty. We apologize for sending the messenger to fetch you—but my grandson worries after my health." An attempt at a smile. "To my chagrin."

Ren ignored his grandfather and pushed off the mantel, his boot-steps the only sound as he rounded the table. "You knew," he breathed to Aedion.

Lysandra, wisely, shut the door and bid Evangeline and Fleetfoot to stand by the window—to watch for any peering eyes. Aedion gave Ren a little smile. "Surprise."

Before the young lord could retort, Rowan stepped to Aelin's side and pulled back his hood.

The men stiffened as the Fae warrior was revealed in his undimmed glory—glazed violence already in his eyes. Already focused on Lord Darrow.

"Now, that is a sight I have not seen for an age," Darrow murmured.

Murtaugh mastered his shock—and perhaps a bit of fear—enough to extend a hand toward the empty chairs across from them. "Please, sit. Apologies for the mess. We hadn't realized the messenger might retrieve you so swiftly." Aelin made no move to sit. Neither did her companions. Murtaugh added, "We can order fresh food if you wish. You must be famished." Ren shot his grandfather an incredulous look that told her everything she needed to know about the rebel's opinion of her.

Lord Darrow was watching her again. Assessing.

Humility—gratitude. She should try; she *could* try, damn it. Darrow had sacrificed for her kingdom; he had men and money to offer in the upcoming battle with Erawan. *She* had called this meeting; *she* had asked these lords to meet them. Who cared if it was in another location? They were all here. It was enough.

Aelin forced herself to walk to the table. To claim the chair across from Darrow and Murtaugh.

Ren remained standing, monitoring her with dark fire in his eyes.

She said quietly to Ren, "Thank you—for helping Captain Westfall this spring."

A muscle flickered in Ren's jaw, but he said, "How does he fare? Aedion mentioned his injuries in his letter."

"Last I heard, he was on his way to the healers in Antica. To the Torre Cesme."

"Good."

Lord Darrow said, "Would you care to enlighten me on how you know each other, or shall I be required to guess?"

Aelin began counting to ten at the tone. But it was Aedion who said as he claimed a seat, "Careful, Darrow."

Darrow interlaced his gnarled but manicured fingers and set them on the table. "Or what? Shall you burn me to ash, Princess? Melt my bones?"

Lysandra slipped into a chair beside Aedion and asked with the sweet, unthreatening politeness that had been trained into her, "Is there any water left in that pitcher? Traveling through the storm was rather taxing."

Aelin could have kissed her friend for the attempt at dulling the razor-sharp tension.

"Who, pray tell, are you?" Darrow frowned at the exquisite beauty, the uptilted eyes that did not shy from his despite her gentle words. Right—he had not known who traveled with her and Aedion. Or what gifts they bore.

"Lysandra," Aedion answered, unbuckling his shield and setting it on the floor behind them with a heavy thunk. "Lady of Caraverre."

"There is no Caraverre," Darrow said.

Aelin shrugged. "There is now." Lysandra had settled on the name a week ago, whatever it meant, bolting upright in the middle of the night and practically shouting it at Aelin once she'd mastered herself long enough to shift back into her human form. Aelin doubted she'd soon forget the image of a wide-eyed ghost leopard trying to speak. She smiled a bit at Ren, still watching her like a hawk. "I took the liberty of buying the land your family yielded. Looks like you'll be neighbors."

"And what bloodline," Darrow asked, his mouth tightening at the brand across Lysandra's tattoo, the mark visible no matter what form she took, "does Lady Lysandra hail from?"

"We didn't arrange this meeting to discuss bloodlines and heritage," Aelin countered evenly. She looked to Rowan, who gave a confirming nod that the inn staff was far from the room and no one was within hearing range.

Her Fae Prince stalked to the serving table against the wall to fetch the water Lysandra had asked for. He sniffed it, and she knew his magic swept through it, probing the water for any poison or drug, while he floated four glasses over to them on a phantom wind.

The three lords watched in wide-eyed silence. Rowan sat and casually poured the water, then summoned a fifth cup, filled it, and floated it to Evangeline. The girl beamed at the magic and went back to staring out the rain-splattered window. Listening while pretending to be pretty, to be useless and small, as Lysandra had taught her.

Lord Darrow said, "At least your Fae warrior is good for something other than brute violence."

"If this meeting is interrupted by unfriendly forces," Aelin said smoothly, "you'll be glad for that brute violence, Lord Darrow."

"And what of your particular skill set? Should I be glad of that, too?"

She didn't care how he'd learned. Aelin cocked her head, choosing each word, forcing herself to think it through for once. "Is there a skill set that you would prefer I possess?"

Darrow smiled. It didn't reach his eyes. "Some control would do Your Highness well."

On either side of her, Rowan and Aedion were taut as bowstrings. But if *she* could keep her temper leashed, then they could—

Your Highness. Not *Majesty*.

"I'll take that into consideration," she said with a little smile of her own. "As for why my court and I wished to meet with you today—"

"Court?" Lord Darrow raised his silver brows. Then he slowly raked his stare over Lysandra, then Aedion, and finally Rowan. Ren was gaping at them all, something like longing—and dismay—on his face. "This is what you consider a court?"

"Obviously, the court will be expanded once we're in Orynth—"

"And for that matter, I do not see how there can even *be* a court, as you are not yet queen."

She kept her chin high. "I'm not sure I catch your meaning."

Darrow sipped from his tankard of ale. The plunk as he set it down echoed through the room. Beside him, Murtaugh had gone still as death. "Any ruler of Terrasen must be approved by the ruling families of each territory."

Ice, cold and ancient, cracked through her veins. Aelin wished she could blame it on the thing hanging from her neck.

"Are you telling me," she said too quietly, fire flickering in her gut, dancing along her tongue, "that even though I am the last living Galathynius, my throne does not yet belong to me?"

She felt Rowan's attention fix upon her face, but she didn't look away from Lord Darrow.

"I am telling you, Princess, that while you might be the last living direct descendant of Brannon, there are other possibilities, other directions to go in, should you be deemed unfit."

"Weylan, please," Murtaugh cut in. "We did not accept the offer to meet for this. It was to discuss rebuilding, to *help* her and work with her."

They all ignored him.

"Other possibilities such as yourself?" Aelin asked Darrow. Smoke curled in her mouth. She swallowed it down, nearly choking on it.

Darrow didn't so much as flinch. "You can hardly expect us to allow a nineteen-year-old assassin to parade into our kingdom and start yapping orders, regardless of her bloodline."

Think it through, take a deep breath. Men, money, support from your already-broken people. That's what Darrow offers, what you can stand to gain, if you just control your rutting temper.

She stifled the fire in her veins into murmuring embers. "I understand that my personal history might be considered problematic—"

"I find everything about you, Princess, to be problematic. The least of which is your choice in friends and *court* members. Can you explain to me why a common whore is in your company and being passed as a lady? Or why one of Maeve's minions is now sitting at your side?" He tossed a sneer in Rowan's direction. "Prince Rowan, is it?" He must have pieced it together from what the messenger had whispered in his ear upon arriving. "Oh, yes, we've heard of you. What an interesting turn of events, that when our kingdom is weakest and its heir so young, one of Maeve's most trusted warriors manages to gain a foothold, after so many years of gazing at our kingdom with such longing. Or perhaps the better question is, why serve at Maeve's feet when you could rule beside Princess Aelin?"

It took considerable effort to keep her fingers from curling into fists. "Prince Rowan is my *carranam*. He is above any doubt."

"*Carranam*. A long-forgotten term. What other things did Maeve teach you in Doranelle this spring?"

She bit back her retort as Rowan's hand grazed hers beneath the table—his face bored, uninterested. The calm of a feral, frozen storm. *Permission to speak,* Majesty*?*

She had a feeling Rowan would very, very much enjoy the task of shredding Darrow into little pieces. She also had the feeling that she'd very, very much enjoy joining him.

Aelin gave a slight nod, at a loss for words herself as she struggled to keep her flames at bay.

Honestly, she felt slightly bad for Darrow as the Fae Prince gave him a look laced with three hundred years of cold violence. "Are you accusing me of taking the blood oath to my queen with dishonor?"

Nothing human, nothing merciful in those words.

To his credit, Darrow didn't shrink. Rather, he raised his brows at Aedion, then turned and shook his head at Aelin. "You gave away the sacred oath to this . . . male?"

Ren gaped a bit as he surveyed Aedion, that scar stark against his tan skin. She had not been there to protect him from it. Or to protect Ren's sisters when their magic academy became a slaughterhouse during Adarlan's invasion. Aedion caught Ren's surprise and subtly shook his head, as if to say, *I'll explain later.*

But Rowan leaned back in his chair with a faint smile—and it was a horrifying, terrible thing. "I have known many princesses with kingdoms to inherit, Lord Darrow, and I can tell you that absolutely none of them were ever stupid enough to allow a male to manipulate them that way, least of all my queen. But if I were going to scheme my way onto a throne, I'd pick a far more peaceful and prosperous kingdom." He shrugged. "But I do not think my brother and sister in this room would allow me to live for very long if they suspected I meant their queen ill—or their kingdom."

Aedion gave a grim nod, but beside him, Lysandra straightened—not in anger or surprise, but pride. It broke Aelin's heart as much as it lightened it.

Aelin smiled slowly at Darrow, flames banking. "How long did it take you to come up with a list of every possible thing to insult me with and accuse me of during this meeting?"

Darrow ignored her and jerked his chin at Aedion. "You're rather quiet tonight."

"I don't think you particularly want to hear my thoughts right now, Darrow," Aedion replied.

"Your blood oath is stolen by a foreign prince, your queen is an assassin who appoints common whores to serve her, and yet you have nothing to say?"

Aedion's chair groaned, and Aelin dared a look—to find him gripping the sides of it so hard his knuckles were white.

Lysandra, though stiff-backed, did not give Darrow the pleasure of blushing with shame.

And she was done. Sparks danced at her fingertips beneath the table.

But Darrow went on before Aelin could speak or incinerate the room.

"Perhaps, Aedion, if you hope to still gain an official position in Terrasen, you could see if your kin in Wendlyn have reconsidered the betrothal proposition of so many years ago. See if they'll recognize you as family. What a difference it might have made, if you and our beloved Princess Aelin had been betrothed—if Wendlyn had not rejected the offer to formally unite our kingdoms, likely at Maeve's behest." A smile in Rowan's direction.

Her world tilted a bit. Even Aedion had paled. No one had ever hinted that there had been an official attempt at betrothing them. Or that the Ashryvers had truly left Terrasen to war and ruin.

"Whatever will the adoring masses say of their savior princess," Darrow mused, putting his hands flat on the table, "when they hear of how she has spent her time while they suffered?" A slap in the face, one after another. "But," Darrow added, "you've always been good at whoring yourself out, Aedion. Though I wonder if Princess Aelin knows what—"

Aelin lunged.

Not with flame, but steel.

The dagger shuddering between Darrow's fingers flickered with the light of the crackling hearth.

She snarled in the old man's face, Rowan and Aedion half out of their chairs, Ren reaching for a weapon, but looking sick—sick at the sight of the ghost leopard now sitting where Lysandra had been a moment ago.

Murtaugh gaped at the shape-shifter. But Darrow glared at Aelin, his face white with rage.

"You want to sling insults at me, Darrow, then go ahead," Aelin hissed, her nose almost touching his. "But you insult my own again, and I won't miss next time." She flicked her eyes to the dagger between the old man's splayed fingers, a hairsbreadth separating the blade from his speckled flesh.

"I see you inherited your father's temper," Darrow sneered. "Is this how you plan to rule? When you don't like someone, you'll threaten them?" He slid his hand from the blade and pulled back far enough to cross his arms. "What would Orlon think of this behavior, this bullying?"

"Choose your words wisely, Darrow," Aedion warned.

Darrow lifted his brows. "All the work I have done, all that I have sacrificed these past ten years, has been in Orlon's name, to honor him and to save his kingdom—*my* kingdom. I do not plan to let a spoiled, arrogant child destroy that with her temper tantrums. Did you enjoy the riches of Rifthold these years, Princess? Was it very easy to forget us in the North when you were buying clothes and serving the monster who butchered your family and friends?"

Men, and money, and a unified Terrasen.

"Even your cousin, despite his whoring, helped us in the North. And Ren Allsbrook"—a wave of the hand in Ren's direction—"while you were living in luxury, did you know that Ren and his grandfather were scraping together every copper they could, all to find a way to keep the rebel effort alive? That they squatted in shanties and slept under horses?"

"That's enough," Aedion said.

"Let him go on," Aelin said, sitting back in her seat and crossing her arms.

"What else is there to say, Princess? Do you think the people of Terrasen will be glad to have a queen who served their enemy? Who shared a bed with the son of their enemy?"

Lysandra snarled softly, rattling the glasses.

Darrow was unfazed. "And a queen who now undoubtedly shares a bed with a Fae Prince who served the other enemy at our backs—what do you suppose our people will make of *that*?"

She didn't want to know how Darrow had guessed, what he'd read between them.

"Who shares my bed," she said, "is none of your concern."

"And that is why you are not fit to rule. Who shares the queen's bed is *everyone's* concern. Will you lie to our people about your past, deny that you served the deposed king—and served his son, too, in a different manner?"

Beneath the table, Rowan's hand shot out to grip her own, his fingers coated in ice that soothed the fire starting to flicker at her nails. Not in warning or reprimand—just to tell her that he, too, was struggling with the effort to keep from using the pewter food platter to smash in Darrow's face.

So she didn't break Darrow's stare, even as she laced her fingers with Rowan's.

"I will tell *my* people," Aelin said quietly but not weakly, "the entire truth. I will show them the scars on my back from Endovier, the scars on my body from my years as Celaena Sardothien, and I will tell them that the new King of Adarlan is not a monster. I will tell them that we have one enemy: the bastard down in Morath. And Dorian Havilliard is the only chance for survival—and future peace between our two kingdoms."

"And if he is not? Will you shatter his stone castle as you shattered the glass one?"

Chaol had mentioned this—months ago. She should have considered it more, that ordinary humans might demand checks against her power. Against the power of the court gathering around her. But let Darrow believe she'd shattered the glass castle; let him believe she'd killed the king. Better than the potentially disastrous truth.

"Should you still wish to be a part of Terrasen," Darrow continued when none of them replied, "I'm sure Aedion can find some use for you in the Bane. But I will have no use for you in Orynth."

She flicked her brows up. "Is there anything else that you have to say to me?"

His gray eyes turned flinty. "I do not recognize your right to rule; I do not recognize you as the rightful Queen of Terrasen. Neither do the Lords Sloane, Ironwood, and Gunnar, who make up the remaining surviving majority of what was once your uncle's court. Even if the Allsbrook family sides with you, that is still one vote against four. General Ashryver has no lands or title here—and no say as a result. As for *Lady* Lysandra, Caraverre is not a recognized territory, nor do we recognize her lineage or your *purchase* of those lands." Formal words, for a formal declaration. "Should you return to Orynth and seize your throne without our invitation, it will be considered an act of war and treason." Darrow pulled a piece of paper from his jacket—lots of fancy writing and four different signatures on the bottom. "As of this moment, until it is otherwise decided, you shall remain a princess by blood—but not queen."

CHAPTER 5

Aelin stared and stared at that piece of paper, at the names that had been signed long before tonight, the men who had decided against her without meeting her, the men who had changed her future, her kingdom, with just their signatures.

Perhaps she should have waited to call this meeting until she was in Orynth—until her people saw her return and it would have been harder to kick her to the curb of the palace.

Aelin breathed, "Our doom gathers in the South of Adarlan—yet this is what you focus on?"

Darrow sneered, "When we have need of your . . . skill set, we will send word."

No fire burned in her, not even an ember. As if Darrow had clenched it in his fist, snuffed it out.

"The Bane," Aedion said with a hint of that legendary insolence, "will answer to none but Aelin Galathynius."

"The Bane," Darrow spat, "is now ours to command. In the event that there is no fit ruler on the throne, the lords control the armies of Terrasen." He again surveyed Aelin, as if sensing the vague plan to publicly return to her city, to make it harder for him to shut her out, glimmering as it formed. "Set foot in Orynth, girl, and you will pay."

"Is that a threat?" Aedion snarled, a hand darting to grip the hilt of the Sword of Orynth sheathed at his side.

"It is the law," Darrow said simply. "One generations of Galathynius rulers have honored."

There was such a roaring in her head, and such a still emptiness in the world beyond.

"The Valg march on us—a Valg *king* marches on us," Aedion pushed, the general incarnate. "And *your queen*, Darrow, might be the only person capable of keeping them at bay."

"War is a game of numbers, not magic. You know this, Aedion. You fought at Theralis." The great plain before Orynth, host to the final, doomed battle as the empire had swept down upon them. Most of Terrasen's forces and commanders had not walked away from the bloodbath, so thorough streams ran red for days afterward. If Aedion had fought in it . . . Gods, he must have been barely fourteen. Her stomach turned. Darrow concluded, "Magic failed us once before. We will not trust in it again."

Aedion snapped, "We will need allies—"

"There are no allies," Darrow said. "Unless Her Highness decides to be useful and gain us men and arms through marriage"—a sharp glance at Rowan—"we are alone."

Aelin debated revealing what she knew, the money she'd schemed and killed to attain, but—

Something cold and oily clanged through her. Marriage to a foreign king or prince or emperor.

Would this be the cost? Not just in blood shed, but in dreams yielded?

To be a princess eternal, but never a queen? To fight with not just magic, but the other power in her blood: royalty.

She could not look at Rowan, could not face those pine-green eyes without being sick.

She had laughed once at Dorian—*laughed* and scolded him for admitting that the thought of marriage to anyone but his soul-bonded was abhorrent. She'd chided him for choosing love over the peace of his kingdom.

Perhaps the gods did hate her. Perhaps this was her test. To escape one form of enslavement only to walk into another. Perhaps this was the punishment for those years in Rifthold's riches.

Darrow gave her a small, satisfied smile. "Find me allies, Aelin Galathynius, and perhaps we shall consider your role in Terrasen's future. Think on it. Thank you for asking us to meet."

Silently, Aelin rose to her feet. The others did as well. Save for Darrow.

Aelin plucked up the piece of paper he had signed and examined the damning words, the scribbled signatures. The crackling fire was the only sound.

Aelin silenced it.

And the candles. And the wrought-iron chandelier over the table.

Darkness fell, cleaved only by twin sharp inhales of breath—Murtaugh and Ren. The patter of rain filled the black room.

Aelin spoke into the dark, toward where Darrow was seated. "I suggest, Lord Darrow, that you become accustomed to this. For if we lose this war, darkness will reign forever."

There was a scratch and a hiss—then a match sputtered as it lit a candle on the table. Darrow's wrinkled, hateful face flickered into view. "Men can make their own light, Heir of Brannon."

Aelin stared at the sole flame Darrow had sparked. The paper in her hands wilted into ashes.

Before she could speak, Darrow said, "That is our law—our right. You ignore that decree, Princess, and you defile all that your family stood and died for. The Lords of Terrasen have spoken."

Rowan's hand was solid against her lower back. But Aelin looked to Ren, his face tight. And over the roaring in her head, she said, "Whether or not you vote in my favor, there is a spot for you in this court. For what you helped Aedion and the captain do. For Nehemia." Nehemia, who had worked with Ren, fought with him. Something like pain rippled in Ren's eyes, and he opened his mouth to speak, but Darrow cut him off.

"What a waste of a life that was," Darrow spat. "A princess actually dedicated to her people, who fought until her last breath for—"

"One more word," Rowan said softly, "and I don't care how many lords support you or what your laws are. One more word about that, and I will gut you before you can get up from that chair. Understand?"

For the first time, Darrow looked into Rowan's eyes and blanched at the death he found waiting there. But the lord's words had found their mark, leaving a shuddering sort of numbness in their wake.

Aedion snatched Aelin's dagger off the table. "We'll take your thoughts into consideration." He scooped up his shield and put a hand on Aelin's shoulder to guide her from the room. It was only the sight of that dented and scarred shield, the ancient sword hanging at his side, that set her feet moving, slicing through that thick numbness.

Ren moved to open the door, stepping into the hall beyond to scan it, giving Lysandra a wide berth as she padded past, Evangeline and Fleetfoot on her fluffy tail, secrecy be damned.

Aelin met the young lord's eyes and drew in breath to say something, when Lysandra snarled down the hall.

A dagger was instantly in Aelin's hand, angled and ready.

But it was Darrow's messenger, hurtling for them.

"Rifthold," he panted as he skidded to a stop, flinging rain on them. "One of the scouts from the Ferian Gap just raced past. The Ironteeth host flies for Rifthold. They mean to sack the city."

Aelin stood in a clearing just past the inn's glow, the cold rain plastering her hair and raising bumps on her skin. Soaking them all, because Rowan now buckled on the extra blades she handed him, conserving each drop of his magic for what he was about to do.

They'd let the messenger spill the information he'd received—not much at all.

The Ironteeth host lingering in the Ferian Gap were now flying for Rifthold. Dorian Havilliard would be their target. Dead or alive.

They'd be upon the city by nightfall tomorrow, and once Rifthold was taken . . . Erawan's net across the middle of the continent would be complete. No forces from Melisande, Fenharrow, or Eyllwe could reach them—and none of Terrasen's forces could get to them, either. Not without wasting months to trek around the mountains.

"There's nothing to be done for the city," Aedion said, his voice cutting through the rain. The three of them lingered under the cover of a large oak, all keeping an eye on Ren and Murtaugh, who were speaking with Evangeline and Lysandra, now back in her human form. Her cousin went on, rain pinging against the shield across his back, "If the witches fly on Rifthold, then Rifthold already is gone."

Aelin wondered if Manon Blackbeak would be leading the attack—if it'd be a blessing. The Wing Leader had saved them once before, but only as a payment for a life debt. She doubted the witch would feel obliged to throw them a bone anytime soon.

Aedion met Rowan's gaze. "Dorian must be saved at all costs. I know Perrington's—Erawan's—style. Don't believe any promises they make, and don't let Dorian be taken again." Aedion dragged a hand through his rain-soaked hair and added, "Or yourself, Rowan."

They were the most hideous words she'd ever heard. Rowan's confirming nod made her knees buckle. She tried not to think about the two glass vials Aedion had handed the prince moments before. What they contained. She didn't even know when or where he'd acquired them.

Anything but that. Anything but—

Rowan's hand brushed hers. "I will save him," he murmured.

"I wouldn't ask this of you unless it was . . . Dorian is vital. Lose him, and we lose any support in Adarlan." And one of the few magic-wielders who could stand against Morath.

Rowan's nod was grim. "I serve you, Aelin. Do not apologize for putting me to use."

Because only Rowan, riding the winds with his magic, could reach Rifthold in time. Even now, he might be too late. Aelin swallowed hard, fighting the feeling that the world was being ripped from under her feet.

A glimmer of movement near the tree line caught her eye, and Aelin schooled her face into neutrality as she studied what had been left by little, spindly hands at the base of a gnarled oak. None of the others so much as blinked in its direction.

Rowan finished with his weapons, glancing between her and Aedion with a warrior's frankness. "Where do I meet you once I've secured the prince?"

Aedion said, "Run north. Stay clear of the Ferian Gap—"

Darrow appeared at the other end of the clearing, barking an order for Murtaugh to come to him.

"No," Aelin said. Both warriors turned.

She stared northward into the roiling rain and lightning.

She would not set foot in Orynth; she would not see her home.

Find me allies, Darrow had sneered.

She didn't dare glance at what the Little Folk had left in the shadow of that rain-lashed tree mere feet away.

Aelin said to Aedion, "If Ren is to be trusted, you tell him to get to the Bane, and to be ready to march and press from the North. If we are not to lead them, then they will have to work around Darrow's orders as best they can."

Aedion's brows rose. "What are you thinking?"

Aelin jerked her chin at Rowan. "Get a boat and travel south with Dorian. Land is too risky, but your winds on the seas can get you there in a few days. To Skull's Bay."

"Shit," Aedion breathed.

But Aelin pointed with a thumb over a shoulder to Ren and Murtaugh as she said to her cousin, "You told me that they were in communication with Captain Rolfe. Get one of them to write a letter of recommendation for us. Right now."

"I thought *you* knew Rolfe," Aedion said.

Aelin gave him a grim smile. "He and I parted on . . . bad terms, to say the least. But if Rolfe can be turned to our side . . ."

Aedion finished for her, "Then we'd have a small fleet that could unite North and South—brave the blockades."

And it was a good thing she'd taken all that gold from Arobynn to pay for it. "Skull's Bay might be the only safe place for us to hide—to contact the other kingdoms." She didn't dare tell them that Rolfe might have far more than a fleet of blockade runners to offer them, if she played it right. She said to Rowan, "Wait for us there. We'll strike out for the coast tonight, and sail to the Dead Islands. We'll be two weeks behind you."

Aedion clasped Rowan on the shoulder in farewell and headed for Ren and Murtaugh. A heartbeat later, the old man was hobbling into the inn, Darrow on his heels, demanding answers.

As long as Murtaugh wrote that letter to Rolfe, she didn't care.

Alone with Rowan, Aelin said, "Darrow expects me to take this order lying down. But if we can rally a host in the South, we can push Erawan right onto the blades of the Bane."

"It still might not convince Darrow and the others—"

"I'll deal with that later," she said, spraying water as she shook her head. "For now, I have no plans to lose this war because some old bastard has learned he likes playing king."

Rowan's grin was fierce, wicked. He leaned in, grazing his mouth against hers. "I have no plans to let him keep that throne, either, Aelin."

She only breathed, "Come back to me." The thought of what awaited him down in Rifthold struck her again. Gods—oh, gods. If anything happened to him . . .

He brushed a knuckle down her wet cheek, tracing her mouth with his thumb. She put a hand on his muscled chest, right where those two vials of poison were now hidden. For a heartbeat, she debated turning the deadly liquid within into steam.

But if Rowan was caught, if Dorian was caught . . . "I can't—I can't let you go—"

"You can," he said with little room for argument. The voice of her prince-commander. "And you will." Rowan again traced her mouth. "When you find me again, we will have that night. I don't care where, or who is around." He pressed a kiss to her neck and said onto her rain-slick skin, "You are my Fireheart."

She grabbed his face in both hands, drawing him down to kiss her.

Rowan wrapped his arms around her, crushing her against him, his hands roaming as if he were branding the feel of her into his palms. His kiss was savage—ice and fire twining together. Even the rain seemed to pause as they at last drew away, panting.

And through the rain and fire and ice, through the dark and lightning and thunder, a word flickered into her head, an answer and a challenge and a truth she immediately denied, ignored. Not for herself, but for him—for *him*—

Rowan shifted in a flash brighter than lightning.

When she finished blinking, a large hawk was flapping up through the trees and into the rain-tossed night. Rowan loosed a shriek as he banked right—toward the coast—the sound a farewell and a promise and a battle cry.

Aelin swallowed the tightness in her throat as Aedion approached and gripped her shoulder. "Lysandra wants Murtaugh to take Evangeline. For 'lady training.' The girl refuses to go. You might need to . . . help."

The girl was indeed clinging to her mistress, shoulders shaking with the force of her weeping. Murtaugh looked on helplessly, now back from the inn.

Aelin stalked through the mud, the ground squelching. How far away, how long ago, their merry morning now seemed.

She touched Evangeline's soaked hair, and the girl pulled back long enough for Aelin to say to her, "You are a member of my court. And as such, you answer to me. You are wise, and brave, and a joy—but we are headed into dark, horrible places where even I fear to tread."

Evangeline's lip wobbled. Something in Aelin's chest strained, but she let out a low whistle, and Fleetfoot, who had been cowering from the rain under their horses, slunk over.

"I need you to care for Fleetfoot," Aelin said, stroking the hound's damp head, her long ears. "Because in those dark, horrible places, a dog would be in peril. You are the only one I trust with her safety. Can you look after her for me?" She should have cherished them more—those happy, calm, boring moments on the road. Should have savored each second they were all together, all safe.

Above the girl, Lysandra's face was tight—her eyes shone with more than just the rain. But the lady nodded at Aelin, even as she surveyed Murtaugh once more with a predator's focus.

"Stay with Lord Murtaugh, learn about this court and its workings, and protect my friend," Aelin said to Evangeline, squatting to kiss Fleetfoot's sodden head. Once. Twice. The dog absently licked the rain off her face. "Can you do that?" Aelin repeated.

Evangeline stared at the dog, at her mistress. And nodded.

Aelin kissed the girl's cheek and whispered into her ear, "Work your magic on these miserable old men while you're at it." She pulled away to wink at the girl. "Win me back my kingdom, Evangeline."

But the girl was beyond smiles, and nodded again.

Aelin kissed Fleetfoot one last time and turned to her awaiting cousin as Lysandra knelt in the mud before the girl, brushing back her wet hair and speaking too low for her Fae ears to detect.

Aedion's mouth was a hard line as he dragged his eyes away from Lysandra and the girl and inclined his head toward Ren and Murtaugh. Aelin fell into step beside him, pausing a few feet from the Allsbrook lords.

"Your letter, Majesty," Murtaugh said, extending a wax-sealed tube.

Aelin took it, bowing her head in thanks.

Aedion said to Ren, "Unless you want to swap one tyrant for another, I suggest you get the Bane and any others ready to push from the North."

Murtaugh answered for his grandson, "Darrow means well—"

"Darrow," Aedion interrupted, "is now a man of limited days."

They all looked to her. But Aelin watched the inn flickering through the trees—and the old man once again storming for them, a force of nature in his own right. She said, "We don't touch Darrow."

"What?" Aedion snapped.

Aelin said, "I'd bet all my money that he's already taken the steps to ensure that if he meets an untimely death, we never set foot in Orynth again." Murtaugh gave her a grim, confirming nod. Aelin shrugged. "So we don't touch him. We play his game—play by rules and laws and oaths."

Several feet away, Lysandra and Evangeline still spoke softly, the girl now crying in her mistress's arms, Fleetfoot anxiously nuzzling her hip.

Aelin met Murtaugh's stare. "I do not know you, Lord, but you were loyal to my uncle—to my family these long years." She slid a dagger free of a hidden sheath along her thigh. They flinched as she sliced into her palm. Even Aedion started. Aelin clenched her bloodied palm into a fist, holding it in the air between them. "Because of that loyalty, you will understand what blood promises mean to *me* when I say if that girl comes to harm, physical or otherwise, I do not care what laws exist, what rules I will break." Lysandra had now turned to them, her shifter senses detecting blood. "If Evangeline is hurt, you will burn. *All* of you."

"Threatening your loyal court?" sneered a cold voice as Darrow halted a few feet away. Aelin ignored him. Murtaugh was wide-eyed—so was Ren.

Her blood seeped into the sacred earth. "Let this be your test."

Aedion swore. He understood. If the Lords of Terrasen could not keep one child safe in their kingdom, could not find it in themselves to save Evangeline, to look after someone who could do them no good, gain them no wealth or rank . . . they would deserve to perish.

Murtaugh bowed again. "Your will is mine, Majesty." He added quietly, "I lost my granddaughters. I will not lose another." With that, the old man walked toward where Darrow waited, pulling the lord aside.

Her heart strained, but Aelin said to Ren, that scar hidden by the shadows of his rain-drenched hood, "I wish we had time to speak. Time for me to explain."

"You're good at walking away from this kingdom. I don't see why now would be different."

Aedion let out a snarl, but Aelin cut him off. "Judge me all you like, Ren Allsbrook. But do not fail this kingdom."

She saw the unspoken retort flash in Ren's eyes. *Like you did for ten years.*

The blow struck low and deep, but she turned away. As she did, she noted how Ren's eyes fell on the little girl—on the brutal scars across Evangeline's face. Near-twins to the ones on his own. Something in his gaze softened, just a bit.

But Darrow was now thundering toward Aelin, pushing past Murtaugh, his face white with anger. "You—" he started.

Aelin held up a hand, flame leaping at her fingertips, rain turning to steam above it. Blood snaked down her wrist from the deep cut, sibling to the other on her right hand, bright as Goldryn's ruby, peeking over her shoulder. "I'll make one more promise," she said, folding her bloodied hand into a fist as she lowered it before them. Darrow tensed.

Her blood dripped onto the sacred soil of Terrasen, and her smile turned lethal. Even Aedion held his breath beside her.

Aelin said, "I promise you that no matter how far I go, no matter the cost, when you call for my aid, I will come. I promise you on my blood, on my family's name, that I will not turn my back on Terrasen as you have turned your back on me. I promise you, Darrow, that when the day comes and you crawl for my help, I will put my kingdom before my pride and not kill you for this. I think the true punishment will be seeing me on the throne for the rest of your miserable life."

His face had gone from white to purple.

She just turned away.

"Where do you think you're going?" Darrow demanded. So Murtaugh had not filled him in on her plan to go to the Dead Islands. Interesting.

She looked over her shoulder. "To call in old debts and promises. To raise an army of assassins and thieves and exiles and commoners. To finish what was started long, long ago."

Silence was his answer.

So Aelin and Aedion strode to where Lysandra now monitored them, solemn-faced in the rain, Evangeline hugging herself as Fleetfoot leaned against the silently weeping girl.

Aelin said to the shape-shifter and the general, locking out the sorrow from her heart, locking out the pain and worry from her mind, "We travel now."

And when they dispersed to gather the horses, Aedion brushing a kiss to Evangeline's soaked head before Murtaugh and Ren led her back to the inn with considerable gentleness, Darrow striding ahead with no farewell whatsoever, when Aelin was alone, she finally approached that shadowed, gnarled tree.

The Little Folk had known about the wyvern attack this morning.

So she'd supposed that this little effigy, already falling apart under the torrent of rain, was another message of sorts. One just for her.

Brannon's temple on the coast had been rendered carefully—a clever little contraption of twigs and rocks to form the pillars and altar . . . And on the sacred rock in its center, they'd created a white stag from raw sheep's wool, his mighty antlers no more than curling thorns.

An order—where to go, what she needed to obtain. She was willing to listen, play along. Even if it had meant telling the others only half the truth.

Aelin broke apart the temple reconstruction but left the stag in her palm, the wool deflating in the rain.

Horses nickered as Aedion and Lysandra hauled them closer, but Aelin felt him a heartbeat before he emerged between the distant, night-veiled trees. Too far in the wood to be anything but a ghost, a figment of an ancient god's dream.

Barely breathing, she watched him for as long as she dared, and when Aelin mounted her horse, she wondered if her companions could tell that it was not rain gleaming on her face as she tugged on her black hood.

Wondered if they, too, had spied the Lord of the North standing watch deep in the forest, the white stag's immortal glow muted in the rain, come to bid Aelin Galathynius farewell.

Chapter 6

Dorian Havilliard, King of Adarlan, hated the silence.

It had become his companion, walking beside him through the near-empty halls of his stone castle, crouching in the corner of his cluttered tower room at night, sitting across the table at each meal.

He had always known he would one day be king.

He had not expected to inherit a shattered throne and vacant stronghold.

His mother and younger brother were still ensconced in their mountain residence in Ararat. He had not sent for them. He'd given the order to remain, actually.

If only because it would mean the return of his mother's preening court, and he'd gladly take the silence over their tittering. If only because it would mean looking into his mother's face, his brother's face, and lying about who had destroyed the glass castle, who had slaughtered most of their courtiers, and who had ended his father.

Lying about *what* his father had been—the demon that had dwelled inside him.

A demon that had reproduced with his mother—not once, but twice.

Standing on the small stone balcony atop his private tower, Dorian gazed at the glittering sprawl of Rifthold beneath the setting sun, at the sparkling ribbon of the Avery as it wended inland from the sea, curving around the city like the coils of a snake, and then flowing straight through the continent's heart.

He lifted his hands before the view, his palms callused from the exercises and swordplay he'd made himself start learning once more. His favorite guards—Chaol's men—were all dead.

Tortured and killed.

His memories of his time beneath the Wyrdstone collar were dim and blurred. But in his nightmares, he sometimes stood in a dungeon far beneath this castle, blood that was not his own coating his hands, screams that were not his own ringing in his ears, begging him for mercy.

Not him, he told himself. The Valg prince had done it. His *father* had done it.

He'd still had difficulty meeting the stare of the new Captain of the Guard, a friend of Nesryn Faliq, as he'd asked the man to show him how to fight, help him become stronger, faster.

Never again. Never again would he be weak and useless and frightened.

Dorian cast his gaze southward, as if he could see all the way to Antica. He wondered if Chaol and Nesryn had gotten there—wondered if his friend was already at the Torre Cesme, having his broken body healed by its gifted masters.

The demon inside his father had done that, too—snapped Chaol's spine.

The man fighting inside his father had kept the blow from being fatal.

Dorian had possessed no such control, no such strength, when he watched the demon use his own body—when the demon had tortured and killed and taken what it wanted. Maybe his father had been the stronger man in the end. The better man.

Not that he'd ever had a chance to know him as a man. As a human.

Dorian flexed his fingers, frost sparking in his palm. Raw magic—yet there was no one here to teach him. No one he dared ask.

He leaned against the stone wall beside the balcony door.

He lifted his hand toward the pale band marking his throat. Even with the hours he'd spent outside training, the skin where the collar had once laid had not darkened to a golden tan. Maybe it always would remain pale.

Maybe his dreams would always be haunted by that demon prince's hissing voice. Maybe he would always wake up with his sweat feeling like Sorscha's blood on him, like Aelin's blood as he stabbed her.

Aelin. Not a word from her—or from anyone regarding the queen's return to her kingdom. He tried not to worry, to contemplate why there was such silence.

Such silence, when Nesryn and Chaol's scouts now brought him news that Morath was stirring.

Dorian glanced inside, toward the pile of papers on his cluttered desk, and winced. He still had a disgusting amount of paperwork to do before sleep: letters to sign, plans to read—

Thunder murmured across the city.

Perhaps a sign that he should get to work, unless he wanted to be up until the black hours of the morning once again. Dorian turned inside, sighing sharply through his nose, and thunder boomed again.

Too soon, and the sound too short-lived.

Dorian scanned the horizon. No clouds—nothing but the red-and-pink-and-gold sky.

But the city lounging at the foot of the castle's hill seemed to pause.

Even the muddy Avery seemed to halt its slithering as the *boom* sounded again.

He had heard that sound before.

His magic roiled in his veins, and he wondered what it sensed as ice coated his balcony against his will, so swift and cold the stones groaned.

He tried to reel it back in—as if it were a ball of yarn that had tumbled from his hands—but it ignored him, spreading thicker, faster over the stones. Along the arch of the doorway behind him, down the curving face of the tower—

A horn sounded in the west. A high, bleating note.

It was cut off before it finished.

With the angle of the balcony, he couldn't see its source. He rushed into his room, leaving his magic to the stones, and hurtled for the open western window. He was halfway through the pillars of books and papers when he spied the horizon. When his city began screaming.

Spreading into the distance, blotting out the sunset like a storm of bats, flew a legion of wyverns.

Each bore armed witches, roaring their battle cries to the color-stained sky.

Manon and her Thirteen had been flying without stop, without sleep. They'd left the two escort covens behind yesterday, their wyverns too exhausted to keep up. Especially when the Thirteen had been going on all those extra runs and patrols for months—and had quietly, solidly built up their stamina.

They flew high to keep hidden, and through gaps in the clouds, the continent had flashed below in varying shades of summer green and butter yellow and sparkling sapphire. Today had been clear enough that no clouds concealed them as they hurtled for Rifthold, the sun beginning its final descent toward the west.

Toward her lost homeland.

With the height and distance, Manon fully beheld the carnage as the horizon at last revealed the sprawl of the capital city.

The attack had begun without her. Iskra's legion was still falling upon it, still spearing for the palace and the glass wall that crested over the city at its eastern edge.

She nudged Abraxos with her knees, a silent command to go faster.

He did—but barely. He was drained. They all were.

Iskra wanted the victory for herself. Manon had no doubt the Yellowlegs heir had received orders to yield . . . but only once Manon arrived. Bitch. *Bitch* to get here first, not to wait—

Closer and closer they swept for the city.

The screams reached them soon enough. Her red cape became a millstone.

Manon aimed Abraxos for the stone castle atop the hill, barely peeking above that shining glass wall—the wall she had been ordered to bring down—and hoped she had not been too late in one regard.

And that she knew what the hell she was doing.

CHAPTER 7

Dorian had sounded the alarm, but the guards already knew. And when he'd gone to rush down the tower stairs, they blocked his path, telling him to stay in his tower. He tried to go again, to help—but they begged him to stay. *Begged* him, so that they would not lose him.

It was the desperation, how *young* their voices were, that kept him in the tower. But not useless.

Dorian stood atop his balcony, a hand raised before him.

From the distance, he could do nothing as the wyverns unleashed hell beyond the glass wall. They shredded through buildings, ripping apart roofs with their talons, snatching up people—*his* people—from the street.

They covered the skies like a blanket of fangs and claws, and though arrows from the city guards hit true, the wyverns did not pause.

Dorian rallied his magic, willing it to obey, summoning ice and wind to his palm, letting it build.

He should have trained, should have asked Aelin to teach him *something* when she was here.

The wyverns sailed closer to the castle and the glass wall still around it, as if they'd wanted to show him precisely how powerless he was before they came for him.

Let them come. Let them get close enough for his magic.

He might not have Aelin's long range, might not be able to encircle the city with his power, but if they got close enough . . .

He would not be weak or cowering again.

The first of the wyverns crested the glass wall. Huge—so much bigger than the white-haired witch and her scarred mount. Six of them flapped for his castle, for his tower. For its king.

He'd give them a king.

He let them draw nearer, clenching his fingers into a fist, burrowing down, down, down into his magic. Many witches lingered at the glass wall, slamming their wyverns' tails into it, cracking that opaque glass bit by bit. Like the six who sailed for the castle were all it would take to sack it.

He could see their figures now—see their iron-studded leather, the setting sun glinting on the massive breastplates of the wyverns as they raced over the still-healing castle grounds.

And when Dorian could see their iron teeth as they grinned at him, when the shouts of the guards so valiantly firing arrows from the castle doors and windows became a din in his ears, he extended his hand toward the witches.

Ice and wind tore into them, shredding through beast and rider.

The guards shouted in alarm—then fell into a stunned silence.

Dorian gasped for breath, gasped to remember his name and what he was as the magic drained out of him. He'd killed while enslaved, but never of his own free will.

And as the dead meat rained down, thudding on the castle grounds, as their blood misted the air . . . *More*, his magic moaned, spiraling down and up at the same time, dragging him again into its icy eddies.

Beyond the cracking glass wall, his city was bleeding. Screaming in terror.

Four more wyverns crossed the now-crumbling glass wall, banking as the riders beheld their shredded sisters. Cries shattered from their immortal throats, the tendrils of the yellow bands across their brows snapping in the wind. They shot their wyverns into the sky, as if they'd rise and rise and then plunge down directly atop him.

A smile danced on Dorian's lips as he unleashed his magic again, a two-pronged whip snapping for the ascending wyverns.

More blood and chunks of wyvern and witch fell to the ground, all coated with ice so thick they shattered upon the courtyard flagstones.

Dorian tunneled deeper. Maybe if he could get into the city, he could cast a wider net—

That was when the other attack hit. Not from ahead or above or below.

But from behind.

His tower rocked to the side, and Dorian was flung forward, slamming into the stone balcony, narrowly avoiding flipping over the edge.

Stone cracked and wood splintered, and he was spared from a crushing bit of rock only by the magic he'd flung around himself as he covered his head.

He whirled toward the interior of his bedroom. A giant, gaping hole had been ripped into the side and roof. And perched on the broken stone, a solidly built witch now smiled at him with flesh-shredding iron teeth, a faded band of yellow leather around her brow.

He rallied his magic, but it sputtered to a flicker.

Too soon, too fast, he realized. Too uncontrolled. Not enough time to draw up the full depths of his power. The wyvern's head snaked into the tower.

Behind him, six other wyverns crested the wall, soaring for his exposed back. And the wall itself . . . Aelin's wall . . . Beneath those frantic, furious claws and tails . . . it collapsed entirely.

Dorian eyed the door to the tower stairs, where the guards should have already been charging through. Only silence waited.

So close—but getting to it would require passing in front of the wyvern's maw. Exactly why the witch was smiling.

One chance—he'd have one chance to do this.

Dorian clenched his fingers, not granting the witch time to study him further.

He flung out a hand, ice shattering from his palm and into the eyes of the wyvern. It roared, rearing back, and he ran.

Something sharp nicked his ear and embedded in the wall before him. A dagger.

He kept sprinting for the door—

The tail whipped through his vision a heartbeat before it slammed into his side.

His magic was a film around him, shielding his bones, his skull, as he was hurled against the stone wall. Hard enough that the stones cracked. Hard enough that most humans would have been dead.

Stars and darkness danced in his vision. The door was so close.

Dorian tried to rise, but his limbs wouldn't obey.

Stunned; stunned by—

Wet warmth leaked just below his ribs. Blood. Not a deep cut, but enough to hurt, courtesy of one of the spines on that tail. Spines coated in a greenish sheen.

Venom. Some sort of venom that weakened and paralyzed before it killed—

He wouldn't be taken again, not to Morath, not to the duke and his collars—

His magic thrashed against the venom's paralyzing, lethal kiss.

Healing magic. But slow, weakened by his careless expenditure moments before.

Dorian tried to crawl for the door, panting through his gritted teeth.

The witch barked a command to her wyvern, and Dorian rallied enough to crane his head. To see her draw her swords and begin to dismount.

No, no, *no*—

The witch didn't make it to the ground.

One heartbeat she was perched in her saddle, swinging a leg over.

The next, her head was gone, her blood spraying her wyvern as it roared and turned—

And was slammed off the tower by another, smaller wyvern. Scarred and vicious, with glimmering wings.

Dorian didn't wait to see what happened, didn't wonder.

He crawled for the door, his magic devouring the venom that should have killed him, a raging torrent of light fighting with all of its considerable force against that greenish darkness.

Cleaved skin, muscle, and bone itched as they slowly knit together—and that spark flickered and guttered in his veins.

Dorian was reaching for the door handle when the small wyvern landed in the ruined hole of his tower, its enormous fangs dripping blood onto the scattered paperwork he'd been grousing over mere minutes ago. Its armored, lithe rider nimbly leaped off, the arrows in the quiver across her back clacking against the hilt of the mighty sword now strapped alongside it.

She hauled away the helmet crowned with slender, lancelike blades.

He knew her face before he remembered her name.

Knew the white hair, like moonlight on water, that spilled over her dark, scalelike armor; knew the burnt-gold eyes.

Knew that impossibly beautiful face, full of cold bloodlust and wicked cunning.

"Get up," Manon Blackbeak snarled.

Shit.

The word was a steady chant in Manon's head as she stalked across the ruins of the king's tower, armor thundering against the fallen stones, fluttering paper, and scattered books.

Shit, shit, shit.

Iskra was nowhere to be found—not by the castle, at least. But her coven was.

And when Manon had spied that Yellowlegs sentinel perched inside the tower, readying to claim this kill for herself . . . a century of training and instinct had barreled into Manon.

All it had taken was one swipe of Wind-Cleaver as Abraxos flew by, and Iskra's sentinel was dead.

Shit, shit, shit.

Then Abraxos attacked the remaining mount, a dull-eyed bull who hadn't even the chance to roar before Abraxos's teeth were clamped around his broad throat and blood and flesh were flying as they tumbled through the air.

She didn't have a heartbeat to spare to marvel that Abraxos had not balked at the fight, that he had not yielded. Her warrior-hearted wyvern. She'd give him an extra ration of meat.

The young king's dark, bloody jacket was coated in dust and dirt. But his sapphire eyes were clear, if not wide, as she snarled again over the screaming city, "Get up."

He reached a hand toward the iron door handle. Not to call for help or flee, she realized, now a foot from him, but to raise himself.

Manon studied his long legs, more muscled than the last time she'd seen him. Then she noted the wound peeking through the side of his torn jacket. Not deep and not gushing, but—

Shit, shit, shit.

The venom of the wyvern's tail was deadly at worst, paralyzing at best. Paralyzing with just a scratch. He should be dead. Or dying.

"What do you want?" he rasped, eyes darting between her and Abraxos, who was busy monitoring the skies for any other attackers, his wings rustling with impatience.

The king was buying himself time—while his wound healed.

Magic. Only the strongest magic could have kept him from death. Manon snapped, "Quiet," and hauled him to his feet.

He didn't flinch at her touch, or at the iron nails that snagged and ripped through his jacket. He was heavier than she'd estimated—as if he'd packed on more muscle beneath those clothes, too. But with her immortal strength, heaving him to a standing position required little energy.

She'd forgotten how much taller he was. Face-to-face, Dorian panted as he stared down at her and breathed, "Hello, witchling."

Some ancient, predatory part of her awoke at the half smile. It sat up, cocking its ears toward him. Not a whiff of fear. Interesting.

Manon purred back, "Hello, princeling."

Abraxos gave a warning growl, and Manon whipped her head to discover another wyvern sailing hard and fast for them.

"*Go*," she said, letting him support himself as she hauled open the tower door. The screams of the men levels below rose to meet them. Dorian sagged against the wall, as if focusing all his attention on staying upright. "Is there another exit? Another way out?"

The king assessed her with a frankness that had her snarling.

Behind them, as if the Mother had stretched out her hand, a mighty wind buffeted the wyvern and rider away from the tower, sending them tumbling into the city. Even Abraxos roared, clinging to the tower stones so hard the rock cracked beneath his claws.

"There are passages," the king said. "But you—"

"Then find them. Get out."

He didn't move from his spot against the wall. "Why."

The pale line still sliced across his throat, so stark against the golden tan of his skin. But she did not take questioning from mortals. Not even kings. Not anymore.

So she ignored his question and said, "Perrington is not as he seems. He is a demon in a mortal body, and has shed his former skin to don a new one. A golden-haired man. He breeds evil in Morath that he plans to unleash any day now. This is a taste." She flicked an iron-tipped hand to the destruction around them. "A way to break your spirits and win favor from other kingdoms by casting you as the enemy. Rally your forces before he is given a chance to grow his numbers to an unconquerable size. He means to take not just this continent, but the whole of Erilea."

"Why would his crowned rider tell me this?"

"My reasons are none of your concern. Flee." Again, that mighty wind blasted the castle, shoving back any approaching forces, setting the stones groaning. A wind that smelled of pine and snow—a familiar, strange scent. Ancient and clever and cruel.

"You killed that witch." Indeed, the sentinel's blood freckled the stones. It coated Wind-Cleaver and her discarded helmet. *Witch Killer.*

Manon shoved the thought away, along with his implied question. "You owe me a life debt, King of Adarlan. Prepare yourself for the day I come to claim it."

His sensuous mouth tightened. "Fight with us. Now—fight with us *now* against him."

Through the doorway, screams and battle cries rent the air. Witches had managed to land somewhere—had infiltrated the castle. It'd be a matter of moments before they were found. And if the king was not gone . . . She yanked him off the wall and shoved him into the stairwell.

His legs buckled, and he braced a tan hand against the ancient stone wall as he shot her a glare over a broad shoulder. A *glare*.

"Do you not know death when you see it?" she hissed, low and vicious.

"I have seen death, and worse," he said, those sapphire eyes frozen as he surveyed her from head to armored boot-tip and back again. "The death you'd offer is kind compared to that."

It struck something in her, but the king was already limping down the stairs, a hand braced on the wall. Moving so damn slowly while that poison worked its way out of him, his magic surely battling with everything it had to keep him on this side of life.

The door at the base of the tower shattered.

Dorian halted at the four Yellowlegs sentinels who rushed in, snarling up the hollow center of the tower. The witches paused, blinking at their Wing Leader.

Wind-Cleaver twitched in her hand. Kill him—kill him now, before they could spread the word that she'd been spotted with him . . . *Shit, shit, shit.*

Manon didn't have to decide. In a whirlwind of steel, the Yellowlegs died before they could turn toward the warrior who exploded through the doorway.

Silver hair, tattooed face and neck, and slightly pointed ears. The source of that wind.

Dorian swore, staggering down a step, but the Fae warrior's eyes were on her. Only lethal rage flickered there.

The air in Manon's throat choked away into nothing.

A strangled sound came out of her, and she stumbled back, clawing at her throat as if she could carve an airway. But the male's magic held firm.

He'd kill her for what she'd tried to do to his queen. For the arrow Asterin had shot, meaning to strike the queen's heart. An arrow he had jumped in front of.

Manon crashed to her knees. The king was instantly at her side, studying her for a heartbeat before he roared down the stairs, "*NO!*"

That was all it took. Air flooded her mouth, her lungs, and Manon gasped, back arching as she drank it in.

Her kind had no magical shields against attacks like that. Only when most desperate, most enraged, could a witch summon the core of magic in her—with devastating consequences. Even the most bloodthirsty and soulless of them only whispered of that act: the Yielding.

Dorian's face swam in her watery vision. Manon still gasped for that fresh, lifesaving air as he said, "Find me when you change your mind, Blackbeak."

Then the king was gone.

CHAPTER 8

Rowan Whitethorn had flown without food or water or rest for two days.

He'd still reached Rifthold too late.

The capital was in chaos under the claws of the witches and their wyverns. He'd seen enough cities fall over the centuries to know that this one was done for.

Even if the people rallied, it would only be to meet their deaths head-first. The witches had already brought down Aelin's glass wall. Another calculated move by Erawan.

It had been an effort to leave the innocent to fight on their own, to race hard and fast for the stone castle and the king's tower. He had one order, given to him by his queen.

He'd still come too late—but not without a glimmer of hope.

Dorian Havilliard stumbled as they hurried down the castle hallway, Rowan's keen ears and sense of smell keeping them from areas where the fighting raged. If the secret tunnels were watched, if they could not reach the sewers . . . Rowan calculated plan after plan. None ended well.

"This way," the king panted. It was the first thing Dorian had said since rushing down the stairs. They were in a residential part of the palace Rowan had only seen from his own scouting outside—in hawk form. The queen's quarters. "There's a secret exit from my mother's bedroom."

The pale white doors to the queen's suite were locked.

Rowan blasted through them with half a thought, wood splintering and impaling the lavish furniture, the art on the walls. Baubles and valuables shattered. "Sorry," Rowan said to the king—not sounding like it at all.

His magic flickered, a distant flutter to let him know it was draining. Two days of riding the winds at breakneck speed, then fighting off those wyverns outside, had taken its toll.

Dorian surveyed the casual damage. "Someone would have done it anyway." No feeling, no sorrow behind it. He hurried through the room, limping a bit. If the king had possessed a fraction less magic, he might have succumbed to the wyvern's venomous tail.

Dorian reached a large, gilded portrait of a beautiful auburn-haired young woman with a sapphire-eyed babe in her arms.

The king looked at it for a heartbeat longer than necessary, enough to tell Rowan everything. But Dorian hauled the painting toward him. It pulled away to reveal a small trapdoor.

Rowan saw to it that the king went inside first, candle in hand, before using his magic to float the painting back into its resting place, then shutting the door behind them.

The hall was cramped, the stones dusty. But the wind ahead whispered of open spaces, of dampness and mold. Rowan sent a tendril of magic to probe the stairs they now strode down and the many halls ahead. No sign of the cave-in from when they'd destroyed the clock tower.

No signs of enemies lying in wait, or the corrupt reek of the Valg and their beasts. A small mercy.

His Fae ears picked up the muffled screams and shouts of the dying above them.

"I should stay," Dorian said softly.

A gift of the king's magic, then—the enhanced hearing. Raw magic that could grant him any gifts: ice, flame, healing, heightened senses and strength. Perhaps shape-shifting, if he tried.

"You are more useful to your people alive," Rowan said, his voice rough against the stones. Exhaustion nagged at him, but he shoved it aside. He'd rest when they were safe.

The king didn't respond.

Rowan said, "I have seen many cities fall. I have seen entire kingdoms fall. And the destruction I saw as I flew in was thorough enough that even with your considerable gifts, there is nothing you could have done." He wasn't entirely sure what they'd do if that destruction were brought to Orynth's doorstep. Or why Erawan was waiting to do it. He'd think about that later.

"I should die with them," was the king's answer.

They reached the bottom of the stairs, the passage now widening into breathable chambers. Rowan again snaked his magic through the many tunnels and stairs. The one to the right suggested a sewer entrance lay at its bottom. Good.

"I was sent here to keep you from doing just that," Rowan said at last.

The king glanced over his shoulder at him, wincing a bit as the motion stretched his still-healing skin. Where Rowan suspected a gaping wound had been minutes before, now only an angry red scar peeked through the side of his torn jacket. Dorian said, "You were going to kill her."

He knew whom the king meant. "Why did you tell me not to?"

So the king told him of the encounter as they descended deeper into the castle's bowels. "I wouldn't trust her," Rowan said after Dorian had finished, "but perhaps the gods will throw us a bone. Perhaps the Blackbeak heir will join our cause."

If her crimes weren't discovered first. But even if they only had thirteen witches and their wyverns, if that coven was the most skilled of all the Ironteeth . . . it could mean the difference between Orynth falling or standing against Erawan.

They reached the castle sewers. Even the rats were fleeing through the small stream entrance, as if the bellowing of the wyverns were a death knell.

They passed an archway sealed off by collapsed stones—no doubt from the hellfire eruption this summer.

Aelin's passageway, Rowan realized with a tug deep in his chest. And a few steps ahead, an old pool of dried blood stained the stones along the water's edge. A human reek lingered around it, tainted and foul.

"She gutted Archer Finn right there," Dorian said, following his stare.

Rowan didn't let himself think about it, or that these fools had unwittingly given an assassin a room that connected to their queen's chambers.

There was a boat moored to a stone post, its hull almost rotted through, but solid enough. And the grate to the little river snaking past the castle remained open.

Rowan again speared his magic into the world, tasting the air beyond the sewers. No wings cleaved it, no blood scented its path. A quiet, eastern part of the castle. If the witches had been smart, they'd have sentries monitoring every inch of it.

But from the screaming and pleading going on above, Rowan knew the witches were too lost in their bloodlust to think straight. At least for a few minutes.

Rowan jerked his chin to the boat. "Get in."

Dorian frowned at the mold and rot. "We'll be lucky if it doesn't collapse around us."

"You," Rowan corrected. "Around you. Not me. Get in."

Dorian heard his tone and wisely got in. "What are you—"

Rowan yanked off his cloak and threw it over the king. "Lie down, and put that over you."

Face a bit pale, Dorian obeyed. Rowan snapped the ropes with a flash of his knives.

He shifted, wings flapping loudly enough to inform Dorian what had happened. Rowan's magic groaned and strained while it pushed what looked like an empty, meandering vessel out of the sewers, as if someone had accidentally loosed it.

Flying through the sewer mouth, he shielded the boat with a wall of hard air—containing the king's scent and keeping any stray arrows from piercing it.

Rowan looked back only once as he flew down the little river, high above the boat.

Only once, at the city that had forged and broken and sheltered his queen.

Her glass wall was no more than chunks and shards gleaming in the streets and the grass.

These past weeks of travel had been torture—the need to claim her, taste her, driving him out of his wits. And given what Darrow had said . . . perhaps, despite his promise when he'd left, it had been a good thing that they had not taken that final step.

It had been in the back of his mind long before Darrow and his horseshit decrees: he was a prince, but in name only.

He had no army, no money. The substantial funds he possessed were in Doranelle—and Maeve would never allow him to claim them. They'd likely already been distributed amongst his meddlesome cousins, along with his lands and residences. It wouldn't matter if some of them—the cousins he'd been raised with—might refuse to accept out of typical Whitethorn loyalty and stubbornness. All Rowan now had to offer his queen were the strength of his sword, the depth of his magic, and the loyalty of his heart.

Such things did not win wars.

He'd scented the despair on her, though her face had hidden it, when Darrow had spoken. And he knew her fiery soul: she would do it. Consider marriage to a foreign prince or lord. Even if this thing between them . . . even if he knew it was not mere lust, or even just love.

This thing between them, the force of it, could devour the world.

And if they picked it, picked *them*, it might very well cause the end of it.

It was why he had not uttered the words he'd meant to tell her for some time, even when every instinct was roaring for him to do it as they parted. And maybe having Aelin only to lose her was his punishment for letting his mate die; his punishment for finally letting go of that grief and loathing.

The lap of waves was barely audible over the roar of wyverns and the innocents screaming for help that would never come. He shut out the ache in his chest, the urge to turn around.

This was war. These lands would endure far worse in the coming days and months. His queen, no matter how he tried to shield her, would endure far worse.

By the time the boat drifted down the little river snaking toward the Avery delta, a white-tailed hawk soaring high above it, the walls of the stone castle were bathed in blood.

CHAPTER 9

Elide Lochan knew she was being hunted.

For three days now, she'd tried to lose whatever tracked her through the endless sprawl of Oakwald. And in the process, she herself had become lost.

Three days hardly sleeping, barely stopping long enough to scavenge for food and water.

She'd turned south once—to backtrack and shake it off her trail. She'd wound up heading a day in that direction. Then west, toward the mountains. Then south, possibly east; she couldn't tell. She'd been running then, Oakwald so dense that she could hardly track the sun. And without a clear view of the stars, not daring to stop and find an easy tree to climb, she couldn't find the Lord of the North—her beacon home.

By noon on the third day, she was close to weeping. From exhaustion, from rage, from bone-deep fear. Whatever took its time hunting her would surely take its time killing her.

Her knife trembled in her hand as she paused in a clearing, a swift, nimble stream dancing through it. Her leg ached—her ruined, useless leg. She'd offer the dark god her soul for a few hours of peace and safety.

Elide dropped the knife into the grass beside her, falling to her knees before the stream and drinking swift and deep. Water filled the gaps in her belly left by berries and roots. She refilled her canteen, hands shaking uncontrollably.

Shaking so hard she dropped the metal cap into the stream.

She swore, plunging into the cold water up to her elbows as she fumbled for the cap, patting the rocks and slick tendrils of river weed, begging for one solitary *break*—

Her fingers closed on the cap as the first howl sounded through the forest.

Elide and the forest went still.

She had heard dogs baying, had listened to the unearthly choruses of wolves when she'd been hauled from Perranth down to Morath.

This was neither. This was . . .

There had been nights in Morath when she'd been yanked from sleep because of howls like that. Howls she'd believed were imagined when they didn't sound again. No one ever mentioned them.

But there was the sound. *That* sound.

We shall create wonders that will make the world tremble.

Oh, gods. Elide blindly screwed the cap onto the canteen. Whatever it might be, it was closing in fast. Maybe a tree—high up a tree—might save her. Hide her. Maybe.

Elide twisted to shove her canteen into her bag.

But a warrior was crouched across the stream, a long, wicked knife balanced on his knee.

His black eyes devoured her, his face harsh beneath equally dark, shoulder-length hair as he said in a voice like granite, "Unless you want to be lunch, girl, I suggest you come with me."

A small, ancient voice whispered in her ear that she'd at last found her relentless hunter.

And they'd now both become someone else's prey.

Lorcan Salvaterre listened to the rising snarls in the ancient wood and knew they were likely about to die.

Well, the girl was about to die. Either at the claws of whatever pursued them or at the end of Lorcan's blade. He hadn't yet decided.

Human—the cinnamon-and-elderberries scent of her was utterly human—and yet that *other* smell remained, that tinge of darkness fluttering about her like a hummingbird's wings.

He might have suspected she'd summoned the beasts were it not for the tang of fear staining the air. And for the fact that he'd been tracking her for three days now, letting her lose herself in the tangled labyrinth of Oakwald, and had found little to indicate she was under Valg thrall.

Lorcan rose to his feet, and her dark eyes widened as she took in his towering height. She remained kneeling by the stream, a dirty hand reaching for the dagger she'd foolishly discarded in the grass. She wasn't stupid or desperate enough to lift it against him. "Who are you?"

Her hoarse voice was low—not the sweet, high thing he'd expected from her delicate, fully curved frame. Low and cold and steady.

"If you want to die," Lorcan said, "then go ahead: keep asking questions." He turned away—northward.

And that was when the second set of snarling began. From the other direction.

Two packs, closing in. Grass and cloth rustled, and when he looked, the girl was on her feet, dagger angled, face sickly pale as she realized what was happening: they were being herded.

"East or west," Lorcan said. In the five centuries he'd been slaughtering his way across the world, he'd never heard snarls like that from any manner of beast. He thumbed free his hatchet from where it was strapped at his side.

"East," the girl breathed, eyes darting to either direction. "I—I was told to stay out of the mountains. Wyverns—large, winged beasts—patrol them."

"I know what a wyvern is," he said.

Some temper snapped in her dark eyes at his tone, but the fear washed it away. She began backing toward the direction she'd chosen. One of the creatures loosed a keening cry. Not a canine sound. No, this was high-pitched, screeching—like a bat. But deeper. Hungrier. "Run," he said.

She did.

Lorcan had to give the girl credit: despite the still-injured leg, despite the exhaustion that had made her sloppy these past few days, she bolted like a doe through the trees, her terror likely leeching away any pain. Lorcan leaped the wide stream in an easy movement, closing the distance between them in mere heartbeats. Slow; these humans were so damned slow. Her breathing was already ragged as she hauled herself up a hill, making enough noise to alert their trackers.

Crashing from the brush behind them—from the south. Two or three from the sound of it. Big, from the snapping branches and thudding of footfalls.

The girl hit the top of the hill, stumbling. She stayed upright, and Lorcan eyed the leg again.

There was no point in having tracked her for so long if she died now. For a heartbeat, he contemplated the weight in his jacket—the Wyrdkey tucked away. His magic was strong, the strongest of any demi-Fae male in any kingdom, any realm. But if he used the key—

If he used the key, then he'd deserve the damnation it'd call down upon him.

So Lorcan flung out a net of his power behind them, an invisible barrier wafting black tendrils of wind. The girl stiffened, whipping her head to him as the power rippled away in a wave. Her skin blanched further, but she continued, half falling, half running down the hill.

The impact of four massive bodies against his magic struck a moment later.

The tang of her blood as she sliced herself open on rock and root shoved itself up his nose. She was nowhere near fast enough.

Lorcan opened his mouth to order her to hurry when the invisible wall snapped.

Not snapped, but *cracked*, as if those beasts had cleaved it.

Impossible. No one could get through those shields. Not even Rowan-rutting-Whitethorn.

But sure enough, the magic had been sundered.

The girl hit the gully at the bottom of the hill, near-sobbing at the flat expanse of forest sprawling ahead. She sprinted, dark braid thrashing, pack bouncing against her slim back. Lorcan moved after her, eyeing the trees to either side as the snarling and rustling began again.

They were being herded, but toward what? And if these things had ripped his magic apart . . .

It had been a long, long while since he'd had a new enemy to study, to break.

"Keep going," he growled, and the girl didn't so much as look over her shoulder as Lorcan slammed to a stop between two towering oaks. He'd been spiraling down into his magic for days, planning to use it on the human-but-not girl when he grew bored of stalking her. Now his body was rife with it, the power aching to get out.

Lorcan flipped his axe in his hand—once, twice, the metal singing through the dense forest. A chill wind edged in black mist danced between the fingers of his other hand.

Not wind like Whitethorn's, and not light and flame like Whitethorn's bitch-queen. Not even raw magic like the new King of Adarlan.

No, Lorcan's magic was that of will—of death and thought and destruction. There was no name for it.

Not even his queen had known what it was, where it had come from. A gift from the dark god, from Hellas, Maeve had mused—a dark gift, for her dark warrior. And left it at that.

A wild smile danced on Lorcan's lips as he let his magic rise to the surface, let its black roar fill his veins.

He had crumbled cities with this power.

He did not think these beasts, however fell, would fare much better.

They slowed as they closed in, sensing a predator was waiting—sizing him up.

For the first time in a damn long while, Lorcan had no words for what he saw.

Maybe he should have killed the girl. Death at his hand would be a mercy compared to what snarled before him, crouching low on massive, flesh-shredding claws. Not a Wyrdhound. No, these things were far worse.

Their skin was a mottled blue, so dark as to be almost black. Each long, lightly muscled limb had been ruthlessly crafted and honed. For the long claws at the end of their hands—five-fingered hands—now curled as if in anticipation of a strike.

But it was not their bodies that stunned him.

It was the way the creatures halted, smiling beneath their smashed in, bat-like noses to reveal double rows of needlelike teeth, and then stood on their hind legs.

Stood to their full height, as a crawling man might rise. They dwarfed him by a foot at least.

And the physical attributes that seemed unnervingly familiar were confirmed when the one closest to him opened its hideous mouth and said, "We have not tasted your kind's flesh yet."

Lorcan's axe twitched up. "I can't say I've had the pleasure, either."

There were very, very few beasts who could speak in the tongues of mortal and Fae. Most had developed it through magic, ill-gained or blessed.

But there, slitted with pleasure in anticipation of violence, gleamed dark, human eyes.

Whitethorn had warned of what was occurring in Morath—had mentioned the Wyrdhounds might be the first of many awful things to be unleashed. Lorcan hadn't realized those things would be nearly eight feet tall and part human, part whatever Erawan had done to turn it into *this*.

The closest one dared a step but hissed—hissed at the invisible line he'd drawn. Lorcan's power flickered and throbbed at the poisoned claw-tips of the creature as it prodded the shield.

Four against one. Usually easy odds for him.

Usually.

But he bore the Wyrdkey they sought, and that golden ring he'd stolen from Maeve, then given to and stolen from Aelin Galathynius. Athril's ring. And if they brought either to their master . . .

Then Erawan would possess all three Wyrdkeys. And would be able to open a door between worlds to unleash his awaiting Valg hordes upon them all. And as for Athril's golden ring . . . Lorcan had no doubt Erawan would destroy the ring forged by Mala herself—the one object in Erilea that granted immunity to its bearer against Wyrdstone . . . and the Valg.

So Lorcan moved. Faster than even they could detect, he hurled his axe at the creature farthest from him, its focus pinned on its companion as it prodded his shield.

They all whirled toward their companion as the axe slammed into its neck, deep and permanent. All turned away to see it fall. Lethal by nature, but untrained.

The beasts' attention diverted for a heartbeat, Lorcan's next two knives flew.

Both blades embedded to the hilt in their ridged foreheads, their heads reeling back as the blows sent them clattering to their knees.

The one in the center, the one who had spoken, loosed a primal scream that set Lorcan's ears ringing. It lunged for the shield.

It rebounded, the magic denser this time. Lorcan drew his long-sword and a knife.

And could only watch as the thing roared at the shield and slammed against it with both ruined, clawed hands . . . and his magic, his shield, *melted* under its touch.

It stepped through his shield like it was a doorway. "Now we'll play."

Lorcan crouched into a defensive stance, wondering how far the girl had made it, if she'd even turned to look at what pursued them. The sounds of her flight had faded away.

Behind the creature, its companions were twitching.

No—reviving.

They each lifted a strong, clawed hand to the daggers through their skulls—and yanked them out. Metal rasped on bone.

Only the one with its head now attached by a few tendons remained down. Beheading, then.

Even if it meant getting close enough to do so.

The creature before him smiled in savage delight.

"What are you?" Lorcan ground out.

The two others were now on their feet, the wounds in their heads already healed, bristling with menace.

"We are hunters for His Dark Majesty," the leader said with a mock bow. "We are the ilken. And we have been sent to retrieve our quarry."

Those witches had dispatched these beasts for him? Cowards, not to do their own hunting.

The ilken went on, stepping toward him on legs that bent backward. "We were going to let you have a quick death—a gift." Its broad nostrils flared, scenting the silent forest. "But as you have stood between us and our prey . . . we will savor your long end."

Not him. He was not what the wyverns had been stalking these days, what these creatures had come to claim. They had no idea what he bore—who he was.

"What do you want with her?" he asked, monitoring the creeping approach of the three.

"It is none of your concern," the leader said.

"If there is a reward in it, I will help you."

Dark, soulless eyes flashed toward him. "You do not protect the girl?"

Lorcan gave a shrug, praying they couldn't scent his bluff as he bought her more time, bought himself time to work out the puzzle of their power. "I don't even know her name."

The three ilken looked at one another, a glance of question and decision. Their leader said, "She is important to our king. Retrieve her, and he will fill you with power far greater than feeble shields."

Was that the price for the humans they'd once been—magic that was somehow immune to what flowed naturally in this world? Or had the choice been taken from them, as surely as their souls had been stolen, too?

"Why is she important?"

They were now within spitting range. He wondered how long it'd take to replenish the supply of whatever power allowed them to cleave through magic. Perhaps they were buying themselves time, too.

The ilken said, "She is a thief and a murderer. She must be brought to our king for justice."

Lorcan could have sworn an invisible hand touched his shoulder.

He knew that touch—had trusted it his entire life. It had kept him alive this long.

A touch on his back to go forward, to fight and kill and breathe in death. A touch on his shoulder to instead run. To know that only doom waited ahead, and life lay behind.

The ilken smiled once more, its teeth bright in the gloom of the wood.

As if in answer, a scream shattered from the forest behind him.

CHAPTER 10

Elide Lochan stood before a creature birthed from a dark god's nightmares.

Across the clearing, it towered over her, its talons digging into the loam of the forest floor. "There you are," it hissed through teeth sharper than a fish's. "Come with me, girl, and I will grant you a quick end."

Lies. She saw how it sized her up, claws curling as if it could already feel them shredding into her soft belly. The thing had appeared in her path as if a cloud of night had dropped it there, and had laughed when she screamed. Her knife shook as she raised it.

It stood like a man—spoke like one. And its eyes . . . Utterly soulless, yet the shape of them . . . They were human, too. Monstrous—what terrible mind had dreamed up such a thing?

She knew the answer.

Help. She needed help. But that man from the stream was likely dead at the claws of the other beasts. She wondered how long that magic of his had held out.

The creature stepped toward her, its muscled legs closing the distance too quickly. She backed toward the trees, the direction she'd come from.

"Is your blood as sweet as your face, girl?" Its grayish tongue tasted the air between them.

Think, think, think.

What would Manon do before such a creature?

Manon, she remembered, came equipped with claws and fangs of her own.

But a small voice whispered in her ear, *So do you. Use what you have.*

There were other weapons than those made of iron and steel.

Though her knees shook, Elide lifted her chin and met the black, human eyes of the creature.

"Careful," she said, dropping her voice into the purr Manon had so often used to frighten the wits out of everyone. Elide reached into the pocket of her coat, pulling out the shard of stone and clenching it in her fist, willing that otherworldly presence to fill the clearing, the world. She prayed the creature wouldn't look at her fist, wouldn't ask what was in it as she drawled, "Do you think the Dark King will be pleased if you harm me?" She looked down her nose at it. Or as best as she could while standing several feet shorter. "I have been sent to look for the girl. Do not interfere."

The creature seemed to recognize the fighting leathers then.

Seemed to scent that strange, *off* scent surrounding the rock.

And it hesitated.

Elide kept her face a mask of cold displeasure. "Get out of my sight."

She almost vomited as she began stalking toward it, toward sure death. But she stomped along, prowling as Manon had so often done. Elide made herself look up into the bat-like, hideous face as she passed. "Tell your brethren that if you interfere again, I will personally oversee what delights you experience upon Morath's tables."

Doubt still danced in its eyes—along with real fear. A lucky guess, those words and phrases, based on what she'd overheard. She didn't let herself consider what had been done to make such a creature quake at the mention.

Elide was five paces from the creature, keenly aware that her spine was now vulnerable to those shredding claws and teeth, when it asked, "Why did you flee at our approach?"

She said without turning, in that cold, vicious voice of Manon Blackbeak, "I do not tolerate the questions of underlings. You have already disrupted my hunt and injured my ankle with your useless attack. Pray that I do not remember your face when I return to the Keep."

She knew her mistake the moment it sucked in a hissing breath.

Still, she kept her legs moving, back straight.

"What a coincidence," it mused, "that our prey is similarly lamed."

Anneith save her. Perhaps it had not noticed the limp until then. Fool. *Fool.*

Running would do her no good—running would proclaim the creature had won, that it was right. She halted, as if her temper had yanked on its leash, and snapped her face toward the creature. "What is that you're hissing about?"

Utter conviction, utter rage.

Again the creature paused. One chance—just one chance. It'd learn soon enough that it had been duped.

Elide held its gaze. It was like staring a dead snake in the eyes.

She said with that lethal quiet the witches liked to use, "Do not make me reveal what His Dark Majesty put inside *me* on that table."

As if in response, the stone in her hand throbbed, and she could have sworn darkness flickered.

The creature shuddered, backing away a step.

Elide didn't consider what she held as she sneered one last time and stalked away.

She made it perhaps half a mile before the forest was again full of chittering life.

She fell to her knees and vomited.

Nothing but bile and water came out. She was so busy hurling up her guts with stupid fear and relief that she didn't notice anyone's approach until it was too late.

A broad hand clamped on her shoulder, whirling her around.

She drew her dagger, but too slowly. The same hand released her to slap the blade to the grass.

Elide found herself staring into the dirt-splattered face of the man from the stream. No, not dirt. Blood that reeked—black blood.

"How?" she said, stumbling away a step.

"*You first*," he snarled, but whipped his head toward the forest behind them. She followed his gaze. Saw nothing.

When she looked at his harsh face, a sword lay against her throat.

She tried to fall back, but he gripped her arm, holding her as steel bit into her skin. "Why do you smell of one of them? Why do they chase you?"

She'd pocketed the stone, or else she might have shown him. But movement might cause him to strike—and that small voice whispered to keep the stone concealed.

She offered another truth. "Because I have spent the past several months in Morath, living amongst that scent. They seek me because I managed to get free. I flee north—to safety."

Faster than she could see, he lowered his blade—only to slice it across her arm. A scratch, barely more than a whisper of pain.

They both watched as her red blood surged and dribbled.

It seemed answer enough for him.

"You can call me Lorcan," he said, though she hadn't asked. And with that, he hauled her over his broad shoulder like a sack of potatoes and ran.

Elide knew two things within seconds:

That the remaining creatures—however many there were—had to be on their trail and closing in fast. Had to have realized she'd bluffed her way free.

And that the man, moving swift as a wind between the oaks, was demi-Fae.

Lorcan ran and ran, his lungs gobbling down great gulps of the forest's stifling air. Slung over his shoulder, the girl didn't even whimper as the miles passed. He'd carried packs heavier than her over entire mountain ranges.

Lorcan slowed when his strength at last began to flag, spent quicker thanks to the magic he'd used to get those three beasts into a stranglehold, battering past their natural-born immunity to it, then kill two while he pinned the other long enough to sprint for the girl.

He'd been lucky.

The girl, it seemed, had been smart.

He jogged into a stop, setting her down hard enough that she winced—winced and hopped a bit on that hurt ankle. Her blood had flowed red instead of the reeking black that implied Valg possession, but it still didn't explain how she'd been able to intimidate that ilken into submission.

"Where are we going?" she said, swinging her pack to pull out her canteen. He waited for the tears and prayers and begging. She just unscrewed the cap of the leather-coated container and swigged deep. Then, to his surprise, offered him some.

Lorcan didn't take it. She merely drank again.

"We're going to the edge of the forest—to the Acanthus River."

"Where—where are we?" The hesitation said enough: she'd calculated the risk of revealing how vulnerable she was with that question . . . and decided she was too desperate for the answer.

"What is your name?"

"Marion." She held his gaze with a sort of unflinching steel that had him angling his head.

An answer for an answer. He said, "We're in the middle of Adarlan. You were about a day's hike from the Avery River."

Marion blinked. He wondered if she even knew that—or had considered how she'd cross the mighty body of water that had claimed ships captained by the most seasoned of men and women.

She said, "Are we running, or can I sit for a moment?"

He listened to the sounds of the forest for any hint of danger, then jerked his chin.

Marion sighed as she sat on the moss and roots. She surveyed him. "I thought all the Fae were dead. Even the demi-Fae."

"I'm from Wendlyn. And you," he said, brows rising slightly, "are from Morath."

"Not from. *Escaping* from."

"Why—and how."

Her narrowed eyes told him enough: she knew he still didn't believe her, not entirely, red blood or no. Yet she didn't answer, instead leaning over her legs to unlace a boot. Her fingers trembled a bit, but she got through the laces, yanking off the boot, removing the sock, and rolling up her leather pant leg to reveal—

Shit. He'd seen plenty of ruined bodies in his day, had done plenty of ruining himself, but rarely were they left so untreated. Marion's leg was a mess of scar tissue and twisted bone. And right above her misshapen ankle lay still-healing wounds where shackles had unmistakably been.

She said quietly, "Allies of Morath are usually whole. Their dark magic could surely cure a cripple—and they surely would have no use for one."

That was why she'd managed so well with the limp. She'd had years to master it, from the coloring of the scar tissue.

Marion rolled her pant leg back down but left her foot bare, massaging it. She hissed through her teeth.

He sat on a fallen log a few feet away, taking off his own pack to rifle through it. "Tell me what you know of Morath," he said, and chucked her a tin of salve straight from Doranelle.

The girl stared at it, those sharp eyes putting together what he was, where he was from, and what that tin likely contained. When she lifted them to his face, she nodded silently in agreement of his offer: relief from the pain for answers. She unscrewed the lid, and he caught the way her mouth parted as she breathed in the pungent herbs.

Pain and pleasure danced across her face as she began rubbing the salve into her old injuries.

And as she worked, she spoke.

Marion told him of the Ironteeth host, of the Wing Leader and the Thirteen, of the armies camped around the mountain Keep, of the places where only screaming echoed, of the countless forges and blacksmiths. She described her own escape: without warning, she didn't know how, the castle had exploded. She'd seen it as her chance, disguising herself in a witch's attire, grabbing one of their packs, and running. In the chaos, no one had chased her.

"I've been running for weeks," she said. "Apparently, I've barely covered half the distance."

"To where?"

Marion looked northward. "Terrasen."

Lorcan stifled a snarl. "You're not missing much."

"Have you news of it?" Alarm filled those eyes.

"No," he said, shrugging. She finished rubbing her foot and ankle. "What's in Terrasen? Your family?" He had not asked why she'd been brought to Morath. He didn't particularly care to hear her sad story. Everyone had one, he'd found.

The girl's face tightened. "I owe a debt to a friend—someone who helped me get out of Morath. She bade me to find someone named Celaena Sardothien. So that is my first task: learning who she is, where she is. Terrasen seems like a better place to start than Adarlan."

No guile, no whisper of this meeting being anything but chance.

"And then," the girl went on, the brightness in her eyes growing, "I need to find Aelin Galathynius, the Queen of Terrasen."

It was an effort not to go for his sword. "Why?"

Marion glanced toward him, as if she'd somehow even forgotten he was there. "I heard a rumor that she's raising an army to stop the one in Morath. I plan to offer my services."

"Why?" he said again. Aside from the wits that had kept her out of the ilken's claws, he saw no other reason for the bitch-queen to need the girl.

Marion's full mouth tightened. "Because I am from Terrasen and believed my queen dead. And now she is alive, and fighting, so I will fight with her. So that no other girls will be taken from their homes and brought to Morath and forgotten."

Lorcan debated telling her what he knew: that her two quests were one and the same. But that would lead to questions from her, and he was in no mood—

"Why do you wish to go to Morath? Everyone else is fleeing from it."

"I was sent by my mistress to stop the threat it poses."

"You're one man—male." Not an insult, but Lorcan stared her down anyway.

"I have my skills, just as you have yours."

Her eyes darted to his hands, now crusted in dried black blood. He wondered, though, if she was imagining the magic that had sparked there.

He waited for Marion to ask more, but she pulled on her sock, then her boot, and laced it up. "We shouldn't rest for long." Indeed.

She eased to her feet, wincing a bit, but gave an appreciative frown toward her leg. Lorcan took that as answer enough regarding the salve's efficiency. She bent down to retrieve the tin, her dark curtain of hair sweeping over her face. At some point, it had come free of its braid.

She rose, chucking him the tin. He caught it in one hand. "Once we reach the Acanthus, what then?"

He pocketed the tin in his cloak. "There are countless merchants' caravans and seasonal carnivals wandering the plains—I passed many on my way down here. Some might even be trying to cross the river. We'll get in with one of them. Hide out. Once we've crossed and wandered far enough onto the grasslands, you'll take one north; I'll head south."

Her eyes narrowed slightly. But Marion said, "Why travel with me at all?"

"There are more details regarding Morath's interior that I want from you. I'll keep you from danger, and you'll provide them for me."

The sun began its final descent, bathing the woods in gold. Marion frowned slightly. "You swear it? That you will protect me?"

"I didn't leave you to the ilken today, did I?"

She eyed him with a clarity and frankness that made him pause. "Swear it."

He rolled his eyes. "I promise." The girl had no idea that for the past five centuries, promises were the only currency he really traded in. "I will not abandon you."

She nodded, seemingly satisfied with that. "Then I will tell you what I know."

He started eastward, slinging his pack over his shoulder.

But Marion said, "They'll be hunting for us at every crossing, searching wagons. If they could find me here, they'll find me on any main road."

And find him, too, if the witches were still out for his blood.

Lorcan said, "And you have some idea around this?"

A faint smile danced around her rosebud mouth, despite the horrors they'd escaped, her misery in the woods. "I might."

CHAPTER 11

Manon Blackbeak landed in Morath more than ready to start slitting throats.

Everything had gone to shit.

Everything.

She'd ended that Yellowlegs bitch and her wyvern, saved the sapphire-eyed king, and watched the Fae Prince slaughter those four other Yellowlegs sentinels.

Five. Five Yellowlegs witches now lay dead, either by her hand or through her inaction. Five members of Iskra's coven.

In the end, she'd barely participated in Rifthold's destruction, leaving it to the others. But she'd again donned her crowned helm, then ordered Abraxos to sail to the highest spire of the stone castle and roar his victory—and command.

Even at the distant white walls of the city, ripping apart the guards and fleeing folk, the wyverns had paused at his order to stand down. Not one coven disobeyed.

The Thirteen had found her moments later. She didn't tell them what had happened, but both Sorrel and Asterin stared closely at her: the former to inspect for any cuts or wounds received during the "attack" Manon had claimed occurred, the latter because she had been with Manon that day they'd flown to Rifthold and painted a message to the Queen of Terrasen in Valg blood.

With the Thirteen perched on the castle towers, some draped along them like cats or serpents, Manon had waited for Iskra Yellowlegs.

As Manon now stalked down the dim, reeking halls of Morath, that crowned helm tucked into the crook of her arm, Asterin and Sorrel on her heels, she went over that conversation again.

Iskra had landed on the only space left: a lower bit of roofing below Manon. The positioning had been intentional.

Iskra's brown hair had come untangled from her tight braid, and her haughty face was splattered with human blood as she'd snarled at Manon, "*This was my victory.*"

Her face veiled in shadow beneath the helm, Manon had said, "The city is mine."

"Rifthold was *mine* to take—you were only to oversee." A flash of iron teeth. On the spire to Manon's right, Asterin growled in warning. Iskra cast her dark eyes on the blond sentinel and snarled again. "Get your pack of bitches out of my city."

Manon sized up Fendir, Iskra's bull. "You've left your mark enough. Your work is noted."

Iskra trembled with rage. Not from the words.

The wind had shifted, blowing toward Iskra.

Blowing Manon's scent at her.

"Who?" Iskra seethed. *"Who of mine did you butcher?"*

Manon had not yielded, had not allowed one flicker of regret or worry to shine through. "Why should I know any of your names? She attacked me as I closed in on my prey, wanting to get the king for herself and willing to strike an heir for it. She deserved her punishment. Especially because my prey slipped away while I dealt with her."

Liar liar liar.

Manon bared her iron teeth, the only bit of her face visible beneath that crowned helm. "Four others lie dead inside the castle—at the hand of the Fae Prince who came to rescue the king while *I* dealt with your unruly bitch. Consider yourself lucky, Iskra Yellowlegs, that I do not take that loss out of your hide as well."

Iskra's tan face had gone pale. She surveyed Manon, all of the Thirteen assembled. Then she said, "Do what you want with the city. It's yours." A flash of a smile as she lifted her hand and pointed at Manon. The Thirteen tensed around her, arrows silently drawn and aimed at the Yellowlegs heir. "But *you*, Wing Leader . . ." That smile grew and she reined her wyvern, preparing to take to the skies. "You are a liar, *Witch Killer.*"

Then she was gone.

Soaring not for the city, but the skies.

Within minutes, she'd vanished from sight—sailing toward Morath.

Toward Manon's grandmother.

Manon now glanced at Asterin, then at Sorrel, as they slowed to a stop before turning the corner that would lead to Erawan's council chamber. Where she knew Iskra, and her grandmother, and the other Matrons would be waiting. Indeed, a glance around the corner revealed the Thirds and Fourths of several covens on guard, eyeing one another as suspiciously as the blank-faced men posted beside the double doors.

Manon said to her Second and Third, "This will be messy."

Sorrel said quietly, "We'll deal with it."

Manon clenched the helmet a bit harder. "If it goes poorly, you are to take the Thirteen and leave."

Asterin breathed, "You cannot go in there, Manon, accepting defeat. Deny it until your last breath." Whether Sorrel had realized Manon had killed that witch to save their enemy, she didn't let on. Asterin demanded, "Where would we even go?"

Manon said, "I don't know or care. But when I am dead, the Thirteen will be targeted by anyone with a score to settle." A very, very long list. She held her Second's stare. "You get them out. At any cost."

They glanced at each other. Sorrel said, "We will do as you ask, Wing Leader."

Manon waited—waited for any objection from her Second, but Asterin's dark eyes were bright as she bowed her head and murmured her agreement.

A knot in Manon's chest loosened, and she rolled her shoulders once before turning away. But Asterin gripped her hand. "Be careful."

Manon debated snapping to not be a spineless fool, but . . . she'd seen what her grandmother was capable of. It was carved into Asterin's flesh.

She would not go into this looking guilty, looking like a liar. No—she'd make Iskra crawl by the end.

So Manon took a solid breath before she resumed her usual storming pace, red cape flapping behind her on a phantom wind.

Everyone stared as they approached. But that was to be expected.

Manon didn't deign to acknowledge the Thirds and Fourths assembled, though she took them in through her peripheral vision. Two young ones from Iskra's coven. Six old ones, iron teeth flecked with rust, from the covens of the Matrons. And—

There were two other young sentinels in the hall, braided bands of dyed blue leather upon their brows.

Petrah Blueblood had come.

If the heirs and their Matrons were all assembled . . .

She did not have room for fear in her husk of a heart.

Manon flung open the doors, Asterin on her heels, Sorrel falling back to join the others in the hall.

Ten witches turned toward Manon as she entered. Erawan was nowhere in sight.

And though her grandmother was in the center of where they all stood in the room, her own Second against the stone wall behind Manon, lined up with the four other Seconds gathered, Manon's attention went to the golden-haired heir.

To Petrah.

She had not seen the Blueblood heir since the day of the War Games, when Manon had saved her life from a sure-kill fall. Saved her life, but was unable to save the life of Petrah's wyvern—whose throat had been ripped to shreds by Iskra's bull.

The Blueblood heir stood beside her mother, Cresseida, both of them tall and thin. A crown of iron stars sat upon the Matron's pale brow, the face below unreadable.

Unlike Petrah's. Caution—warning shone in her deep blue eyes. She wore her riding leathers, a cloak of midnight blue hanging from bronze clasps at her shoulders, her golden braid snaking over her chest. Petrah had always been odd, head in the clouds, but that was the way of the Bluebloods. *Mystics*, *fanatics*, *zealots* were among the pleasanter terms used to describe them and their worship of the Three-Faced Goddess.

But there was a hollowness in Petrah's face that had not been there months ago. Rumor had claimed that losing her wyvern had broken the heir—that she had not gotten out of bed for weeks.

Witches did not mourn, because witches did not love enough to allow it to break them. Even if Asterin, now taking up her place by the Blackbeak Matron's Second, had proved otherwise.

Petrah nodded, a slight dip of the chin—more than a mere acknowledgment of an heir to an heir. Manon turned toward her grandmother before anyone could notice.

Her grandmother stood in her voluminous black robes, her dark hair plaited over the crown of her head. Like the crown her grandmother sought for them—for her and Manon. *High Queens of the Wastes*, she'd once promised Manon. Even if it meant selling out every witch in this room.

Manon bowed to her grandmother, to the other two Matrons assembled.

Iskra snarled from beside the Yellowlegs Matron, an ancient, bent-backed crone with bits of flesh still in her teeth from lunch. Manon fixed the heir with a cool stare as she straightened.

"Three stand gathered," her grandmother began, and every bone in Manon's body went stiff. "Three Matrons, to honor the three faces of our Mother." Maiden, Mother, Crone. It was why the Yellowlegs Matron was always ancient, why the Blackbeak was always a witch in her prime, and why Cresseida, as the Blueblood Matron, still looked young and fresh.

But Manon did not care about that. Not when the words were being spoken.

"The Crone's Sickle hangs above us," Cresseida intoned. "Let it be the Mother's blade of justice."

This was not a meeting.

This was a trial.

Iskra began smiling.

As if a thread wove between them, Manon could feel Asterin straightening behind her, feel her Second readying for the worst.

"Blood calls for blood," the Yellowlegs crone rasped. "We shall decide how much is owed."

Manon kept still, not daring to show one inch of fear, of trepidation.

Witch trials were brutal, exact. Usually, problems were settled with the three blows to face, ribs, and stomach. Rarely, only in the gravest circumstances, did the three Matrons gather to mete out judgment.

Manon's grandmother said, "You stand accused, Manon Blackbeak, of cutting down a Yellowlegs sentinel with no provocation beyond your own pride."

Iskra's eyes positively burned.

"And, as the sentinel was a part of the Yellowlegs' heir's own coven, it is also a crime against Iskra." Her grandmother's face was tight with rage—not for what Manon had done, but for getting caught. "Through either your own neglect or ill-planning, the lives of four other coven members were ended. Their blood, too, stains your hands." Her grandmother's iron teeth shone in the candlelight. "Do you deny these charges?"

Manon kept her back straight, looked each of them in the eye. "I do not deny that I killed Iskra's sentinel when she tried to claim my rightful prize. I do not deny that the other four were slaughtered by the Fae Prince. But I do deny any wrongdoing on my part."

Iskra hissed. "You can smell Zelta's blood on her—smell the fear and *pain*."

Manon sneered, "You smell that, Yellowlegs, because your sentinel had a coward's heart and attacked another sister-in-arms. When she realized she would not win our fight, it was already too late for her."

Iskra's face contorted with fury. *"Liar—"*

"Tell us, Blackbeak Heir," Cresseida said, "what happened in Rifthold three days past."

So Manon did.

And for the first time in her century of miserable existence, she lied to her elders. She wove a fine tapestry of falsehoods, *believing* the stories she told them. As she finished, she gestured to Iskra Yellowlegs. "It's common knowledge the Yellowlegs heir has long coveted my position. Perhaps she rushed back here to fling accusations at me so she might steal my place as Wing Leader, just as her sentinel tried to steal my prey."

Iskra bristled but kept her mouth shut. Petrah took a step forward, however, and spoke. "I have questions for the Blackbeak heir, if it would not be an impertinence."

Manon's grandmother looked like she'd rather have her own nails ripped out, but the other two nodded.

Manon straightened, bracing herself for whatever Petrah thought she was doing.

Petrah's blue eyes were calm as she met Manon's stare. "Would you consider me your enemy or rival?"

"I consider you an ally when the occasion demands it, but always a rival, yes." The first true thing Manon had said.

"And yet you saved me from sure death at the War Games. Why?"

The other Matrons glanced at one another, faces unreadable.

Manon lifted her chin. "Because Keelie fought for you as she died. I would not allow her death to be wasted. I could offer a fellow warrior nothing less."

At the sound of her dead wyvern's name, pain flickered across Petrah's face. "You remember her name?"

Manon knew it wasn't an intended question. But she nodded all the same.

Petrah faced the Matrons. "That day, Iskra Yellowlegs nearly killed me, and her bull slaughtered my mare."

"We have dealt with that," Iskra cut in, teeth flashing, "and dismissed it as accidental—"

Petrah held up a hand. "I am not finished, Iskra Yellowlegs."

Nothing but brutal steel in those words as she addressed the other heir. A small part of Manon was glad not to be on the receiving end of it.

Iskra saw the unfinished business that waited in that tone and backed down.

Petrah lowered her hand. "Manon Blackbeak had the chance to let me die that day. The easier choice would have been to let me die, and she would not be standing accused as she is now. But she risked her life, and the life of her mount, to spare me from death."

A life debt—that was what lay between them. Did Petrah think to fill it by speaking in her favor now? Manon reined in her sneer.

Petrah went on, "I do not comprehend why Manon Blackbeak would save me only to later turn on her Yellowlegs sisters. You crowned her Wing Leader for her obedience, discipline, and brutality—do not let the anger of Iskra Yellowlegs sully the qualities you saw in her then, and which still shine forth today. Do not lose your Wing Leader over a misunderstanding."

The Matrons again glanced among them as Petrah bowed, backing into her place at her mother's right. But the three witches continued that unspoken discussion waging between them. Until Manon's grandmother stepped forward, the other two falling back—yielding the decision to her. Manon almost sagged in relief.

She'd corner Petrah the next time the heir was foolish enough to be out alone, get her to admit why she'd spoken in Manon's favor.

Her grandmother's black-and-gold gaze was hard. Unforgiving.

"Petrah Blueblood has spoken true."

That tense, tight string between Manon and Asterin loosened, too.

"It would be a waste to lose our obedient, *faithful* Wing Leader."

Manon had been beaten before. She could endure her grandmother's fists again.

"Why should the heir of the Blackbeak Witch-Clan yield her life for that of a mere sentinel? Wing Leader or not, it is still the word of heir against heir in this matter. But the blood has still been shed. And blood must be paid."

Manon again gripped her helm. Her grandmother smiled a little.

"The blood shed must be equal," her grandmother intoned. Her attention flicked over Manon's shoulder. "So you, Granddaughter, will not die for this. But one of your Thirteen will."

For the first time in a long, long while, Manon knew what fear, what human helplessness, tasted like as her grandmother said, triumph lighting her ancient eyes, "Your Second, Asterin Blackbeak, shall pay the blood debt between our clans. She dies at sunrise tomorrow."

CHAPTER 12

Without Evangeline slowing them down, Aelin, Aedion, and Lysandra traveled with little rest as they hauled ass for the coast.

Aelin remained in her Fae form to keep up with Aedion, who she begrudgingly admitted was by far the better rider, while Lysandra shifted in and out of various bird shapes to scout the land ahead for any danger. Rowan had been instructing her on how to do it, what things to note and what to avoid or get a closer look at, while they'd been on the road these weeks. But Lysandra found little to report from the skies, and Aelin and Aedion encountered few dangers on the ground as they crossed the valleys and plains of Terrasen's lowlands.

So little remained of the once-rich territory.

Aelin tried not to dwell on it too much—on the threadbare estates, the abandoned farms, the gaunt-faced people whenever they ventured into town, cloaked and disguised, for desperately needed supplies. Though she had faced darkness and emerged full of light, a voice whispered in her head, *You did this, you did this, you did this.*

That voice often sounded like Weylan Darrow's icy tones.

Aelin left gold pieces in her wake—tucked under a mug of watery tea offered to her and Aedion on a stormy morning; dropped in the bread box of a farmer who'd given them slices and a bit of meat for Lysandra in falcon form; slipped into the coin drawer of an innkeeper who had offered them a free extra bowl of stew upon seeing how swiftly they devoured their lunches.

But that gold didn't ease the cracking in her heart—that hideous voice that haunted her waking and dreaming thoughts.

By the time they reached the ancient port town of Ilium a week later, she'd stopped leaving gold behind.

It'd started to feel more like a bribe. Not to her people, who had no inkling she'd been among them, but to her own conscience.

The green flatlands eventually yielded to rocky, arid coastline miles before the white-walled town rose between the thrashing turquoise sea and the broad mouth of the Florine River snaking inland, all the way to Orynth. The town of Ilium was as ancient as Terrasen itself, and would likely have already been forgotten by traders and history were it not for the crumbling temple at the northeastern edge of the city, drawing enough pilgrims to keep it thriving.

The Temple of the Stone, it was called, had been built around the very rock where Brannon had first placed his foot upon the continent before sailing up the Florine to its source at the base of the Staghorns. How the Little Folk had known how to render the temple for her, she had no idea.

Ilium's stout, sprawling temple had been erected on a pale cliff with commanding views of the storm-worn, pretty town behind it and the endless ocean beyond—so blue that it reminded Aelin of the tranquil waters of the South.

Waters where Rowan and Dorian should now be headed, if they were lucky. Aelin tried not to dwell on that, either. Without the Fae Prince at her side, there was a horrible, endless silence.

Almost as quiet as the white walls of the town—and the people inside. Hooded and armed to the teeth beneath their heavy cloaks, Aelin and Aedion rode through the open gates, no more than two cautious pilgrims on their way to the temple. Disguised for secrecy—and for the little fact that Ilium was now under Adarlanian occupation.

Lysandra had brought the news that morning after flying ahead, lingering in human form only long enough to inform them.

"We should have gone north to Eldrys," Aedion murmured as they rode past a cluster of hard-faced sentries in Adarlanian armor, the soldiers only glancing their way to note the sharp-eyed, sharper-beaked falcon perched on Aelin's shoulder. None marked the shield hidden amongst Aedion's saddlebags, carefully veiled by the folds of his cloak. Or the swords they'd both concealed as well. Damaris remained where she'd stored it these weeks on the road: strapped beneath the heavy bags containing the ancient spell-books she'd *borrowed* from Dorian's royal library in Rifthold. "We can still turn around."

Aelin shot him a glare beneath the shadows of her hood. "If you think for one moment I'm leaving this city in Adarlan's hands, you can go to hell." Lysandra clicked her beak in agreement.

The Little Folk had not been wrong to send the message to come here, their rendering of the temple near-perfect. Through whatever magic they possessed, they had foreseen the news long before it ever reached Aelin on the road: Rifthold had indeed fallen, its king vanished and the city sacked by witches. Emboldened by this, and by the rumor that *she* was not taking back her throne but rather running as well, the Lord of Meah, Roland Havilliard's father and one of the most powerful lords in Adarlan, had marched his garrison of troops just over the border into Terrasen. And claimed this port for himself.

"Fifty soldiers are camped here," Aedion warned her and Lysandra.

The shifter only puffed out her feathers as if to say, *So?*

His jaw clenched. "Believe me, I want a piece of them, too. But—"

"I am not hiding in my own kingdom," Aelin cut in. "And I am not going to leave without sending a reminder of who this land belongs to."

Aedion kept quiet as they rounded a corner, aiming for the small seaside inn Lysandra had also scouted that morning. On the other side of the city from the temple.

The temple the soldiers had the *nerve* to use as their barracks.

"Is this about sending a message to Adarlan, or to Darrow?" Aedion asked at last.

"It is about freeing my people, who have dealt with these Adarlanian pieces of shit for too long," Aelin snapped, reining her mare in to a halt before the inn courtyard. Lysandra's talons dug into her shoulder in silent agreement. Mere feet beyond the weatherworn courtyard wall, the sea gleamed sapphire-bright. "We move at nightfall."

Aedion remained quiet, his face partially hidden as the inn's owner scuttled out and they secured a room for the night. Aelin let her cousin brood a bit, wrangling her magic under control. She hadn't released any of it this morning, wanting it to be at full force for what they were to do tonight, but the strain now tugged at her, an itch with no relief, an edge she could not dull.

Only when they were ensconced in their tiny, two-bed chamber, Lysandra perched on the windowsill, did Aedion say, "Aelin, you know I'll help—you know I want these bastards out of here. But the people of Ilium have lived here for centuries, aware that in war, they are the first to be attacked."

And these soldiers could easily return as soon as they left, he didn't need to add.

Lysandra pecked the window—a quiet request. Aelin strode over, shoved open the window to let the sea breeze flit in. "Symbols have power, Aedion," she said, watching the shifter fan her speckled wings. She'd read books and books on it during that ridiculous competition in Rifthold.

He snorted. "I know. Believe me—I've wielded them to my advantage as often as I can." He patted the bone pommel of the Sword of Orynth for emphasis. "Come to think of it, I said the same exact thing once to Dorian and Chaol." He shook his head at the memory.

Aelin just leaned against the windowsill. "Ilium used to be the stronghold of the Mycenians."

"The Mycenians are nothing more than a myth—they were banished three hundred years ago. If you're looking for a symbol, they're fairly outdated—and divisive."

She knew that. The Mycenians had once ruled Ilium not as nobility, but crime lords. And during some long-ago war, their lethal fleet had been so crucial in winning that they'd been turned legitimate by whatever king ruled at the time. Until they had been exiled centuries later for their refusal to come to Terrasen's aid in another war.

She met Lysandra's green-eyed stare as the shifter lowered her wings, sufficiently cooled. She'd been distant on the road this week, preferring feathers or fur to skin. Perhaps because some piece of her heart now rode for Orynth with Ren and Murtaugh. Aelin stroked her friend's silken head. "The Mycenians abandoned Terrasen so they would not die in a war they did not believe in."

"And they disbanded and vanished soon after that, never to be seen again," Aedion countered. "What's your point? You think liberating Ilium will summon them again? They're long gone, Aelin, their sea dragons with them."

Indeed, there was no sign anywhere in this city of the legendary fleet and warriors who had sailed to wars across distant, violent seas, who had defended these borders with their own blood spilled upon the waves beyond the windows. And the blood of their sea dragons, both allies and weapons. Only when the last of the dragons had died, heartsick to be banished from Terrasen's waters, had the Mycenians truly been lost. And only when the sea dragons returned would the Mycenians, too, come home. Or so their ancient prophecies claimed.

Aedion began removing the extra blades hidden in their saddlebags, save for Damaris, and strapped them on, one by one. He double-checked that Rowan's knife was securely buckled at his side before he said to Aelin and Lysandra, still by the window, "I know you two are of the opinion that we males are here to provide you with a pretty view and meals, but I *am* a general of Terrasen. We need to find a real army—not spend our time chasing ghosts. If we don't get a host to the North by mid-fall, the winter storms will keep it away by land and sea."

"If you're so versed in symbols wielding such power, Aedion," she said, "then you know why Ilium is vital. We can't allow Adarlan to hold it. For a dozen reasons." She was certain her cousin had already calculated all of them.

"So take back the town," Aedion challenged. "But we need to sail by dawn." Her cousin's eyes narrowed. "The temple. It's also that they took the temple, isn't it?"

"That temple is my birthright," Aelin said. "I cannot allow that insult to go unchecked." She rolled her shoulders. Revealing her plans, explaining herself . . . It would take some getting used to. But she'd promised she'd try to be more . . . open about her plotting. And for this matter, at least, she could be. "Both for Adarlan and for Darrow. Not if I am to one day reclaim my throne."

Aedion considered. Then snorted, a hint of a smile on his face. "An undisputed queen of not just blood, but also of legends." His face remained contemplative. "You would be the undisputed queen if you got the kingsflame to bloom again."

"Too bad Lysandra can only shift herself and not things," Aelin muttered. Lysandra clicked her beak in agreement, puffing her feathers.

"They say the kingsflame bloomed once during Orlon's reign," Aedion mused. "Just one blossom, found in Oakwald."

"I know," Aelin said quietly. "He kept it pressed within glass on his desk." She still remembered that small red-and-orange flower, so simple in its make, but so vibrant it had always snatched her breath away. It had bloomed in fields and across mountains throughout the kingdom the day Brannon set foot on this continent. And for centuries afterward, if a solitary blossom was ever found, the current sovereign was deemed blessed, the kingdom truly at peace.

Before the flower was found in Orlon's second decade of kingship, the last one had been spotted ninety-five years earlier. Aelin swallowed hard. "Did Adarlan—"

"Darrow has it," Aedion said. "It was the only thing of Orlon's he managed to grab before the soldiers took the palace."

Aelin nodded, her magic flickering in answer. Even the Sword of Orynth had fallen into Adarlan's hands—until Aedion had won it back. Yes, her cousin understood perhaps more than anyone else the power a single symbol could wield. How the loss or reclaiming of one could shatter or rally an army, a people.

Enough—it was *enough* destruction and pain inflicted on her kingdom.

"Come on," she said to Lysandra and Aedion, heading for the door. "We'd better eat before we raise hell."

CHAPTER 13

It had been a long while since Dorian had seen so many stars.

Far behind them, smoke still stained the sky, the plumes illuminated by the crescent moon overhead. At least the screams had faded miles ago. Along with the thump of mighty wings.

Seated behind him in the one-masted skiff, Prince Rowan Whitethorn gazed over the calm black expanse of the sea. They'd sail south, pushed by the prince's own magic, to the Dead Islands. The Fae warrior had gotten them quickly to the coast, where he'd had no qualms about stealing this boat while its owner was focused on the panicking city to the west. And all the while, Dorian had been silent, useless. As he had been while his city was destroyed, his people murdered.

"You should eat," Rowan said from the other end of the small boat.

Dorian glanced toward the sack of supplies Rowan had also stolen. Bread, cheese, apples, dried fish . . . Dorian's stomach turned.

"You were impaled by a poisoned barb," Rowan said, his voice no louder than the waves lapping against their boat as the swift wind pushed them from behind. "Your magic was drained keeping you alive and walking. You need to eat, or else it won't replenish." A pause. "Didn't Aelin warn you about that?"

Dorian swallowed. "No. She didn't really have the time to teach me about magic." He looked toward the back of the boat, where Rowan sat with a hand braced on the rudder. The sight of those pointed ears was still a shock, even months after meeting the male. And that silver hair—

Not like Manon's hair, which was the pure white of moonlight on snow.

He wondered what had become of the Wing Leader—who had killed for him, spared him.

Not spared him. Rescued him.

He wasn't a fool. He knew she'd done it for whatever reasons were useful to her. She was as alien to him as the warrior sitting at the other end of the boat—more so.

And yet, that darkness, that violence and stark, honest way of looking at the world . . . There would be no secrets with her. No lies.

"You need to eat to keep up your strength," Rowan went on. "Your magic feeds on your energy—feeds on *you.* The more rested you are, the greater the strength. More important, the greater the control. Your power is both part of you and its own entity. If left to its own devices, it will consume you, wield *you* like a tool." A flash of teeth as Rowan smiled. "A certain person we know likes to siphon off her power, use it on frivolous things to keep its edge dull." Dorian could feel Rowan's stare pin him like a physical blow. "The choice is yours how much you allow it into your life, how to use it—but go any longer without mastering it, Majesty, and it will destroy you."

A chill went down Dorian's spine.

And maybe it was the open ocean, or the endless stars above them, but

Dorian said, "It wasn't enough. That day . . . that day Sorscha died, it wasn't enough to save her." He spread his hands on his lap. "It only wishes to destroy."

Silence fell, long enough that Dorian wondered if Rowan had fallen asleep. He hadn't dared ask when the prince himself had last slept; he'd certainly eaten enough for a starved man.

"I was not there to save my mate when she was murdered, either," Rowan said at last.

Dorian straightened. Aelin had told him plenty of the prince's history, but not this. He supposed it wasn't her secret, her sorrow to share. "I'm sorry," Dorian said.

His magic had felt the bond between Aelin and Rowan—the bond that went deeper than blood, than their magic, and he'd assumed it was just that they were mates, and hadn't announced it to anyone. But if Rowan already had a mate, and had lost her . . .

Rowan said, "You're going to hate the world, Dorian. You are going to hate yourself. You will hate your magic, and you will hate any moment of peace or happiness. But I had the luxury of a kingdom at peace and no one depending upon me. You do not."

Rowan shifted the rudder, adjusting their course farther out to sea as the coastline jutted to meet them, a rising wall of steep cliffs. He'd known they were traveling swiftly, but they had to be almost halfway to the southern border—and traveling far faster than he'd realized under the cover of darkness.

Dorian said at last, "I am the sovereign of a broken kingdom. My people do not know who rules them. And now that I am fleeing . . ." He shook his head, exhaustion gnawing on his bones. "Have I yielded my kingdom to Erawan? What—what do I even *do* from here?"

The ship's creaking and the rush of water were the only sounds. "Your people will have learned by now that you were not among the dead. It is upon you to tell them how to interpret it—if they are to see you as abandoning them, or if they are to see you as a man who is leaving to find help—to save them. You must make that clear."

"By going to the Dead Islands."

A nod. "Aelin, unsurprisingly, has a fraught history with the Pirate Lord. You don't. It's in your best interest to make him see you as an advantageous ally. Aedion told me the Dead Islands were once overrun by General Narrok and several of Erawan's forces. Rolfe and his fleet fled—and though Rolfe is now once more ruler of Skull's Bay, that disgrace might be your way in with him. Convince him you are not your father's son—and that you'll grant Rolfe and his pirates privileges."

"You mean turn them into privateers."

"You have gold, we have gold. If promising Rolfe money and free rein to loot Erawan's ships will secure us an armada in the South, we'd be fools to shy from it."

Dorian considered the prince's words. "I've never met a pirate."

"You met Aelin when she was still pretending to be Celaena," Rowan said drily. "I can promise you Rolfe won't be much worse."

"That's not reassuring."

A huffed laugh. Silence fell between them again. At last, Rowan said, "I'm sorry—about Sorscha."

Dorian shrugged, and hated himself for the gesture, as if it diminished what Sorscha had meant, how brave she'd been—how special. "You know," he said, "sometimes I wish Chaol were here—to help me. And then sometimes I'm glad he's not, so he wouldn't be at risk again. I'm glad he's in Antica with Nesryn." He studied the prince, the lethal lines of his body, the predatory stillness with which he sat, even as he manned their boat. "Could you—could you teach me about magic? Not everything, I mean, but . . . what you can, whenever we can."

Rowan considered for a moment, and then said, "I have known many kings in my life, Dorian Havilliard. And it was a rare man indeed who asked for help when he needed it, who would put aside pride."

Dorian was fairly certain his pride had been shredded under the claws of the Valg prince.

"I'll teach you as much as I can before we arrive in Skull's Bay," Rowan said. "We may find someone there who escaped the butchers—someone to instruct you more than I can."

"You taught Aelin."

Again, silence. Then, "Aelin is my heart. I taught her what I knew, and it worked because our magics understood each other deep down—just as our souls did. You are . . . different. Your magic is something I have rarely encountered. You need someone who grasps it, or at least how to train you in it. But I can teach you control; I can teach you about spiraling down into your power, and taking care of yourself."

Dorian nodded his thanks. "The first time you met Aelin, did you know . . . ?"

A snort. "No. Gods, no. We wanted to kill each other." The amusement flickered. "She was . . . in a very dark place. We both were. But we led each other out of it. Found a way—together."

For a heartbeat, Dorian could only stare. As if reading his mind, Rowan said, "You will find your way, too, Dorian. You'll find your way out."

He didn't have the right words to convey what was in his heart, so he sighed up at the starry, endless sky. "To Skull's Bay, then."

Rowan's smile was a slash of white in the darkness. "To Skull's Bay."

CHAPTER 14

Clothed in battle-black from head to toe, Aedion Ashryver kept to the shadows of the street across from the temple and watched his cousin scale the building beside him.

They'd already secured passage on a ship for tomorrow morning, along with another messenger ship to sail to Wendlyn, bearing letters beseeching the Ashryvers for aid and signed by both Aelin and Aedion himself. Because what they'd learned today . . .

He'd been to Ilium enough times over the past decade to know his way around. Usually, he and his Bane had camped outside the town walls and enjoyed themselves so thoroughly at the taverns that he'd wound up puking in his own helmet the next morning. A far cry from the stunned silence as he and Aelin had walked down the pale, dusty streets, disguised and unsociable.

In all those visits to the town, he'd never imagined traversing these streets with his queen—or that her face would be so grave as she took in the frightened, unhappy people, the scars of war.

No flowers thrown in their path, no trumpets singing their return. Just the crash of the sea, the howl of the wind, and the beating sun overhead. And the rage rippling off Aelin at the sight of the soldiers stationed around the town . . .

All strangers were watched enough that they'd had to be careful about securing their ship. To the town, the world, they'd be boarding the *Summer Lady* at midmorning, heading north to Suria. But they would instead be sneaking onto the *Wind-Singer* just before sunrise to sail south come dawn. They'd paid in gold for the captain's silence.

And for his information. They had been about to leave the man's cabin when he'd said, "My brother is a merchant. He specializes in goods from distant lands. He brought me news last week that ships were spotted rallying along the western coast of the Fae territory."

Aelin had asked, "To sail here?" at the same time Aedion had demanded, "How many ships?"

"Fifty—all warships," the captain had said, looking them over carefully. No doubt assuming they were agents of one of the many crowns at play in this war. "An army of Fae warriors camped on the beach beyond. They seemed to be waiting for the order to sail."

The news would likely spread fast. Panic the people. Aedion had made a note to send warning to his Second to brace the Bane for it—and counter any wild rumors.

Aelin's face had gone a bit bloodless, and he'd braced a steadying hand between her shoulder blades. But she had only stood straighter at his touch and asked the captain, "Did your brother get the sense that Queen Maeve has allied with Morath, or that she is coming to assist Terrasen?"

"Neither," the captain had cut in. "He was only sailing past, though if the armada was out like that, I doubt it was secret. We know nothing else—perhaps the ships were for another war."

His queen's face yielded nothing in the dimness of her hood. Aedion made his do the same.

Except her face had remained like that the entire walk back, and in the hours since, when they'd honed their weapons and then slipped back onto the streets under cover of darkness. If Maeve was indeed rallying an army to stand against them . . .

Aelin paused atop the roof, Goldryn's bright hilt wrapped in cloth to hide its gleaming, and Aedion glanced between her shadowy figure and the Adarlan watch patrolling the temple walls mere feet below.

But his cousin turned her head toward the nearby ocean, as if she could see all the way to Maeve and her awaiting fleet. If the immortal bitch allied with Morath . . . Surely Maeve would not be so stupid. Perhaps the two dark rulers would destroy each other in their bid for power. And likely destroy this continent in the process.

But a Dark King and a Dark Queen united against the Fire-Bringer . . .

They had to act quickly. Cut off one snake's head before dealing with the other.

Cloth on skin hissed, and Aedion glanced at where Lysandra waited behind him, on the lookout for Aelin's signal. She was in her traveling clothes—a bit worn and dirty. She'd been reading an ancient-looking book all afternoon. *Forgotten Creatures of the Deep* or whatever it had been called. A smile tugged at his lips as he wondered whether she'd borrowed or stolen the title.

The lady looked to where Aelin still stood on the roof, no more than a shadow. Lysandra cleared her throat a bit and said too softly for anyone to hear, either the queen or the soldiers across the street, "She's accepted Darrow's decree too calmly."

"I'd hardly call any of this calm." But he knew what the shifter meant.

Since Rowan had gone, since word of Rifthold's fall had arrived, Aelin had been half present. Distant.

Lysandra's pale green eyes pinned him to the spot. "It's the calm before the storm, Aedion."

Every one of his predatory instincts perked.

Lysandra's eyes again drifted to Aelin's lithe figure. "A storm is coming. A great storm."

Not the forces lurking in Morath, not Darrow plotting in Orynth or Maeve assembling her armada—but the woman on that roof, hands braced on the edge as she crouched down.

"You're not frightened of . . . ?" He couldn't say the rest. He'd somehow grown accustomed to having the shifter guard Aelin's back—had found the idea mighty appealing. Rowan at her right, Aedion at her left, Lysandra at her back: nothing and no one would get to their queen.

"No—no, never," Lysandra said. Something eased in his chest. "But the more I think about it, the more . . . the more it seems like this was all planned, laid out long ago. Erawan had decades before Aelin was born to strike—decades during which no one with her powers, or Dorian's powers, existed to challenge him. Yet, as fate or fortune would have it, he moves now. At a time when a Fire-Bringer walks the earth."

"What are you getting at?" He'd considered all this before, during those long watches on the road. It was all horrifying, impossible, but—so much of their lives defied logic or normalcy. The shifter next to him proved that.

"Morath is unleashing its horrors," Lysandra said. "Maeve stirs across the sea. Two goddesses walk hand in hand with Aelin. More than that, Mala and Deanna have watched over her the entirety of her life. But perhaps it wasn't watching. Perhaps it was . . . shaping. So they might one day unleash her, too. And I wonder if the gods have weighed the costs of that storm. And deemed the casualties worth it."

A chill snaked down his spine.

Lysandra went on, so quietly that Aedion wondered if she feared not the queen hearing, but those gods. "We have yet to see the full extent of Erawan's darkness. And I think we have yet to see the full extent of Aelin's fire."

"She's not some unwitting pawn." He'd defy the gods, find a way to slaughter them, if they threatened Aelin, if they deemed these lands a worthy sacrifice to defeat the Dark King.

"Is it really *that* hard for you to just agree with me for once?"

"I never *disagree*."

"You always have an answer to everything." She shook her head. "It's insufferable."

Aedion grinned. "Good to know I'm finally getting under your skin. Or is it skins?"

That staggeringly beautiful face turned positively wicked. "Careful, Aedion. I bite."

Aedion leaned in a bit closer. He knew there were lines with Lysandra—knew there were boundaries he wouldn't cross, wouldn't push at. Not after what she'd endured since childhood, not after she'd regained her freedom. Not after what he'd been through, too.

Even if he hadn't yet told Aelin about it. How could he? How could he explain what had been done to him, what he'd been forced to do in those early years of conquest?

But flirting with Lysandra was harmless—for both him and the shifter. And gods, it was good to talk to her for more than a minute between forms. So he snapped his teeth at her and said, "Good thing I know how to make women purr."

She laughed softly, but the sound died as she looked toward their queen again, the sea breeze shifting her dark silken hair. "Any minute now," she warned him.

Aedion didn't give a shit what Darrow thought, what he sneered about. Lysandra had saved his life—had fought for their queen and put everything on the line, including her ward, to rescue him from execution and reunite him with Aelin. He'd seen how often the shifter's eyes had darted behind them the first few days—as if she could see Evangeline with Murtaugh and Ren. He knew even now part of her remained with the girl, just as part of Aelin remained with Rowan. He wondered if he'd ever feel it—that degree of love.

For Aelin, yes—but . . . it was a part of him, as his limbs were a part of him. It had never been a choice, as Lysandra's selflessness with that little girl had been, as Rowan and Aelin had chosen each other. Perhaps it was stupid to consider, given what he'd been trained to do and what awaited them in Morath, but . . . He'd never tell her this in a thousand years, but looking at Aelin and Rowan, he sometimes envied them.

He didn't even want to think about what else Darrow had implied—that a union between Wendlyn and Terrasen *had* been attempted over ten years ago, with marriage between him and Aelin the asking price, only to be rejected by their kin across the sea.

He loved his cousin, but the thought of touching her like that made his stomach turn. He had a feeling she returned the sentiment.

She hadn't shown him the letter she'd written to Wendlyn. It hadn't occurred to him until now to ask to see it. Aedion stared up at the lone figure before the vast, dark sea.

And realized he didn't want to know.

He was a general, a warrior honed by blood and rage and loss; he had seen and done things that still drew him from his sleep, night after night, but . . . He did not want to know. Not yet.

Lysandra said, "We should leave before dawn. I don't like the smell of this place."

He inclined his head toward the fifty soldiers camped inside the temple walls. "Obviously."

But before she could speak, blue flames sparked at Aelin's fingertips. The signal.

Lysandra shifted into a ghost leopard, and Aedion faded into the shadows as she loosed a roar that set the nearby homes tumbling awake. People spilled out of their doors just as the soldiers threw open the gates to the temple to see what the commotion was about.

Aelin was off the roof in a few nimble maneuvers, landing with feline grace as the soldiers shoved into the street, weapons out and eyes wide.

Those eyes grew wider as Lysandra slunk up beside Aelin, snarling. As Aedion fell into step on her other side. Together, they pulled off their hoods. Someone gasped behind them.

Not at their golden hair, their faces. But at the hand wreathed in blue flame as Aelin lifted it above her head and said to the soldiers pointing crossbows at them, "Get the hell out of my temple."

The soldiers blinked. One of the townsfolk behind them began weeping as a crown of fire appeared atop Aelin's hair. As the cloth smothering Goldryn burned away and the ruby glowed bloodred.

Aedion smiled at the Adarlanian bastards, unhooked his shield from across his back, and said, "My lady gives you a choice: leave now . . . or never leave at all."

The soldiers exchanged glances. The flame around Aelin's head burned brighter, a beacon in the dark. *Symbols have power indeed.*

There she was, crowned in flame, a bastion against the gathered night. So Aedion drew the Sword of Orynth from its sheath along his spine. Someone cried out at the sight of that ancient, mighty blade.

More and more soldiers filled the open temple courtyard beyond the gate. And some dropped their weapons outright, lifting their hands. Backing away.

"You bleeding cowards," a soldier snarled, shoving to the front. A commander, from the decorations on his red-and-gold uniform. Human. No black rings on any of them. His lip curled as he beheld Aedion, the shield and sword he held angled and ready for bloodletting. "The Wolf of the North." The sneer deepened. "And the fire-breathing bitch herself."

Aelin, to her credit, only looked bored. And she said one last time to the human soldiers gathered there, shifting on their feet, "Live or die; it's your choice. But make it now."

"Don't listen to the bitch," the commander snapped. "Simple parlor tricks, Lord Meah said."

But five more soldiers dropped their weapons and ran. Outright sprinted into the streets. "Anyone else?" Aelin asked softly.

Thirty-five soldiers remained, weapons out, faces hard. Aedion had fought against and alongside such men. Aelin looked to him in question. Aedion nodded. The commander had his claws in them—they would only retreat when the man did.

"Come on, then. Let's see what you have to offer," the commander taunted. "I've got a lovely farmer's daughter I want to finish—"

As if she were blowing out a candle, Aelin exhaled a breath toward the man.

First the commander went quiet. As if every thought, every feeling had halted. Then his body seemed to stiffen, like he'd been turned to stone.

And for a heartbeat, Aedion thought the man *had* been turned to stone as his skin, his Adarlanian uniform, turned varying shades of gray.

But as the sea breeze brushed past, and the man simply *fell* apart into nothing but ashes, Aedion realized with no small amount of shock what she had done.

She'd burned him alive. From the inside out. Someone screamed.

Aelin merely said, "I warned you." A few soldiers now bolted.

But most held their ground, hate and disgust shining in their eyes at the magic, at his queen—at him.

And Aedion smiled like the wolf he was as he lifted the Sword of Orynth and unleashed himself upon the line of soldiers raising weapons on the left, Lysandra lunging to the right with a guttural snarl, and Aelin rained down flames of gold and ruby upon the world.

They took back the temple in twenty minutes.

It was only ten before they had control of it, the soldiers either dead or, if they'd surrendered, hauled to the town dungeon by the men and women who had joined the fight. The other ten minutes were spent scouring the place for any ambushers. But they found only their trappings and refuse, and the sight of the temple in such disrepair, the sacred walls carved with the names of Adarlanian brutes, the ancient urns of never-ending fire extinguished or used for chamber pots . . .

Aelin had let them all see when she sent a razing fire through the place, gobbling up any trace of those soldiers, removing years of dirt and dust and gull droppings to reveal the glorious, ancient carvings beneath, etched into every pillar and step and wall.

The temple complex comprised three buildings around a massive courtyard: the archives, the residence for the long-dead priestesses, and the temple proper, where the ancient Rock was held. It was in the archives, the most defensible area by far, that she left Aedion and Lysandra to find anything suitable for bedding, a wall of flame now encompassing the entire site.

Aedion's eyes still shone with the thrill of battle when she claimed she wanted a moment alone by the Rock. He'd fought beautifully—and she'd made sure to leave some men alive for him to take down. She was not the only symbol here tonight, not the only one watched.

And as for the shifter who had ripped into those soldiers with such feral savagery . . . Aelin left her again in falcon form, perched on a rotting beam in the cavernous archives, staring at the enormous rendering of a sea dragon carved into the floor, at last revealed by that razing fire. One of many similar carvings throughout, the heritage of a people long since exiled.

From every space inside the temple, the crashing of waves on the shore far below whispered or roared. There was nothing to absorb the sound, to soften it. Great, sprawling rooms and courtyards where there should have been altars and statues and gardens of reflection were wholly empty, the smoke of her fire still lingering.

Good. Fire could destroy—but also cleanse.

She crept across the darkened temple-complex grounds to where the innermost, holiest of sanctuaries sprawled to the lip of the sea. Golden light leaked onto the rocky ground before the inner sanctum's steps—light from the now-eternally-burning vats of flame to honor Brannon's gift.

Still clothed in black, Aelin was little more than a shadow as she dimmed those fires to sleepy, murmuring embers and entered the heart of the temple.

A great sea wall had been built to push back the wrath of storms from the stone itself, but even then, the space was damp, the air thick with brine.

Aelin cleared the massive antechamber and strode between the two fat pillars that framed the inner sanctuary. At its far end, open to the wrath of the sea beyond, arose the massive black Rock.

It was smooth as glass, no doubt from the reverent hands that had touched it over the millennia, and perhaps as big as a farmer's market wagon. It jutted upward, overhanging the sea, and starlight bounced off its pocked surface as Aelin extinguished every flame but the sole white candle fluttering in the center of the Rock.

The temple carvings revealed no Wyrdmarks or further messages from the Little Folk. Just swirls and stags.

She'd have to do this the old-fashioned way, then.

Aelin mounted the small stairs that allowed pilgrims to gaze upon the sacred Rock—then stepped onto it.

CHAPTER 15

The sea seemed to pause.

Aelin tugged the Wyrdkey from her jacket, letting it rest between her breasts as she took a seat on the overhanging lip of the stone and peered out into the night-veiled sea.

And waited.

The sliver of crescent moon was beginning to descend when a deep male voice said behind her, "You look younger than I thought."

Aelin stared at the sea, even as her stomach tightened. "But just as good-looking, right?"

She did not hear any footsteps, but the voice was definitely closer as he said, "At least my daughter was right about your humility."

"Funny, she never implied you had a sense of humor."

A whisper of wind to her right, then long, muscled legs beneath ancient armor appeared beside hers, sandaled feet dangling into the surf. She finally dared to turn her head, finding that armor continued to a powerful male body and a broad-boned, handsome face. He might have fooled anyone into thinking he was flesh and blood—were it not for the pale glimmer of blue light along his edges.

Aelin bowed her head slightly to Brannon.

A half smile was his only acknowledgment, his red-gold hair shifting in the moonlight. "A brutal but efficient battle," he said.

She shrugged. "I was told to come to this temple. I found it occupied. So I unoccupied it. You're welcome."

His lips twitched toward a smile. "I cannot stay long."

"But you're going to manage to cram in as many cryptic warnings as you can, right?"

Brannon's brows rose, his brandy-colored eyes crinkling with amusement. "I had my friends send you a message to come for a reason, you know."

"Oh, I'm sure of it." She wouldn't have risked reclaiming the temple otherwise. "But first tell me about Maeve." She'd had enough of waiting until *they* dumped their message into her lap. She had her own gods-damned questions.

Brannon's mouth tightened. "Specify what you need to know."

"Can she be killed?"

The king's head whipped toward her. "She is old, Heir of Terrasen. She was old when I was a child. Her plans are far-reaching—"

"I know, I know. But will she die if I shove a blade into her heart? Cut off her head?"

A pause. "I don't know."

"What?"

Brannon shook his head. "I don't know. All Fae may be killed, yet she has outlived even our extended life spans, and her power . . . no one really understands her power."

"But you journeyed with her to get the keys back—"

"I do not know. But she long feared my flame. And yours."

"She's not Valg, is she?"

A low laugh. "No. As cold as one, but no." Brannon's edges began to blur a bit.

But he saw the question in her eyes and nodded for her to go on.

Aelin swallowed, her jaw clenching a bit as she forced out a breath. "Does the power ever get easier to handle?"

Brannon's gaze softened a fraction. "Yes and no. How it impacts your relationships with those around you becomes harder than managing the power—yet is tied to it as well. Magic is no easy gift in any form, yet fire . . . We burn not just within our magic, but also in our very souls. For better or worse." His attention flicked to Goldryn, peeking over her shoulder, and he laughed in quiet surprise. "Is the beast in the cave dead?"

"No, but he told me that he misses you and you should pay him a visit. He's lonely out there."

Brannon chuckled again. "We would have had fun together, you and I."

"I'm starting to wish they'd sent you to deal with me instead of your daughter. The sense of humor must skip a generation."

Perhaps it was the wrong thing to say. For that sense of humor instantly faded from that beautiful tan face, those brandy eyes going cold and hard. Brannon gripped her hand, but his fingers went through hers—right down to the stone itself. "The Lock, Heir of Terrasen. I summoned you here for it. In the Stone Marshes, there lies a sunken city—the Lock is hidden there. It is needed to bind the keys back into the broken Wyrdgate. It is the *only* way to get them back into that gate and seal it permanently. My daughter begs you—"

"What Lock—"

"Find the Lock."

"*Where* in the Stone Marshes? It's not exactly a small—"

Brannon was gone.

Aelin scowled and shoved the Amulet of Orynth back into her shirt. "Of course there's a gods-damned lock," she muttered.

She groaned a bit as she eased to her feet, and frowned at the night-dark sea crashing mere yards away. At the ancient queen across it, readying her armada.

Aelin stuck out her tongue.

"Well, if Maeve wasn't already poised to attack, that'll certainly set her off," Aedion drawled from the shadows of a nearby pillar.

Aelin stiffened, hissing.

Her cousin grinned at her, his teeth moon white. "You think I didn't know you had something else up your sleeve for why we took back this temple? Or that this spring in Rifthold taught me nothing about your tendency to be planning a few things at once?"

She rolled her eyes, stepping off the sacred stone and stomping down the stairs. "I assume you heard everything."

"Brannon even winked at me before he vanished."

She clenched her jaw.

Aedion leaned his shoulder against the carved pillar. "A Lock, eh? And when, precisely, were you going to inform us about this new shift in direction?"

She stalked up to him. "When I rutting felt like it, that's when. And it's not a shift in direction—not yet. Allies remain our goal, not cryptic commands from dead royals."

Aedion just smiled. A ripple in the murky shadows of the temple snagged her attention, and Aelin heaved a sigh. "You two are honestly insufferable."

Lysandra flapped onto the top of a nearby statue and clicked her beak rather saucily.

Aedion slid an arm around Aelin's shoulders, guiding her back toward the ramshackle residence within the compound. "New court, new traditions, you said. Even for *you*. Starting with fewer schemes and secrets that take years off my life every time you do a grand reveal. Though I certainly enjoyed that new trick with the ash. Very artistic."

Aelin jabbed him in the side. "Do *not*—"

The words halted as footsteps crunched on the dry earth from the nearby courtyard. The wind drifted by, carrying a scent they knew too well.

Valg. A powerful one, if he'd walked through her wall of flame.

Aelin drew Goldryn as Aedion's own blade whined softly, the Sword of Orynth gleaming like freshly forged steel in the moonlight. Lysandra remained aloft, ducking deeper into the shadows.

"Sold out or shit-poor luck?" Aedion murmured.

"Likely both," Aelin muttered back as the figure appeared through two pillars.

He was stocky, slightly overweight—not at all the impossible beauty that the Valg princes preferred when inhabiting a human body. But the inhuman reek, even with that collar on his wide neck . . . So much stronger than usual.

Of course, Brannon couldn't have been bothered to warn her.

The Valg stepped into the light of the sacred braziers.

The thoughts eddied from her head as she saw his face.

And Aelin knew that Aedion had been right: her actions tonight *had* sent a message. An outright declaration of her location. Erawan had been waiting for this meeting far longer than a few hours. And the Valg king knew both sides of her history.

For it was the Chief Overseer of Endovier who now grinned at them.

She still dreamt of him.

Of that ruddy, common face leering at her, at the other women in Endovier. Of his laughter when she was stripped to the waist and whipped in the open, then left to hang from her shackles in the bitter cold or blazing sun. Of his smile as she was shoved into those lightless pits; the grin still stretching wide when they removed her from them days or weeks later.

Goldryn's hilt became slimy in her hand. Flame instantly burned along the fingers of her other. She cursed Lorcan for stealing back the golden ring, for taking away that one bit of immunity, of redemption.

Aedion was glancing between them, reading the recognition in her eyes.

The Overseer of Endovier sneered at her, "Aren't you going to introduce us, slave?"

The utter stillness that crept over her cousin's face told her enough about what he'd pieced together—along with the glance at the faint scars on her wrists where shackles had been.

Aedion slid a step between them, no doubt reading every sound and shadow and scent to see if the man was alone, estimating how hard and long they'd have to fight their way out of here. Lysandra flapped to another pillar, poised to shift and pounce at a single word.

Aelin tried to rally the swagger that had shielded and bluffed her way out of everything. But all she saw was the man dragging those women behind the buildings; all she heard was the slam of that iron grate over her lightless pit; all she smelled were the salt and the blood and the unwashed bodies; all she felt was the burning, wet slide of blood down her ravaged back—

I will not be afraid; I will not be afraid—

"Have they run out of pretty boys in the kingdoms for you to wear?" Aedion drawled, buying them time to figure out the odds.

"Come a bit closer," the overseer smirked, "and we'll see if you make a better fit, General."

Aedion let out a low chuckle, the Sword of Orynth lifting a bit higher. "I don't think you'd walk away from it."

And it was the sight of that blade, her father's blade, the blade of her people . . .

Aelin lifted her chin, and the flames encircling her left hand flickered brighter.

The overseer's watery blue eyes slid to hers, narrowing with amusement. "Too bad you didn't have that little gift when I put you in those pits. Or when I painted the earth with your blood."

A low snarl was Aedion's answer.

But Aelin made herself smile. "It's late. I just trounced your soldiers. Let's get this chat out of the way so I can have some rest."

The overseer's lip curled. "You'll learn proper manners soon enough, girl. All of you will."

The amulet between her breasts seemed to grumble, a flicker of raw, ancient power.

Aelin ignored it, shutting out any thought of it. If the Valg, if Erawan, got one whiff that she possessed what he so desperately sought—

The overseer again opened his mouth. She attacked.

Fire blasted him into the nearest wall, surging down his throat, through his ears, up his nose. Flame that did not burn, flame that was mere light, blindingly white—

The overseer roared, thrashing as her magic swept into him, melded with him.

But there was nothing inside to grab on to. No darkness to burn out, no remaining ember to breathe life into. Only—

Aelin reeled back, magic vanishing and knees buckling as if struck. Her head gave a throb, and nausea roiled in her gut. She knew that feeling—that taste.

Iron. As if the man's core was made of it. And that oily, hideous aftertaste . . . Wyrdstone.

The demon inside the overseer let out a choked laugh. "What are collars and rings compared to a solid heart? A heart of iron and Wyrdstone, to replace the coward's heart beating within."

"Why," she breathed.

"I was planted here to demonstrate what is waiting should you and your court visit Morath."

Aelin slammed her fire into him, scouring his insides, striking that core of pure darkness inside. Again, again, again. The overseer kept roaring, but Aelin kept attacking, until—

She vomited all over the stones between them. Aedion hauled her upright.

Aelin lifted her head. She'd burned off his clothes, but not touched the skin.

And there—pulsing against his ribs as if it were a fist punching through—was his heart.

It slammed into his skin, stretching bone and flesh.

Aelin flinched back. Aedion threw a hand in her path as the overseer arched in agony, his mouth open in a silent scream.

Lysandra flapped down from the rafters, shifting into leopard form at their side and snarling.

Again, that fist struck from inside. And then bones snapped, punching outward, ripping through muscle and skin as if his chest cavity were the petals of a blooming flower. There was nothing inside. No blood, no organs.

Only a mighty, ageless darkness—and two flickering golden embers at its core.

Not embers. Eyes. Simmering with ancient malice. They narrowed in acknowledgment and pleasure.

It took every ounce of her fire to steel her spine, to tilt her head at a jaunty angle and drawl, "At least you know how to make a good entrance, Erawan."

CHAPTER 16

The overseer spoke, but the voice was not his. And the voice was not Perrington's.

It was a new voice, an old voice, a voice from a different world and lifetime, a voice that fed on screams and blood and pain. Her magic thrashed against the sound, and even Aedion swore softly, still trying to herd her behind him.

But Aelin stood fast against the darkness peering at them from the man's cracked chest. And she knew that even if his body hadn't been irreparably broken, there was nothing left inside him to save anyway. Nothing worth saving to begin with.

She flexed her fingers at her sides, rallying her magic against the darkness that coiled and swirled inside the man's shattered chest.

Erawan said, "I would think gratitude is in order, Heir of Brannon."

She flicked her brows up, tasting smoke in her mouth. *Easy,* she murmured to her magic. Careful—she'd have to be so careful he did not see the amulet around her neck, sense the presence of the final Wyrdkey inside. With the first two already in his possession, if Erawan suspected that the third key was in this temple, and that his utter dominance over this land and all others was close enough to grab . . . She had to keep him distracted.

So Aelin snorted. "Why should I thank you, exactly?"

The embers of eyes slid upward, as if surveying the hollow body of the overseer. "For this small warning present. For ridding the world of one more bit of vermin."

And for making you realize how fruitless standing against me will be, that voice whispered right into her skull.

She slammed fire outward in a blind maneuver, stumbling back into Aedion at the caress in that hideous, beautiful voice. From her cousin's pale face, she knew he'd heard it, too, felt its violating touch.

Erawan chuckled. "I'm surprised you tried to save him first. Given what he did to you at Endovier. My prince could scarcely stand to be inside his mind, it was already so vile. Do you find pleasure in deciding who shall be saved and who is beyond it? So easy, to become a little, burning god."

Nausea, true and cold, struck her.

But it was Aedion who smirked, "I'd think you'd have better things to do, Erawan, than taunt us in the dead hours of the morning. Or is this all just a way to make yourself feel better about Dorian Havilliard slipping through your nets?"

The darkness hissed. Aedion squeezed her shoulder in silent warning. End it now. Before Erawan might strike. Before he could sense that the Wyrdkey he sought was mere feet away.

So Aelin inclined her head to the force staring at them through flesh and bone. "I suggest you rest and gather your strength, Erawan," she purred, winking at him with every shred of bravado left in her. "You're going to need it."

A low laugh as flames started to flicker in her eyes, heating her blood with welcome, delicious warmth. "Indeed. Especially considering the plans I have for the would-be King of Adarlan."

Aelin's heart stopped.

"Perhaps you should have told your lover to disguise himself before he snatched Dorian Havilliard out of Rifthold." Those eyes narrowed to slits. "What was his name . . . Oh, yes," Erawan breathed, as if someone had whispered it to him. "Prince Rowan Whitethorn of Doranelle. What a prize he shall be."

Aelin plummeted down into fire and darkness, refusing to yield one inch to the terror creeping over her.

Erawan crooned, "My hunters are already tracking them. And I am going to hurt them, Aelin Galathynius. I am going to hone them into my most loyal generals. Starting with your Fae Prince—"

A battering ram of hottest blue slammed into that pit in the man's chest cavity, into those burning eyes.

Aelin kept her magic focused on that chest, on the bones and flesh melting away, leaving only that heart of iron and Wyrdstone untouched. Her magic flowed around it like a stream surging past a rock, burning his body, that *thing* inside him—

"Don't bother saving any part of him," Aedion snarled softly.

Her magic roaring out of her, Aelin glanced over a shoulder. Lysandra was now in human form beside Aedion, teeth gritted at the overseer—

The look cost her.

She heard Aedion's shout before she felt Erawan's punch of darkness crash into her chest.

Felt the air snap against her as she was hurled back, felt her body bark against the stone wall before the agony of that darkness really sank in. Her breath stalled, her blood halted—

Get up get up get up.

Erawan laughed softly as Aedion was instantly at her side, dragging her to her feet as her mind, her body tried to reorder itself—

Aelin threw out her power again, letting Aedion believe she allowed him to hold her upright simply because she forgot to step away, not because her knees were shaking so violently she wasn't sure she *could* stand.

But her hand remained steady, at least, as she extended it.

The temple around them shuddered at the force of the power she hurled out of herself. Dust and kernels of debris trickled from the ceiling high above; columns swayed like drunken friends.

Aedion's and Lysandra's faces glowed in the blue light of her flame, their features wide-eyed but set with solid determination—and wrath. She leaned farther into Aedion as her magic roared from her, his grip tightening at her waist.

Each heartbeat was a lifetime; each breath ached.

But the overseer's body at last ripped apart under her power—the dark shields around it yielding to her.

And some small part of her realized that it only did so when Erawan deigned to leave, those amused, ember-like eyes guttering into nothing.

When the man's body was only ashes, Aelin reeled back her magic, cocooned her heart in it. She gripped Aedion's arm, trying not to breathe too loudly, lest he hear the rasp of her battered lungs, realize how hard that single plume of darkness had hit.

A heavy *thud* echoed through the silent temple as the lump of iron and Wyrdstone fell.

That was the cost—Erawan's plan. To realize that the only mercy she might offer her court would be death.

If they were ever captured . . . he'd make her watch as they were all carved apart and filled with his power. Make her look into their faces when he'd finished, and find no trace of their souls within. Then he'd get to work on her.

And Rowan and Dorian . . . If Erawan was hunting them at this very moment, if he learned that they were in Skull's Bay, and how hard he'd actually struck her—

Aelin's flames banked to a quiet ember, and she finally found enough strength in her legs to push away from Aedion's grip.

"We need to be on that ship before dawn, Aelin," he said. "If Erawan wasn't bluffing . . ."

Aelin only nodded. They had to get to Skull's Bay as fast as the winds and currents could carry them.

But as she turned toward the archway out of the temple, heading for the archives, she glanced at her chest—utterly untouched, though Erawan's power had hit her like a hurled spear.

He'd missed. By three inches, Erawan had narrowly missed hitting the amulet. And possibly sensing the Wyrdkey inside it.

Yet the blow still reverberated against her bones in brutal ripples.

A reminder that she might be the heir of fire . . . but Erawan was King of the Darkness.

Chapter 17

Manon Blackbeak watched the black skies above Morath bleed to rotted gray on the last morning of Asterin's life.

She had not slept the entirety of the night; had not eaten or drank; had done nothing but sharpen Wind-Cleaver in the frigid openness of the wyvern's aerie. Over and over, she had honed the blade, leaning against Abraxos's warm side, until her fingers were too stiff with cold to grip sword or stone.

Her grandmother had ordered Asterin locked in the deepest bowels of the Keep's dungeon, so heavily guarded that escape was impossible. Or rescue.

Manon had toyed with the idea for the first few hours after the sentence had been given. But to rescue Asterin would be to betray her Matron, her Clan. Her mistake—it was *her* own mistake, her own damned choices, that had led to this.

And if she stepped out of line again, the rest of the Thirteen would be put down. She was lucky she hadn't been stripped of her title as Wing Leader. At least she could still lead her people, protect them. Better than allowing someone like Iskra to take command.

The Ferian Gap legion's assault on Rifthold under Iskra's command had been sloppy, chaotic—not the systematic, careful sacking Manon would have planned had they asked her. It made no difference now whether the city was in full or half ruin. It didn't alter Asterin's fate.

So there was little to be done, other than to sharpen her ancient blade and memorize the Words of Request. Manon would have to utter them at the right moment. This last gift, she could give her cousin. Her only gift.

Not the long, slow torture and beheading that was typical of a witch execution.

But the swift mercy of Manon's own blade.

Boots scuffed on stone and crunched the hay littering the aerie floor. Manon knew that step—knew it as well as Asterin's own gait. "What," she said to Sorrel without looking behind her.

"Dawn approaches," her Third said.

Soon to be Second. Vesta would become Third, and . . . and maybe Asterin would at last see that hunter of hers, see the stillborn witchling they'd had together.

Never again would Asterin ride the winds; never again would Asterin soar on the back of her sky-blue mare. Manon's eyes slid to the wyvern across the aerie—shifting on her two legs, awake when the others were not.

As if she could sense her mistress's doom beckoning with each passing moment.

What would become of the mare when Asterin was gone?

Manon rose to her feet, Abraxos nudging the backs of her thighs with his snout. She reached down, brushing his scaly head. She didn't know who it was meant to comfort. Her crimson cape, as bloody and filthy as the rest of her, was still clasped at her collarbone.

The Thirteen would become twelve.

Manon met Sorrel's gaze. But her Third's attention was on Wind-Cleaver, bare in Manon's hand.

Her Third said, "You mean to make the Words of Request."

Manon tried to speak. But she could not open her mouth. So she only nodded.

Sorrel stared toward the open archway beyond Abraxos. "I wish she had the chance to see the Wastes. Just once."

Manon forced herself to lift her chin. "We do not wish. We do not hope," she said to her soon-to-be Second. Sorrel's eyes snapped to her, something like hurt flashing there. Manon took the inner blow. She said, "We will move on, adapt."

Sorrel said quietly, but not weakly, "She goes to her death to keep your secrets."

It was the closest Sorrel had ever come to outright challenge. To resentment.

Manon sheathed Wind-Cleaver at her side and strode for the stairwell, unable to meet Abraxos's curious stare. "Then she will have served me well as Second, and will be remembered for it."

Sorrel said nothing.

So Manon descended into the gloom of Morath to kill her cousin.

The execution was not to be held in the dungeon.

Rather, her grandmother had selected a broad veranda overlooking one of the endless drops into the ravine curled around Morath. Witches were crowded onto the balcony, practically thrumming with bloodlust.

The Matrons stood before the gathered group, Cresseida and the Yellowlegs Matron flanked by each of their heirs, all facing the open doors through which Manon and the Thirteen exited the Keep proper.

Manon did not hear the murmur of the crowd; did not hear the roaring wind ripping between the high turrets; did not hear the strike of hammers in the forges of the valley below.

Not when her attention went to Asterin, on her knees before the Matrons. She, too, was facing Manon, still in her riding leathers, her golden hair limp and knotted, flecked with blood. She lifted her face—

"It was only fair," Manon's grandmother drawled, the crowd silencing, "for Iskra Yellowlegs to also avenge the four sentinels slaughtered on your watch. Three blows apiece for each of the sentinels killed."

Twelve blows total. But from the cuts and bruises on Asterin's face, the split lip, from the way she cradled her body as she bent over her knees . . . It had been far more than that.

Slowly, Manon looked at Iskra. Cuts marred her knuckles—still raw from the beating she'd given Asterin in the dungeon.

While Manon had been upstairs, brooding.

Manon opened her mouth, her rage a living thing thrashing in her gut, her blood. But Asterin spoke instead.

"Be glad to know, Manon," her Second rasped with a faint, cocky smile, "that she had to chain me up to beat me."

Iskra's eyes flashed. "You still screamed, bitch, when I whipped you."

"Enough," Manon's grandmother cut in, waving a hand.

Manon barely heard the order.

They had *whipped* her sentinel like some underling, like some mortal beast—

Someone snarled, low and vicious, to her right.

The breath went out of her as she found Sorrel—unmovable rock, unfeeling stone—baring her teeth at Iskra, at those assembled here.

Manon's grandmother stepped forward, brimming with displeasure. Behind Manon, the Thirteen were a silent, unbreakable wall.

Asterin began scanning their faces, and Manon realized her Second understood that it was the last time she'd do so.

"Blood shall be paid with blood," Manon's grandmother and the

Yellowlegs Matron said in unison, reciting from their eldest rituals. Manon steeled her spine, waiting for the right moment. "Any witch who wishes to extract blood in the name of Zelta Yellowlegs may come forward."

Iron nails slid out from the hands of the entire Yellowlegs coven.

Asterin only stared at the Thirteen, her bloody face unmoved, eyes clear.

The Yellowlegs Matron said, "Form the line."

Manon pounced.

"I invoke the right of execution."

Everyone froze.

Manon's grandmother's face went pale with rage. But the other two Matrons, even Yellowlegs, just waited.

Manon said, head high, "I claim the right to my Second's head. Blood shall be paid with blood—but at my sword's edge. She is mine, and so shall her death be mine."

For the first time, Asterin's mouth tightened, eyes gleaming. Yes, she understood the only gift Manon could give her, the only honor left.

It was Cresseida Blueblood who cut in before the other two Matrons could speak. "For saving my daughter's life, Wing Leader, it shall be granted."

The Yellowlegs Matron whipped her head to Cresseida, a retort on her lips, but it was too late. The words had been spoken, and the rules were to be obeyed at any cost.

The Crochan's red cape fluttering behind her in the wind, Manon dared a look at her grandmother. Only hatred glowed in those ancient eyes—hatred, and a flicker of satisfaction that Asterin would be ended after decades of being deemed an unfit Second.

But at least this death was now hers to give.

And in the east, slipping over the mountains like molten gold, the sun began to rise.

A hundred years she'd had with Asterin. She'd always thought they'd have a hundred more.

Manon said softly to Sorrel, "Turn her around. My Second shall see the dawn one last time."

Sorrel obediently stepped forward, pivoting Asterin to face the High Witches, the crowd by the rail—and the rare sunrise piercing through Morath's gloom.

Blood soaked through the back of her Second's leathers.

And yet Asterin knelt, shoulders square and head high, as she looked not at the dawn—but at Manon herself while she stalked around her Second to take a place a few feet before the Matrons.

"Sometime before breakfast, Manon," her grandmother said from a few feet behind.

Manon drew Wind-Cleaver, the blade singing softly as it slid free of its sheath.

The sunlight gilded the balcony as Asterin whispered, so softly that only Manon could hear, "Bring my body back to the cabin."

Something in Manon's chest broke—broke so violently that she wondered if it was possible for no one to have heard it.

Manon lifted her sword.

All it would take was one word from Asterin, and she could save her own hide. Spill Manon's secrets, her betrayals, and she'd walk free. Yet her Second uttered no other word.

And Manon understood in that moment that there were forces greater than obedience, and discipline, and brutality. Understood that she had not been born soulless; she had not been born without a heart.

For there were both, begging her not to swing that blade.

Manon looked to the Thirteen, standing around Asterin in a half circle.

One by one, they lifted two fingers to their brows.

A murmur went through the crowd. The gesture not to honor a High Witch.

But a Witch-Queen.

There had not been a Queen of Witches in five hundred years, either among the Crochans or the Ironteeth. Not one.

Forgiveness shone in the faces of her Thirteen. Forgiveness and understanding and loyalty that was not blind obedience, but forged in pain and battle, in shared victory and defeat. Forged in hope for a better life—a better world.

At last, Manon found Asterin's gaze, tears now rolling down her Second's face. Not from fear or pain, but in farewell. A hundred years—and yet Manon wished she'd had more time.

For a heartbeat, she thought of that sky-blue mare in the aerie, the wyvern that would wait and wait for a rider who would never return. Thought of a green rocky land spreading to the western sea.

Hand trembling, Asterin pressed her fingers to her brow and extended them. "Bring our people home, Manon," she breathed.

Manon angled Wind-Cleaver, readying for the strike.

The Blackbeak Matron snapped, "Be done with it, Manon."

Manon met Sorrel's eyes, then Asterin's. And Manon gave the Thirteen her final order.

"Run."

Then Manon Blackbeak whirled and brought Wind-Cleaver down upon her grandmother.

CHAPTER 18

Manon saw only the flash of her grandmother's rusted iron teeth, the glimmer of her iron nails as she raised them to ward against the sword—but too late.

Manon slashed Wind-Cleaver down, a blow that would have cut most men in half.

Yet her grandmother darted back fast enough that the sword sliced down her torso, ripping fabric and skin as it cut between her breasts in a shallow line. Blue blood sprayed, but the Matron was moving, blocking Manon's next blow with her iron nails—iron so hard that Wind-Cleaver bounced off.

Manon did not look to see if the Thirteen obeyed. But Asterin was roaring; roaring and shouting to *stop.* The cries grew more distant, then echoed, as if she were now inside the hall, being dragged away.

No sounds of pursuit—as if the onlookers were too stunned. Good.

Iskra and Petrah had swords out, iron teeth down as they stepped between their Matrons and Manon, herding their two High Witches away.

The Blackbeak Matron's coven lunged forward, only to be halted by a hand. "Stay back," her grandmother commanded, panting as Manon circled her. Blue blood leaked down her grandmother's front. An inch closer, and she'd have been dead.

Dead.

Her grandmother bared her rusted teeth. "She's mine." She jerked her chin at Manon. "We do this the ancient way."

Manon's stomach roiled, but she sheathed her sword.

A flick of her wrists had her nails out, and a snap of her jaw had her teeth descending.

"Let's see how good you are, Wing Leader," her grandmother hissed, and attacked.

Manon had never seen her grandmother fight, never trained with her.

And some small part of Manon wondered if it was because her grandmother did not want others to know how skilled she was.

Manon could hardly move fast enough to avoid the nails ripping into her face, her neck, her gut, yielding step after step after step.

She only had to do this long enough to buy the Thirteen time to get to the skies.

Her grandmother slashed for her cheek, and Manon blocked the blow with an elbow, slamming the joint down hard into her grandmother's forearm. The witch barked in pain, and Manon spun out of reach, circling again.

"It is not so easy to strike now is it, Manon Blackbeak?" her grandmother panted as they surveyed each other. No one around them dared move; the Thirteen had vanished—every last one of them. She almost sagged with relief. Now to keep her grandmother occupied long enough to avoid her giving the onlookers the order to pursue. "So much easier with a blade, the weapon of those cowardly humans," her grandmother seethed. "With the teeth, the nails . . . You have to *mean* it."

They lunged for each other, some fundamental part of her cracking with every slash and swipe and block. They darted apart again.

"As pathetic as your mother," her grandmother spat. "Perhaps you'll die like her, too—with my teeth at your throat."

Her mother, whom she'd killed coming out of, who had died birthing her—

"For years, I tried to train her weakness out of you." Her grandmother spat blue blood onto the stones. "For the good of the Ironteeth, I made you into a force of nature, a warrior equal to none. And this is how you repay me—"

Manon didn't let the words unnerve her. She went for the throat, only to feint and slash.

Her grandmother barked in pain—genuine *pain*—as Manon's claws shredded her shoulder.

Blood showered her hand, flesh clinging to her nails—

Manon staggered back, bile burning her throat.

She saw the blow coming, but still didn't have time to stop it as her grandmother's right hand slashed across her belly.

Leather, cloth, and skin ripped. Manon screamed.

Blood, hot and blue, rushed out of her before her grandmother had darted back.

Manon shoved a hand against her abdomen, pushing against the shredded skin. Blood dribbled through her fingers, splattering onto the stones.

High above, a wyvern roared.

Abraxos.

The Blackbeak Matron laughed, flicking Manon's blood off her nails. "I'm going to dice your wyvern into tiny pieces and feed him to the hounds."

Despite the agony in her belly, Manon's vision honed. "Not if I kill you first."

Her grandmother chuckled, still circling, assessing. "You are stripped of your title as Wing Leader. You are stripped of your title as heir." Step after step, closer and closer, an adder looping around its prey. "From this day, you are Manon Witch Killer, Manon Kin Slayer."

The words pelted her like stones. Manon backed toward the balcony rail, pushing against the wound in her stomach to keep the blood in. The crowd parted like water around them. Just a little longer—just another minute or two.

Her grandmother paused, blinking toward the open doors, as if realizing the Thirteen had vanished. Manon attacked again before she could give the order to pursue.

Swipe, lunge, slash, duck—they moved in a whirlwind of iron and blood and leather.

But as Manon twisted away, the wounds in her stomach gave more, and she stumbled.

Her grandmother didn't miss a beat. She struck.

Not with her nails or teeth, but with her foot.

The kick to Manon's stomach set her screaming, a roar again answered by Abraxos, locked high above. Soon to die, as she would. She prayed the Thirteen would spare him, let him join them wherever they would flee.

Manon slammed into the stone rail of the balcony and crumpled to the black tiles. Blue blood leaked from her, staining the thighs of her pants.

Her grandmother slowly approached, panting.

Manon grabbed the balcony rail, hauling herself to her feet one last time.

"Do you want to know a secret, Kin Slayer?" her grandmother breathed.

Manon slumped against the balcony rail, the drop below endless and a relief. They'd take her to the dungeons—either use her for Erawan's breeding, or torture her until she begged for death. Maybe both.

Her grandmother spoke so softly that even Manon could barely hear over her own gasps for air. "As your mother labored to push you out, she confessed who your father was. She said you . . . *you* would be the one who broke the curse, who saved us. She said your father was a rare-born Crochan Prince. And she said that your mixed blood would be the key." Her grandmother lifted her nails to her mouth and licked off Manon's blue blood.

No.

No.

"So you have been a Kin Slayer your whole life," her grandmother purred. "Hunting down those Crochans—your *relatives.* When you were a witchling, your father searched the lands for you. He never stopped loving your mother. *Loving* her," she spat. "And loving you. So I killed him."

Manon gazed at the drop below, the death that beckoned.

"His despair was delicious when I told him what I'd done to her. What I would make you into. Not a child of peace—but war."

Made.

Made.

Made.

Manon's iron nails chipped on the dark stone of the balcony rail. And then her grandmother said the words that broke her.

"Do you know why that Crochan was spying in the Ferian Gap this spring? She had been sent to find *you.* After a hundred and sixteen years of searching, they had finally learned the identity of their dead prince's lost child."

Her grandmother's smile was hideous in its absolute triumph. Manon willed strength to her arms, to her legs.

"Her name was Rhiannon, after the last Crochan Queen. And she was your half sister. She confessed it to me upon our tables. She thought it'd save her life. And when she saw what you had become, she chose to let the knowledge die with her."

"I am a Blackbeak," Manon rasped, blood choking her words.

Her grandmother took a step, smiling as she crooned, "You are a Crochan. The last of their royal bloodline with the death of your sister at your own hand. You are a Crochan *Queen*."

Absolute silence from the witches gathered.

Her grandmother reached for her. "And you're going to die like one by the time I'm finished with you."

Manon didn't let her grandmother's nails touch her.

A boom sounded nearby.

Manon used the strength she'd gathered in her arms, her legs, to hurl herself onto the stone ledge of the balcony.

And roll off it into the open air.

Air and rock and wind and blood—

Manon slammed into a warm, leathery hide, screaming as pain from her wounds blacked out her vision.

Above, somewhere far away, her grandmother was shrieking orders—

Manon dug her nails into the leathery hide, burying her claws deep. Beneath her, a bark of discomfort she recognized. Abraxos.

But she held firm, and he embraced the pain as he banked to the side, swerving out of Morath's shadow—

She felt them around her.

Manon managed to open her eyes, flicking the clear lid against the wind into place.

Edda and Briar, her Shadows, were now flanking her. She knew they'd been there, waiting in the shadows with their wyverns, had heard every one of those damning last words. "The others have flown ahead. We were sent to retrieve you," Edda, the eldest of the sisters, shouted over the roar of the wind. "Your wound—"

"It's shallow," Manon snapped, forcing the pain aside to focus on the task at hand. She was on Abraxos's neck, the saddle a few feet behind her. One by one, every breath an agony, she released her nails from his skin and slid toward the saddle. He evened out his flight, offering smooth air to buckle herself into the harness.

Blood leaked from the gouges in her belly—soon the saddle was slick with it.

Behind them, several roars set the mountains trembling.

"We can't let them get to the others," Manon managed to say.

Briar, black hair streaming behind her, swept in closer. "Six Yellowlegs on our tail. From Iskra's personal coven. Closing in fast."

With a score to settle, they'd no doubt been given free rein to slaughter them.

Manon surveyed the peaks and ravines of the mountains around them.

"Two apiece," she ordered. The Shadows' black wyverns were enormous—skilled at stealth, but devastating in a fight. "Edda, you drive two to the west; Briar, you slam the other two to the east. Leave the last two to me."

No sign of the rest of the Thirteen in the gray clouds or mountains.

Good—they had gotten away. It was enough.

"You kill them, then you find the others," Manon ordered, an arm draped over her wound.

"But, Wing Leader—"

The title almost sapped her will. But Manon barked, "*That's an order.*"

The Shadows bowed their heads. Then, as if sharing one mind, one heart, they banked to either direction, peeling away from Manon like petals in the wind.

Bloodhounds on a scent, four Yellowlegs split from their group to deal with each Shadow.

The two in the center flew faster, harder, spreading apart to close in on Manon. Her vision blurred.

Not a good sign—not a good sign at all.

She breathed to Abraxos, "Let's make it a final stand worthy of song."

He bellowed in answer.

The Yellowlegs swept near enough for Manon to count their weapons. A battle cry shattered from the one to her right.

Manon dug her left heel into Abraxos's side.

Like a shooting star, he blasted down toward the peaks of the ashy mountains. The Yellowlegs dove with them.

Manon aimed for a ravine running through the spine of the mountain range, her vision flashing black and white and foggy. A chill crept into her bones.

The walls of the ravine closed around them like the maw of a mighty beast, and she pulled on the reins once.

Abraxos flung out his wings and coasted along the side of the ravine before catching a current and leveling out, flapping like hell through the heart of the crevasse, pillars of stone jutting from the floor like lances.

The Yellowlegs, too ensnared in their bloodlust, their wyverns too large and bulky, balked at the ravine—at the sharp turn—

A boom and a screech, and the whole ravine shuddered.

Manon swallowed her bark of agony to peer behind. One of the wyverns had panicked, too big for the space, and slammed into a stone column. Broken bone and blood rained down.

But the other wyvern had managed to bank, and now sailed toward them, wings so wide they nearly grazed either side of the ravine.

Manon panted through her bloody teeth, "*Fly, Abraxos.*"

And her gentle, warrior-hearted mount flew.

Manon focused on keeping to the saddle, on keeping the arm pressed against her wound to hold the blood in, keep that lethal cold away.

She'd gotten enough injuries to know her grandmother had struck deep and true.

The ravine swerved right, and Abraxos took the turn with expert skill. She prayed for the boom and roar of the pursuing wyvern to hit the walls, but none came.

But Manon knew these deadly canyons. She'd flown this path countless times on the endless, inane patrols these months. The Yellowlegs, sequestered in the Ferian Gap, did not.

"To the very end, Abraxos," she said. His roar was his only confirmation.

One shot. She'd have one shot. Then she could gladly die, knowing the Thirteen wouldn't be pursued. Not today, at least.

Turn after turn, Abraxos hurtled through the ravine, snapping his own tail against the rock to send debris flying into the Yellowlegs sentinel.

The rider dodged the rocks, her wyvern bobbing on the wind. Closer—Manon needed her closer. She tugged on Abraxos's reins, and he checked his speed.

Turn after turn after turn, black rock flashing by, blurring like her own fading vision.

The Yellowlegs was near enough to throw a dagger.

Manon looked over a shoulder with her failing eyesight in time to see her do just that.

Not one dagger—but two, metal gleaming in the dim canyon light.

Manon braced herself for the impact of metal in flesh and bone.

Abraxos took the final turn as the sentinel hurled her daggers at Manon. A towering, impenetrable wall of black stone arose, mere feet away.

But Abraxos soared up, catching the updraft and sailing out of the heart of the ravine, so close Manon could touch the dead-end wall.

The two daggers struck the rock where Manon had been moments before.

And the Yellowlegs sentinel, on her bulky, heavy wyvern, did as well.

Rock groaned as wyvern and rider splattered against it. And fell to the ravine floor.

Panting, her breath a wet, bloody rasp, Manon patted Abraxos's side. Even the motion was feeble. "Good," she managed to say.

Mountains became small again. Oakwald spread before her. Trees—the cover of trees might hide her . . . "Oak . . . ," she rasped.

Manon didn't finish the command before the Darkness swept in to claim her.

Chapter 19

Elide Lochan kept quiet during the two days she and Lorcan trekked through the eastern edges of Oakwald, heading for the plains beyond.

She had not asked him the questions that seemed to matter the most, letting him think her a foolish girl, blinded by gratitude that he had saved her.

He'd quickly forgotten that though he'd carried her out, she'd saved herself. And he'd accepted her name—her *mother's* name—without question. If Vernon was on her trail . . . It had been a fool's mistake, but there was no undoing it, not without raising Lorcan's suspicions.

So she kept her mouth shut, swallowed her questions. Like why he'd been hunting her. Or who his mistress was to command such a powerful warrior—why he wanted to get into Morath, why he kept touching some object beneath his dark jacket. And why he had looked so surprised—though he'd tried to hide it—when she'd mentioned Celaena Sardothien and Aelin Galathynius.

Elide had no doubt the warrior was keeping secrets of his own, and that despite his promise to protect her, the moment he got every answer he needed, that protection would end.

But she still slept soundly these last two nights—thanks to the belly full of meat courtesy of Lorcan's hunting. He'd scrounged up two rabbits, and when she'd devoured all of hers in minutes, he'd given her half of what was left of his. She hadn't bothered being polite by refusing.

It was midmorning by the time the light in the forest turned brighter, the air fresher. And then the roaring of mighty waters—the Acanthus.

Lorcan stalked ahead, and Elide could have sworn even the trees leaned away from him as he held up a hand in a silent motion to wait.

She obeyed, lingering in the gloom of the trees, praying he wouldn't make them return to the tangle of Oakwald, that she wouldn't be denied this step into the bright, wide-open world . . .

Lorcan motioned again—to come forward. All was clear.

Elide was silent as she stepped, blinking at the flood of sunshine, from the last line of trees to stand beside Lorcan on a high, rocky riverbank.

The river was enormous, shades of rushing gray and brown—the last of the ice melt from the mountains. So wide and wild that she knew she could not swim it, and that the crossing had to be somewhere else. But past the river, as if the water were a boundary between two worlds . . .

Hills and meadows of high emerald grasses swayed on the other side of the Acanthus, like a hissing sea under a cloudless blue sky, stretching away forever to the horizon.

"I can't remember," she murmured, the words barely audible over the roaring song of the river, "the last time I saw . . ." In Perranth, locked in that tower, she'd only had a view of the city, perhaps the lake if the day was clear enough. Then she'd been in that prison wagon, then in Morath, where it was only mountains and ash and armies. And during the flight with Manon and Abraxos, she had been too lost in terror and grief to notice anything at all. But now . . . She could not remember the last time she'd seen sunlight dancing on a meadow, or little brown birds bobbing and swooping on the warm breeze over it.

"The road is about a mile upriver," Lorcan said, his dark eyes unmoved by the Acanthus or the rippling grasses beyond. "If you want your plan to work, now would be the time to prepare."

She cut him a glance. "You need the most work." A flick of black brows. Elide clarified, "If this ruse is to succeed, you at least need to . . . pretend to be human."

Nothing about the man suggested his human heritage held sway.

"Hide more of your weapons," she went on. "Leave only the sword."

Even the mighty blade would be a dead giveaway that Lorcan was no ordinary traveler.

She fished an extra strap of leather out of her jacket pocket. "Tie back your hair. You'll look less . . ." She trailed off at the faint amusement tinged with warning in his eyes. "Savage," she made herself say, dangling the leather strap between them. Lorcan's broad fingers closed around it, a frown on his lips as he obeyed. "And unbutton your jacket," she said, rummaging through her mental catalog of traits she had noted seemed less threatening, less intimidating. Lorcan obeyed that order, too, and soon the dark gray shirt beneath his tight-fitting black jacket was showing, revealing the broad, muscled chest. It looked more inclined for solid labor than killing fields, at least.

"And you?" he said, brows still high.

Elide surveyed herself, and set down her pack. First, she removed the leather jacket, even though it left her feeling like a layer of skin had peeled off, then she rolled up the sleeves of her white shirt. But without the tight leather, the full size of her breasts could be seen—marking her as a woman and not a slip of a girl that people assumed she was. She then took to her hair, ruffling it out of its braid and restyling it into a knot atop her head. A married woman's hairstyle, not the free-flowing locks or plait of youth.

She stuffed her jacket into her pack, standing up straight to face Lorcan.

His eyes traveled from her feet to her head, and he frowned again. "Bigger tits won't prove or hide anything."

Her cheeks heated. "Perhaps they'll keep men distracted just enough that they won't ask questions."

With that, she started upstream, trying not to think about the men who had touched and sneered in that cell. But if it got her safely across the river, she'd use her body to her advantage. Men would see what they wanted to: a pretty young woman who did not bristle at their attention, who spoke kindly and warmly. Someone trustworthy, someone sweet yet unremarkable.

Lorcan trailed, then caught up to walk beside her like an actual companion and not some promise-bound escort for the final half mile around the bend of the river.

Horses and wagons and shouts greeted them before the sight did.

But there it was: a broad if worn stone bridge, wagons and carts and riders lined up in droves on either side. And about two dozen guards in Adarlanian colors monitoring either bank, collecting tolls, and—

Checking wagons, inspecting every face and person.

The ilken had known about her limp.

Elide slowed, keeping close to Lorcan as they neared the two-story, derelict barracks on their side of the river. Down the road, flanked by the trees, a few equally sorry-looking buildings were a flurry of activity. An inn and a tavern. For travelers to wait out the lines with a drink or meal, or perhaps rent a room during inclement weather.

So many people—humans. No one appeared panicked or hurt or sickly. And the guards, despite their uniforms, moved like men while they searched the wagons passing the barracks that served as tollhouse and sleeping quarters.

She said quietly to Lorcan as they headed for the dirt road and the distant back of the line, "I don't know what magic you possess, but if you can make my limp less noticeable—"

Before she could finish, a force like a cool night wind pushed against her ankle and calf, then wrapped around it in a solid grip. A brace.

Her steps evened out, and she had to bite back her urge to gawk at the feeling of walking straight and sure. She didn't allow herself to enjoy it, savor it, not when it would likely only last until they cleared the bridge.

Merchants' wagons idled, crammed with goods from those who hadn't wanted to risk the Avery river to the north, their drivers tight-faced at the wait and impending inspections. Elide scanned the drivers, the merchants, the other travelers . . . Each one of them made her instincts shout that they'd be betrayed the second they asked to ride or offered a coin to keep quiet.

To trawl the line would catch the eye of the guards, so Elide used every step to study it while seemingly heading toward the back. But she reached the end of the line empty-handed.

Lorcan, however, gave a pointed glance behind her—toward the tavern, whitewashed to no doubt hide the near-crumbling stones. "Let's get a bite before we wait," he said, loud enough for the wagon in front of them to hear and dismiss it.

She nodded. Someone else might be inside, and her stomach was grumbling. Except—

"I don't have any money," she murmured as they approached the pale wooden door. Lie. She had gold and silver from Manon. But she wasn't about to flash it in front of Lorcan, promise or no.

"I've got plenty," he said tightly, and she delicately cleared her throat.

He lifted his brows.

"You'll win us no allies looking like that," she said, and gave him a sweet little smile. "Walk in there looking like a warrior and you'll get noticed."

"And what am I to be, then?"

"Whatever we need you to be when the time comes. But . . . don't glower."

He opened the door, and by the time her eyes adjusted to the glow of the wrought-iron chandeliers, Lorcan's face *had* changed. His eyes might never be warm, but a bland smile was on his face, his shoulders relaxed—as if he were slightly inconvenienced by the wait but eager for a good meal.

He almost looked human.

The tavern was packed, the noise so deafening that she could barely speak loudly enough to the nearest barmaid to order lunch. They squeezed between crammed tables, and Elide noticed that more than a few pairs of eyes went to her chest, then her face. And lingered.

She pushed against the crawling feeling and kept her steps unhurried as she aimed for a table tucked against the back wall that a weary-looking couple had just vacated.

A boisterous party of eight was crammed around the table a few feet away, a middle-aged woman with a booming laugh instantly singling herself out as their leader. The others at the table—a beautiful, raven-haired woman; a barrel-chested bearded man whose hands were as large as dinner plates; and a few rough-looking people—all kept looking to the older woman, gauging her responses and listening carefully to what she had to say.

Elide slid into the worn wooden chair, Lorcan claiming the one across from her—his size earning him a look from the bearded man and the middle-aged woman at the table.

Elide weighed that look.

Assessment. Not for a fight; not for a threat. But in appreciation and calculation.

Elide wondered for a heartbeat if Anneith herself had nudged that other couple to move away—to free up this one table for them. For that very look.

Elide laid her hand out on the table, palm up, and gave Lorcan a sleepy smile she'd once seen a kitchen maid give a Morath cook. "Husband," she said sweetly, wriggling her fingers.

Lorcan's mouth tightened, but he took her hand—her fingers dwarfed in his.

His calluses scraped against her own. He noticed it at the same moment she did, sliding his hand to cup hers so he might inspect her palm. She closed her hand, rotating it to grip his again.

"Brother," Lorcan murmured so no one else could hear. "I am your brother."

"You are my husband," she said with equal quiet. "We have been married three months. Follow my lead."

He glanced around, not having noticed the assessing stare they'd been given. Doubt still danced in his eyes, along with a silent question.

She said simply, "Men will not fear the threat of a brother. I would still be unclaimed—still be open for . . . invitations. I have seen how little respect men have for anything they think they are entitled to. So you are my husband," she hissed, "until I say otherwise."

A shadow flickered in Lorcan's eyes, along with another question. One she didn't want to and couldn't answer. His hand tightened on hers, demanding she look at him. She refused.

Their food arrived, mercifully, before Lorcan could ask it.

Stew—root vegetables and rabbit. She dug in, nearly melting the roof of her mouth at the first bite.

The group behind them began talking again, and she listened as she ate, selecting bits and pieces as if they were shells on a shore.

"Maybe we'll offer them a performance and they'll cut the toll fee in half." From the blond, bearded man.

"Unlikely," the leader said. "Those pricks would charge *us* to perform. Worse, they enjoy our performance and demand we stay awhile. We can't afford that wait. Not when other companies are already on the move. We don't want to hit all the plains towns after everyone else."

Elide almost choked on her stew. Anneith *must* have freed this table, then. Her plan had been to find a troupe or carnival to fall into, disguise themselves as workers, and this . . .

"We pay full price on that toll," the beautiful woman said, "and we might get to that first town half starved and barely able to perform at all."

Elide lifted her eyes to Lorcan's—he gave a nod.

She took a sip of her stew, steeling herself, thinking of Asterin Blackbeak. Charming, confident, fearless. She'd always had her head at a jaunty angle, a looseness to her limbs, a hint of a smile on her lips. Elide took a breath, letting those memories sink into muscle and flesh and bone.

Then she pivoted in her chair, an arm draped around the back as she leaned toward their table and said with a grin, "Sorry to interrupt your meal, but I couldn't help but overhear your conversation." They all turned toward her, brows high, the eyes of the leader going right to Elide's face. She saw the assessment: young, pretty, unblemished by a hard life. Elide kept her own expression pleasant, willed her eyes to brighten. "Are you some sort of performing troupe?" She motioned to Lorcan with a tilt of her head. "My husband and I have been looking to fall in with one for weeks with no luck—everyone's full."

"So are we," their leader said.

"Right," Elide replied merrily. "But that toll is steep—for anyone. And if we were to be in business together, perhaps on a temporary basis . . ." Lorcan's knee brushed hers in warning. She ignored him. "We'd be glad to chip in on the fee—make up any difference owed."

The woman's assessment turned wary. "We are a carnival indeed. But we have no need of new members."

The bearded man and beautiful woman shot glances at the woman, reprimand in their eyes.

Elide shrugged. "All right, then. But in case you change your mind before you depart, my husband"—a gesture to Lorcan, who was giving his best attempt at an easy smile—"is an expert sword-thrower. And in our previous troupe, he made good coin matching himself against men who sought to best him in feats of strength."

The leader turned her keen eyes on Lorcan—on the height and muscles and posture.

Elide knew she'd guessed right on the vacancy they'd needed filled when the woman said to her, "And what did you do for them?"

"I worked as a fortune-teller—they called me their oracle." A shrug. "Mostly just shadows and guesswork." It'd have to be, considering the little fact that she couldn't read.

The woman remained unimpressed. "And what was your troupe's name?"

They likely knew them—knew every troupe that patrolled the plains.

She scanned her memory for anything helpful, anything—

Yellowlegs. The witches in Morath had once mentioned Baba Yellowlegs, who had traveled in a carnival to avoid detection, who had died in Rifthold this winter with no explanation. . . . Detail after detail, buried in the catacombs of her memory, poured out.

"We were in the Carnival of Mirrors," Elide said. Recognition—surprise, respect—sparked in the leader's eyes. "Until Baba Yellowlegs, our owner, was killed in Rifthold this past winter. We left, and have been looking for work since."

"Where did you come from, then?" the bearded man asked.

It was Lorcan who replied, "My family lives on the western side of the Fangs. We've spent the past few months with them—waited until the snows melted, since the pass was so treacherous. Strange things happening," he added, "in the mountains these days."

The company stilled.

"Indeed," the raven-haired woman said. She looked to their leader. "They could help pay the toll, Molly. And since Saul left, that act has been empty . . ." Likely their sword-thrower.

"Like I said," Elide chimed in with Asterin's pretty smile, "we'll be here for a little while, so if you change your minds . . . let us know. If not . . ." She saluted with her dented spoon. "Safe travels."

Something flashed in Molly's eyes, but the woman looked them over once more. "Safe travels," she murmured.

Elide and Lorcan returned to their meal.

And when the barmaid came to take their money for it, Elide reached into her inner pocket and pulled out a silver coin.

The barmaid's eyes were wide, but it was the sharp eyes of Molly, of the others at that table, that Elide noted as the girl slipped away and brought back their change.

Lorcan kept silent as Elide left a generous tip on the table, but they both offered pleasant smiles to the troupe as they vacated their table and the tavern.

Elide went right to the back of the line, still keeping that smile on her face, her back straight.

Lorcan sidled up close, not at all noteworthy for the front they were putting on. "You have no money, do you?"

She gave him a sidelong glance. "Looks like I was mistaken."

A flash of white teeth as he smiled—genuinely this time. "Well, you'd better hope you and I have enough, Marion, because Molly's about to make you an offer."

Elide turned at the crunch of dirt beneath black boots and found Molly before them, the others lingering—some slipping around the corner of the tavern, to no doubt retrieve the wagons.

Molly's hard face was flushed—as if they'd been arguing. But she just clicked her tongue and said, "Temporary stint. If you're shit, you're out, and we won't pay back the money for the toll."

Elide smiled, not entirely faking it. "Marion and Lorcan, at your service, madam."

His wife. Gods above.

He was over five hundred years old—and this . . . this girl, young woman, she-devil, whatever she was, had just bluffed and lied her way into a job. A sword-thrower indeed.

Lorcan lingered outside the tavern, Marion at his side. A small troupe—hence the lack of funds—and one that had seen better days, he realized as the two yellow-painted wagons clattered and wobbled into view, pulled by four nags.

Marion carefully observed Molly climb into the driver's seat beside the raven-haired beauty, who paid Lorcan absolutely no heed.

Well, having Marion as his gods-damned *wife* certainly put an end to anything more than appreciation of the stunning woman.

It was an effort not to growl. He hadn't been with a woman in months now. And of course—*of course*—he'd have the time and interest in one . . . only to be shackled by another one's lies.

His wife.

Not that Marion was hard on the eyes, he noted as she obeyed Molly's barked order to climb into the back of the second wagon. Some of the other party members followed on piss-poor horses.

Marion took the bearded man's extended hand and he easily hauled her into the wagon. Lorcan trailed, assessing everyone in the party, everyone in the makeshift little town. A number of men, and some women, had noticed Marion when she strode by.

The sweet face paired with sinful curves—and without the limp, with her hair out of her face . . . She knew exactly what she was doing. Knew people would notice those things, think about those things, instead of the cunning mind and lies she fed them.

Lorcan ignored the hand the bearded man offered and jumped into the back of the wagon, reminding himself to sit close to Marion, to put an arm around her bony shoulders and look relieved and happy to have a troupe again.

Supplies filled the wagon, along with five other people who all smiled at Marion—and then quickly looked away from him.

Marion put a hand on his knee, and Lorcan avoided the urge to flinch. It had been a shock, earlier, to feel how rough those delicate hands were.

Not just a prisoner in Morath—but a slave.

The calluses were old and dense enough that she'd likely worked for years. Hard labor, from the looks of it—and with that ruined leg . . .

He tried not to think about that tang of fear and pain he'd sensed when she'd told him how little she believed in the kindness and decency of men. He didn't let his imagination delve too deep regarding why she might feel that way.

The wagon was hot, the air soaked with human sweat, hay, the shit of the horses lined up before them, the tang of iron from the weapons.

"Not much by way of belongings?" asked the bearded man—Nik, he'd called himself.

Shit. He'd forgotten humans traveled with baggage as if they were moving somewhere—

"We lost most of it on our trip out of the mountains. My *husband*," Marion said with charming annoyance, "insisted we ford a rushing stream. I'm lucky he even bothered to help *me* out, since he certainly didn't go after our supplies."

A low chuckle from Nik. "I suspect he was more focused on saving you than on the packs."

Marion rolled her eyes, patting Lorcan's knee. He nearly cringed at every touch.

Even with his lovers, outside the bed itself, he didn't like casual, careless contact. Some found that intolerable. Some thought they could break him into a decent male who just wanted a home and a good female to work beside him. Not one of them had succeeded.

"I can save myself," Marion said brightly. "But his throwing swords, our cooking supplies, my *clothes* . . ." A shake of the head. "His act might be a bit lackluster until we can find somewhere to purchase more supplies."

Nik met Lorcan's eyes, holding them for longer than most men dared. What he did for the carnival, Lorcan wasn't sure. Sometime performer—but definitely security. Nik's smile faded a bit. "The land beyond the Fangs isn't kind. Your people must be hardy folk to live out there."

Lorcan nodded. "A rougher life," he said, "than I want for my wife."

"Life on the road isn't much better," Nik countered.

"Ah," Marion chimed in, "but isn't it? A life of open skies and roads, of wandering where the wind takes you, answering to no one and nothing? A life of freedom . . ." She shook her head. "What more could I ask than to live a life unchecked by cages?"

Lorcan knew the words were no lie. He had seen her face when they beheld the grassy plain.

"Spoken like someone who has spent long enough on the road," Nik said. "It always goes either way with our kind: you settle down and never travel again, or you wander forever."

"I want to see life—see the world," Marion said, her voice softening. "I want to see everything."

Lorcan wondered if Marion would even get to do that if he failed in his task, if the Wyrdkey he carried wound up in the wrong hands.

"Best not wander too far," Nik said, frowning. "Not with what happened in Rifthold—or what's brewing down in Morath."

"What happened in Rifthold?" Lorcan cut in, sharply enough that Marion squeezed his knee.

Nik idly scratched his wheat-colored beard. "Whole city's been sacked—overrun, they say, by flying terrors and demon-women as their riders. Witches, if one is to believe the rumors. Ironteeth, straight out of legend." A shudder.

Holy gods. The destruction would have been a sight to behold. Lorcan forced himself to listen, to concentrate and not begin calculating casualties and what it would mean for this war, as Nik continued, "No word on the young king. But the city belongs to the witches and their beasts. They say to travel north is to now face a death trap; to travel south is another death trap . . . So"—a shrug—"we'll head east. Maybe we can find a way to bypass whatever's waiting in either direction. Maybe war will come and we'll all scatter to the winds." Nik looked him over. "Men like you and me might be conscripted."

Lorcan bit back a dark chuckle. No one could force him into anything—save for one person, and she . . . His chest tightened. It was best not to think of his queen.

"You think either side would do that? Force men to fight?" Marion's words were breathless.

"Don't know," Nik said, the scent and sound of the river now overwhelming enough that Lorcan knew they were near the toll. He reached into his jacket for the money Molly had demanded. Far more than their fair share, but he didn't care. These people could go to hell the moment they were safely hidden deep in the endless plains. "Duke Perrington's forces might not even want us, if they've got witches and beasts on their side."

And much worse, Lorcan wanted to say. Wyrdhounds and ilken and the gods knew what.

"But Aelin Galathynius," Nik mused. Marion's hand went limp on Lorcan's knee. "Who knows what she will do. She has not called for aid, has not asked soldiers to come to her. Yet she held Rifthold in her grip—killed the king, destroyed his castle. But gave the city back."

The bench beneath them groaned as Marion leaned forward. "What do you know of Aelin?"

"Rumors, here and there," Nik said, shrugging. "They say she's beautiful as sin—and colder than ice. They say she's a tyrant, a coward, a whore. They say she's gods-blessed—or gods-damned. Who knows? Nineteen seems awfully young to have such burdens . . . Rumor claims her court is strong, though. A shape-shifter guards her back—and two warrior-princes flank her on either side."

Lorcan thought of that shape-shifter, who had so unceremoniously vomited not once, but twice, all over him; thought of those two warrior-princes . . . One of them Gavriel's son.

"Will she save or damn us all?" Nik considered, now monitoring the snaking line behind their wagon. "I don't know if I much like the thought of everything resting in her hands, but . . . if she wins, perhaps the land will get better—life will get better. And if she fails . . . perhaps we all deserve to be damned anyway."

"She will win," Marion said with quiet strength. Nik's brows rose.

Men shouted, and Lorcan said, "I'd save talk of her for another time."

Boots crunched, and then uniformed men were peering into the back of the wagon. "Out," one ordered. "Line up." The man's eyes snagged on Marion.

Lorcan's arm tightened around her as an ugly, too-familiar light filled the soldier's eyes.

Lorcan bit back his snarl as he said to her, "Come, wife."

The soldier noticed him, then. The man backed away a step, a bit pale, then ordered the supplies be searched.

Lorcan jumped out first, bracing his hands on Marion's waist as he helped her off the wagon. When she made to step away, he tugged her back against him, an arm across her abdomen. He met each soldier's stare as they passed and wondered who was looking after the dark-haired beauty in the front.

A moment later, she and Molly came around. A dark, rimmed hat was slung over the beauty's head, half of her light brown face obscured, her body concealed in a heavy coat that drew the eye away from any feminine curves. Even the cast of her mouth was unpleasant—as if the woman had slipped into another person's skin entirely.

Still, Molly nudged the woman between Lorcan and Nik. Then took the money pouch from Lorcan's free hand without so much as a thank-you.

The dark-haired beauty leaned forward to murmur to Marion, "Don't look them in the eye, and don't talk back."

Marion nodded, chin dipping as she focused on the ground. Against him, he could feel her racing heart—wild, despite the calm submission written over every line of her body.

"And you," the beauty hissed at him as the soldiers searched their wares—and took what they wanted. "Molly says if you get into a fight, you're gone, and we're not bailing you out of prison. So let them talk and laugh, but don't interfere."

Lorcan debated saying he could slaughter this entire garrison if he pleased, but nodded.

After five minutes, another order was shouted. Molly handed over Lorcan's money and her own to pay the toll, plus more for "expedited passage." Then they were all back in the wagon again, none of them daring to see what had been pilfered. Marion was shaking slightly against where he kept her tucked into his side, but her face was blank, bored.

The guards hadn't so much as questioned them—hadn't asked after a woman with a limp.

The Acanthus roared beneath them as they crossed the bridge, wagon wheels clattering on ancient stones. Marion kept shaking.

Lorcan studied her face again—the hint of red along her high cheekbones, her tight mouth.

Not shaking from fear, he realized as he caught a whiff of her scent. A slight tang of it, perhaps, but mostly something red-hot, something wild and raging and—

Anger. It was boiling rage that made her shake. At the inspection, at the leering of the guards.

An idealist—that's what Marion was. Someone who wanted to fight for her queen, who believed, as Nik did, that this world could be better.

As they cleared the other side of the bridge, the soldiers letting them pass without fuss, as they meandered past the line on *that* side, and emerged onto the plains themselves, Lorcan wondered at that anger—at that belief in a better world.

He didn't feel like telling either Marion or Nik that their dream was a fool's one.

Marion relaxed enough to peer out the back of the wagon—at the grasses flanking the wide dirt road, at the blue sky, at the roaring river and the looming sprawl of Oakwald behind them. And for all her rage, a tentative sort of wonder grew in her dark eyes. He ignored it.

Lorcan had seen the worst and best in men for five hundred years.

There was no such thing as a better world—no such thing as a happy end.

Because there were no endings.

And there would be nothing waiting for them in this war, nothing waiting for an escaped slave girl, but a shallow grave.

CHAPTER 20

Rowan Whitethorn just needed a place to rest. He didn't give a shit if it was a bed or a pile of hay or even beneath a horse in a stable. As long as it was quiet and there was a roof to keep out the driving veils of rain, he didn't care.

Skull's Bay was what he expected, and yet not. Ramshackle buildings, painted every color but mostly in cracking disrepair, were bustling as residents shuttered windows and hauled in clotheslines against the storm that had chased Rowan and Dorian into the harbor minutes ago.

Hooded and cloaked, no one had asked them any questions once Rowan had flipped a five-copper mark to the dockmaster. Enough to keep his mouth shut, but not enough to warrant any of the would-be thieves monitoring the docks to come after them.

Dorian had mentioned twice now that he wasn't sure how Rowan was still functioning. To be honest, Rowan wasn't, either. He'd allowed himself to doze only for hours at a time over the past few days. The burnout loomed—steadily fraying his grip on his magic, his focus.

When Rowan hadn't been wrangling the winds to propel their skiff through the vibrant warm waters of the Dead Islands' archipelago, he'd been soaring high above to monitor for approaching enemies. He'd seen none. Just turquoise ocean and white sands flecked with dark, volcanic stone. All of it ringing the dense emerald foliage crusting mountainous islands that spread as far as even a hawk's eye could see.

Thunder grumbled across Skull's Bay, and the turquoise sea beyond the harbor seemed to glow brighter, as if a distant lightning strike had lit up the entire ocean. Along the docks, a cobalt-painted tavern remained lightly guarded, even with the storm bearing down on them.

The Sea Dragon. Rolfe's own headquarters, named after his ship, from Aelin's reports. Rowan debated going right up to it, no more than two lost travelers seeking shelter from the storm.

But he and the young king had chosen another route, during the many hours he'd made good on his promise to teach Dorian about magic. They'd worked for only minutes at a time—since it'd be no use if the king wrecked their little boat should his power slip its leash. So it had been exercises with ice: summoning a ball of frost to his palm, letting it melt. Over and over.

Even now, standing like a stone amid the stream of people hauling in wares from the storm's fury, the king was curling and relaxing his fingers, letting Rowan glean their bearings while he gazed across the horseshoe-shaped bay to the colossal chain stretched across its mouth—currently beneath the surface.

Ship-Breaker, the chain was called. Crusted with barnacles and draped in scarves of seaweed, it was connected to a watchtower on either side of the bay, where guards would raise and lower the chain to let ships out. Or keep ships in until they'd paid the hefty tolls. They'd been lucky that the chain had already been lowered in anticipation of the storm.

Since their plan for announcing themselves would be . . . calm. Diplomatic.

Which it would need to be, given that the last time Aelin had set foot in Skull's Bay, two years ago, she'd wrecked that chain. And taken out one of the now-rebuilt watchtowers (Rolfe, it seemed, had added a sister-tower across the bay since then), plus half the town. And disabled the rudders on every ship in the harbor, including Rolfe's prized one, the *Sea Dragon*.

Rowan wasn't surprised, but seeing the *scope* of the hell she had unleashed . . . Holy gods.

So Dorian's announcement of his arrival would be the opposite of *that*. They'd take rooms at a reputable inn and then request an audience with Rolfe. Proper and dignified.

Lightning flashed, and Rowan swiftly scanned the street ahead, a hand gripping his hood to keep the wind from revealing his Fae heritage.

An emerald-painted inn lay at the other end of the block, its gilded sign clacking in the wild wind. THE OCEAN ROSE.

The nicest inn in town, the dockmaster had claimed when they asked. Since they at least needed to appear like they could make good on the money they'd offer Rolfe.

And get some rest, if only for a few hours. Rowan stepped toward it, nearly sagging with relief, and looked over a shoulder to motion the king to follow.

But as if the gods themselves wanted to test him, a gust of rain-cooled wind sprayed into their faces, and some sense pricked in its wake. A shift in the air. Like a great pocket of power gathered close, beckoning.

The knife at his side was instantly in his soaked hand as he searched the rooftops, revealing only plumes of rain. Rowan quieted his mind, listening to the city and storm around them.

Dorian swept his dripping hair out of his face, mouth open to speak—until he noted the knife. "You feel it, too."

Rowan nodded, rain sliding down his nose. "What do you sense?"

The king's raw power might pick up different feelings, different clues, than what his wind and ice and instinct could detect. But without the training, it might not be clear.

"It feels . . . old." Dorian winced, and said over the storm, "Feral. Ruthless. I can't glean anything more."

"Does it remind you of the Valg?"

If there was one person who'd know, it'd be the king before him.

"No," Dorian said, gaze shuttering. "They were abhorrent to my magic. This thing out there . . . It just makes my magic curious. Wary, but curious. But it's concealed—somehow."

Rowan sheathed his knife. "Then stay close and keep alert."

Dorian had never been in such a place as Skull's Bay.

Even with the heavy rain lashing them as they hunted the source of that power down the main street, he'd marveled at the blend of lawlessness and complete order of the island-city. It bowed to no king of royal blood—yet was ruled by a Pirate Lord who had clawed his way to power thanks to hands tattooed with a map of the world's oceans.

A map, rumor claimed, that had revealed where enemies, treasure, and storms awaited him. The cost: his eternal soul.

Aelin had once confirmed that Rolfe was indeed soulless *and* indeed tattooed. As for the map . . . She'd shrugged, saying Rolfe claimed it stopped moving when magic fell. Dorian wondered if that map now indicated that he and Rowan walked through his city—if it marked them as enemies.

Perhaps Aelin's arrival would be known well before she set foot on this island.

Cloaked and hooded and thoroughly soaked, Dorian and Rowan made a wide circuit of the surrounding streets. People had quickly vanished, and the ships in the harbor rocked wildly with the waves lapping over the broad quay and onto the cobblestones. Palms thrashed and hissed, and not even gulls stirred.

His magic remained dormant, rumbling when he'd stiffen at a loud noise from within the taverns, inns, homes, and shops they passed. At his side, Rowan plowed through the storm, the rain and wind seeming to part for him.

They reached the quay, Rolfe's massive prize ship looming out in the heaving waters, sails tied down against the storm.

At least Rolfe was here. At least that had gone right.

Dorian was so busy observing the ship that he nearly slammed into Rowan's back as the warrior-prince halted.

He staggered back, Rowan mercifully not commenting on it, then scanned the building that had snagged the prince's attention.

His magic perked up like a startled deer.

"I shouldn't even be surprised," Rowan grumbled, and the blue-painted sign clattered in the winds above the tavern entrance. THE SEA DRAGON.

Two guards stood halfway down the block—guards not for any uniform, but for the fact that they were standing in this storm, hands on their swords.

Rowan angled his head in a way that told Dorian the prince was likely contemplating whether it was worth it to chuck the men into the roiling harbor. But no one stopped them as Rowan gave Dorian a warning look and opened the door to the Pirate Lord's personal tavern. Golden light, spices, polished wood floors and walls greeted them.

It was empty, despite the storm. Utterly empty, save for the dozen or so tables.

Rowan shut the door behind Dorian, scanning the room, the small stairs in the back. From where they stood, Dorian could see the letters covering most of the tables.

Storm-Chaser. Lady Ann. Tiger-Star.

The sterns of ships. Every table was made from them.

They hadn't been taken from wrecks. No, this was a trophy room—a reminder to those who met with the Pirate Lord of how, exactly, he had gained his crown.

All the tables seemed centered around one in the back, bigger and more worn than the others. *Thresher.* The enormous slats were flecked with burn marks and gouges—but the lettering remained clear. As if Rolfe never wanted to forget what ship was used as his personal dining table.

But as for the man himself and that power they'd felt . . . No sign of either.

A door behind the bar opened, and a slim, brown-haired young woman stepped out. Her apron marked her as the barmaid, but her shoulders were back, head high—gray eyes sharp and clear as she scanned them and remained unimpressed. "He was wondering when you two would come snooping," she said, her accent rich and thick—like Aedion's.

Rowan said, "Oh?"

The barmaid jerked her delicate chin toward the narrow wood stairs in the back. "Captain wants to see you—in his office. One flight up, second door down."

"Why."

Even Dorian knew not to ignore that tone. But the girl just grabbed a glass, held it to the candlelight to inspect for smudges, and pulled a rag from her apron. Twin tattoos of roaring gray sea dragons snaked around her tan forearms, the beasts seeming to slither as her muscles shifted with the movement.

Their scales, he realized, matched her eyes perfectly as she flicked her stare over Dorian and Rowan once more and said coolly, "Don't keep him waiting."

Dorian murmured to Rowan as they ascended the creaky, dim stairs, "It could be a trap."

"Possibly," Rowan said with equal quiet. "But consider that we were allowed to come to him. If it was a trap, the smarter move would have been to catch us unawares."

Dorian nodded, something in his chest easing. "And you—your magic is . . . better?"

That hard face yielded nothing. "I'll manage." Not an answer.

Along the second-level hallway, four steely-eyed young men had been stationed, each armed with fine swords whose hilts were fashioned after attacking sea dragons—surely the mark of their captain. None bothered to speak as he and Rowan made for the indicated door.

The Fae Prince knocked once. A grunt was all they got in response.

Dorian didn't know what he expected from the Lord of Pirates.

But a dark-haired man, a day past thirty if that, lounging on a red velvet chaise before the rain-splattered curve of windows was not it.

Chapter 21

The Pirate Lord of Skull's Bay did not turn from where he was sprawled on the chaise, piles of papers littering the worn cobalt rug beneath it. From the neat columns that Dorian could barely make out from where he and Rowan stood a few feet into the man's office, the papers seemed crammed with tallies of goods or expenses—ill-gained or otherwise.

But Rolfe continued monitoring the ships tilting and bobbing in the harbor, the shadow of Ship-Breaker's sagging chain cleaving the storm-tossed world beyond them.

Rolfe had likely learned of their arrival not due to any magic map, but from sitting here. Indeed, dark leather gloves adorned his hands—the material scarred and cracked with age. Not a hint of the legendary tattoos lurking beneath.

Rowan didn't move; barely blinked as he took in the captain, the office. Dorian himself had been part of enough political maneuverings to know the uses of silence—the power in who spoke first. The power in making someone wait.

The rain drumming on the windows and the muffled dripping of their own soaked clothes on the threadbare carpet filled the quiet.

Captain Rolfe tapped a gloved finger on the arm of the chaise, watching the harbor for a heartbeat longer—as if to make sure the *Sea Dragon* still floated—and finally turned to them.

"Take off your hoods. I want to know who I'm talking to."

Dorian stiffened at the command, but Rowan said, "Your barmaid implied that you know damn well who we are."

A wry half smile tugged on Rolfe's lips, the upper-left corner flecked with a small scar. Hopefully not from Aelin. "My barmaid talks too much."

"Then why keep her?"

"Easy on the eyes—hard to come by around here," Rolfe said, uncoiling to his feet. He was about Dorian's height and clothed in simple but well-made black. An elegant rapier hung at his side, along with a matching parrying knife.

Rowan snorted, but to Dorian's surprise, removed his hood.

Rolfe's sea-green eyes flared—no doubt at the silver hair, pointed ears, and slightly elongated canines. Or the tattoo. "A man who likes ink as much as I do," Rolfe said with an appreciative nod. "I think you and I will get along just fine, Prince."

"Male," Rowan corrected. "Fae males are not human men."

"Semantics," Rolfe said, flicking his attention to Dorian. "So you're the king everyone's in such a tizzy over."

Dorian finally tugged back his hood. "What of it?"

With that gloved hand, Rolfe pointed toward a paper-covered desk and two upholstered chairs before it. Like the man himself, it was elegant, but worn—either from age, use, or battles past. And those gloves . . . To cover the maps inked there?

Rowan gave Dorian a nod to sit. The flames on the candles burning throughout guttered as they passed, and claimed their seats.

Rolfe edged around the stacks of papers on the floor and took up his spot at the desk. His carved, high-backed chair might very well have been a throne from some distant kingdom. "You seem remarkably calm for a king who's just been declared a traitor to his crown and robbed of his throne."

Dorian was glad he was in the process of sitting down.

Rowan lifted a brow. "According to whom?"

"According to the messengers who arrived yesterday," Rolfe said, leaning back in his seat and crossing his arms. "Duke Perrington—or should I call him King Perrington now?—issued a decree, signed by the majority of Adarlan's lords and ladies, naming *you*, Majesty, an enemy to your kingdom, and claiming that he liberated Rifthold from *your* claws after you and the Queen of Terrasen slaughtered so many innocents this spring. It also claims that any ally"—a nod toward Rowan—"is an enemy. And that you will be crushed under his armies if you do not yield."

Silence filled his head. Rolfe went on, perhaps a bit more gently, "Your brother has been named Perrington's heir and Crown Prince."

Oh gods. Hollin was a child, but still . . . something had rotted in him, festered—

He had left them there. Rather than deal with his mother and brother, he'd told them to stay in those mountains. Where they were now as good as lambs surrounded by a pack of wolves.

He wished Chaol were with him. Wished for time to just . . . *stop* so he might sort out all these fractured pieces of himself, put them into some kind of order, if not back together entirely.

Rolfe said, "From the look on your face, I'm guessing your arrival indeed has something to do with the fact that Rifthold now lies in ruin, its people fleeing wherever they can."

Dorian shoved out the insidious thoughts and drawled, "I came to learn what side of the line you stand on, Captain, in regard to this conflict."

Rolfe sat forward, resting his forearms on the desk. "You must be desperate indeed, then." A glance at Rowan. "And is your queen equally desperate for my aid?"

"My queen," Rowan said, "is not a part of this discussion."

Rolfe only grinned at Dorian. "You wish to know what side of the line I stand on? I stand on the side that keeps the hell out of my territory."

"Rumor has it," Rowan countered smoothly, "that the easternmost part of this archipelago is no longer your territory at all."

Rolfe held Rowan's gaze. A heartbeat passed. Then another. A muscle flickered in Rolfe's jaw.

Then he pulled off those gloves to reveal hands tattooed from fingertip to wrist. He turned them palm up, revealing a map of the archipelago, and what—

Dorian and Rowan leaned forward as the blue waters did indeed flow, little dots among it sailing by. And in the easternmost tip of the archipelago, curving out to sea . . .

Those waters were gray, the islands a ruddy brown. But nothing moved—no dots indicated ships. As if the map had frozen.

"They have magic that shields them—even from this," Rolfe said. "I can't get a count of their ships, or men, or beasts. Scouts never return. This winter, we'd hear roaring from the islands—some almost-human, some definitely not. Often, we'd spy . . . things standing out on those rocks. Men, but not. We let it go unchecked for too long—and paid the price."

"Beasts," Dorian said. "What sort of beasts?"

A grim smile, scar stretching. "Ones to make you consider fleeing this continent, Majesty."

The condescension snapped something loose in Dorian's temper. "I have walked through more nightmares than you realize, Captain."

Rolfe snorted, but his eyes went to that pale line across Dorian's throat.

Rowan leaned back in his chair with lazy grace—the War Commander incarnate. "It must be a solid truce you hold, then, if you're still camped here with minimal ships in your harbor."

Rolfe simply tugged on his worn gloves. "My fleet does have to do a little pirating every now and then, you know. Bills to pay and all that."

"I'm sure. Especially when you employ four guards to watch your hallway."

Dorian caught Rowan's train of thought and said to the Fae Prince, "I didn't scent the Valg in town." No, whatever that power had been . . . it had flickered into nothing now.

"That's because," Rolfe drawled, cutting them off, "we killed most of them."

Wind rattled the windows, smearing the rain across them.

"And as for the four men in the hall—they are all that's left of my crew. Thanks to the battle we had early this spring to reclaim this island after Perrington's general stole it from us."

Dorian swore low and viciously. The captain nodded.

"But I am again Pirate Lord of Skull's Bay, and if the eastern islands are as far as Morath plans to go, then Perrington and his beasts can have them. The Dead End is barely more than caves and rock anyway."

"What manner of beasts," Dorian said again.

Rolfe's pale green eyes darkened. "Sea-wyverns. Witches rule the skies with their wyverns—but these waters are now ruled by beasts bred for naval battle, foul corruptions of an ancient template. Imagine a creature half the size of a first-rate ship—faster than a racing dolphin—and the damage it can cause with tooth and claw and a poisoned tail big as a mast. Worse, if you kill one of their vicious offspring, the adults will hunt you to the ends of the earth." Rolfe shrugged. "So you will find, Majesty, that I have no interest in disturbing the eastern islands if they do not disturb me any further. I have no interest in doing anything but continuing to profit from my endeavors." He waved a vague hand to the papers scattered throughout.

Dorian held his tongue. The offer he'd been planning to make . . . His coffers belonged to Morath now. He doubted privateers would volunteer based on credit.

Rowan gave him a look that said the same. Another route to win Rolfe to their cause, then. Dorian surveyed the office, the taste leaning toward finery and yet so little that was not worn. The half-wrecked town around them. The four surviving crew. The way Rolfe had looked at that band of white along his throat.

Rowan opened his mouth, but Dorian said, "They weren't just killed, your crew. Some were taken, weren't they?"

Rolfe's sea-green eyes went cold.

Dorian pushed, "Captured, along with others, and taken into the Dead Islands. Used for information about how and where to strike you. The only way to free them when they were sent back to you, demons wearing their bodies, was to behead them. Burn them."

Rowan asked roughly, "Was it rings or collars they wore, Captain?"

Rolfe's throat bobbed once. After a long moment, he said, "Rings. They said they'd been set free. But they weren't the men who . . ." A shake of the head. "Demons," he breathed, as if it explained something. "That's what he put in them."

So Rowan told him. Of the Valg, their princes, and of Erawan, the last Valg king.

Even Rolfe had the wits to look unnerved as Rowan concluded, "He has cast off the disguise as Perrington. He is only Erawan now—King Erawan, apparently."

Rolfe's eyes again drifted to Dorian's neck, and it was an effort not to touch the scar there. "How did you survive it? We even cut the rings off—but my men . . . they were gone."

Dorian shook his head. "I don't know." No answer didn't make Rolfe's men sound . . . lesser for not having survived. Maybe he'd been infested by a Valg prince who'd savored taking his time.

Rolfe shifted a piece of paper on his desk, reading it again for a heartbeat—as if it were a mere distraction while he thought. He said at last, "Wiping what's left of them from the Dead Islands won't do shit against the might of Morath."

"No," Rowan countered, "but if we hold the archipelago, we can use these islands to wage a battle from the seas while we strike from the land. We can use these islands to house fleets from other kingdoms, other continents."

Dorian added, "My Hand is currently in the southern continent—in Antica itself. He will persuade them to send a fleet." Chaol would do nothing less for him, for Adarlan.

"None will come," Rolfe said. "They didn't come ten years ago; they certainly won't come now." He surveyed Rowan and added with a small smirk, "Especially not with the latest news."

This couldn't end well, Dorian decided as Rowan asked flatly, "What news?"

Rolfe didn't answer, instead watching the stormy bay, or whatever out there held his interest. A rough few months for the man, Dorian realized. Someone holding on to this place through sheer arrogance and will. And all those tables below, assembled from the wreckage of conquered ships . . . How many enemies were circling, waiting for a shot at revenge?

Rowan opened his mouth, no doubt to demand an answer, when Rolfe thumped his booted foot thrice on the worn floorboards. An answering thump on the wall sounded.

Silence fell. Given Rolfe's hatred for the Valg, Dorian doubted Morath was about to spring shut a trap, but . . . he slid deep into his magic as footsteps thudded down the hall. From the tight cast of Rowan's tattooed face, he knew the prince was doing the same. Especially as Dorian felt his magic reach toward the Fae Prince's, as it had done that day with Aelin atop the glass castle.

Those footsteps paused outside the office door, and again, that pulse of foreign, mighty magic rose up. Rowan's hand slid into casual distance of the hunting knife at his thigh.

Dorian focused on his breathing, on hauling up lines and pieces of his magic. Ice bit into his palms as the office door opened.

Two golden-haired males appeared in the doorway.

Rowan's snarl reverberated through the floorboards and along Dorian's feet as he took in the muscle, the pointed ears, the gaping mouths that revealed elongated canines . . .

The two strangers, the source of that power . . . They were Fae.

The one with night-dark eyes and an edged grin looked Rowan over and drawled, "I liked your hair longer."

A dagger embedding itself in the wall not an inch from the male's ear was Rowan's only answer.

CHAPTER 22

Dorian didn't see the Fae Prince throw the dagger until the blade thudded into the wooden wall, its hilt still bobbing with the impact.

But the dark-eyed, bronze-skinned male—so handsome that Dorian blinked—smirked at the dagger shivering beside his head. "Was your aim that shitty when you cut your own hair?"

The other male beside him—tan, tawny-eyed, with a steady sort of quiet to him—lifted his broad, tattooed hands. "Rowan, put your blades down. We're not here for you."

For there were already more weapons gripped in Rowan's hands. Dorian hadn't even heard him stand, let alone draw the sword, or the elegant hatchet in the other hand.

Dorian's magic writhed in his veins as it studied the two strangers. *Here you are*, it sang.

Alone with Rowan, his magic had become accustomed to the prince's staggering abyss of power, but the three of these males together, ancient and powerful and primal . . . They were their own maelstrom. They could wreck this city without even trying. He wondered if Rolfe realized it.

The Pirate Lord said drily, "I take it you know each other."

The solemn, golden-eyed one nodded, his pale clothes so like the ones Rowan favored: layered, efficient fabric, fit for battlefields. A band of black tattoos encircled the male's muscled neck. Dorian's stomach lurched. From a distance, it might very well have been another sort of black collar.

Rowan said tightly, "Gavriel and Fenrys used to . . . work with me."

Rolfe's sea-green eyes darted among them all, assessing, weighing.

Fenrys—Gavriel. Dorian knew those names. Rowan had mentioned them during their journey here . . . Two members of Rowan's cadre.

Rowan explained to Dorian, "They are blood-sworn to Maeve. As I used to be."

Meaning they were here under her orders. And if Maeve had sent not one, but *two* of her lieutenants to this continent, when Lorcan was already here . . .

Rowan said through his teeth but sheathed his weapons, "What is your business with Rolfe?"

Dorian released his magic into himself. It settled into his core like a bit of dropped ribbon.

Rolfe waved a hand to the two males. "They're the bearer of the news I promised you—among other things."

"And we were just sitting down to lunch," Fenrys said, those dark eyes dancing. "Shall we?"

Fenrys didn't wait for them as he ducked back into the hall and walked out.

The tattooed one—Gavriel—sighed quietly. "It's a long tale, Rowan, and one you and the King of Adarlan"—a flick of tawny eyes in his direction—"must hear." He gestured to the hall and said, utterly stone-faced, "You know how cranky Fenrys gets when he doesn't eat."

"I heard that," called a deep male voice from the hall.

Dorian reined in his smile, watching Rowan for his reaction instead. But the Fae Prince only jerked his head at Gavriel in silent order to lead the way.

None of them, not even Rolfe, spoke as they descended into the main room. The barmaid was gone, only sparkling glasses behind the bar hinting that she'd been there. And, indeed digging into a steaming bowl of what smelled like fish stew, Fenrys now waited for them at a table in the back.

Gavriel slid into a seat beside the warrior, his mostly full bowl sloshing a bit as the table shifted, and said to Rowan when the prince halted halfway through the room, "Is . . ." The Fae warrior paused, as if weighing the words and how Rowan might react if the question was posed poorly. Dorian knew why the exact next moment. "Is Aelin Galathynius with you?"

Dorian didn't know where to look: at the warriors now at the table, at Rowan beside him, or at Rolfe, brows raised as he leaned against the stair banister, with no idea that the queen was his great enemy.

Rowan shook his head once, a swift, cutting move. "My queen is not in our company."

Fenrys flicked his brows up but continued devouring his meal, his gray jacket unbuttoned to reveal the muscled brown chest peeking through the vee of his white shirt. Gold embroidery swirled along the lapels of the jacket—the only sign of wealth among them.

Dorian didn't quite know what had happened this past spring with Rowan's cadre, but . . . they obviously hadn't parted on good terms. At least on Rowan's end.

Gavriel rose to drag over two chairs—closest to the exit, Dorian noticed. Perhaps Gavriel was the one who kept the peace among the cadre.

Rowan didn't make a move for them. It was so easy to forget that the prince had centuries of handling foreign courts—had gone to war and back again. With these males.

Rowan didn't bother with diplomacy, however, as he said, "Tell me whatever the hell this news is."

Fenrys and Gavriel exchanged a look. The former just rolled his eyes and gestured with his spoon for Gavriel to speak.

"Maeve's armada sails for this continent."

Dorian was glad he didn't have anything in his stomach.

Rowan's words were guttural as he asked, "Is that bitch allying with Morath?" He cut what Dorian considered to be the definition of an icy stare at Rolfe. "Are *you* allying with her?"

"No," Gavriel said evenly.

Rolfe, to his credit, just shrugged. "I told you, I want no part in this war."

"Maeve isn't the sort to share power," Gavriel cut in calmly. "But before we left, she was readying her armada to leave—for Eyllwe."

Dorian whooshed out a breath. "Why Eyllwe? Is it possible she could be sending aid?"

From the look on Rowan's face, Dorian could tell the prince was already cataloging and marking, analyzing what he knew of his former queen, of Eyllwe, and how it tied to everything else.

Dorian tried to control his thundering heart, knowing they could likely hear its shift in rhythm.

Fenrys set down his spoon. "I doubt she's sending aid to anyone at all—at least not where this continent is concerned. And again, she didn't tell us her specific reasons."

"She always tells us," Rowan countered. "She's never contained information like that."

Fenrys's dark eyes flickered. "That was before you humiliated her by leaving her for Aelin of the Wildfire. And before Lorcan abandoned her as well. She trusts none of us now."

Eyllwe . . . Maeve had to know how dear the kingdom was to Aelin. But to launch an armada . . . There had to be something there, something worth her while. Dorian ran through every lesson he'd been taught, every book he'd read on the kingdom. But nothing sparked.

Rowan said, "Maeve cannot believe she can conquer Eyllwe—at least not for any extended period of time, not without drawing all her armies here, and leaving her realm undefended."

But perhaps it'd spread Erawan thin, even if the cost of Maeve's invasion would be steep . . .

"*Again*," Fenrys drawled, "we don't know details. We only told him"—a jerk of the chin toward where Rolfe still leaned against the banister with crossed arms—"as a courtesy warning—among other things."

Dorian noted that Rowan didn't ask if they'd have extended the courtesy to them had they not been here. Or what, exactly, those other *things* were. The prince said to Rolfe, "I need to dispatch messages. Immediately."

Rolfe studied his gloved hands. "Why bother? Won't the recipient arrive soon enough?"

"What?" Dorian braced himself at the simmering temper in Rowan's tone.

Rolfe smiled. "Rumor has it Aelin Galathynius destroyed General Narrok and his lieutenants over in Wendlyn. And that she accomplished this with a Fae Prince at her side. Impressive."

Rowan's canines flashed. "And your point is, Captain?"

"I just wish to know whether Her Majesty, Queen of Fire, expects a grand parade when she arrives."

Dorian doubted Rolfe would very much like her other title—Adarlan's Assassin.

Rowan's snarl was soft. "Again, she's not coming here."

"Oh? You mean to tell me that her lover goes to rescue the King of Adarlan, and instead of taking him north, he brings him *here*—and it doesn't somehow mean I'm to soon play host to her?"

At the mention of *lover*, Rowan gave Fenrys a lethal stare. The beautiful male—really, there was no way to describe him other than that—just shrugged.

But Rowan said to Rolfe, "She asked me to bring King Dorian to persuade you to join our cause. But as you have no interest in any agenda but your own, it seems our trip was wasted. So we have no further use for you at this table, especially if you're incapable of dispatching messengers." Rowan flicked his eyes toward the stairs behind Rolfe. "You're dismissed."

Fenrys choked on a dark laugh, but Gavriel straightened as Rolfe hissed, "I don't care who you are and what power you wield. You don't give me orders in my territory."

"You'd better get used to taking them," Rowan said, his voice calm in that way that made Dorian's every instinct prepare to run. "For if Morath wins this war, they will not be content to let you flounce about these islands, pretending to be king. They will lock you out of every port and river, deny you trade with cities that you have come to depend upon. Who shall your buyers be when there are none left to purchase your goods? I doubt Maeve will bother—or remember you."

Rolfe snapped, "If these islands are sacked, we will sail to others—and others. The seas are my haven—upon the waves, we will always be free."

"I'd hardly call squatting in your tavern in fear of Valg assassins free."

Rolfe's gloved hands flexed and unfurled, and Dorian wondered if he'd go for the rapier at his side. But then the Pirate Lord said to Fenrys and Gavriel, "We will meet here tomorrow at eleven." When his gaze shifted to Rowan, it hardened. "Send however many damn messages you want. You may stay until your queen arrives, which I have no doubt she *will*. At that time, I will hear what the legendary Aelin Galathynius has to say for herself. Until then, *get the hell out*." He jerked his chin toward Gavriel and Fenrys. "You can talk to the *princes* at their own damn lodgings." Rolfe stalked to the front door, yanking it open to reveal a wall of rain and the four young but hard-looking men lingering on the soaked quay. Their hands shot to their weapons, but Rolfe made no move to summon them. He only pointed out the door.

Rowan stared down the man for a moment, then said to his former companions, "Let's go."

They weren't stupid enough to argue.

This was bad. Undeniably bad.

Rowan's magic frayed apart as he worked to keep the shields around him and Dorian intact. But he didn't let Fenrys or Gavriel get a whiff of that exhaustion, didn't reveal one bit of the effort it took to hold the magic *and* concentrate.

Rolfe might very well be a lost cause against Erawan or Maeve—especially once he saw Aelin. If Aelin had been present during this conversation, Rowan had a feeling it would have ended with the *Sea Dragon*—both the inn and the ship anchored in the harbor—aflame. But those sea-wyverns . . . And Maeve's armada . . . He'd think about that later. But shit. Just—*shit.*

The no-nonsense innkeeper at the Ocean Rose asked no questions as Rowan purchased two rooms—the best the inn had to offer. Not when he laid a gold piece on the counter. Two weeks' accommodations, plus all meals, plus stabling of their horses if they had them, and unlimited laundry, she'd offered with a knowing look at his clothes.

And whatever guests he wished, she added as Rowan whistled sharply, and Dorian, Fenrys, and Gavriel crossed the flagstone courtyard, hoods on as they edged around the burbling fountain. Rain pattered on the potted palms, rustling the magenta bougainvillea crawling up the walls toward the white-painted balconies, still shuttered against the storm.

Rowan asked the woman to send up what was likely enough food for eight people, then stalked for the polished stairs at the back of the dim dining room, the others falling in behind him. Fenrys, mercifully, kept his mouth shut until they reached Rowan's room, discarded their cloaks, and Rowan lit a few candles. The act alone left a hole in his chest.

Fenrys sank into one of the cushioned chairs before the dark fireplace, running a finger down the black-painted arm. "Such fine accommodations. Which of the royals is paying, then?"

Dorian, who had been about to claim the seat by the small desk before the shuttered windows, stiffened. Gavriel gave Fenrys a look that said, *Please no brawling.*

"Does it make a difference?" Rowan asked as he went wall to wall, lifting the framed pictures of lush flora for any spy holes or access points. Then he checked beneath the white-sheeted bed, its posts of twirled black wood kissed with the candlelight, trying not to consider that for all his resolutions . . . she'd share this room with him. This bed.

The space was secure—serene, even, with the beat of the rain in the courtyard and on the roof, the smell of sweet fruit heavy in the air.

"Someone's got to have money to finance this war," Fenrys purred, watching Rowan at last lean against a low dresser beside the door. "Though maybe considering yesterday's decree from Morath, you'll be moving to more . . . economical quarters."

Well, that said enough about what Fenrys and Gavriel knew regarding Erawan's decree concerning Dorian and his allies. "Worry over your own business, Fenrys," Gavriel said.

Fenrys snorted, toying with a small curl of golden hair at his nape. "How you even manage to walk with that much steel on you, Whitethorn, has always been a mystery to me."

Rowan said smoothly, "How no one has ever cut out your tongue just to shut you up has always been a mystery to me as well."

An edged chuckle. "I've been told it's my best feature. At least the women think so."

A low laugh escaped Dorian—the first sound like it Rowan had witnessed from the king.

Rowan braced his hands on the dresser. "How did you keep your scents hidden?"

Gavriel's tawny eyes darkened. "A new trick of Maeve's—to keep us nearly invisible in a land that does not receive our kind warmly." He jerked his chin at Dorian and Rowan. "Though it seems it's not wholly effective."

Rowan said, "You two better have a damn good explanation for why you're here—and why you dragged Rolfe into whatever it is."

Fenrys drawled, "You get everything you want, Rowan, yet you're still a stone-cold bastard. Lorcan would be proud."

"Where's Connall?" was Rowan's mocking reply, naming Fenrys's twin.

Fenrys's face tightened. "Where do you think? One of us is always the anchor."

"She'd stop keeping him as collateral if you didn't make your discontent so obvious."

Fenrys had always been a pain in his ass. And Rowan had not forgotten that it was Fenrys who had wanted the task of handling Aelin Galathynius this past spring. Fenrys loved anything that was wild and beautiful, and to dangle Aelin before him . . . Maeve had known it was torture.

Perhaps it was torture, too, for Fenrys to be so far from Maeve's grip—but to know that his twin was back in Doranelle, that if Fenrys never came back . . . Connall would be punished in unspeakable ways. It was how the queen had ensnared them in the first place: offspring were rare among the Fae—but twins? Even rarer. And for twins to be born gifted with strength, to grow into males whose dominance rivaled that of warriors centuries older than them . . .

Maeve had coveted them. Fenrys had refused the offer to join her service. So she'd gone after Connall—the dark to Fenrys's gold, quiet to Fenrys's roar, thoughtful to Fenrys's recklessness.

Fenrys got what he wanted: women, glory, wealth. Connall, though skilled, was forever in his twin's shadow. So when the queen approached him about the blood oath, at a time when Fenrys, not Connall, had been selected to fight in the war with the Akkadians . . . Connall had sworn it.

And when Fenrys returned to find his brother bound to the queen, and learned what Maeve forced him to do behind closed doors . . . Fenrys had bargained: he'd swear the oath, but only to get Maeve to back off his brother. For over a century now, Fenrys had served in the queen's bedroom, had sat chained by invisible shackles beside her dark throne.

Rowan might have liked the male. Respected him. If it weren't for that damned mouth of his.

"So," Fenrys said, well aware he had not answered Rowan's demand for information, "are we soon to call you King Rowan?"

Gavriel murmured, "Gods above, Fenrys." He gave the sigh of the long-suffering and added before Fenrys could open that stupid mouth, "Your arrival, Rowan, was a fortunate turn of events."

Rowan faced the male beside him—second-in-command for Maeve now that Rowan had vacated the title. As if the golden-haired warrior read the name from his eyes, Gavriel asked, "Where is Lorcan?"

Rowan had been debating how to answer that question from the moment he'd seen them. That Gavriel had asked . . . Why *had* they come to Skull's Bay?

"I don't know where Lorcan is," Rowan said. Not a lie. If they were lucky, his former commander would get the other two Wyrdkeys, realize Aelin had tricked him, and come running—delivering the two keys for Aelin to then destroy.

If they were lucky.

Gavriel said, "You don't know where he is—but you've seen him." Rowan nodded.

Fenrys snorted. "Are we really going to play truths and lies? Just tell us, you bastard."

Rowan pinned Fenrys with a look. The White Wolf of Doranelle smiled right back at him.

Gods help them all if Fenrys and Aedion ever sat in a room together.

Rowan said, "Are you here on Maeve's command—ahead of the armada?"

Gavriel shook his head. "Our presence has nothing to do with the armada sailing. She sent us to hunt him. You already know the crime he committed."

An act of love—though only in the twisted way that Lorcan could love things. Only in the twisted way he loved Maeve.

"He claims to be doing it in her best interest," Rowan said casually, aware of the king seated beside him. Rowan knew most underestimated the sharp intelligence under that disarming smile. Knew that Dorian's value wasn't his godlike magic, but his mind. He'd latched on to Rolfe's fear and trauma at the hands of the Valg and laid the foundation—one he'd make sure Aelin would exploit.

"Lorcan's always been arrogant that way," Fenrys drawled. "This time, he crossed the line."

"So you've been sent here to bring Lorcan back?"

Those tattoos on Gavriel's throat—marks Rowan himself had inked—bobbed with each word as he said, "We've been sent here to kill him."

CHAPTER 23

Holy gods.

Rowan froze. "That explains the two of you, then."

Fenrys tossed his hair out of his dark eyes. "Three, actually. Vaughan left yesterday afternoon to fly north—while we take the South." Vaughan, with his osprey form, could cover the far harsher terrain more easily. "We landed in this shithole town to see if Rolfe had dealings with Lorcan—to bribe him to tip us off if Lorcan should come through here again, looking to hire a boat." Skull's Bay would be one of the few ports where Lorcan could do such a thing without questions. "Warning Rolfe about Maeve's armada was part of convincing the bastard to help us. We're to make our way onto the continent from here—start our hunt in the South. And since these lands are rather large . . ." A flash of white teeth in a feral smile. "Any inkling about his general whereabouts would be much appreciated, *Prince*."

Rowan debated it. But if they caught Lorcan, and the commander had possession of even one of the Wyrdkeys . . . If they brought both commander and keys back to Maeve, especially if she was already sailing for Eyllwe for whatever reasons of her own . . .

Rowan shrugged. "I washed my hands of you all this spring. Lorcan's business is his own."

"You *prick*—" Fenrys snarled.

Gavriel cut in, "If we could bargain?"

There was something like pain—and regret—in Gavriel's eyes. Of all of them, Gavriel had probably been his only friend.

Rowan debated if he should tell him about the son who now was making his way here. Debated if Aedion would like the chance to meet his father . . . perhaps before war made corpses of them all.

But Rowan said, "Has Maeve given you leave to bargain on her behalf?"

"We only received our orders," Fenrys drawled, "and the permission to use any means necessary to kill Lorcan. She did not mention your queen at all. So that amounts to a *yes*."

Rowan crossed his arms. "You send me an army of Doranelle warriors, and I'll tell you where Lorcan is, and where he plans to go."

Fenrys let out a harsh laugh. "Mother's tits, Rowan. Even if we could, the armada's already in use."

"I suppose I'll have to make do with you two, then."

Dorian had the good sense not to look as surprised as Rowan's former brothers-in-arms.

Fenrys burst out laughing. "What—work for your queen? Fight in your battles?"

"Isn't that what you want, Fenrys?" Rowan fixed him with a stare. "To serve my queen? You've been pulling on the leash for months. Well, here's your shot."

All amusement faded from Fenrys's beautiful face. "You're a bastard, Rowan."

Rowan turned to Gavriel. "I'm assuming Maeve didn't specify *when* you had to do this." A shallow nod was his only confirmation. "And you will technically be fulfilling her command to you." The blood oath operated on specific, clear demands. And relied on close physical contact to enable that *tug* to get the body to yield. This far away . . . they had to obey Maeve's orders—but could use any loopholes in the language to their own advantage.

"Lorcan might very well be gone by the time you've considered our bargain fulfilled," Fenrys countered.

Rowan smiled a bit. "Ah, but the thing is . . . Lorcan's path will eventually lead him right back to me. To my queen. Who knows how long it will take, but he will find us again. At which time, he'll be yours." He tapped a finger against his bicep. "People are going to be talking about this war for a thousand years. Longer." Rowan jerked his chin at Fenrys. "You've never shied from a fight."

"That's if we survive," Fenrys said. "And what of Brannon's gifts? How long will a single flame last against the darkness that gathers? Maeve hid her motives about the armada and Eyllwe, but she at least told us who really reigns in Morath."

When Rowan had walked through the door of the Sea Dragon, he'd wondered what god had sent the storm that had pushed them to arrive in Skull's Bay on this day, at this time.

Together, he and the cadre had taken on a legion of Adarlan's forces this spring and won—easily.

And even if Lorcan, Vaughan, and Connall weren't with them . . . One Fae warrior was as good as a hundred mortal soldiers. Maybe more.

Terrasen needed more troops. Well, here was a three-male army.

And against the aerial Ironteeth legions, they would need Fae speed and strength and centuries of experience.

Together, they had sacked cities and kingdoms for Maeve; together, they had waged war and ended it.

Rowan said, "Ten years ago, we did nothing to stop this. If Maeve had sent a force, we might have kept it from growing so out of control. Our brethren were hunted and killed and tortured. Maeve let it happen for spite, because Aelin's mother would not yield to her wishes. So yes—my Fireheart is one flame in the sea of darkness. But she is willing to fight, Fenrys. She is willing to take on Erawan, take on Maeve and the gods themselves, if it means peace can be had."

Across the room, Dorian's eyes had shuttered. Rowan knew the king would fight—and go down swinging—and that his gift could make a difference between victory and defeat. Yet . . . he was untrained. Still untried, despite all he'd endured.

"But Aelin is one person," Rowan went on. "And even her gifts might not be enough to win. Alone," he breathed, meeting Fenrys's stare, then Gavriel's, "she will die. And once that flame goes out, it is done. There is no second chance. Once that fire extinguishes, we are all doomed, in every land and every world."

The words were poison on his tongue, his very bones aching at the thought of that death—what he'd do if it should happen.

Gavriel and Fenrys looked at each other, speaking in that silent way he used to do with them. There was one card Rowan had to play to convince them—to convince Gavriel.

Even if the specificity of Maeve's command might allow it, she could very well punish them for acting *around* her orders. She'd done it before; they all bore scars from it. They knew the risk of it as well as Rowan did. Gavriel shook his head slightly at Fenrys.

Before they could turn to say no, Rowan said to Gavriel, "If you do not fight in this war, Gavriel, then you doom your son to die."

Gavriel froze.

Fenrys spat, "Bullshit." Even Dorian was gaping a bit.

Rowan wondered just how pissed Aedion would be as he said, "Think on my proposal. But know that your son makes for Skull's Bay. You may want to wait to decide until you meet him."

"Who . . ." Rowan wasn't sure Gavriel was breathing properly. The warrior's hands were clenched so tightly the scars over his knuckles were moon white. "I have a son?"

Some part of Rowan felt like the prick Fenrys claimed he was and not the male that Aelin believed him to be as he nodded.

The information would have gotten out sooner or later.

If Maeve had learned first, she might have schemed to ensnare Aedion—might have sent the cadre to kill or steal him. But now, Rowan supposed, he'd ensnared the cadre himself. It was only a matter of how desperately Gavriel wanted to meet his son . . . and how afraid they were of failing Maeve should they not find Lorcan.

So Rowan said coldly, "Stay out of our way until they arrive and we'll stay out of yours."

Putting his back to them went against every instinct, but Rowan kept his shields tight, his magic spread to alert him if either so much as breathed wrong while he twisted to open the bedroom door in silent dismissal. He had much to do. Starting with writing a warning to the Eyllwe royals and Terrasen's forces. Ending with trying to figure out how the hell they could fight two wars at once.

Gavriel rose, slack-faced, pale—something like devastation written there.

Rowan caught the spark of realization that flashed across Dorian's eyes a heartbeat before the king buried it. Yes—at first glance, Aedion and Aelin looked like siblings, but it was Aedion's smile that gave away his heritage. Gavriel would know in a heartbeat . . . if Aedion's scent didn't give it away first.

Fenrys stepped closer to the male, a hand on his shoulder as they entered the hallway. For both Rowan and Fenrys, Gavriel had always been their sounding board. Never each other—no, he and Fenrys . . . it was easier to be at each other's throats instead.

Rowan said to both of his former companions, "If you so much as hint about Gavriel's son to Maeve, our bargain is over. You'll never find Lorcan. And if Lorcan does show up . . . I'll gladly help him kill you." Rowan prayed it wouldn't come to it—to a fight that brutal and devastating.

This was war, though. And he had no intention of losing it.

CHAPTER 24

The *Wind-Singer* left Ilium at dawn, its crew and captain unaware that the two hooded individuals—and their pet falcon—who had paid in gold had no intention of going the entire journey to Leriba. Whether they pieced together that those two individuals were also the general and queen who had liberated their town the night before, they didn't let on.

It was considered an easy trip down the coast of the continent, though Aelin wondered if voicing that statement would guarantee it *wasn't* an easy trip. First, there was the matter of sailing through Adarlan's waters—near Rifthold, specifically. If the witches patrolled far out to sea . . .

But they had no other choice, not with the net Erawan had stretched across the continent. Not with his threat to find and capture Rowan and Dorian still ringing fresh in her mind, along with the throbbing of the deep purple bruise on her chest, right over her heart.

Standing on the deck of the ship, the rising sun staining the turquoise bay of Ilium with gold and pink, Aelin wondered if the next time she'd see these waters, they'd be red. Wondered how long the Adarlanian soldiers would remain on their side of the border.

Aedion stepped to her side, finished with his *third* inspection. "Everything looks fine."

"Lysandra said all was clear." Indeed, from high up on the mainmast of the ship, Lysandra's falcon eyes missed nothing.

Aedion frowned. "You know, you ladies *can* let us males do things every now and then."

Aelin lifted a brow. "Where would the fun be in that?" But she knew this would be an ongoing argument—stepping back so that others, so that Aedion, might fight for her. It'd been bad enough in Rifthold, bad enough knowing that those rings and collars might enslave them—but what Erawan had done to that overseer . . . as an *experiment*.

Aelin glanced toward the scurrying crew, biting back her demand to *hurry*. Every minute delayed could be one that Erawan closed in on Rowan and Dorian. It was only a matter of time before a report reached him regarding where they'd been spotted. Aelin tapped her foot on the deck.

The rocking of the ship on the calm waves echoed the beat of her foot. She'd always loved the smell and feel of the sea. But now . . . even the lapping of those waves seemed to say, *Hurry, hurry*.

"The King of Adarlan—and Perrington, I suppose—had me in their grasp for years," Aedion said. His voice was tight enough that Aelin turned from the sea to face him. He'd gripped the wooden railing, the scars on his hands stark against his summer-tanned skin. "They met with me in Terrasen, in Adarlan. He had me in his rutting *dungeon*, gods above. And yet he didn't do *that* to me. He offered me the ring but didn't notice I wore a fake instead. Why not cleave me open and corrupt me? He had to know—he *had* to know that you'd come for me."

"The king left Dorian alone for as long as he could—perhaps that goodness extended to you, too. Perhaps he knew that if you were gone, I might very well have decided to let this world go to hell and never free him for spite."

"Would you have done that?"

The people you love are just weapons that will be used against you, Rowan had once told her. "Don't waste your energy worrying about what could have been." She knew she hadn't answered his question.

Aedion didn't look at her as he said, "I knew what happened in Endovier, Aelin, but seeing that overseer, hearing what he said . . ." His throat bobbed. "I was so close to the salt mines. That year—I was camped with the Bane right over the border for three months."

She whipped her head to him. "We're not starting down this road. Erawan sent that man for a reason—for *this* reason. He knows my past—*wants* me to know he's aware of it—and will use it against me. Against us. He'll use everyone we know, if he needs to."

Aedion sighed. "Would you have told me what happened last night if I hadn't been there?"

"I don't know. I bet you would have awoken as soon as I unleashed my power on him."

He snorted. "It's hard to miss."

The crying of gulls swooping overhead filled the quiet that followed. Despite her declaration not to linger in the past, Aelin said carefully, "Darrow claimed you fought at Theralis." She'd been meaning to ask for weeks, but hadn't worked up the nerve.

Aedion fixed his stare on the churning water. "It was a long time ago."

She swallowed against the burning in her throat. "You were barely fourteen."

"I was." His jaw tightened. She could only imagine the carnage. And the horror—not just of a boy killing and fighting, but seeing the people they cared for fall. One by one.

"I'm sorry," she breathed. "That you had to endure it."

Aedion turned toward her. No hint of the haughty arrogance and insolence. "Theralis is the battlefield I see the most—in my dreams." He scratched at a fleck on the rail. "Darrow made sure I stayed out of the thick of it, but we were overwhelmed. It was unavoidable."

He'd never told her—that Darrow had tried to shield him. She put a hand atop Aedion's and squeezed. "I'm sorry," she said again. She couldn't bring herself to ask more.

He shrugged with a shoulder. "My life as a warrior was chosen long before that battlefield."

Indeed, she couldn't imagine him without that sword and shield—both currently strapped across his back. She couldn't decide if it was a good thing.

Silence settled between them, heavy and old and weary.

"I don't blame him," Aelin said at last. "I don't blame Darrow for blocking me from Terrasen. I would do the same, judge the same, if I were him."

Aedion frowned. "I thought you were going to fight his decree."

"I am," she swore. "But . . . I understand why Darrow did it."

Aedion observed her before nodding. A grave nod, from one soldier to another.

She put a hand against the amulet beneath her clothes. Its ancient, otherworldly power rubbed up against her, and a shiver went down her spine. *Find the Lock.*

Good thing Skull's Bay was on their way to the Stone Marshes of Eyllwe.

And good thing that its ruler possessed a magical map inked on his hands. A map that revealed enemies, storms . . . and hidden treasure. A map to find things that did not wish to be found.

Aelin lowered her hand, propping both on the rail and examining the scar across each palm. So many promises and oaths made. So many debts and favors to still call in.

Aelin wondered what answers and oaths she might find waiting in Skull's Bay.

If they got there before Erawan did.

CHAPTER 25

Manon Blackbeak awoke to the sighing of leaves, the distant call of wary birds, and the reek of loam and ancient wood.

She groaned as she opened her eyes, squinting at the dappled sunlight through heavy canopy cover.

She knew these trees. Oakwald.

She was still strapped in the saddle, Abraxos sprawled beneath her, neck craned so he could monitor her breaths. His dark eyes widened with panic as she moaned, trying to sit up. She'd fallen flat onto her back, had undoubtedly lain here for some time, judging by the blue blood coating Abraxos's sides.

Manon lifted her head to peer at her stomach and bit back a cry as muscles pulled.

Wet warmth trickled from her abdomen. The wounds had barely set, then, if they were tearing so easily.

Her head pounded like a thousand forges. And her mouth was so dry she could barely shift her tongue.

First order of business: get out of this saddle. Then try to assess herself. Then water.

A stream babbled nearby, close enough that she wondered if Abraxos had chosen this spot for it.

He huffed, shifting in worry, and she hissed as her stomach tore more. "Stop," she rasped. "I'm . . . fine."

She wasn't fine, not even close.

But she wasn't dead.

And that was a start.

The other bullshit—her grandmother, the Thirteen, the Crochan claim . . . She'd deal with it once she didn't have one foot in the Darkness.

Manon lay there for long minutes, breathing against the pain.

Clean the wound; staunch the bleeding.

She had nothing on her but her leathers—but her shirt . . . She didn't have the strength to boil the linen first.

She'd just have to pray that the immortality gracing her blood would drive off any infection.

The Crochan blood in her—

Manon sat up in a sudden jerk, not giving herself time to balk, biting down on her scream so hard her lip bled, a coppery tang filling her mouth.

But she was up. Blood dribbled from beneath her flying leathers, but she focused on unstrapping the harness, one buckle at a time.

She was not dead.

The Mother still had some use for her.

Free of the harness, Manon stared at the drop off Abraxos onto the mossy ground.

Darkness save her, this was going to hurt.

Just shifting her body to pivot her leg over one side made her clench her teeth against the sobbing. If her grandmother's nails had been poisoned, she'd be dead.

But they had been left jagged—jagged instead of honed, and full of rust.

A large head nudged at her knee, and she found Abraxos there, neck stretched—his head just below her feet, the offer in his eyes.

Not trusting consciousness to keep its grip much longer, Manon slid onto his wide, broad head, breathing through the ripples of fiery pain. His breath warmed her chilled skin as he gently lowered her onto the grassy clearing.

She lay on her back, letting Abraxos nose her, a faint whine breaking from him.

"Fine . . . ," she breathed. "I'm . . ."

Manon awoke at twilight.

Abraxos was curled around her, his wing angled to form a makeshift covering.

At least she was warm. But her thirst . . .

Manon groaned, and the wing instantly snapped back, revealing a leathery head and concerned eyes. "You . . . mother hen," she gasped out, sliding her arms beneath her and pushing up.

Oh gods, oh gods, oh gods—

But she was in a sitting position.

Water. That stream . . .

Abraxos was too big to reach it through the trees—but she needed water. Soon. How many days had it been? How much blood had she lost?

"Help," she breathed.

Powerful jaws closed around the collar of her tunic, hoisting her up with such gentleness Manon's chest tightened. She swayed, bracing a hand on his leathery side, but stayed upright.

Water—then she could sleep more.

"Wait here," she said, stumbling to the nearest tree, a hand on her belly, Wind-Cleaver a weight on her back. She debated leaving the sword behind, but any extra movement, even unbuckling the belt from across her chest, was unthinkable.

Tree to tree, she staggered, nails digging into each trunk to keep herself upright, her ragged breathing filling the silent forest.

She was alive; she was alive . . .

The stream was barely more than a trickle through some mossy boulders. But it was clear and fast and the most beautiful thing she'd ever seen.

Manon surveyed the water. If she knelt, could she get back up?

She'd sleep here if she had to. Once she drank.

Carefully, muscles trembling, she knelt at the bank. She swallowed her cry as she bowed over the stream, as more blood slid out. She drank the first few handfuls without stop—then slowed, her stomach aching inside and out now.

A twig snapped, and Manon was on her feet, instinct overriding pain so fast the agony hit her a breath later. But she scanned the trees, the rocks and canopy and little hills.

A cool female voice said from across the stream, "It seems you have fallen far from your aerie, Blackbeak."

Manon couldn't place who it belonged to, what witch she'd met . . .

From behind the shadows of a tree, a stunning young woman emerged.

Her body was supple yet lithe—her unbound auburn hair draping to partially cover her nakedness. Not a stitch of clothing covered that cream-colored skin. Not a scar or mark marred flesh as pure as snow. The woman's silken hair moved with her as she stepped closer.

But the woman was no witch. And her blue eyes . . .

Run. *Run*.

Eyes of glacier blue gleamed even in the shadowed wood. And a full red mouth made for the bedroom parted in a too-white smile as she took in Manon, the blood, the injury. Abraxos roared in warning, shaking the ground, the trees, the leaves.

"Who are you," Manon said, her voice raw.

The young woman cocked her head—a robin studying a writhing worm. "The Dark King calls me his Bloodhound."

Manon made every breath count as she rallied her strength.

"Never heard of you," Manon rasped.

Something too dark to be blood slithered under the cream-colored skin of the woman's abdomen, then vanished. She traced a small, beautiful hand over where it had squirmed across the curve of her taut belly. "You would not have heard of me. Until your treachery, I was kept beneath those other mountains. But when he honed the power within my own blood . . ." Those blue eyes pierced Manon, and it was madness that glittered there. "He could do much with you, Blackbeak. So much. He sent me to bring his crowned rider to his side once more . . ."

Manon backed away a step—just one.

"There is nowhere to flee. Not with your belly barely inside you." She tossed her auburn hair over a shoulder. "Oh, what fun we'll have now that I've found you, Blackbeak. All of us."

Manon braced herself, drawing Wind-Cleaver as the woman's form glowed like a black sun, then rippled, the edges expanding, morphing, until—

The woman had been an illusion. A glamour. The creature that stood before her had been birthed in darkness, so white she doubted it had ever felt the kiss of the sun until now. And the mind that had invented it . . . The imagination of someone born in another world—one where nightmares prowled the dark, cold earth.

The body and face were vaguely human. But—Bloodhound. Yes, that was fitting. The nostrils were enormous, the eyes so large and lidless she wondered if Erawan himself had spread her eyelids apart, and her mouth . . . The teeth were black stumps, the tongue thick and red—for tasting the air. And spreading from that white body—the method of Manon's transportation: wings.

"You see," the Bloodhound purred. "You see what he can give you? I can now taste the wind; smell its very marrow. Just as I smelled you across the land."

Manon kept an arm cradled over her belly as the other trembled, lifting Wind-Cleaver.

The Bloodhound laughed, low and soft. "I shall enjoy this, I think," she said—and pounced.

Alive—she was *alive*, and she would stay that way.

Manon jumped back, sliding between two trees, so close that the creature hit them, a wall of wood in her way. Those calf eyes narrowed in rage, and her white hands—tipped with earth-digging claws—sank into the wood as she backtracked—

Only to be stuck.

Maybe the Mother was watching over her.

The Bloodhound had lodged herself between the two trees, half in, half out, thanks to those wings, wood squeezing—

Manon ran. Pain ripped at her with each step, and she sobbed through her teeth as she sprinted between the trees. A snap and crash of wood and leaves from behind.

Manon pushed herself, a hand shoved against her wound, gripping Wind-Cleaver tight enough it shook. But there was Abraxos, eyes wild, wings already flapping, preparing for flight.

"*Go*," she rasped, flinging herself at him as wood crunched behind her.

Abraxos launched for her as she leaped for him—not onto him, but into his claws, into the mighty talons that wrapped her under her breasts, her stomach tearing a bit more as he hefted her up, up, up, through wood and leaf and nest.

The air snapped beneath her boots, and Manon, eyes streaming, peered down to see the Bloodhound's claws reaching wildly. But too late.

A shriek of rage on her lips, the Bloodhound backed a few steps to the edge of the clearing, preparing to get a running leap into the air, as Abraxos's wings beat like hell—

They cleared the canopy, his wings shattering branches, raining them onto the Bloodhound.

The wind tore at Manon as Abraxos sailed with her, higher and higher, heading east, toward the plains—east and south . . .

The thing wouldn't be detained long. Abraxos realized it, too.

Had planned for it.

A flicker of white broke through the canopy below them.

Abraxos lunged, a swift, lethal dive, his roar of rage making Manon's head buzz.

The Bloodhound didn't have time to bank as Abraxos's mighty tail slammed into her, poison-coated steel barbs hitting home.

Black festering blood sprayed; ivory membranous wings sundered.

Then they were sweeping back up and the Bloodhound was tumbling down through the canopy—dying or injured, Manon didn't care.

"*I will find you*," the Bloodhound screeched from the forest floor.

It was miles before the screamed words faded.

Manon and Abraxos paused only long enough for her to crawl onto his back and strap herself in. No signs of other wyverns in the skies, no hint of the Bloodhound pursuing them. Perhaps that poison would keep her down for a while—if not permanently.

"To the coast," Manon said over the wind as the sky bled crimson into a final blackness. "Somewhere safe."

Blood trickled from between her fingers—faster, stronger than before—only a moment before the Darkness claimed her again.

CHAPTER 26

Even after two weeks in Skull's Bay, being utterly ignored by Rolfe despite their requests to meet with him, Dorian still wasn't entirely used to the heat and humidity. It hounded him day and night, driving him from sleep to wake drenched in sweat, chasing him inside the Ocean Rose when the sun was at its zenith.

And since Rolfe refused to see them, Dorian tried to fill his days with things *other* than complaining about the heat. Mornings were for practicing his magic in a jungle clearing a few miles away. Worse, Rowan made him run there and back; and when they returned at lunch, he had the "choice" of eating before or after one of Rowan's grueling workouts.

Honestly, Dorian had no idea how Aelin had survived months of this—let alone fallen in love with the warrior while she did. Though he supposed both the queen and prince possessed a sadistic streak that made them compatible.

Some days, Fenrys and Gavriel met them in the inn's courtyard to either exercise or give unwanted pointers on Dorian's technique with a sword and dagger. Some days, Rowan let them stay; others, he kicked them out with a snarl.

The latter, Dorian realized, usually happened when even the heat and sun couldn't drive away the shadows of the past few months—when he awoke with his sweat feeling like Sorscha's blood, when he couldn't abide even the brush of his tunic against his neck.

He wasn't sure whether to thank the Fae Prince for noticing or to hate him for the kindness.

During the afternoons, he and Rowan prowled the city for gossip and news, watching Rolfe's men as closely as they were watched. Only seven captains of Rolfe's depleted armada were on the island—eight including Rolfe, with fewer ships anchored in the bay. Some had fled after the Valg attack; some now slept with the fishes at the bottom of the harbor, their ships with them.

Reports poured in from Rifthold: of the city under witch command, of most of it in ruin, its nobility and merchants fleeing to country estates and leaving the poor to fend for themselves. The witches controlled the city gates and the docks—nothing and no one got in without them knowing. Worse, ships from the Ferian Gap were sailing down the Avery toward Rifthold, carrying strange soldiers and beasts that turned the city into their own personal hunting ground.

Erawan was no fool with planning this war. Those ships prowling the Avery were too small, Rowan had claimed, and there was no way the force at the Dead End was the entirety of Erawan's armada. So where had Adarlan's fleet been all this time?

Rowan discovered the answer five days into their stay: the Gulf of Oro. Some of the fleet had been positioned near Eyllwe's northwestern coast, some hidden in Melisande's ports, where, rumor had it, their queen was allowing Morath soldiers in through any direction they pleased. Erawan had skillfully divided his fleet, placing it in enough key locations that Rowan informed Dorian they'd have to sacrifice land, allies, and geographical advantages in order to hold others.

Dorian had hated to admit to the Fae warrior that he'd never heard any of these plans these past years—his council meetings had all been on policy and trade and slaves. A distraction, he realized—a way to keep the lords and rulers of the continent focused on one thing while other plans were set in motion. And now . . . if Erawan summoned the fleet from the gulf, they'd likely sail around Eyllwe's southern coast and sack every city until they reached Orynth's doorstep.

Perhaps they'd get lucky and Erawan's fleet would collide with Maeve's. Not that they'd heard anything of the latter. Not even a whisper of where and how fast her ships sailed. Or a whisper of where Aelin Galathynius had gone. It was for news of her, Dorian knew, that Rowan hunted through the city streets.

So Dorian and Rowan collected kernels of information and would return to the inn each night to analyze them over spiced prawns from the warm waters of the archipelago and steaming rice from traders in the southern continent, their glasses of orange-infused water resting atop the maps and charts they'd purchased in town. Information was mostly second- or third-hand—and a common whore patrolling the streets seemed to know as much as the sailors laboring at the docks.

But none of the whores or the sailors or the traders had news of Prince Hollin's or Queen Georgina's fates. War was coming—and the fate of a child and a flippant queen who had never bothered to take power for herself was of little concern to anyone but Dorian, it seemed.

On a particularly steamy afternoon, cooling off now thanks to a dazzling thunderstorm, Dorian set down his fork beside his plate of steamed reef fish and said to Rowan, "I find I'm tired of waiting for Rolfe to meet with us."

Rowan's fork clinked against his plate as he lowered it—and waited with preternatural stillness. Where Gavriel and Fenrys were for the afternoon, he didn't care. Dorian was actually grateful for their absence as he said, "I need some paper—and a messenger."

Rolfe summoned them and the cadre to the Sea Dragon tavern three hours later.

Rowan had been teaching him about shielding these past few days—and Dorian erected one around himself as Rolfe led the four of them along the upstairs hall of the tavern, heading for his office.

His idea had unfolded smoothly—perfectly.

No one had noticed that the letter Rowan mailed after lunch was the same one that was later delivered to Dorian at the inn.

But Rolfe's spies noticed the shock that Dorian displayed while reading it—the dismay and fear and rage at whatever news he'd received. Rowan, true to form, had paced and snarled at the *news* he'd attained. They made sure the servant washing the hallway had overheard their mention of the war-altering information, that Rolfe himself could gain much from it—or lose everything.

And now, striding for the man's office, Dorian couldn't tell if it pleased or unnerved him that they were so closely watched that his plan had worked. Gavriel and Fenrys, thankfully, asked no questions.

The Pirate Lord, clad in a faded blue-and-gold jacket, paused before the oak door to his office. His gloves were on, his face a bit haggard. He doubted that expression would improve when Rolfe realized there was no news whatsoever—and he'd have this meeting whether he wanted to or not.

Dorian caught the three Fae males assessing Rolfe's each breath, his posture, listening to the sounds of the first mate and quartermaster a level below. All three exchanged barely perceptible nods. Allies—at least until Rolfe heard them out.

Rolfe unlocked the door, muttering, "This had better be worth my time," and stalked into the awaiting dimness beyond. Then stopped dead.

Even in the watery light, Dorian could perfectly see the woman sitting at Rolfe's desk, her black clothes dirty, weapons gleaming, and her feet propped on the dark wooden surface.

Aelin Galathynius, her hands laced behind her head, grinned at them all and said, "I like this office far better than your other one, Rolfe."

CHAPTER 27

Dorian didn't dare move as Rolfe let out a snarl. "I have a distinct memory, Celaena Sardothien, of saying that if you set foot in my territory again, your life was forfeit."

"Ah," Aelin said, lowering her hands but leaving her feet still propped on Rolfe's desk, "but where would the fun be in that?"

Rowan was still as death beside him. Aelin's grin became feline as she finally lowered her feet and ran her hands along either side of the desk, assessing the smooth wood as if it was a prize horse. She inclined her head to Dorian. "Hello, Majesty."

"Hello, Celaena," he said as calmly as he could, well aware that two Fae males behind him could hear his thundering heart. Rolfe whipped his head toward him.

Because it was Celaena who sat here—for whatever purpose, it was Celaena Sardothien in this room.

She jerked her chin at Rolfe. "You've seen better days, but considering half your fleet has abandoned you, I'd say you look decent enough."

"Get out of my chair," Rolfe said too quietly.

Aelin did no such thing. She just gave Rowan a sultry sweep from foot to face. Rowan's expression remained unreadable, eyes intent—near-glowing. And then Aelin said to Rowan with a secret smile, "You, I don't know. But I'd like to."

Rowan's lips tugged upward. "I'm not on the market, unfortunately."

"Pity," Aelin said, cocking her head as she noticed a bowl of small emeralds on Rolfe's desk. *Don't do it, don't—*

Aelin swiped up the emeralds in a hand, picking them over as she glanced at Rowan beneath her lashes. "She must be a rare, staggering beauty to make you so faithful."

Gods save them all. He could have sworn Fenrys coughed behind him.

Aelin chucked the emeralds into the metal dish as if they were bits of copper, their plunking the only sound. "She must be clever"—*plunk*—"and fascinating"—*plunk*—"and very, *very* talented." *Plunk, plunk, plunk* went the emeralds. She examined the four gems remaining in her hand. "She must be the most wonderful person who ever existed."

Another cough from behind him—from Gavriel this time. But Aelin only had eyes for Rowan as the warrior said to her, "She is indeed that. And more."

"Hmmm," Aelin said, rolling the emeralds in her scarred palm with expert ease.

Rolfe growled, "What. Are. You. Doing. Here."

Aelin dumped the emeralds into their dish. "Is that any way to speak to an old friend?"

Rolfe stalked toward the desk, and Rowan trembled with restraint as the Pirate Lord braced his hands on the wooden surface. "Last I heard, your master was dead and you sold the Guild to his underlings. You're a free woman. What are you doing in *my* city?"

Aelin met his sea-green eyes with an irreverence that Dorian wondered if she had been born with or had honed through skill and blood and adventure. "War is coming, Rolfe. Am I not allowed to weigh my options? I thought to see what *you* planned to do."

Rolfe looked over his broad shoulder at Dorian. "Rumor has it she was your Champion this fall. Do you wish to deal with *this*?"

Dorian said smoothly, "You will find, Rolfe, that one does not *deal* with Celaena Sardothien. One survives her."

A flash of a grin from Aelin. Rolfe rolled his eyes and said to the assassin-queen, "So, what is the plan, then? You made a bargain to get out of Endovier, became the King's Champion, and now that he is dead, you wish to see how you might profit?"

Dorian tried not to flinch. Dead—his father was dead, at his own hands.

"You know how my tastes run," Aelin said. "Even with Arobynn's fortune and the sale of the Guild . . . War can be a profitable time for people who are smart with their business."

"And where is the sixteen-year-old self-righteous brat who wrecked six of my ships, stole two of them, and destroyed my town, all for the sake of two hundred slaves?"

A shadow flickered in Aelin's eyes that sent a chill down Dorian's spine. "Spend a year in Endovier, Rolfe, and you quickly learn how to play a different sort of game."

"I told you"—Rolfe seethed with quiet venom—"that you'd one day pay for that arrogance."

Aelin's smile became lethal. "Indeed I did. And so did Arobynn Hamel."

Rolfe blinked—just once, then straightened. "Get out of my seat. And put back that emerald you slipped up your sleeve."

Aelin snorted, and with a flash of her fingers, an emerald—the fourth one Dorian had forgotten—appeared between her fingers. "Good. At least your eyesight isn't failing in your old age."

"And the other one," Rolfe said through clenched teeth.

Aelin grinned again. And then leaned back in Rolfe's chair, tipped up her head, and spat out an emerald she'd somehow kept hidden under her tongue. Dorian watched the gem arc neatly through the air.

Its plunk in the dish was the only sound.

Dorian glanced at Rowan. But delight shone in the prince's eyes—delight and pride and simmering lust. Dorian quickly looked away.

Aelin said to the Pirate Lord, "I have two questions for you."

Rolfe's hand twitched toward his rapier. "You're in no rutting position to ask questions."

"Aren't I? After all, I made you a promise two and a half years ago. One that you signed."

Rolfe snarled.

Aelin propped her chin on a fist. "Have you or have any of your ships bought, traded, or transported slaves since that . . . unfortunate day?"

"No."

A satisfied little nod. "And have you provided sanctuary for them here?"

"We haven't gone out of our way, but if any arrived, yes." Each word was tighter than the last, a spring about to burst forward and throttle the queen. Dorian prayed the man wouldn't be dumb enough to draw on her. Not with Rowan watching his every breath.

"Good and good," Aelin said. "Smart of you, not to lie to me. As I took it upon myself when I arrived this morning to look into your warehouses, to ask around in the markets. And then I came here . . ." She ran her hands over the papers and books on the desk. "To see your ledgers for myself." She dragged a finger down a page containing various columns and numbers. "Textiles, spices, porcelain dining ware, rice from the southern continent, and various contraband, but . . . no slaves. I have to say, I'm impressed. Both at you honoring your word and at your thorough record keeping."

A low snarl. "Do you know what your stunt cost me?"

Aelin flicked her eyes toward a piece of parchment on the wall, various daggers, swords, and even scissors embedded in it—target practice, apparently, for Rolfe. "Well, there's the bar tab I left unpaid . . . ," she said of the document, which was indeed a list of items, and—holy gods, that was a large sum of money.

Rolfe turned to Rowan, Fenrys, and Gavriel. "You want my assistance in this war? Here's the cost. Kill her. Now. Then my ships and men are yours."

Fenrys's dark eyes glittered, but not at Rolfe, as Aelin rose to her feet. Her black clothes were travel-worn, her golden hair gleaming in the gray light. And even in a room of professional killers, she took the lion's share of air. "Oh, I don't think they will," she said. "Or even can."

Rolfe whirled to her. "You'll find that you are not so skilled in the face of Fae warriors."

She pointed to one of the chairs before the desk. "You might want to sit."

"Get the *hell* out of—"

Aelin let out a low whistle. "Allow me to introduce to you, Captain Rolfe, the *incomparable*, the beautiful, and the absolutely and all-around flawless Queen of Terrasen."

Dorian's brows creased. But footsteps sounded, and then—

The males shifted as Aelin Galathynius indeed strode into the room, clad in a dark green tunic of equal wear and dirt, her golden hair unbound, her turquoise-and-gold eyes laughing as she strode past a slack-jawed Rolfe and perched on the arm of Aelin's chair.

Dorian couldn't tell—without a Fae's sense of smell, he couldn't tell.

"What—what devilry is this," Rolfe hissed, yielding a single step.

Aelin and Aelin looked at each other. The one in black grinned up at the newcomer. "Oh, you *are* gorgeous, aren't you?"

The one in green smiled, but for all its delight, all its wicked mischief . . . It was a softer smile, made with a mouth that was perhaps less used to snarling and teeth-baring and getting away with saying hideous, swaggering things. Lysandra, then.

The two queens faced Rolfe.

"Aelin Galathynius had no twin," he growled, a hand on his sword.

Aelin in black—the true Aelin, who had been among them all along—rolled her eyes. "Ugh, Rolfe. You ruin my fun. *Of course* I don't have a twin."

She jerked her chin at Lysandra, and the shifter's flesh glowed and melted, hair becoming a heavy, straight fall of dark tresses, her skin sun-kissed, her uptilted eyes a striking green.

Rolfe barked in alarm and staggered back—only for Fenrys to steady him with a hand on his shoulder as the Fae warrior stepped forward, eyes wide. "A shifter," Fenrys breathed.

Aelin and Lysandra fixed the warrior with an unimpressed look that would have sent lesser men running.

Even Gavriel's placid face was slack at the sight of the shape-shifter—his tattoos bobbing as he swallowed. Aedion's father. And if Aedion was here with Aelin . . .

"As intrigued as I am to see that the cadre is present," Aelin said, "will you verify to His Pirateness that I am who I say I am, and we can move on to more pressing matters?"

Rolfe's face was white with fury as he realized they'd all known who truly sat before them.

Dorian said, "She is Aelin Galathynius. And Celaena Sardothien."

But it was to Fenrys and Gavriel, the outside party, that Rolfe turned. Gavriel nodded, Fenrys's eyes now fixed on the queen. "She is who she says she is."

Rolfe turned to Aelin, but the queen frowned up at Lysandra as the shifter handed her a wax-sealed tube. "You made your hair shorter."

"You try hair that long and see if you last more than a day," Lysandra said, fingering the hair brushing her collarbone.

Rolfe gaped at them. Aelin grinned at her companion and faced the Pirate Lord.

"So, Rolfe," the queen drawled, tossing the tube from hand to hand, "let's discuss this little business of you refusing to aid my cause."

CHAPTER 28

Aelin Galathynius didn't bother to contain her smugness as Rolfe pointed to the large table on the right side of his office—far grander than the piece-of-shit office where he'd once had her and Sam meet him.

She managed all of one step toward her designated seat before Rowan was at her side, a hand on her elbow.

His face—oh, gods, she'd missed that harsh, unyielding face—was tight as he leaned in to whisper with Fae softness, "The cadre is working with us on the condition that it'll lead them to Lorcan, since Maeve sent them to kill him. I refused to divulge his whereabouts. Most of Adarlan's fleet is in the Gulf of Oro thanks to some foul agreement with Melisande to use their ports, and Maeve's own armada sails for Eyllwe—whether to attack or aid, we don't know."

Well, it was nice to know absolute hell awaited them and that the information about Maeve's armada was correct. But then Rowan added, "And I missed you like hell."

She smiled despite what he'd told her, pulling back to look at him. Untouched, unharmed.

It was more than she could have hoped for. Even with the news he'd delivered.

Aelin decided she didn't particularly give a shit who was watching and rose up on her toes to brush her mouth against his. It had taken all her wits and abilities to avoid leaving traces of her scent today for him to detect—and the shocked delight on his face had been utterly worth it.

Rowan's hand on her arm tightened as she pulled away. "The feeling, Prince," she murmured, "is mutual."

The others were doing their best not to watch them—save for Rolfe, who was still seething.

"Oh, don't look so put out, Captain," she said, turning away from Rowan and sliding into a seat across from Rolfe. "You hate me, I hate you, we *both* hate being told what to do by busybody, overlording empires—it's a perfect pairing."

Rolfe spat, "You nearly wrecked everything I've worked for. Your silver tongue and arrogance won't get you through this."

Just for the hell of it, she smiled and stuck out her tongue. Not the real thing—but a forked tongue of silver fire that wriggled like a snake's in the air.

Fenrys choked on a dark laugh. She ignored him. She'd deal with *their* presence later. She just prayed she'd be able to warn Aedion before he ran into his father—who was now sitting two seats down from her, gawking at her as if she had ten heads.

Gods, even the expression was like Aedion's. How hadn't she noticed that this spring in Wendlyn? Aedion had been a boy the last time she'd seen him—but as a man . . . With Gavriel's immortality, they even looked the same age. Different in many ways, but that look . . . it was a reflection.

Rolfe wasn't smiling. "A queen who plays with fire is not one who makes a solid ally."

"And a pirate whose men abandoned him at the first test of allegiance makes for a shit naval commander, yet here I am, at this table."

"Careful, girl. You need me more than I need you."

"Do I?" A dance—that was all this was. Long before she'd set foot on this horrible island, it had been a dance, and she was now to enter into its second movement. She set Murtaugh's sealed letter of recommendation on the table between them. "The way I see it, I have the gold, and I have the ability to raise you up from a common criminal to a respectable, established businessman. Fenharrow can dispute who owns these islands, but . . . what if I were to throw my support behind you? What if I were to make you not a Pirate Lord but a Pirate King?"

"And who would verify the word of a nineteen-year-old princess?"

She jerked her chin at the wax-sealed tube. "Murtaugh Allsbrook would. He wrote you a nice, long letter about it."

Rolfe picked up the tube, studied it, and chucked it in a neat arc—right into his rubbish bin. The thud echoed through the office.

"And I would," Dorian said, leaning forward before Aelin could snarl at the ignored letter. "We win this war, and you have the two largest kingdoms on this continent proclaiming you the undisputed King of all Pirates. Skull's Bay and the Dead Islands become not a hideout for your people, but a proper home. A new kingdom."

Rolfe let out a low laugh. "The talk of young idealists and dreamers."

"The world," Aelin said, "will be saved and remade by the dreamers, Rolfe."

"The world will be saved by the warriors, by the men and women who will spill their blood for it. Not for empty promises and gilded dreams."

Aelin laid her hands flat on the table. "Perhaps. But if we win this war, it will be a new world—a free world. That is my promise—to you, to anyone who will march under my banner. A better world. And you will have to decide where your place in it shall be."

"That is the promise of a little girl who still doesn't know how the world truly works," Rolfe said. "Masters are needed to maintain order—to keep things running and profitable. It will not end well for those who seek to upend it."

Aelin purred, "Do you want gold, Rolfe? Do you want a title? Do you want glory or women or land? Or is it just the bloodlust that drives you?" She gave a pointed glance at his gloved hands. "What was the cost for the map? What was the end goal if that sacrifice had to be made?"

"There is nothing you can offer or say, Aelin Galathynius, that I cannot attain myself." A sly smile. "Unless you plan to offer me your hand and make me king of your territory . . . which might be an interesting proposition."

Bastard. Self-serving, awful bastard. He'd seen her with Rowan. He was drinking in the stillness with which both of them now sat, the death in Rowan's eyes.

"Looks like you bid on the wrong horse," Rolfe crooned. He flicked his eyes to Dorian. "What news did you receive?"

But that wrong horse cut in smoothly, "There was none. But you'll be glad to know your spies at the Ocean Rose are certainly doing their job. And that His Majesty is quite an accomplished actor." Aelin held in her laugh.

Rolfe's face darkened. "Get out of my office."

Dorian said coldly, "For a petty grudge, you'd refuse to consider allying with us?"

Aelin snorted. "I'd hardly call wrecking his shit-poor city and ships a 'petty grudge.'"

"You have two days to get yourselves off this island," Rolfe said, teeth flashing. "After that, my promise from two and a half years ago still holds." A sneer at her companions. "Take your . . . menagerie with you."

Smoke curled in her mouth. She had expected debate, but . . . It was time to regroup—time to see what Rowan and Dorian had done and plan out the next steps.

Let Rolfe think she was leaving the dance unfinished for now.

Aelin hit the narrow hallway, a wall of muscle at her back and by her side, and faced another dilemma: Aedion.

He was loitering outside the inn to monitor for any unfriendly forces. If she stormed right to him, she'd bring him face-to-face with his long-lost, completely oblivious father.

Aelin made it all of three steps down the hall when Gavriel said behind her, "Where is he?"

Slowly, she looked back. The warrior's tan face was tight, his eyes full of sorrow and steel.

She smirked. "If you are referring to sweet, darling Lorcan—"

"You know who I'm referring to."

Rowan took a step between them, but his harsh face yielded nothing. Fenrys slipped into the hall, shutting Rolfe's office door, and monitored them with dark amusement. Oh, Rowan had told her lots about him. A face and body women and men would kill to possess. What Maeve made him do, what he'd given for his twin.

But Aelin sucked on a tooth and said to Gavriel, "Isn't the better question '*Who* is he?'"

Gavriel didn't smile. Didn't move. Buy herself time, buy Aedion time . . .

"You don't get to decide when and where and how you meet him," Aelin said.

"He's my gods-damned son. I think I do."

Aelin shrugged. "You don't even get to decide if you're allowed to call him that."

Those tawny eyes flashed; the tattooed hands curled into fists. But Rowan said, "Gavriel, she does not intend to keep you from him."

"Tell me where my son is. *Now.*"

Ah—there it was. The face of the Lion. The warrior who had felled armies, whose reputation made wintered soldiers shudder. Whose fallen warriors were tattooed all over him.

But Aelin picked at her nails, then frowned at the now-empty hall behind her. "Hell if I know where he's gone off to."

They blinked, then started as they beheld where Lysandra had once been. To where she had now vanished, flying or slithering or crawling out of the open window. To get Aedion away.

Aelin just said to Gavriel, her voice flat and cold, "Don't ever give me orders."

Aedion and Lysandra were already waiting at the Ocean Rose, and as they entered the pretty courtyard, Aelin barely dragged up the energy to remark to Rowan that she was shocked he hadn't opted for warrior-squalor.

Dorian, a few steps behind, laughed quietly—which was good, she supposed. Good that he was laughing. He had not been the last time she saw him.

And it had been weeks since she'd laughed herself, felt that weight lift long enough to do so.

She gave Rowan a look that told him to meet her upstairs, and halted halfway across the courtyard. Dorian, sensing her intent, paused as well.

The evening air was heavy with sweet fruit and climbing flowers, the fountain in the center gurgling softly. She wondered if the owner of the inn hailed from the Red Desert—if they'd seen the use of water and stone and greenery at the Keep of the Silent Assassins.

But Aelin murmured to Dorian, "I'm sorry. About Rifthold."

The king's summer-tanned face tightened. "Thank you—for the help."

Aelin shrugged. "Rowan's always looking for an excuse to show off. Dramatic rescues give him purpose and fulfillment in his dull, immortal life."

There was a pointed cough from the open balcony doors above them, sharp enough to inform her that Rowan had heard and wouldn't forget that little quip when they were alone.

She held in her smile. It had been a surprise and a delight, she supposed, that an easy, respectful calm flowed between Rowan and Dorian on their walk over here.

She motioned for the king to continue with her and said quietly, well aware of how many spies Rolfe employed within the building, "It seems you and I are currently without crowns, thanks to a few bullshit pieces of paper."

Dorian didn't return her smile. The stairs groaned beneath them as they headed for the second floor. They were almost to the room Dorian had indicated when he said, "Maybe that's a good thing."

She opened and closed her mouth—and opted, for once, to keep quiet, shaking her head a bit as she entered the chamber.

Their meeting was hushed, thorough. Rowan and Dorian laid out in precise detail what had happened to them, Aedion pushing for counts of the witches, their armor, how they flew, what formations they used. Anything to feed to the Bane, to amplify their northern defenses, regardless of who commanded them. The general of the North—who would take all those pieces and build their resistance. But the sheer ease with which the Ironteeth legion had taken the city . . .

"Manon Blackbeak," Aedion mused, "would be a valuable ally, if we can get her to turn."

Aelin glanced at Rowan's shoulder—where a faint scar now marred the golden skin beneath his clothes.

"Perhaps getting Manon to turn on her kin would ignite an internal battle among the witches," she said. "Maybe they'll save us the task of killing them and just destroy each other."

Dorian straightened in his chair, but only cold calculation swirled in his eyes as he countered, "But what is it that they want? Beyond our heads, I mean. Why ally with Erawan at all?"

And all of them then looked to the thin necklace of scars marring the base of Aelin's throat—where the scent permanently marked her as a Witch Killer. Baba Yellowlegs had visited the castle this winter for that alliance, but had there been anything else?

"We can contemplate the whys and hows of it later," Aelin declared. "If we encounter any of the witches, we take them alive. I want some questions answered."

Then she explained what they'd witnessed in Ilium. The order Brannon had given her: Find the Lock. Well, he and his little quest could get in line.

It was never-ending, she supposed while they dined that night on peppered crab and spiced rice. This burden, these threats.

Erawan had been planning this for decades. Maybe for centuries, while he'd slept, he'd planned all this out. And she was to be given nothing more than obscure commands by long-dead royals to find a way to stop it, nothing more than gods-damned *months* to rally a force against him.

She doubted it was a coincidence that Maeve was sailing for Eyllwe at the same moment Brannon had commanded she go to the Stone Marshes on its southwestern peninsula. Or that the gods-damned Morath fleet was squatting in the Gulf of Oro—right on its other side.

There was not enough time, not enough *time* to do what she needed to, to *fix* things.

But . . . small steps.

She had Rolfe to deal with. The little matter of securing his people's alliance. And the map she still needed to persuade him to use to assist her in tracking down that Lock.

But first . . . best to ensure that infernal map actually worked.

CHAPTER 29

Too many animals loitering about the streets at this hour would attract the wrong sort of attention.

But Aedion still wished that the shifter was wearing fur or feathers compared to . . . this.

Not that she was sore on the eyes as an auburn-haired and green-eyed young woman. She could have passed for one of the lovely mountain maidens of northern Terrasen with that coloring. It was *who* Lysandra was supposed to be as they waited just inside an alley. Who *he* was supposed to be, too.

Lysandra leaned against the brick wall, a foot propped against it to reveal a length of creamy-white thigh. And Aedion, with his hand braced against the wall beside her head, was no more than an hourly customer.

No sound in the alley but scuttling rats digging through rotten, discarded fruit. Skull's Bay was precisely the shithole he expected it to be, right down to its Pirate Lord.

Who now unwittingly held the only map to the Lock that Aelin had been commanded to find. When Aedion had complained that *of course* it was a map they could not steal, Rowan had been the one to suggest this . . . plan. Trap. Whatever it was.

He glanced at the delicate gold chain dangling around Lysandra's pale throat, tracing its length down the front of her bodice, to where the Amulet of Orynth was now hidden beneath.

"Admiring the view?"

Aedion snapped his eyes up from the generous swells of her breasts. "Sorry."

But the shifter somehow saw the thoughts churning in his head. "You think this won't work?"

"I think there are plenty of valuable things on this island—why would Rolfe bother to go after this?" Storms, enemies, and treasure—that was what the map showed. And since he and Lysandra were not the first two . . . only one, it seemed, would be able to appear on that map inked on Rolfe's hands.

"Rowan claimed Rolfe would find the amulet interesting enough to go after it."

"Rowan and Aelin have a tendency to say one thing and mean something else entirely." Aedion heaved a breath through his nose. "We've already been here an hour."

She arched an auburn brow. "Do you have somewhere else to be?"

"You're tired."

"We're all tired," she said sharply.

He shut his mouth, not wanting his head ripped off just yet.

Each shift took something out of Lysandra. The bigger the change, the bigger the animal, the steeper the cost. Aedion had witnessed her morph from butterfly to bumblebee to hummingbird to bat within the span of a few minutes. But going from human to ghost leopard to bear or elk or horse, she'd once demonstrated, took longer between shifts, the magic having to draw up the strength to *become* that size, to fill the body with all its inherent power.

Casual footsteps sounded, accented by a two-note whistle. Lysandra's breath brushed against his jaw at the sound. Aedion, however, stiffened slightly as those steps grew closer, and he found himself staring at the son of his great enemy. King, now.

But still a face he'd hated, sneered at, debated cutting into tiny pieces for many, many years. A face he'd seen drunk out of his mind at parties mere seasons ago; a face he'd seen buried against the necks of women whose names he'd never bothered to learn; a face that had taunted him in that dungeon cell.

That face was now hooded, and for all the world, he looked like he was here to inquire about Lysandra's services—once Aedion had finished with her. The general clenched his teeth. "What?"

Dorian looked over Lysandra, as if surveying the goods, and Aedion fought the urge to bristle. "Rowan sent me to see if you had any developments." The prince and Aelin were back at the inn, drinking in the dining room—where all of Rolfe's spying eyes might see and report them. Dorian blinked at the shifter, starting. "And gods above—you really *can* take on any human form."

Lysandra shrugged, the irreverent street whore debating her rate. "It's not as interesting as you'd think. I'd like to see if I could become a plant. Or a bit of wind."

"Can you . . . *do* that?"

"Of course she can," Aedion said, pushing off the wall and crossing his arms.

"No," Lysandra said, cutting a glare in Aedion's direction. "And there's nothing to report. Not even a whiff of Rolfe or his men."

Dorian nodded, sliding his hands into his pockets. Silence.

Aedion's ankle barked in pain as Lysandra subtly kicked him.

He reined in his scowl as he said to the king, "So, you and Whitethorn didn't kill each other."

Dorian's brows scrunched. "He saved my life, nearly got himself burned out to do it. Why should I be anything but grateful?" Lysandra gave Aedion a smug smile.

But the king asked him, "Are you going to see your father?"

Aedion cringed. He'd been glad for their venture tonight to avoid deciding. Aelin hadn't brought it up, and he had been content to come out here, even if it put him at risk of running into the male.

"Of course I'll see him," Aedion said tightly. Lysandra's moon-white face was calm, steady as she watched him, the face of a woman trained to listen to men, to never show surprise—

He did not resent what she had been, what she portrayed now, only the monsters who had seen the beauty the child would grow into and taken her into that brothel. Aelin had told him what Arobynn had done to the man she'd loved. It was a miracle the shifter could smile at all.

Aedion jerked his chin at Dorian. "Go tell Aelin and Rowan we don't need their hovering. We can manage on our own."

Dorian stiffened, but backed down the alley, no more than a disgruntled would-be customer.

Lysandra shoved a hand against Aedion's chest and hissed, "That man has endured *enough*, Aedion. A little kindness wouldn't kill you."

"He *stabbed* Aelin. If you knew him as I have, you wouldn't be so willing to fawn over—"

"No one expects you to fawn over him. But a kind word, some *respect*—"

He rolled his eyes. "Keep your voice down."

She did—but went on, "He was enslaved; he was *tortured* for months. Not just by his father, but by that *thing* inside of him. He was *violated*, and even if you cannot draw up forgiveness for stabbing Aelin against his own will, then try to have some compassion for *that*." Aedion's heart stuttered at the anger and pain on her face. And that word she'd used—

He swallowed hard, checking the street behind them. No sign of anyone hunting for the treasure they bore. "I knew Dorian as a reckless, arrogant—"

"I knew your queen as the same. We were children then. We are allowed to make mistakes, to figure out who we wish to be. If you will allow Aelin the gift of your acceptance—"

"I don't care if he was as arrogant and vain as Aelin, I don't *care* if he was enslaved to a demon that took his mind. I look at him and see my family *butchered*, see those tracks to the river, and hear Quinn tell me that Aelin was drowned and *dead*." His breathing was uneven, and his throat burned, but he ignored it.

Lysandra said, "Aelin forgave him. Aelin never once held it against him."

Aedion snarled at her. Lysandra snarled right back and held his stare with the face not trained or built for bedrooms, but the true one beneath—wild and unbroken and indomitable. No matter what body she wore, she was the Staghorns given form, the heart of Oakwald.

Aedion said hoarsely, "I'll try."

"Try harder. Try better."

Aedion braced his palm against the wall again and leaned in to glower in her face. She did not yield an inch. "There is an order and rank in our court, *lady*, and last I checked, you were *not* number three. You don't give me commands."

"This isn't a battlefield," Lysandra hissed. "Any ranks are formalities. And the last *I* checked . . ." She poked his chest, right between his pectorals, and he could have sworn the tip of a claw pierced the skin beneath his clothes. "*You* weren't pathetic enough to enforce rank to hide from being in the wrong."

His blood sparked and thrummed. Aedion found himself taking in the sensuous curves of her mouth, now pressed thin with anger.

The hot temper in her eyes faded, and as she retracted her finger as if she'd been burned, he froze at the panic that filled her features instead. Shit. *Shit*—

Lysandra backed away a step, too casual to be anything but a calculated move. But Aedion tried—for her sake, he tried to stop thinking about her mouth—

"You truly want to meet your father?" she asked calmly. Too calmly.

He nodded, swallowing hard. Too soon—she wouldn't want a man's touch for a long time. Maybe forever. And he'd be damned if he pushed her into it before she wanted to. And gods above, if Lysandra ever looked at *any* man with interest like that . . . he'd be glad for her. Glad she was choosing for herself, even if it wasn't him she picked—

"I . . ." Aedion swallowed, forcing himself to remember what she'd asked. His father. Right. "Did he want to see me?" was all he could think to ask.

She cocked her head to the side, the movement so feline he wondered if she was spending too much time in that ghost leopard's fur. "He nearly bit Aelin's head off when she refused to tell him where and who you are." Ice filled his veins. If his father had been rude to her—"But I got the sense," Lysandra quickly clarified as he tensed, "that he is the sort of male who would respect your wishes if you chose not to see him. Yet in this small town, with the company we're keeping . . . that might prove impossible."

"Did you also get the sense that it could persuade him to help us? Knowing me?"

"I don't think Aelin would ever ask that of you," Lysandra said, laying a hand on the arm still braced beside her head.

"What do I even say to him?" Aedion murmured. "I've heard so many stories about him—the Lion of Doranelle. He's a gods-damned white knight. I don't think he'll approve of a son most people call Adarlan's Whore." She clicked her tongue, but Aedion pinned her with a look. "What would you do?"

"I can't answer that question. My own father . . ." She shook her head.

He knew about that—the shifter-father who had either abandoned her mother or not even known she was pregnant. And then the mother who had thrown Lysandra into the street when she discovered her heritage. "Aedion, what do *you* want to do? Not for us, not for Terrasen, but for *you*."

He bowed his head a bit, glancing sidelong at the quiet street again. "My whole life has been . . . not about what I want. I don't know how to choose those things."

No, from the moment he'd arrived in Terrasen at age five, he'd been trained—his path chosen. And when Terrasen had burned beneath Adarlan's torches, another hand had gripped the leash of his fate. Even now, with war upon them . . . Had he truly never wanted something for himself? All he'd wanted had been the blood oath. And Aelin had given that away to Rowan. He didn't resent her for it, not anymore, but . . . He had not realized he had asked for so little.

Lysandra said quietly, "I know. I know what that feels like."

He lifted his head, finding her green eyes again in the darkness. He sometimes wished Arobynn Hamel were still alive—just so he could kill the assassin-king himself.

"Tomorrow morning," he murmured. "Will you come with me? To see him."

She was quiet for a moment before she said, "You really want me to go with you?"

He did. He couldn't explain why, but he wanted her there. She got under his skin so damn easily, but . . . Lysandra steadied him. Perhaps because she was something new. Something he had not encountered, had not filled with hope and pain and wishes. Not too many of them, at least.

"If you wouldn't mind . . . yes. I want you there."

She didn't respond. He opened his mouth, but steps sounded.

Light. Too casual.

They ducked deeper into the shadows of the alley, its dead-end wall looming behind them. If this went poorly . . .

If it went poorly, he had a shape-shifter capable of shredding apart droves of men at his side. Aedion flashed Lysandra a grin as he leaned over her once more, his nose within grazing distance of her neck.

Those steps neared, and Lysandra loosed a breath, her body going pliant.

From the shadows of his hood, he monitored the alley ahead, the shadows and shafts of moonlight, bracing himself. They'd picked the dead-end alley for a reason.

The girl realized her mistake a step too late. "Oh."

Aedion looked up, his own features hidden within his hood, as Lysandra purred to the young woman who perfectly matched Rowan's description of Rolfe's barmaid, "I'll be done in two minutes, if you want to wait your turn."

Color stained the girl's cheeks, but she gave them a flinty look, scanning them from head to toe. "Wrong turn," she said.

"You sure?" Lysandra crooned. "A bit late in the evening for a stroll."

Rolfe's barmaid fixed them with that sharp stare and sauntered back down the street.

They waited. A minute. Five. Ten. No others came.

Aedion at last pulled away, Lysandra now watching the alley entrance. The shifter wound an auburn curl around her finger. "She seems an unlikely thief."

"Some would say similar things about you and Aelin." Lysandra hummed in agreement. Aedion mused, "Perhaps she was just a scout—Rolfe's eyes."

"Why bother? Why not just come take the thing?"

Aedion glanced again at the amulet that disappeared beneath Lysandra's bodice. "Maybe she thought she was looking for something else."

Lysandra, wisely, didn't fish the Amulet of Orynth out from her dress. But his words hung between them as they carefully picked their way back to the Ocean Rose.

CHAPTER 30

After two weeks of inching across the muddy open plains, Elide was tired of using her mother's name.

Tired of constantly being on alert to hear it barked by Molly to clean up after every meal (a mistake, no doubt, to have ever told the woman she had some experience washing dishes in busy kitchens), tired of hearing Ombriel—the dark-haired beauty not a carnival act at all but Molly's niece and their money-keeper—use it when questioning about how she'd hurt her leg, where her family came from, and how she'd learned to observe others so keenly that she could turn a coin as an oracle.

At least Lorcan barely used it, as they'd hardly spoken while the caravan trudged through the mud-laden fields. The ground was so saturated with the daily afternoon summer rain that the wagons often became stuck. They'd barely covered any distance at all, and when Ombriel would catch Elide gazing northward, she'd ask—yet another recurring question—what lay in the North to draw her attention so frequently.

Elide always lied, always evaded. The sleeping situation between Elide and her *husband*, fortunately, was more easily avoided.

With the sodden earth, sleeping on it was nearly impossible. So the women laid out wherever they could in the two wagons, leaving the men to draw straws each night for who would get any remaining space and who would sleep on the ground atop a makeshift floor of reeds. Lorcan, somehow, always got the short straw, either by his own devices, sleight of hand from Nik, who ran security and the nightly straw-drawing, or simply from sheer bad luck.

But at least it kept Lorcan far, far away from her, and kept their interactions to a minimum.

Those few conversations they'd had—held when he escorted her to draw water from a swollen stream or gather whatever firewood could be found on the plain—weren't much to bother her, either. He pressed her for more details regarding Morath, more information about the guards' clothes, the armies camped around it, the servants and witches.

She'd started at the top of the Keep—with the aeries and wyverns and witches. Then she'd descended, floor by floor. It had taken them these two weeks to work their way down to the sublevels, and their companions had no idea that while the young, married couple snuck off for more "firewood," whispering sweet nothings was the last thing on their minds.

When the caravan stopped that night, Elide aimed for a copse of trees in the heart of the field to see what could be used at their large campfire. Lorcan trailed at her side, as quiet as the hissing grasses around them. The nickering of the horses and clamor of their companions readying for the evening meal faded behind, and Elide frowned as her boot sank deep into a pocket of mud. She yanked on it, ankle barking at bearing her weight, and gritted her teeth until—

Lorcan's magic pushed against her leg, an invisible hand freeing her boot, and she tumbled into him. His arm and side were as hard and unyielding as the magic he'd used, and she rebounded away, tall grass crunching beneath her. "Thank you," she murmured.

Lorcan stalked ahead and said without looking back, "We finished at the three dungeons and their entrances yesterday night. Tell me about what's inside them."

Her mouth went a bit dry as she recalled the cell she'd squatted in, the darkness and tight air . . .

"I don't know what's inside," she lied, following him. "Suffering people, no doubt."

Lorcan stooped, his dark head disappearing beneath a wave of grass. When he emerged, two sticks were gripped in his massive hands. He snapped them with little effort. "You described everything else with no problem. Yet your scent changed just now. Why?"

She strode past him, bending over and over to collect whatever scattered wood she could find. "They did horrible things down there," she said over a shoulder. "You could sometimes hear people screaming." She prayed Terrasen would be better. It *had* to be.

"Who did they keep down there? Enemy soldiers?" Potential allies, no doubt, for whatever he planned to do.

"Whoever they wanted to torture." The hands of those guards, their sneers— "I assume you're going to leave as soon as I finish describing the last pit of Morath?" She plucked up stick after stick, ankle objecting with each shift in her balance.

"Is there a problem if I do? That was our bargain. I've stayed longer than I intended."

She turned, finding him with an armful of larger sticks. He unceremoniously dumped them into the small pile in her arms and thumbed free the hatchet at his side before prowling to the curving, fallen branch behind him. "So, am I just to play the abandoned wife, then?"

"You're already playing the oracle, so what difference does another role make?" Lorcan brought his hatchet down upon the branch with a solid *thwack!* The blade sank unnervingly deep; wood groaned. "Describe the dungeons."

It was only fair, and it had been their bargain, after all: his protection and help to get her out of harm's way, in exchange for what she knew. And he'd been complacent in all the lies she'd spun to their company—quiet, but he'd gone along with it.

"The dungeons are gone," Elide managed to say. "Or most of them should be. Along with the catacombs."

Thwack, thwack, thwack. Lorcan severed the branch, the wood yielding with a splintering cry. He set to cutting another section apart. "Taken out in that blast?" He lifted his axe, the muscles in his powerful back shifting beneath his dark shirt, but paused. "You said you were near the courtyard when the blast happened—how do you know the dungeons are gone?"

Fine. She had lied about it. But . . . "The explosion came from the catacombs and took out some of the towers. One would assume the dungeons would be in its path, too."

"I don't make plans based on assumptions." He resumed hacking apart the branch, and Elide rolled her eyes at his back. "Tell me the layout of the northern dungeon."

Elide turned toward the sinking sun staining the fields with orange and gold beyond them. "Figure it out yourself."

The thud of metal on wood halted. Even the wind in the grasses died down.

But she had endured death and despair and terror, and she had told him enough—turned over every horrible stone, looked around every dark corner at Morath for him. His rudeness, his arrogance . . . He could go to hell.

She had barely set one foot into the swaying grasses when Lorcan was before her, no more than a lethal shadow himself. Even the sun seemed to avoid the broad planes of his tan face, though the wind dared ruffle the silken black strands of his hair across it.

"We have a bargain, girl."

Elide met that depthless gaze. "You did not specify when I had to tell you. So I may take as much time as I wish to recall details, if you desire to wring every last one of them from me."

His teeth flashed. "Do *not* toy with me."

"Or what?" She stepped around him as if he were no more than a rock in a stream. Of course, walking with temper was a bit difficult when every other step was limping, but she kept her chin high. "Kill me, hurt me, and you'll still be out of answers."

Faster than she could see, his arm lashed out—gripping her by the elbow. "Marion," he growled.

That *name*. She looked up at his harsh, wild face—a face born in a different age, a different world. "Take your hand off me."

Lorcan, to her surprise, did so immediately.

But his face did not change—not a flicker—as he said, "You will tell me what I wish to know—"

The thing in her pocket began thrumming and beating, a phantom heartbeat in her bones.

Lorcan yielded a step, his nostrils flaring delicately. As if he could sense that stone awakening. "What are you," he said quietly.

"I am nothing," she said, voice hollow. Maybe once she found Aelin and Aedion, she'd find some purpose, some way to be of use to the world. For now, she was a messenger, a courier of this stone—to Celaena Sardothien. However Elide might find one person in such an endless, vast world. She had to get north—and quickly.

"Why do you go to Aelin Galathynius?"

The question was too tense to be casual. No, every inch of Lorcan's body seemed restrained. Leashed rage and predatory instincts.

"You know the queen," she breathed.

He blinked. Not in surprise, but to buy himself time.

He did know—and he was considering what to tell her, how to tell her—

"Celaena Sardothien is in the queen's service," he said. "Your two paths are one. Find one and you'll find the other."

He paused, waiting.

Would this be her life, then? Wretched people, always looking out for themselves, every kindness coming at a cost? Would her own queen at least gaze at her with warmth in her eyes? Would Aelin even remember her?

"Marion," he said again—the word laced with a growl.

Her mother's name. Her mother—and her father. The last people who had looked at her with true affection. Even Finnula, all those years locked in that tower, had always watched her with some mixture of pity and fear.

She couldn't remember the last time she'd been held. Or comforted. Or smiled at with any genuine love for who she was.

Words were suddenly hard, the energy to dredge up a lie or retort too much to bother with. So Elide ignored Lorcan's command and headed back toward the cluster of painted wagons.

Manon had come for her, she reminded herself with each step. Manon, and Asterin, and Sorrel. But even they had left her alone in the woods.

Pity, she reminded herself—self-pity would do her no good. Not with so many miles between her and whatever shred of a future she stood a chance of finding. But even when she arrived, handed over her burden, and found Aelin . . . what could she offer? She couldn't even read, gods above. The mere thought of explaining that to Aelin, to anyone—

She'd think on it later. She'd wash the queen's clothes if she had to. At least she didn't need to be literate for that.

Elide didn't hear Lorcan this time as he approached, arms laden with massive logs.

"You will tell me what you know," he said through his teeth. She almost sighed, but he added, "Once you are . . . better."

She supposed that, to him, sorrow and despair would be some sort of sickness.

"Fine."

"Fine," he said right back.

Their companions were smiling when she and Lorcan returned. They had found dry ground on the other side of the wagons—solid enough for tents.

Elide spied the one that had been raised for her and Lorcan and wished it would rain.

Lorcan had trained enough warriors to know when not to push. He'd tortured enough enemies to know when they were one slice or snap away from breaking in ways that would make them useless.

So Marion, when her scent had changed, when he'd felt even the strange, otherworldly power hidden in her blood shift to sorrow . . . worse, to hopelessness . . .

He'd wanted to tell her not to bother with hope anyway.

But she was barely into womanhood. Perhaps hope, foolish as it was, had gotten her out of Morath. At least her cleverness had, lies and all.

He'd dealt with enough people, killed and bedded and fought alongside enough people, to know Marion wasn't wicked, or conniving, or wholly selfish. He wished she was, because it'd make it easier—make his task so much easier.

But if she didn't tell him about Morath, if he broke her from pushing too much . . . He needed every advantage when he slipped into that Keep. And when he slipped out again.

She'd done it once. Perhaps Marion was the only person alive who had managed to escape.

He was about to explain that to her when he saw what she was staring at—the tent.

Their tent.

Ombriel came forward, throwing her usual wary glance his way, and slyly informed Elide they'd finally have a night *alone* together.

Arms full of logs, Lorcan could only watch as that pale face of sorrow and despair transformed into youth and mischief, into blushing anticipation, as easily as if Marion had held up a mask. She even gave him a flirting glance before beaming at Ombriel and rushing to dump her armful of sticks and twigs into the pit they'd cleared for the nightly fire.

He possessed the good sense to at least smile at the woman who was supposed to be his wife, but by the time he'd followed to drop his own burden into the fire pit, she'd stalked off for the tent set a good distance away from the others.

It was small, he realized with no tiny amount of horror. Probably meant for the sword-thrower who'd last used it. Marion's slim figure slipped through the white canvas flaps with hardly a ripple. Lorcan just frowned a bit before ducking inside.

And remained ducking slightly. His head would go straight through the canvas if he stood to his full height. Woven mats atop gathered rushes covered the stuffy interior, and Marion stood on the other side of the tent, cringing at the sleeping roll on the makeshift floor.

The tent probably had enough room for a proper bed and table, if need be, but unless they were camping longer than a night, he doubted they'd get any of those things.

"I'll sleep on the ground," he offered blandly. "You take the roll."

"What if someone comes in?"

"Then you'll say we got into a fight."

"Every night?" Marion pivoted, her rich eyes meeting his. The cold, weary face was back.

Lorcan considered her words. "If someone walks into our tent without permission tonight, no one here will make the same mistake again."

He'd punished men in his war camps for less.

But her eyes remained weary—wholly unimpressed and unmoved. "Fine," she said again.

Too close—far too close to the edge of snapping entirely. "I could find some buckets, heat water, and you could bathe in here, if you want. I'll stand watch outside."

Creature comforts—to get her to trust him, be grateful to him, to want to help him. To ease that dangerous brittleness.

Indeed, Marion peered down at herself. The white shirt that was now dirt-flecked, the brown leather pants that were filthy, the boots . . .

"I'll offer Ombriel a coin to wash it all for you tonight."

"I have no other clothes to wear."

"You can sleep without them."

Wariness faded in a flash of dismay. "With you in here?"

He avoided the urge to roll his eyes.

She blurted, "What about your own clothes?"

"What of them?"

"You . . . they're filthy, too."

"I can wait another night." She'd likely beg to sleep in the wagon if he was naked in here—

"Why should I be the only one naked? Wouldn't the ruse work better if you and I both took the opportunity at once?"

"You are very young," he said carefully. "And I am very old."

"How old?"

She'd never asked.

"Old."

She shrugged. "A body is a body. You reek as badly as I do. Go sleep outside if you won't wash."

A test—not driven by any desire or logic, but . . . to see if he'd listen to her. Who was in control. Get her a bath, do as she asked . . . Let her get a sense of control over the situation. He gave her a thin smile. "Fine," he echoed.

When Lorcan pushed through the tent again, laden with water, he discovered Marion seated on the bedroll, boots off, that ruined ankle and foot stretched out before her. Her small hands were braced on the mangled, discolored flesh, as if she'd been rubbing the ache from it.

"How badly does it hurt every day?" He sometimes used his magic to brace the ankle. *When* he remembered. Which wasn't often.

Marion's focus, however, went right to the steaming cauldron he'd set on the floor, then the bucket he'd hauled over a shoulder for her to use as well.

"I've had it since I was a child," she said distantly, as if hypnotized by the clean water. She rose on uneven feet, wincing at her wrecked leg. "I learned to live with it."

"That's not an answer."

"Why do you even care?" The words were barely more than a breath as she unbraided her long, thick hair, still fixated on the bath.

He was curious; he wanted to know how and when and why. Marion was beautiful—surely marring her like that had been done with some ill intent. Or to prevent something worse.

She at last cut him a glance. "You said you'd stand watch. I thought you meant *outside*."

He snorted. Indeed he did. "Enjoy yourself," he said, pushing out of the tent once more.

Lorcan stood in the grasses, monitoring the busy camp, the wide bowl of the darkening sky. He hated the plains. Too much open space; too much visibility.

Behind him, his ears picked up the sigh and hiss of leather sliding down skin, the rustle of rough-woven cloth being peeled off. Then fainter, softer sounds of more delicate fabric sliding away. Then silence—followed by a very, very quiet rustling. Like she didn't want even the gods hearing what she was doing. Hay crunched. Then a thud of the mattress roll lifting and falling—

The little witch was hiding something. The hay snapped again as she returned to the cauldron.

Hiding something under the mattress—something she'd been carrying with her and didn't want him knowing about. Water splashed, and Marion let out a moan of surprising depth and sincerity. He shut out the sound.

But even as he did, Lorcan's thoughts drifted toward Rowan and his bitch-queen.

Marion and the queen were about the same age—one dark, one golden. Would the queen bother at all with Marion once she arrived? Likely, if her curiosity was piqued about why she wished to see Celaena Sardothien, but . . . what about after?

It wasn't his concern. He'd left his conscience on the cobblestones of the back streets of Doranelle five centuries ago. He'd killed men who had begged for their lives, wrecked entire cities and never once looked back at the smoldering rubble.

Rowan had, too. Gods-damned Whitethorn had been his most effective general, assassin, and executioner for centuries. They had laid waste to kingdoms and then drunk and bedded themselves into stupors in the following days-long celebrations on the ruins.

This winter, he'd had a damn fine commander at his disposal, brutal and vicious and willing to do just about anything Lorcan ordered.

The next time he'd seen Rowan, the prince had been roaring, desperate to fling himself into lethal darkness to save the life of a princess with no throne. Lorcan had known—in that moment.

Lorcan had known, as he'd pinned Rowan into the grass outside Mistward, the prince thrashing and screaming for Aelin Galathynius, that everything was about to change. Knew that the commander he'd valued was altered irrevocably. No longer would they glut themselves on wine and women; no longer would Rowan gaze toward a horizon without some glimmer of longing in his eyes.

Love had broken a perfect killing tool. Lorcan wondered if it would take him centuries more to stop being so pissed about it.

And the queen—princess, whatever Aelin called herself . . . She was a fool. She could have bartered Athril's ring for Maeve's armies, for an alliance to wipe Morath off the earth. Even not knowing what the ring was, she could have used it to her advantage.

But she'd chosen Rowan. A prince with no crown, no army, no allies. They deserved to perish together.

Marion's soaked head popped out of the tent, and Lorcan twisted to see the heavy wool blanket wrapped around her like a gown. "Can you bring the clothes now?" She chucked her pile out. She'd bundled her underthings in her white shirt, and the leathers . . . They'd never be dry before morning—and would likely shrink beyond use if washed improperly.

Lorcan stooped, picking up the bundle of clothes and trying not to peer into the tent to learn what she'd hidden beneath the bedroll. "What about standing guard?"

Her hair was plastered to her head, heightening the sharp lines in her cheekbones, her fine nose. But her eyes were bright again, her full lips once more like a rosebud, as she said, "Please get them washed. Quickly."

Lorcan didn't bother confirming as he carried her clothes away from the tent, leaving her to sit in partial nakedness inside. Ombriel was in the middle of cooking whatever was in the pot over the fire. Likely rabbit stew. Again. Lorcan examined the clothes in his hands.

Thirty minutes later, he returned to the tent, plate of food in hand. Marion was perched on the bedroll, foot stretched out before her, blanket tucked under her shoulders.

Her skin was so pale. He'd never seen such white unmarred skin.

As if she'd never been let outside.

Her dark brows furrowed at the plate—then at the bundle under his arm.

"Ombriel was busy—so I washed your clothes myself."

She flushed.

"A body is a body," he repeated simply to her. "So are undergarments."

She frowned, but her attention was again riveted on the plate. He set it down before her. "I got you dinner, since I assumed you didn't want to sit among everyone in your blanket." He dumped the pile of clothes on her bedroll. "And I got you clothes from Molly. She's charging you, of course. But at least you won't sleep naked."

She dug into the stew without so much as thanking him.

Lorcan was about to leave when she said, "My uncle . . . He is a commander at Morath."

Lorcan froze. And looked right to the bedroll.

But Marion continued between bites, "He . . . locked me in the dungeon once."

The wind in the grasses died; the campfire far beyond their tent flickered, the people around it huddling closer together as the nighttime insects went silent and the small, furred creatures of the plains scampered into their burrows.

Marion either didn't notice the surge of his dark power, the magic kissed by Death himself, or didn't care. She said, "His name is Vernon, and he is clever and cruel, and he will likely try to keep you alive if you are caught. He wields people to gain power for himself. He has no mercy, no soul. There is no moral code that guides him."

She went back to her food, done for the night.

Lorcan said quietly, "Would you like me to kill him for you?"

Her limpid, dark eyes rose to his face. And for a moment, he could see the woman she'd become—was already becoming. Someone who, regardless of where she'd been born, any queen would prize at her side. "Would there be a cost?"

Lorcan hid his smile. Smart, cunning little witch. "No," he said, and meant it. "Why did he lock you in the dungeon?"

Marion's white throat bobbed once. Twice. She seemed to hold his stare through effort of will, through a refusal not to back down from him, but from her own fears. "Because he wished to see if his bloodline could be crossed with the Valg. That was why I was brought to Morath. To be bred like a prize mare."

Every thought emptied out of Lorcan's head.

He had seen and dealt and endured many, many unspeakable things, but this . . .

"Did he succeed?" he managed to ask.

"Not with me. There were others before me who . . . Help came too late for them."

"That explosion was not accidental, was it."

A small shake of the head.

"You did it?" He glanced to the bedroll—to whatever she hid beneath.

Again that shake of the head. "I will not say who, or how. Not without risking the lives of the people who saved me."

"Are the ilken—"

"No. The ilken are not the creatures that were bred in the catacombs. Those . . . those came from the mountains around Morath. Through far darker methods."

Maeve had to know. She had to know what they were doing in Morath. The horrors being bred there, the army of demons and beasts to rival any from legend. She would never ally with such evil—never be foolish enough to ally with the Valg. Not when she warred with them millennia ago. But if she did not fight . . . How long would it be before these beasts were howling around Doranelle? Before it was his own continent under siege?

Doranelle could hold out. But he would likely be dead, once he found some way to destroy the keys and Maeve punished him. And with him dead and Whitethorn likely carrion, too . . . how long would Doranelle last? Decades? Years?

A question snagged in Lorcan's mind, drawing him to the present, to the stuffy little tent. "Your foot has been ruined for years, though. He locked you in the dungeon that long?"

"No," she said, not even flinching at his rough description. "I was only in the dungeon for a week. The ankle, the chain . . . He did that to me long before."

"What chain."

She blinked. And he knew she'd meant to avoid telling him that one particular detail.

But now that he looked . . . he could make out, among the mass of scars, a white band. And there, around her perfect, lovely other ankle, was its twin.

A wind laced with the dust and coldness of a tomb gnawed through the field.

Marion merely said, "When you kill my uncle, ask him yourself."

CHAPTER 31

Well, on the one hand, at least Rolfe's map worked.

It had been Rowan's idea, actually. And she might have felt slightly guilty for letting Aedion and Lysandra believe the Pirate Lord had only gone after the Amulet of Orynth, but . . . at least they now knew his unholy map functioned. And that the Pirate Lord was indeed living in terror of the Valg returning to this harbor.

She wondered what Rolfe made of it—what his map had shown him of the Wyrdkey. If it revealed the difference between it and the Wyrdstone rings his men had been enslaved with. Whatever the reason, the Pirate Lord had sent his barmaid to scout for any hint of the Valg, not realizing Rowan had selected that dead-end alley to ensure *only* someone sent by Rolfe would venture so far down it. And since Aelin had no doubt whatsoever that Aedion and Lysandra had snuck through the streets unnoticed . . . Well, at least that part of her evening had gone right.

As for the rest of it . . . It was just past midnight when Aelin wondered how the hell she and Rowan would ever go back to normalcy if they survived this war. If there'd be a day when it wasn't easy to leap over rooftops as if they were stones on a stream, to break into someone's room and hold a blade to the occupant's throat.

They did the first two within the span of fifteen minutes.

And as they found Gavriel and Fenrys waiting for them in their shared room in the Sea Dragon inn, Aelin supposed she needn't bother with the third. Even if both she and Rowan kept their hands within casual reach of their daggers while they leaned against the wall beside the now-shut window. They'd unlocked it with Rowan's wind—only to have a candle ignite the moment the window swung away. Revealing two stone-faced Fae warriors, both dressed and armed.

"You could have used the door," Fenrys said, arms crossed—a bit too casually.

"Why bother when a dramatic entrance is so much more fun?" Aelin countered.

Fenrys's beautiful face twitched with amusement that didn't quite meet his onyx eyes. "What a shame it'd be for you to miss out on any of that."

She grinned at him. He grinned at her.

She supposed both of their smiles were less of a grin and more . . . teeth-exposing.

She snorted. "You two look like you enjoyed your summer in Doranelle. How's sweet Aunt Maeve?"

Gavriel's tattooed hands closed into loose fists. "You deny me the right to see my son and yet you barge into our room in the dead of the night to demand we divulge information about our blood-sworn queen."

"One, *I* did not deny you anything, kitty-cat."

Fenrys let out what might have been a choking sound.

"It's your son's decision, not mine. I don't have enough time to oversee or really care." Lies.

"It must be hard to find the time to care at all," Fenrys cut in, "when you are facing a mortal life span." A sly, cutting glance at Rowan. "Or is she due to Settle soon?"

Oh, he was a bastard. A bitter, hard-edged bastard, the laughing side of the coin to Lorcan's sullen brooding. Maeve certainly had a type.

Rowan's face yielded nothing. "The matter of Aelin's Settling is none of your concern."

"Isn't it? Knowing if she's immortal changes things. Many things."

"Fenrys," Gavriel warned.

She knew enough about it—the transition pureblooded Fae, and some demi-Fae, went through once their bodies locked into immortal youth. It was a rough process, their bodies and magic needing months to adjust to the sudden freezing and reordering of their aging process. Some Fae had no control over their power—some lost it entirely during the time it took to Settle.

And demi-Fae . . . some might be longer-lived, some might have the true immortal gift given to them. Like Lorcan. And possibly Aedion. They'd find out in the next few years if he'd take after his mother . . . or the male sitting across the room from her. If they survived the war.

And as for her . . . She did not let herself think about it. Precisely for the reasons Fenrys claimed. "I don't see what it would change," she said to him. "There's already one immortal queen. Surely a second would be nothing new."

"And will you hand out blood oaths to males who catch your eye, or will it just be Whitethorn at your side?"

She could feel the aggression beginning to pour off Rowan, and she was half tempted to grumble, *They're your friends. Deal with them.* But he kept quiet, containing himself, as she said, "You didn't seem nearly so interested in me that day at Mistward."

"Trust me, he was," Gavriel muttered.

Aelin lifted a brow. But Fenrys was giving Gavriel a look that promised a slow death.

Rowan explained, "Fenrys was the one who . . . volunteered to train you when Maeve told us you'd come to Wendlyn."

Was he, now. Interesting. "Why?"

Rowan opened his mouth, but Fenrys cut him off. "It would have gotten me out of Doranelle. And we likely would have had far more fun, anyway. I know what a bastard Whitethorn can be when it comes to training."

"You two would have stayed on that rooftop in Varese and drunk yourselves to death," Rowan said. "And as for training . . . You're alive today because of that training, boyo."

Fenrys rolled his eyes. Younger, she realized. Still old by human standards, but Fenrys was and felt younger. Wilder.

"Speaking of Varese," Aelin said with cool amusement. "And Doranelle . . ."

"I will warn you," Gavriel said quietly, "that there is little we know regarding Maeve's plans, and less still we can reveal with the blood oath's constraints."

"How does she do it?" Aelin asked baldly. "With Rowan, it's not . . . Every order I give him, even casual ones, are his to decide what to do with. Only when I actively pull on the bond can I get him to . . . yield. And even then it's more of a suggestion."

"It is different with her," Gavriel said softly. "Dependent on the ruler it is sworn to. You two took the oath to each other with love in your hearts. You had no desire to own or rule him."

Aelin tried not to flinch at the truth of that word—*love.* That day . . . when Rowan had looked into her eyes as he drank her blood . . . she'd started to realize what it was. That the feeling that passed between them, so powerful there was no language to describe it . . . It was not mere friendship, but something born of and strengthened by it.

"Maeve," Fenrys added, "offers it with those things in mind. And so the bond itself is born of obedience to her—no matter what. She orders, we submit. For whatever she wishes." Shadows danced in those eyes, and Aelin's fingers curled into fists. That Maeve felt the need to force any of them into her bed . . . Rowan had told her their familial bloodline, while distant, was still close enough that it had kept Maeve from seeking him out, but the others . . .

"So you couldn't break it on your own."

"Never—if we did so, the magic that binds us to her would kill us in the process," Fenrys said. She wondered if he'd tried. How many times. He angled his head to the side, the movement purely lupine. "Why are you asking this?"

Because if Maeve somehow can claim ownership over Aedion's life thanks to his bloodline, I can't do a damn thing to help him.

Aelin shrugged. "Because you sidetracked me." She gave him a little smile that she knew drove Rowan and Aedion insane, and—yes. It seemed it was a surefire way to piss off *any* Fae male, because ire flashed across Fenrys's stupidly perfect face.

She picked at her nails. "I know you two are old and up past your bedtime, so I'll keep this quick: Maeve's armada sails for Eyllwe. We are now allies. But my path might take me into direct conflict with that fleet, maybe with her, whether I desire it or not." Rowan had tensed slightly, and she wished it wouldn't look weak to glance at him, try to read whatever had sparked the reaction.

Fenrys looked to Rowan—as if it were habit. "I think the bigger concern is whether Maeve sails to join Erawan. She could go either way."

"Our—her network of information is too vast," Rowan countered. "There's not a chance she doesn't already know the empire's fleet is camped out in the Gulf of Oro."

Aelin wondered how often her Fae Prince had to silently correct himself about what terms to use. *Our*, *her* . . . Wondered if he ever missed the two males frowning at them.

"Maeve could be going to intercept it," Gavriel mused. "Vanquish Morath's fleet as proof of her intentions to assist you, then . . . play it into whatever agenda she has beyond that."

Aelin clicked her tongue. "Even with Fae soldiers on those ships, she couldn't be stupid enough to risk such catastrophic losses just to get into my good graces again." No matter that Aelin knew she'd accept any offer of aid from Maeve, risk or no.

Fenrys's edged smile flashed. "Oh, the losses of Fae lives would be of little concern to her. It likely just increases her excitement about it."

"Careful," Gavriel said. Gods, he nearly sounded identical to Aedion with that tone.

Aelin went on, "Regardless. You two know what we face with Erawan; you know what Maeve wanted from me in Doranelle. What Lorcan left to do." Their faces had resumed their warrior-calm and didn't so much as flicker as she asked, "Did Maeve give you an order to take those keys from Lorcan as well? And the ring? Or is it just his life you'll be claiming?"

"If we say she gave us the order to take everything," Fenrys drawled, bracing his hands behind him on the bed, "will you kill us, Heir of Fire?"

"It'll depend on how useful you prove to be as an ally," Aelin simply said.

The weight hanging between her breasts beneath her shirt rumbled as if in answer.

"Rolfe has weapons," Gavriel said quietly. "Or will be receiving them."

Aelin lifted a brow. "And will hearing about it cost me?"

Gavriel wasn't stupid enough to ask for Aedion. The warrior just said, "They're called firelances. Alchemists in the southern continent developed them for their own territory wars. More than that, we don't know, but the device can be wielded by one man—to devastating effect."

And with magic-users still so new to their returned gifts, or mostly dead thanks to Adarlan . . .

She would not be alone. Not the only fire-wielder on that battlefield.

But only if Rolfe's armada became hers. If he did what she was carefully, so carefully, guiding him to do. Reaching out to the southern continent could take months she didn't have. But if Rolfe had already ordered a supply . . . Aelin nodded at Rowan once more, and they pushed off the wall.

"That's it?" Fenrys demanded. "Do we get to know what you plan to do with this information, or are we just your lackeys, too?"

"You don't trust me; I don't trust you," Aelin said. "It's easier that way." She nudged open the window with her elbow. "But thank you for the information."

Fenrys's brows rose high enough that she wondered if Maeve had uttered those words in his hearing. And she honestly wished she'd melted her aunt that day in Doranelle.

She and Rowan leaped and climbed the rooftops of Skull's Bay, the ancient shingles still slick from the day's rain.

When the Ocean Rose glittered like a pale jewel a block ahead, Aelin paused in the shadows beside a chimney and murmured, "There is no room for error."

Rowan laid a hand on her shoulder. "I know. We'll make it count."

Her eyes burned. "We're playing a game against two monarchs who have ruled and schemed longer than most kingdoms have existed." And even for her, the odds of outsmarting and outmaneuvering them . . . "Seeing the cadre, how Maeve contains them . . . She came so close to separating us this spring. So close."

Rowan traced his thumb over her mouth. "Even if Maeve had kept me enslaved, I would have fought her. Every day, every hour, every breath." He kissed her softly and said onto her lips, "I would have fought for the rest of my life to find a way to return to you again. I knew it the moment you emerged from the Valg's darkness and smiled at me through your flames."

She swallowed the tightness in her throat and raised a brow. "You were willing to do that before all this? So few benefits back then."

Amusement and something deeper danced in his eyes. "What I felt for you in Doranelle and what I feel for you now are the same. I just didn't think I'd ever get the chance to act on it."

She knew why she needed to hear it—he knew, too. Darrow's and Rolfe's words danced around in her head, an endless chorus of bitter threats. But Aelin only smirked at him. "Then act away, Prince."

Rowan let out a low laugh, and said nothing else as he claimed her mouth, nudging her back against the crumbling chimney. She opened for him, and his tongue swept in, thorough, lazy.

Oh, gods—this. This was what drove her out of her mind—this fire between them.

They could burn the entire world to ashes with it. He was hers and she was his, and they had found each other across centuries of bloodshed and loss, across oceans and kingdoms and war.

Rowan pulled back, breathing heavily, and whispered against her lips, "Even when you're in another kingdom, Aelin, your fire is still in my blood, my mouth." She let out a soft moan, arching into him as his hand grazed her backside, not caring if anyone spotted them in the streets below.

"You said you wouldn't take me against a tree the first time," she breathed, sliding her hands up his arms, across the breadth of his sculpted chest. "What about a chimney?"

Rowan huffed another laugh and nipped at her bottom lip. "Remind me again why I missed you."

Aelin chuckled, but the sound was quickly silenced as Rowan claimed her mouth again and kissed her deeply in the moonlight.

CHAPTER 32

Aedion had been up half the night, debating the merits of every possible place to meet his father. On the beach seemed like it was asking for a private conversation he wasn't entirely sure he wanted to have; in Rolfe's headquarters felt too public; the inn courtyard felt too formal . . . He'd tossed and turned on his cot, nearly asleep when he heard Aelin and Rowan *returning* well past midnight. Not surprising they'd snuck out without telling anyone. But at least she'd gone with the Fae Prince.

Lysandra, sleeping like the dead, hadn't stirred as their steps had creaked in the hall outside. She'd barely made it through the door hours earlier, Dorian already asleep on his cot, before she'd shifted back into her usual body and swayed on her feet.

Aedion had hardly noticed her nakedness—not when she teetered and he lunged to grab her before she ate carpet.

She'd blinked dazedly at him, her skin drained of color. So he'd gently set her on the edge of the bed, grabbed the throw across it, and draped it around her.

"You've seen naked women plenty," she'd said, not bothering to hold it in place. "It's too hot for wool."

So the blanket slid off her back as she leaned forward, bracing her forearms on her knees and breathing deep. "Gods, it makes me so dizzy."

Aedion put a hand on her bare back and gently stroked. She stiffened at the touch, but he made broad, light circles over that velvet-soft skin. After a moment, she let out a sound that might have been a purr.

The silence went on for long enough that Aedion realized she'd somehow fallen asleep. And not normal sleep, but the sleep that Aelin and Rowan sometimes went into in order to let their magic recover. So deep and thorough no training could pierce it, no instincts could override it. The body had claimed what it needed, at any cost, at any vulnerability.

Easing her into his arms before she could fall right onto her face, Aedion hauled her over a shoulder and carried her around to the head of the bed. He flipped back the crisp cotton sheets with one hand and then laid her down, her once-again long hair covering her high, firm breasts. So much smaller than the ones he'd first seen her with. He didn't care what size they were—they were beautiful in both forms.

She hadn't awoken again, and he'd drifted to his own cot. He only slept once the light had shifted to the watery gray trickle before dawn, awoke just past sunrise, and gave up on sleep entirely. He doubted any sort of rest would come until this meeting was past him.

So Aedion bathed and dressed, debating if it made him a fool to brush his hair for his father.

Lysandra was awake as he padded back into the room, the color mercifully returned to her cheeks, the king still asleep on his cot.

But the shifter looked Aedion over and said, "*That's* what you're wearing?"

Lysandra made him change out of his dirty travel clothes, barged into Aelin and Rowan's room wearing no more than her own bedsheet, and took whatever she wanted from the Fae Prince's armoire.

Aelin's barked *Get out!* was likely heard from across the bay, and Lysandra was smirking with feline wickedness as she returned, chucking the green jacket and pants at him.

When he emerged from the bathing room, the lady was in clothes of her own—where she'd gotten them, he had no idea. They were simple: black, tight pants, knee-high boots, and a tucked-in white shirt. She'd left her hair half down, half up, and now twisted the silken mass of it over a shoulder. Lysandra surveyed him with an approving smirk. "Much better. Much more princely and less . . . derelict."

Aedion gave her a mocking bow.

Dorian stirred, a cool breeze fluttering in as if his magic awoke as well, squinted at them both, then at the clock atop the mantel. He hauled the pillow over his eyes and went back to sleep.

"Very kingly," Aedion told him, heading for the door.

Dorian grumbled something through the pillow that Aedion chose not to hear.

He and Lysandra grabbed a quiet breakfast in the dining room—though he had to force half the food down. The shifter asked no questions, either from consideration or because she was so busy stuffing her face with every single morsel offered at the buffet table.

Gods, the females in his court ate more than he did. He supposed the magic burned through their energy reserves so fast it was a miracle they weren't constantly biting his head off.

They walked to Rolfe's tavern in silence, too, the sentries out front stepping aside without so much as a question. He reached for the handle when Lysandra finally said, "You're sure?"

He nodded. And that was that.

Aedion opened the door, finding the cadre precisely where he'd guessed they'd be at this hour: eating breakfast in the taproom. The two males halted as they entered.

And Aedion's eyes went right to the golden-haired man—one of two, but . . . there was no denying which one was . . . his.

Gavriel set his fork on his half-eaten plate.

He wore clothes like Rowan's—and like the Fae Prince, he was heavily armed, even at breakfast.

Aelin was the other side of his fair coin, but Gavriel was a murky reflection. The honed, broad features; the harsh mouth—that was where he'd gotten them from. The cropped golden hair was different; more sunshine to Aedion's shoulder-length honey gold. And Aedion's skin was Ashryver golden—not the sun-kissed, deep tan.

Slowly, Gavriel stood. Aedion wondered if he'd also inherited that grace, the predatory stillness, the unreadable, intent face—or if they'd both been trained that way.

The Lion incarnate.

He'd wanted to do it this way, little more than an ambush, so his father wouldn't have time to prepare pretty speeches. He wanted to see what his father would do when confronted with him, what sort of male he was, how he reacted to *anything*—

The other warrior, Fenrys, was glancing between them, a fork still raised to his open mouth.

Aedion made himself walk, knees surprisingly steady, even if his body felt as if it belonged to someone else. Lysandra kept at his side, solid and bright-eyed. With every step he took, his father surveyed him, face yielding nothing, until—

"You look . . . ," Gavriel breathed, sinking into his chair. "You look so much like her."

Aedion knew Gavriel didn't mean Aelin. Even Fenrys looked at the Lion now, at the grief rippling in those tawny eyes.

But Aedion barely remembered his mother. Barely recalled anything more than her dying, wrecked face.

So he said, "She died so your *queen* wouldn't get her claws on me."

He wasn't sure his father was breathing. Lysandra stepped closer, a solid rock in the thrashing sea of his rage.

Aedion pinned his father with a look, not sure where the words came from, the wrath, but there they were, snapping from his lips like whips. "They could have cured her in the Fae compounds, but she wouldn't go near them, wouldn't let them come for fear of Maeve"—he spat the name—"knowing I existed. For fear I'd be enslaved to her as *you* were."

His father's tan face had drained of all color. Whatever Gavriel had suspected until now, Aedion didn't care. The Wolf snarled at the Lion, "She was twenty-three years old. She never married, and her family shunned her. She refused to tell anyone who'd sired me, and took their disdain, their humiliation, without an ounce of self-pity. She did it because she loved *me*, not you."

And he suddenly wished he'd asked Aelin to come, so he could tell her to burn this warrior into ashes like that commander in Ilium, because looking at the face—*his face* . . . he hated him. He hated him for the twenty-three-year-old his mother had been, younger than he now was when she'd died, alone and sorrowful.

Aedion growled, "If your bitch of a queen tries to take me, I'll slit her throat. If she hurts my family any more than she already has, I'll slit yours, too."

His father rasped, "Aedion."

The sound of the name his mother had given him on his lips . . . "I want nothing from you. Unless you plan to help us, in which case I will not object to the . . . assistance. But beyond that, I want nothing from you."

"I'm sorry," his father said, those Lion's eyes full of such grief Aedion wondered if he'd just struck a male already down.

"I'm not the one you need to apologize to," he said, turning toward the door.

His father's chair scraped against the floor. "Aedion."

Aedion kept walking, Lysandra falling into place beside him.

"Please," his father said as Aedion's hand clamped down on the handle.

"Go to hell," Aedion said, and left.

He didn't return to the Ocean Rose. And he couldn't stand to be around people, to be around their sounds and smells. So he strode for the dense mountain above the bay, losing himself in the jungle of leaves and shade and damp soil. Lysandra stayed a step behind him, silent as he was.

It wasn't until he'd found a rocky outcropping jutting from the side of the mountain to overlook the bay, the town, the pristine waters beyond, that he paused. That he sat. And breathed.

Lysandra sat beside him on the flat rock, crossing her legs beneath her.

He said, "I didn't expect to say any of that."

She was gazing toward the nearby watchtower nestled at the base of the mountain. He watched her green eyes survey the lower level where Ship-Breaker was wrapped around a massive wheel, the spiraling exterior staircase up the tower itself, all the way up to the upper levels, where a catapult, and a turret-mounted, massive harpoon—or was it a giant crossbow?—was locked into place, its wielder's seat and arrow aimed at an invisible enemy in the bay below. With the size of the weapon and the machine that had been rigged to launch it into the bay, he had no doubt it could smash through a hull and do lethal damage to a ship. Or spear three men on it.

Lysandra said simply, "You spoke from your heart. Perhaps it's good he heard that."

"We need them to work with us. I might have made an enemy of him."

She tucked her hair over a shoulder. "Trust me, Aedion, you have not. If you'd told him to crawl over hot coals, he would have."

"He'll realize soon enough who, exactly, I am, and perhaps not be so desperate."

"Who, exactly, do you think you are?" She frowned at him. "Adarlan's Whore? Is that what you still think of yourself? The general who held his kingdom together, who saved his people when they were forgotten even by their own queen—that's the man I know." She snarled softly, and not at him. "And if he starts pointing fingers, I'll remind him that he's served that bitch in Doranelle for centuries without question."

Aedion snorted. "I'd pay good money to see you go toe-to-toe with him. And Fenrys."

She nudged him with an elbow. "You say the word, General, and I'll transform into the face of their nightmares."

"And what creature is that?"

She gave him a knowing little smile. "Something I've been working on."

"I don't want to know, do I?"

White teeth flashed. "No, you really don't."

He laughed, surprised he could even do so. "He's a handsome bastard, I'll give him that."

"I think Maeve likes to collect pretty men."

Aedion snorted. "Why not? She has to deal with them for eternity. They might as well be pleasant to look at."

She laughed again, and the sound loosed a weight from his shoulders.

Bearing both Goldryn and Damaris for once, Aelin walked into the Sea Dragon two hours later and wished for the days when she could sleep without the dread or urgency of *something* pulling at her.

Wished for the days when she might have had the time to bed

her gods-damned lover and not choose to catch a few hours of sleep instead.

She'd meant to. Last night, they'd returned to the inn, and she'd bathed faster than she'd ever washed before. She'd even emerged from the bathing room naked . . . and found her Fae Prince asleep atop the glowingly white bed, still clothed, looking for all the world like he'd intended to close his eyes while she washed.

And the heavy exhaustion on him . . . She let Rowan rest. Had curled up beside him above the blankets, still naked, and had been unconscious before her head had settled against his chest. There would be a time, she knew, when they would not be able to sleep so safely, so soundly.

A grand total of five minutes before Lysandra barged in, Rowan had awoken—and begun the process of awakening her, too. Slowly, with taunting, proprietary strokes down her bare torso, her thighs, accented with little biting kisses to her mouth, her ear, her neck.

But as soon as Lysandra had thundered through the room to steal clothes for Aedion, as soon as she'd explained *where* Aedion was going . . . the interruption had lasted. Made her remember what, exactly, she needed to accomplish today. With a man currently inclined to kill her and a scattered, petrified fleet.

Gavriel and Fenrys were now sitting with Rolfe at the table in the back of the taproom, no sign of Aedion, both a bit wide-eyed as she swaggered in.

She might have preened at the look, had Rowan not prowled in right behind her, already prepared to slit their throats.

Rolfe shot to his feet. "What are you doing here?"

"I would be very, very careful how you speak to her today, Captain," Fenrys said with more wariness and consideration than she'd seen him use yesterday. His eyes were fixed on Rowan, who was indeed watching Rolfe as if he were dinner. "Choose your words wisely."

Rolfe glanced at Rowan, saw his face, and seemed to get it.

Maybe that caution would make Rolfe more inclined to agree to her request today. If she played it right. If she'd played all of it right.

Aelin gave Rolfe a little smile and leaned against the vacant table beside theirs, the chipped gold lettering on the slats reading *Mist-Cutter*. Rowan took up a spot beside her, his knee brushing hers. Like even a few feet of distance was unbearable.

But she smiled a bit wider at Rolfe. "I came to see if you'd changed your mind. About my alliance."

Rolfe drummed his tattooed fingers on the table, right over some gilded letters that read *Thresher*. And beside it . . . a map of the continent had been spread between Rolfe and the Fae warriors.

Not the map she really, truly needed now that she knew the damn thing worked, but—Aelin stiffened at what she beheld.

"What is that," she said, noting the silver figurines camped across the middle of the continent, an impenetrable line from the Ferian Gap to the mouth of the Avery. And the additional figures in the Gulf of Oro. And in Melisande and Fenharrow and near Eyllwe's northern border.

Gavriel, looking a bit like someone had knocked him in the head—gods, how had the meeting with Aedion gone?—said before Rolfe could get his throat ripped out by Rowan with whatever response he had brewing, "Captain Rolfe received word this morning. He wanted our counsel."

"What *is* this," she said, stabbing a finger near the main line of figures stretched across the middle of the continent.

"It's the latest report," Rolfe drawled, "of the locations of Morath's armies. They have moved into position. Aid to the North is now impossible. And they stand poised to strike Eyllwe."

CHAPTER 33

"Eyllwe has no standing army," Aelin said, feeling the blood drain from her face. "There is nothing and no one to fight after this spring—save for rebel militia bands."

Rowan said to Rolfe, "Do you have exact numbers?"

"No," the captain said. "The news was given only as a warning—to keep any shipments away from the Avery. I wanted their opinions"—a nod of the chin toward the cadre—"for handling it. Though I suppose I should have invited you, too, since they seem intent on telling you my business."

None of them deigned to respond. Aelin scanned that line—that line of *armies*.

Rowan said, "How fast do they move?"

"The legions departed Morath nearly three weeks ago," Gavriel supplied. "They moved faster than any army I've ever seen."

The timing of it . . .

No. No—no, it couldn't be because of Ilium, because she'd taunted him . . .

"It's an extermination," Rolfe said baldly.

She closed her eyes, swallowing hard. Even the captain didn't dare speak.

Rowan slid a hand along her lower back, a silent comfort. He knew—was piecing it together, too.

She opened her eyes, that line burning into her vision, her heart, and said, "It's a message. For me." She unfurled her fist, gazing at the scar there.

"Why attack Eyllwe, though?" Fenrys asked. "And why move into position but not sack it?"

She couldn't say the words aloud. That she'd brought this upon Eyllwe by mocking Erawan, because he knew who Celaena Sardothien had cared for, and he wanted to break her spirit, her heart, by showing her what his armies could do. What they *would* do, whenever he now felt like it. Not to Terrasen . . . but to the kingdom of the friend she'd loved so dearly.

The kingdom she had sworn to protect, to save.

Rowan said, "We have personal ties to Eyllwe. He knows it matters to her."

Fenrys's eyes lingered on her, scanning. But Gavriel, voice steady, said, "Erawan now holds everything south of the Avery. Save for this archipelago. And even here, he has a foothold in the Dead End."

Aelin stared at that map, at the space that now seemed so small to the north.

To the west, the vast expanse of the Wastes spread beyond the mountainous continental divide. And her gaze snagged on a small name along the western coast.

Briarcliff.

The name clanged through her, shuddering her awake, and she realized they'd been talking, debating how such an army might move so quickly over the terrain.

She rubbed her temple, staring at that speck on the map.

Considering the life debt owed to her.

Her gaze dragged down—south. To the Red Desert. Where another life debt, many life debts, waited for her to claim them.

Aelin realized they had asked her something, but she didn't care to figure it out as she said quietly to Rolfe, "You're going to give me your armada. You're going to arm it with those firelances I know you've ordered, and you will ship any extras to the Mycenian fleet when they arrive."

Silence.

Rolfe barked a laugh and sat again. "Like hell I am." He waved that tattooed hand over the map, the waters inked on it churning and changing in some pattern she wondered if only he could read. A pattern she *needed* him to be able to read, to find that Lock. "This just shows how utterly outmatched you are." He chewed over her words. "The Mycenian fleet is little more than a myth. A bedside tale."

Aelin looked to the hilt of Rolfe's sword, to the inn itself and his ship anchored just outside.

"You are the heir of the Mycenian people," Aelin said. "And I have come to claim the debt you owe my bloodline on that account, too."

Rolfe did not move, did not blink.

"Or were all the sea dragon references from some personal fetish?" Aelin asked.

"The Mycenians are gone," Rolfe said flatly.

"I don't think so. I think they have been hiding here, in the Dead Islands, for a long, long time. And you somehow managed to claw your way back to power."

The three Fae males were glancing between them.

Aelin said to Rolfe, "I have liberated Ilium from Adarlan. I took back the city—your ancient home—for you. For the Mycenians. It is yours, if you dare to claim your people's inheritance."

Rolfe's hand shook slightly. He fisted it, tucking it beneath the table.

She allowed a flicker of her magic to rise to the surface then, allowed the gold in her eyes to glow like bright flame. Gavriel and Fenrys straightened as her power filled the room, filled the city. The Wyrdkey between her breasts began thrumming, whispering.

She knew there was nothing human, nothing mortal on her face.

Knew it because Rolfe's golden-brown skin had paled to a sickly sheen.

She closed her eyes and loosed a breath.

The tendril of power she'd gathered rippled away in an invisible line. The world shuddered in its wake. A city bell chimed once, twice, in its force. Even the waters in the bay shivered as it swept past and out into the archipelago.

When Aelin opened her eyes, the mortality had returned.

"What the rutting hell was that?" Rolfe at last demanded.

Fenrys and Gavriel became *very* interested in the map before them.

Rowan said smoothly, "Milady has to release bits of her power daily or it can consume her."

Despite herself, despite what she'd done, she decided she wanted Rowan to call her *milady* at least once every day.

Rowan continued on, pressing Rolfe about the moving army. The Pirate Lord, who Lysandra had confirmed weeks ago *was* Mycenian thanks to Arobynn's own spying on his business partners, seemed barely able to speak, thanks to the offer she'd laid out for him. But Aelin merely waited.

Aedion and Lysandra arrived after some time—and her cousin only spared Gavriel a passing glance as he stood over the map and fell into that general's mindset, demanding details large and minute.

But Gavriel silently stared up at his son, watching her cousin's eyes dart over the map, listening to the sound of his voice as if it were a song he was trying to memorize.

Lysandra drifted to the window, monitoring the bay.

Like she could see that ripple Aelin had sent out into the world.

The shifter had told Aedion by now—of why they had truly gone to

Ilium. Not only to see Brannon, not only to save its people . . . but for this. She and the shifter had hatched the plan during the long night watches together on the road, considering all pitfalls and benefits.

Dorian strolled in ten minutes later, his eyes going straight to Aelin. He'd felt it, too.

The king gave a polite greeting to Rolfe, then remained silent as he was briefed on the positioning of Erawan's armies. Then he slid into a seat beside her while the other males continued discussing supply routes and weapons, being led in circle after circle by Rowan.

Dorian just gave her an unreadable glance and folded his ankle over a knee.

The clock struck eleven, and Aelin rose to her feet in the middle of whatever Fenrys had been saying about various armor and Rolfe possibly investing in the ore to supply the demand.

Silence fell again. Aelin said to Rolfe, "Thank you for your hospitality."

And then turned away. She made it a step before he demanded, "That's it?"

She looked over her shoulder, Rowan approaching her side. Aelin let a bit of that flame rise to the surface. "Yes. If you will not give me an armada, if you will not unite what is left of the Mycenians and return to Terrasen, then I'll find someone else who will."

"There is no one else."

Again, her eyes went to the map on his table. "You once said I would pay for my arrogance. And I did. Many times. But Sam and I took on your entire city and fleet and destroyed it. All for two hundred lives you deemed less than human. So perhaps I've been underestimating myself. Perhaps I do not need you after all."

She turned again, and Rolfe sneered, "Did Sam die still pining after you, or did you finally stop treating him like filth?"

There was a choking sound, and a slam and rattle of glasses. She looked slowly to find Rowan with his hand around Rolfe's neck, the captain pressed onto the map, the figures scattered everywhere, Rowan's snarling teeth close to ripping off Rolfe's ear.

Fenrys smirked a bit. "I told you to choose your words carefully, Rolfe."

Aedion seemed to be doing his best to ignore his father as he said to the captain, "Nice to meet you." Then he strolled toward where Aelin, Dorian, and Lysandra waited by the door.

Rowan leaned in, murmuring something in Rolfe's ear that made him blanch, then shoved him a bit harder into the table before stalking for Aelin.

Rolfe set his hands on the table, pushing up to bark some surely stupid words at them, but went rigid. As if some pulse thrashed through his body.

He turned his hands over, fitting the edges of his palms together.

His eyes lifted—but not to her. To the windows.

To the bells that had begun ringing in the twin watchtowers flanking the mouth of the bay.

The frantic pealing set the streets beyond them halting, silencing.

Each bleat's meaning was clear enough.

Rolfe's face went pale.

Aelin watched as black—darker than the ink that had been etched there—spread across his fingers, to his palms. Black such as only the Valg could bring.

Oh, there was no doubt now that the map worked.

She said to her companions, "We leave. Now."

Rolfe was already storming toward her—toward the door. He said nothing as he flung it open, striding onto the quay, where his first mate and quartermaster were already sprinting for him.

Aelin shut the door behind Rolfe and surveyed her friends. And the cadre.

It was Fenrys who spoke first, rising to his feet and watching through the window as Rolfe and his men rushed about. "Remind me never to get on your bad side."

Dorian said quietly, "If that force reaches this town, these people—"

"It won't," Aelin said, meeting Rowan's stare. Pine-green eyes held her own.

Show them why you're my blood-sworn, she silently told him.

A hint of a wicked smile. Rowan turned to them. "Let's go."

"Go," Fenrys blurted, pointing to the window. "Where?"

"There's a boat," Aedion said, "anchored on the other side of the island." He inclined his head toward Lysandra. "You'd think they'd notice a skiff being tugged out to sea by a shark last night, but—"

The door banged open, and Rolfe's towering figure filled it. "*You.*"

Aelin put a hand on her chest. "Me?"

"*You* sent that magic out there; *you* summoned them."

She barked a laugh, pushing off the table. "If I ever learn such a useful talent, I'd use it for summoning my allies, I think. Or the Mycenians, since you seem so adamant they don't exist." She glanced over his shoulder—the sky was still clear. "Good luck," she said, stepping around him.

Dorian blurted, "What?"

Aelin looked the King of Adarlan over. "This isn't our battle. And I won't sacrifice my kingdom's fate over a skirmish with the Valg. If you have any sense, you won't, either." Rolfe's face contorted with wrath—even as fear, deep and true, shone in his eyes. She took a step toward the chaotic streets but paused, turning to the Pirate Lord. "I suppose the cadre will be coming with me, too. Since they're now my allies."

Silently, Fenrys and Gavriel approached, and she could have sighed with relief that they did so without question, that Gavriel was willing to do whatever it took to stay near his son.

Rolfe hissed, "You think withholding your assistance will sway me into helping you?" But far beyond the bay, between the distant, humped islands, a cloud of darkness gathered.

"I meant what I said, Rolfe. I can do fine without you, armada or no. Mycenians or no. And this island has now become dangerous for my cause." She inclined her head toward the sea. "I'll offer a prayer to Mala for you." She patted the hilt of Goldryn. "A bit of advice, from one professional criminal to the other: cut off their heads. It's the only way to kill them. Unless you burn them alive, but I bet most would jump ship and swim to shore before your flaming arrows can do much damage."

"And what of your idealism—what of that *child* who stole two hundred slaves from me? You'd leave the people of this island to perish?"

"Yes," she said simply. "I told you, Rolfe, that Endovier taught me some things."

Rolfe swore. "Do you think *Sam* would stand for this?"

"Sam is dead," she said, "because men like you and Arobynn have power. But Arobynn's reign is now over." She smiled at the darkening horizon. "Seems like yours might end rather soon as well."

"You *bitch*—"

Rowan snarled, taking all of a step before Rolfe flinched away.

Rushing footsteps sounded, then Rolfe's quartermaster filled the doorway. He panted as he rested a hand on the threshold, the other gripping the sea dragon-shaped pommel of his sword. "We are knee-deep in shit."

Aelin paused. Rolfe's face tightened. "How bad?" the captain asked.

He wiped the sweat from his brow. "Eight warships teeming with soldiers—at least a hundred on each, more on the lower levels I couldn't see. They're flanked by two sea-wyverns. All moving so fast that it's like storm winds carry them."

Aelin cut a glance at Rowan. "How quickly can we get to that boat?"

Rolfe was gazing at the few ships in his harbor, his face deathly pale. At Ship-Breaker out in the bay, the chain currently beneath the calm surface. Fenrys, seeing the captain's stare, observed, "Those sea-wyverns will snap that chain. Get your people off this island. Use every skiff and sloop you have and get them *out*."

Rolfe slowly turned to Aelin, his sea-green eyes simmering with hate. And resignation. "Is this an attempt to call my bluff?"

Aelin toyed with the end of her braid. "No. It's convenient timing, but no."

Rolfe surveyed them all—the power that could level this island if they chose. His voice was hoarse as he at last spoke. "I want to be admiral. I want this entire archipelago. I want Ilium. And when this war is over, I want *Lord* in front of my name, as it was before my ancestors' names long ago. What of my payment?"

Aelin surveyed him in turn, the entire room deathly quiet compared to the chaos of outside. "For every Morath ship you sack, you can keep whatever gold and treasure is aboard it. But weapons and ammunition go to the front. I'll give you land, but no royal titles beyond those of Lord of Ilium and King of the Archipelago. If you bear any offspring, I will recognize them as your heirs—as I would any children Dorian might bear."

Dorian nodded gravely. "Adarlan will recognize you and your heirs, and this land as yours."

Rolfe ground out, "You send those bastards down to the inky black, and my fleet is yours. I cannot guarantee the Mycenians will rise, though. We've been scattered too far and too long. Only a small number live here, and they will not stir without proper . . . motivation." He glanced toward the bar, as if he'd expected to see someone behind it.

But Aelin held out her hand, smiling faintly. "Leave that to me."

Tattooed skin met scarred flesh as Rolfe shook her hand. Hard enough to break bones, but she did it right back. Sent a little flame searing into his fingers.

He hissed, pulling back his hand, and Aelin grinned. "Welcome to Her Majesty's army, Privateer Rolfe." She gestured to the open door. "Shall we?"

Aelin was insane, Dorian realized. Brilliant and wicked, but insane.

And perhaps the greatest, most unremorseful liar he'd ever encountered.

He'd felt her summons sweep through the world. Felt fire hum against his skin. There was no mistaking who it belonged to. And there was no mistaking that it had gone right to the Dead End, where the forces dwelling there would know there was one person alive with that kind of flame at her disposal, and track the magic back here.

He didn't know what had triggered it, why she'd chosen now, but—

But Rowan had informed Aelin how the Valg haunted Rolfe. How he had this city watched day and night, terrified of their return. So Aelin had used it to her advantage. The Mycenians—holy gods. They were little more than a bedtime story and cautionary tale. But here they were, carefully hidden away. Until Aelin had smoked them out.

And as the Pirate Lord and Queen of Terrasen shook hands and she grinned at Rolfe, Dorian realized he . . . perhaps he could do with a bit more wickedness and insanity, too.

This war would not be won on smiles and manners.

It would be won by a woman willing to gamble with an entire *island* full of people to get what she needed to save them all. A woman whose friends were equally willing to play along, to rip their souls to shreds if it meant saving the greater population. They knew the weight of the lives panicking around them if they gambled wrong. Aelin perhaps more than anyone else.

Aelin and Rolfe stalked through the open tavern doorway and into the street beyond. Behind him, Fenrys let out a low whistle. "Gods help you, Rowan, that woman is . . ."

Dorian didn't wait to hear the rest as he followed the pirate and the queen into the street, Aedion and Lysandra trailing. Fenrys kept at a distance from the others, but Gavriel remained close, his gaze still fixed on his son. Gods, they looked so much alike, *moved* alike, the Lion and the Wolf.

Rolfe barked to his men waiting in a line before him, "Every ship that can bear men sails *now*." He rattled off orders, delegating his men to various ships long bereft of crew to run them, including his own, while Aelin stood there, hands braced on her hips, watching them all.

She said to the captain, "What's your fastest ship?"

He pointed at his own.

She held his stare, and Dorian waited for the wild, reckless plan. But she said without looking at any of them, "Rowan, Lysandra, Fenrys, and Gavriel, you're with me. Aedion, you get on the northern watchtower and man the mounted harpoon. Any ship gets too close to the chain, you blast a hole through their gods-damned side." Dorian stiffened as she at last addressed him, seeing the orders already in her eyes. He opened his mouth to object, but Aelin said simply, "This battle is no place for a king."

"And it's one for a queen?"

There was no amusement, nothing but icy calm as she handed him a sword he hadn't realized she'd been carrying at her side. Damaris.

Goldryn was still strapped across her back, its ruby glowing like a living ember as she said, "One of us has to live, Dorian. You take the southern watchtower—stay at the base, and get your magic ready. Any forces that try to cross the chain, you take them out."

Not with steel, but magic. He fastened Damaris to his sword belt, its weight foreign. "And what are you going to do?" he demanded. As if in answer, his power writhed in his gut, like an asp curling to strike.

Aelin glanced at Rowan, at his tattooed hand. "Rolfe, get whatever iron chains you have left from your slave-mongering. We're going to need them."

For her—for Rowan. As a check against their magic, if it got out of control.

Because Aelin . . . Aelin was going to sail that ship right into the heart of the enemy fleet and blow them all out of the water.

CHAPTER 34

She was a liar, and a murderer, and a thief, and Aelin had a feeling she'd be called much worse by the end of this war. But as that unnatural darkness gathered on the horizon, she wondered if she might have bitten off more than she and all her fanged friends could chew.

She did not give her fear an inch of space.

Did not do anything but let black fire ripple through her.

Securing this alliance was only part of it. The other part, the bigger part . . . was the message. Not to Morath.

But to the world.

To any potential allies watching this continent, contemplating if it was indeed a lost cause.

Today her message would thunder across the realms.

She was not a rebel princess, shattering enemy castles and killing kings.

She was a force of nature. She was a calamity and a commander of immortal warriors of legend. And if those allies did not join with her . . .

she wanted them to think of today, of what she would do, and wonder if they might find her on their shores, in their harbors, one day, too.

They had not come ten years ago. She wanted them to know she had not forgotten it.

Rolfe finished barking orders to his men and rushed aboard the *Sea Dragon*, Aedion and Dorian hurtling for horses to carry them to their respective watchtowers. Aelin turned to Lysandra, the shifter calmly monitoring all. Aelin said quietly, "Do you know what I need you to do?"

Lysandra's moss-green eyes were bright as she nodded.

Aelin did not allow herself to embrace the shifter. Did not allow herself to so much as touch her friend's hand. Not with Rolfe watching. Not with the citizens of this town watching, the lost Mycenians among them. So Aelin merely said, "Good hunting."

Fenrys let out a choked sound, as if he realized what she had indeed demanded of the shape-shifter. Beside him, Gavriel was still too busy staring after Aedion, who hadn't so much as glanced at his father before fastening his shield and sword across his back, mounting a sorry-looking mare, and galloping for the watchtower.

Aelin said to Rowan, the wind already dancing in the silver hair of her warrior-prince, "We move now."

So they did.

People were panicking in the streets as the dark force took shape on the horizon: massive ships with black sails, converging on the bay as if they were indeed carried on a preternatural wind.

But Aelin, Lysandra close to her, stalked for the towering *Sea Dragon*, Rowan and his two companions falling into step behind them.

People halted and gawked while they ascended the gangway, securing and rearranging their weapons. Knives and swords, Rowan's hatchet gleaming while he hooked it at his side, a bow and quiver full of black-feathered arrows that Aelin assumed Fenrys could fire with deadly accuracy, and more blades. As they prowled onto the gently rocking deck of the *Sea Dragon*, the wood meticulously polished, Aelin supposed that together they formed a walking armory.

Gavriel had no sooner set foot on board than the gangway was hauled up by Rolfe's men. The others, seated on benches flanking the deck, lifted oars, two men to a seat. Rowan jerked his chin at Gavriel and Fenrys, and the two wordlessly went to join the men, his cadre falling into rank and rhythms that were older than some kingdoms.

Rolfe stalked out a door that no doubt led to his chambers, two men behind him bearing enormous iron chains.

Aelin strode for them. "Anchor them to the mainmast and make sure there's enough room for them to reach right . . . here." She pointed to where she now stood in the heart of the deck. Enough space clear of everyone, enough space for her and Rowan to work.

Rolfe barked an order to begin rowing, glancing once at Fenrys and Gavriel—who each manned an oar themselves, teeth bared as they threw their considerable strength into the motion.

Slowly, the ship began moving—the others around them stirring as well.

But they had to be out of the bay first, had to get past the boundary of Ship-Breaker.

Rolfe's men looped the chains around the mast, leaving enough length to reach Aelin.

Iron would provide a bite, an anchor to remind her who she was, what she was. Iron would keep her tethered when the sheer vastness of her magic, of Rowan's magic, threatened to sweep her away.

The *Sea Dragon* inched over the harbor, the call and grunting of Rolfe's men as they rowed drowning out the din of the town behind them.

She flicked a glance toward either watchtower to see Dorian arrive—then Aedion's golden hair racing up the outer spiral staircase to the enormous mounted harpoon at the top. Her heart strained for a moment as she flashed between now and a time when she'd seen Sam running up those same stairs—not to defend this town, but to wreck it.

She shook off the icy grip of memory and turned to Lysandra, standing at the deck rail, watching her cousin as well. "Now."

Even Rolfe paused his ordering at the word.

Lysandra gracefully sat on the broad wooden railing, pivoted her legs over the side . . . and dropped into the water.

Rolfe's men rushed to the rail. People in boats flanking them did the same, spotting the woman plunge into the vivid blue.

But it was not a woman who came out.

Below, deep down, Aelin could make out the glow and shift and spread. Men began cursing.

But Lysandra kept growing and growing beneath the surface, along the sandy harbor floor.

Faster, the men rowed.

But the ship's speed was nothing compared to the speed of the creature that emerged from the waves.

A broad jade-green snout, peppered with shredding white teeth, huffed a mighty breath then arced back under the water, revealing a flash of a massive head and cunning eyes as she disappeared.

Some men screamed. Rolfe braced a hand on the wheel. His first mate, that sea dragon sword freshly polished at his side, dropped to his knees.

Lysandra dove, and she let them see the long, powerful body that broke the surface bit by bit as she plunged down, her jade scales gleaming like jewels in the blinding midday sun. See the legend straight from their prophecies: the Mycenians would only return when the sea dragons did.

And so Aelin had ensured that one appeared right in their gods-damned harbor.

"Holy gods," Fenrys muttered from where he rowed.

Indeed, that was about the only reaction Aelin could muster as the sea dragon dove down deep, then swam ahead.

For those were mighty fins—*wings* that Lysandra spread beneath the water, tucking in her small front arms and back legs, her massive, spiked tail acting as a rudder.

Some of Rolfe's men were murmuring, "A dragon—a dragon to defend our own ship . . . The legends of our fathers . . ." Indeed, Rolfe's face was pale as he stared toward where Lysandra had vanished into the blue, still clutching the wheel as if it'd keep him from falling.

Two sea-wyverns . . . against one sea dragon.

For all the fire in the world would not work beneath the sea. And if they were to stand a chance of decimating those ships, there could be no interference from beneath the surface.

"Come on, Lysandra," Aelin breathed, and sent a prayer to Temis, the Goddess of Wild Things, to keep the shifter swift and unfaltering beneath the waves.

Aedion chucked off the shield from his back and slammed into the seat before the giant iron harpoon, its length perhaps a hand taller than him, its head bigger than his own. There were only three spears. He'd have to make his shots count.

Across the bay, he could just make out the king taking up a position along the battlement on the lowest level of the tower. In the bay itself, Rolfe's ship rowed closer and closer to Ship-Breaker's lowered chain.

Aedion stomped on one of the three operating pedals that allowed him to pivot the mounted launcher, gripping the handles on either side that positioned the spear into place. Carefully, precisely, he aimed the harpoon toward the very outer edge of the bay, where the two branches of the island leaned toward each other to provide a narrow passage into the harbor.

Waves broke just beyond—a reef. Good for breaking ships against—and no doubt where Rolfe would plant his ship, in order to fool Morath's fleet into skewering themselves on it.

"What the hell is that?" one of the sentries manning the gunner breathed, pointing toward the bay waters.

A mighty, long shadow swept under the water ahead of the *Sea Dragon*, faster than the ship, faster than a dolphin. Its long, serpentine body soared through the sea, carried on wings that might have also been fins.

Aedion's heart stopped dead. "It's a sea dragon," he managed to say.

Well, at least he now knew what secret form Lysandra had been working on.

And why Aelin had insisted on getting inside Brannon's temple. Not just to see the king, not just to reclaim the city for the Mycenians and Terrasen, but . . . for Lysandra to study the life-size, detailed carvings of those sea dragons. To become a living myth.

The two of them . . . Oh, those crafty, scheming devils. A queen of legends indeed.

"How . . . how . . ." The sentry turned toward the others, babbling among themselves. "It's gonna defend us?"

Lysandra approached Ship-Breaker, still lowered under the surface, twirling and arcing, banking along rocks as if getting a feel for her new form. Getting a feel for it in whatever little time they had. "Yes," Aedion breathed as terror flooded his veins. "Yes, she is."

The water was warm, and quiet, and ageless.

And she was a scaled shadow that set the jewel-colored fish darting into their coral homes; she was a soaring menace through the water that made the white birds bobbing on the surface scatter into flight as they sensed her passing below.

Sunbeams streamed in pillars through the water, and Lysandra, in the small part of her that remained human, felt as if she were gliding through a temple of light and shadow.

But there—far out, carried on echoes of sound and vibration—she felt them.

Even the larger predators of these waters flitted off, taking to the open seas beyond the islands. Not even the promise of water stained red could keep them in the path of the two forces about to collide.

Ahead, the mighty links of Ship-Breaker sagged into the deep, like the colossal necklace of some goddess leaning down to drink the sea.

She had been reading about them—the long-forgotten and long-dead sea dragons—at Aelin's behest. Because her friend had known that strong-arming Rolfe with the Mycenians would only get them so far, but if they were to wield the power of myth instead . . . its people might rally around it. And with a home to finally offer them, among these islands and in Terrasen . . .

Lysandra had studied the carvings of the sea dragons at the temple, once Aelin had burned away the dirt on them. Her magic had filled in gaps the carvings didn't show. Like the nostrils that picked apart each scent on the current, the ears that unraveled varying layers of sound.

Lysandra swept for the reef just beyond the parted lips of the island. She'd have to retract the wings, but here . . . here she would make her stand.

Here she would have to unleash every wild instinct, yielding the part of her that felt and cared.

These beasts, however they were made, were only that: beasts. Animals.

They would not fight with morals and codes. They would fight to the death, and fight for survival. There would be no mercy, no compassion.

She would have to fight as they did. She had done so before—had turned feral not just that day the glass castle had shattered, but the night she'd been captured and those men had tried to take Evangeline. This would be no different.

Lysandra dug her bone-shredding, curved talons into the reef shelf to hold her position against the current's nudging, and peered into the silent blue stretching endlessly ahead.

So she began her death vigil.

CHAPTER 35

Perched on the rail of the *Sea Dragon*, gripping the rope ladder flowing from the looming mast, Aelin savored the cooling spindrift that sprayed her face as the ship plowed through the waves. Once the ship was clear of the others, Rowan had let his winds fill its sails, setting the *Sea Dragon* flying toward the mammoth chain.

It was hard not to look back as they passed over the submerged chain . . . and then Ship-Breaker began to rise from the water.

Sealing them out of the bay—where Rolfe's other ships would wait safely behind the chain's line—to guard the town now silently watching them.

If all went well, they would only need this boat, she'd told Rolfe.

And if it went badly, then his ships wouldn't make a difference anyway.

Tightly grasping the rope, Aelin leaned out, the vibrant blue and white below passing in a swift blur. *Not too fast*, she'd told Rowan. *Don't waste your strength—you barely slept last night.*

He'd just leaned in to nip at her ear before sliding onto Gavriel's bench to concentrate.

He was still there, his power letting the men cease their rowing and prepare for what swept toward them. Aelin again looked ahead—toward those black sails blotting the horizon.

The Wyrdkey at her chest murmured in response.

She could feel them—her magic could *taste* their corruption on the wind. No sign of Lysandra, but she was out there.

The sun was blinding on the waves as Rowan's magic slowed, bringing them into a steady glide toward the two peaks of the island that curved toward each other.

It was time.

Aelin swung off the railing, boots thudding on the soaked wood of the deck. So many eyes turned to her, to the chains spread across the main deck.

Rolfe stalked toward her, descending from the raised quarterdeck, where he'd been manning the wheel himself.

She picked up a heavy iron chain, wondering who it'd previously held. Rowan rose to his feet in a steady, graceful movement. He reached her when Rolfe did.

The captain demanded, "What now?"

Aelin jerked her chin toward the ships near enough to make out figures crammed onto the various decks. Many, *many* figures. "We draw them in as close as we can. When you can see the whites of their eyes, you shout at us."

Rowan added, "And then you lay anchor off the starboard side. Swing us around."

"Why?" Rolfe asked as Rowan helped her fasten the manacle around her wrist.

She balked at the iron, her magic twisting. Rowan gripped her chin between his thumb and forefinger, making her meet his unflinching gaze, even as he said to Rolfe, "Because we don't want the masts in the way when we open fire. They seem like a rather important part of the ship."

Rolfe growled and stalked off.

Rowan's fingers slid to cup her jaw, his thumb brushing her cheek. "We draw out our power, slow and steady."

"I know."

He angled his head, brows lifting. A half smile curved his sinful mouth. "You've been spiraling down into your power for days now, haven't you?"

She nodded. It had taken most of her focus, had been such an effort to stay in the present, to stay active and aware while she was burrowing down and down, drawing up as much of her power as she could without attracting any notice. "I didn't want to take any chances here. Not if you were drained from saving Dorian."

"I've recovered, I'll have you know. So this morning's little display . . ."

"A way to take off the power's full edge," she said wryly. "And make Rolfe piss himself." He chuckled and released her face to pass her the other manacle. She hated its ancient, hideous touch on her skin, on his, as she clamped it around his tattooed wrist.

"Hurry," Rolfe said from where he'd returned to his spot at the wheel.

Indeed, the ships were gaining on them. No sign of those sea-wyverns—though the shifter also remained out of sight.

Rowan palmed his hunting knife, the steel bright in the blazing sun. High noon.

Precisely why she'd gone into Rolfe's office nearly two hours beforehand.

She'd practically rung the dinner bell for the host in the Dead End. She'd gambled that they wouldn't wait until nightfall, but they apparently feared the wrath of their master if she slipped their nets more than they feared the light itself. Or were too stupid to realize Mala's heir would be at her most powerful.

"Do you want to do the honors, or should I?" Rowan said. Fenrys and Gavriel had risen to their feet, blades out as they monitored from a safe distance. Aelin held out her free hand, her palm scarred, and took the knife from him. A quick slice had her skin stinging, warm blood heating her seawater-sticky skin.

Rowan had the knife a heartbeat later, and the scent of his blood filled her nose, set her senses on edge. But she extended her bloodied palm.

Her magic swirled into the world with it, crackling in her veins, her ears. She reined in the urge to tap her foot on the ground, to roll her shoulders.

"Slow," Rowan repeated, as if sensing the hair-trigger that her power was now on, "and steady." His shackled arm slid around her waist to hold her to him. "I'll be with you every step of the way."

She lifted her head to study his face, the harsh planes and the curving tattoo. He leaned in to brush a kiss to her mouth. And as his lips met hers, he joined their bleeding palms.

Magic jolted through her, ancient and wicked and cunning, and she arched against him, knees buckling as his cataclysmic power roared into her.

All anyone on deck saw, she knew, was two lovers embracing.

But Aelin tunneled down, down, down into her power, felt him doing the same with his, felt every ounce of ice and wind and lightning go slamming from him into her. And when it reached her, the core of his power yielded to her own, melted and became embers and wildfire. Became the molten heart of the earth, shaping the world and birthing new lands.

Deeper and deeper, she went.

Aelin had a vague sense of the ship rocking beneath them, felt the faint bite of the iron as it rejected her magic, felt the presence of Fenrys and Gavriel flickering around them like candles.

It had been months since she'd drawn from so deep in the abyss of her power.

During the time she'd trained with Rowan in Wendlyn, her power's limit had been self-imposed. And then that day with the Valg, she'd broken through it—had discovered an entire hidden level beneath. She had drawn from it when she'd encircled Doranelle with her power, had taken a whole day to tunnel that far, to draw up what she needed.

Aelin had begun this descent three days ago.

She'd expected it to stop after the first day. To hit that bottom she'd sensed once before.

She had not.

And now . . . now with Rowan's power joining hers . . .

Rowan's arm still held her tightly against him, and she had the distant, murky sensation of his coat scratching lightly against her face, of the hardness of the weapons strapped beneath, the scent of him washing over her, soothing her.

She was a stone plunked into the sea of her power—their power.

Down

and

down

and

down

There—there was the bottom. The ash-lined bottom, the pit of a dormant crater.

Only the feeling of her own feet against the wood deck kept her from sinking into that ash, learning what might slumber beneath it.

Her magic whispered to start digging through that ash and silt. But Rowan's grip tightened on her waist. "Easy," he murmured in her ear. "Easy."

Still more of his power flowed into her, wind and ice churning with her power, eddying into a maelstrom.

"Close now," Rolfe warned from nearby—from another world.

"Aim for the middle of the fleet," Rowan ordered her. "Send the flanking ships scattering onto the reef." Where they'd founder, leaving any survivors to be picked off with arrows shot by Fenrys and Rolfe's men. Rowan had to be alert, then—watching the approaching force.

She could feel them—feel her magic's hackles rise in response to the blackness gathering beyond the horizon of her consciousness.

"Almost in range," Rolfe called.

She began pulling up, dragging the abyss of flame and embers with her.

"Steady," Rowan murmured.

Higher, higher, Aelin rose, back toward the sea and sunlight.

Here, that sunlight seemed to beckon. *To me.*

Her magic surged for it, for that voice.

"*Now!*" Rolfe barked.

And like a feral beast freed of its leash, her magic erupted.

She'd been doing well as Rowan had handed over his power to her.

She'd balked and bobbed a few times, but . . . she had the descent under control.

Even if her power . . . the well had gone deeper than before. It was easy to forget she was still growing—that her power would mature with her.

And when Rolfe shouted, *Now!* Rowan knew he had forgotten to his detriment.

A pillar of flame that did not burn erupted from Aelin, slamming into the sky, turning the world into red and orange and gold.

Aelin was ripped from his arms with the force of it, and Rowan grabbed her hand in a crushing grip, refusing to let her break that line of contact. Men around them stumbled back, falling onto their asses as they gawked upward in terror and wonder.

Higher, that column of flame swirled, a maelstrom of death and life and rebirth.

"Holy gods," Fenrys whispered behind him.

Still Aelin's magic poured into the world. Still she burned hotter, wilder.

Her teeth were gritted, her head arched back as she panted, eyes shut.

"Aelin," Rowan warned. The pillar of flame began expanding, laced now with blue and turquoise. Flame that could melt bone, crack the earth.

Too much. He had given her too much, and she had delved too deep into her power—

Through the flames encasing them, Rowan glimpsed the frantic enemy fleet, now hurling themselves into motion to flee, to get out of range.

Aelin's ongoing display was not for them.

Because there was no escape, not with the power she'd dragged up with her.

The display was for the others, for the city watching them.

For the world to know she was no mere princess playing with pretty embers.

"Aelin," Rowan said again, trying to tug on that bond between them.

But there was nothing.

Only the gaping maw of some immortal, ancient beast. A beast that had opened an eye, a beast that spoke in the tongue of a thousand worlds.

Ice flooded his veins. She was wearing the Wyrdkey.

"*Aelin.*" But Rowan felt it then. Felt that bottom of her power crack open as if the beast within that Wyrdkey stomped its foot, and ash and crusted rock crumbled away beneath it.

And revealed a roiling, molten core of magic beneath it.

As if it were the fiery heart of Mala herself.

Aelin plunged into that power. Bathed in it.

Rowan tried to move, tried to scream at her to stop—

But Rolfe, eyes wide with what could only be terror and awe, roared at her, "*Open fire!*"

She heard that. And as violently as it had pierced the sky, that pillar of fire shot down, shot back into *her*, coiling and wrapping inside her, fusing into a kernel of power so hot it sizzled into him, searing his very soul—

The flames winked out at the same second she reached into Rowan with burning hands and *tore* the last remnants of his power from him.

Just as she ripped her hand from his. Just as her power and the Wyrdkey between her breasts merged.

Rowan collapsed to his knees, and there was a crack inside his head, as if thunder cleaved through him.

As Aelin opened her eyes, he realized it wasn't thunder—but the sound of a door slamming open.

Her face turned expressionless. Cold as the gaps between the stars. And her eyes . . .

Turquoise burned bright . . . around a core of silver. No hint of gold to be found.

"That's not Aelin," Fenrys breathed.

A faint smile blossomed on her full mouth, born of cruelty and arrogance, and she examined the iron chain wrapped around her wrist.

The iron melted away, molten ore sizzling through the wooden deck and into the dark below. The creature that stared out through Aelin's eyes furled her fingers into a fist. Light leaked through her clenched fingers.

Cold white light. Tendrils flickered—silver flame . . .

"Get away," Gavriel warned him. *"Get away and don't look."*

Gavriel was indeed on his knees, head bowed and eyes averted. Fenrys followed suit.

For what gazed at the dark fleet assembled, what had filled his beloved's body . . . He knew. Some primal, intrinsic part of him knew.

"Deanna," Rowan whispered. She flicked her eyes to him in question and confirmation.

And she said to him, in a voice that was deep and hollow, young and old, "Every key has a lock. Tell the Queen Who Was Promised to retrieve it soon, for all the allies in the world shall make no difference if she does not wield the Lock, if she does not put those keys back with it. Tell her flame and iron, together bound, merge into silver to learn what must be found. A mere step is all it shall take." Then she looked away again.

And Rowan realized what the power in her hand was. Realized that the flame she would unleash would be so cold it burned, realized it was the cold of the stars, the cold of stolen light.

Not wildfire—but moonfire.

One moment she was there. And then she was not.

And then she was shoved aside, locked into a box with no key, and the power was not hers, her body was not hers, her name was not hers.

And she could feel the Other there, filling her, laughing silently as she marveled at the heat of the sun on her face, at the damp sea breeze coating her lips with salt, at the pain of the hand now healed of its wound.

So long—it had been so long since the Other had felt such things, felt them *wholly* and not as something in between and diluted.

And those flames—*her* flames and her beloved's magic . . . they belonged to the Other now.

To a goddess who had walked through the temporary gate hanging between her breasts and seized her body as if it were a mask to wear.

She had no words, for she had no voice, no self, *nothing*—

And she could only watch as if through a window as she felt the goddess, who had perhaps not protected her but *hunted* her the entirety of her life, for this moment, this opportunity, examine the dark fleet ahead.

So easy to destroy it.

But more life glimmered—*behind*. More life to obliterate, to hear their dying cries with her own ears, to witness firsthand what it was to cease to be in a way the goddess never could . . .

She watched as her own hand, wreathed in pulsing white flame, began to move from where it had been aimed toward the dark fleet.

Toward the unprotected city at the heart of the bay.

Time slowed and stretched as her body pivoted toward that town, as her own arm lifted, her fist aimed toward the heart of it. There were people on the docks, the scions of a lost clan, some running from the display of fire she'd unleashed moments ago. Her fingers began to unfurl.

"No!"

The word was a roar, a plea, and silver and green flashed in her vision.

A name. A name clanged through her as he hurled himself in the path of that fist, that moonfire, not just to save those innocents in the city, but to spare *her* soul from the agony if she destroyed them all—

Rowan. And as his face became clear, his tattoo stark in the sun, as that fist full of unimaginable power now opened toward *his* heart—

There was no force in any world that could keep her contained.

And Aelin Galathynius remembered her own name as she shattered through the cage that goddess had shoved her into, as she grabbed that goddess by the damned *throat* and hurled her *out, out, out* through that gaping hole where she had infiltrated her, and sealed it—

Aelin snapped into her body, her power.

Fire like ice, fire stolen from the stars—

Rowan's hair was still moving as he slammed into a stop before her uncoiling fist.

Time launched again, full and fast and unrelenting. Aelin had only enough of it to throw herself sideways, to angle that now-open fist away from him, point it *anywhere* but at him—

The ship beneath her, the center and left flank of the dark fleet beyond her, and the outer edge of the island behind it blew apart in a storm of fire and ice.

CHAPTER 36

There was such quiet beneath the waves, even as the muffled sounds of shouting, of collision, of death echoed toward her.

Aelin drifted down, as she had drifted into her power, the weight of the Wyrdkey around her neck like a millstone—

Deanna. She didn't know how, didn't know why—

The Queen Who Was Promised.

Her lungs constricted and burned.

Shock. Perhaps this was shock.

Down she drifted, trying to feel her way back into her body, her mind.

Salt water stung her eyes.

A large, strong hand gripped the back of her collar and *yanked*, hauling her up in tugs—in steady strokes.

What had she done what had she done what had she done—

Light and air shattered around her, and that hand grasping her collar now banded around her chest, tugging her against a hard male body, keeping her head above the roiling waves.

"I've got you," said a voice that was not Rowan's.

Others. There had been others on the ship, and she had as good as killed them all—

"Majesty," the male said, a question and quiet order.

Fenrys. That was his name.

She blinked, and her name, her title, her gutted power came thrashing back into her—the sea and the battle and the threat of Morath swarming.

Later. Later, she'd deal with that rutting goddess who had thought to use *her* like some temple priestess. Later, she'd contemplate how she'd shred through every world to find Deanna and make her pay.

"Hold on," Fenrys said over the chaos now filtering in: the screaming of men, the groaning of breaking things, the crackle of flames. "Don't let go."

Before she could remember how to speak, they vanished into—nothing. Into darkness that was both solid and insubstantial as it squeezed her tightly.

Then they were in the water again, bobbing beneath the waves as she reoriented herself and sputtered for air. He'd moved them, somehow—jumped between distances, judging by the wholly different flotsam spinning around them.

Fenrys held her against him, his panting labored. As if whatever magic he possessed to leap between short distances took everything he had. He sucked in a deep breath.

Then they were gone again, into that dark, hollow, yet squeezing space. Only a handful of heartbeats passed before the water and sky returned.

Fenrys grunted, arm tightening around her as he swam with the other toward the shore, shoving aside debris. His breathing was a wet rasp now. Whatever that magic was, it was spent.

But Rowan—where was *Rowan*—

She made a sound that might have been his name, might have been a sob.

Fenrys panted, "He's on the reef—he's fine."

She didn't believe him. Thrashing against the Fae warrior's arm until he released her, she slid into the cold open water and twisted toward where Fenrys had been headed. Another small sound cracked from her as she beheld Rowan standing knee-deep in water atop the reef. His arm was already outstretched, even though thirty yards still separated them.

Fine. Unscathed. Alive. And an equally soaked Gavriel stood beside him, facing—

Oh, gods, oh, gods.

Blood stained the water. There were bodies everywhere. And Morath's fleet . . .

Most of it was gone. Nothing more than black wood splintered across the archipelago and burning bits of canvas and rope. But three ships remained.

Three ships now converging on the ruins of the *Sea Dragon* as it took on water, looming like thunderclouds—

"You have to swim," Fenrys growled beside her, his sodden golden hair plastered to his head. "Right now. As fast as you can."

She whipped her head toward him, blinking away burning seawater.

"Swim *now*," Fenrys snapped, canines flashing, and she didn't let herself consider what was prowling *beneath* them as he grabbed her collar again and practically *threw* her ahead of him.

Aelin didn't wait. She focused on Rowan's outstretched hand as she swam, his face so carefully calm—the commander on a battlefield. Her magic was barren, her magic was a wasteland, and his . . . She had stolen his power from him—

Think of that later. Aelin shoved through and ducked under larger bits of debris, past . . .

Past men. Rolfe's men. Dead in the water. Was the captain among them somewhere?

She'd likely killed her first and only human ally in this war—and her only direct path to that Lock. And if news of the former spread—

"*Faster!*" Fenrys barked.

Rowan sheathed his sword, his knees bent—

Then he was swimming to her, fast and smooth, cutting between and beneath the waves, the water seeming to part for him. She wanted to growl she could make it herself, but—

He reached her, saying nothing before he slipped behind her. Guarding with Fenrys.

And what could he do in the water with no magic, against a gaping maw of a sea-wyvern?

She ignored the crushing tightness in her chest and hurtled for the reef, Gavriel now waiting where Rowan had been. Beneath her, the shelf of the coral at last spread, and she nearly sobbed, her muscles trembling as Gavriel crouched so she could reach his outstretched hand.

The Lion easily hauled her out of the water. Her knees buckled as her boots steadied on the uneven coral heads, but Gavriel kept his grip on her, subtly letting her lean against him. Rowan and Fenrys were out a heartbeat later, and the prince instantly was there, hands on her face, slicking back her soaked hair, scanning her eyes.

"I'm fine," she rasped, her voice hoarse. From the magic or the goddess or the salt water she'd swallowed. "I'm me."

That was good enough for Rowan, who faced the three ships now bearing down on them.

On her other side, Fenrys had doubled over, hands on his knees as he panted. He lifted his head at her gaze, hair dripping, but said to Rowan, "I'm out—we'll have to either wait for it to replenish or swim to shore."

Rowan gave him a sharp nod that Aelin interpreted as understanding and thanks, and she glanced behind them. The reef seemed to be an extension of the black rocky shore far behind, but with the tide out, they'd indeed have to swim in spots. Have to risk what was beneath the water . . .

Beneath the water. With Lysandra.

There was no sign of wyvern or dragon.

Aelin didn't know if that was a good or bad thing.

Aelin and the Fae males had made it to the reef and now stood knee-deep in water atop it.

Whatever had happened . . . it had gone horribly wrong. So wrong that Lysandra could have sworn the feral, wild presence who had never once forgotten her had ducked into her long shadow as the world above exploded.

She'd tumbled off the coral, the current cleaving and eddying. Wood and rope and canvas rained onto the surface, some plunging deep. Then bodies and arms and legs.

But—there were the captain and his first mate thrashing against the flotsam that tangled them, trying to drag them down to the sandy floor.

Shaking off her shock, Lysandra swept for them both.

Rolfe and his man froze at her approach, reaching for weapons at their sides beneath the waves. But she ripped away the debris surely drowning them, then let herself go still—let them grab on to her. She didn't have much time . . .

Rolfe and his first mate latched on to her legs, clinging like barnacles as she propelled them through the water—past the now-scorched ruin. The work of a minute had her depositing them onto a rocky shelf, and she emerged only long enough to gulp down a breath before diving.

There were more men struggling in the water. She aimed for them, dodging debris, until—

Blood laced the current. And not the puffs that had been staining the water since the ship exploded.

Great, roiling clouds of blood. As if massive jaws clamped around a body and squeezed.

Lysandra launched forward, mighty tail snapping back and forth, body undulating, racing for the three boats bearing down on the survivors. She had to act *now*, while the wyverns were distracted with glutting themselves.

The stench of the black boat reached her even under the waves. As if the dark wood had been soaked in rotted blood.

And as she approached the closest ship's fat underbelly, two mighty shapes took form out in the blue.

Lysandra felt their attention lock on her the moment she slammed her tail into the hull.

Once. Twice.

Wood cracked. Muffled shouts reached her from above.

She drifted back, coiling, and slammed her tail into the hull a third time.

Wood tore and ripped into her, peeling away scales, but the damage was done. Water sucked in past her, more and more, tearing through the wood as its death-wound grew and grew. She backtracked out of the water's pull—flipping down, down, down as the two wyverns feasting on frantic men paused.

Lysandra raced for the next ship. Get the ships sinking, then their allies could pick off the struggling soldiers one by one as they swam to shore.

The second ship was wiser.

Spears and arrows whizzed through the water, lancing for her. She dove to the sandy floor, then shot up, up, up, aiming for the vulnerable belly of the ship, body bracing for impact—

She didn't reach the ship before another impact came.

Faster than she could sense, slipping around the side of the ship, the sea-wyvern slammed into her.

Talons tore and sliced, and she flipped on instinct, whipping her tail so hard that the wyvern went tumbling out into the water.

Lysandra lunged back, getting an eyeful of it as it stared her down.

Oh, gods.

It was nearly double her size, made of the deepest blue, its underside white and speckled with paler blue. The body was almost serpentine, wings little more than fins along its sides. Built not for speed or cruising through oceans, but . . . but for the long, curving talons, for the maw that was now open, tasting the blood and salt and scent of her, revealing teeth as narrow and sharp as an eel's.

Hooked teeth. For clamping down and shredding.

Behind the wyvern, the other fell into formation.

Men were splashing and screaming above her. If she did not get those enemy ships down . . .

Lysandra tucked her wings in tight. She wished she had taken a bigger gulp of air, had filled these lungs to capacity. Fanning her tail in the current, she let the blood still leaking from where the ship's wood had pierced her hide drift to them.

She knew the moment it reached the wyverns.

The moment they realized she was not just an ordinary animal.

And then Lysandra dove.

Fast and smooth, she plunged into the deep. If they had been bred for brute killing, then she'd use speed.

Lysandra swept beneath them, passing under their dark shadows before they could so much as pivot. Toward the open ocean.

Come on, come on, come on—

Like hounds after a hare, they gave chase.

There was a sandbar flanked by reefs just to the north.

She aimed for it, swimming like hell.

One of the wyverns was faster than the other, swift enough that its snapping maw rippled the water at her tail—

The water became clearer, brighter. Lysandra shot straight for the reef looming up out of the deep, a pillar of life and activity gone still. She curved around the sandbar—

The other wyvern appeared in front of her, the second still close on her tail.

Clever things.

But Lysandra threw herself to the side—into the shallows of the sandbar, and let momentum flip her, over and over, closer and closer to that narrow spit of sand. She dug her claws in deep, slowing to a stop, sand spraying and crusting her, and had her tail lifted, her body so much heavier out of the water—

The wyvern that had thought to catch her off guard by swimming around the other way launched itself out of the water and onto the sandbar.

She struck, fast as an asp.

Its neck exposed, she clamped her jaws around it and bit down.

It bucked, tail slashing, but she slammed her own onto its spine. Cracking its back as she cracked its neck.

Black blood that tasted of rancid meat flooded her throat.

Dropping the dead wyvern, she scanned the turquoise seas, the flotsam, the two remaining ships and harbor—

Where was the second wyvern? Where the hell was it?

Clever enough, she realized, to know when death was upon it and to seek an easier quarry.

For that was a spiked dorsal fin now submerging. Heading toward . . .

Toward where Aelin, Rowan, Gavriel, and Fenrys stood atop the reef, swords out. Surrounded by water on all sides.

Lysandra plunged into the waves, sand and blood washing away. One more—just one more wyvern, then she could wreck the boats . . .

The remaining wyvern reached the coral outcropping, gathering speed, as if it'd leap from the water and swallow the queen down whole.

It didn't get within twenty feet of the surface.

Lysandra hurled into it, both of them hitting the coral so hard it shuddered beneath them. But her claws were in its spine, her mouth around the back of its neck, shaking, yielding wholly to the song of survival, to the screaming demands of this body to *kill, kill, kill*—

They tumbled into open water, the wyvern still fighting, her grip on its neck loosening—

No. A warship loomed overhead, and Lysandra dug down deep, rallying her strength one last time as she spread those wings and flapped *up*—

She slammed the sea-wyvern into the hull of the boat now above them. The beast roared its fury. She slammed it again, and again. The hull snapped. And so did the sea-wyvern's body.

She watched the beast go limp. Watched the water rush into the cleaved belly of the ship. Listened to the soldiers aboard begin shouting.

She eased her claws from the beast and let it drift to the bottom of the sea.

One more ship. Just one more . . .

She was so tired. Shifting afterward might not even be possible for a few hours.

Lysandra broke the surface, drawing down air, bracing herself.

Aelin's screaming hit her before she could submerge again.

Not in pain . . . but warning. One word, over and over. One word for her.

Swim.

Lysandra craned her head toward where the queen stood atop the reef. But Aelin was pointing behind Lysandra. Not at the remaining ship . . . but the open water.

Where three massive forms raged through the waves, aiming right for her.

CHAPTER 37

Aedion's queen was on the reef, Rowan beside her, his father and Fenrys flanking them. Rolfe and most of his men had made it to the opposite side of the narrow bay mouth—atop the reef there.

And through the channel between them . . .

One warship.

One sea dragon.

And three sea-wyverns.

Adult sea-wyverns. The first two . . . they hadn't been full-grown.

"Oh, shit," the sentry beside Aedion on the watchtower began chanting. "Oh, shit. Oh, shit. Oh, shit."

The sea-wyverns that, Rolfe had claimed, would go to the ends of the earth to slaughter whoever killed their offspring. Only being in the heart of the continent might save you—but even then, waterways would never be safe.

And Lysandra had just killed two.

It seemed they had not come alone. And from the cheering of the Valg soldiers on that remaining warship . . . it had been a trap. The offspring had been the bait.

They had been only slightly bigger than Lysandra. The adults—the bulls—were thrice her size.

Longer than the warship now sitting there, archers firing at the men trying to swim ashore in the channel that had become a death trap for the green sea dragon.

The green sea dragon who now stood between the three monstrous creatures and his queen, stranded on those rocks with not even an ember of magic left in her veins. His queen, screaming over and over and over at Lysandra to *swim*, to *shift*, to *run*.

But Aedion had seen Lysandra take on the two offspring.

By the second, she'd been lagging. And he'd seen her change shapes so often these past months to know she couldn't shift fast enough now, perhaps might not have enough strength left to do it at all.

She was stranded in her form, as surely as his companions were stuck on the reef. And if Lysandra even tried to climb onto shore . . . He knew the bulls would reach her before she could so much as haul her body out of the shallows.

Faster and faster, those three bulls closed in. Lysandra remained at the mouth of the bay.

Holding the line.

Aedion's heart stopped.

"She's dead," one of the sentries hissed. "Oh, gods, she's dead—"

"*Shut your rutting mouth*," Aedion snarled, scanning the bay, slipping into that cold, calculating place that allowed him to make decisions in battle, to weigh the costs and risks.

Dorian, however, got the idea before he did.

Across the bay, hand uplifted and flickering bright as a star, Dorian signaled Lysandra again and again with his power. *Come to me, come to me, come to me*, the king seemed to call.

The three bulls sank beneath the waves.

Lysandra turned, plunging down—

But not toward Dorian.

Aelin stopped shouting. And Dorian's magic winked out.

Aedion could only watch as the shape-shifter's shadow soared toward the three bulls, meeting them head-on.

The three wyverns spread out, so huge Aedion's throat went dry.

And for the first time, he hated his cousin.

He hated Aelin for asking this of Lysandra, both to defend them and to secure the Mycenians to fight for Terrasen. Hated the people who had left such scars on the shifter that Lysandra was so willing to throw her life away. Hated . . . hated himself for being stuck in this useless tower, with a war machine only capable of firing one shot at a time.

Lysandra aimed for the wyvern in the middle, and when only a hundred yards separated them, she veered left.

They broke formation, one diving low, one keeping to the surface, and the other falling back. They were going to herd her. Herd her to a spot where they'd surround her from every angle and then rip her to shreds. It would be messy and vicious.

But Lysandra shot across the channel. Headed—

Headed right for the final remaining warship.

Arrows rained down on her.

Blood bloomed as some found their mark through her jade scales.

She kept swimming, her blood sending the bull closest to her, the one near the surface, into a frenzy, pushing himself faster to grab her, bite her—

Lysandra neared the ship, taking arrow after arrow, and leaped out of the water.

She crashed into soldiers and wood and the mast, rolling, writhing, and bucking, the twin masts snapping under her tail.

She hit the other side, flipping down into the water, red blood shining everywhere—

Just as the wyvern on her ass leaped onto the ship in a mighty arc that took Aedion's breath away. But with the jagged stumps of the masts jutting up like lances . . .

The bull landed atop them with a crunch that Aedion heard across the bay.

He bucked, but—that was wood now piercing through his back.

And beneath his enormous weight . . . the ship began to crack and sink.

Lysandra wasted no time in getting clear, and Aedion could barely draw breath as she shot across the bay again, the two bulls so horribly close that their wakes merged.

One dove, the depths swallowing him from sight. But the second one, still on her tail . . .

Lysandra led that one right into Dorian's range.

She drew in as close to the shore and looming tower as she could get, bringing the second bull with her. The king stretched out both hands.

The bull raged past—only to halt as ice lashed across the water. Solid ice, such as there had never been here.

The sentries beside Aedion fell silent. The bull roared, trying to wrest himself free—but the king's ice grew thicker, trapping the wyvern within its frozen grip. When the beast stopped moving, hoarfrost like scales covered him from snout to tail.

Dorian loosed a battle cry.

And Aedion had to admit the king wasn't that useless after all as the catapult behind Dorian sprang free, and a rock the size of a wagon jettisoned into the bay.

Right atop the frozen wyvern.

Rock met ice and flesh. And the wyvern shattered into a thousand pieces.

Rolfe and some of his men were cheering—people were cheering from the docks in town.

But there was one bull left in the harbor. And Lysandra was . . .

She had no idea where the bull was.

The long green body thrashed in the water, dipping beneath the waves, near-frantic.

Aedion scanned the bay, rotating in the gunner chair as he did, searching for any hint of that colossal dark shadow—

"*YOUR LEFT!*" Gavriel roared across the bay, magic no doubt amplifying his voice.

Lysandra twisted—and there the bull was, speeding out of the depths, as if he were a shark ambushing prey.

Lysandra threw herself into movement. A field of floating debris lay around her, the sinking ships of their enemy like islands of death, and there was the chain . . . If she could maybe get on it and climb high . . . No, she was too heavy, too slow.

She again streaked past Dorian's tower, but the bull wouldn't get near. He knew doom awaited him there. He kept just out of range, playing with her as she launched back into the field of debris between the enemy ships. Toward the open sea.

Aelin and the others watched helplessly from the reef outcropping as the two monsters swept by, the bull sending bits of broken hulls and masts into the air—aiming at the shifter.

One struck Lysandra in the side, and she went down.

Aedion shot out of his seat, a roar on his lips. But there she was, blood streaming from her as she swam and swam, as she led that bull through the heart of debris, then cut back—sharply. The bull followed through the blood clouding the water, blasting through debris that she nimbly dodged.

She'd worked him into a blood-frenzy.

And Lysandra, damn her, led him to the remnants of enemy ships, where Valg soldiers were trying to save themselves. The bull exploded through soldier and wood as if they were veils of gossamer.

Leaping through the water, twining around debris and coral and bodies, the sunlight glinting on green scales and ruby blood, Lysandra led the bull into a dance of death.

Each movement slower as more of her blood leaked into the water.

And then she changed course. Heading into the bay. To the chain.

And cut north—toward him.

Aedion examined the massive bolt before him.

Three hundred yards of open water separated her from the range of his arrow.

"*SWIM*," Aedion roared, even if she couldn't hear. "*SWIM, LYSANDRA!*"

Silence fell across the entirety of Skull's Bay as that jade sea dragon swam for her life.

The bull gained on her, diving down.

Lysandra passed under the links of the chain, and the shadow of the bull spread beneath her.

So small. She was so small compared to him—one bite was all it would take.

Aedion slammed himself back into the gunner chair, gripping the levers and pivoting the machine as she swam and swam for him.

One shot. That was all he'd have. One gods-damned shot.

Lysandra hurled herself forward, and Aedion knew she was aware of the death that loomed. Knew she was pushing that sea dragon's heart to near-stopping. Knew that the bull had reached the bottom and now launched himself up, up, up toward her vulnerable belly.

Only a few more yards, only a few more heartbeats.

Sweat slid down Aedion's brow, his own heart hammering so violently all he could hear was its thunder. He shifted the spear, slightly, adjusting his aim.

The bull raged up from the deep, maw open, ready to rip her in half with one blow.

Lysandra passed into range and leaped—leaped clean out of the water, all sparkling scales and blood. The bull jumped with her, water streaming from his open jaws as they arced up.

Aedion fired, slamming his palms into the lever.

Lysandra's long body arched away from those jaws as the bull lifted clean out of the water, baring his white throat—

As Aedion's massive spear went clean through it.

Blood spurted from the open jaws, and the creature's eyes went wide as he reared back.

Lysandra slammed into the water, sending a plume so high it blocked out the sight of both of them as they crashed into the sea.

When it subsided, there was only the shadow of them—and a growing pool of black blood.

"You . . . you . . . ," the sentry babbled.

"*Load another one*," he ordered, standing from his seat to scan the bubbling water.

Where was she, where was she—

Aelin was perched on Rowan's shoulders, scanning the bay.

And then a green head shot from the water, black blood spraying like spindrift as she hurled the severed head of the bull across the waves.

Cheering—riotous, wild cheering—exploded from every corner of the bay.

But Aedion was already up and running, half leaping down the stairs that would take him toward the beach that Lysandra now swam for, her own blood replacing the black ichor that stained the water.

So slow, each of her movements was so painfully slow. He lost track of her as he descended below the tree line, his chest heaving.

Roots and stones wrenched at him, but his Fae-swift feet flew over the loam until it turned to sand, until light broke through the trees and there she was, sprawled on the beach, bleeding everywhere.

Beyond them, out in the bay, Ship-Breaker dropped low, and Rolfe's fleet swept out to pick off the surviving soldiers—and save any of their own still out there.

He vaguely noted Aelin and the others diving into the sea, swimming hard for land.

Aedion dropped to his knees, wincing as sand sprayed onto her. Her scaled head was nearly as big as he was, but her eyes . . . those green eyes, the same color as her scales . . .

Full of pain. And exhaustion.

He lifted a hand toward her, but she showed her teeth—a low snarl slipping out of her.

He held up his hands, scooting back.

It was not the woman who looked at him, but the beast she'd become. As if she had given herself so fully to its instincts, that it had been the only way to survive.

There were gashes and slices everywhere. All dribbling blood, soaking the white sand.

Rowan and Aelin—one of them could help. If they could summon any power after what the queen had done. Lysandra closed her eyes, her breathing shallow.

"Open your gods-damned eyes," Aedion snarled.

She snarled back but cracked open an eye.

"You made it this far. Don't die on the rutting beach."

The eye narrowed—with a hint of female temper. He had to get the woman back. Let her take control. Or else the beast would never allow them near enough to help.

"You can thank me when your sorry ass is healed."

Again, that eye watched him warily, temper flickering. But an animal remained.

Aedion drawled, even as his relief began to crumble his mask of arrogant calmness, "The useless sentries in the watchtower are now all half in love with you," he lied. "One said he wanted to marry you."

A low snarl. He yielded a foot but held eye contact with her as he grinned. "But you know what I told them? I said that they didn't stand a chance in hell." Aedion lowered his voice, holding her pained, exhausted stare. "Because *I* am going to marry you," he promised her. "One day. I am going to marry you. I'll be generous and let you pick when, even if it's ten years from now. Or twenty. But one day, you are going to be my wife."

Those eyes narrowed—in what he could only call female outrage and exasperation.

He shrugged. "Princess Lysandra Ashryver sounds nice, doesn't it?"

And then the dragon huffed. In amusement. Exhaustion, but . . . amusement.

She opened her jaws, as if she'd try to speak, but realized she couldn't in this body. Blood leaked through her enormous teeth, and she shuddered in pain.

Brush snapped and crashed, and there were Aelin and Rowan, and his father and Fenrys. All of them soaked, covered in sand, and gray as death.

His queen staggered for Lysandra with a sob, flinging herself onto the sand before Aedion could bark a warning.

But Lysandra only winced as the queen laid a hand on her, saying over and over, "I'm so sorry, I'm so sorry."

Fenrys and Gavriel, who had maybe saved her life with that amplified shout about the bull's location, lingered near the tree line as Rowan approached, surveying the wounds.

Fenrys spotted Aedion's glance, spotted the warning wrath on his face if either of them got near the shifter, and said, "That was one hell of a shot, boyo." His father nodded in silent agreement.

Aedion ignored them both. Whatever well of magic his cousin and Rowan had depleted was already refilling. The shifter's wounds knitted closed, one by one. Slowly—painfully slowly, but . . . the bleeding stopped.

"She lost a lot of blood," Rowan observed to none of them in particular. "Too much."

"I've never seen anything like that in my life," Fenrys murmured. None of them had.

Aelin was trembling, a hand on her friend—face so white and drawn that any harsh words he'd reserved for her were unnecessary. His queen knew the cost. It had taken her so damn long to trust any of them to do anything. If Aedion roared at her now, even if he still yearned to . . . Aelin might never delegate again. Because if Lysandra hadn't been in the water when things had gone so, so badly . . .

"What happened?" he breathed, catching Aelin's eye. "What the hell happened out there?"

"I lost control," Aelin said hoarsely. As if she couldn't help it, her hand drifted to her chest. Where, through the white of her shirt, he could make out the Amulet of Orynth.

He knew then. Knew precisely what Aelin carried. What would have snagged Rolfe's interest on that map of his—similar enough to the Valg essence to get him to come running.

Knew why it had been so important, so vital, she risk everything to get it from Arobynn Hamel. Knew that she had used a *Wyrdkey* today, and it had almost killed them all—

He was shaking now, that rage indeed taking over. But Rowan snarled at him, low and vicious, "Save it for later." Because Fenrys and Gavriel had tensed—watching.

Aedion growled right back at him. Rowan gave him a cold, steady look that said if he so much as began to hint at what their queen carried, he'd rip out his tongue. Literally.

Aedion shoved down the anger. "We can't carry her, and she's too weak to shift."

"Then we wait here until she can," Aelin said. But her eyes drifted to the bay, where Rolfe was now being helped onto those rescue ships. And to the city beyond, still cheering.

A victory—but very nearly a loss. The remnants of the Mycenians, saved by one of their long-lost sea dragons. Aelin and Lysandra had woven ancient prophecies into tangible fact.

"I'll stay," Aedion said. "You deal with Rolfe."

His father offered from behind him, "I can get some supplies from the watchtower."

"Fine," he said.

Aelin groaned, getting to her feet, but stared down at him before she took Rowan's extended hand. She said softly, "I'm sorry."

Aedion knew she meant it. He still didn't bother replying.

Lysandra groaned, the reverberations running up his knees and straight into his gut, and Aedion whirled back to the shifter.

Aelin left without further good-bye.

The Lion lingered in the brush, keeping out of sight and sound as the Wolf watched over the dragon still sprawled across the beach.

For hours, the Wolf remained there. While the outgoing tide cleared the harbor of blood. While the Pirate Lord's ships sent any remaining enemy bodies to the crushing blue. While the young queen returned to the city in the heart of the bay to handle any fallout.

Once the sun had begun to set, the dragon stirred, and slowly, her form shimmering and shrinking, scales were smoothed into skin, a snout melted back into a flawless human face, and stumpy limbs lengthened into golden legs. Sand crusted her naked body, and she tried and failed to rise. The Wolf moved then, slinging his cloak around her and sweeping her into his arms.

The shifter didn't object, and her eyes were again closed by the time the Wolf began striding up the beach to the trees, her head leaning against his chest.

The Lion remained out of sight and held in the offer of help. Held in the words he needed to say to the Wolf, who had downed a sea-wyvern with one arrow. Twenty-four years old and already a myth whispered over campfires.

Today's events would no doubt be told around fires in lands even the Lion had not roamed in all his centuries.

The Lion watched the Wolf vanish into the trees, heading for the town at the end of the sandy road, the shifter unconscious in his arms.

And the Lion wondered if he himself would ever be mentioned in those whispered stories—if his son would ever allow the world to know who had sired him. Or even care.

CHAPTER 38

The meeting with Rolfe once the harbor was again safe was quick. Frank.

And Aelin knew if she didn't get the hell out of this city for an hour or two, she might very well explode again.

Every key has a lock, Deanna had said, a little reminder of Brannon's order. Using *her* voice. And had called her that title . . . that title that struck some chord of horror and understanding in her, so deep she was still working out what it meant. *The Queen Who Was Promised*.

Aelin stormed onto a spit of beach on the far side of the island, having run here, needing to get her blood roaring, needing it to silence the thoughts in her head. Behind her, Rowan's steps were quiet as death.

Only the two of them had been in that meeting with Rolfe. Bloodied, soaked, the Pirate Lord had met them in the main room of his inn, the name of it now a permanent reminder of the ship she'd wrecked. He demanded, "What the *hell* happened?"

And she had been so tired, so pissed off and full of disgust and despair, that it had been nearly impossible to muster the swagger. "When you are blessed by Mala, you find that sometimes your control can slip."

"*Slip?* I don't know what you fools were talking about down there, but from where I was standing, it looked like you lost your gods-damned mind and were about to fire on *my* town."

Rowan, leaning against the edge of a nearby table, explained, "Magic is a living thing. When you are that deep in it, remembering yourself, your purpose, is an effort. That my queen did so before it was too late is a feat in itself."

Rolfe wasn't impressed. "It looks to me like you were a little girl playing with power too big for you to handle, and only your prince jumping in your path made you decide *not* to slaughter my innocent people."

Aelin closed her eyes for a heartbeat, the image of Rowan leaping in front of that fist of moonfire flashing before her. When she opened her eyes, she let the crackling assuredness fade into something frozen and hard. "It looks to *me*," she said, "like the Pirate Lord of Skull's Bay and long-lost Mycenian heir has just allied with a young queen so powerful she can decimate *cities* if she wishes. It looks to me like you have made yourself untouchable with that alliance, and any fool who seeks to harm you, usurp you, will have *me* to contend with. So I suggest you salvage what you can of your precious ship, mourn the dozen men I take full responsibility for losing and whose families I will compensate accordingly, and shut your rutting mouth."

She turned toward the door, exhaustion and rage nipping at her bones.

Rolfe said to her back, "Do you want to know what the cost of this map was?"

She halted, Rowan glancing between them, face unreadable.

She smirked over her shoulder. "Your soul?"

Rolfe let out a hoarse laugh. "Yes—in a way. When I was sixteen, I was barely more than a slave on one of these festering ships, my Mycenian heritage just a one-way ticket to a beating." He laid a tattooed hand on the *Thresher*'s lettering. "Every coin I earned came back here—to my mother and sister. And one day the ship I was on got caught in a storm. The captain was a haughty bastard, refused to find safe harbor, and the ship was destroyed. Most of the crew drowned. I drifted for a day, washed up on an island at the edge of the archipelago, and awoke to find a man staring down at me. I asked if I was dead, and he laughed and inquired what I wanted for myself. I was so delirious I told him that I wanted to be captain—I wanted to be Pirate Lord of Skull's Bay and make the arrogant fools like the captain who had killed my friends *bow* before me. I thought I was dreaming when he explained that if he were to grant me the skills to do it, there would be a price. What I valued most in the world, he would have. I said I'd pay it—whatever it was. I had no belongings, no wealth, no people anyway. A few coppers would be nothing. He smiled before he vanished into sea mist. I awoke with the ink on my hands."

Aelin waited.

Rolfe shrugged. "I made it back here, finding friendly ships using the map the stranger had inked there. A gift from a god—or so I thought. But it wasn't until I saw the black sheets over my cottage's windows that I began to worry. And it wasn't until I learned that my mother and sister had used their little money to hire a skiff to go looking for me—and that the skiff had returned to harbor but they had not—that I realized the price I'd handed over. That's what the sea claimed. What *he* claimed. And it made me soulless enough that I loosed myself upon this city, this archipelago." Rolfe's green eyes were as merciless as the Sea God who had gifted and damned him. "That was the price of my power. What shall yours be, Aelin Galathynius?"

She didn't reply to him before storming out. Though Deanna's voice had echoed in her mind.

The Queen Who Was Promised.

Now, standing on that empty beach and monitoring the glimmering expanse of the sea as the last of the sun vanished, Rowan said beside her, "Did you willingly use the key?"

No hint of judgment, of condemnation. Just curiosity—and concern.

Aelin rasped, "No. I don't know what happened. One minute it was us . . . then *she* came." She rubbed at her chest, avoiding the touch of the golden chain against it. Her throat tightened as she took in that spot on his own chest, right between his pectorals. Where her fist had been aimed.

"How could you?" she breathed, a tremor running through her. "How could you put yourself in front of me like that?"

Rowan took a step closer but no farther. The crashing of waves and cries of gulls heading home for the night filled the space between them. "If you had destroyed that city, it would have destroyed *you*, and any sort of hope at an alliance."

Shaking began in her hands, spreading to her arms, her chest, her knees. Flame and ash curled on her tongue. "If I had killed you," she hissed, but choked on the words, unable to finish the thought, the idea of it. Her throat burned, and she squeezed her eyes shut, warm flames rippling around her. "I thought I'd found the bottom of my power," she admitted, magic already overflowing, so soon, too soon after she'd emptied herself. "I thought what I found in Wendlyn was the bottom. I had no idea it was all just an . . . antechamber."

Aelin lifted her hands, opening her eyes to find her fingers wreathed in flame. Darkness spread over the world. Through the veil of gold and blue and red, she looked at her prince. She raised her burning hands helplessly between them. "*She stole me*—she *took* me. And I could feel her—feel her consciousness. It was like she was a spider, waiting in a web for *decades*, knowing I'd one day be strong and stupid enough to use my magic and the key together. I might as well have rung the dinner bell." Her fire burned hotter, brighter, and she let it build and rise and flicker.

A wry, bitter smile. "It seems she wants us to make finding this Lock a priority, if you were given the message *twice*."

Indeed. "Isn't it enough to contend with Erawan and Maeve, to do the bidding of Brannon and Elena? Now I have to face the gods breathing down my neck about it as well?"

"Perhaps it was a warning—perhaps Deanna wished to show you how a not-so-friendly god might use you if you're not careful."

"She enjoyed every rutting second of it. She *wanted* to see what my power might do, what she could do with my body, with the key." Her flames burned hotter, shredding through her clothes until they were ash, until she was naked and clothed in only her own fire. "And what she called me—the Queen Who Was Promised. Promised when? To whom? To do what? I've never heard that phrase in my life, not even before Terrasen fell."

"We'll figure it out." And that was that.

"How can you be so . . . *fine* with this?" Embers sprayed from her like a swarm of fireflies.

Rowan's mouth tightened. "Trust me, Aelin, I am anything but *fine* with the idea that you are fair game to those immortal bastards. I am anything but *fine* with the idea that you could be taken from me like that. If I could, I would hunt Deanna down and pay her back for it."

"She's the Goddess of the Hunt. You might be at a disadvantage." Her flames eased a bit.

A half smile. "She's a haughty immortal. She's bound to slip up. And besides . . . " A shrug. "I have her sister on my side." He angled his head, studying her fire, her face. "Perhaps that's why Mala appeared to me that morning, why she gave me her blessing."

"Because you're the only one arrogant and insane enough to hunt a goddess?"

Rowan shucked off his boots, tossing them onto the dry sand behind him. "Because I'm the only one arrogant and insane enough to ask Mala Fire-Bringer to let me stay with the woman I love."

Her flames turned to pure gold at the words—at that word. But she said, "Perhaps you're just the only one arrogant and insane enough to love *me*."

That unreadable mask cracked. "This new depth to your power, Aelin, changes nothing. What Deanna did changes nothing. You are still young; your power is still growing. And if this new well of power gives us even the slightest advantage against Erawan, then thank the rutting darkness for it. But you and I will learn to manage your power together. You do not face this alone; you do not decide that you are unlovable because you have powers that can save *and* destroy. If you start to resent that power . . ." He shook his head. "I do not think we will win this war if you start down that road."

Aelin strode into the lapping waves and sank to her knees in the surf, steam rising around her in great plumes. "Sometimes," she admitted over the hissing water, "I wish someone else could fight this war."

Rowan stepped into the bubbling surf, his magic shielding against the heat of her. "Ah," he said, kneeling beside her as she still gazed out over the dark sea, "but who else would be able to get under Erawan's skin? Never underestimate the power of that insufferable swagger."

She chuckled, starting to feel the cool kiss of the water on her naked body. "As far as memory serves, Prince, it was that insufferable swagger that won your cranky, immortal heart."

Rowan leaned into the thin veil of flame now melting into night-sweet air and nipped her lower lip. A sharp, wicked bite. "There's my Fireheart."

Aelin let him pivot her in the surf and sand to face him fully, let him slide his mouth along her jaw, the curve of her cheekbone, the point of her Fae ear.

"These," he said, nibbling at her earlobe, "have been tempting me for months." His tongue traced the delicate tip, and her back arched. The strong hands at her hips tightened. "Sometimes, you'd be sleeping beside me at Mistward, and it'd take all my concentration *not* to lean over and bite them. Bite you all over."

"Hmmm," she said, tipping back her head to grant him access to her neck.

Rowan obliged her silent demand, pressing kisses and soft, growling nips to her throat. "I've never taken a woman on a beach," he purred against her skin, sucking gently on the space between her neck and shoulder. "And look at that—we're far from any sort of . . . collateral." One hand drifted from her hip to caress the scars on her back, the other sliding to cup her backside, drawing her fully against him.

Aelin spread her hands over his chest, tugging his white shirt over his head. Warm waves crashed against them, but Rowan held her fast—unmovable, unshakable.

Aelin remembered herself enough to say, "Someone might come looking for us."

Rowan huffed a laugh against her neck. "Something tells me," he said, his breath skittering along her skin, "you might not mind if we were discovered. If someone saw how thoroughly I plan to worship you."

She felt the words dangling there, felt herself dangling there, off the edge of the cliff. She swallowed. But Rowan had caught her each time she had fallen—first, when she had plummeted into that abyss of despair and grief; second, when that castle had shattered and she had plunged to the earth. And now this time, this third time . . . She was not afraid.

Aelin met Rowan's stare and said clearly and baldly and without a speckle of doubt, "I love you. I am in love with you, Rowan. I have been for a while. And I know there are limits to what you can give me, and I know you might need time—"

His lips crushed into hers, and he said onto her mouth, dropping words more precious than rubies and emeralds and sapphires into her heart, her soul, "I love you. There is no limit to what I can give to you, no time I need. Even when this world is a forgotten whisper of dust between the stars, I will love you."

Aelin didn't know when she started crying, when her body began shaking with the force of it. She had never said such words—to anyone. Never let herself be that vulnerable, never felt this burning and unending *thing*, so consuming she might die from the force of it.

Rowan pulled back, wiping away her tears with his thumbs, one after another. He said softly, barely audible over the crashing waves around them, "Fireheart."

She sniffed back tears. "Buzzard."

He roared a laugh and she let him lay her down on the sand with a gentleness near reverence. His sculpted chest heaved slightly as he ran an eye over her bare body. "You . . . are so beautiful."

She knew he didn't just mean the skin and curves and bones.

But Aelin still smiled, humming. "I know," she said, lifting her arms above her head, setting the Amulet of Orynth onto a safe, high part of the beach. Her fingers dug into the soft sand as she arched her back in a slow stretch.

Rowan tracked every movement, every flicker of muscle and skin. When his gaze lingered on her breasts, gleaming with seawater, his expression turned ravenous.

Then his gaze slid lower. Lower. And when it lingered on the apex of her thighs and his eyes glazed, Aelin said to him, "Are you going to stand there gawking all night?"

Rowan's mouth parted slightly, his breathing shallow, his body already showing her precisely where this was going to end.

A phantom wind hissed through the palms, whispered over the sand. Her magic tingled as she felt, more than saw, Rowan's shield fall into place around them. She sent her own power tracing over it, knocking and tapping at the shield in sparks of flame.

Rowan's canines gleamed. "Nothing is getting past that shield. And nothing is going to hurt me, either."

Something tight in her chest eased. "Is it that different? With someone like me."

"I don't know," Rowan admitted. Again, his eyes slid along her body, as if he could see through skin to her burning heart beneath. "I've never been with . . . an equal. I've never allowed myself to be that unleashed."

For every bit of power she threw at him, he'd throw back at her. She braced herself on her elbows, lifting her mouth to the new scar on his shoulder, the wound small and jagged—as broad as an arrowhead. She kissed it once, twice.

Rowan's body was so tense above hers she thought his muscles would snap. But his hands were gentle as they drifted to her back, stroking her scars and the tattoos he'd inked over them.

The waves tickled and caressed her, and he made to settle over her, but she lifted a hand to his chest—halting him dead. She smiled against his mouth. "If we're equals, then I don't understand why you're still half clothed."

She didn't give him the chance to explain as she traced her tongue over the seam of his lips, as her fingers unlatched the buckle of his worn sword belt. She wasn't sure he was breathing.

And just to see what he'd do, she palmed him through his pants.

Rowan barked a curse.

She laughed quietly, kissed his newest scar again, and dragged a finger down lazily, indolently, holding his gaze for every single inch she touched.

And when Aelin laid her palm flat on him again, she said, "You are mine."

Rowan's breathing started again, jagged and savage as the waves breaking around them. She flicked open the top button of his pants. "I'm yours," he ground out.

Another button popped free. "And you love me," she said. Not a question.

"To whatever end," he breathed.

She popped the third and final button free, and he let go of her to toss his pants into the sand nearby, taking his undershorts with them. Her mouth went dry as she took in the sight of him.

Rowan had been bred and honed for battle, and every inch of him was pure-blooded warrior.

He was the most beautiful thing she'd ever seen. Hers—he was *hers*, and—

"You are mine," Rowan breathed, and she felt the claiming in her bones, her soul.

"I am yours," she answered.

"And you love me." Such hope and quiet joy in his eyes, beneath all that fierceness.

"To whatever end." For too long—for too long had he been alone and wandering. No longer.

Rowan kissed her again. Slow. Soft. A hand slid up the plane of her torso while he lowered himself over her, his hips nestling against hers. She gasped a bit at the touch, gasped a bit more as his knuckle grazed the heavy, aching underside of her breast. As he leaned down to kiss the other.

His teeth grazed over her nipple, and her eyes drifted closed, a moan slipping out of her.

Oh, gods. Oh, burning, rutting gods. Rowan knew what he was doing; he really gods-damned did.

His tongue flicked against her nipple, and her head tipped back, her fingers digging into his shoulders, urging him to take more, take *harder*.

Rowan growled his approval, her breast still in his mouth, on his tongue, his hand making lazy strokes from her ribs down her waist, down her thighs, then back up. She arched in silent demand—

A phantom touch, like the northern wind given form, flicked over her bare breast.

Aelin burst into flames.

Rowan laughed darkly at the reds and golds and blues that erupted around them, illumining the palms that towered over the edge of the beach, the waves breaking behind him. She might have panicked, might have been mortified, had he not lifted his mouth to hers, had those phantom hands of ice-kissed wind not kept working her breasts, had his own hand not continued stroking, closer and closer to where she needed him. "You're magnificent," he murmured onto her lips, his tongue sliding into her mouth.

The hardness of him pushed against her, and she bucked her hips, needing to grind herself against him, to do anything to ease the building ache between her legs. Rowan groaned, and she wondered if there was any other male in the world who would be so naked and prone with a woman on fire, who would not look at those flames with any ounce of fear.

She slid her hand between them, and when she closed her fingers around him, marveling at the velvet-wrapped steel, Rowan groaned again, pushing into her hand. She pulled her mouth from his, staring into those pine-green eyes as she slid her hand along him. He lowered his head—not to kiss her, but to watch where she stroked him.

A roaring wind full of ice and snow blasted around them. And it was her turn to huff a laugh. But Rowan gripped her wrist, drawing her hand away. She opened her mouth in protest, wanting to touch more, *taste* more. "Let me," Rowan growled onto the sea-slick skin between her breasts. "Let me touch you." His voice trembled enough that Aelin lifted his chin with her thumb and forefinger.

A flicker of fear and relief shone beneath the glazed lust. As if doing this, touching her, was as much to remind him that she had made it today, that she was safe, as it was to pleasure her. She leaned up, brushing her mouth against his. "Do your worst, Prince."

Rowan's smile was nothing short of wicked as he pulled away to run a broad hand from her throat down to the juncture of her thighs. She shuddered at the sheer possession in the touch, her breath coming in tight pants as he gripped either thigh and spread her legs, baring her fully for him.

Another wave crashed, parting around them, the cool water like a thousand kisses along her skin. Rowan kissed her navel, then her hip.

Aelin couldn't take her eyes from his silver hair shining with salt water and moonlight, from the hands holding her wide for him as his head dipped between her legs.

And as Rowan tasted her on that beach, as he laughed against her slick skin while her hoarse cries of his name shattered across palm trees and sand and water, Aelin let go of all pretense at reason.

She moved, hips undulating, begging him to *go, go,* go. So Rowan did, sliding a finger into her as his tongue flicked that one spot, and oh, gods, she was going to explode into starfire—

"Aelin," he growled, her name a plea.

"Please," she moaned. *"Please."*

The word was his undoing. Rowan rose over her again, and she let out a sound that might have been a whimper, might have been his name.

Then Rowan had a hand braced in the sand beside her head, fingers twining in her hair, while the other guided himself into her. At the first nudge of him, she forgot her own name. And as he slid in with gentle, rolling thrusts, filling her inch by inch, she forgot that she was queen and that she had a separate body and a kingdom and a world to look after.

When Rowan was seated deep in her, trembling with restraint as he let her adjust, she lifted her burning hands to his face, wind and ice tumbling and roaring around them, dancing across the waves with ribbons of flame. There were no words in his eyes; none in hers, either.

Words did not do it justice. Not in any language, in any world.

He leaned in, claiming her mouth as he began to move, and they let go entirely.

She might have been crying, or it might have been his tears on her face, turning to steam amid her flames.

She dragged her hands down his powerful, muscled back, over scars from battles and terrors long since past. And as his thrusts turned deeper, she dug in her fingers, dragging her nails across his back, claiming him, marking him. His hips slammed home at the blood she drew, and she arched, baring her throat to him. For him—only him.

Rowan's magic went wild, though his mouth on her neck was so careful, even as his canines dragged along her skin. And at the touch of those lethal teeth against her, the death that hovered nearby and the hands that would always be gentle with her, always love her—

Release blasted through her like wildfire. And though she could not remember her name, she remembered Rowan's as she cried it while he kept moving, wringing every last ounce of pleasure from her, fire searing the sand around them to glass.

Rowan's own release barreled through him at the sight of it, and he groaned her name so that she remembered it at last, lightning joining wind and ice over the water.

Aelin held him through it, sending the fire-opal of her magic to twine with his power. On and on, as he spilled himself in her, lightning and flame danced on the sea.

The lightning continued to strike, silent and lovely, even after he stilled. The sounds of the world came pouring back in, his breathing as ragged as the hiss of the crashing waves while he brushed lazy kisses to her temple, her nose, her mouth. Aelin drew her eyes away from the beauty of their magic, the beauty of *them*, and found his face to be the most beautiful of all.

She was trembling—and so was Rowan as he remained in her. He buried his face in the crook of her neck and shoulder, his uneven breath warming her skin. "I never . . . ," he tried, voice hoarse. "I didn't know it could be . . ."

She ran her fingers down his scarred back, over and over. "I know," she breathed. "I know."

Already, she wanted more, already she was calculating how long she'd have to wait. "You once told me that you don't bite the females of other males." Rowan stiffened a bit. But she went on coyly, "Does that mean . . . you'll bite your own female, then?"

Understanding flashed in those green eyes as he raised his head from her neck to study the spot where those canines had once pierced her skin. "That was the first time I really lost control around you, you know. I wanted to chuck you off a cliff, yet I bit you before I knew what I was doing. I think my body knew, my magic knew. And you tasted . . ." Rowan loosed a jagged breath. "So good. I hated you for it. I couldn't stop thinking about it. I'd wake up at night with that taste on my tongue—wake up thinking about your foul, beautiful mouth." He traced his thumb over her lips. "You don't want to know the depraved things I've thought about this mouth."

"Hmmm, likewise, but you didn't answer my question," Aelin said, even as her toes curled in the wet sand and warm water.

"Yes," Rowan said thickly. "Some males enjoy doing it. To mark territory, for pleasure . . ."

"Do females bite males?"

He began to harden again inside her as the question lingered. Oh, gods—Fae lovers. Everyone should be so damn lucky to have one. Rowan rasped, "Do you *want* to bite me?"

Aelin eyed his throat, his glorious body, and the face she had once so fiercely hated. And she wondered if it were possible to love someone enough to die from it. If it were possible to love someone enough that time and distance and death were of no concern. "Am I limited to your neck?"

Rowan's eyes flared, and his answering thrust was answer enough.

They moved together, undulating like the sea before them, and when Rowan roared her name again into the star-flecked black, Aelin hoped the gods themselves heard it and knew their days were now numbered.

CHAPTER 39

Rowan didn't know whether to be amused, thrilled, or slightly terrified that he'd been blessed with a queen and lover who had so little care for public decency. He'd taken her three times on that beach—twice in the sand, then a third out in the warm waters. And yet his very blood was still electrified. And yet he still wanted more.

They'd swum into the shallows to wash off the sand crusted on them, but Aelin had wrapped her legs around his waist, kissed his neck, then licked his ear the way he'd nibbled hers, and he was buried in her again. She knew why he needed the contact, why he'd needed to taste her on his tongue, and then with the rest of his body. She'd needed the same.

He still needed it. When they'd finished after that first time, he'd been left reeling, to pull his sanity back together after the joining that had . . . unleashed him. Broken and remade him. His magic had been a song, and she had been . . .

He'd never had anything like her. Everything he'd given her, she'd given right back to him. And when she had bit him during that second coupling in the sand . . . His magic had left six nearby palm trees in splinters as he'd climaxed hard enough that he thought his body would shatter.

But once they were finished, when she'd actually made to walk back to Skull's Bay in nothing but her flames, he'd given her his shirt and belt. Which did little to cover her up, especially those beautiful legs, but at least it was less likely to start a riot.

Barely, though. And it'd be obvious what they'd done on that beach the moment they stepped within scenting range of anyone with a preternatural sense of smell.

He'd marked her—richer than the scent that had clung to her before. Marked her deep and true, and there was no undoing it, no washing it away. She'd claimed him, and he'd claimed her, and he knew she was well aware of what that claiming meant—just as he knew . . . He knew it had been a choice on her part. A final decision regarding the matter of who would be in her royal bed.

He would try to live up to that honor—try to find *some* way to prove he deserved it. That she hadn't bet on the wrong horse. Somehow. He'd earn it. Even with so little to offer beyond his own magic and heart.

But he also knew his queen. And knew that despite the enormity of what they'd done, Aelin had also kept him on that beach to avoid the others. Avoid answering their questions and demands. But he made it one foot inside the Ocean Rose, saw the light in Aedion's room, and knew their friends would not be so easily deterred.

Indeed, Aelin was scowling up at the light—though worry quickly replaced it as she remembered the shifter who had been so thoroughly unconscious. Her bare feet were silent on the stairs and hallway as she hurried for the room, not bothering to knock before flinging open the door.

Rowan loosed a sharp breath, trying to draw up his magic to cool the fire still in his blood. To calm the instincts roaring and raging at him. Not to take her—but to eliminate any other threat.

A dangerous time, for any Fae male, when they first took a lover. Worse, when it meant something more.

Dorian and Aedion sat in the two armchairs before the darkened fireplace, arms crossed.

And her cousin's face went pale with what might have been terror as he scented Aelin—the markings both seen and invisible on them.

Lysandra sat in bed, face drawn but eyes narrowed at the queen. It was the shifter who purred, "Enjoy your ride?"

Aedion didn't dare move and was giving Dorian a warning look to do the same. Rowan bit down against the rage at the sight of other males near his queen, reminding himself that they were his friends, but—

That primal rage stumbled as he felt Aelin's shuddering relief upon finding the shifter mostly healed and lucid. But his queen only shrugged. "Isn't that all these Fae males are good for?"

Rowan raised his brows, chuckling as he debated reminding her how she'd begged him throughout, how she'd said words like *please*, and *oh, gods*, and then a few extra *please*s thrown in for good measure. He'd enjoy wringing those rarely seen manners from her again.

Aelin shot him a glare, daring him to say it. And despite just having her, despite the fact that he could still taste her, Rowan knew that whenever they found their bed again, she would not get the rest she wanted.

Color stained Aelin's cheeks, as if she saw his plans unfold, but she lifted the amulet from around her neck, dropped it onto the low-lying table between Aedion and Dorian, and said, "I learned that this was the third Wyrdkey when I was still in Wendlyn."

Silence.

Then, as if she hadn't shattered any sense of safety they still possessed, Aelin withdrew the mangled Eye of Elena from her pack, chucked it once in the air, and jerked her chin at the King of Adarlan. "I think it's time you met your ancestor."

Dorian listened to Aelin's story.

About the Wyrdkey she'd secretly carried, about what had happened today in the bay, about how she'd tricked Lorcan and how it would eventually lead the warrior back to them—hopefully with the other two keys in his hands. And, if they were lucky, they would have already found this Lock she had been ordered twice now to retrieve from the Stone Marshes—the only thing capable of binding the Wyrdkeys back into the gate from which they'd been hewn and ending the threat of Erawan forever.

No number of allies would make a difference if they could not stop Erawan from using those keys to unleash the Valg hordes from his own realm upon Erilea. His possession of two keys had already led to such darkness. If he gained the third, gained mastery over the Wyrdgate and could open it to any world at will, use it to summon any conquering army . . . They had to find that Lock to nullify those keys.

When the queen was done, Aedion was silently fuming, Lysandra was frowning, and Aelin was now snuffing out the candles in the room with hardly a wave of her hand. Two ancient tomes, withdrawn from Aedion's crammed saddlebags, lay open on the table. He knew those books—he had no idea she'd taken them from Rifthold. The warped metal of the Eye of Elena amulet sat atop one of them as Aelin double-checked the markings on an age-spotted page.

Darkness fell as she used her own blood to etch those markings on the wooden floor.

"Looks like our bill of damages to this city is going to rise," Lysandra muttered.

Aelin snorted. "We'll just move the rug to cover it." She finished making a mark—a Wyrdmark, Dorian realized with a chill, and stepped back, plucking up the Eye in her fist.

"Now what?" Aedion said.

"Now we keep our mouths shut," Aelin said sweetly.

The moonlight spread on the floor, devoured by the dark lines she'd etched. Aelin drifted over to where Rowan sat on the edge of the bed, still shirtless thanks to the queen currently *wearing* his shirt, and took up a spot beside him, a hand on his knee.

Lysandra was the first to notice.

She sat up in the bed, green eyes glowing with animal brightness as the moonlight on the blood-marks seemed to shimmer. Aelin and Rowan jerked to their feet. Dorian just stared at the marks, at the moonlight, at the beam of it shining through the open balcony doors.

As if the light itself were a doorway, the shaft of moonlight turned into a humanoid figure.

It flickered, its form barely there. Like a figment of a dream.

The hair on Dorian's arms rose. And he had the good sense to slide out of his chair and onto a knee as he bowed his head.

He was the only one who did so. The only one, he realized, who had spoken to Elena's mate, Gavin. Long ago—another lifetime ago. He tried not to consider what it meant that he now carried Gavin's sword, Damaris. Aelin had not asked for it back—did not seem inclined to do so.

A muffled female voice, as if it were calling from far away, flickered in and out with the image. "Too—far," a light, young voice said.

Aelin stepped forward and shut those ancient spellbooks before stacking them with a thump. "Well, Rifthold isn't exactly available, and your tomb is trashed, so *tough luck*."

Dorian's head lifted as he glanced between the flickering figure of moonlight and the young queen of flesh and blood.

Elena's roughly formed body vanished, then reappeared, as if the wind itself disturbed her. "Can't—hold—"

"Then I'll make it quick." Aelin's voice was sharp as a blade. "No more games. No more half-truths. *Why* did Deanna arrive today? I get it:

finding the Lock is important. But *what* is it? And tell me what she meant by calling me the Queen Who Was Promised."

As if the words jolted the dead queen like lightning, his ancestor appeared, fully corporeal.

She was exquisite: her face young and grave, her hair long and silvery-white—like Manon's—and her eyes . . . Startling, dazzling blue. They now fixed on him, the pale gown she wore fluttering on a phantom breeze. "Rise, young king."

Aelin snorted. "Can we not play the holier-than-thou-ancient-spirit game?"

But Elena surveyed Rowan, Aedion. Her slender, fair neck bobbed.

And Aelin, gods above, snapped her fingers at the queen—once, twice—drawing her attention back to her. "Hello, Elena," she drawled, "so nice to see you. It's been a while. Care to answer some questions?"

Irritation flickered in the dead queen's eyes. But Elena's chin remained high, her slender shoulders back. "I do not have much time. The connection is too hard to maintain so far from Rifthold."

"What a surprise."

The two queens stared each other down.

Elena, Wyrd damn him, broke first. "Deanna is a god. She does not have rules and morals and codes the way we do. *Time* does not exist for her the way it does for us. You let your magic touch the key, the key opened a door, and Deanna happened to be watching at that exact moment. That she spoke to you at all is a gift. That you managed to shove her out before she was ready . . . She will not soon forget that insult, *Majesty*."

"She can get in line," Aelin said.

Elena shook her head. "There is . . . there is so much I did not get to tell you."

"Like the fact that you and Gavin never killed Erawan, lied to everyone about it, and then left him for us to deal with?"

Dorian risked a glance at Aedion, but his face was hard, calculating, ever the general—fixed on the dead queen now standing in this room with them. Lysandra—Lysandra was gone.

No, in ghost leopard form, slinking through the shadows. Rowan's hand was resting casually on his sword, though Dorian's own magic swept the room and realized the weapon was to be the physical distraction from the magical blow he'd deal Elena if she so much as looked funny at Aelin. Indeed, a hard shield of air now lay between the two queens—and sealed this room, too.

Elena shook her head, her silver hair flowing. "You were meant to retrieve the Wyrdkeys before Erawan could get this far."

"Well, I didn't," Aelin snapped. "Forgive me if you weren't entirely *clear* on your directions."

Elena said, "I do not have time to explain, but know it was the *only* choice. To save us, to save Erilea, it was the *only* choice I could make." And for all their snapping at each other, the queen exposed her palms to Aelin. "Deanna and my father spoke true. I'd thought . . . I'd thought it was broken, but if they told you to find the Lock . . ." She bit her lip.

Aelin said, "Brannon said to go to the Stone Marshes of Eyllwe to find the Lock. *Where*, precisely, in the marshes?"

"There was once a great city in the heart of the marshes," Elena breathed. "It is now half drowned on the plain. In a temple at its center, we laid the remnants of the Lock. I didn't . . . My father attained the Lock at terrible cost. The cost . . . of my mother's body, her mortal life. A Lock for the Wyrdkeys—to seal shut the gate, and bind the keys inside them forever. I did not understand what it had been intended for; my father never told me about any of it until it was too late. All I knew was that the Lock was only able to be used once—its power capable of sealing *anything* we wished. So I stole it. I used it for myself, for my people. I have been paying for that crime since."

"You used it to seal Erawan in his tomb," Aelin said quietly.

The pleading faded from Elena's face. "My friends died in the valley of the Black Mountains that day so I might have the chance to stop him. I heard their screaming, even in the heart of Erawan's camp. I will not apologize for trying to end the slaughter so that the survivors could have a future. So *you* could have a future."

"So you used the Lock, then chucked it into a ruin?"

"We placed it inside the holy city on the plain—to be a commemoration of the lives lost. But a great cataclysm rocked the land decades later . . . and the city sank, the marsh water flowed in, and the Lock was forgotten. No one ever retrieved it. Its power had already been used. It was just a bit of metal and glass."

"And now it's not?"

"If both my father and Deanna mentioned it, it must be vital in stopping Erawan."

"Forgive me if I do not trust the word of a goddess who tried to use me like a puppet to blow this town into smithereens."

"Her methods are roundabout, but she likely meant you no harm—"

"Bullshit."

Elena flickered again. "Get to the Stone Marshes. Find the Lock."

"I told Brannon, and I'll tell you: we have more pressing matters at hand—"

"My mother *died* to forge that Lock," Elena snapped, eyes blazing bright. "She let go of her mortal body so that she could forge the Lock for my father. I was the one who broke the promise for how it was to be used."

Aelin blinked, and Dorian wondered if he should indeed be worried when even she was speechless. But Aelin only whispered, "Who was your mother?"

Dorian ransacked his memory, all his history lessons on his royal house, but couldn't recall.

Elena made a sound that might have been a sob, her image fading into cobwebs and moonlight. "She who loved my father best. She who blessed him with such mighty gifts, and then bound herself in a mortal body and offered him the gift of her heart."

Aelin's arms slackened at her sides.

Aedion blurted, "Shit."

Elena laughed humorlessly as she said to Aelin, "Why do you think you burn so brightly? It is not just Brannon's blood that is in your veins. But Mala's."

Aelin breathed, "Mala Fire-Bringer was your mother."

Elena was already gone.

Aedion said, "Honestly, it's a miracle you two didn't kill each other."

Dorian didn't bother to correct him that it was technically impossible, given that one of them was already dead. Rather, he weighed all that the queen had said and demanded. Rowan, remaining silent, seemed to be doing the same. Lysandra sniffed around the blood-marks, as if testing for whatever remnants of the ancient queen might be around.

Aelin stared out the open balcony doors, eyes hooded and mouth a tight line. She unfurled her fist and examined the Eye of Elena, still held in her palm.

The clock struck one in the morning. Slowly, Aelin turned to them. To him.

"Mala's blood flows in our veins," she said hoarsely, fingers closing around the Eye before she slipped it into the shirt's pocket.

He blinked, realizing that it indeed did. That perhaps both of them had been so considerably gifted because of it. Dorian said to Rowan, if only because he might have heard or witnessed something in all his travels, "Is it truly possible—for a god to become mortal like that?"

Rowan, who had been watching Aelin a bit warily, twisted to him. "I've never heard of such a thing. But . . . Fae have given up their immortality to bind their lives to that of their mortal mates." Dorian had the distinct feeling Aelin was deliberately examining a spot on her shirt. "It's certainly possible Mala found a way to do it."

"It's not just possible," Aelin murmured. "She *did* it. That . . . pit of power I uncovered today . . . That was from Mala herself. Elena might be many things, but she wasn't lying about that."

Lysandra shifted back into her human form, swaying enough that she set herself down on the bed before Aedion could move to steady her. "So what do we do now?" she asked, her voice gravelly. "Erawan's fleet squats in the Gulf of Oro; Maeve sails for Eyllwe. But neither knows that we possess this Wyrdkey—or that this Lock exists . . . and lies directly between their forces."

For a heartbeat, Dorian felt like a useless fool as they all, including him, looked to Aelin. He was King of Adarlan, he reminded himself. Equal to her. Even if his lands and people had been stolen, his capital captured.

But Aelin rubbed her eyes with her thumb and forefinger, loosing a long breath. "I really, really hate that old windbag." She lifted her head, surveying them all, and said simply, "We sail for the Stone Marshes in the morning to hunt down that Lock."

"Rolfe and the Mycenians?" Aedion asked.

"He takes half his fleet to find the rest of the Mycenians, wherever they're hiding. Then they all sail north to Terrasen."

"Rifthold lies between here and there, with wyverns patrolling it," Aedion countered. "And this plan depends on *if* we can trust Rolfe to actually follow through on his promise."

"Rolfe knows how to stay out of range," Rowan said. "We have little choice but to trust him. And he honored the promise he made to Aelin regarding the slaves two and a half years ago." No doubt why Aelin had made him confirm it so thoroughly.

"And the other half of Rolfe's fleet?" Aedion pushed.

"Some remain to hold the archipelago," Aelin said. "And some come with us to Eyllwe."

"You can't fight Maeve's armada with a fraction of Rolfe's fleet," Aedion said, crossing his arms. Dorian bit back his own agreement, leaving the general to it. "Let alone Morath's forces."

"I'm not going there to pick a fight," was all Aelin said. And that was that.

They dispersed then, Aelin and Rowan slipping off to their own room.

Dorian lay awake, even when his companions' breathing became deep and slow. He mulled over each word Elena had uttered, mulled over that long-ago appearance of Gavin, who had awoken him to stop Aelin from opening that portal. Perhaps Gavin had done it not to spare Aelin from damnation, but to keep those waiting, cold-eyed gods from seizing her as Deanna had today.

He tucked the speculation away to consider when he was less prone to leaping to conclusions. But the threads lay in a lattice across his mind, in hues of red and green and gold and blue, glimmering and thrumming, whispering their secrets in languages not spoken in this world.

An hour past dawn, they departed Skull's Bay on the swiftest ship Rolfe could spare. Rolfe didn't bother to say good-bye, already preoccupied with readying his fleet, before they sailed out of the sparkling harbor and into the lush archipelago beyond. He did grant Aelin one parting gift: vague coordinates for the Lock. His map had found it—or rather, the general location. Some sort of wards must be placed around it, the captain warned them, if his tattoo could not pinpoint its resting place. But it was better than nothing, Dorian supposed. Aelin had grumbled as much.

Rowan circled high above in hawk form, scouting behind and ahead. Fenrys and Gavriel were at the oars, helping row them out of the harbor—Aedion doing so as well, at a comfortable distance from his father.

Dorian himself stood at the wheel beside the surly, short captain—an older woman who had no interest in speaking to him, king or not. Lysandra swam in the surf below in some form or another, guarding them from any threats beneath the surface.

But Aelin stood alone on the prow, her golden hair unbound and flowing behind her, so still that she might have been the twin to the figurehead mere feet beneath. The rising sun cast her in shimmering gold, no hint of the moonfire that had threatened to destroy them all.

But even as the queen stood undimming before the shadows of the world . . . a lick of cold traced the contours of Dorian's heart.

And he wondered if Aelin was somehow watching the archipelago, and the seas, and the skies, as if she might never see them again.

Three days later, they were nearly out of the archipelago's strangling grasp. Dorian was again at the helm, Aelin at the prow, the others scattered on various rounds of scouting and resting.

His magic felt it before he did. A sense of awareness, of warning and awakening.

He scanned the horizon. The Fae warriors fell silent before the others.

It looked like a cloud at first—a wind-tossed little cloud on the horizon. Then a large bird.

When the sailors began rushing for their weapons, Dorian's mind at last spat out a name for the beast that swept toward them on shimmering, wide wings. *Wyvern.*

There was only one. And only one rider atop it. A rider who did not move, whose white hair was unbound—listing toward the side. As the rider now was.

The wyvern dropped lower, skimming over the water. Lysandra was instantly ready, waiting for the queen's order to shift into whatever form would fight it—

"No." The word ripped from Dorian's lips before he could think. But then it came out, over and over, as the wyvern and rider sailed closer to the ship.

The witch was unconscious, her body leaning to the side because she was not awake, because that was blue blood all over her. *Don't shoot; don't shoot—*

Dorian was roaring the order as he hurtled for where Fenrys had drawn his longbow, a black-tipped arrow aimed at the witch's exposed neck. His words were swallowed by the shouting of the sailors and their captain. Dorian's magic swelled as he unsheathed Damaris—

But then Aelin's voice cut over the fray—*Hold your fire!*

All of them halted. The wyvern sailed close, then banked, circling the boat.

Blue blood crusted the beast's scarred sides. So much blood. The witch was barely in the saddle. Her tan face was leeched of color, her lips paler than whale bone.

The wyvern completed its circle, sweeping lower this time, readying to land as near the boat as possible. Not to attack . . . but for help.

One moment, the wyvern was soaring smoothly over the cobalt waves. Then the witch listed so far that her body seemed to go boneless. As if in that heartbeat, when help was mere feet away, whatever luck had kept her astride at last abandoned her.

Silence fell on the ship as Manon Blackbeak tumbled from her saddle, falling through wind and spindrift, and hit the water.

PART TWO

Fireheart

CHAPTER 40

The smoke had been stinging Elide's eyes for the better part of the gray muggy morning.

Just farmers burning fields left to fallow, Molly had claimed, so the ashes might fertilize the earth for next year's harvest. They had to be miles away, but the smoke and ash would travel far on the brisk northward wind. The wind that led home to Terrasen.

But they weren't headed to Terrasen. They were headed due east, straight toward the coast.

Soon she'd have to cut northward. They had passed through one town—only one, and its denizens had already been fatigued of roving carnivals and performers. Even with the night barely under way, Elide already knew they would likely only make enough money to cover their expenses for staying.

She had attracted a grand total of four customers to her little tent so far, mostly young men looking to know which of the village girls fancied them, barely noticing that Elide—beneath the makeup pasted thick as cream on her face—was no older than they were. They'd scampered off when their friends had rushed by, whispering through the star-painted flaps that a swordsman was putting on the show of a lifetime, and his arms were nearly the size of tree trunks.

Elide had glowered, both at the feckless young men who vanished—one without paying—and at Lorcan, for stealing the show.

She waited all of two minutes before shoving out of the tent, the enormous, ridiculous headdress Molly had plunked on her hair snagging on the flaps. Bits of dangling beads and charms hung from the arching crest, and Elide batted them out of her eyes, nearly tripping over her matching bloodred robes as she went to see what all the fuss was about.

If the young men of the town had been impressed by Lorcan's muscles, it was nothing on what those muscles were doing to the young women.

And older women, Elide realized, not bothering to squeeze through the tightly packed crowd before the makeshift stage on which Lorcan stood, juggling and throwing swords and knives.

Lorcan was not a natural performer. No, he had the gall to actually look *bored* up there, bordering on outright sullen.

But what he lacked in charm he made up for with his shirtless, *oiled* body. And holy gods . . .

Lorcan made the young men who had visited her tent look like . . . children.

He balanced and hurled his weapons as if they were nothing, and she had the feeling the warrior was merely going through one of his daily exercise routines. But the crowd still *ooh*ed and *aah*ed at every twist and toss and catch, and coins still trickled into the pan at the edge of the stage.

With the torches around him, Lorcan's dark hair seemed to swallow the light, his onyx eyes flat and dull. Elide wondered if he was contemplating the murder of everyone drooling over him like dogs around a bone. She couldn't blame him.

A trickle of sweat slid through the crisp spattering of dark hair on his sculpted chest. Elide watched, a bit transfixed, as that bead of sweat wended down the muscled grooves of his stomach. Lower.

No better than those ogling women, she said to herself, about to head back into her tent when Molly observed from beside her, "Your husband could just be sitting up there, fixing your stockings, and women would empty their pockets for the chance to stare at him."

"He had that effect wherever we went with our former carnival," Elide lied.

Molly clicked her tongue. "You're lucky," she murmured as Lorcan hurled his sword high in the air and people gasped, "that he still looks at you the way he does."

Elide wondered if Lorcan would look at her at all if she told him what her name was, who she was, what she carried. He'd slept on the floor of the tent each night—not that she'd ever once bothered to offer him the roll. He usually came in after she'd fallen asleep, and left before she awoke. To do what, she had no idea—perhaps exercise, since his body was . . . like that.

Lorcan chucked three knives in the air, bowing without one bit of humility or amusement to the crowd. They gasped again as the blades aimed for his exposed spine.

But in an easy, beautiful maneuver, Lorcan rolled, catching each blade, one after another.

The crowd cheered, and Lorcan coolly looked at his pan of coins.

More copper—and some silver—flowed, like the patter of rain.

Molly let out a low laugh. "Desire and fear can loosen any purse strings." A sharp glance. "Shouldn't you be in your tent?"

Elide didn't bother responding as she left, and could have sworn she felt Lorcan's gaze narrow on her, on the headdress and swaying beads, on the long, voluminous robes. She kept going, and endured a few more young men—and some young women—asking about their love lives before she found herself again alone in that silly tent, the dark only illuminated by dangling crystal orbs with tiny candles inside.

She was waiting for Molly to finally shout the carnival was over when Lorcan shouldered through the flaps, wiping his face with a scrap of fabric that was most definitely not his shirt.

Elide said, "Molly will be begging you to stay, you realize."

He slid into the folding chair before her round table. "Is that your professional prediction?"

She swatted at a strand of beads that swayed into her eyes. "Did you sell your shirt, too?"

Lorcan gave a feral grin. "Got ten coppers from a farmer's wife for it."

Elide scowled. "That's disgusting."

"Money is money. I suppose you don't need to worry about it, with all the gold you've got stashed."

Elide held his stare, not bothering to look pleasant. "You're in a rare good mood."

"Having two women and one man offer a spot in their beds tonight will do that to a person."

"Then why are you here?" It came out sharper than she intended.

He surveyed the hanging orbs, the woven carpet, the black tablecloth, and then her hands, scarred and calloused and small, gripping the edge of the table. "Wouldn't it ruin your ruse if I slipped off into the night with someone else? You'd be expected to throw me out on my ass—to be heartbroken and raging for the rest of your time here."

"You might as well enjoy yourself," she said. "You're going to leave soon anyway."

"So are you," he reminded her.

Elide tapped a finger on the tablecloth, the rough fabric scratching against her skin.

"What is it?" he demanded. As if it were an inconvenience to be polite.

"Nothing."

It wasn't nothing, though. She knew why she'd been delaying that turn northward, the inevitable departure from this group and final trek on her own.

She could barely make an impact at a backwater carnival. What the hell would she do in a court of such powerful people—especially without being able to read? While Aelin could destroy kings and save cities, what the hell would she do to prove her worth? Wash their clothes? Clean their dishes?

"Marion," he said roughly.

She looked up, surprised to find him still there. Lorcan's dark eyes were unreadable in the dimness. "You had plenty of young men unable to stop staring at you tonight. Why not have some fun with them?"

"Why?" she snapped. The thought of a stranger touching her, of some faceless, nameless man pawing at her in the dark . . .

Lorcan stilled. He said too calmly, "When you were in Morath, did someone—"

"No." She knew what he meant. "No—it didn't get that far." But the memory of those men touching her, laughing at her nakedness . . . She shoved it away. "I've never been with a man. Never had the chance or the interest."

He cocked his head, his dark, silken hair sliding over his face. "Do you prefer women?"

She blinked at him. "No—I don't think so. I don't know what I prefer. Again, I've never . . . I've never had the opportunity to feel . . . that." Desire, lust, she didn't know. And she didn't know how or why they'd wound up talking about this.

"Why?" And with all of Lorcan's considerable focus honed in on her, with the way he'd glanced at her red-painted mouth, Elide wanted to tell him. About the tower, and Vernon, and her parents. About why, if she were to ever feel desire, it'd be a result of trusting someone so much that those horrors faded away, a result of knowing they would fight tooth and claw to keep her free and never lock her up or hurt her or leave her.

Elide opened her mouth. Then the screaming started.

Lorcan didn't know why the hell he was in Marion's ridiculous little oracle's tent. He needed to wash, needed to clean away the sweat and oil and *feel* of all those ogling eyes on him.

But he'd spotted Marion in the crowd while he'd finished up his piss-poor performance. He hadn't seen her earlier in the evening before she'd put on that headdress and those robes, but . . . maybe it was the cosmetics, the heavy kohl around her eyes, the way the red-painted lips made her mouth look like a fresh piece of fruit, but . . . he'd noticed her.

Noticed the way the men had spotted her, too. Some had outright gawked, wonder and lust written across their bodies, as Marion lingered, oblivious, at the edge of the crowd and watched Lorcan instead.

Beautiful. After a few weeks of eating, of safety, the terrified, gaunt young woman had somehow gone from pretty to beautiful. He'd ended his performance sooner than he'd intended, and by the time he looked up again, Marion was gone.

Like a gods-damned dog, he'd picked up her scent among the crowd and followed her back to this tent.

In the shadows and glowing lights within, with the headdress and dangling beads and dark red robes . . . the oracle incarnate. Serene, exquisite . . . and utterly forbidden.

And he'd been so focused on cursing himself for staring at that ripe, sinful mouth while she admitted she was still untouched, that he hadn't detected anything amiss until the screaming started.

No, he'd been too busy contemplating what sounds might come from that full mouth if he slowly, gently, taught her the art of the bedroom.

The attack, Lorcan supposed, was Hellas's way of telling him to keep his cock in his pants and mind out of the gutter.

"*Get under a wagon and stay there*," he snapped before hurtling out of the tent. He didn't wait to see if she obeyed. Marion was smart—she knew she'd stand a better chance at survival if she listened to him and found shelter.

Lorcan loosed his gift through the panicking carnival site—a wave of dark, terrible power sweeping out in a ripple, then rushing back to tell him what it sensed. His power was gleeful, breathless in a way he knew too well: death.

At one end of the field lay the outskirts of the little town. At the other, a copse of trees and endless night—and wings.

Towering, sinewy forms plunged down from the skies—his magic picked up four. Four ilken as they landed, claws out and baring those flesh-shredding teeth. The leathery wings, it seemed, marked them as some slight variation of the ones who had tracked them in Oakwald. A variation—or a refining of an already ruthless hunter.

People ran, screaming—toward the town, toward the cover of the dark fields beyond.

Those distant fires had not been set by farmers to burn their idle fields.

They had been set to cloud the skies, to hide the scent of these beasts. From him. Or any other gifted warriors.

Marion. They were hunting Marion.

The carnival was in chaos, the horses were shrieking and bucking. Lorcan plunged toward where the four ilken had landed in the heart of the camp, right where he'd been performing minutes before, in time to see one land atop a fleeing young man and flip him onto his back.

The young man was still screaming for gods who would not answer as the ilken leaned down, flicking free a long talon, and opened up his belly in a smooth swipe. He was still screaming when the ilken lowered his mutilated face and feasted.

"What in burning hell *are* those beasts?" It was Ombriel, a long-sword out—and gripped in a way that told him she knew how to wield it. Nik came thundering up behind her, two rough, near-rusted blades in his meaty hands.

"Soldiers from Morath," was all Lorcan supplied. Nik was eyeing the blade and hatchet Lorcan had drawn, and he didn't think to pretend to not know how to use either, to be a simple man from the wilds, as he said with cold precision, "They're naturally able to cut through most magic—and only beheading will keep them down."

"They're nearly eight feet," Ombriel said, face pale.

Lorcan left them to their assessments and fear, stepping into the ring of light in the heart of the camp as the four ilken finished playing with the young man. The human was still alive, silently mouthing pleas for help.

Lorcan lashed out with his power and could have sworn the young man had gratitude in his eyes as death kissed him in greeting.

The ilken looked up as one, hissing softly. Blood slid from their teeth.

Lorcan tunneled into his power, preparing to distract and addle them, if their resistance to magic held true. Perhaps Marion would have time to run. The ilken who had ripped open the belly of the young man said to him, laughter dancing on its gray tongue, "Are you the one in charge?"

Lorcan simply said, "Yes."

It told him enough. They did not know who he was, his role in Marion's escape.

The four ilken smiled. "We seek a girl. She murdered our kin—and several others."

They blamed her for the ilken's death those weeks ago? Or was it an excuse to further their own ends? "We tracked her to the Acanthus crossing . . . She may be hiding here, among your people." A sneer.

Lorcan willed Nik and Ombriel to keep their mouths shut. If they so much as started to reveal them, the hatchet in his hands would move.

"Check another carnival. We've had this crew for months."

"She is small," it went on, those too-human eyes flickering. "Crippled on one leg."

"We don't know anyone like that."

They'd hunt her to the ends of the earth.

"Then line up your crew so we might . . . inspect them."

Make them walk. Look them over. Look for a dark-haired young woman with a limp and whatever other markers her uncle had provided.

"You've scared them all away. It might be days before they return. And, again," Lorcan said, hatchet flicking a bit higher, "there is no one in my caravan who matches such a description." Behind him, Nik and Ombriel were silent, their terror a reek that shoved itself up his nose. Lorcan willed Marion to remain hidden.

The ilken smiled—the most hideous smile Lorcan had beheld in all his centuries. "We have gold." Indeed, the ilken beside it had a hip-pouch sagging with it. "Her name is Elide Lochan. Her uncle is Lord of Perranth. He will reward you handsomely to turn her over."

The words hit Lorcan like stones. Marion—*Elide* had . . . lied. Had managed to keep him from even sniffing the lie on her, had used enough truths and her own general fear to keep the scent of it hidden—

"We know no one by such a name," Lorcan said again.

"Pity," the sentinel crooned. "For if you had her in your company, we would have taken her and left. But now . . ." The ilken smiled at its three companions, and their dark wings rustled. "Now it seems we have flown a very long way for nothing. And we are very hungry."

CHAPTER 41

Elide had squeezed herself into a hidden floor compartment in the largest of the wagons and prayed that no one discovered her. Or began burning things. Her frantic breathing was the only sound. The air grew tight and hot, her legs trembled and cramped from staying curled in a ball, but still she waited, still she kept hidden.

Lorcan had run out—he'd just run into the fray. She'd fled the tent in time to see four ilken—*winged* ilken—descend upon the camp. She had not lingered long enough to see what happened after.

Time passed—minutes or perhaps hours, she couldn't tell.

She had done this. She had brought these things here, to these people, to the caravan . . .

The screaming grew louder, then faded. Then nothing.

Lorcan might be dead. Everyone might be dead.

Her ears strained, and she tried to quiet her breathing to *listen* for any sounds of life, of action beyond her small, hot hiding space. No doubt, it was usually reserved for smuggling contraband—not at all intended for a human being.

She couldn't stay hidden much longer. If the ilken slaughtered them all, they'd search for any survivors. Could likely sniff her out.

She would have to make a run for it. Have to break out, observe what she could, and sprint for the dark fields and pray no others waited out there. Her feet and calves had gone numb minutes before and now tingled incessantly. She might very well not even be able to walk, and her stupid, useless leg—

She listened again, praying to Anneith to turn the ilken's attention elsewhere.

Only silence greeted her. No more screaming.

Now. She should go *now*, while she had the cover of darkness.

Elide did not give her fear another heartbeat to whisper its poison into her blood. She had survived Morath, survived weeks alone. She'd make it, she *had* to make it, and she wouldn't at all mind being the queen's gods-damned dishwasher if it meant she could *live*—

Elide uncoiled, shoulders aching as she quietly eased the trapdoor up, the little area rug sliding back. She scanned the interior of the wagon—the empty benches on either side—then studied the night beckoning beyond. Light spilled from the camp behind her, but ahead . . . a sea of blackness. The field was perhaps thirty feet away.

Elide winced as the wood groaned while she hefted the trapdoor high enough for her to slither, belly-down, over the floorboards. But her robe snagged, yanking her into a stop. Elide gritted her teeth, tugging blindly. But it had caught inside the crawl space. Anneith save her—

"Tell me," drawled a deep male voice behind her, from near the driver's seat. "What would you have done if I were an ilken soldier?"

Relief turned her bones to liquid, and Elide held in her sob. She twisted to find Lorcan covered in black blood, sitting on the bench behind the driver's seat, legs spread before him. His axe and sword lay discarded beside him, coated in that black blood as well, and Lorcan idly chewed on a long stalk of wheat as he gazed at the canvas wall of the wagon.

"The first thing I might have done in your place," Lorcan mused, still not looking at her, "would have been to ditch the robe. You'd fall flat on your face if you ran—and the red would be as good as ringing the dinner bell."

She tugged at the robe again, and the fabric ripped at last. Scowling, she patted where it had come free and found a loose bit of wood paneling.

"The second thing I might have done," Lorcan went on, not even bothering to wipe away the blood splattered on his face, "is tell me the gods-damned truth. Did you know those ilken beasts *love* to talk with the right encouragement? And they told me some very, very interesting things." Those dark eyes at last slid to her, utterly vicious. "But you didn't tell me the truth, did you, Elide?"

Her eyes were wide, her face leeched of color beneath the cosmetics. She'd lost the headdress somewhere, and her dark sheet of hair slid free of some of its pins as she climbed from the hidden compartment. Lorcan watched every movement, assessing and weighing and debating what, exactly, to do with her.

Liar. Cunning little liar.

Elide Lochan, rightful Lady of Perranth, crawled out, slamming the trapdoor shut and glaring at him from where she knelt on the floor. He glared right back. "Why should I have trusted you," she said with impressive coldness, "when you were stalking me for *days* in the forest? Why should I have told you a thing about me when you could have sold me to the highest bidder?"

His body ached; his head throbbed from the slaughter he'd barely managed to survive. The ilken had gone down—but not willingly. And the one he'd kept alive, the one Nik and Ombriel had begged him to kill and be done with, had told him very little, actually.

But Lorcan had decided his *wife* didn't need to know that. Decided it was time to see what she might reveal if he let some lies of his own fool her.

Elide glanced at his weapons, at the reeking blood coating him like oil. "You killed them all?"

He lowered the wheat stalk from his mouth. "Do you think I'd be sitting here if I hadn't?"

Elide Lochan wasn't some mere human trying to return to her homeland and serve her queen. She was a royal-blooded *lady* who wanted to get back to that fire-breathing bitch in the North to offer whatever aid she could. She and Aelin would be well suited for each other, he decided. The sweet-faced liar and the insufferable, haughty princess.

Elide slumped onto the bench, massaging her feet and calves.

"I'm risking my neck for you," he said too quietly, "and yet you decided not to tell me that your uncle isn't just a mere commander at Morath, but Erawan's right hand—and *you* are his prized possession."

"I told you enough of the truth. Who I am makes no difference. And I am no one's possession."

His temper yanked at the leash he'd been careful to keep short before tracking her scent to this wagon. Outside, the others were hurriedly packing, readying to flee into the night before the villagers decided to blame them for the disaster. "It does make a difference who you are. With your queen on the move, your uncle knows she'd pay a steep price to get you back. You are not a mere breeding asset—you are a negotiation tool. You might very well be what brings that bitch to her knees."

Rage flashed in her fine-boned face. "You keep plenty of secrets, too, *Lorcan*." She spat his name like a curse. "And I still haven't been able to decide if I find it insulting or amusing that you think I'm too stupid to notice. That you thought I was some fear-addled girl, too grateful for the presence of such a strong, brooding warrior to even question why you were there or what you wanted or what your stake in all this is. I gave you exactly what you wanted to see: a lost young woman in need of help, perhaps a bit skilled at lying and deceit, but ultimately not worth more than a few seconds' consideration. And you, in all your immortal arrogance, didn't think twice. Why should you, when humans are so useless? Why should you even bother, when you planned to abandon me the moment you got what you needed?"

Lorcan blinked, bracing his feet on the floor. She didn't back down an inch.

He couldn't remember the last time anyone had spoken to him like that. "I would be careful what you say to me."

Elide gave him a hateful little smile. "Or what? You'll sell me to Morath? Use me as your ticket in?"

"I hadn't thought to do that, but thank you for the idea."

Her throat bobbed, the only sign of her fear. And she said clearly and without a hint of hesitation, "If you try to bring me to Morath, I will end my own life before you can carry me over the Keep's bridge."

It was the threat, the promise, that checked his anger, his utter *rage* that . . . that she had indeed played into his expectations of her, his arrogance and prejudices. He said carefully, "What is it that you're carrying that makes them hunt you so relentlessly? Not your royal blood, not your magic and use for breeding. The object you carry with you—what is it?"

Perhaps it was a night for truth, perhaps death hovered close enough to make her a bit reckless, but Elide said, "It's a gift—for Celaena Sardothien. From a woman kept imprisoned in Morath, who had waited a long time to repay her for a past kindness. More than that, I don't know."

A gift for an assassin—not the queen. Perhaps nothing of note, but— "Let me see it."

"No."

They stared each other down again. And Lorcan knew that if he wanted, he could wait until she was asleep, take it for himself, and vanish. See what might make her so protective of it.

But he knew . . . some small, stupid part of him knew that if he took from this woman who had already had too much stolen from her . . . He didn't know if there was any coming back from that. He'd done such despicable, vicious things over the centuries and hadn't thought twice. He'd reveled in them, relished them, the cruelty.

But this . . . there was a line. Somehow . . . somehow there was a gods-damned line here.

She seemed to pick up on his decision—with whatever gift she had. Her shoulders slumped, and she stared blankly at the canvas wall as the sounds of their group now grew closer, their urging to hurry and pack, leave what could be spared.

Elide said quietly, "Marion was my mother's name. She died defending Aelin Galathynius from her assassin. My mother bought Aelin time to run—to get away so she could one day return to save us all. My uncle, Vernon, watched and smiled as my father, the Lord of Perranth, was executed outside our castle. Then he took my father's title and lands and home. And for the next ten years, my uncle locked me in the highest tower of Perranth Castle, with only my nursemaid for company. When I broke my foot and ankle, he did not trust healers enough to let them treat it. He kept bars on the tower windows to keep me from killing myself, and shackled my ankles to keep me from running. I left for the first time in a decade when he shoved me into a prison wagon and dragged me down to Morath. There, he made me work as a servant—for the humiliation and terror he delights in. I planned and dreamed of escaping every day. And when the time came . . . I took my chance. I did not know about the ilken, had only heard rumors of fell things being bred in the mountains beyond the Keep. I have no lands, no money, no army to offer Aelin Galathynius. But I will find her—and help her in whatever way I can. If only to keep just one girl, just *one*, from ever enduring what I did."

He let the truth in her words sink into him. Let them adjust his view of her. His . . . plans.

Lorcan said roughly, "I am over five hundred years old. I am blood-sworn to Queen Maeve of the Fae, and I am her second-in-command. I have done great and terrible things in her name, and I will do more before death comes to claim me. I was born a bastard on the streets of Doranelle, ran wild with the other discarded children until I realized my talents were different. Maeve noticed, too. I can kill faster—I can sense when death is near. I think my magic *is* death, given to me by Hellas himself. I am in these lands on behalf of my queen—though I came without her permission. She might very well hunt me down and kill me for it. If her sentinels arrive looking for me, it is in your best interest to pretend not to know who and what I am." There was more, but . . . Elide had remaining secrets, too. They'd offered each other enough for now.

No fear tainted her scent—not even a trace of it. All Elide said was, "Do you have a family?"

"No."

"Do you have friends?"

"No." His cabal of warriors didn't count. Gods-damned Whitethorn hadn't seemed to care when he abandoned them to serve Aelin Galathynius; Fenrys made no secret he hated the bond; Vaughan was barely around; he couldn't stand Gavriel's unbreakable restraint; and Connall was too busy rutting Maeve like an animal most of the time.

Elide angled her head, her hair sliding across her face. He almost lifted a hand to brush it back and read her dark eyes. But his hands were covered in that filthy blood. And he had the feeling Elide Lochan did not wish to be touched unless she asked to be.

"Then," she murmured, "you and I are the same in that regard, at least."

No family, no friends. It hadn't seemed quite so pathetic until she said it, until he suddenly saw himself through her eyes.

But Elide shrugged, rising to her feet as Molly's voice barked from nearby. "You should clean up—you look like a warrior again."

He wasn't sure if she meant it as a compliment. "Nik and Ombriel, unfortunately, realized you and I are perhaps not what we seem."

Alarm flashed in her eyes. "Should we leave—"

"No. They'll keep our secrets." If only because they'd seen Lorcan lay into those ilken, and knew precisely what he could do to them if they so much as breathed wrong in their direction. "We can stay awhile yet—until we get clear of this."

Elide nodded, her limp deep as she headed for the back of the wagon. She sat on the edge before climbing off, her wrecked ankle too weak and painful to ever jump. Yet she moved with quiet dignity, hissing a little as her foot made contact with the ground.

Lorcan watched her limp into the night without so much as a backward glance at him.

And he wondered what the hell he was doing.

CHAPTER 42

Death smelled like salt and blood and wood and rot.

And it hurt.

Darkness embrace her, it hurt like hell. The Ancient Ones had lied that it cured all ills, if the slice of pain across her abdomen was any indication. Not to mention the pounding headache, the sheer dryness of her mouth, the burning sting in the other cut on her arm.

Perhaps the Darkness was another world, another realm. Perhaps she'd gone to the hell-realm the humans so feared.

She hated Death.

And Death could go to hell, too—

Manon Blackbeak cracked open eyelids that were too heavy, too burning, and squinted against the flickering lantern light that swayed upon the wood panels of the room in which she lay.

Not a real bedroom, she realized by the reek of salt and rocking and creaking of the world around her. A cabin—on a ship.

A small, dingy one, with barely space for this bed, a porthole too small for her shoulders to even squeeze through—

She bolted upright. Abraxos. Where was *Abraxos*—

"Relax," drawled a too-familiar female voice from the shadowed space near the foot of the bed.

Pain flared in Manon's belly, a delayed response to her sudden movement, and she glanced between the white bandages that now scratched against her fingers and the young queen, lounging in the chair by the door. Glanced between the woman and the chains now around Manon's wrists, around her ankles—anchored into the walls with what appeared to be freshly drilled holes.

"Looks like you owe me a life debt once more, Blackbeak," Aelin Galathynius said, cold humor in her turquoise eyes. *Elide.* Had Elide made it here—

"Your fussy nursemaid of a wyvern is fine, by the way. I don't know how you wound up with a sweet thing like that for a mount, but he's content to sprawl in the sun on the foredeck. Can't say it makes the sailors particularly happy—especially cleaning up after him."

Find somewhere safe, she'd told Abraxos. Had he somehow found the queen? Somehow known this was the only place she might stand a chance of surviving?

Aelin braced her feet on the floor, boots thudding softly. There was a frank sort of impatience with any sort of bullshit that had not been there the last time Manon had seen the woman. As if the warrior who had laughed her way through their battle atop Temis's temple had lost a bit of that wicked amusement but gained more of the cunning cruelty.

Manon's belly gave a throb of pain that made her bite her lip to keep from hissing.

"Whoever gave you that wound wasn't joking," the queen said. "Trouble at home?"

It wasn't the queen's business, or anyone else's. "Let me heal, and then I'll be on my way," Manon rasped, her tongue a dried, heavy husk.

"Oh, no," Aelin purred. "You're not going anywhere. Your mount may do whatever he pleases, but you are now officially our prisoner."

Manon's head started spinning, but she forced herself to say, "Our?"

A knowing little smile. Then the queen rose gracefully. Her hair was longer, face leaner, those turquoise eyes hard and haunted. The queen said simply, "Here are the rules, Blackbeak. You try to escape, you die. You hurt anyone, you die. You somehow bring any of us into trouble . . . I think you get where I'm going with this. You step one foot out of line, and I'll finish what we started that day in the forest, life debt or no. This time I don't need steel to do it."

As she spoke, gold flames seemed to flicker in her eyes. And Manon realized with no small thrill, even with her pain, that the queen could indeed end her before she'd get close enough to kill.

Aelin turned for the door, her scarred hand on the knob. "I found iron splinters in your belly before I healed you. I suggest you don't lie to whoever can tolerate being around you long enough to get the full story." She jerked her chin toward the floor. A pitcher and cup lay there. "Water's next to the bed. If you can reach it."

Then she was gone.

Manon listened to her steady footsteps fade. No other voices or sounds beyond the lap of waves against the ship, the groan of the wood, and—gulls. They had to still be within range of the coast, then. Sailing to where . . . she'd have to figure that out.

Once she healed. Once she got out of these irons. Once she got onto Abraxos.

But to go where? To whom?

There was no aerie to receive her, no Clan who would shield her from her grandmother. And the Thirteen . . . Where were they now? Had they been hunted down?

Manon's stomach burned, but she reached for the water. Pain lashed her hard enough that she gave up after a heartbeat.

They had heard, no doubt—what she was. The Thirteen had heard.

Not just a half-blooded Crochan . . . but the last Crochan Queen.

And her sister . . . her half sister . . .

Manon stared at the shadowed, wooden ceiling.

She could feel that Crochan's blood on her hands. And her cape . . . that red cape was draped over the edge of the bed. Her sister's cape. That her grandmother had made her wear, knowing who it belonged to, knowing whose throat Manon had slit.

No longer the Blackbeak heir, Crochan blood or no.

Despair curled like a cat around the pain in Manon's belly. She was no one and nothing.

She did not remember falling asleep.

The witch slept for three days after Aelin reported that she had awakened. Dorian went into that cramped cabin with Rowan and the queen every time they healed a little bit more of her, observing the way their magic worked, but not daring to try it on the unconscious Blackbeak.

Even unconscious, Manon's every breath, every twitch, was a reminder that she was a born predator, her agonizingly beautiful face a careful mask to lure the unwary to their doom.

It felt fitting, somehow, considering that *they* were likely sailing to their own doom.

As Rolfe's two ships had escorted them down the coast of Eyllwe, they'd kept well away from the shore. A wicked storm had them mooring among the small cluster of islands off Leriba's waters, and they'd only survived thanks to Rowan's own winds shielding them. Most of them had still spent the entirely of it with their head in a bucket. Himself included.

They were nearing Banjali now—and Dorian had tried and failed not to think of his dead friend with every league closer to the lovely city. Tried and failed not to consider if Nehemia would have been with them on this very ship had things not gone so terribly wrong. Tried and failed not to contemplate if that touch she'd once given him—the Wyrdmark she'd sketched over his chest—had somehow . . . awakened that power of his. If it had been a curse as much as a blessing.

He hadn't had the nerve to ask what Aelin was feeling, though he found her frequently staring toward the coast—even if they couldn't see it, even if they wouldn't get close.

Another week—perhaps less, if Rowan's magic helped—would have them at the eastern edge of the Stone Marshes. And once they were in range . . . they'd have to trust Rolfe's vague directions to guide them.

And avoid Melisande's armada—Erawan's armada now, he supposed—waiting just around the peninsula in the Gulf of Oro.

But for now . . . Dorian was on watch in Manon's room, none of them taking any risks where the Blackbeak heir was concerned.

He cleared his throat as her eyelids shifted, her dark lashes bobbing up—then lifting wholly.

Gold sleep-murky eyes met his.

"Hello, witchling," he said.

Her full, sensuous mouth tightened slightly, either in a repressed grimace or smile, he couldn't tell. But she sat up, her moon-white hair sliding forward—her chains clanking. "Hello, princeling," she said. Gods, her voice was like sandpaper.

He glanced at the water jug. "Care for a drink?"

She had to be parched. They'd barely been able to get a trickle down her throat, not wanting to risk her choking or freeing those iron teeth from wherever she kept them.

Manon studied the pitcher, then him. "Am I your prisoner, too?"

"My life debt is paid," he said simply. "You're nothing to me at all."

"What happened," she rasped. An order—and one he allowed her to make.

But he filled the glass, trying not to look like he was calculating her range in those chains as he handed it to her. No sign of her iron nails as her slim fingers wrapped around the cup. She winced slightly, winced a bit more as she lifted it to her still-pale lips—and drank. And drank.

She drained the glass. Dorian silently refilled it for her. Once. Twice. Thrice.

When she at last finished, he said, "Your wyvern flew straight as an arrow for us. You tumbled off the saddle and into the water barely fifty yards from our ship. How he found us, we don't know. We got you out of the water—Rowan himself had to temporarily bind your stomach on the deck before we could even move you down here. It's a miracle you're not dead from blood loss alone. Never mind infection. We had you down here for a week, Aelin and Rowan working on you—they had to cut you open again in some spots to get the bad flesh out. You've been in and out of it since."

Dorian didn't feel like mentioning that he'd been the one who'd jumped into the water. He'd just . . . acted, as Manon had acted when she'd saved him in his tower. He owed her nothing less. Lysandra, in sea dragon form, had caught up to them moments later, and he'd held the water-heavy Manon in his arms as he'd climbed onto the shifter's back. The witch had been so pale, and the wound on her stomach . . . He'd almost lost his breakfast at the sight of it. She looked like a fish who'd been sloppily gutted.

Gutted, Aelin had confirmed an hour later when she held up a small sliver of metal, by someone with very, very sharp iron nails.

None of them had mentioned that it might have been punishment—for saving him.

Manon was assessing the room with eyes quickly clearing. "Where are we."

"On the sea."

Aelin had ordered he not give her any information about their plans and whereabouts.

"Are you hungry?" he asked, wondering what, exactly, she might eat.

Indeed, those gold eyes slashed to his throat.

"Really?" He lifted a brow.

Her nostrils flared slightly. "Only for sport."

"Aren't you . . . partially human, at least?"

"Not in the ways that count."

Right—because the other parts . . . Fae, Valg . . . It was Valg blood that had shaped the witches. The very prince that had infested him shared blood with her. From the black pit of his memory, images and words slithered out—of that prince seeing the gold eyes Dorian now met, screeching at him to get away . . . Eyes of the Valg kings. He said carefully, "So would you consider yourself more Valg than human, then?"

"The Valg are my enemy—Erawan is my enemy."

"And does that make us allies?"

She revealed no indication either way. "Is there a young woman in your company named Elide?"

"No." Who in hell was that? "We've never encountered anyone with that name."

Manon closed her eyes for a heartbeat. Her slender throat bobbed. "Have you heard news of my Thirteen?"

"You're the first rider and wyvern we've seen in weeks." He contemplated why she'd asked, why she'd gone so still. "You don't know if they're alive."

And with those iron shavings in her gut . . .

Manon's voice was flat and cold as death. "Tell Aelin Galathynius not to bother using me for negotiations. The Blackbeak Matron will not acknowledge me, either as heir or witch, and all you will get out of it is revealing your precise location."

His magic flickered. "What happened after Rifthold?"

Manon lay back down, angling her head away from him. Spindrift from the open porthole caught in her white hair and set it shimmering in the dim cabin. "Everything has a price."

And it was those words, the fact that the witch had turned her face away and seemed to be waiting for death to claim her, that made him croon, "I once told you to find me again—it seems like you couldn't wait to see my handsome face."

Her shoulders stiffened slightly. "I'm hungry."

He smiled slowly.

As if she'd heard that smile, Manon glared. "*Food.*"

But there was still an edge—a too-fragile edge limning every line of her body. Whatever had happened, whatever she had endured . . . Dorian draped an arm along the back of his chair. "It's coming in a few minutes. I'd hate for you to waste away into nothing. It'd be a shame to lose the most beautiful woman in the world so soon into her immortal, wicked life."

"I am not a woman," was all she said. But hot temper laced those molten gold eyes.

He gave her an indolent shrug, perhaps only because she was indeed in chains, perhaps because, even though the death she radiated thrilled him, it did not strike a chord of fear. "Witch, woman . . . as long as the parts that matter are there, what difference does it make?"

She eased into a sitting position, disbelief and exhausted outrage on that perfect face. She bared her teeth in a silent snarl.

Dorian offered a lazy grin in return. "Believe it or not, this ship has an unnatural number of attractive men and women on board. You'll fit right in. And fit in with the cranky immortals, I suppose."

She glanced toward the door moments before he heard approaching footsteps. They were silent until the knob turned, revealing Aedion's frowning face. "Awake and ready to rip out throats, it seems," the general said by way of greeting. Dorian rose, taking the tray of what looked to be fish stew from him. He wondered if he should test it for poison from the look Aedion was giving Manon. She glared right back at the golden-haired warrior.

Aedion said, "I would have shot you and your runt of a wyvern clean out of the sky if given my way. Be grateful my queen finds you more useful alive."

Then he was gone.

Dorian set the tray within Manon's reach and watched her sniff at it. She took a slow, cautious bite—as if letting it slide into her healing belly and seeing how it settled there. As if indeed testing it for poison. While she waited, Manon said, "You don't give orders on this ship?"

It was a focused effort not to bristle. "You know my circumstances. I am now at the mercy of my friends."

"And the Queen of Terrasen is your friend?"

"There is no one else I'd want guarding my back." Other than Chaol, but . . . it was no use even thinking about him, missing him.

Manon at last took another bite of her fish stew. Then another. And another.

And he realized she was avoiding speaking to him. Enough so that he asked, "It was your grandmother who did that to you, wasn't it?"

Her spoon stilled in the chipped wooden bowl. Slowly, she turned her face toward him. Unreadable, a face crafted of nightmares and midnight fantasies.

"I'm sorry," he admitted, "if the cost of saving me that day in Rifthold was . . . was this."

"Find out if my Thirteen are alive, princeling. Do that, and I am yours to command."

"Where did you last see them?"

Nothing. She swallowed another spoonful.

He pushed, "Were they present when your grandmother did that to you?"

Her shoulders curved a bit, and she scooped another spoonful of cloudy liquid but didn't sip. "The cost of Rifthold was the life of my Second. I refused to pay it. So I bought my Thirteen time to run. The moment I swung my sword at my grandmother, my title, my legion, was forfeit. I lost the Thirteen while I fled. I do not know if they are alive, or if they have been hunted down." Her eyes snapped to his, bright from more than the steam of her stew. "*Find them* for me. Learn if they live or if they have returned to the Darkness."

"We're in the middle of the ocean. There won't be news of anything for a while."

She went back to eating. "They are all I have left."

"Then I suppose you and I are both heirs without crowns."

A humorless snort. Her white hair shifted in the sea breeze.

Dorian rose and walked to the door. "I'll do what I can."

"And—Elide."

Again, that name. "Who is she?"

But Manon was back at her stew. "Just tell Aelin Galathynius that Elide Lochan is alive—and looking for her."

The conversation with the king took everything out of her. Once that food was in her belly, once she'd downed more water, Manon lay back in bed and slept.

And slept.

And slept.

The door banged open at one point, and she had the vague recollection of the Queen of Terrasen, then her general-prince, demanding answers about something. Elide, perhaps.

But Manon had lain there, half awake, unwilling to think or speak.

She wondered if she would have stopped bothering to breathe, if her body hadn't done it all on its own.

She had not realized how impossible the survival of the Thirteen might indeed have been until she was practically begging Dorian Havilliard to find them for her. Until she had found herself desperate enough to sell her sword for any news of them.

If they even wanted to serve her after everything. A Blackbeak—and a Crochan.

And her parents . . . murdered by her grandmother. They had promised the world a child of peace. And she had let her grandmother hone her into a child of war.

The thoughts swirled and eddied, sapping her strength, muting colors and sounds. She awoke and saw to her needs when necessary, ate when food was left, but she let that heavy, meaningless sleep take hold.

Sometimes, Manon dreamed that she was in that room in the Omega, her half sister's blood on her hands and in her mouth. Sometimes, she stood beside her grandmother, a witch fully grown and not the witchling she'd been at the time, and helped the Matron carve up a handsome, bearded man who begged for her life—his offspring's life. Sometimes, she flew over a lush green land, the song of a western wind singing her home.

Often, the dream was that a great cat, pale and speckled like old snow on granite, sat in the cabin with her, its long tail slashing back and forth when it noticed her glazed attention. Sometimes, it was a grinning white wolf. Or a calm-eyed golden mountain lion.

Manon wished they'd put their jaws around her throat and crunch down.

They never did.

So Manon Blackbeak slept. And so she dreamed.

CHAPTER 43

Lorcan was still wondering what the hell he was doing three days later. They'd left that plains town far behind them, but the terror of that night lay draped over the carnival caravan like a heavy blanket with each mile the wagons hurried down the roads.

The others hadn't wised up to how, exactly, they'd survived the ilken—hadn't realized the ilken were near-impossible to kill, and no mere mortal could have slain one, let alone four. Nik and Ombriel gave him and Elide a wide berth—and only catching their wary, examining stares at the dinner campfire every night revealed they were still piecing together who and what he was.

Elide kept well away from him, too. They hadn't had a chance to set up their usual tents thanks to fleeing so quickly, but tonight, safely within the walls of a small plains town, they'd have to share a room at the cheap inn Molly had begrudgingly paid for.

It was hard not to watch Elide as she took in the town, then the inn—the keen-eyed observation, the hint of surprise and confusion that sometimes crossed her face.

He used a tendril of his magic to keep her foot stabilized. She never commented on it. And sometimes that dark, fell magic of his would brush up against whatever it was she carried—the gift from a dying woman to a hotheaded assassin—and recoil.

Lorcan hadn't pushed to see it since that night, though he'd spent a great deal of time contemplating what might have come out of Morath. Collars and rings were likely the start of it.

Whitethorn and the bitch-queen had no idea about the ilken—perhaps about the majority of horrors Elide had shared with him. He wondered what a wall of wildfire would do to the creatures—wondered if the ilken were somehow training against Aelin Galathynius's arsenal. If Erawan was smart, he'd have something in mind.

While the others trudged into the ramshackle inn in search of food and rest, Elide informed Molly that she was going on a walk along the river, and headed into the cobblestone streets. And though his stomach was grumbling, Lorcan trailed her, ever the husband wishing to guard his beautiful wife in a town that had seen better days—decades. No doubt caused by Adarlan's relentless road-building across the continent and the fact that this town had been left far from any artery through the land.

The thunderstorm he'd scented building on the horizon lumbered toward the stone-wrought town, the light shifting from gold to silver. Within minutes, the thick humidity was washed away by a sweep of welcome coolness. Lorcan gave Elide all of three blocks before he fell into step beside her and said, "It's going to rain."

She slid a flat glance at him. "I do know what thunder means."

The walled town had been built on either side of a small, half-forgotten river—two large water gates on either end demanding tolls to enter the city and tracking the goods that passed through. Old water, fish, and rotting wood reached him before the sight of the muddy, calm waters did, and it was precisely at the edge of the river docks that Elide paused.

"What are you looking for?" he asked at last, an eye on the darkening skies. The dockworkers, sailors, and merchants monitored the clouds, too, as they scurried about. Some lingered to tie up the long, flat-bellied barges and latch down the smooth poles they used to navigate the river. He'd seen a kingdom, perhaps three hundred years ago, that relied on barges to sail its goods from one end to another. Its name eluded him, lost to the catacombs of his memory. Lorcan wondered if it still existed, tucked away between two mountain ranges on the other side of the world.

Elide's bright eyes tracked a group of well-dressed men heading into what looked to be a tavern. "Storms mean looking for shelter," she murmured. "Shelter means being stuck inside with nothing to do but gossip. Gossip means news from merchants and sailors about the rest of the land." Those eyes cut to him, dry humor dancing there. "*That* is what thunder means."

Lorcan blinked as she followed after the men who'd entered the dockside tavern. The first fat drops of the storm plunked onto the moss-speckled cobblestones of the quay.

Lorcan followed Elide inside the tavern, some part of him admitting that for all his five hundred years of surviving and killing and serving, he'd never quite encountered someone so . . . unimpressed with him. Even gods-damned Aelin had some sense of the threat he posed. Maybe living with monsters had stripped away a healthy fear of them. He wondered how Elide hadn't become one in the process.

Lorcan took in the details of the taproom by instinct and training, finding nothing worth a second thought. The reek of the place—unwashed bodies, piss, mold, wet wool—threatened to suffocate him. But in the span of a few moments, Elide had grabbed herself a table near a cluster of those people from the docks and ordered two tankards of ale and whatever was the lunch special.

Lorcan slid into the ancient wooden chair beside hers, wondering if the damn thing would collapse under him as it groaned. Thunder cracked overhead, and all eyes shifted to the bay of windows overlooking the quay. Rain fell in earnest, setting the barges bobbing and swaying.

Lunch was dropped before them, the bowls clattering and sending the goopy brown stew splashing over the chipped rims. Elide didn't so much as look at it, or touch the ales that were plunked down with equal disinterest for a tip, as she scanned the room.

"Drink," Elide commanded him.

Lorcan debated telling her not to give him orders, but . . . he liked seeing this small, fine-boned creature in action. Liked seeing her size up a room of strangers and select her prey. Because it was a hunt—for the best and safest source of information. The person who wouldn't report to a town garrison still under Adarlan's control that a dark-haired young woman was asking questions about enemy forces.

So Lorcan drank and watched her while she watched others. So many calculating thoughts beneath that pale face, so many lies ready to spill from those rosebud lips. Part of him wondered if his own queen could find her useful—if Maeve would also pick up on the fact that it was perhaps Anneith herself who'd taught the girl to look and listen and lie.

Part of him dreaded the thought of Elide in Maeve's hands. What she'd become. What Maeve would ask her to do as a spy or courtier. Perhaps it was good that Elide was mortal, life span too short for Maeve to bother honing her into quite possibly her most vicious sentinel.

He was so damn busy thinking about it that he nearly didn't notice when Elide leaned back casually in her chair and interrupted the table of merchants and captains behind them. "What do you mean, Rifthold is gone?"

Lorcan snapped to attention. But they'd heard the news weeks ago.

The captain nearest them—a woman in her early thirties—sized up Elide, then Lorcan, then said, "Well, it's not gone, but . . . witches now control it, on behalf of Duke Perrington. Dorian Havilliard's been ousted."

Elide, the cunning little liar, looked outright shocked. "We've been in the deep wild for weeks. Is Dorian Havilliard dead?" She whispered the words, as if in horror . . . and as if to avoid being heard.

Another person at the table—an older, bearded man—said, "They never found his body, but if the duke's declaring him not to be king anymore, I'd assume he's alive. No use making proclamations against a dead man."

Thunder rattled, almost drowning out her whisper as she said, "Would he—would he go to the North? To . . . her?"

They knew precisely who Elide meant. And Lorcan knew exactly why she'd come here.

She was going to leave. Tomorrow, whenever the carnival rolled out. She'd likely hire one of these boats to take her northward, and he . . . he would go south. To Morath.

The companions swapped glances, weighing the appearance of the young woman—and then Lorcan. He attempted to smile, to look bland and unthreatening. None of them returned the look, though he must have done something right, because the bearded man said, "She's not in the North."

It was Elide's turn to go still.

The bearded man went on, "Rumor has it, she was in Ilium, trouncing soldiers. Then they say she was in Skull's Bay last week, raising hell. Now she's sailing elsewhere—some say to Wendlyn, some say to Eyllwe, some say she's fleeing to the other side of the world. But she's not in the North. Won't be for a while, it seems. Not wise to leave your home undefended, if you ask me. But she's barely a woman; she can't know much about warfare at all."

Lorcan doubted that, and doubted the bitch didn't make a move without Whitethorn or Gavriel's son weighing in. But Elide loosed a shuddering breath. "Why leave Terrasen at all?"

"Who knows?" The woman turned back to her food and company. "Seems like the queen has a habit of showing up where she's least expected, unleashing chaos, and vanishing again. There's good money to be had from the betting pool about where she'll show up next. I say Banjali, in Eyllwe—Vross here says Varese in Wendlyn."

"Why Eyllwe?" Elide pushed.

"Who knows? She'd be a fool indeed to announce her plans." The woman gave Elide a sharp look as if to say to keep quiet about it.

Elide returned to her food and ale, the rain and thunder drowning the chatter in the room.

Lorcan watched her drink the entire tankard in silence. And when it seemed the least suspicious, she rose and left.

Elide went to two other taverns in the town—followed the same exact pattern. The news shifted slightly with each recounting, but the general consensus was that Aelin was on the move, perhaps south or east, and no one knew what to expect.

Elide walked out of the third tavern, Lorcan on her heels. They hadn't spoken once since she'd gone into that first inn. He'd been too lost in contemplating what it would be like to suddenly travel on his own again. To leave her . . . and never see her again.

And now, staring up at the rain and the thunder, Elide said, "I was supposed to go north."

Lorcan found himself not wanting to confirm or object. Like a useless fool, he found himself . . . hesitating to push her toward that original path.

She lowered her face, water and light gilding her high cheekbones. "Where do I head now? How do I find her?"

He dared say, "What did you glean from the rumors?" He'd been analyzing each tidbit of information, but wanted to see that clever mind at work.

And some small part of him wanted to see what she'd decide about their splitting ways, too.

Elide said softly, "Banjali—in Eyllwe. I think she's going to Banjali."

He tried not to look too relieved. He'd arrived at the same conclusion, if only because it was what Whitethorn would have done—and he'd trained the prince himself for a few decades.

She scrubbed at her face. "How . . . how far is it?"

"Far."

She lowered her hands, her features stark and bone white. "How do I get there? How do . . ." She rubbed at her chest.

"I can get you a map," he found himself saying. Just to see if she'd ask him to stay.

Her throat bobbed, and she shook her head, her black hair flowing. "It'd be no use."

"Maps are always useful."

"Not if you can't read."

Lorcan blinked, wondering if he'd heard her right. But color stained her pale cheeks, and that was indeed shame and despair clouding her dark eyes. "But you . . ." There had been no opportunity for it these weeks, he realized—no chance where she might have revealed it.

"I learned my letters, but when—when everything happened," she said, "and I was put in that tower . . . My nursemaid was illiterate. So I never learned more. So I forgot what I did know."

He wondered if he would have ever noticed if she hadn't told him. "You seem to have survived rather impressively without it."

He spoke without considering, but it seemed to be the right thing to say. The corners of her mouth twitched upward. "I suppose I have," she mused.

Lorcan's magic picked up on the garrison before he heard or scented them.

It slithered along their swords—rudimentary, half-rusted weapons—and then bathed in their rising fear, excitement, perhaps even a tinge of bloodlust.

Not good. Not when they were headed right to them.

Lorcan closed the distance to Elide. "It seems our friends at the carnival wanted to make an easy silver coin."

The helpless desperation on her face sharpened into wide-eyed alertness. "Guards are coming?"

Lorcan nodded, the footsteps now close enough for him to count how many approached from the garrison in the heart of the town, no doubt meant to trap them between their swords and the river. If he were the betting sort, he'd gamble that the two bridges that spanned the river—ten blocks up on either side of them—were already full of guards.

"You get a choice," he said. "Either I can end this matter here, and we can go back to the inn to learn if Nik and Ombriel wanted to get rid of us . . ." Her mouth tightened, and he knew her choice before he offered, "Or we can get on one of those barges and get the hell out right now."

"The second," she breathed.

"Good," was his only reply as he gripped her hand and tugged her forward. Even with his power supporting her leg, she was too slow—

"Just do it," she snapped.

So Lorcan hauled her over a shoulder, freeing his hatchet with his other hand, and ran for the water.

Elide bounced and slammed into Lorcan's broad shoulder, craning her head enough to watch the street behind them. No sign of guards, but . . . that little voice who often whispered in her ear now tugged and begged her to go. To get out.

"The gates at the city entrance," she gasped as muscle and bone pummeled into her gut. "They'll be there, too."

"Leave them to me."

Elide tried not to imagine what that meant, but then they were at the docks, Lorcan sprinting for a barge, thundering down the steps of the quay and onto the long wooden dock. The barge was smaller than the others, its one-room chamber in the center painted bright green. Empty—aside from a few boxes of cargo on its prow.

Lorcan pocketed the axe he'd thumbed free, and Elide gripped his shoulder, fingers digging into muscle, as he set her over the high lip of the barge and onto the wooden planks. She stumbled a step as her legs adjusted to the bobbing of the river, but—

Lorcan was already whirling toward the reed-slim man who barreled toward them, a knife out. "That's *my* boat," he bleated. He realized who, exactly, he would be fighting as he cleared the short wooden ladder onto the dock and took in Lorcan's size, the hatchet *and* sword now in the warrior's broad hands, and the expression of death surely on his face.

Lorcan said simply, "It's our boat now."

The man glanced between them. "You—you won't clear the bridges or the city walls—"

Moments. They had only moments before the guards came—

Lorcan said to the man, "Get in. *Now.*"

The man began backing away.

Elide braced her hand on the broad, raised side of the boat and said calmly, "He will kill you before you clear the ladder. Get us out of the city, and I swear you'll be set free once we're clear."

"You'll slit my throat then, as good as you will now," the man said, gulping in air.

Indeed, Lorcan's hatchet bobbed in that way she'd learned meant he was about to throw it.

"I would ask you to reconsider," Elide said.

Lorcan's wrist twitched ever so slightly. He'd do it—he'd kill this innocent man, just to get them free—

The man's knife drooped, then vanished into the sheath at his side. "There's a bend in the river past the town. Drop me off there."

That was all Elide needed to hear as the man rushed toward them, untying lines and leaping into the boat with the ease of someone who'd done it a thousand times. He and Lorcan grabbed the poles to push out into the river, and as soon as they were loose, Lorcan hissed, "If you betray us, you'll be dead before the guards can even board." The man nodded, now steering them toward the eastern exit of the town, as Lorcan dragged her into the one-room cabin.

The cabin interior was lined with windows, all clean enough to suggest the man took some pride in his boat. Lorcan half shoved her under a table in its center, the embroidered cloth covering it shielding her from anything but sounds: Lorcan's footsteps going silent, though she could feel him taking up a hiding place to monitor the proceedings from within the cabin; the patter of rain on the flat roof; the thud of the pole as it occasionally knocked into the side of the barge.

Her body soon ached from holding herself still and quiet.

Was this to be her life for the foreseeable future? Hunted and hounded across the world?

And finding Aelin . . . How would she ever do that? She could go back to Terrasen, but she didn't know who ruled from Orynth. If Aelin had not taken back her throne . . . Perhaps it was an unspoken message that danger lay there. That all was not well in Terrasen.

But to go to Eyllwe on a bit of speculation . . . Of all the rumors Elide had listened to in the past two hours, that captain's reasons had been the wisest.

The world seemed to still with some unspoken tension, a ripple of fear.

But then the man's voice was calling out again, and metal groaned—a gate. The city gates.

She stayed under the table, counting her breaths, thinking through all that she'd heard. She doubted the carnival would miss them.

And she'd bet all the money in her boot that Nik and Ombriel had been the ones who'd set the guards on them, deciding she and Lorcan were too much of a threat—especially with the ilken hunting her. She wondered if Molly had known all along, from that very first meeting, that they were liars and had let Nik and Ombriel sell them out when the bounty was too good to pass up, the cost of loyalty too great.

Elide sighed through her nose. A splash sounded, but the boat ambled onward.

At least she'd taken the little bit of stone with her, though she'd miss her clothes, shabby as they were. These leathers were growing stuffy in the oppressive heat, and if she were to go to Eyllwe, they'd be sweltering—

Lorcan's footsteps sounded. "Get out."

Wincing as her ankle barked in pain, she crawled from under the table and peered around. "No trouble?"

He shook his head. He was splattered with rain or river water. She peered around him to where the man had been steering the boat. No one there—or in the rear of the boat.

"He swam to shore back at the bend," Lorcan explained.

Elide loosed a breath. "He might very well run to town and tell them. It won't take long for them to catch up."

"We'll deal with it," Lorcan said, turning away. Too fast. He avoided her eyes too fast—

She took in the water, the stains now on the sleeves of his shirt. Like . . . like he'd washed his hands quickly, sloppily.

She glanced at the hatchet at his side as he strode out of the cabin. "You killed him, didn't you?" That was what the splash had been. A body being dumped over the side.

Lorcan halted. Looked over a broad shoulder. There was nothing human in his dark eyes. "If you want to survive, you have to be willing to do what is necessary."

"He might have had a family depending on him." She'd seen no wedding ring, but it didn't mean anything.

"Nik and Ombriel didn't give us that consideration when they reported us to the garrison." He stalked onto the deck, and she stormed after him. Lush trees lined the river, a living shield around them.

And there—there was a *stain* on the planks, shining and dark. Her stomach rose.

"You planned to lie to me about it," she seethed. "But how would you explain *that*?"

A shrug. Lorcan took up the pole and moved with fluid grace to the side of the barge, where he pushed them away from an approaching sandbank.

He had *killed* that man— "I *swore* to him he'd be set free."

"You swore it, not me."

Her fingers curled into fists. And that thing—that stone—wrapped in that bit of cloth inside her jacket began to stir.

Lorcan stilled, the pole gripped tight in his hands. "What is that," he said too softly.

She held her ground. Like hell she'd back down from him, like hell she'd allow him to intimidate her, overrule her, *kill people* so they could escape—

"What. Is. That."

She refused to speak, to even touch the lump in her pocket. It thrummed and grumbled, a beast opening an eye, but she didn't dare to reach out, to so much as acknowledge that strange, otherworldly presence.

Lorcan's eyes widened slightly, then he was setting down the pole and stalking across the deck and into the cabin. She lingered by the edge, unsure whether to follow or perhaps jump into the water and swim to shore, but—

There was a thud of metal on metal, as if something was being cracked open, and then—

Lorcan's roar shook the boat, the river, the trees. Long-legged river birds hauled themselves into flight.

Then Lorcan flung open the door, so violently it nearly ripped off its hinges, and hurled what looked to be the shards of a broken amulet into the river. Or he tried to. Lorcan threw it hard enough that it cleared the river entirely and slammed into a tree, gouging out a chunk of wood.

He whirled, and Elide's anger stumbled a step at the blistering wrath twisting his features. He prowled for her, grabbing the pole as if to keep from throttling her, and said, "*What is it that you carry?*"

And the demand, the violence and entitlement and arrogance, had her seeing red, too. So Elide said with quiet venom, "Why don't you just slit my throat and find out for yourself?"

Lorcan's nostrils flared. "If you have a problem with my killing someone who *reeked* of itching to betray us the moment he got the chance, then you are going to *love* your queen."

For a while now, he'd hinted that he knew of her, that he knew of her well enough to call her horrible things, but— "What do you mean?"

Lorcan, gods above, looked as if his temper had at last slipped its leash as he said, "Celaena Sardothien is a nineteen-year-old assassin—who calls herself the best in the world." A snort. "She killed and reveled and shopped her way through life and never once apologized for it. She gloried in it. And then this spring, one of *my* sentinels, Prince Rowan Whitethorn, was tasked to deal with her when she washed up on Wendlyn's shores. Turns out, he fell in love with her instead, and she with him. Turns out, whatever they were doing up in the Cambrian Mountains got her to stop calling herself Celaena and start going by her true name again." A brutal smile. "Aelin Galathynius."

Elide could barely feel her body. "What?" was about the only word she could manage.

"Your fire-breathing queen? She's a gods-damned assassin. Trained to be a killer from the moment your mother died defending her. Trained to be no better than the man who butchered your mother and your royal family."

Elide shook her head, her hands slackening. "What?" she said again.

Lorcan laughed mirthlessly. "While you were locked in that tower for ten years, she was indulging in the riches of Rifthold, spoiled and coddled by her master—the King of the Assassins—whom she murdered in cold blood this spring. So you'll find that your long-lost savior is little better than I am. You'll find that she would have killed that man the same as I did, and would have as little tolerance for your whining as I do."

Aelin . . . an assassin. Aelin—the same person she'd been tasked to give the stone to . . .

"You knew," she said. "This whole time we've been together—you knew I was looking for the same person."

"I told you that to find one would be to find the other."

"You *knew*, and you didn't tell me. Why?"

"You still haven't told me your secrets. I don't see why I should tell all of mine, either."

She squeezed her eyes shut, trying to ignore the dark stain on the wood—trying to soothe the sting of his words and seal the hole that had opened beneath her feet. What had been in that amulet? Why had he roared and—

"Your little queen," Lorcan sneered, "is a murderer, and a thief, and a liar. So if you're going to call me such things, then be prepared to fling them at her, too."

Her skin was too tight, her bones too brittle to bear the anger that took control. She scrambled for the right words to hurt him, wound him, as if they were fistfuls of rocks that she could hurl at Lorcan's head.

Elide hissed, "I was wrong. I said you and I were the same—that we had no family, no friends. But I have none because land and circumstance separate me from them. You have none because no one can stomach being around you." She tried—and succeeded, if the ire that rippled in his eyes was any indication—to look down her nose at him, even with him towering over her. "And you know what is the biggest lie you tell everyone, Lorcan? It's that you prefer it that way. But what I hear, when you rant about my *bitch-queen*? All I hear are the words of someone who is deeply, deeply jealous, and lonely, and *pathetic*. All I hear are the words of someone who saw Aelin and Prince Rowan fall in love and resented them for their happiness—because *you* are so unhappy." She couldn't stop the words once they started flinging out. "So call Aelin a murderer and a thief and a liar. Call her a bitch-queen and a fire-breather. But forgive me if I take it upon myself to be the judge of those things when I meet her. Which I *will* do." She pointed to the muddy gray river flowing around them. "I'm going to Eyllwe. Take me ashore and I'll wash my hands of you as easily as you washed the blood of that man off yours."

Lorcan looked her over, teeth bared enough to show those slightly elongated canines. But she didn't care about his Fae heritage, or his age, or his ability to kill.

After a moment, he went back to pushing the pole against the river bottom—not to bring them to shore, but to guide them along.

"Did you not hear what I said? *Take me to shore.*"

"No."

Her rage overcame any sort of common sense, any warning from Anneith as she stormed over to him. *"No?"*

He let the pole drag in the water and turned his face to her. No emotion—not even anger lingered there. "The river veered southward two miles ago. From the map in the cabin, we can take it straight south, then find the fastest route to Banjali." She wiped the rain from her dripping brow as Lorcan brought his face close enough for them to share breath. "Turns out, I now have business with Aelin Galathynius, too. Congratulations, Lady. You just got yourself a guide to Eyllwe."

A cold, killing light was in his eyes, and she wondered what the hell he'd roared about.

But those eyes dipped to her mouth, clamped tight in her rage. And a part of her that had nothing to do with fear went still at the attention, even as other parts went a bit molten.

Lorcan's eyes at last found her own, and his voice was a midnight growl as he said, "As far as anyone's concerned, you're still my wife."

Elide didn't object—even as she walked back into the cabin, his insufferable magic helping with her limp, and slammed the door shut so hard the glass rattled.

Storm clouds drifted away to reveal a star-flecked night and a moon bright enough for Lorcan to navigate the narrow, sleepy river.

He steered them hour after hour, contemplating precisely how he was going to murder Aelin Galathynius without Elide or Whitethorn getting in the way, and then how he was going to slice up her corpse and feed it to the crows.

She had lied to him. She *and* Whitethorn had tricked him that day the prince had handed over the Wyrdkey.

There'd been nothing inside the amulet but one of those rings—an utterly useless Wyrdstone ring, wrapped in a bit of parchment. And on it was written in a feminine scrawl:

> *Here's hoping you discover more creative terms than "bitch" to call me when you find this.*
>
> *With all my love,*
>
> *A.A.G.*

He'd kill her. Slowly. Creatively. He'd been forced to swear a blood promise that Mala's ring truly offered immunity from the Valg when it was worn—he hadn't thought to demand that their Wyrdkey was real, too.

And Elide—what Elide carried, what had made him realize it . . . He'd think about that later. Contemplate what to do with the Lady of Perranth later.

His only consolation was that he'd stolen Mala's ring back, but the little *bitch* still had the key. And if Elide needed to go to Aelin anyway . . . Oh, he'd find Aelin for Elide.

And he'd make the Queen of Terrasen crawl before the end of it.

CHAPTER 44

The world began and ended in fire.

A sea of fire with no room for air, for sound beyond the cascading molten earth. The true heart of fire—the tool of creation and destruction. And she was drowning in it.

Its weight smothered her as she thrashed, seeking a surface or a bottom to push off from. Neither existed.

As it flooded her throat, surging into her body and melting her apart, she began screaming noiselessly, begging it to halt—

Aelin.

The name, roared into the core of flame at the heart of the world, was a beacon, a summons. She'd been born waiting to hear that voice, had blindly sought it her whole life, would follow it unto the ending of all things—

"AELIN."

Aelin bowed off the bed, flame in her mouth, her throat, her eyes. Real flame.

Golds and blues wove among simmering swaths of reds. Real flame, erupting from her, the sheets scorched, the room and the rest of the bed spared from incineration, the *ship in the middle of the sea* spared from incineration, by an uncompromising, unbreakable wall of air.

Hands wrapped in ice squeezed her shoulders, and through the flame, Rowan's snarling face appeared, commanding her to breathe—

She took a breath. More flame rushed down her throat.

There was no tether, no leash to bring her magic to heel. Oh, gods—oh, gods, she couldn't even feel a burnout threatening nearby. There was nothing but this flame—

Rowan gripped her face in his hands, steam rippling where his ice and wind met her fire. "You are its master; *you* control it. Your fear grants it the right to take over."

Her body arced off the mattress again, utterly naked. She must have burned her clothes—Rowan's favorite shirt. Her flames burned wilder.

He gripped her hard, forcing her to meet his eyes as he snarled, "I see you. I see every part of you. And I am not afraid."

I will not be afraid.

A line in the burning brightness.

My name is Aelin Ashryver Galathynius . . .

And I will not be afraid.

As surely as if she grabbed it in her hand, the leash appeared.

Darkness flowed in, blessed and calm where that burning pit of flame had raged.

She swallowed once, twice. "Rowan."

His eyes gleamed with near-animal brightness, scanning every inch of her.

His heartbeat was rampant, thundering—panicked. "Rowan," she repeated.

Still he did not move, did not stop staring at her, searching for signs of harm. Something in her own chest shifted at his panic.

Aelin grasped his shoulder, digging in her nails at the violence rampant on every line of his body, as if he'd loosed whatever leashes he kept on himself in anticipation of fighting to keep *her* in this body and not some goddess or worse. "Calm down. *Now.*"

He did no such thing. Rolling her eyes, she tugged his hands from her face to lean over and throw the sheets off them. "I am fine," she said, enunciating each word. "You saw to that. Now, get me some water. I'm thirsty."

A basic, easy command. To serve, in the way he'd explained that Fae males *liked* to be needed, to fulfill some part of them that wanted to fuss and dote. To drag him back up to that level of civilization and reason.

Rowan's face was still harsh with feral wrath—and the insidious terror running beneath it.

So Aelin leaned in, nipped his jaw, making sure her canines scratched, and said onto his skin, "If you don't start acting like a prince, you can sleep on the floor."

Rowan pulled back, his savage face not wholly of this world, but slowly, as if the words sank in, his features softened. He was still looking pissy, but not so near *killing* that invisible threat against her, as he leaned in, nipping her jaw in return, and said into her ear, "I'm going to make you regret using such threats, Princess."

Oh, gods. Her toes curled, but she gave him a simpering smile as he rose to his feet, every muscle in his naked body rippling with the movement, and watched him pad with feline grace to the washstand and ewer atop it.

The bastard had the nerve to look her over as he lifted the jug. And then give her a satisfied, male smile as he poured a glass right to the brim, halting with expert precision.

She debated sending a lick of flame to burn his bare ass as he set down the jug with emphasized care and calm. And then stalked back to the bed, eyes on her every step of the way, and set the water on the small table beside it.

Aelin rose on surprisingly steady knees and faced him.

Only the creaking of the ship and hissing of the waves against it filled the room.

"What was that?" she asked quietly.

His eyes shuttered. "It was . . . me losing control."

"Why?"

He glanced at the porthole and moon-kissed sea beyond. So rare for him to avoid her stare.

"Why?" she pushed.

Rowan at last met her gaze. "I didn't know if she'd taken you again." No matter that the Wyrdkey now lay beside the bed and not around her neck. "Even when I realized you were just in the magic's thrall, I still . . . The magic took you away. It's been a long time since I wasn't certain . . . since I didn't know how to get you back." He bared his teeth, loosing a jagged breath, the wrath now directed inward. "Before you call me a territorial Fae bastard, allow me to apologize and explain that it is *very* difficult—"

"Rowan." He stilled. She crossed the small lingering distance between them, every step like the answer to some question she'd asked from the moment her soul had sparked into existence. "You are not human. I do not expect you to be."

He almost seemed to recoil. But she put a hand on his bare chest, over his heart. It still thundered beneath her palm.

She said softly, feeling that heart beneath her hand, "I do not care if you are Fae, or human, if you are Valg or a gods-damned skinwalker. You are what you are. And what I want . . . what I *need*, Rowan, is someone who does not apologize for it. For who they are. You have never once done so." She leaned forward to kiss the bare skin where her hand had been. "Please don't start doing it now. Yes, sometimes you piss me the hell off with that Fae territorial nonsense, but . . . I heard your voice. It woke me up. It led me out of that . . . place."

He bowed his head until his brow leaned against hers. "I wish I had more to offer you—during this war, and beyond it."

She slid her arms around his bare waist. "You offer me more than I ever hoped for." He seemed to object, but she said, "And I figured since both Darrow and Rolfe informed me I needed to sell my hand in marriage for the sake of this war, I should do the opposite."

A snort. "Typical. But if Terrasen needs—"

"Here is the way I see it," she said, pulling back to examine his harsh face. "We do not have the luxury of time. And a marriage to a foreign kingdom, with its contracts and distances, plus the months it takes to raise and send an army . . . we do not *have* that time. We only have *now*. And what I don't need is a husband who will try to get into a pissing contest with me, or who I'll have to cloister somewhere for his own safety, or who will hide in a corner when I wake up with flames all around me." She kissed his tattooed chest again, right over that mighty, thundering heart. "This, Rowan—*this* is all I need. Just this."

The reverberations of his deep, rattling breath echoed into her cheek, and he stroked a hand over her hair, along her bare back. Lower. "A court that can change the world."

She kissed the corner of his mouth. "We'll find a way—together." The words he'd given her once, the words that had begun the healing of her shattered heart. And his own. "Did I hurt—" Her words were a rasp.

"No." He brushed a thumb over her cheekbone. "No, you didn't hurt me. Or anything else."

Something in her chest caved in, and Rowan gathered her in his arms as she buried her face in his neck. His calloused hands caressed her back, over each and every scar and the tattoos he'd inked on her.

"If we survive this war," she murmured after a while onto his bare chest, "you and I are going to have to learn how to relax. To sleep through the night."

"If we survive this war, Princess," he said, running a finger down the groove of her spine, "I'll be happy to do anything you want. Even learn how to relax."

"And if we never have a moment's peace, even after we get the Lock, the keys, and send Erawan back to his hellhole realm?"

The amusement faded, replaced by something more intent as his fingers stilled on her back. "Even if we have threats of war every other day, even if we have to host fussy emissaries, even if we have to visit god-awful kingdoms and play nice, I'll be happy to do it, if you're at my side."

Her lips trembled. "Och, you. Since when did you learn to make such pretty speeches?"

"I just needed the right excuse to learn," he said, kissing her cheek.

Her body went taut and molten in all the right places as his mouth moved lower, pressing gentle, biting kisses to her jaw, her ear, her neck. She dug her fingers into his back, baring her throat as his canines scratched lightly.

"I love you," Rowan breathed onto her skin, and flicked his tongue over the spot where his canines had scratched. "I'd walk into the burning heart of hell itself to find you."

He almost had mere minutes ago, she wanted to say. But Aelin only arched her back a bit more, a small, needy noise coming out of her. This—*him* . . . Would it ever stop—the wanting? The need to not only be near him, but to have him so deep in her she felt their souls twining, their magic dancing . . . The tether that had led her out of that burning core of madness and destruction.

"Please," she breathed, nails digging into his lower back in emphasis.

Rowan's low groan was his only answer as he hoisted her up. She wrapped her legs around his waist, letting him carry her not to the bed, but to the wall, and the sensation of the cool wood against her back, compared to the heat and hardness of him pushing into her front—

Aelin panted through her gritted teeth as he again dragged his tongue over that spot on her neck. "*Please.*"

She felt his smile against her skin as Rowan thrust into her in a long, powerful stroke—and bit down on her neck.

A claiming, mighty and true, that she understood he so desperately needed. That *she* needed, and with his teeth in her, his body in her . . . She was going to combust, she was going to splinter apart from the overwhelming *need*—

Rowan's hips began to move, setting a lazy, smooth pace as he kept his canines buried in her neck. As his tongue slid along the twin points of pleasure edged with finest pain, and he tasted her very essence as if it were wine.

He laughed, low and wicked, as release had her biting down on his shoulder to keep from screaming loud enough to wake the creatures sleeping on the bottom of the sea.

When Rowan finally drew his mouth away from her neck, his magic healing the small holes he'd left, his hands tightened on her thighs, pinning her to the wall as he moved deeper, harder.

Aelin only dragged her fingers through his hair as she gave him a savage kiss, and tasted her own blood on his tongue.

She whispered onto his mouth, "I'll always find a way back to you."

This time, when Aelin went over the edge, Rowan plummeted with her.

Manon Blackbeak awoke.

There had been no sound, no smell, no hint of *why* she'd awoken, but those predatory instincts had sensed something amiss and sent her tumbling from sleep.

She blinked as she sat up, her wound now a dull ache—and found her head clear of whatever that haze had been.

The room was near-black, save for the moonlight that trickled through the porthole to illuminate her cramped cabin. How long had she been lost to sleep and hideous melancholy?

She listened carefully to the creaking of the ship. A faint grumbling sounded from above—Abraxos. Still alive. Still—sleeping, if she knew that drowsy, wheezing grumble.

She tested the manacles on her wrists, lifting them to peer at the lock. A clever sort of contraption, the chains thick and anchored soundly into the wall. Her ankles were no better.

She couldn't remember the last time she'd been in chains. How had Elide endured it for a decade?

Maybe she'd find the girl once she got out of here. She doubted the Havilliard king had any news of the Thirteen anyway. She'd sneak onto Abraxos's back, fly for the coast, and find Elide before tracking down her coven. And then . . . she didn't know what she'd do. But it was better than lying here like a worm in the sun, letting whatever despair had seized control these days or weeks wreak havoc on her.

But as if she'd summoned him, the door opened.

Dorian stood there, a candle in his—

Not a candle. Pure flame wreathed his fingers. It set his sapphire eyes glowing bright as he found her lucid. "Was it you—who sent that ripple of power?"

"No." Though it didn't take much guessing to suspect who it'd been, then. "Witches don't have magic like that."

He angled his head, his blue-black hair stained gold by his flames. "But you're long-lived."

She nodded, and he took that as an invitation to slide into his usual chair. "It's called the Yielding," she said, a chill brushing down her spine. "The bit of magic we have. We usually cannot summon or wield, but for one moment in a witch's life, she can summon great power to unleash upon her enemies. The cost is that she is incinerated in the blast, her body yielded to the Darkness. In the witch wars, witches on both sides made Yieldings during every battle and skirmish."

"It's suicide—to blow yourself into smithereens . . . and take enemies with you."

"It is, and it's not pretty. As the Ironteeth witch yields life to the Darkness, its power fills her, and unleashes from her in an ebony wave. A manifestation of what lies in our souls."

"Have you seen it done?"

"Once. By a scared young witch who knew she wouldn't win glory any other way. Only, she took out half our Ironteeth force as well as the Crochans."

Her mind snagged on the word. *Crochans.* Her people—

Not her people. She was a gods-damned Blackbeak—

"Will the Ironteeth use it on us?"

"If you're facing lower-level covens, yes. Older covens are too arrogant, too skilled to choose the Yielding instead of fighting their way out. But younger, weaker covens get spooked, or wish to win valor through sacrifice."

"It's murder."

"It's war. War is sanctioned murder, no matter what side you're on." Ire flickered on his face, and she asked, "Have you ever killed a man?"

He opened his mouth to say no, but the light in his hand died.

He had. When he'd been collared, she guessed. The Valg inside him had done it. Multiple times. And not cleanly.

"Remember what they made you do," Manon said, "when you face them again."

"I doubt I'll ever forget it, witchling." He stood, heading for the door.

Manon said, "These chains are rubbing my skin raw. Surely you've some sympathy for chained things." Dorian paused. She lifted her hands, displaying the chains. "I'll give my word not to do any harm."

"It's not my call. Now that you're talking again, maybe telling Aelin what she's been pushing you about will get you on her good side."

Manon had no idea what the queen had been demanding of her. None.

"The longer I stay in here, *princeling*, the more likely I am to do something stupid when you release me. Let me at least feel the wind on my face."

"You've got a window. Go stand in front of it."

Part of her sat up straight at the harshness, the *maleness* in that tone, in the set of those broad shoulders. She purred, "If I had been asleep, would you have lingered to stare at me for a while?"

Icy amusement gleamed there. "Would you have objected?"

And perhaps she was reckless and wild and still a bit stupid from blood loss, but she said, "If you plan to sneak in here in the darkest hours of the night, you should at least have the decency to ensure I get something out of it."

His lips twitched, though the smile was cold and sensuous in a way that made her wonder what playing with a king blessed with raw magic might be like. If he'd make her beg for the first time in her long life. He looked capable of it—perhaps willing to let a little cruelty into the bedroom. Her blood thrummed. "As tempting as seeing you naked and chained might be . . ." A soft lover's laugh. "I don't think you'd enjoy the loss of control."

"And you've been with so many women to be able to judge a witch's wants so easily?"

That smile turned lazy. "A gentleman never tells."

"How many?" He was only twenty—though he was a prince, now a king. Women had likely been falling over themselves for him since his voice had deepened.

"How many men have *you* been with?" he countered.

She smirked. "Enough to know how to handle the needs of mortal princelings. To know what will make you beg." Never mind that she was contemplating the opposite.

He drifted across the room, past the range of her chains, right into her own breathing space. He leaned over her, nearly nose-to-nose, nothing at all amused in his face, in the cut of his cruel, beautiful mouth, as he said,

"I don't think you can handle the sort of things I need, witchling. And I am never begging for anything again in my life."

And then he left. Manon stared after him, a hiss of rage slipping from her own lips. At the opportunity she hadn't taken to grab him, hold him hostage, and demand her freedom; at the arrogance in his assumption; at the heat that had gathered in her core and now throbbed insistently enough that she clamped her legs together.

She had never been denied. Men had fallen to pieces, sometimes literally, to crawl into her bed. And she . . . She didn't know what she would have done if he had taken up her offer, if she would have decided to learn what the king could do, exactly, with that beautiful mouth and toned body. A distraction—and an excuse to loathe herself even more, she supposed.

She was still seething at the door when it opened again.

Dorian leaned against the aged wood, his eyes still glazed in a way she couldn't tell was lust or hatred or both. He slid the lock shut without looking at it.

Her heartbeat picked up, her entire immortal focus narrowed to his steady, unhurried breathing, the unreadable face.

His voice was rough as he said, "I won't waste my breath telling you how stupid it would be to try to take me hostage."

"I won't waste mine telling you to take only what I offer you and nothing more."

Her ears strained to listen, but even his damned heart was a solid beat. Not a whiff of fear. He said, "I need to hear you say yes." His eyes flicked to the chains.

It took her a moment to comprehend, but she let out a low laugh. "So considerate, princeling. But yes. I do this of my own free will. It can be our little secret."

She was nothing and no one now anyway. Sharing a bed with her enemy was nothing compared to the Crochan blood that flowed in her veins.

She began to unbutton the white shirt she'd been wearing for gods knew how long, but he growled, "I'll do it myself."

Like hell he would. She touched the second button.

Invisible hands wrapped around her wrists, tightly enough that she dropped the shirt.

Dorian prowled to her. "I said that I'd do it." Manon took in each inch of him as he towered over her, and a shiver of pleasure rippled through her. "I suggest you listen."

The pure male *arrogance* in that statement alone—

"You're courting death if you—"

Dorian lowered his mouth to hers.

It was a featherlight graze, barely a whisper of touch. Intent, calculated, and so unexpected she arched into it a bit.

He kissed the corner of her mouth with the same silken gentleness. Then the other corner. She didn't move, didn't even breathe—like every part of her body was waiting to see what he'd do next.

But Dorian pulled back, studying her eyes with a cool detachment. Whatever he beheld there made him step away.

The invisible fingers on her wrists vanished. The door unlatched. And that cocky grin returned as Dorian shrugged with one shoulder and said, "Maybe another night, witchling."

Manon almost bellowed as he slipped out the door—and didn't return.

CHAPTER 45

The witch was lucid but pissed off.

Aedion had the pleasure of serving her breakfast and tried not to note the lingering scent of female arousal in the cabin, or that Dorian's scent was entwined among it.

The king was entitled to move on, Aedion reminded himself hours later as he scanned the late afternoon horizon from the ship's helm. In the quiet hours of his watches, he'd often mulled over the thorough scolding Lysandra had given him regarding his anger and cruelty toward the king. And maybe—just maybe—Lysandra was right. And maybe the fact that Dorian could even look at a female with interest after seeing Sorscha beheaded was a miracle. But . . . the witch? *That* was what he wanted to tangle with?

He asked Lysandra as much when she joined him thirty minutes later, still soaked from patrolling the waters ahead. All clear.

Lysandra finger-combed her inky sheet of hair, frowning. "I had clients who lost their wives or lovers, and wanted something to distract them. Wanted the opposite of who their beloved had been, perhaps to make the act feel wholly separate. What he went through would change anyone. He might very well find himself now attracted to dangerous things."

"He already had a penchant for them," Aedion murmured, glancing to where Aelin and Rowan sparred on the main deck, sweat gleaming golden as the afternoon light shifted toward evening. Dorian perched on the nearby steps up to the quarterdeck, Damaris braced over his knees, half awake in the heat. Part of Aedion smiled, knowing Rowan would no doubt kick his ass for it.

"Aelin was dangerous, but still human," Lysandra observed. "Manon is . . . not. He probably likes it that way. And I'd stay out of it if I were you."

"I'm not getting in the middle of that disaster, don't worry. Though I wouldn't let those iron teeth near my favorite part if I were him." Aedion grinned as Lysandra tipped her head back and laughed. He added, "Besides, watching Aelin and the witch go head-to-head this morning about Elide was enough to remind me to stay the hell back and enjoy the spectacle."

Little Elide Lochan—alive and out there, searching for them. Gods above. The look on Aelin's face when Manon had revealed detail after detail, what Vernon had tried to do to the girl . . .

There would be a reckoning in Perranth for that. Aedion himself would hang the lord by his intestines. While Vernon was still breathing. And then he'd get started on paying Vernon back for the ten years of horror Elide had endured. For the maimed foot and the chains. For the tower.

Locked in a tower—in a city he'd visited so many times in the past ten years he had no count. She might have even watched the Bane from that spire as they came and left the city. Possibly thinking he'd forgotten or didn't care about her, either.

And now she was out there. Alone.

With a permanently mangled foot, no training, and no weapons. If she was lucky, perhaps she'd run into the Bane first. His commanders would recognize her name, protect her. That is, if she dared to reveal herself at all.

It had taken all his self-control not to strangle Manon for abandoning the girl in the middle of Oakwald, for not flying her right to Terrasen.

Aelin, however, hadn't bothered with restraint.

Two strikes, both so fast even the Wing Leader didn't see them.

A backhanded blow to Manon's face. For leaving Elide.

And then a ring of fire around Manon's throat, slamming her into the wood, as Aelin made her swear the information was correct.

Rowan had drily reminded Aelin that Manon was responsible for Elide's escape and rescue, too. Aelin had merely said if Manon hadn't been, the fire would already be down her throat.

And that was that.

Aelin, from the fervor with which she sparred with Rowan across the deck, was still pissed.

The witch, from the snarling and scent in her cabin, was still pissed.

Aedion was more than ready to get to the Stone Marshes—even if what awaited them there might not be so pleasant.

Three more days lay between them and the eastern coast. And then . . . then they'd all see how much Rolfe's alliance was worth, if the man could be trusted.

"You can't avoid him forever, you know," Lysandra said, drawing his attention to the *other* reason he needed to get off this ship.

His father sat near where Abraxos had curled along the prow, guarding and observing the wyvern. Learning how to kill them—where to strike.

No matter that the wyvern was little more than an oversized hound, docile enough that they hadn't bothered to chain him. They had none big enough anyway, and the beast would likely refuse to leave this ship until Manon did. Abraxos only moved to hunt for fish or larger game, Lysandra escorting him in sea dragon form beneath the waves. And when the beast was sprawled on the deck . . . the Lion kept him company.

Aedion had barely spoken to Gavriel since Skull's Bay.

"I'm not avoiding him," Aedion said. "I just have no interest in talking to him."

Lysandra flipped her wet hair over a shoulder, frowning at the damp splotches on her white shirt. "I, for one, would like to hear the story of how he crossed paths with your mother. He's kind—for one of Maeve's cadre. Better than Fenrys."

Indeed, Fenrys made Aedion want to shatter things. That laughing face, the swaggering, dark arrogance . . . It was another mirror, he realized. But one who tracked Aelin everywhere like some dog. Or wolf, he supposed.

Aedion hadn't pitted himself against the male in the sparring ring, but he'd carefully watched Fenrys take on Rowan and Gavriel, both of whom had trained the male. Fenrys fought as he'd expect a warrior with centuries of training by two lethal killers to fight. But he had not glimpsed another whisper of the magic that allowed Fenrys to leap between places as if walking through some invisible doorway.

As if his thoughts summoned the immortal warrior, Fenrys swaggered out from the shadows below deck and smirked at them all before taking up his sentry position near the foremast. They were all on a schedule of watches and patrols, Lysandra and Rowan usually tasked with flying far out of sight to survey behind and ahead or communicate with the two escort ships. Aedion hadn't dared tell the shifter that he often counted the minutes until she returned, that his chest always felt unbearably tight until he spotted whatever winged or finned form she wore returning to them.

Like his cousin, he had no doubt the shifter wouldn't take well to his *fussing.*

Lysandra was carefully watching Aelin and Rowan, their blades like quicksilver, as they met each other blow for blow. "You've been doing well with your lessons," Aedion told the shifter.

Lysandra's green eyes crinkled. They'd all been taking turns walking the shifter through handling various weapons and hand-to-hand combat. Lysandra knew some from her time with Arobynn—he'd taught her as a way of ensuring the survival of his *investment*, she'd told him.

But she wanted to know more. How to kill men in a myriad of ways. It shouldn't have thrilled him as much as it had. Not when she'd laughed off the claim Aedion had made on the beach that day in Skull's Bay. She hadn't mentioned it again. He hadn't been stupid enough to, either.

Aedion trailed Lysandra, unable to help it, as she drifted toward where the queen and prince sparred, Dorian scooting over on the steps to silently offer her a space. Aedion marked the gesture and the king's respect, shoving aside his own warring feelings about it as he lingered above them, and focused on his cousin and Rowan.

But they'd worked themselves into an impasse—enough so that Rowan called it off and sheathed his sword. Then flicked Aelin's nose when she looked pissy at not winning. Aedion laughed under his breath, glancing to the shifter as the queen and prince strode for the water jug and glasses against the stair railing and helped themselves.

He was about to offer Lysandra a final round in the ring before the sun set when Dorian braced his arms on his knees and said to Aelin through the stair railing, "I don't think she'll do anything if we let her out."

Aelin took a dainty sip of her water, still breathing hard. "Did you arrive at that conclusion before, during, or after you visited her in the middle of the night?"

Oh, gods. It was going to be that sort of conversation.

Dorian gave a half smile. "You have a preference for immortal warriors. Why can't I?"

It was the faint click of her glass on the small table that made Aedion brace himself—really start calculating the layout of the various decks. Fenrys still monitored them from the foremast, Lysandra remained on

Dorian's other side. He supposed that, standing above Dorian on the stairs and Aelin beside them, he'd be right in the middle.

Exactly where he'd sworn not to be.

Rowan, on the other side of Aelin, said to Dorian, "Is there a reason, Majesty, that you believe the witch should be free?"

Aelin shot him a look of pure flame. Good—let the prince deal with her wrath. Even days after the claiming that had left everyone pretending they didn't notice the two puncture wounds on Rowan's neck or the delicate, vicious scratches over his shoulders, the Fae Prince still looked like a male who had barely survived a storm and had enjoyed every wild second of it.

Not to mention the twin wounds on Aelin's neck this morning. He'd almost begged her to find a scarf.

"Why don't we lock one of you in a room"—Dorian pointed with his chin at the Fae warriors across the deck, at Lysandra to his right—"and see how well you fare after so much time."

Aelin said, "Every inch of her has been designed to ensnare men. To make them think she's harmless."

"Trust me, Manon Blackbeak is anything but harmless."

Aelin charged on, "She and her kind are killers. They are raised without conscience. Regardless of what her grandmother did to her, she will always be that way. I will not endanger the lives of the people on this ship so you can sleep better at night." Her eyes shone with the unspoken jab.

They all shifted, and Aedion was about to ask Lysandra to spar, conversation closed, when Dorian said a bit too quietly, "I am king, you know."

Turquoise-and-gold eyes snapped to Dorian. Aedion could almost see the words Aelin fought to think through, her temper begging her to shut down the challenge. With a few choice sentences, she could fillet his spirit like a fish, further shredding the scraps of the man who remained after the Valg prince had violated him. And in doing so, lose a strong ally she'd need not just in this war, but if they survived it. And—those eyes softened a bit. A friend. She'd lose that, too.

Aelin rubbed at the scars on her wrists, stark in the golden light of the setting sun. Ones that made Aedion sick to look at. She said to Dorian after a moment, "Controlled movements. If she leaves the room, she stays under guard—one of the Fae at any given time, plus one of us. Shackles on her wrists, not feet. No chains for the room, but a guard outside the door."

Aedion caught the thumb Rowan brushed over one of those scars on her wrist.

Dorian just said, "Fine."

Aedion debated telling the king that a compromise from Aelin should be outright celebrated.

Aelin's voice dropped to that lethal purr. "After you finished flirting with her that day in Oakwald, she and her coven tried to kill me."

"You provoked her," Dorian countered. "And I sit here today because of what she risked when she came to Rifthold *twice*."

Aelin wiped the sweat from her brow. "She has her own reasons, and I highly doubt it was because she, in her one hundred years of killing, decided your pretty face would turn her good."

"Yours turned Rowan from three centuries of a blood oath."

It was Aedion's father who said calmly as he left his perch near Abraxos on the prow to approach them, "I'd suggest, Majesty, that you pick another argument."

Indeed, Aedion's every instinct came to attention at the frozen anger now limning the prince's every muscle.

Dorian noticed it, too, and said, perhaps a bit guiltily, "I meant no offense, Rowan."

Gavriel angled his head, golden hair sliding over his broad shoulder, and said with a ghost of a smile, "Don't worry, Majesty. Fenrys has given Whitethorn enough shit for it to last him another three centuries."

Aedion blinked at the humor, the hint of a smile.

But Aelin saved him the effort of deciding whether or not to answer that smile by saying to Dorian, “Well? Let’s see if the Wing Leader would like to take a turn about the deck before dinner.”

Dorian was right to look wary, Aedion decided. But Aelin was already heading for the opposite side of the deck, Fenrys peeling off from his post by the foremast, that edged, bitter gaze sliding over them all while they passed.

But Fenrys would follow, no doubt. Like hell would they unleash the witch without all of them there. Even the cadre seemed to understand that.

So Aedion trailed after his queen into the dimness of the ship, night setting in above them, and prayed Aelin and Manon weren’t about to rip the boat to shreds.

Climbing into bed with a witch. Aelin ground her teeth as she headed for Manon’s room.

Dorian had once been notorious when it came to women, but *this* . . . Aelin snorted, wishing Chaol were present, if only to see the look on *his* face.

Even if it eased something tight in her chest to know Chaol and Faliq were in the South. Perhaps raising an army to cross the Narrow Sea and march northward. If they were all lucky.

If. Aelin hated that word. But . . . her friendship with Dorian was precarious enough. She’d yielded to his request partially out of some scrap of kindness, but mostly because she knew there was more Manon had to tell them about Morath. About Erawan. Lots more.

And she doubted the witch would be forthcoming—especially when Aelin had lost her temper just a *little* bit this morning. And maybe it made her a conniving, hideous person for using Dorian’s interest as a veil to butter up the witch, but . . . it was war.

Aelin flexed her hand as she neared the witch’s room, the lights swaying in the rougher waves they’d encountered since midday.

Rowan had healed the bruise on the back of her knuckles from the blow she'd dealt the witch—and she'd thanked him by locking the door to their room and getting on her knees before him. She could still feel his fingers fisted in her hair, still hear his groan—

Rowan, now a step beside her, whipped his head in her direction. *What the hell are you thinking about?*

But his pupils had flared enough that she was well aware he knew precisely where her mind had gone as they walked down to the witch's cabin. That Fenrys hung far back down the hall told her enough about the change in her scent.

The usual things, she shot back at Rowan with a simpering smile. *Killing, crocheting, how to make you emit those noises again—*

Rowan's face took on a pained expression that had her grinning. Especially as his throat bobbed while he swallowed—hard. *Round two*, he seemed to say. *As soon as this is dealt with. We're having round two. This time,* I *get to see what noises you make.*

Aelin nearly walked into the doorpost of Manon's open cabin. Rowan's low laugh made her focus, made her stop smiling like a lust-addled, love-sick idiot—

Manon was sitting upright in bed, golden eyes darting between Rowan and Dorian and her.

Fenrys slid in behind them, his attention going right to the witch. No doubt stunned by the beauty, the grace, the *blah-blah-blah* perfectness of her.

Manon said, low and flat, "Who is this?"

Dorian lifted a brow, following her gaze. "You've met him before. He's Fenrys—sworn warrior of Queen Maeve."

It was the narrowing of Manon's eyes that had some instinct pricking. The flare of the witch's nostrils as she scented the male, his smell barely detectable in the cramped cabin—

"No, he's not," Manon said.

The witch's iron nails flashed out a heartbeat before Fenrys struck.

CHAPTER 46

It was still instinct to go for a knife before Aelin went for her magic.

And as Fenrys leaped for Manon with a snarl, it was Rowan's power that sent him slamming through the room.

Before the male had finished sliding across the floor, Aelin had a wall of flame up between them. "What the *hell*," she spat.

On his knees, Fenrys clawed at his throat—at the air Rowan was choking off.

The cabin was too small for them all to fit without getting too close. Ice danced at Dorian's fingertips as he slid beside Manon, still chained by the bed.

"What did you mean, that's not Fenrys?" Aelin said to the witch without taking her eyes off him. Rowan let out a grunt behind her.

And Aelin watched with a mix of horror and fascination as Fenrys's chest expanded in a mighty breath. As he got to his feet and surveyed that wall of flame.

As if Rowan's magic had worn off.

And as Fenrys's skin seemed to glow and melt away, as a creature as pale as fresh snow emerged from the vanishing illusion, Aelin gave Aedion a subtle look over her shoulder.

Her cousin instantly moved, keys to Manon's chains appearing from his pocket.

But Manon didn't move as the thing took form, all the spindly limbs, its wings tucked in tight; the hideous warped face sniffing them—

Manon's chains clanked free.

Aelin said to the thing beyond her wall of flame, "What are you?"

Manon answered for it. "Erawan's Bloodhound."

The thing smiled, revealing rotted black stumps of teeth. "At your service," it said. *She* said, Aelin realized as she noted the small, shriveled breasts on its narrow chest. "So your guts stayed in," it purred to Manon.

"Where is Fenrys?" Aelin demanded.

The Bloodhound's smile didn't falter. "On patrol of the ship, on another level, I assume. Unaware, just as you were unaware, that one of your own wasn't truly with you while I—"

"Ugh, another talker," Aelin said, flipping her braid over a shoulder. "Let me guess: you killed a sailor, took his place, learned what you needed to about how to get Manon off this ship and our patrols, and . . . what? You planned to carry her off into the night?" Aelin frowned at the thing's thin body. "You look like you could barely lift a fork—and haven't in months."

The Bloodhound blinked at her—then hissed.

Manon let out a low laugh.

Aelin said, "Honestly? You could have just snuck in here and saved yourself a thousand stupid steps—"

"*Shifter*," the thing hissed, hungrily enough that Aelin's words stumbled.

Its enormous eyes had gone right to Lysandra, snarling softly in the corner in ghost leopard form.

"*Shifter*," it hissed again, that longing twisting its features.

And Aelin had a feeling she knew what this thing had begun as. What Erawan had trapped and mutilated in the mountains around Morath.

"As I was saying," Aelin drawled as best she could, "you really brought this upon yourself—"

"I came for the Blackbeak heir," the Bloodhound panted. "But look at you all: a trove worth your weight in gold."

Its eyes went murky, as if it were no longer here, as if it had drifted into another room—

Shit.

Aelin attacked with her flame.

The Bloodhound screamed—

And Aelin's flame melted away into steam.

Rowan was instantly there, shoving her back, sword out. Her magic—

"You should have given me the witch," the Bloodhound laughed, and ripped the porthole clean out of the side of the ship. "Now he knows who you travel with, what ship you sail . . ."

The creature lunged for the hole it had hewn in the side of the ship, spindrift misting in.

A black-tipped arrow slammed into its knee, then another one.

The Bloodhound went down an inch from freedom.

Snarling as he stepped into the room, Fenrys fired another, pinning its shoulder into the wood planks.

Apparently, he didn't take well to being impersonated. He gave Rowan a seething look that said as much. And that demanded how they all hadn't noticed the difference.

But the Bloodhound wrenched herself up, black blood spraying the room, filling it with her reek. Aelin had a dagger angled, ready to fly; Manon was about to pounce; Rowan's hatchet was cocked—

The Bloodhound chucked a strap of black leather into the center of the room.

Manon stopped dead.

"Your Second screamed when Erawan broke her," the Bloodhound said. "His Dark Majesty sends this to remember her by."

Aelin didn't dare take her eyes off the creature. But she could have sworn Manon swayed.

And then the Bloodhound said to the witch, "A gift from a King of the Valg . . . to the last living Crochan Queen."

Manon stared and stared at that braided leather band—the one Asterin had worn every day, even when battle did not demand it—and did not care what the Bloodhound had declared to the others. Did not care if she was heir to the Blackbeak Witch-Clan or Queen of the Crochans. Did not care if—

Manon did not finish the thought over the roar that silenced everything in her head.

The roar that came out of her mouth as she launched herself at the Bloodhound.

The arrows through the beast scratched at Manon as she tackled that dewy, bony body into the wood. Claws and teeth slashed for her face, but Manon got her hands around that neck, and iron tore through damp skin.

Then those claws were pinned in the wood beneath phantom hands as Dorian sauntered over, face so unyieldingly unmoved. The Bloodhound thrashed, those claws trying to wrench free—

The creature screamed as those invisible hands crunched down on bone.

Then through it.

Manon gaped at the severed hands a moment before the Bloodhound screamed, so loud her own ears rang. But Dorian crooned, "Be done with it."

Manon lifted her other hand, wanting iron to shred her and not steel.

The others watched behind them, weapons ready.

But the Bloodhound panted, "Don't you want to know what your Second said before she died? What she *begged* for?"

Manon hesitated.

"What a horrible brand on her stomach—*unclean*. Did you do that yourself, Blackbeak?"

No. No, no, no—

"A baby; she said she'd birthed a stillborn witchling."

Manon froze entirely.

And didn't particularly care as the Bloodhound lunged for her throat, teeth bared.

It was not flame or wind that snapped the Bloodhound's neck.

But invisible hands.

The crunch echoed through the room, and Manon whirled on Dorian Havilliard. His sapphire eyes were utterly merciless. Manon snarled. "How *dare* you take my kill—"

Men on the deck began screaming, and Abraxos roared.

Abraxos.

Manon turned on her heel and sprinted through the wall of warriors, careening down the hall, up the stairs—

Her iron nails tore chunks out of the slippery wood as she hauled herself up, stomach aching. Muggy night air hit her, then the sea's scent, then—

There were six of them.

Their skin was not bone white like the Bloodhound's, but rather a mottled darkness—bred for shadows and stealth. Winged, all with humanoid faces and bodies—

Ilken, one of them hissed as it disemboweled a man in one swipe of its claws. *We are the ilken, and we have come to feast.* Indeed, pirates were dead on the deck, blood a coppery tang that filled her senses as she raced for where Abraxos's roar had sounded.

But he was airborne, flapping high, tail swinging.

The shape-shifter in wyvern form at his side.

Taking on three of the smaller figures, so much more nimble as they—

Flame blasted into the night, along with wind, and ice.

One ilken melted. The second had its wings snapped. And the third—the third froze into a solid block and shattered upon the deck.

Eight more ilken landed, one ripping into a screaming sailor's neck on the foredeck—

Manon's iron teeth snapped down. Flame blasted again, spearing for the approaching terrors.

Only for them to sail through it.

The ship became a melee as wings and talons tore into delicate human hides, as the immortal warriors unleashed themselves upon the ilken that landed on the deck.

Aedion hurtled after Aelin the moment the wyvern roared.

He got as far as the main deck before those *things* attacked.

Before Aelin's flame ruptured from the deck ahead, and he realized his cousin could look after herself because *shit*, the Valg king had been busy. *Ilken*, they'd called themselves.

There were two of them now before him on the quarterdeck, where he'd run to spare the first mate and captain from having their organs ripped out of their bellies. Both beasts were nearly eight feet and born of nightmares, but in their eyes . . . those were human eyes. And their scents . . . like rotted meat, but . . . human. Partially.

They stood between him and the stairs back to the main deck. "What a bounty this hunt has yielded," one said.

Aedion didn't dare take his attention off them, though he vaguely heard Aelin ordering Rowan to go help the other ships. Vaguely heard a wolf and a lion's snarl, and felt the kiss of cold as ice slammed into the world.

Aedion gripped his sword, flipping it once, twice. Had the Pirate Lord sold them out to Morath? The way that Bloodhound had looked at Lysandra—

His rage became a song in his blood.

They sized him up, and Aedion flipped his sword again. Two against one—he might stand a chance.

That was when the third lunged from the shadows behind him.

Aelin killed one with Goldryn. Beheading.

The other two . . . They hadn't been too pleased by it, if their incessant shrieking in the moments following was any indication.

A lion's roar cleaved the night, and Aelin prayed Gavriel was with Aedion somewhere—

The two in front of her, blocking the way belowdecks, finally stopped their hissy fits long enough to ask, "Where are your flames now?"

Aelin opened her mouth. But then Fenrys leaped out of a patch of night as if he'd simply run through a doorway, and slammed into the one nearest. He had a score to settle, it seemed.

Fenrys's jaws went around the ilken's throat, and the other whirled, claws out.

She was not fast enough to stop it as two sets of claws slashed through the white coat, through the shield he kept on himself, and Fenrys's cry of pain barked across the water.

Twin swords of flame plunged through two ilken necks.

Heads rolled onto the blood-slick deck.

Fenrys staggered back, making it all of a step before he crashed to the planks. Aelin surged for him, swearing.

Blood and bone and greenish slime—poison. Like those on the wyverns' tails.

Like blowing out a thousand candles, she pushed aside her flame, rallied that healing water. Fenrys shifted back into a male, his teeth clenched, swearing low and vicious, a hand against his torn ribs. "*Don't move,*" she told him.

She'd immediately sent Rowan to the other ships, and he'd tried to argue, but . . . had obeyed. She had no idea where the Wing Leader was—the *Crochan Queen*. Holy gods.

Aelin readied her magic, trying to calm her raging heart—

"The others," panted Aedion, limping for them, coated in black blood, "are fine." She almost sobbed in relief—until she noticed the way her cousin's eyes shone, and that . . . that Gavriel, bloodied and limping worse than Aedion, was a step behind his son. What the hell had happened?

Fenrys groaned, and she focused on his wounds, that poison slithering into his blood. She opened her mouth to tell Fenrys to lower his hand when wings flapped.

Not the kind she loved.

Aedion was instantly before them, sword out, grimacing in pain—but one of the ilken lifted a claw-tipped hand. *Parley.*

Her cousin halted. But Gavriel shifted imperceptibly closer to the ilken as it sniffed at Fenrys and smiled.

"Don't bother," the thing told Aelin, laughing quietly. "He won't have much longer to live."

Aedion snarled, palming his fighting knives. Aelin rallied her flame. Only the hottest of her fire could kill them—anything less and they remained unscathed. She'd think about the long-term implications of it later.

"I was sent to deliver a message," the ilken said, smiling over a shoulder toward the horizon. "Thank you for confirming in Skull's Bay that you carry what His Dark Majesty seeks."

Aelin's stomach dropped to her feet.

The key. Erawan knew she had the Wyrdkey.

CHAPTER 47

Rowan hauled ass back to their ship, his magic near-flinging him through the air.

The other two ships had been left undisturbed—they'd even had the nerve to demand what the hell all the shouting was about.

Rowan hadn't bothered to explain other than an enemy attack and to drop anchor until it was over before he'd left. He'd returned to carnage.

Returned with his heart beating so wildly he thought he'd vomit with relief as he swept in for the landing and beheld Aelin kneeling on the deck. Until he saw Fenrys bleeding beneath her hands.

Until that last ilken landed before them.

His rage honed itself into a lethal spear, his magic rallying as he dove through the sky, aiming for the deck. Concentrated bursts, he'd discovered, could get through whatever repellant had been bred into them.

He'd rip the thing's head right off.

But then the ilken laughed right as Rowan landed and shifted, looking over its thin shoulder. "Morath looks forward to welcoming you," the creature smirked, and launched skyward before Rowan could lunge for it.

But Aelin wasn't moving. Gavriel and Aedion, bloodied and limping, were barely moving. Fenrys, his chest a bloody mess with greenish slime—*poison* . . .

Power glowed at Aelin's hands as she knelt over Fenrys, concentrating on that bit of water she'd been given, a drop of water in a sea of fire . . .

Rowan opened his mouth to offer to help when Lysandra panted from the shadows, "Is anyone going to deal with that thing, or should I?"

Indeed, the ilken was flapping for the distant coast, barely more than a bit of blackness against the darkened sky, hurtling for the coast, no doubt to fly right to Morath to report.

Rowan snatched up Fenrys's fallen bow and quiver of black-tipped arrows.

None of them stopped him as he strode to the railing, blood splashing beneath his boots.

The only sounds were the tapping waves, the whimpering of the injured, and the groan of the mighty bow as he nocked an arrow and drew back the string. Farther and farther. His arms strained, but he honed in on that dark speck flapping away.

"A gold coin says he misses," Fenrys rasped.

"Save your breath for healing," Aelin snapped.

"Make it two," Aedion said behind him. "I say he hits."

"You can all go to hell," Aelin snarled. But then added, "Make it five. Ten says he downs it with the first shot."

"Deal," Fenrys groaned, his voice thick with pain.

Rowan gritted his teeth. "Remind me why I bother with any of you."

Then he fired.

The arrow was nearly invisible as it sailed through the night.

And with his Fae sight, Rowan saw with perfect clarity as that arrow found its mark.

Right through the thing's head.

Aelin laughed quietly as it hit the water, its splash visible even from the distance.

Rowan turned and scowled down at her. Light shimmered at her fingertips as she held them over Fenrys's ravaged chest. But he turned his glare on the male, then on Aedion, and said, "Pay up, pricks."

Aedion chuckled, but Rowan caught the shadow in Aelin's eyes as she resumed healing his former sentinel. Understood why she'd made light of it, even with Fenrys injured before her. Because if Erawan now knew their whereabouts . . . they had to move. Fast.

And pray Rolfe's directions to the Lock weren't wrong.

Aedion was sick of surprises.

Sick of feeling his heart stop dead in his chest.

As it had when Gavriel had leaped to save his ass with the ilken, the Lion tearing into them with a ferocity that had left Aedion standing there like a novice with his first practice sword.

The stupid bastard had injured himself in the process, earning a swipe down his arm and ribs that set the male roaring in pain. The venom coating those claws, mercifully, had been used up on other men.

But it was the tang of his father's blood that launched Aedion into action—that coppery, mortal scent. Gavriel had only blinked at him as Aedion had ignored the throbbing pain in his leg, courtesy of a blow moments before right above his knee, and they'd fought back-to-back until those creatures were nothing but twitching heaps of bone and flesh.

He hadn't said a word to the male before sheathing sword and shield across his back and stalking to find Aelin.

She still knelt over Fenrys, offering Rowan nothing more than a pat on his thigh as he stormed past to help with the other wounded. A pat on the thigh—for making a shot that Aedion was fairly certain most of his Bane would have judged to be impossible.

Aedion set down the pail of water she'd asked him to get for Fenrys, trying not to wince as she wiped away the green poison that oozed out. A few feet away, his father was tending to a blubbering pirate—who had barely more than a tear to the thigh.

Fenrys hissed, and Aelin let out a grunt of pain herself. Aedion pushed in. "What?"

Aelin shook her head once, a sharp dismissal. But he watched as she locked eyes with Fenrys—locked and held them in a way that told Aedion whatever she was about to do would hurt. He'd seen that same look pass between healer and soldier a hundred times on killing fields and in the healers' tents afterward.

"Why," Fenrys panted, "didn't"—another pant—"you just melt them?"

"Because I wanted to get some information out of them before you charged in, you bossy Fae bastard." She gritted her teeth again, and Aedion braced a hand on her back as the poison no doubt brushed against her magic. As she tried to wash it out. She leaned a bit into his touch.

"Can heal on my own," Fenrys rasped, noting the strain. "Get to the others."

"Oh, please," she snapped. "You're all insufferable. That thing had *poison* on its claws—"

"The others—"

"Tell me how your magic works—how you can leap between places like that." A clever, easy way to keep him focused elsewhere.

Aedion scanned the deck, making sure he wasn't needed, and then carefully sopped up the blood and poison leaking from Fenrys's chest. It had to hurt like hell. The insistent throbbing in his leg was likely nothing by comparison.

"No one knows where it comes from—what it is," Fenrys said between shallow breaths, fingers curling and uncurling at his sides. "But it lets me slip between folds in the world. Only short distances, and only a few times before I'm drained, but . . . it's useful on a killing field." He panted through his clenched teeth as the outer edges of his gash began to reach for each other. "Aside from that, I've got nothing special. Speed, strength, swift healing . . . more than the average Fae, but the same stock of gifts. I can shield myself and others, but can't summon an element."

Aelin's hand wavered slightly over his wound. "What's your shield made of, then?"

Fenrys tried and failed to shrug. But Gavriel muttered from where he worked on the still-whimpering pirate, "Arrogance."

Aelin snorted, but didn't dare take her eyes off Fenrys's injury as she said, "So you do have a sense of humor, Gavriel."

The Lion of Doranelle gave a wary smile over his shoulder. The rare-sighted, restrained twin to Aedion's own flashing grins. Aelin had called him *Uncle Kitty-Cat* all of one time before Aedion had snarled viciously enough to make her think carefully before using the term again. Gavriel, to his credit, had merely given Aelin a long-suffering sigh that seemed to be used only when she or Fenrys were around.

"That sense of humor only appears about once every century," Fenrys rasped, "so you'd better hope you Settle, or else that's the last time you'll see it." Aelin chuckled, though it faded quickly. Something cold and oily slid into Aedion's gut. "Sorry," Fenrys added, wincing either at the words or the pain.

Aelin asked before Aedion let his words sink in, "Where did you come from? Lorcan, I know, was a bastard in the slums."

"Lorcan was a bastard in Maeve's palace, don't worry," Fenrys smirked, his bronze face wan. Aelin's lips twitched toward a smile. "Connall and I were the sons of nobles who dwell in the southeastern part of Maeve's lands . . ." He hissed.

"Your parents?" Aedion pressed when Aelin herself seemed to be straining for words. He'd seen her heal little cuts, and slowly repair Manon's wound over days, but . . .

"Our mother was a warrior," Fenrys said, each word labored. "She trained us as such. Our father was, too, but was often away at war. She was tasked with defending our home, our lands. And reporting to Maeve." Rasping, laboring breaths from both of them. Aedion shifted so that Aelin could lean wholly against him, biting down on the weight it put on his already-swollen knee. "When Con and I were thirty, we were straining at the leash to go to Doranelle with her—to see the city, meet the queen, and do . . . what young males like to do with money in their pockets and youth on their sides. Only Maeve took one look at us and . . ." He needed longer to catch his breath this time. "It didn't go well from there."

Aedion knew the rest; so did Aelin.

The last of the green slime slid out of Fenrys's chest. And Aelin breathed, "She knows you hate the oath, doesn't she?"

"Maeve knows," Fenrys said. "And I have no doubt she sent me here, hoping I'd be tortured by the temporary freedom."

Aelin's hands were shaking, her body shuddering against his own. Aedion slipped an arm around her waist. "I'm sorry you're bound to her," was all Aelin managed.

The wounds in Fenrys's chest began knitting together. Rowan stalked over as if sensing she was fading.

Fenrys's face was still grayish, still taut, as he glanced up at Rowan and said to Aelin, "This is what we are meant to do—protect, serve, cherish. What Maeve offers is . . . a mockery of that." He surveyed the wounds now healing on his chest, mending so slowly. "But it is what calls to a Fae male's blood, what guides him. What we're all looking for, even when we say we're not."

Aedion's father had gone still over the wounded pirate.

Aedion, surprising even himself, said over his shoulder to Gavriel, "And do you find Maeve fulfills that—or are you like Fenrys?"

His father blinked, about all the shock he'd show, and then straightened, the wounded sailor before him now sleeping off the healing. Aedion bore the brunt of his tawny stare, tried to shut out the kernel of hope that shone in the Lion's eyes. "I come from a noble house as well, the youngest of three brothers. I wouldn't inherit or rule, so I took to soldiering. It earned Maeve's eye, and her offer. There was—is no greater honor."

"That's not an answer," Aedion said quietly.

His father rolled his shoulders. Fidgeting. "I only hated it once. Only wanted to leave once."

He didn't continue. And Aedion knew what the unspoken words were.

Aelin brushed a strand of hair out of her face. "You loved her that much?"

Aedion tried not to let his gratitude that she'd asked for him show.

Gavriel's hands were white-knuckled as they folded into fists. "She was a bright star in centuries of darkness. I would have followed that star to the ends of the earth, if she had let me. But she didn't, and I respected her wishes to stay away. To never seek her out again. I went to another continent and didn't let myself look back."

The ship's creaking and the groaning of the injured were the only sounds. Aedion clamped down on the urge to stand and walk away. He'd look like a child—not a general who'd fought his way through knee-deep gore on killing fields.

Aelin said, again because Aedion couldn't bring himself to say the words, "You would have tried to break the blood oath for her? For them?"

"Honor is my code," Gavriel said. "But if Maeve had tried to harm either you or her, Aedion, I would have done everything in my power to get you out."

The words hit Aedion, then flowed through him. He didn't let himself think about it, the truth he'd felt in each word. The way his name had sounded on his father's lips.

His father checked the injured pirate for any lingering injuries, then moved on to another. Those tawny eyes slid to Aedion's knee, swollen beneath his pants. "You need to tend to that, or it'll be too stiff to function in a few hours."

Aedion felt Aelin's attention snap to him, scanning him for injury, but he held his father's gaze and said, "I know how to treat my own injuries." The battlefield healers and the Bane had taught him enough over the years. "Tend to your own wounds." Indeed, the male had blood crusting his shirt. Lucky—so lucky the venom had already been wiped off those claws. Gavriel blinked down at himself, his band of tattoos bobbing as he swallowed, then continued without another word.

Aelin pushed off Aedion at last, trying and failing to get to her feet. Aedion reached for her as the focus went out of her now-dull eyes, but Rowan was already there, smoothly sweeping her up before she kissed the planks. Too fast—she must have drained her reserves too fast, and without any food in her system.

Rowan held his stare, Aelin's hair limp as she rested her head against his chest. The strain—Aedion's guts twisted at it. Morath knew what it was going up against. *Who* it was going up against. Erawan had built his commanders accordingly. Rowan nodded as if in confirmation of Aedion's thoughts, but only said, "Elevate that knee."

Fenrys had slipped into a light sleep before Rowan carried Aelin below.

So Aedion kept his own company for the rest of the night: first on watch, then sitting against the mast on the quarterdeck for a few hours, knee indeed elevated, unwilling to descend into the cramped, dim interior.

Sleep was finally starting to tug at him when wood groaned a few feet behind, and he knew it did so only because she willed it, to keep from startling him.

The ghost leopard sat beside him, tail twitching, and met his eyes for a moment before she laid her enormous head on his thigh.

In silence, they watched the stars flicker over the calm waves, Lysandra nuzzling her head against his hip.

The starlight stained her coat with muted silver, and a smile ghosted Aedion's lips.

CHAPTER 48

They worked through the night, weighing anchor only long enough for the crew to patch up the hole in Manon's room. It would hold for now, the captain told Dorian, but gods help them if they hit another storm before they got to the marshes.

They tended to the wounded for hours, and Dorian was grateful for the little healing magic Rowan had taught him as he pieced flesh back together. Pretending it was a puzzle, or bits of torn cloth, kept his meager dinner from coming back up. But the poison . . . He left that to Rowan, Aelin, and Gavriel.

By the time the morning had shifted into a sickly gray, their faces were sallow, dark smudges etched deep beneath their eyes. Fenrys, at least, was limping around, and Aedion had let Aelin tend to his knee only long enough to get him walking again, but . . . They'd seen better days.

Dorian's legs were wobbling a bit as he scanned the blood-soaked deck. Someone had dumped the creatures' bodies overboard, along with the worst of the gore, but . . . If what the Bloodhound had said was true, they didn't have the luxury of pulling into a harbor to fix the rest of the damage to the ship.

A low, rumbling growl sounded, and Dorian looked across the deck, to the prow.

The witch was still there. Still tending to Abraxos's wounds, as she had been all night. One of the creatures had bit him a few times—thankfully, no poison in their teeth, but . . . he'd lost some blood. Manon had not let anyone near him.

Aelin had tried once, and when Manon snarled at her, Aelin had cursed enough to make everyone else halt, saying she'd rutting deserve it if the beast died. Manon had threatened to rip out her spine, Aelin had given her a vulgar gesture, and Lysandra had been forced to monitor the space between them for an hour, perched in the rigging of the mainmast in ghost leopard form, tail swaying in the breeze.

But now . . . Manon's white hair was limp, the warm morning wind tugging lazily at the strands as she leaned against Abraxos's side.

Dorian knew he was toeing a dangerous line. The other night, he'd been ready to slowly strip her naked, to put those chains to good use. And when he'd found her gold eyes devouring him as intently as he wanted to devour other parts of her . . .

As if sensing his stare, Manon peered over at him.

Even from across the deck, every inch between them went taut.

Of course, Aedion and Fenrys instantly noted it, pausing where they now washed blood off the deck, and the latter snorted. Both had healed enough to walk, but neither moved to interfere as Manon prowled toward him. If she hadn't fled or attacked yet, they must have decided she wasn't going to bother doing so now.

Manon took up a space at the rail, gazing out at the endless water, the wisps of pink clouds smeared along the horizon. Dark blood stained her shirt, her palms. "Do I have you to thank for this freedom?"

He braced his forearms on the wooden rail. "Maybe."

Gold eyes slid to him. "The magic—what is it?"

"I don't know," Dorian said, studying his hands. "It felt like an extension of me. Like real hands I could command."

For a heartbeat, he thought of how they'd felt pinning her wrists—how her body had reacted, loose and tense where he usually liked it to be, while his mouth had barely caressed hers. Her golden eyes flared as if recalling it as well, and Dorian found himself saying, "I wouldn't harm you."

"You liked killing the Bloodhound, though."

He didn't bother keeping the ice from his eyes. "Yes."

Manon stepped close enough to brush a finger over the pale band around his throat, and he forgot that there was a ship full of people watching. "You could have made her suffer—you went for a clean blow instead. Why?"

"Because even with our enemies, there's a line."

"Then you have your answer."

"I didn't ask a question."

Manon snorted. "You've had that look in your eyes all night—if you're becoming a monster like the rest of us. The next time you kill, remind yourself of that line."

"Where do you stand on that line, witchling?"

She met his gaze, as if willing him to see a century of all that she'd done. "I am not mortal. I do not play by your rules. I have killed and hunted men for sport. Do not mistake me for a human woman, *princeling*."

"I have no interest in human women," he purred. "Too breakable."

Even as he said it, the words struck some deep, aching wound in him.

"The ilken," he said, pushing past that pain. "Did you know about them?"

"I assume they are a part of whatever is in those mountains."

A hoarse female voice snapped, "What do you mean, *whatever is in those mountains*?"

Dorian nearly leaped out of his skin. Aelin, it seemed, had been taking some notes from her ghost leopard friend. Even Manon blinked at the blood-drenched queen now behind them.

Manon eyed Aedion and Fenrys as they heard Aelin's demand and came over, followed by Gavriel. Fenrys's shirt was still hanging in strips. At least Rowan was now keeping watch from the rigging, and Lysandra was off flying overhead, scouting for danger.

The witch said, "I never saw the ilken. Only heard of them—heard their screaming as they died, then their roaring as they were remade. I didn't know that's what they were. Or that Erawan would send them so far from their aerie. My Shadows caught a glimpse of them, just once. Their description matches what attacked last night."

"Are the ilken mostly scouts or warriors?" Aelin said.

The fresh air seemed to have made Manon amenable to divulging information, because she leaned her back against the railing, facing the cabal of killers around them. "We don't know. They used the cloud cover to their advantage. My Shadows can find anything that doesn't want to be found, and yet they could not hunt or track these things."

Aelin tensed a bit, scowling at the water flowing past them. And then she said nothing, as if the words had vanished and exhaustion—something heavier than that—had set in.

"Snap out of it," Manon said.

Aedion loosed a warning growl.

Aelin slowly lifted her eyes to the witch, and Dorian braced himself.

"So you miscalculated," Manon said. "So they tracked you. Don't get distracted with the minor defeats. This is war. Cities will be lost, people slaughtered. And if I were you, I would be more concerned about *why* they sent so few of the ilken."

"If you were me," Aelin murmured in a tone that had Dorian's magic rising, ice cooling his fingertips. Aedion's hand slid to his sword. "If you were me." A low, bitter laugh. Dorian had not heard that sound since . . . since a blood-soaked bedroom in a glass castle that no longer existed. "Well, you are *not* me, Blackbeak, so I'll trust you to keep your musings on the matter to yourself."

"I am not a Blackbeak," Manon said.

They all stared at her. But the witch merely watched the queen.

Aelin said with a wave of her scar-flecked hand, "Right. *That* matter of business. Let's hear the story, then."

Dorian wondered if they would come to blows, but Manon simply waited a few heartbeats, looked toward the horizon again, and said, "When my grandmother stripped me of my title as heir and Wing Leader, she also stripped my heritage. She told me that my father was a Crochan Prince, and she had killed my mother and him for conspiring to end the feud between our peoples and break the curse on our lands."

Dorian glanced to Aedion. The Wolf of the North's face was taut, his Ashryver eyes shining bright, churning at the possibilities of all that Manon implied.

Manon said a bit numbly, as if it was the first time she'd even spoken it to herself, "I am the last Crochan Queen—the last direct descendant of Rhiannon Crochan herself."

Aelin only sucked on a tooth, brows lifting.

"And," Manon continued, "whether my grandmother acknowledges it or not, I am heir to the Blackbeak Clan. My witches, who have fought at my side for a hundred years, have spent most of it killing Crochans. Dreaming of a homeland that *I* promised to return them to. And now I am banished, my Thirteen scattered and lost. And now I am heir to our enemy's crown. So you are not the only one, *Majesty*, who has plans that go awry. So get yourself together and figure out what to do next."

Two queens—there were two queens among them, Dorian realized.

Aelin closed her eyes and let out a rough, breathy laugh. Aedion again tensed, as if that laugh might easily end in violence or peace, but Manon stood there. Weathering the storm.

When Aelin opened her eyes, her smile subdued but edged, she said to the Witch-Queen, “I knew I saved your sorry ass for a reason.”

Manon’s answering smile was terrifying.

The males all seemed to loosen a tight breath, Dorian himself included.

But then Fenrys pulled at his lower lip, scanning the skies. “What I don’t get is why wait so long to do any of this? If Erawan wants you lot dead”—a nod toward Dorian and Aelin—“why let you mature, grow powerful?”

Dorian tried not to shudder at the thought. How unprepared they’d been.

“Because I escaped Erawan,” Aelin said. Dorian tried not to remember that night ten years ago, but the memory of it snapped through him, and her, and Aedion. “He thought I was dead. And Dorian . . . his father shielded him. As best he could.”

Dorian shut out that memory, too. Especially as Manon angled her head in question.

Fenrys said, “Maeve knew you were alive. Odds are, so did Erawan.”

“Maybe she told Erawan,” Aedion said.

Fenrys whipped his head to the general. “She’s never had any contact with Erawan, or Adarlan.”

“As far as you know,” Aedion mused. “Unless she’s a talker in the bedroom.”

Fenrys’s eyes darkened. “Maeve does not share power. She saw Adarlan as an inconvenience. Still does.”

Aedion countered, “Everyone can be bought for a price.”

“Nameless is the price of Maeve’s allegiance,” Fenrys snapped. “It can’t be purchased.”

Aelin went utterly still at the warrior’s words.

She blinked at him, her brows narrowing as her lips silently mouthed the words he’d said.

"What is it?" Aedion demanded.

Aelin murmured, "Nameless is my price." Aedion opened his mouth, no doubt to ask what had snagged her interest, but Aelin frowned at Manon. "Can your kind see the future? See it as an oracle can?"

"Some," Manon admitted. "The Bluebloods claim to."

"Can other Clans?"

"They say that for the Ancients, past and present and future bleed together."

Aelin shook her head and walked toward the door that led to the hall of cramped cabins. Rowan swooped off the rigging and shifted, his feet hitting the planks just as he finished. He didn't so much as look at them as he followed her into the hall and shut the door behind them.

"What was that about?" Fenrys asked.

"An Ancient," Dorian mused, then murmured to Manon, "Baba Yellowlegs."

They all turned to him. But Manon's fingers brushed against her collarbone—where the necklace of Aelin's scars from Yellowlegs still ringed her neck in stark white.

"This winter, she was at your castle," Manon said to him. "Working as a fortune-teller."

"And what—she said something to that degree?" Aedion crossed his arms. He'd known of the visit, Dorian recalled. Aedion had always kept an eye on the witches—on all the power players of the realm, he'd once said.

Manon stared the general down. "Yellowlegs *was* a fortune-teller—a powerful oracle. I bet she knew who the queen was the moment she saw her. And saw things she planned to sell to the highest bidder." Dorian tried not to flinch at the memory. Aelin had butchered Yellowlegs when she'd threatened to sell *his* secrets. Aelin had never implied a threat against her own. Manon continued, "Yellowlegs wouldn't have told the queen anything outright, only in veiled terms. So it'd drive the girl mad when she figured it out."

A pointed glance at the door through which Aelin had vanished.

None of them said anything else, even as they later ate cold porridge for breakfast.

The cook, it seemed, hadn't made it through the night.

Rowan knocked on the door of their private bathing room. She'd locked it. Walked into their room, then into the bathing room, and locked him out.

And now she was puking her guts up.

"Aelin," he growled softly.

A ragged intake of breath, then retching, then—more vomiting.

"*Aelin*," he snarled, debating how long until it was socially acceptable for him to break down the door. *Act like a prince*, she'd snarled at him the other night.

"I don't feel well," was her muffled response. Her voice was hollow, flat in a way he hadn't heard for some time now.

"Then let me in so I can take care of you," he said as calmly and rationally as he could.

She'd locked him out—*locked him out.*

"I don't want you to see me like this."

"I've seen you wet yourself. I can handle vomiting. Which I have *also* seen you do before."

Ten seconds. Ten more seconds seemed like a fair enough amount of time before he crunched down on the handle and splintered the lock.

"Just—give me a minute."

"What was it about Fenrys's words that set you off?" He'd heard it all from his post on the mast.

Utter silence. Like she was spooling the raw terror back into herself, shoving it down into a place where she wouldn't look at it or feel it or acknowledge it. Or tell him about it.

"Aelin."

The lock turned.

Her face was gray, her eyes red-rimmed. Her voice broke as she said, "I want to talk to Lysandra."

Rowan looked at the bucket she'd half filled, then at her bloodless lips. At the sweat beaded on her brow.

His heart stopped dead in his chest as he contemplated that . . . that she might not be lying.

And why she might be ill. He tried to scent her, but the vomit was too overpowering, the space too small and full of brine. He stumbled back a step, shutting out the thoughts. Without another word, he left their room.

He was numb as he hunted down the shifter, now returned and in human form as she devoured a cold, soggy breakfast. With a concerned look, Lysandra silently did as he commanded.

Rowan shifted and soared so high that the ship turned into a bobbing speck below. Clouds cooled his feathers; the wind roared over the pure panic thundering in his heart.

He planned to lose himself in the awakening sky while scouting for danger, to sort himself out before he returned to her and started asking questions that he might not be ready to hear the answers to.

But the coast appeared—and only his magic kept him from tumbling out of the sky at what the first rays of the sun revealed.

Broad, sparkling rivers and snaking streams flowed throughout the undulating emerald and gold of the grasslands and reeds lining them, the burnt gold of the sandbanks flanking either side.

And where little fishing villages had once watched over the sea . . . Fire.

Dozens of those villages burning.

On the ship beneath him, the sailors began to shout, calling to one another as the coast at last broke over the horizon and the smoke became visible.

Eyllwe.

Eyllwe was burning.

CHAPTER 49

Elide didn't speak to Lorcan for three days.

She wouldn't have spoken to him for another three, maybe for three damn months, if necessity hadn't required them to break their hateful silence.

Her cycle had come. And through whatever steady, healthy diet she'd been consuming this past month, it had gone from an inconsistent trickle to the deluge she'd awoken to this morning.

She'd hurtled from the narrow bed in the cabin to the small privy on board, rifled through every drawer and box she could find, but . . . clearly, a woman had never spent any time on this infernal boat. She resorted to ripping up the embroidered tablecloth for liners, and by the time she'd cleaned herself up, Lorcan was awake and already steering the boat.

She said flatly to him, "I need supplies."

"You still reek of blood."

"I suspect I *will* reek of blood for several more days, and it will get worse before it gets better, so I *need* supplies. *Now*."

He turned from his usual spot near the prow, sniffing once. Her face was burning, her stomach a knotted mess of cramping. "I'll stop at the next town."

"When will that be?" The map was of no use to her.

"By nightfall."

They'd sailed right through every town or outpost along the river, surviving on the fish Lorcan had caught. She'd been so annoyed at her own helplessness that after the first day, she'd started copying his movements—and had earned herself a fat trout in the process. She'd made him kill it and gut it and cook it, but . . . she'd at least caught the thing.

Elide said, "Fine."

Lorcan said, "Fine."

She aimed for the cabin to find some other fabrics to tide her over, but Lorcan said, "You barely bled the last time."

The last thing she wanted to do was have this conversation. "Perhaps my body finally felt safe enough to be normal."

Because even with him murdering that man, lying, and then spitting the truth about Aelin in her face . . . Lorcan would go up against any threat without a second thought. Perhaps for his own survival, but he'd promised her protection. She was able to sleep through the night because he lay on the floor between her and the door.

"So . . . there's nothing wrong, then." He didn't bother to look at her as he said it.

But she cocked her head, studying the hard muscles of his back. Even while refusing to speak to him, she'd watched him—and made excuses to watch as he went through his exercises each day, usually shirtless.

"No, there's nothing wrong," she said. At least, she hoped. But Finnula, her nursemaid, had always clicked her tongue and said her cycles were spotty—too light and irregular. For this one to have come precisely a month later . . . She didn't feel like wondering about it.

Lorcan said, "Good. It'd delay us if it were otherwise."

She rolled her eyes at his back, not at all surprised by the answer, and limped into the cabin.

He'd needed to stop anyway, Lorcan told himself as he watched Elide barter with an innkeeper in town for the supplies she needed.

She'd wrapped her dark hair in a discarded red kerchief she must have scrounged up on that pitiful little barge, and even used a nasally accent while she spoke to the woman, her entire countenance a far cry from the graceful, quiet woman he'd spent three days ignoring.

Which had been fine. He'd used these three days to sort out his plans for Aelin Galathynius, how he'd return the favor she'd dealt him.

The inn seemed safe enough, so Lorcan left Elide to her bartering—turned out, she wanted new *clothes*, too—and wandered the ramshackle streets of the backwater town in search of supplies.

The streets were abuzz with river traders and fisherfolk mooring for the night. Lorcan managed to intimidate his way into buying a crate of apples, dried venison, *and* some oats for half their usual price. Just to get him away, the merchant along the crumbling quay threw in a few pears—for the lovely lady, he'd said.

Lorcan, arms full of his wares, was almost to the barge when the words echoed in his head, an off-kilter pealing.

He hadn't taken Elide past that section of the quay. Hadn't spied the man while he'd been docking, or when they'd left. Rumor could account for it, but this was a river town: strangers were always coming and going, and paid for their anonymity.

He hurried back to the barge. Fog had rippled in from the river, clouding the town and the opposite bank. By the time he dumped the crate and wares onto the boat, not even bothering to tie them down, the streets had emptied.

His magic stirred. He scanned the fog, the splotches of gold where candles shone in windows. *Not right, not right, not right*, his magic whispered.

Where was she?

Hurry, he willed her, counting the blocks they'd taken to the inn. She should have been back by now.

The fog pressed in. Squeaking sounded at his boots.

Lorcan snarled at the cobblestones as rats streamed past—toward the water. They flung themselves into the river, crawling and clawing over one another.

Something wasn't coming—something was *here*.

The innkeeper insisted she try on the clothes before she bought them. She bundled them in Elide's arms and pointed her toward a room in the back of the inn.

Men stared at her—too eagerly—as she passed and strode down a narrow hall. Typical of Lorcan to leave her while he sought whatever he needed. Elide shoved into the room, finding it black and chilled. She twisted, scanning for a candle and flint.

The door snapped shut, sealing her in.

Elide lunged for the handle as that little voice whispered, *Run run run run run run*.

She slammed into something muscled, bony, and leathery.

It reeked of spoiled meat and old blood.

A candle sparked to life across the room. Revealing a wooden table, an empty hearth, sealed windows, and . . .

Vernon. Sitting on the other side of the table, smiling at her like a cat.

Strong hands tipped in claws clamped on her shoulders, nails cutting through her leathers. The ilken held her firmly as her uncle drawled, "What an adventure you've had, Elide."

CHAPTER 50

"How did you find me?" Elide breathed, the reek of the ilken nearly enough to make her vomit.

Her uncle rose to his feet in a fluid, unhurried movement, straightening his green tunic. "Asking questions to buy yourself time? Clever, but expected." He jerked his chin to the creature. It loosed a low, guttural clicking sound.

The door opened behind it, revealing two other ilken now crowding the hall with their wings and hideous faces. Oh gods. Oh, gods.

Think think think think think.

"Your companion, last we heard, was putting supplies on his boat and unmooring it. You probably should have paid him more."

"He's my husband," she hissed. "You have no right to take me from him—*none*." Because once she was married, Vernon's wardenship over her life ended.

Vernon let out a low laugh. "Lorcan Salvaterre, Maeve's second-in-command, is your husband? Really, Elide." He waved a lazy hand to the ilken. "We depart now."

Fight now—now, before they had the chance to move her, to get her away.

But where to run? The innkeeper had sold her out, someone had betrayed their location on this river—

The ilken tugged at her. She planted her heels onto the wooden slats, little good it would do.

It let out a low laugh and brought its mouth to her ear. "Your blood smells clean."

She recoiled, but it gripped her hard, its grayish tongue tickling the side of her neck. Thrashing, she still could do nothing as it twisted them into the hall and toward the two waiting ilken in it. To the back door, not ten feet away, already open to the night beyond.

"You see what I shielded you from at Morath, Elide?" Vernon crooned, falling into step behind them. She slammed her feet into the wooden floor, over and over, straining for the wall, for anything to have leverage to push and fight against it—

No.

No.

No.

Lorcan had left—he'd gotten everything he needed from her and left. She'd slowed him down, had brought enemy after enemy after him.

"And whatever will you do back at Morath," Vernon mused, "now that Manon Blackbeak is dead?"

Elide's chest cracked open at the words. *Manon*—

"Gutted by her own grandmother and thrown off the side of the Keep for her disobedience. Of course, I'll shield you from your *relatives*, but . . . Erawan will be interested to learn what you've been up to. What you . . . took from Kaltain."

The stone in her jacket's breast pocket.

It thrummed and whispered, awakening as she bucked.

No one in the now-silent inn at the opposite end of the hall bothered to come around the corner and investigate her wordless shouting. Another ilken stepped into view just beyond the open back door.

Four of them. And Lorcan had left—

The stone at her breast began to seethe.

But a voice that was young and old, wise and sweet, whispered, *Do not touch it. Do not use it. Do not acknowledge it.*

It had been inside Kaltain—had driven her mad. Had made her into that . . . shell.

A shell for something else to fill.

The open door loomed.

Think think think.

She couldn't breathe enough to think, the ilken reek around her promising the sort of horrors she'd endure when they got her back to Morath—

No, she wouldn't go. She wouldn't let them take her, break and use her—

One shot. She'd have one shot.

No, whispered the voice in her head. *No*—

But there was a knife at her uncle's side as he strolled ahead and out the door. It was all she'd need. She'd seen Lorcan do it enough while hunting.

Vernon paused in the back courtyard, a large, rectangular iron box waiting before him.

There was a small window in it.

And handles on two of its edges.

She knew what the ilken were for as the three others fell into place around it.

They'd shove her inside, lock the door, and *fly* her back to Morath.

The box was little bigger than a coffin standing upright.

Its door was already open.

The ilken would have to release her to throw her inside. For a heartbeat, they'd let go. She'd have to use it to her advantage.

Vernon loitered beside the box. She didn't dare look at his knife.

A sob broke from her throat. She'd die here—in this filthy courtyard, with these awful things around her. She'd never see the sun again, or laugh, or hear music—

The ilken stirred around the box, wings rustling.

Five feet. Four. Three.

No, no, no, the wise voice begged her.

She would not be taken back to Morath. She would not let them touch her and corrupt her—

The ilken shoved her forward, a violent thrust meant to send her staggering into the box.

Elide twisted, slamming face-first into the edge instead, her nose crunching, but she whirled on her uncle. Her ankle roared as she set her weight on it to lunge for the knife at his side.

Vernon didn't have time to realize what she intended as she whipped the knife free from its sheath at his hip. As she flipped the knife in her fingers, her other hand wrapping around the hilt.

As her shoulders curved inward, her chest caving, and she drove the blade home.

Lorcan had the kill shot.

Hidden in the fog, the four ilken couldn't detect him as the man he was certain was Elide's uncle had that ilken haul her toward that prison-box.

It was on him that Lorcan had trained his hatchet.

Elide was sobbing. In terror and despair.

Each sound whetted his rage into something so lethal Lorcan could barely see straight.

Then the ilken threw her into that iron box.

And Elide proved she wasn't bluffing in her claim to never return to Morath.

He heard her nose break as she hit the rim of the box, heard her uncle's cry of surprise as she rebounded and lunged for him—

And grabbed his dagger. Not to kill him.

For the first time in five centuries, Lorcan knew true fear as Elide turned that knife on herself, the blade angled to plunge up and into her heart.

He threw his hatchet.

As the tip of that dagger pierced the leather over her ribs, the wooden handle of his hatchet slammed into her wrist.

Elide went down with a cry, the dagger flying wide—

Lorcan was already moving as they whirled toward where he'd perched on the rooftop. He leaped to the nearest one, to the weapons he'd positioned there minutes before, knowing they'd emerge from this door—

His next knife went through the wing of an ilken. Then another to keep it down before they pinpointed his location. But Lorcan was already sprinting to the third rooftop flanking the courtyard. To the sword he'd left there. He hurled it right through the face of the closest one.

Two left, along with Vernon, screaming now to get the girl in the box—

Elide was running like hell for the narrow alley out of the courtyard, not the broad street. The alley, too small for the ilken to fit, especially with all the debris and trash littered throughout. Good girl.

Lorcan leaped and rolled onto the next roof, to the two remaining daggers—

He threw them, but the ilken had already learned his aim, his throwing style.

They hadn't learned Elide's.

She hadn't just gone into the alley to save herself. She'd gone after the hatchet.

And Lorcan watched as that woman crept up behind the distracted ilken and drove the hatchet into its wings.

With an injured wrist. With her nose leaking blood down her face.

The ilken screamed, thrashing to grab her, even as it crashed to its knees.

Where she wanted it.

The axe was swinging again before its scream finished sounding.

The sound was cut off a heartbeat later as its head bounced to the stones.

Lorcan hurtled off the roof, aiming for the one remaining ilken now seething at her—

But it pivoted and ran to where Vernon was cowering by the door, his face bloodless.

Sobbing, her own blood sprayed on the stones, Elide whirled toward her uncle, too. Axe already lifting.

But the ilken reached her uncle, snatched him up in its strong arms, and launched them both into the sky.

Elide threw the hatchet anyway.

It missed the ilken's wing by a whisper of wind.

The axe slammed to the cobblestones, taking out a chunk of rock. Right near the ilken with the shredded wings—now crawling toward the courtyard exit.

Lorcan watched as Elide picked up his axe and walked toward the hissing, broken beast.

It lashed at her with its claws. Elide easily sidestepped the swipe.

It screamed as she stomped on its wrecked wing, halting its crawl to freedom.

When it fell silent, she said in a quiet, merciless voice he'd never heard her use, clear despite the blood clogging one nostril, "I want Erawan to know that the next time he sends you after me like a pack of dogs, I'll return the favor. I want Erawan to know that the next time I see him,

I will carve Manon's name on his gods-damned heart." Tears rolled down her face, silent and unending as the wrath that now sculpted her features into a thing of mighty and terrible beauty.

"But it seems like tonight isn't really your night," Elide said to the ilken, lifting the hatchet again over a shoulder. The ilken might have been whimpering as she smiled grimly. "Because it takes only one to deliver a message. And your companions are already on their way."

The axe fell.

Flesh and bone and blood spilled onto the stones.

She stood there, staring at the corpse, at the reeking blood that dribbled from its neck.

Lorcan, perhaps a bit numbly, walked over and took the axe from her hands. How she'd been able to use it with the sore wrist—

She hissed and whimpered at the movement. As if whatever force had rushed through her blood had vanished, leaving only pain behind.

She clutched her wrist, utterly silent as he circled the dead ilken and severed their heads from their bodies. One after another, retrieving his weapons as he went.

People inside the inn were stirring, wondering at the noise, wondering if it was safe to come out to see what had happened to the girl they'd so willingly betrayed.

For a heartbeat, Lorcan debated ending that innkeeper.

But Elide said, "Enough death."

Tears streaked through the splattered black blood on her cheeks—blood that was a mockery of the smattering of freckles. Blood, crimson and pure, ran from her nose down her mouth and chin, already caking.

So he sheathed the hatchet and scooped her into his arms. She didn't object.

He carried her through the fog-wrapped town, to where their boat was tied. Already, onlookers had gathered, no doubt to scavenge their supplies when the ilken left. A snarl from Lorcan had them skittering into the mist.

As he stepped onto the barge, the boat rocking beneath him, Elide said, "He told me you'd left."

Lorcan still didn't set her down, holding her aloft with one arm as he untied the ropes. "You believed him."

She wiped at the blood on her face, then winced at the tender wrist—and broken nose. He'd have to tend to that. Even then, it might very well be slightly crooked forever. He doubted she'd care.

Knew she'd perhaps see that crooked nose as a sign that she'd fought and survived.

Lorcan put her down at last, atop the crate of apples—right where he could see her. She sat silently as he took up the pole and pushed them away from the dock, from that hateful town, glad for the cover of mist as they drifted downstream. They could perhaps afford two more days on the river before they'd have to cut inland to shake any enemies trailing them. Good thing they were close enough to Eyllwe now to make it in a matter of days on foot.

When there was nothing but wafting mist and the lapping of the river against the boat, Lorcan spoke again. "You wouldn't have stopped that dagger."

She didn't respond, and the silence went on long enough that he turned to where she perched on the crate.

Tears rolled down her face as she stared at the water.

He didn't know how to comfort, how to soothe—not in the way she needed.

So he set down the pole and sat beside her on the crate, the wood groaning. "Who is Manon?"

He'd heard most of what Vernon had hissed inside that private dining room while he'd been setting his trap in the courtyard, but some details had evaded him.

"The Wing Leader of the Ironteeth legion," Elide said, voice trembling, the words snagging on the blood clogging her nose.

Lorcan took a shot in the dark. "She was the one who got you out. That day—she was why you're in witch leathers, why you wound up wandering in Oakwald."

A nod.

"And Kaltain—who was she?" The person who'd given her that thing she carried.

"Erawan's mistress—his slave. She was my age. He put the stone inside her arm and made her into a living ghost. She bought me and Manon time to run; she incinerated most of Morath in the process, and herself."

Elide reached into her jacket, her breathing thick with tears still sliding down her face. Lorcan's breath caught as she pulled out a scrap of dark fabric.

The scent clinging to it was female, foreign—broken and sad and cold. But there was another scent beneath it, one he knew and hated . . .

"Kaltain said to give this to Celaena—not to Aelin," Elide said, shaking with her tears. "Because Celaena . . . she gave her a warm cloak in a cold dungeon. And they wouldn't let Kaltain take the cloak with her when they brought her to Morath, but she managed to save this scrap. To remember to repay Celaena for that kindness. But . . . what sort of gift is this thing? What *is* this?" She pulled back the fold of cloth, revealing a dark sliver of stone.

Every drop of blood in his body went cold and hot, awake and dead.

She was sobbing quietly. "Why is this payment? My very bones say to not touch it. My—a voice told me not to even think about it . . ."

It was wrong. The thing in her beautiful, filthy hand was wrong. It did not belong here, should not *be* here—

The god who had watched over him his whole life had recoiled.

Even death feared it.

"Put it away," he said roughly. "Right now."

Hand shaking, she did so. Only when it was hidden inside her jacket did he say, "Let's clean you up first. Set that nose and wrist. I'll tell you what I know while I do."

She nodded, gaze on the river.

Lorcan reached out, grasping her chin and forcing her to look at him. Hopeless, bleak eyes met his. He brushed away a stray tear with his thumb. "I made a promise to protect you. I will not break it, Elide."

She made to pull away, but he gripped her a little harder, keeping her eyes on him.

"I will always find you," he swore to her.

Her throat bobbed.

Lorcan whispered, "I promise."

Elide sifted through all Lorcan had told her while he cleaned her face, inspected her nose and wrist, bound the latter in soft cloth, and quickly, but not viciously, set her nose.

Wyrdkeys. Wyrdgates.

Aelin had one Wyrdkey. Was looking for the other two.

Soon to be only one more, once Elide gave her the key she carried.

Two keys—against one. Perhaps they would win this war.

Even if Elide didn't know how Aelin could use them and not destroy herself. But . . . she'd leave it up to her. Erawan might have the armies, but if Aelin had two keys . . .

She tried not to think about Manon. Vernon had lied about Lorcan leaving—to break her spirit, to get her to come willingly. Perhaps Manon was not dead, either.

She wouldn't believe it until she had proof. Until the whole world screamed at her that the Wing Leader was gone.

Lorcan was back at the prow by the time she'd changed into one of his own shirts while her leathers dried. Her wrist throbbed, a dull, insistent ache, her face was no better and Lorcan had promised she'd likely have a black eye from it, but . . . her head was clear.

She came up beside him, watching him push the pole against the mucky bottom of the river. "I killed those things."

"You did a fine job of it," he said.

"I don't regret it."

Dark, depthless eyes slid to her. "Good."

She didn't know why she said it, why she felt a need or like it was worth anything to him at all, but Elide stood on her toes, kissed his stubble-rough cheek, and said, "I will always find you, too, Lorcan."

She felt him staring at her, even when she'd climbed into bed minutes later.

When she awoke, clean strips of linen for her cycle were next to the bed.

His own shirt, washed and dried overnight—now cut up for her to use as she would.

CHAPTER 51

Eyllwe's coast was burning.

For three days, they sailed past village after village. Some still burning, some only cinders. And at each of them, Aelin and Rowan had labored to put out those flames.

Rowan, in his hawk form, could fly in, but . . . It killed her. Absolutely killed her that they could not afford to halt long enough to go to shore. So she did it from the ship, burrowing deep into her power, stretching it as far as it could go across sea and sky and sand, to wink out those fires one by one.

By the end of the third day, she was flagging, so thirsty that no amount of water was able to slake it, her lips chapped and peeling.

Rowan had gone to shore three times now to ask who had done it.

Each time the answer was the same: darkness had swept over them in the night, the kind that blotted out the stars, and then the villages were burning beneath flaming arrows not spotted until they had found their targets.

But where that darkness, where Erawan's forces were . . . there was no sign of them.

No sign of Maeve, either.

Rowan and Lysandra had flown high and wide, searching for either force, but . . . nothing.

Ghosts, some villagers were now claiming, had attacked them. The ghosts of their unburied dead, raging home from distant lands.

Until they started whispering another rumor.

That Aelin Galathynius herself was burning Eyllwe, village by village. For vengeance that they had not aided her kingdom ten years ago.

No matter that she was putting out the flames. They did not believe Rowan when he tried to explain who soothed their fires from aboard the distant ship.

He told her not to listen, not to let it sink in. So she tried.

And it had been during one of those times that Rowan had run his thumb over the scar on her palm, leaning to kiss her neck. He'd breathed her in, and she knew he detected an answer to the question that had caused him to flee that morning on the ship. No, she was not carrying his child.

They had only discussed the matter once—last week. When she'd crawled off him, panting and coated in sweat, and he'd asked if she was taking a tonic. She merely told him no.

He'd gone still.

And then she had explained that if she'd inherited so much of Mab's Fae blood, she might very well have inherited the Fae's struggle to conceive. And even if the timing was horrible . . . if this was to be the one shot she had of providing Terrasen a bloodline, a future . . . she would not waste it. His green eyes turned distant, but he'd nodded, kissing her shoulder. And that had been that.

She hadn't mustered the nerve to ask if he wanted to sire her children. If he *wanted* to have children, given what had happened to Lyria.

And during that brief moment before he'd flown back to shore to put out more flames, she hadn't possessed the nerve to explain why she'd hurled her guts up that morning, either.

The past three days had been a blur. From the moment Fenrys had uttered those words, *Nameless is my price*, everything had been a blur of smoke and flame and waves and sun.

But as the sun set on the third day, Aelin again shoved those thoughts away as the escort ship began signaling ahead, the crew frantically working to drop anchor.

Sweat beaded on her brow, her tongue parchment-dry. But she forgot her thirst, her exhaustion, as she beheld what Rolfe's men had spied moments ago.

A flat, waterlogged land under a cloudy sky spread inland as far as the eye could see. Moldy green and bone-white grasses crusted the bumps and hollows, little islands of life among the mirror-smooth gray water between them. And among them all, jutting up from brackish water and humped land like the limbs of an ill-buried corpse . . . ruins. Great, crumbling ruins, a once-lovely city drowned on the plain.

The Stone Marshes.

Manon let the humans and Fae meet with the captains of the other two ships.

She heard the news soon enough: what they sought lay about a day and a half inland. Precisely where, they didn't know—or how long it'd take to find its exact location. Until they returned, the ships would remain anchored here.

And Manon, it seemed, would join them on their trip inland. As if the queen suspected that if she were left behind, their little fleet would not be intact when they returned.

Clever woman.

But that was the other problem. The one facing Manon right now, already looking anxious and put-out.

Abraxos's tail lashed a bit, the iron spikes scraping and scratching the pristine ship deck. As if he'd heard the queen's order a minute ago: *the wyvern has to go.*

On the flat, open expanse of the marshes, he'd be too noticeable.

Manon placed a hand on his scarred snout, meeting those depthless black eyes. "You need to lie low somewhere."

A warm, sorrowful huff into her palm.

"Don't whine about it," Manon said, even as something twisted and roiled in her belly. "Stay out of sight, keep alert, and come back in four days' time." She allowed herself to lean forward, resting her brow against his snout. His growl rumbled her bones. "We've been a pair, you and I. A few days is nothing, my friend."

He nudged her head with his own.

Manon swallowed hard. "You saved my life. Many times. I never thanked you for it."

Abraxos let out another low whine.

"You and me," she promised him. "From now until the Darkness claims us."

She made herself pull away. Made herself stroke his snout just once more. Then backed a step. Then another. "Go."

He didn't move. She bared her iron teeth. *"Go."*

Abraxos gave her a look full of reproach, but his body tensed, wings lifting.

And Manon decided she had never hated anyone more than she hated the Queen of Terrasen and her friends. For making him leave. For causing this parting, when so many dangers had not been able to cleave them.

But Abraxos was airborne, the sails groaning in the wind of his wings, and Manon watched until he was a speck on the horizon, until the longboats were being readied to bring them to the high grasses and stagnant gray water of the marshes beyond.

The queen and her court readied, donning weapons like some people adorned themselves with jewelry, moving about in question and answer to one another. So similar, to her Thirteen—similar enough that she had to turn away, ducking into the shadows of the foremast and schooling her breathing into an even rhythm.

Her hands trembled. Asterin was not dead. The Thirteen were not dead.

She'd kept the thoughts about it at bay. But now, with that flower-smelling wyvern vanishing over the horizon . . .

The last piece of the Wing Leader had vanished with him.

A muggy wind tugged her inland—toward those marshes. Dragging her red cape with it.

Manon ran a finger down the crimson cloak she'd made herself wear this morning.

Rhiannon.

She'd never heard a whisper that the Crochan royal bloodline had walked off that final killing field five centuries ago. She wondered if any of the Crochans beyond her half sister knew the child of Lothian Blackbeak and a Crochan Prince had survived.

Manon unfastened the brooch clasping the cloak at her shoulders. She weighed the thick bolt of red fabric in her hands.

A few easy swipes of her nails had her clutching a long, thin strip of the cloak. A few more motions had her tying it around the end of her braid, the red stark against the moon white of her hair.

Manon stepped out of the shadows behind the foremast and peered over the edge of the ship.

No one commented when she dumped her half sister's cloak into the sea.

The wind carried it a few feet over the waves before it fluttered like a dying leaf to land atop the swells. A pool of blood—that's how it looked from the distance as the tide carried it out, out, out into the ocean.

She found the King of Adarlan and Queen of Terrasen waiting at the railing of the main deck, their companions climbing into the awaiting longboat bobbing on the waves.

She met eyes of sapphire, then those of turquoise and gold.

She knew they'd seen it. Perhaps not understood what the cloak had meant, but . . . understood the gesture for what it was.

Manon flicked her iron teeth and nails back into their slits as she approached them.

Aelin Galathynius said quietly, "You never stop seeing their faces."

It was only when they were rowing for the shore, spindrift soaking them, that Manon realized the queen hadn't meant the Thirteen. And Manon wondered if Aelin, too, had watched that cloak floating out to sea and thought it looked like spilled blood.

CHAPTER 52

They didn't get to Leriba. Or to Banjali. They didn't even get close.

Lorcan felt the push on his shoulder that had guided and shaped the course of his life—that invisible, insistent hand of shadow and death. So they went south, then west, sailing swiftly down the network of waterways through Eyllwe.

Elide didn't object or question when he explained that if Hellas himself was nudging him, that the queen they hunted was likely in that direction. Wherever it would lead. There were no cities out there, only endless grasslands that skirted Oakwald's southernmost tip, then marshes. The abandoned peninsula full of ruins among the marshes.

But if that was where he was told to go . . . The dark god's touch on his shoulder had never steered him wrong. So he'd see what he'd find.

He did not let himself dwell too long on the fact that Elide carried a Wyrdkey. That she was trying to bring it to his enemy. Perhaps his power's summons would lead them both to it—to her.

And then he'd have two keys, if he played his cards right.

If he was smarter and faster and more ruthless than the others.

Then the most dangerous part of all: traveling with two keys in his possession, into the heart of Morath, to hunt down the third. Speed would be his best ally and only shot at survival.

And he'd likely never see Elide or any of the others again.

They'd at last abandoned their barge that morning, cramming whatever supplies would fit into their packs before setting off through the rippling grasses. Hours later, Elide's breathing was ragged as they ascended a steep hill deep in the plain. He'd been scenting brine for two days now—they had to be close to the edge of the marshes. Elide swallowed hard, and he passed her the canteen as they crested the summit of the hill.

But Elide halted, arms slackening at her sides.

And Lorcan himself froze at what spread before them.

"What is this place?" Elide breathed, as if fearful the land itself would hear.

As far as the eye could see, flowing into the horizon, the land had sunk a good thirty feet—a severe, brutal crack from the edge of the cliff, not hill, on which they stood, as if some furious god had stomped a foot across the plain and left an imprint.

Silvery brackish water covered most of it, still as a mirror, interrupted only by grassy islands and mounds of earth—and crumbling, exquisite ruins.

"This is a bad place," Elide whispered. "We shouldn't be here."

Indeed, the hair on his arms had risen, every instinct on alert as he scanned the marshes, the ruins, the brambles, and thick foliage that had choked some of the islands.

Even the god of death halted his nudging and ducked behind Lorcan's shoulder.

"What do you sense?"

Her lips were bloodless. "Silence. Life, but such . . . silence. As if . . ."

"As if what?" he pushed.

Her words were a shudder of breath. "As if all the people who once lived here, long ago, are still trapped inside—still . . . beneath." She pointed to a ruin—a curved, broken dome of what had likely been a ballroom attached to the spire. A palace. "I don't think this is a place for the living, Lorcan. The beasts in these waters . . . I do not think they tolerate trespassers. Nor do the dead."

"Is it the stone or the goddess who watches you telling you such things?"

"It's my heart that murmurs a warning. Anneith is silent. I don't think she wants to be anywhere near. I don't think she will follow."

"She came to Morath, but not here?"

"What is inside these marshes?" she asked instead. "Why is Aelin headed into them?"

That, it seemed, was the question. For if they picked up on it, surely the queen and Whitethorn would sense it, too—and only a great reward or threat would drive them here.

"I don't know," he admitted. "No towns or outposts exist anywhere nearby." Yet this was where the dark god had led him—and where that hand still pushed him to venture, even if it quaked.

Nothing but ruins and dense foliage on those too-small islands of safety from whatever dwelled beneath the glassy water.

But Lorcan obeyed the nudging god at his shoulder and led the Lady of Perranth onward.

"Who lived here?" Elide asked, staring at the weather-worn face of the statue jutting from a near-collapsed stone wall. It teetered on the outer edge of the little island they were standing on, and the moss-speckled woman carved there had no doubt once been beautiful, as well as a bit of support for beams and a roof that had since rotted away. But the veil she'd been carved wearing now seemed like a death shroud. Elide shivered.

"This place was forgotten and wrecked centuries before I was even born," Lorcan said.

"Did it belong to Eyllwe?"

"It was a part of a kingdom that is now gone, a lost people who wandered and merged with those of different lands."

"They must have been very talented, to have made such beautiful buildings."

Lorcan grunted in agreement. It had been two days of inching across the marshes—no sign of Aelin. They had slept in the shelter of the ruins, though neither of them really got true rest. Elide's dreams had been filled with the pale, milky-eyed faces of people she'd never met, crying out in supplication as water shoved down their throats, their noses. Even waking, she could see them, hear their cries on the wind.

Just the breeze through the stones, Lorcan grumbled that first day.

But she'd seen it in his eyes. He heard the dead, too.

Heard the thunder of the cataclysm that had dropped the land right from underneath them, heard the rushing water that devoured them all before they could run. Curious beasts from sea and swamp and river had converged in the years following, making the ruins a hunting ground, feasting on one another when the waterlogged corpses ran out. Changing, adapting—growing fatter and cleverer than their ancestors had been.

It was thanks to those beasts that it took so long to cross the marshes. Lorcan would scan the too-still water between those islands of safety. Sometimes it was clear to wade through the chest-deep, salty water. Sometimes it was not.

Sometimes even the islands were not safe. Twice now, she'd spotted a long, scaled tail—plated like armor—sliding behind a stone wall or broken pillar. Thrice, she'd seen great golden eyes, slitted down the pupil, watching from the reeds.

Lorcan had hauled her over a shoulder and run whenever they realized they were not alone.

Then there were the snakes—who liked to dangle from the wraithlike trees draining an existence from the islands. And the incessant, biting midges, who were nothing compared to the clouds of mosquitoes that sometimes hounded them for hours. Or until Lorcan sent a wave of his dark power into them and they all dropped to the earth in a dark rain.

But every time he killed . . . she felt the earth shudder. Not in fear of him . . . but as if it were awakening. Listening.

Wondering who dared walk across it.

On the fourth night, Elide was so tired, so on edge, she wanted to whimper as they curled into a rare sanctuary: a ruined hall, with part of its mezzanine intact. It was open to the sky, and vines choked the three walls, but the stone stair had been solid—and was high enough off the island that nothing might crawl out of the water to prey upon them. Lorcan had rigged the base and top of the stairs with trip wires of vines and branches—to alert them if any beasts slithered up the steps.

They didn't dare risk a fire, but it was warm enough that she didn't miss one. Lying beside Lorcan, his body a solid wall between her and the stone to her left, Elide watched the flickering stars, the drowsy buzz of insects a constant drone in her ears. Something roared in the distance.

The insects paused. The marsh seemed to turn its attention toward that feral, deep roar.

Slowly, life resumed again—though quieter. Lorcan murmured, "Sleep, Elide."

She swallowed, her fear thick in her blood. "What was that?"

"One of the beasts—either a mating call or territorial warning."

She didn't want to know how big they were. Glimpses of eyes and tails were enough.

"Tell me about her," Elide whispered. "Your queen."

"I doubt it'll help you sleep any better."

She turned onto her other side, finding him lying on his back, watching the sky. "Will she truly kill you for what you've done?" A nod.

"Yet you risk it—for her sake." She propped her head up with a fist. "Do you love her?"

Those eyes, darker than the gaps between the stars, slid to her. "I have been in love with Maeve since I first laid eyes on her."

"Are you—are you her lover?" She had not dared ask it, hadn't really wanted to know.

"No. I offered once. She laughed at me for the insolence." His mouth tightened. "So I have made myself invaluable in other ways."

Again, that roar in the distance that silenced the world for a few heartbeats. Was it closer, or had she imagined it? When she glanced back at him, Lorcan's eyes were on her mouth.

She said, "Perhaps she uses your love to her own advantage. Perhaps it's in her best interest to drag you along. Maybe she'll change her mind when you seem the most likely to . . . leave."

"I am blood-sworn to her. I will never leave."

Her chest hurt at that. "Then she can rest assured knowing you'll pine after her for eternity."

The words came out sharper than she intended, and she made to look at the stars, but Lorcan gripped her chin, faster than she could detect. He peered into her eyes, scanning them. "Do not make the mistake of believing me to be a romantic fool. I do not hold any shred of hope for her."

"Then that does not seem like love at all."

"And what do you know of love?" He was so close—had neared without her realizing it.

"I think love should make you happy," Elide said, remembering her mother and father. How often they had smiled and laughed, how they had gazed at each other. "It should make you into the best possible version of yourself."

"Are you implying I am neither of those things?"

"I don't think you even know what happiness is."

His face grew grave—thoughtful. "I do not mind . . . being around you."

"Is that a compliment?"

A half smile cut across his granite-hewn face. And she wanted . . . wanted to touch it. That smile, that mouth. With her fingers, her own lips. It made him younger, made him . . . handsome.

So she reached up with trembling fingers and touched his lips.

Lorcan froze, still half above her, his eyes solemn and intent.

But she traced the contours of his mouth, finding the skin there soft and warm, such a contrast to the harsh words that usually came out of it.

She reached the outer corner of his lips, and he turned his face into her hand, resting his rough cheek against her palm. His eyes grew heavy-lidded as she brushed a thumb over the hard plane of his cheekbone.

Elide whispered, "I would hide you. In Perranth. If you . . . if you do what you need to do, and need somewhere to go . . . You would have a place there. With me."

His eyes snapped open, but there was nothing hard, nothing cold, about the light shining in them. "I would be a dishonored male—it'd reflect poorly upon you."

"If anyone thinks that, they would have no place in Perranth."

His throat bobbed. "Elide, you need to—"

But she rose up slightly, replacing her mouth where her fingers had been.

The kiss was soft, and quiet, and brief. Barely a grazing of her lips against his.

She thought Lorcan might have been trembling as she pulled back. As heat bloomed across her cheeks. But she made herself say, surprised to find her voice steady, "You don't need to answer me now. Or ever. You could show up on my doorstep in ten years, and the offer would still stand. But there is a place for you, in Perranth—if you should ever need or wish for it."

Something like agony rippled in his eyes, the most human expression she'd seen him make.

But he leaned forward, and despite the marshes, despite what gathered in the world, for the first time in ten years, Elide found herself not at all afraid as Lorcan caressed her lips with his own. Not afraid of anything as he did it again, kissing one corner of her mouth, then the other.

Such gentle, patient kisses—his hands equally so as they stroked the hair back from her brow, as they trailed over her hips, her ribs. She lifted her own hands to his face and dragged her fingers into his silken hair as she arched up into him, craving the weight of his body on hers.

Lorcan's tongue brushed against the seam of her mouth, and Elide marveled at how natural it felt to open for him, how her body *sang* at the contact, his hardness against her softness. Lorcan groaned at the first caress of his tongue against her own, his hips grinding against hers in a way that made heat scorch through her, made her own body undulate against his in answer and demand.

He kissed her deeper at that request, a hand sliding down to grip her thigh, spreading her legs a bit wider so he could settle fully between them. And as all of him lined up with her . . . She was panting, she realized, as she ground herself against him, as Lorcan tore his mouth from hers and kissed her jaw, her neck, her ear. She was trembling—not with fear, but with *want* as Lorcan breathed her name over and over onto her skin.

Like a prayer, that was how her name sounded on his lips. She took his face in her hands, finding his eyes blazing, his breathing as ragged as her own.

Elide dared to run her fingers from his cheek down his neck, right beneath the collar of his shirt. His skin was like heated silk. He shuddered at the touch, head bowing so that his inky hair spilled onto her brow, and his hips drove into hers just enough that a small gasp came out of her. More, she realized—she wanted *more.*

His eyes met hers in silent question, her hand pausing over the skin above his heart. It was a raging, thunderous beat.

She lifted her head to kiss him, and as her mouth again met his, she whispered her answer—

Lorcan's head snapped up. He was instantly on his feet, whirling toward the northeast.

Where a darkness had begun to spread across the stars, wiping them out one by one.

Any bit of heat, of desire, winked out of her.

"Is that a storm?"

"We need to run," Lorcan said. But it was the dead of the night—dawn was at least six hours off. To cross the marshes now . . . More and more stars were gobbled up by that gathering darkness.

"What is that?" It spread farther with each heartbeat. Far out, even the marsh beasts stopped roaring.

"Ilken," Lorcan murmured. "That is an army of ilken."

Elide knew they weren't coming for her.

CHAPTER 53

Two days into the endless labyrinth of the Stone Marshes—*two*, not the day and a half that gods-damned Rolfe had suggested—Aelin was inclined to burn the whole place to the ground. With the water and humidity, she was never dry, always sweating and sticky. And worse: the insects.

She kept the little demons away with a shield of invisible flame, revealed only by the zinging as they slammed into it. She might have felt bad, had they not tried to eat her alive the first day here. Had she not scratched at the dozens of swollen red bites until her skin bled—and Rowan stepped in to heal them.

After the Bloodhound's attack, her own healing abilities had remained depleted. So Rowan and Gavriel played healer for all of them, tending to the itching bites, the welts from stinging plants, the scratches from submerged, jagged chunks of the ruins that sliced into them if they weren't careful while wading through the brackish water.

Only Manon seemed immune to the marshes' drain, finding the feral, rotting beauty of the marshes to be pleasing. She indeed reminded Aelin of one of the horrid river beasts that ruled this place—with those golden eyes, those sharp, gleaming teeth . . . Aelin tried not to think on it too much. Tried to imagine getting *out* of this place and onto dry, crisp land.

But in the heart of this dead, wretched sprawl was Mala's Lock.

Rowan was scouting ahead in hawk form as the sun inched toward the horizon, Lysandra surveying the waters between the small hills as some slimy, scaled marsh thing that Aelin had grimaced at, eliciting an indignant hiss of a forked tongue before the shifter splashed into the water.

Aelin grimaced again as she trudged up one of those little hills, crusted in thorny brambles and crowned with two fallen pillars. A maze designed to scratch and stub and tear.

So she sent a blast of fire across the hill, turning it to wilting ashes. It clung to her wet boots as she passed over it, a sodden gray mush.

Fenrys chuckled at her side as they descended the hill. "Well, that's one way to get through it." He held out a hand to lead her through the water, and part of her balked at the idea of being escorted, but . . . she'd be damned if she fell into a watery pit. She had a very, very good idea of what was deep beneath them. She had no interest in swimming among the rotted remnants of people.

Fenrys gripped her hand tightly as they waded through the chest-deep water. He hauled her onto the bank first, then climbed out himself. He could no doubt leap the gaps between the islands in wolf form, as could Gavriel. Why they bothered staying in Fae form was beyond her.

Aelin used her magic to dry off as best she could, then used a tendril to dry Fenrys's and Gavriel's clothes, too.

A harmless, casual expenditure of power. Even if using it for three days straight on Eyllwe's burning coast had drained her. Not the flame, but just . . . physically. Mentally. She still felt like she could sleep for a week. But the magic murmured. Incessantly, relentlessly. Even if *she* was tired . . . the power demanded more. Drying their clothes between dips into the marsh water, at least, kept the damn thing quiet. For now.

Lysandra popped her hideous head up from a tangle of brambles, and Aelin yelped, falling back a step. The shifter grinned, revealing two very, very sharp fangs. Fenrys loosed a low laugh, scanning the shifter as she slithered a few feet ahead. "So you can change skin and bone, but the brand remains?"

Lysandra paused a few inches from the water, and on the island ahead, Aedion seemed to go tense, even as he continued on. Good. At least she wasn't the only one who'd rip out anyone's throat if they so much as mocked Lysandra. But her friend shifted, glowing and expanding, until her form became humanoid—Fae.

Until Fenrys was looking at himself, albeit a smaller version to fit into the woman's clothes. Gavriel, clearing the bank behind them, stumbled a step at the sight.

Lysandra said, her voice near-identical to Fenrys's drawl, "I suppose it shall always be my tell." She extended her wrist, pushing back the sleeve of her jacket to reveal his golden-brown skin, marred with that brand.

But she kept peering down at herself as they all continued wading and climbing, and finally remarked, "Your hearing *is* better." Lysandra ran her tongue over the slightly elongated canines. Fenrys cringed a bit. "What's the point of these?" she asked.

Gavriel edged closer and nudged the shape-shifter along, walking a few paces ahead with her. "Fenrys is the last person to ask. If you want an appropriate answer, that is."

Lysandra chuckled, smiling at the Lion as they ascended the hill. Odd—to see her smile on Fenrys's face. Fenrys caught Aelin's eye and grimaced again, no doubt finding it equally unnerving. She chuckled.

Wings flapped ahead, and Aelin took a moment to marvel as Rowan sailed hard and fast to them. Swift, strong—unfaltering.

Gavriel fell back a few paces as Lysandra stilled beside Aedion atop the hill and shifted into her own form. She swayed a bit, and Aelin lunged—only for Aedion to beat her to it, gripping Lysandra gently under her elbow as Rowan landed and shifted himself. They all needed a nice, long rest.

Her Fae Prince said, "Dead ahead—we'll be there by tomorrow afternoon."

Whenever she saw Rolfe again, they'd have a little chat about how, exactly, he calculated distances on that infernal map of his.

But Rowan's face had paled beneath the tattoos. After a moment, he added, "I can feel it—my magic can feel it."

"Tell me it's not under twenty feet of water."

A swift, cutting shake of the head. "I didn't want to risk getting too close. But it reminds me of the Sin-Eater's temple."

"So, a really lovely, welcoming, and relaxing place to be, then," she said.

Aedion laughed under his breath, eyes on the horizon. Dorian and Manon hauled themselves onto the bank below, dripping wet, the witch scanning the sea of islands ahead. If she noted anything, the witch said nothing.

Rowan surveyed the island they stood atop: high, shielded by a crumbling stone wall on one side, thorns on the other. "We'll camp here tonight. It's secure enough."

Aelin nearly sagged in relief. Lysandra uttered a faint thank-you to the gods.

Within minutes, they'd cleared enough of a general area, through physical and magical toiling, to find seats among the huge blocks of stone, and Aedion set about cooking: a rather sad meal of hard bread and the swamp creatures Gavriel and Rowan had hunted, deeming them safe enough to eat. Aelin didn't watch her cousin, preferring not to know what the hell she was about to shove down her throat.

The others seemed inclined to avert their attention as well, and though Aedion managed to wield their meager spices with surprising talent, some of the meat was . . . chewy. Slimy. Lysandra had politely, but thoroughly, gagged at one point.

Night set in, a sea of stars twinkling into existence. Aelin couldn't recall the last time she had been so far from civilization—perhaps on the ocean crossing to and from Wendlyn.

Aedion, seated beside her, passed the too-light skin of wine. She swigged from it, glad for the sour slide that washed away any lingering taste of the meat.

"Don't ever tell me what that was," Aelin murmured to him, watching the others quietly finish up their own food. Lysandra muttered her agreement.

Aedion grinned a bit wickedly, surveying the others as well. A few feet away, half in shadow, Manon monitored it all. But Aedion's gaze lingered on Dorian, and Aelin braced herself. But her cousin's smile turned softer. "He still eats like a fine lady."

Dorian's head snapped up—but Aelin bit back a laugh at the memory. Ten years ago, they'd sat around a table together and she'd told the Havilliard prince what she thought of his table manners. Dorian blinked as the memory no doubt resurfaced, even as the others glanced between them.

The king gave a magnanimous bow. "I'll take that as a compliment." Indeed, his hands were mostly clean, his now-dry clothes immaculate.

Her own hands . . . Aelin fished into a pocket for her handkerchief. The thing was as filthy as the rest of her, but . . . better than using her pants. She plucked out the Eye of Elena from where it was usually wrapped inside, setting it on her knee as she wiped the smear of spices and fat from her fingers, then offered the scrap of silk to Lysandra. Aelin casually ran her fingers over the bent metal of the Eye as the shifter cleaned her hands, the blue stone in its core flickering with cobalt fire.

"As far as I recall," Dorian went on with a sly grin, "you two—"

The attack happened so fast that Aelin didn't sense or see it until it was over.

One moment, Manon was seated at the edge of the fire, the marshes a dark sprawl behind her.

The next, scales and flashing white teeth were snapping for her, erupting from the brush on the bank. And then—stillness and silence as the enormous marsh beast froze in place.

Halted by invisible hands—strong ones.

Manon's sword was half out, her breathing ragged as she stared down the milky-pink maw spread wide enough to snap off her head. The teeth were each as long as Aelin's thumb.

Aedion swore. The others didn't so much as move.

But Dorian's magic held the beast still, frozen with no ice to be seen. The same power as the one he'd wielded against the Bloodhound. Aelin surveyed him for any tether, any gleaming thread of power, and found none. He hadn't even lifted a hand to direct it. Interesting.

Dorian said to Manon, the witch still peering into the yawning death inches before her face, "Shall I kill it or set it free?"

Aelin most certainly had an opinion on the matter, but a warning look from Rowan had her shutting her mouth. And gaping a bit at her prince.

Oh, you crafty old bastard. His harsh, tattooed face revealed nothing.

Manon glanced toward Dorian. "Free it."

The king's face tightened—then the beast went careening off into the dark, as if a god had hurled it across the marshes. A distant splash sounded.

Lysandra sighed. "Aren't they beautiful?"

Aelin cut her a look. The shifter grinned.

But Aelin looked back at Rowan, holding his stare. *How convenient that your shield vanished right as that thing waddled up. What an excellent opportunity for a magic lesson. What if it had gone wrong?*

Rowan's eyes glittered. *Why do you think the hole opened up by the witch?*

Aelin swallowed her laugh of dismay. But Manon Blackbeak was taking in the king, her hand still on her sword. Aelin didn't bother to pretend looking as if she wasn't watching them as the witch shifted those gold eyes to her. To the Eye of Elena still balanced on Aelin's knee.

Manon's lip curled back from her teeth. "Where did you get that."

The hair on Aelin's arms rose. "The Eye of Elena? It was a gift."

But the witch again glanced to Dorian—as if saving her from that thing . . . Oh, Rowan hadn't lowered the shield just for a magic lesson, had he? Aelin didn't dare glance at him this time, not as Manon dipped her fingers into the muddy earth to sketch a shape.

A large circle—and two overlapping circles, one atop the other, within its circumference. "That is the Three-Faced Goddess," Manon said, her voice low. "We call this . . ." She drew a rough line in the centermost circle, in the eye-shaped space where they overlapped. "The Eye of the Goddess. *Not* Elena." She circled the exterior again. "Crone," she said of the outermost circumference. She circled the interior top circle: "Mother." She circled the bottom: "Maiden." She stabbed the eye inside: "And the heart of the Darkness within her."

It was Aelin's turn to shake her head. The others didn't so much as blink.

Manon said again, "That is an Ironteeth symbol. Blueblood prophets have it tattooed over their hearts. And those who won valor in battle, when we lived in the Wastes . . . they were once given those. To mark our glory—our being Goddess-blessed."

Aelin debated chucking the gods-damned amulet into the marsh, but said, "The day I first saw Baba Yellowlegs . . . the amulet turned heavy and warm in her presence. I thought it was in warning. Perhaps it was in . . . recognition."

Manon studied the necklace of scars marring Aelin's throat. "Its power worked even with magic contained?"

"I was told that certain objects were . . . exempt." Aelin's voice strained. "Baba Yellowlegs knew the entire history of the Wyrdkeys and gates. She was the one who told me about them. Is that a part of your history, too?"

"No. Not in those terms," Manon said. "But Yellowlegs was an Ancient—she knew things now lost to us. She ripped down the walls of the Crochan city herself."

"The legends claim the slaughter was . . . catastrophic," Dorian said.

Shadows flickered in Manon's eyes. "That killing field, the last I heard, is still barren. Not a blade of grass grows on it. They say it's from Rhiannon Crochan's curse. Or from the blood that soaked it for the final three weeks of that war."

"What is the curse, exactly?" Lysandra asked, brows furrowing.

Manon examined her iron nails, long enough that Aelin thought she wouldn't answer. Aedion chucked the wineskin back into her lap, and Aelin swigged from it again as Manon at last replied. "Rhiannon Crochan held the gates to her city for three days and three nights against the three Ironteeth Matrons. Her sisters were dead around her, her children slaughtered, her consort spiked to one of the Ironteeth war caravans. The last Crochan Queen, the final hope of their thousand-year dynasty . . . She did not go gently. It was only when she fell at dawn on the fourth day that the city was truly lost. And as she lay dying on that killing field, as the Ironteeth ripped down the walls of the city around her and butchered her people . . . she cursed us. Cursed the three Matrons, and through them, all Ironteeth. She cursed Yellowlegs herself—who gave Rhiannon her finishing blow."

None of them moved or spoke or breathed too loudly.

"Rhiannon swore on her last breath that we would win the war, but not the land. That for what we had done, we would inherit the land only to see it wilt and die in our hands. Our beasts would shrivel and keel over dead; our witchlings would be stillborn, poisoned by the streams and rivers. Fish would rot in lakes before we could catch them. Rabbits and deer would flee across the mountains. And the once-verdant Witch Kingdom would become a wasteland.

"The Ironteeth laughed at it, drunk on Crochan blood. Until the first Ironteeth witchling was born—dead. And then another and another. Until the cattle rotted in the fields, and the crops withered overnight. By the end of the month, there was no food. By the second, the three Ironteeth Clans were turning on one another, ripping themselves to pieces. So the Matrons ordered us all into exile. Separated the Clans to cross the mountains and wander as we would. Every few decades, they would send groups to try to work the land, to see if the curse still held. Those groups never returned. We have been wanderers for five hundred years—the wound made worse by the fact that humans eventually took it for themselves. And the land responded to them."

"But you plan to return to it still?" Dorian asked.

Those golden eyes were not of this earth. "Rhiannon Crochan said there was one way—only one—to break the curse." Manon swallowed and recited in a cold, tight voice, "*Blood to blood and soul to soul, together this was done, and only together it can be undone. Be the bridge, be the light. When iron melts, when flowers spring from fields of blood—let the land be witness, and return home.*" Manon toyed with the end of her braid, the scrap of red cloak she'd tied around it. "Every Ironteeth witch in the world has pondered that curse. For five centuries, we have tried to break it."

"And your parents . . . their union was made in order to break this curse?" Aelin pushed—carefully.

A sharp nod. "I did not know—that Rhiannon's bloodline survived." And now ran through Manon's blue veins.

Dorian mused, "Elena predates the witch wars by a millennium. The Eye had nothing to do with that." He rubbed his neck. "Right?"

Manon didn't reply, only extending a foot to wipe away the symbol she'd traced in the dirt.

Aelin drained the rest of the wine and shoved the Eye back into her pocket. "Maybe now you understand," she said to Dorian, "why I've found Elena just a *bit* difficult to deal with."

The island was wide enough that a conversation could be had without being overheard.

Rowan supposed that was precisely what his former cadre wanted as they found him on watch atop the vine-choked, crumbling spiral stairwell that overlooked the island and its surroundings. Leaning against a section that had once been the curving wall, Rowan demanded, "What?"

Gavriel said, "You should take Aelin a thousand miles from here. Tonight."

A wave of his magic and honed instincts told him all was safe in the immediate vicinity, calming the killing rage he'd slipped into at the thought.

Fenrys said, "Whatever awaits us tomorrow, it has been waiting for a long time, Rowan."

"And how do either of you know this?"

Gavriel's tawny eyes gleamed animal-bright in the darkness. "Your beloved's life and the witch's are entwined. They have been led here, by forces even we cannot understand."

"Think about it," Fenrys pushed. "Two females whose paths crossed tonight in a way we've rarely witnessed. Two queens, who might control either half of this continent, two sides of one coin. Both half-breeds. Manon, an Ironteeth *and* a Crochan. Aelin . . ."

"Human and Fae," Rowan finished for him.

"Between them, they cover the three main races of this earth. Between the two of them, they are mortal and immortal; one worships fire, the other Darkness. Do I need to go on? It feels as if we're playing right into the hands of whoever has been running this game—for eons."

Rowan gave Fenrys a stare that usually had men backing away. Even as he considered it.

Gavriel interrupted to say, "Maeve has been waiting, Rowan. Since Brannon. For someone who would lead her to the keys. For your Aelin."

Maeve had not mentioned the Lock this spring. She hadn't mentioned Mala's ring, either. Rowan said slowly, his words a death promise, "Did Maeve send you because of this Lock, too?"

"No," Fenrys said. "No—she never mentioned that." He shifted on his feet, turning toward a distant, brutal roar. "If Maeve and Aelin go to war, Rowan, if they meet on a battlefield . . ."

He tried not to let himself imagine it. The cataclysmic carnage and destruction.

Perhaps they should have remained in the North, shoring up their defenses.

Fenrys breathed, "Maeve will not allow herself to lose. Already, she's replaced you."

Rowan whirled on Gavriel. "*Who*."

Those lion's eyes darkened. "Cairn."

Rowan's blood iced over, colder than his magic. "Is she insane?"

"She told us of his promotion a day before we left. He was grinning like a cat with a canary in its mouth as we walked out of the palace."

"He's a sadist." Cairn . . . No amount of training, both off the battlefield and on it, had ever broken the Fae warrior of his penchant for cruelty. Rowan had locked him up, flogged him, disciplined him, wielded whatever shred of compassion he could muster in himself . . . nothing. Cairn had been born savoring the suffering of others.

So Rowan had kicked him out of his own army—dumped him into Lorcan's lap. Cairn had lasted about a month with Lorcan before he was packed off to an isolated legion, commanded by a general who was not cadre and had no interest in being one. The tales of what Cairn did to the soldiers and innocents he encountered . . .

There were few laws against murder with the Fae. And Rowan had considered sparing the world of Cairn's vileness every time he'd seen him. For Maeve to appoint him to the cadre, to give him almost unchecked power and influence—

"I'd bet every bit of gold I have that she's going to let Aelin nearly break herself destroying Erawan . . . then strike when she's weakest," Fenrys mused.

For Maeve not to have given either male a gag order through the blood oath . . . She wanted him—wanted Aelin—to have this knowledge. To worry and speculate.

Fenrys and Gavriel swapped wary glances. "We still serve her, Rowan," Gavriel murmured. "And we still have to kill Lorcan when the time comes."

"Why bring this up at all? I won't get in your way. Neither will Aelin, believe me."

"Because," Fenrys said, "Maeve's style isn't to execute. It's to punish—slowly. Over years. But she wants Lorcan *dead*. And not half dead, or throat slit, but irrevocably dead."

"Beheaded and burned," Gavriel said grimly.

Rowan loosed a breath. "Why?"

Fenrys cast his glance over the edge of the stairs—to where Aelin slept, her golden hair shining in the moonlight. "Lorcan and you are the most powerful males in the world."

"You forget Lorcan and Aelin can't even stand to be in the same breathing space. I doubt there's a chance of an alliance between them."

"All we're saying," Fenrys explained, "is that Maeve does not make decisions without considerable motive. Be ready for anything. Sending her armada, wherever it is, is only the start."

The marsh beasts roared, and Rowan wanted to roar right back. If Aelin and Cairn ever encountered each other, if Maeve had some plan beyond her greed for the keys . . .

Aelin turned in her sleep, scowling at the ruckus, Lysandra dozing beside her in ghost leopard form, that fluffy tail twitching. Rowan pushed off the wall, more than ready to join his queen. But he found Fenrys staring at her as well, his face tight and drawn. Fenrys's voice was a broken whisper as he said, "Kill me. If that order is given. Kill me, Rowan, before I have to do it."

"You'll be dead before you can get within a foot of her."

Not a threat—a promise and a plain statement of fact. Fenrys's shoulders slumped in thanks.

"I'm glad, you know," Fenrys said with unusual graveness, "that I got this time. That Maeve unintentionally gave me that. That I got to know what it was like—to be here, as a part of this."

Rowan didn't have words, so he looked to Gavriel.

But the Lion was merely nodding as he stared down at the little camp below. At his sleeping son.

CHAPTER 54

The last leg of the trek the next morning was the longest yet, Manon thought.

Close—so close to this Lock the queen with a witch emblem in her pocket was seeking.

She'd fallen asleep, pondering how it could be connected, but gleaned nothing. They'd all been awake before dawn, dragged to consciousness by the oppressive humidity, so heavy it felt like a blanket weighing on Manon's shoulders.

The queen was mostly quiet from where she walked at the head of their company, her mate scouting overhead, and her cousin and the shape-shifter flanking her, the latter wearing the skin of a truly horrific swamp viper. The Wolf and the Lion brought up the rear, sniffing and listening for anything wrong.

The people who had once dwelled within these lands had not met easy or pleasant ends. She could feel their pain even now, whispering through the stones, rippling through the water. That marsh beast that had snuck up on her last night was the mildest of the horrors here. At her side, Dorian Havilliard's tense tan face seemed to suggest he felt the same.

Manon waded waist-deep through a pool of warm, thick water and asked, if only to get it out of where it rattled in her skull, "How will she use the keys to banish Erawan and his Valg? Or, for that matter, get rid of the things he's created that aren't of his original realm, but are some hybrid?"

Sapphire eyes slid toward her. "What?"

"Is there a way of weeding out who belongs and who doesn't? Or will all those with Valg blood"—she put a hand on her sodden chest—"be sent into that realm of darkness and cold?"

Dorian's teeth gleamed as he clenched them. "I don't know," he admitted, watching Aelin nimbly hop over a stone. "If she does, I assume she'll tell us when it's most convenient for her."

And the least convenient for them, he didn't need to add.

"And she gets to decide, I suppose? Who stays and who goes."

"Banishing people to live with the Valg isn't something Aelin would willingly do."

"But she does decide, ultimately."

Dorian paused atop a little hill. "Whoever holds those keys gets to decide. And you'd better pray to whatever wicked gods you worship that it's Aelin holding them in the end."

"What about you?"

"Why should I wish to go anywhere near those things?"

"You're as powerful as she is. You could wield them. Why not?"

The others were swiftly pulling ahead, but Dorian remained still. Even had the audacity to grip her wrist—hard. "Why not?" There was such unyielding coldness in that beautiful face. She couldn't turn away from it. A hot, humid breeze shoved past, dragging her hair with it. The wind didn't touch him, didn't ruffle one raven-dark hair on his head. A shield—he was shielding himself. Against her, or whatever was in this swamp? He said softly, "Because I was the one who did it."

She waited.

His sapphire eyes were chips of ice. "I killed my father. I shattered the castle. I purged my own court. So if I had the keys, Wing Leader," he finished as he released her wrist, "I have no doubt that I would do the same once more—across this continent."

"Why?" she breathed, her blood chilling.

She was indeed a bit terrified of the icy rage rippling from him as Dorian said, "Because she died. And even before she did, this world saw to it that she suffered, and was afraid, and alone. And even though no one will remember who she was, I do. I will never forget the color of her eyes, or the way she smiled. And I will never forgive them for taking it away."

Too breakable—he'd said of human women. No wonder he'd come to her.

Manon had no answer, and she knew he wasn't looking for one, but she said anyway, "Good."

She ignored the glimmer of relief that flashed across his face as she moved ahead.

Rowan's calculations hadn't been wrong: they reached the Lock by midday.

Aelin supposed that even if Rowan hadn't scouted ahead, it would have been obvious from the moment they beheld the waterlogged, labyrinthine complex of wrecked pillars that the Lock likely lay in the half-crumbling stone dome in its center. Mostly because everything—every choking weed and drop of water—seemed to be leaning *away* from it. Like the complex was the dark, rippling heartbeat of the marshes.

Rowan shifted as he landed before where they had all gathered on a grassy, dry bit of land on the outskirts of the sprawling complex, not even missing a step as he walked to her side. She tried not to look too relieved as he safely returned.

She really tortured them, she realized, by shoving her way into danger whenever she felt like it. Perhaps she'd try to be better about it, if this dread was at all like what they felt.

"This whole place is too quiet," Rowan said. "I probed the area, but . . . nothing."

Aedion drew the Sword of Orynth from across his back. "We'll circle the perimeter, making smaller passes until we get up to the building itself. No surprises."

Lysandra stepped back from them, bracing for the shift. "I'll take the water—if you hear two roars, get to higher ground. One quick roar, and it's clear."

Aelin nodded in confirmation and order to go ahead. By the time Aedion had strode for the outer wall of the complex, Lysandra had slipped into the water, all scales and talons.

Rowan jerked his chin to Gavriel and Fenrys. Both males silently shifted and then trotted ahead, the latter joining Aedion, the former in the opposite direction.

Rowan kept to Aelin's side, Dorian and the witch at her back, as they waited for the all clear.

When Lysandra's solitary, swift roar cleaved the air, Aelin murmured to Rowan, "What's the catch? *Where* is the catch? It's too easy." Indeed, there was nothing and no one here. No threat beyond what might be rotting away in the pits and sinkholes.

"Believe me, I've been considering it."

She could almost feel him sliding into that frozen, raging place—where born instinct and centuries of training had him seeing the world as a killing field, and willing to do anything to eradicate any threats to her. Not just his Fae nature—but *Rowan*'s nature. To protect, to shield, to fight for what and who he loved.

Aelin stepped close and kissed him on the neck. Those pine-green eyes warmed slightly as they shifted from the ruin to scan her face.

"When we get back to civilization," he said, his voice deepening as he kissed her cheek, her ear, her brow, "I'm going to find you the nicest inn on the whole gods-damned continent."

"Oh?" He kissed her mouth. Once, twice.

"With good food, a disgustingly comfortable bed, and a big bathtub."

Even in the marshes, it was easy to become drunk on him, on the taste and smell and sound and feel of him. "How big?" she murmured, not caring what the others thought as they returned.

"Big enough for two," he said onto her lips.

Her blood turned sparkling at the promise. She kissed him once—briefly but deeply. "I have no defenses against such offers. Especially those made by such a pretty male."

He scowled at *pretty*, nipping at her ear with his canines. "I keep a tally, you know, Princess. To remind myself to repay you the next time we're alone for all the truly wonderful things you say."

Her toes curled in her soggy boots. But she patted him on the shoulder, looking him over with absolute irreverence, saying as she walked ahead, "I certainly hope you make me beg for it."

His answering growl from behind made heat bloom in her core.

The feeling lasted for about a minute, however. Within a few turns into the maze of crumbling walls and pillars, leaving Dorian to guard the entrance and Rowan slipping ahead, Aelin found herself beside the witch—who looked more bored than anything. Fair enough. She'd been dragged here, after all.

Wading as quietly as they could into the towering archways and pillars of stone, Rowan signaled from a crossroads ahead. They were getting close.

Aelin unsheathed Goldryn, Manon drawing her own sword in answer.

Aelin lifted her brows as she glanced between their two blades. "What's your sword called?"

"Wind-Cleaver."

Aelin clicked her tongue. "Good name."

"Yours?"

"Goldryn."

A slash of iron teeth as they were bared in a half smile. "Not as good a name."

"Blame my ancestor." She certainly did. For many, many things.

They reached a crossroads—one leading left, one right. Neither offering a hint of the direct path to the center of the ruin.

Rowan said to Manon, "You go left. Whistle if you find anything."

Manon stalked off among the stones and water and reeds, shoulders tight enough to suggest she hadn't appreciated the order, but she wasn't dumb enough to tangle with him.

Aelin smiled a bit at the thought as she and Rowan continued on. Running her free palm over the carved walls they passed, she said casually, "That sunrise Mala appeared to you—what, exactly, did she say?"

He slashed a glance in her direction. "Why?"

Her heart turned thunderous, and maybe it made her a coward to say it now—

Rowan gripped her elbow as he read her body, scented her fear and pain. "Aelin."

She braced herself, nothing but stone and water and bramble around them, and turned a corner.

And there it was.

Even Rowan forgot to demand an answer to what she'd been about to tell him as they surveyed the open space flanked by crumbling walls and punctuated by fallen pillars. And at its northern end . . . "Big surprise," Aelin muttered. "There's an altar."

"It's a chest," Rowan corrected with a half smile. "It's got a lid."

"Even better," she said, nudging him with an elbow. Yes—yes, she'd tell him later.

The water separating them from the chest was still and silver bright—too murky to see if there was a bottom at all beyond the steps up to the dais. Aelin reached for her water magic, hoping it'd whisper of what lay beneath that surface, but her flames were burning too loudly.

Splashing issued across the way, and Manon appeared around an opposite wall. Her focus went to the enormous stone chest at the rear of the space, the stone cracked and overflowing with weeds and vines. She began easing across the water, one step at a time.

Aelin said, "Don't touch the chest."

Manon just gave her a long look and kept heading for the dais.

Trying not to slip on the slick floor, Aelin crossed the space, sloshing water over the dais steps as she mounted them, Rowan close behind.

Manon leaned over the chest to study the lid but did not open it. Studying, Aelin realized, the countless Wyrdmarks carved into the stone.

Nehemia had known how to use the marks. Had been taught them and was fluent enough in them to have wielded their power. Aelin had never asked how or why or when.

But here were Wyrdmarks, deep within Eyllwe.

Aelin stepped up to Manon, examining the lid more closely. "Do you know what those are?"

Manon brushed back her long white hair. "I've never seen such markings."

Aelin examined a few, her memory straining for the translation. "Some of these aren't symbols I've encountered before. Some are." She scratched her head. "Should we throw a rock at it—see what it does?" she asked, twisting to where Rowan peered over her shoulder.

But a hollow throb of air pulsed around them, silencing the incessant buzz of the marshes' inhabitants. And it was that utter silence, the bark of surprise from Fenrys, that had Aelin and Manon shifting into flanking, defensive positions. As if they'd done this a hundred times before.

But Rowan had gone still as he scanned the gray skies, the ruins, the water.

"What is it?" Aelin breathed.

Before her prince could answer, Aelin felt it again. A pulsing, dark wind *demanding* their attention. Not the Valg. No, this darkness was born of something else.

"Lorcan," Rowan breathed, a hand on his sword—but not drawing it.

"Is that his magic?" Aelin shuddered as that death-kissed wind shoved at her. She batted it away as if it were a gnat. It snapped at her in answer.

"It's his warning signal," Rowan murmured.

"For what?" Manon asked sharply.

Rowan was instantly moving, scaling the high walls with ease, even as stone crumbled away. He balanced on its top, surveying the land on the other side of the wall.

Then he smoothly climbed back down, his splash as he landed echoing off the stones.

Lysandra slithered around a cluster of weeds and halted with a swift thrust of her scaled tail as Rowan said too calmly, "There is an aerial legion approaching."

Manon breathed, "Ironteeth?"

"No," Rowan said, meeting Aelin's gaze with an icy steadiness that had seen him through centuries of battle. "Ilken."

"How many?" Aelin's voice turned distant—hollow.

Rowan's throat bobbed, and she knew he'd been taking in the horizon and surrounding lands not for any chance of winning the battle that was sure to come, but for any shot at getting her out. Even if the rest of them had to buy her time with their own lives.

"Five hundred."

CHAPTER 55

Lorcan's breath singed his throat with every inhalation, but he kept running through the marshes, Elide laboring beside him, never complaining, only scanning the skies with wide, dark eyes.

Lorcan sent out another flickering blast of his power. Not toward the winged army that raced not too far ahead, but farther—toward wherever Whitethorn and his bitch-queen might be in this festering place. If those ilken reached them long before Lorcan could arrive, that Wyrdkey the bitch carried would be as good as lost. And Elide . . . He shut out the thoughts.

The ilken flew hard and fast, heading toward what had to be the heart of the marshes. What the hell had brought the queen out here?

Elide flagged, and Lorcan gripped her under an elbow to keep her upright as she stumbled over a bit of pockmarked stone. Faster. If the ilken caught them unawares, if they stole his revenge and that key . . .

Lorcan sent out burst after burst of his power in every direction.

Keys aside, he didn't want to see the look on Elide's face if the ilken got there first. And they found whatever was left of the fire-breather and her court.

There was nowhere to go.

In the heart of this festering plain, there was nowhere to run, or hide.

Erawan had tracked them here. Had sent five hundred ilken to retrieve them. If the ilken had found them on the sea and in this endless wasteland, they'd no doubt be able to find them if they tried hiding among the ruins.

They were all silent as they gathered on a grassy hill at the edge of the ruins, watching that black mass take form. Deep in the ruins behind them, the chest still waited. Untouched.

Aelin knew the Lock couldn't help—other than to waste their time by opening its container. Brannon could get in line to complain.

And Lorcan . . . somewhere out there. She'd think on that later. At least Fenrys and Gavriel had remained, rather than charging off to fulfill Maeve's kill order.

Rowan said, eyes pinned on those swift, leathery wings far on the horizon, "We'll use the ruin to our advantage. Force them to bottleneck in key areas." Like a cloud of locusts, the ilken blocked out the clouds, the light, the sky. A dull, glazed sort of calm swept over Aelin.

Eight against five hundred.

Fenrys quickly tied back his golden hair. "We divide it up, take them out. Before they can get close enough. While they're still in the air." He tapped his foot on the ground, rolling his shoulders—as if shaking off the grip of that blood oath roaring at him to hunt down Lorcan.

Aelin rasped, "There's another way."

"No," was Rowan's response.

She swallowed hard and lifted her chin. "There is nothing and no one out here. The risk of using that key would be minimal—"

Rowan's teeth flashed as he snarled, "No, and that's final."

Aelin said too quietly, "You don't give me orders."

She saw as much as she felt Rowan's temper rise with dizzying speed. "You will have to pry that key out of my cold, dead hands."

He meant it, too—he'd make her kill him before he let her use the key in any capacity beyond wielding the Lock.

Aedion let out a low, bitter laugh. "You wanted to send a message to our enemies about your power, Aelin." Closer and closer that army came, and Rowan's ice and wind licked at her as he tunneled down into his magic. Aedion jerked his chin toward the army approaching. "It seems Erawan sent his answer."

Aelin hissed, "You blame me for this?"

Aedion's eyes darkened. "We should have stayed in the North."

"I had no choice, I'll have you remember."

"You did," Aedion breathed, none of the others, not even Rowan, stepping in. "You've had a choice all along, and you opted to flash your magic around."

Aelin knew very well that her eyes were now flickering with flames as she took a step toward him. "So I guess the 'you're perfect' stage is over, then."

Aedion's lip curled off his teeth. "This isn't a game. This is *war*, and you pushed and pushed Erawan to show his hand. You refused to run your schemes by us first, to let us weigh in, when *we* have fought wars—"

"Don't you *dare* pin this on me." Aelin peered inside herself—to the power there. Down and down it went, to that pit of eternal fire.

"This isn't the time," Gavriel offered.

Aedion threw out a hand in his direction, a silent, vicious order for the Lion to shut his mouth. "Where are our allies, Aelin? Where are our armies? All we have to show for our efforts is a Pirate Lord who might very well change his mind if he hears about this from the wrong lips."

She held in the words. *Time.* She had needed *time*—

"If we're going to stand a chance," Rowan said, "we need to get into position."

Embers sparked at her fingertips. "We do it together." She tried not to look offended at their raised brows, their slightly gaping mouths. "Magic might not last against them. But steel will." She jerked her chin at Rowan, at Aedion. "Plan it."

So they did. Rowan stepped to her side, a hand on her lower back. The only comfort he'd show—when he knew, they both knew, it hadn't been his argument to win. He said to the Fae males, "How many arrows?"

"Ten quivers, fully stocked," Gavriel said, eyeing Aedion as he removed the Sword of Orynth from his back and rebuckled it at his side.

Returned to her human form, Lysandra had drifted to the edge of the bank, back stiff as the ilken gathered on the horizon.

Aelin left the males to sort out their positions and slipped up beside her friend. "You don't have to fight. You can stay with Manon—guard the other direction."

Indeed, Manon was already scaling one of the ruin walls, a quiver with unnervingly few arrows slung over her back beside Wind-Cleaver. Aedion had ordered her to scout the other direction for any nasty surprises. The witch had looked ready to debate—until she seemed to realize that, on this battlefield at least, she was not the apex predator.

Lysandra loosely braided her black hair, her golden skin sallow. "I don't know how they have done this so many times. For *centuries*."

"Honestly, I don't know, either," Aelin said, glancing over a shoulder at the Fae males now analyzing the layout of the marshes, the flow of the wind, whatever else to use to their advantage.

Lysandra rubbed at her face, then squared her shoulders. "The marsh beasts are easily enraged. Like someone I know." Aelin jabbed the shifter with an elbow, and Lysandra snorted, even with the army ahead. "I can rile them up—threaten their nests. So that if the ilken land . . ."

"They won't just have us to deal with." Aelin gave her a grim smile.

But Lysandra's skin was still pale, her breathing a bit shallow. Aelin threaded her fingers through the shifter's and squeezed tightly.

Lysandra squeezed back once before letting go to shift, murmuring, "I'll signal when I'm done."

Aelin just nodded, lingering on the bank for a moment to watch the long-legged white bird flap across the marsh—toward that building darkness.

She turned back to the others in time to see Rowan jerk his chin to Aedion, Gavriel, and Fenrys. "You three herd them—to us."

"And you lot?" Aedion said, sizing up her, Rowan, and Dorian.

"I get the first shot," Aelin said, flames dancing in her eyes.

Rowan inclined his head. "My lady wants the first shot. She gets the first shot. And when they're scattering in a blind panic, we come in."

Aedion gave her a long look. "Don't miss this time."

"Asshole," she snapped.

Aedion's smile didn't reach his eyes as he strode to fetch extra weapons from their packs, grabbing a quiver of arrows in either hand, slinging one of the longbows across his broad back along with his shield. Manon had already stationed herself atop the wall behind them, grunting as she strung Aedion's other bow.

Rowan was saying to Dorian, "Short bursts. Find your targets—the center of groups—and use only what magic is necessary. Don't waste it all at once. Aim for the heads, if you can."

"What about once they start landing?" Dorian asked, sizing up the terrain.

"Shield yourself, attack when you can. Keep the wall to your back at all times."

"I won't be his prisoner again."

Aelin tried to shut out what he'd meant by it.

But Manon said from the wall above them, an arrow now nocked loosely in her bow, "If it comes to that, princeling, I'll kill you before they can."

Aelin hissed, "You will do no such thing."

Both of them ignored her as Dorian said, "Thank you."

"*None* of you are being taken prisoner," Aelin growled, and walked away.

And there would be no second or third shots.

Only the first shot. Only her shot.

Perhaps it was time to see how deep that new well of power went. What lived inside it.

Perhaps it was time for Morath to learn to scream.

Aelin stepped up to the water's edge, then leaped onto the next island of grass and stone. Rowan silently came up beside her, meeting her pace for pace. It wasn't until they reached the next hill that he angled his face toward her, his golden skin stretched taut, his eyes as cold as her own.

Only that anger was directed at her—perhaps more livid than she'd seen him since Mistward. She bared her teeth in a feral, grim smile. "I know, I know. Just add suggesting to use the Wyrdkey to that tally of all the horrible things I do and say."

Leathery, massive wings beat the air, and shrieking cries at last began to trickle toward them. Her knees quaked, but she clamped down on the fear, knowing he could scent it, knowing the others could, too.

So she willed herself to take another step onto the sodden, reed-laden plain—toward that ilken army. They'd be upon them in minutes—less, maybe.

And horrible, miserable Lorcan had bought them that extra time. Wherever the bastard was.

Rowan didn't object as she took another step, then another. She had to put distance between them all—had to make sure that every last ember was capable of reaching that army and that she didn't waste her strength by traveling far to do so.

Which meant striding out into the marshes alone. To wait for those things to be close enough to see their teeth. They had to know who now marched through the reeds toward them. What she'd do to them.

But still the ilken charged.

In the distance, far to the right, marsh creatures began to roar—no doubt in Lysandra's wake. She prayed the beasts were hungry. And that they didn't mind Morath-bred meat.

"Aelin." Rowan's voice cut across water and plant and wind. She paused, looking over a shoulder at where he now stood on the sandbank, as if it'd been impossible *not* to follow her.

The strong, unyielding bones of his face were set with that warrior's brutality. But his pine-green eyes were bright—almost soft—as he said, "Remember who you are. Every step of the way down, and every step of the way back. Remember who you are. And that you're mine."

She thought of the new, delicate scars on his back—marks from her own nails, that he'd refused to heal with his magic, and instead had set with seawater, the salt locking the scars into place before the immortal body could smooth it over. Her claiming marks, he'd breathed into her mouth the last time he'd been inside her. So he and anyone who saw them would know that he belonged to her. That he was hers, just as she was his.

And because he was hers, because they were *all* hers . . .

Aelin turned away from him and sprinted across the plain.

With every step toward the army whose wings she could just make out, she watched for those beasts Lysandra riled, even as she began a swift, deadly descent into the core of her magic.

She had been hovering around the middle ledge of her power for days now, one eye on the churning, molten abyss far below. Rowan knew. Fenrys and Gavriel, definitely. Shielding them, drying their clothes, killing the insects that plagued them . . . all little ways to relieve the strain, to keep herself steady, to grow accustomed to its depth and pressure.

For the deeper she went into her power, the more her body, her mind, squeezed under the pressure of it. That was the burnout—when that pressure won, when the magic was drained too fast or too greedily, when it was spent and still the bearer tried to claw deeper than it should.

Aelin slammed to a stop in the heart of the plain. The ilken had spied her sprinting and now flapped toward her.

Unaware of the three males who crept far out, bows at the ready to push Erawan's soldiers onto her flames.

If she could burn through their defenses. She'd have to drag up every bit of her power to incinerate them all. The true might of Aelin Fire-Bringer. Not an ember less.

So Aelin abandoned every trapping of civilization, of conscience and rules and humanity, and plummeted into her fire.

She flew for that flaming abyss, only distantly aware of the humidity lying thick on her skin, of the pressure building in her head.

She'd shoot straight down—and push off the bottom, bringing all that power with her to the surface. The drag would be enormous. And it would be the test, the true test, of control and strength. Easy—so easy to spear into the heart of fire and ash. The hard part was bringing it up; that was when the cracking would occur.

Deeper and deeper, Aelin shot into her power. Through distant, mortal eyes, she noted the ilken sweeping closer. A mercy—if they had once been human, perhaps obliterating them would be a mercy.

Aelin knew she'd reached the former edge of her power thanks to warning bells in her blood that pealed in her wake. That pealed as she launched herself into the burning depths of hell.

The Queen of Flame and Shadow, the Heir of Fire, Aelin of the Wildfire, Fireheart . . .

She burned through each title, even as she became them, became what those foreign ambassadors had hissed when they reported on a child-queen's growing, unstable power in Terrasen. A promise that had been whispered into the blackness.

The pressure began to build in her head, in her veins.

Far behind, safely out of her range, she felt the flickers of Rowan's and Dorian's magic as they rallied the blasts that would answer her own.

Aelin soared into the uncharted core of her power.

The inferno went on and on.

CHAPTER 56

Lorcan knew they were still too slow, warning signal or not.

Elide was gasping for breath, weaving on her feet as Lorcan halted on the outskirts of a massive, flooded plain. She pushed back a stray strand of hair from her face, Athril's ring glinting on her finger. She hadn't questioned where it had come from or what it did when he'd slipped it onto her finger this morning. He'd only warned her to never take it off, that it might be the one thing to keep her safe from the ilken, from Morath.

The force had swept northward and away from where Lorcan and Elide had hauled ass, no doubt to secure some better approach. And at the far end of the plain, too distant for Elide's human eyes to clearly make out, Whitethorn's silver hair glinted, the King of Adarlan at his side. Magic, bright and cold, swirling around them. And farther out—

Gods above. Gavriel and Fenrys were in the reeds, bows drawn. And Gavriel's son. Aimed at the army approaching. Waiting for—

Lorcan tracked where they were all facing.

Not the army closing in on them.

But the queen standing alone in the heart of the flooded plain.

Lorcan realized a moment too late that he and Elide were on the wrong side of the demarcation line—too far north of where Aelin's companions stood safely behind her.

Realized it the exact heartbeat that Elide's eyes fell on the golden-haired woman facing that army.

Her arms slackened at her sides. Her face drained of color.

Elide staggered one step—one step toward Aelin, a small noise coming out of her.

That's when he felt it.

Lorcan had sensed it once before, that day at Mistward. When the Queen of Terrasen had laid waste to the Valg princes, when her power had been a behemoth surging from the deep, setting the world trembling.

That was nothing—*nothing*—compared to the power that now roared into the world.

Elide stumbled, gaping at the spongy earth as the marsh water rippled.

Five hundred ilken closed in around them. They had taken his warning—and set a trap.

And that power . . . that power Aelin was now dragging up from whatever hellhole was inside her, from whatever fiery pit she'd been damned to endure . . . Its wake would wash over them.

"What is . . . ," Elide breathed, but Lorcan lunged for her, hurling them to the ground, covering her body with his. He threw a shield over them, plummeting hard and fast into his magic, the drop nearly uncontrolled. He didn't have time to do anything but pour every ounce of power into his shield, into the one barrier that would keep them from being melted into nothing.

He shouldn't have wasted the effort warning them. Not when it was now likely to get him and Elide killed.

Whitethorn knew—even at Mistward—that the queen hadn't yet stepped into her birthright. Knew that this sort of power came around once in an eon, and to serve it, to serve *her* . . .

A court that wouldn't just change the world. It would start the world over.

A court that could conquer this world—and any other it wished.

If it wished. If that woman on the plain desired to. And that was the question, wasn't it?

"Lorcan," Elide whispered, her voice breaking in longing for the queen, or terror of her, he didn't know.

Didn't have time to guess, as a feral roar went up from the reeds. A command.

And then a hail of arrows, precisely and brutally aimed, flew from the marshes to strike at the outer flanks of the ilken. He marked Fenrys's shots by the black-tipped arrows that easily found their marks. Gavriel's son didn't miss, either. Ilken tumbled from the sky, and the others panicked, flapping into one another, careening inward.

Right to where the Queen of Terrasen unleashed the full force of her magic upon them.

The moment Lysandra roared to signal that the marsh beasts were riled and she was safely behind their lines again, the moment the ilken got so close Aedion could shoot them out of the sky like geese, his queen erupted.

Even with Aelin's aim away from them, even with Rowan's shield, the heat of that fire *burned*. "Holy gods," Aedion found himself saying as he stumbled back through the reeds, falling farther behind her line of attack. "Holy rutting gods."

The heart of the legion didn't have the chance to scream as they were washed away in a sea of flame.

Aelin was no savior to rally behind, but a cataclysm to be weathered.

The fire grew hotter, his bones groaning as sweat beaded on his brow. But Aedion took up a new spot, glancing to ensure his father and Fenrys had done the same across the drowned plain, and aimed for the ilken veering out of the flame's path. He made his arrows count.

Ashes fell to the earth in a slow, steady snow.

Not fast enough. As if sensing Aelin's dragging pace, ice and wind erupted overhead.

Where gold-and-red flame did not melt Erawan's legion, Dorian and Rowan ripped them apart.

The ilken still held out, as if they were a stain of darkness, harder to wash away.

Still Aelin kept burning. Aedion couldn't even see her in the heart of that power.

There was a cost—there had to be a cost to such power.

She had been born knowing the weight of her crown, her magic. Had felt its isolation long before she'd reached adolescence. And that seemed like punishment enough, but . . . there had to be a price.

Nameless is my price. That was what the witch had said.

Understanding glimmered at the edge of Aedion's mind, just out of grasp. He fired his second-to-last arrow, straight between the eyes of a frantic ilken.

One by one, their own foul-bred resistance to magic yielded to those bursts of ice, and wind, and flame.

And then Whitethorn began walking into the firestorm fifty feet ahead. Toward Aelin.

Lorcan pinned Elide to the earth, throwing every last shadow and pocket of darkness into that shield. The flames were so hot that sweat dripped down his brow, right into her silken hair, spread on the green moss. The marsh water around them boiled.

Boiled. Fish floated belly-up. The grasses dried out and caught fire. The entire world was a hell-realm, with no end and no beginning.

Lorcan's shredded, dark soul tipped its head back and roared in unison to her power's burning song.

Elide was cringing, fists balled in his shirt, face buried against his neck as he gritted his teeth and weathered the firestorm. Not just fire, he realized. But wind and ice. Two other, mighty magics had joined her—shredding the ilken. And his own shield.

Wave after wave, the magic battered his power. A lesser gift might have been broken against it—a lesser magic might have tried to fight back, and not just let the power wash over them.

If Erawan got a collar around Aelin Galathynius's neck . . . it would be over.

To leash that woman, that power . . . Would a collar even be able to contain *that*?

There was movement through the flames.

Whitethorn was prowling across the boiling marshes, his steps unhurried.

The flame swirled around the dome of Rowan's shield, eddying with his icy wind.

Only a male who'd lost his damn mind would wander into that storm.

The ilken died and died and died, slowly and not at all cleanly, as their dark magic failed them. Those that tried to flee the flame or ice or wind were felled by arrows. Those that managed to land were shredded apart by ambushes of claws and fangs and snapping, scaled tails.

They'd made every minute of his warning count. Had easily set a trap for the ilken. That they'd fallen for it so swiftly—

But Rowan reached the queen in the heart of the marshes as her flames winked out. As his own wind died out, and plumes of unforgiving ice shattered the few ilken flapping in the skies.

Ash and glittering ice rained down, thick and swirling as snow, embers dancing between the clumps that had once been the ilken. There were no survivors. Not one.

Lorcan didn't dare lift his shield.

Not as the prince stepped onto the small island where the queen was standing. Not as Aelin turned toward Rowan, and the only flame that remained was a crown of fire atop her head.

Lorcan watched in silence as Rowan slid a hand over her waist, the other cupping the side of her face, and kissed his queen.

Embers stirred her unbound hair as she wrapped her arms around his neck and pressed close. A golden crown of flame flickered to life atop Rowan's head—the twin to the one Lorcan had seen burning that day at Mistward.

He knew Whitethorn. He knew the prince wasn't ambitious—not in the way that immortals could be. He likely would have loved the woman if she'd been ordinary. But this power . . .

In his wasteland of a soul, Lorcan felt that tug. Hated it.

It was why Whitethorn had strode to her—why Fenrys was now halfway across the plain, dazed, attention wholly fixed on where they stood, tangled in each other.

Elide stirred beneath him. "Is—is it over?"

Given the heat with which the queen was kissing her prince, he wasn't entirely sure what to tell Elide. But he let her squirm out from beneath him, twisting to her feet to spy the two figures on the horizon. He rose, watching with her.

"They killed them all," she breathed.

An entire legion—gone. Not easily, but—they'd done it.

Ash continued to fall, clumping on Elide's silky night-dark hair. He gently picked out a bit, then put a shield over her to keep it from landing on her again.

He hadn't touched her since last night. There hadn't been time, and he hadn't wanted to think about what her kiss had done to him. How it had utterly wrecked him and still twisted up his guts in ways he wasn't sure he could live with.

Elide said, "What do we do now?"

It took him a moment to realize what she'd meant. Aelin and Rowan at last pulled apart, though the prince leaned in to nuzzle her neck.

Power called to power among the Fae. Perhaps Aelin Galathynius was unlucky the cadre had been drawn to Maeve's power long before she was born, had chained themselves to her instead.

Perhaps they were the unlucky ones, for not holding out for something better.

Lorcan shook his head to clear the useless, traitorous thoughts.

That was Aelin Galathynius standing there. Drained of her power.

He felt it now—the utter lack of sound or feeling or heat where there had been such a riotous storm moments before. A creeping cold.

She'd emptied her entire cache. They all had. Maybe Whitethorn had gone to her, put his arms around her, not because he wanted to mount her in the middle of the marshes, but to keep her upright once that power was gone. Once she was left vulnerable.

Open to attack.

What do we do now? Elide had asked.

Lorcan smiled slightly. "We go say hello."

She balked at the shift in his tone. "You're not on friendly terms."

Certainly not, and he wasn't about to be, not when the queen was within his sights. Not when she had that Wyrdkey . . . the sibling to the one Elide carried.

"They won't attack me," he said, and began heading for them. The marsh water was near-scalding, and he grimaced at the fish floating, milky eyes open wide to the sky. Frogs and other beasts bobbed among them, wobbling in his ripples.

Elide hissed at entering the hot water but followed after him.

Slowly, Lorcan closed in on his prey, too focused on the fire-breathing bitch to notice that Fenrys and Gavriel had vanished from their positions in the reeds.

CHAPTER 57

Every step toward Aelin was an eternity—and every step was somehow too swift.

Elide had never been more aware of her limp. Of her dirty clothes; of her long, unshaped hair; of her small body and lack of any discernible gifts.

She had imagined Aelin's power, dreamed of how it had shattered the glass castle.

She hadn't considered that the reality of seeing it unleashed would make her bones quail in terror. Or that the others would possess such harrowing gifts as well—ice and wind twining with fire, until only death rained down. She almost felt bad for the ilken they'd slaughtered. Almost.

Lorcan was silent. Tense.

She was able to read his moods now, the little tells that he believed no one could detect. But there—that faint twitch on the left side of his mouth. That was his attempt to suppress whatever rage was now riding him. And there, that slight angle of his head to the right . . . that was his assessing and reassessing every surrounding, every weapon and obstacle within sight. Whatever this meeting was, Lorcan didn't think it would go well.

He expected to fight.

But Aelin—*Aelin*—had now turned toward them from where she stood on that mound of grass. Her silver-haired prince pivoted with her. Took a casual step in front of her. Aelin sidestepped around him. He tried to block her again. She nudged him with an elbow and held her ground at his side. The Prince of Doranelle—her queen's lover. How much sway would his opinion hold over Aelin? If he hated Lorcan, would his contempt and mistrust for her as well be immediate?

She should have thought of it—how it'd look to be with Lorcan. Approach with Lorcan.

"Regretting your choice in allies?" Lorcan said with cutting calm. Like he'd been able to read her tells, too.

"It sends a message, doesn't it?"

She could have sworn something like hurt flashed in his eyes. But it was typical Lorcan—even when she'd ripped into him atop that barge, he'd barely flinched.

He said coolly, "It would seem our bargain with each other is about to end anyway. I'll be sure to explain the terms, don't worry. I'd hate for them to think you were slumming it with me."

"That's not what I meant."

He snorted. "I don't care."

Elide halted, wanting to call him a liar, half because she knew he *was* lying and half because her own chest tightened at the words. But she kept silent, letting him walk ahead, that distance between them yawning wider with his every storming step.

But what would she even say to Aelin? *Hello? How do you do? Please don't burn me? Sorry I'm so filthy and lamed?*

A gentle hand touched her shoulder. *Pay attention. Look around.*

Elide glanced up from where she'd been wincing at her dirty clothes. Lorcan was perhaps twenty feet ahead, the others mere figures near the horizon.

The invisible hand on her shoulder squeezed. *Observe. See.*

See what? Ash and ice rained to the right, ruins rose up on the left, nothing but open marshes spreading ahead. But Elide halted, scanning the world around her.

Something was wrong. Something made any creatures that had survived the maelstrom of magic go silent again. The burnt grasses rustled and sighed.

Lorcan kept walking, his back stiff, though he hadn't reached for his weapons.

See see see.

See *what*? She turned in place but found nothing. She opened her mouth to call to Lorcan.

Golden eyes flickered in the brush not thirty paces ahead.

Enormous golden eyes, fixed on Lorcan as he strode mere feet away. A mountain lion, ready to pounce, to shred flesh and sever bone—

No—

The beast exploded from the burnt grasses.

Elide screamed Lorcan's name.

He whirled, but not to the lion. Toward her, that furious face shooting toward *her*—

But she was running, leg shrieking in pain, as Lorcan finally sensed the attack about to swoop down on him.

The mountain lion reached him, those thick claws going low while its teeth went right for his throat.

Lorcan drew his hunting knife, so fast it was only the glint of gray light on steel.

Beast and Fae male went down, right into the muddy water.

Elide hurtled for him, a wordless scream breaking from her. Not a normal mountain lion. Not even close. Not with the way it knew Lorcan's every move as they rolled through the water, as they dodged and swiped and lunged, blood spurting, magic clashing, shield against shield—

Then the wolf attacked.

A massive white wolf, sprinting out of nowhere, wild with rage and all of it focused on Lorcan.

Lorcan broke from the lion, blood streaming down his arm, his leg, panting. But the wolf had vanished into *nothing*. Where was it, where was it—

It appeared out of thin air, as if it had stepped through an invisible bridge, ten feet from Lorcan.

Not an attack. An execution.

Elide cleared a gap between two mounds of land, icy grass slicing into her palms, something crunching in her leg—

The wolf leaped for Lorcan's vulnerable back, eyes glazed with bloodlust, teeth shining.

Elide surged up the little hill, time spinning out beneath her.

No no no no no no.

Vicious white fangs neared Lorcan's spine.

Lorcan heard her then, heard the shuddering sob as she threw herself into him.

His dark eyes flared in what looked like terror as she slammed into his unprotected back.

As he noticed the death blow not coming from the lion at his front, but the wolf whose jaws closed around her arm instead of Lorcan's neck.

She could have sworn the wolf's eyes flared in horror as it tried to pull back the physical blow, as a dark, hard shield slammed into her, stealing her breath with its unflinching solidity—

Blood and pain and bone and grass and bellowing fury.

The world tilted as she and Lorcan went down, her body thrown over his, the wolf's jaws wrenching out of her arm.

She curled over Lorcan, waiting for the wolf and mountain lion to end it, to take her neck in their jaws and crunch down.

No attack came. Silence cleaved the world.

Lorcan flipped her over, his breathing ragged, his face bloody and pale as he took in her face, her arm. *"ElideElideElide—"*

She couldn't draw breath, couldn't see around the sensation that her arm was mere shredded flesh and splintered bone—

Lorcan grabbed her face before she could look and snapped, "Why did you do that? *Why?*" He didn't wait for an answer. He lifted his head, his snarl so vicious it echoed in her bones, made the pain in her arm surge violently enough that she whimpered.

He growled to the lion and the wolf, his shield a swirling, obsidian wind around them, "You're dead. You're both *dead*—"

Elide shifted her head enough to see the white wolf staring at them. At Lorcan. See the wolf change in a flash of light into the most beautiful man she'd ever beheld. His golden-brown face tightened as he took in her arm. Her arm, her arm—

"Lorcan, we were ordered," said an unfamiliar, gentle male voice from where the lion, too, had transformed into a Fae male.

"Damn your orders to hell, you stupid bastard—"

The wolf-warrior hissed, chest heaving, "We can't fight against the command much longer, Lorcan—"

"Put the shield down," the calmer one said. "I can heal the girl. Let her get away."

"I'll kill you both," Lorcan swore. "I'll *kill you*—"

Elide looked at her arm.

There was a piece missing. From her forearm. There was blood gushing into the burnt remnants of grass. White bone jutting out—

Maybe she started screaming or sobbing or silently shaking.

"*Don't look*," Lorcan snapped, squeezing her face again to draw her eyes to his own. His face was lined with such wrath she barely recognized it, but he made no move against the males.

His power was drained. He'd nearly wiped it out shielding against Aelin's flame and whoever had borne that other magic on the field. This shield . . . this was all Lorcan had left.

And if he lowered it so they could heal her . . . they'd kill him. He had warned them of the attack, and they'd still kill him.

Aelin—where was *Aelin*—

The world was blackening at the edges, her body begging to submit rather than endure the pain that reordered everything in her life.

Lorcan tensed as if sensing the oblivion that threatened. "You heal her," he said to the gentle-eyed male, "and then we continue—"

"No," she got out. Not for this, not for *her*—

Lorcan's onyx eyes were unreadable as he scanned her face. And then he said quietly, "I wanted to go to Perranth with you."

Lorcan dropped the shield.

It was not a hard choice. And it did not frighten him. Not nearly as much as the fatal wound in her arm did.

Fenrys had hit an artery. She'd bleed out in minutes.

Lorcan had been born from and gifted with darkness. Returning to it was not a difficult task.

But letting that glimmering, lovely light before him die out . . . In his ancient, bitter bones, he could not accept it.

She had been forgotten—by everyone and everything. And still she had hoped. And still she had been kind to him.

And still she had offered him a glimpse of peace in the time he'd known her.

She had offered him a home.

He knew Fenrys wouldn't be able to fight Maeve's kill order. Knew Gavriel would stay true to his word and heal her, but Fenrys couldn't hold out against the blood oath's command.

He knew the bastard would regret it. Knew the wolf had been horrified the moment Elide had jumped between them.

Lorcan let go of his shield, praying she wouldn't watch when the bloodletting started. When he and Fenrys went claw-to-claw and fang-to-fang. He'd last against the warrior. Until Gavriel joined back in.

The shield vanished, and Gavriel was instantly kneeling, reaching with his broad hands for her arm. Pain paralyzed her, but she tried telling Lorcan to run, to put the shield back up—

Lorcan stood, shutting out her pleading.

He faced Fenrys. The warrior was trembling with restraint, his hands clenched at his sides to keep from going for any of his blades.

Elide was still sobbing, still begging him.

Fenrys's taut features were lined with regret.

Lorcan just smiled at the warrior.

It snapped Fenrys's leash.

His sentinel leaped for him, sword out, and Lorcan lifted his own, already knowing the move Fenrys planned to use. He'd trained him how to do it. And he knew the guard Fenrys let drop on his left side, just for a heartbeat, exposing his neck—

Fenrys landed before him, swiping low and dodging right.

Lorcan angled his blade for that vulnerable neck.

They were both blown back by an icy, unbreakable wind. Whatever was left of it after the battle.

Fenrys was up, lost to the blood fury, but the wind slammed into him. Again. Again. Holding him down. Lorcan struggled against it, but the shield Whitethorn had thrown over them, the raw power he now used to keep them pinned, was too strong when his own magic was depleted.

Boots crunched on the burnt grass. Sprawled on the bank of a little hill, Lorcan lifted his head. Whitethorn stood between him and Fenrys, the prince's eyes glazed with wrath.

Rowan surveyed Gavriel and Elide, the latter still weeping, still begging for it to stop. But her arm . . .

A scratch marred that moon-white arm, but Gavriel's rough battlefield healing had filled the holes, the missing flesh and broken bones. He must have used all his magic to—

Gavriel swayed ever so slightly.

Whitethorn's voice was like gravel. "This ends now. You two don't touch them. They're under the protection of Aelin Galathynius. If you harm them, it will be considered an act of war."

Specific, ancient words, the only way a blood order could be detained. Not overridden—just delayed for a little while. To buy them all time.

Fenrys panted, but relief flickered in his eyes. Gavriel sagged a bit.

Elide's dark eyes were still glassy with pain, the smattering of freckles on her cheeks stark against the unnatural whiteness of her skin.

Whitethorn said to Fenrys and Gavriel, "Are we clear on what the hell will happen if you step out of line?"

To Lorcan's eternal shock, they lowered their heads and said, "Yes, Prince."

Rowan let the shields drop, and then Lorcan was hurtling to Elide, who struggled to sit up, gaping at her nearly healed arm. Gavriel, wisely, backed away. Lorcan examined her arm, her face, needing to touch her, smell her—

He didn't notice that the light footsteps in the grass didn't belong to his former companions.

But he knew the female voice that said from behind him, "What the rutting hell is going on?"

Elide had no words to express to Lorcan what she'd felt in that moment he'd let the shield drop. What she'd felt when the silver-haired, tattooed warrior-prince had halted that fatal bloodshed.

But she had no breath in her body when she looked over Lorcan's broad shoulder and beheld the golden-haired woman striding toward them.

Young, and yet her face . . . It was an ancient face, wary and cunning and limned with power. Beautiful, with the sun-kissed skin, the vibrant turquoise eyes. Turquoise eyes, with a core of gold around the pupil.

Ashryver eyes.

The same as the golden-haired, handsome man who came up beside her, muscled body tense as he assessed whether he'd need to spill blood, a bow dangling from his hand.

Two sides of the same golden coin.

Aelin. Aedion.

They were both staring at her with those Ashryver eyes.

Aelin blinked. And her golden face crumpled as she said, "Are you Elide?"

It was all Elide could do to nod. Lorcan was taut as a bowstring, his body still half angled over her.

Aelin strode closer, eyes never leaving Elide's face. Young—she felt so young compared to the woman who approached. There were scars all over Aelin's hands, along her neck, around her wrists . . . where shackles had been.

Aelin slid to her knees not a foot away, and it occurred to Elide that she should be bowing, head to the dirt—

"You look . . . so much like your mother," Aelin said, her voice cracking. Aedion silently knelt, putting a broad hand on Aelin's shoulder.

Her mother, who had gone down swinging, who had died fighting so this woman could live—

"I'm sorry," Aelin said, shoulders curving inward, head dropping low as tears slid down her flushed cheeks. "I'm so sorry." How many years had those words been locked up?

Elide's arm ached, but it didn't stop her from touching Aelin's hand, clenched in her lap.

Touching that tanned, scarred hand. Warm, sticky skin met her fingertips.

Real. This was—*Aelin* was—real.

As if Aelin realized the same, her head lifted. She opened her mouth, but her lips wobbled, and the queen clamped them together.

None of the gathered company spoke.

And at last Aelin said to Elide, "She bought me time."

Elide knew who the queen meant.

Aelin's hand began shaking. The queen's voice broke entirely as she said, "I am alive today because of your mother."

Elide only whispered, "I know."

"She told me to tell you . . ." A shuddering inhale. But Aelin didn't break her stare, even as tears continued cutting through the dirt on her cheeks. "Your mother told me to tell you that she loves you—very much. Those were her last words to me. 'Tell my Elide I love her very much.' "

For over ten years, Aelin had been the sole bearer of those final words. Ten years, through death and despair and war, Aelin had carried them across kingdoms.

And here, at the edge of the world, they had found each other again. Here at the edge of the world, just for a heartbeat, Elide felt the warm hand of her mother brush her shoulder.

Tears stung Elide's eyes as they slipped free. But then the grass crunched behind them.

She saw the white hair first. Then the golden eyes.

And Elide sobbed as Manon Blackbeak emerged, smiling faintly.

As Manon Blackbeak saw her and Aelin, knee-to-knee in the grass, and mouthed one word.

Hope.

Not dead. None of them were dead.

Aedion said hoarsely, "Is your arm—"

Aelin grabbed it—gently. Inspecting the shallow cut, the new pink skin that revealed what had been missing mere moments before. Aelin twisted on her knees, snarling at the wolf-warrior.

The golden-haired male averted his eyes as the queen glared her displeasure. "It wasn't his fault," Elide managed to say.

"The bite," Aelin said drily, turquoise eyes livid, "would suggest otherwise."

"I'm sorry," the male said, either to the queen or Elide, she didn't know. His eyes lifted to Aelin—something like devastation there.

Aelin ignored the words. The male flinched. And the silver-haired prince seemed to give him a brief pitying glance.

But if the order hadn't come from Aelin to kill Lorcan . . .

Aelin said to the *other* golden-haired male behind Elide, the one who had healed her—the lion, "I assume Rowan told you the deal. You touch them, you die. You so much as breathe wrong in their direction, and you're dead."

Elide tried not to cringe at the viciousness. Especially when Manon smiled in wicked delight.

Aelin tensed as the witch came at her exposed back but allowed Manon to settle on her right. To look over Elide with those gold eyes. "Well met, witchling," Manon said to her. Manon faced Lorcan just as Aelin did.

Aelin snorted. "You look a bit worse for wear."

"Likewise," Lorcan snapped at her.

Aelin's grin was terrifying. "Got my note, did you?"

Aedion's hand had slid to his sword—

"The Sword of Orynth," Elide blurted, noticing the bone pommel, the ancient markings. Aelin and Lorcan paused being at each other's throats. "The sword . . . you . . ."

Vernon had mocked her about it once. Said it had been taken by the King of Adarlan and melted down. Burned, along with the antler throne.

Aedion's turquoise eyes softened. "It survived. We survived."

The three of them, the remnants of their court, their families.

But Aelin was again sizing up Lorcan, bristling, that wicked grin returning. Elide said softly, "I survived, Majesty, because of him." She pointed with her chin to Manon. "And because of her. I am here because of both of them."

Manon nodded, focus going to the pocket where she'd seen Elide hide that scrap of stone. The confirmation she'd been looking for. The reminder of the third part of the triangle.

"I'm here," Elide said as Aelin fixed those unnervingly vivid eyes on her, "because of Kaltain Rompier." Her throat clogged, but she pushed past it as her trembling fingers fished out the little bit of cloth from her inside pocket. The otherworldly *feel* of it pulsed in her palm.

"She said to give this to you. To Celaena Sardothien, I mean. She didn't know they . . . you were the same. She said it was payment for . . . for a warm cloak offered in a cold dungeon." She wasn't ashamed of the tears that fell, not in honor of what that woman had done. Aelin studied the scrap of cloth in Elide's shaking palm. "I think she kept this as a reminder of kindness," Elide said hoarsely. "They . . . they broke her, and hurt her. And she died alone in Morath. She died alone, so I wouldn't . . . so they couldn't . . ." None of them spoke or moved. She couldn't tell if it made it worse. If the hand that Lorcan laid on her back made her cry harder.

The words tumbled out of Elide's shaking mouth. "She said t-to remember your promise to punish them all. And s-said that you can unlock any door, if you only have the k-key."

Aelin clamped her lips together and closed her eyes.

A beautiful, dark-haired man now approached. He was perhaps a few years older than her, but carried himself so gracefully that she felt small and unmolded before him. His sapphire eyes fixed on Elide, clever and unruffled—and sad. "Kaltain Rompier saved your life? And gave you that?"

He knew her—had known her.

Manon Blackbeak said in a faint, amused voice, "Lady Elide Lochan of Perranth, meet Dorian Havilliard, King of Adarlan." The king lifted his brows at the witch.

"M-majesty," she stammered, inclining her head. She should really get up. Really stop lying on the ground like a worm. But the cloth and stone still lay in her hand.

Aelin wiped her damp face on a sleeve, then straightened. "Do you know what it is you carry, Elide?"

"Y-yes, Majesty."

Turquoise eyes, haunted and weary, lifted to her own. Then slid to Lorcan. "Why didn't you take it?" The voice was hollow and hard. Elide suspected she'd be lucky if it was never used on her.

Lorcan met her gaze without flinching. "It wasn't mine to take."

Aelin now glanced between them, seeing too much. And there was no warmth on the queen's face, but she said to Lorcan, "Thank you—for bringing her to me."

The others seemed to be trying not to look too shocked at the words.

But Aelin turned to Manon. "I lay claim to her. Witch-blood in her veins or no, she is Lady of Perranth, and she is *mine*."

Gold eyes gleamed with the thrill of challenge. "And if I claim her for the Blackbeaks?"

"Blackbeaks—or the Crochans?" Aelin purred.

Elide blinked. Manon—and the Crochans? What *was* the Wing Leader doing here? Where was Abraxos? The witch said, "Careful, Majesty. With your power reduced to embers, you'll have to fight me the old-fashioned way again."

That dangerous grin returned. "You know, I've been hoping for round two."

"Ladies," the silver-haired prince said through clenched teeth.

They both turned, giving Rowan Whitethorn horrifyingly innocent smiles. The Fae Prince, to his credit, only winced after they looked away again.

Elide wished she could hide behind Lorcan as both women fixed that near-feral attention on her again. Manon reached forward, tipping Elide's hand over—to where Aelin's waited. "There you go, over and done with," Manon said.

Aelin cringed slightly but pocketed the cloth and the key inside. A shadow instantly lifted from Elide's heart, a whispering presence now silenced.

Manon ordered, "On your feet. We were in the middle of something."

She reached to pull Elide up, but Lorcan stepped in and did it himself. He didn't let go of Elide's arm, and she tried not to lean into his warmth. Tried not to make it seem like she hadn't just met her queen, her friend, her court, and . . . somehow now found Lorcan to be the safest of them all.

Manon smirked at Lorcan. "Your claim on her, male, is at the very bottom of the list." Iron teeth slid out, turning that beautiful face petrifying. Lorcan didn't let go. Manon crooned in that way that usually meant death, "Don't. Touch. Her."

"You don't give me orders, witch," Lorcan said. "And you have no say in what is between us."

Elide frowned at him. "You're making it worse."

"We like to call it 'territorial male nonsense,'" Aelin confided. "*Or* 'territorial Fae bastard' works just as nicely."

The Fae Prince coughed pointedly behind her.

The queen looked over a shoulder, brows raised. "Am I forgetting another term of endearment?"

The warrior-prince's eyes glowed, even as his face remained set with predatory intent. "I think you covered it."

Aelin winked at Lorcan. "You hurt her, and I'll melt your bones," she merely said, and walked away.

Manon's iron-clad smile grew, and she gave Lorcan a mocking incline of the head as she followed in the queen's wake.

Aedion looked Lorcan over and snorted. "Aelin does whatever she wants, but I think she'd let me see how many of your bones I can break before she melts them." Then he, too, was walking toward the two females. One silver, one gold.

Elide almost screamed as a ghost leopard appeared out of nowhere, twitched its whiskers in Lorcan's direction, and then trotted after the women, its puffy tail swishing behind it.

Then the king left, then the Fae males. Until only Prince Rowan Whitethorn stood there. He gave Elide a Look.

Elide immediately shrugged out of Lorcan's grip. Aelin and Aedion had stopped ahead, waiting for her. Smiling faintly—welcomingly.

So Elide headed for them, her court, and did not look back.

Rowan had kept quiet during the past few minutes, observing.

Lorcan had been willing to die for Elide. Had been willing to put aside his quest for Maeve in order for Elide to live. And had then acted territorial enough to make Rowan wonder if he seemed so ridiculous around Aelin all the time.

Now alone, Rowan said to Lorcan, "How did you find us?"

A cutting smile. "The dark god nudged me toward here. The ilken army did the rest."

The same Lorcan he'd known for centuries, and yet . . . not. Some hard edge had been dulled—no, *soothed*.

Lorcan stared toward the source of that soothing, but his jaw clenched as his focus shifted to where Aelin walked beside her. "That power could just as easily destroy her, you know."

"I know," Rowan admitted. What she'd done minutes ago, the power she'd summoned and unleashed . . . It had been a song that had made his magic erupt in kind.

When the ilken's resistance had finally yielded beneath flame and ice and wind, Rowan hadn't been able to stifle the yearning to walk into the burning heart of that power and see her glowing with it.

Halfway across the plain, he'd realized it wasn't just the allure of it that tugged at him. It was the woman inside it, who might need physical contact with another living being to remind herself that she had a body, and people who loved her, and to pull back from that killing calm that so mercilessly wiped the ilken from the skies. But then the flames had vanished, their enemies raining down as ash and ice and corpses, and she'd looked at him . . . Holy gods, when she'd looked at him, he'd almost fallen to his knees.

Queen, and lover, and friend—and more. He hadn't cared that they had an audience. *He* had needed to touch her, to reassure himself that she was all right, to *feel* the woman who could do such great and terrible things and still look at him with that beckoning, vibrant life in her eyes.

You make me want to live, Rowan.

He wondered if Elide Lochan had somehow made Lorcan want to do the same.

He said to Lorcan, "And what about your mission?"

Any softness vanished from Lorcan's granite-hewn features. "Why don't you tell me why you're in this shithole place, and then we'll discuss *my* plans."

"Aelin can decide what to tell you."

"Such a good dog."

Rowan gave him a lazy smile but refrained from commenting on the delicate, dark-haired young woman who now held Lorcan's own leash.

CHAPTER 58

Kaltain Rompier had just turned the tide in this war.

Dorian had never been more ashamed of himself.

He should have been better. Should have *seen* better. They all should have.

The thoughts swirled and eddied as Dorian kept back in the half-drowned temple complex, silently watching as Aelin studied the chest on the altar as if it were an opponent.

The queen was now flanked by Lady Elide, Manon on the dark-haired girl's other side, Lysandra sprawled in ghost leopard form at the queen's feet.

The power in that cluster alone was staggering. And Elide . . . Manon had murmured something to Aelin on their walk back into the ruins about Elide being watched over by Anneith.

Watched over, as the rest of them seemed to be by other gods.

Lorcan stepped into the ruins, Rowan at his side. Fenrys, Gavriel, and Aedion approached them, hands on their swords, bodies still thrumming with tension as they kept Lorcan within sight. Especially Maeve's warriors.

Another ring of power.

Lorcan—Lorcan, blessed by Hellas himself, Rowan had told him on that skiff ride into the Dead Islands. Hellas, god of death. Who had traveled here with Anneith, his consort.

The hair on Dorian's arms rose.

Scions—each of them touched by a different god, each of them subtly, quietly, guided here. It wasn't a coincidence. It couldn't be.

Manon noticed him standing a few feet away, read whatever wariness was on his face, and broke from the circle of quietly talking women to come to his side. "What?"

Dorian clenched his jaw. "I have a bad feeling about this."

He waited for the dismissal, the mockery. Manon only said, "Explain."

He opened his mouth, but Aelin stepped up to the dais.

The Lock—the Lock that would contain the Wyrdkeys, would allow Aelin to put them back in their gate. Thanks to Kaltain, thanks to Elide, they only needed one more. Wherever Erawan had it. But getting this Lock . . .

Rowan was instantly at the queen's side as she peered into the chest.

Slowly, she looked back at them. At Manon.

"Get up here," the queen said in an unnervingly calm voice.

Manon, wisely, did not refuse.

"This isn't the place or time for exploring it," Rowan said to the queen. "We move it back to the ship, then figure it out from there."

Aelin murmured her agreement, her face paling.

Manon asked them, "Was the Lock ever here to begin with?"

"I don't know." Dorian had never heard Aelin utter the words. It was enough to send him splashing up the stairs, dripping water behind him as he peered in.

There was no Lock. Not in the way that they had expected, not in the way the queen had been promised and instructed to find it.

The stone chest held only one thing:

An iron-bound mirror, the surface near-golden with age, speckled, and covered in grime. And along the twining, intricately carved border, tucked into the upper right corner . . .

The marking of the Eye of Elena. A witch symbol.

"What the hell is it?" Aedion demanded from the steps below.

It was Manon who answered, glancing sidelong at the grim-faced queen, "It's a witch mirror."

"A what?" Aelin asked. The others edged closer.

Manon tapped a nail on the stone rim of the chest. "When you killed Yellowlegs, did she give any hint about why she was there, what she wanted from you or the former king?" Dorian searched his own memory but found nothing.

"No." Aelin glanced to him in question, but Dorian shook his head as well. She asked the witch, "Do *you* know why she was there?"

A hint of a nod. A breath of hesitation. Dorian braced himself. "Yellowlegs was there to meet with the king—to show him how her magic mirrors worked."

"I smashed most of them," Aelin said, crossing her arms.

"Whatever you destroyd were cheap tricks and replicas. Her true witch mirrors . . . You cannot break those. Not easily, at least."

Dorian had a horrible feeling about where this was headed. "What can they do?"

"You can see the future, past, present. You can speak between mirrors, if someone possesses the sister-glass. And then there are the rare silvers—whose forging demands something vital from the maker." Manon's voice dropped low. Dorian wondered if even among the Blackbeaks, these tales had only been whispered at their campfires. "Other mirrors amplify and hold blasts of raw power, to be unleashed if the mirror is aimed at something."

"A weapon," Aedion said, eliciting a nod from Manon. The general must have been piecing things together as well because he asked before Dorian could, "Yellowlegs met with him about those weapons, didn't she?"

Manon went silent for long enough that he knew Aelin was about to push. But Dorian gave her a warning stare to keep quiet. So she did. They all did.

Finally, the witch said, "They've been making towers. Enormous, yet capable of being hauled across battlefields, lined with those mirrors. For Erawan to use with his powers—to incinerate your armies in a few blasts."

Aelin closed her eyes. Rowan laid a hand on her shoulder.

Dorian asked, "Is this . . ." He gestured to the chest, the mirror inside. "One of the mirrors they plan to use?"

"No," Manon said, studying the witch mirror within the chest. "Whatever *this* mirror is . . . I'm not sure what it was meant for. What it can even do. But it surely isn't that Lock you sought."

Aelin fished the Eye of Elena from her pocket, weighing it in her hand, and loosed a sharp sigh through her nose. "I'm ready for today to be over."

Mile after mile, the Fae males carried the mirror between them.

Rowan and Aedion pushed Manon for details on those witch towers. Two were already constructed, but she didn't know how many more were being built. They were stationed in the Ferian Gap, but with others possibly elsewhere. No, she didn't know the mode of transportation. Or how many witches to a tower.

Aelin let their words settle into some deep, quiet part of her. She'd figure it out tomorrow—after she slept. Figure out this damn witch mirror tomorrow, too.

Her magic was exhausted. For the first time in days, that pit of magic now slumbered.

She could sleep for a week. A month.

Each step across the marshes, back toward where those three ships would be waiting, was an effort. Lysandra frequently offered to shift into a horse and carry her, but Aelin refused. The shifter was drained as well. They all were.

She wanted to talk to Elide, wanted to ask about so many things regarding those years apart, but . . . The exhaustion that nagged at her rendered speech nearly impossible. She knew what kind of sleep beckoned—the deep, restorative slumber that her body demanded after too much magic had been spent, after she'd held on to it for too long.

So Aelin hardly spoke to Elide, leaving the lady to lean on Lorcan as they hurried to the coast. As they hauled the mirror with them.

Too many secrets—there were still too many secrets with Elena and Brannon and their long-ago war. Had the Lock ever existed? Or was the witch mirror the Lock? Too many questions with too few answers. She'd figure it out. Once they were back to safety. Once she had a chance to sleep.

Once . . . everything else fell into place, too. So they trudged through the marshes without rest.

It was Lysandra who picked up on it with that leopard's senses, half a mile from the white-sand beach and the calm gray sea beyond, a wall of grassy sand dunes blocking the view ahead.

They all had weapons drawn as they scrambled up the dune, sand slipping from beneath them. Rowan didn't shift—the only proof he'd shown of his utter exhaustion. He made it up the hill first. Drew his sword from across his back.

Aelin's breath burned her throat as she halted beside him, Gavriel and Fenrys gently setting down the mirror on her other side.

Because a hundred gray sails stretched ahead, surrounding their own ships.

They spread toward the western horizon, utterly silent save for the men they could barely make out on board. Ships from the west . . . from the Gulf of Oro.

Melisande's fleet.

And on the beach, waiting for them . . . a party of twenty warriors, led by a gray-cloaked woman. Lysandra's claws slipped free of their sheaths as she let out a low snarl.

Lorcan shoved Elide behind him. "We retreat into the marshes," he said to Rowan, whose face was set in stone as he sized up the party on the beach, the looming fleet. "We can outrun them."

Aelin slid her hands into her pockets. "They're not going to attack."

Lorcan sneered, "You're guessing this based on your many years of experience in war?"

"Watch it," Rowan snarled.

"This is absurd," Lorcan spat, twisting away, as if he'd grab Elide, pale-faced at his side. "Our reservoirs are drained—"

Lorcan was halted from hauling Elide over a shoulder by a paper-thin wall of fire. About as much as Aelin could summon.

And by Manon and her iron nails stepping before him as she growled, "You're not taking Elide anywhere. Not now, and not ever."

Lorcan rose to his full height. And before they could wreck everything with their brawling, Elide laid a delicate hand on Lorcan's arm—his own hand wrapped around the hilt of his sword. "I choose this, Manon."

Manon only glanced at the hand on Lorcan's arm. "We'll discuss this later."

Indeed. Aelin looked Lorcan over and jerked her chin. "Go brood somewhere else." The cloaked woman on the beach, along with her soldiers, was now striding toward them.

Lorcan growled, "It's not over, this business between us."

Aelin smiled a bit. "You think I don't know that?"

But Lorcan prowled to Rowan, his dark power flickering, rippling away across the waves as if in a silent boom of thunder. Taking up a defensive position.

Aelin looked to her stone-faced prince, then to Aedion, her cousin's sword and shield angled and at the ready, then the others. "Let's go say hello."

Rowan started. "Aelin—"

But she was already striding down the dune, doing her best to keep from sliding on the treacherous sand, to keep her head high. The others trailing behind were taut as bowstrings, but their breathing remained even—primed for anything.

The soldiers were in heavy, worn gray armor, their faces rough and scarred, sizing them up as they hit the sand. Fenrys snarled at one of them, and the man averted his eyes.

But the cloaked woman removed her hood as she approached with feline grace, halting perhaps ten feet away.

Aelin knew every detail about her.

Knew that she was twenty years old now. Knew that the medium-length, wine-red hair was her real hair color. Knew the red-brown eyes were the only she'd seen in any land, on any adventure. Knew the wolf's head on the pommel of the mighty sword at her side was her family's crest. She knew the smattering of freckles, the full, laughing mouth, knew the deceptively slim arms that hid rock-hard muscle as she crossed them.

That full mouth slanted into a half grin as Ansel of Briarcliff, Queen of the Wastes, drawled, "Who gave you permission to use my name in pit fights, *Aelin*?"

"I gave myself permission to use your name however I please, *Ansel*, the day I spared your life instead of ending you like the coward you are."

That cocky smile widened. "Hello, bitch," Ansel purred.

"Hello, traitor," Aelin purred right back, surveying the armada spread before them. "Looks like you made it on time after all."

CHAPTER 59

Aelin felt the utter shock of her companions ripple from them as Ansel bowed dramatically, gesturing to the ships behind them, and said, "As requested: your fleet."

Aelin snorted. "Your soldiers look like they've seen better days."

"Oh, they always look like that. I've tried and tried to get them to focus on *outside* appearances as much as improving their inner beauty, but . . . you know how men are."

Aelin chuckled. Even as she sensed her companions' shock turning into something red-hot.

Manon stepped forward, the sea breeze whipping strands of her white hair over her face, and said to Aelin, "Melisande's fleet bows to Morath. You might as well be signing an alliance with Erawan, too, if you're working with this . . . person."

Ansel's face drained of color at the iron teeth, the nails. And Aelin remembered the story the assassin-turned-queen had once told her, whispered atop rolling desert sands and beneath a carpet of stars. A childhood friend—eaten alive by an Ironteeth witch.

Then Ansel herself, after the slaughter of her family, had been spared when she'd stumbled into an Ironteeth witch's camp.

Aelin said to Manon, "She is not from Melisande. The Wastes are allied with Terrasen."

Aedion started, now sizing up the ships, the woman before them.

Manon Blackbeak said in a voice like death, "Who is she to speak for the Wastes?"

Oh, gods above. Aelin schooled her face into bland irreverence and gestured between the two women. "Manon Blackbeak, Heir to the Blackbeak Witch-Clan and now the last Crochan Queen . . . meet Ansel of Briarcliff, assassin and Queen of the Western Wastes."

Roaring filled Manon's head as they rowed back to their ship, interrupted only by the splashing of the oars through the calm waves.

She was going to kill the red-haired bitch. Slowly.

They remained silent until they reached the towering ship, then climbed its side.

No sign of Abraxos.

Manon scanned the skies, the fleet, the seas. Not a scale to be found.

The rage in her gut twisted into something else, something worse, and she took a step for the ruddy-faced captain to demand answers.

But Aelin casually stepped in her path, giving her an adder's smile as she glanced between Manon and the red-haired young woman who now leaned against the stair post. "You two should have a little chat later."

Manon stormed around her. "Ansel of Briarcliff does not speak for the Wastes."

Where was Abraxos—

"But you do?"

And Manon had to wonder if she'd somehow . . . somehow become tangled in whatever plans the queen had woven. Especially as Manon found herself forced to halt again, forced to turn back to the smirking queen and say, "Yes. I do."

Even Rowan blinked at Manon Blackbeak's tone—the voice that was not witch or warrior or predator. Queen.

The last Crochan Queen.

Rowan sized up the potentially explosive fight brewing between Ansel of Briarcliff and Manon Blackbeak.

He remembered all that Aelin had told him of Ansel—the betrayal while the two woman had trained in the desert, the fight to the death that had left Aelin sparing the red-haired woman. A life debt.

Aelin had called in the life debt owed to her.

Ansel, with a swaggering arrogance that completely explained why she and Aelin had become fast friends, drawled to Manon from where she'd perched on the quarterdeck stairs, "Well, last I heard, neither Crochan nor Ironteeth witches bothered to look after the Wastes. I suppose that as someone who has fed and guarded its people these past two years, I do get to speak for them. And decide who we help and how we do it." Ansel smirked at Aelin like the witch wasn't staring at her throat as if she'd rip it out with her iron teeth. "You and I live next door to each other, after all. It'd be un-neighborly of me not to help."

"Explain," Aedion said tightly, his heartbeat thundering loud enough for Rowan to hear. The first word the general had uttered since Ansel had pulled back her hood. Since Aelin's little surprise had been waiting for them on the beach.

Ansel angled her head, the silky red hair catching the light, looking, Rowan realized, like the richest red wine. Exactly as Aelin had once described it. "Well, months ago, I was minding my own business in the Wastes, when I got a message out of the blue. From Aelin. She sent me a message loud and clear from Rifthold. Pit fighting." She chuckled, shaking her head. "And I knew to get ready. To move my army to the edge of the Anascaul Mountains."

Aedion's breathing snagged. Only centuries of training kept Rowan's from doing the same. His cadre remained stalwart behind them all, positions they'd taken hundreds of times over the centuries. Ready for bloodshed—or to fight their way out of it.

Ansel smiled, a winning grin. "Half of them are on their way there now. Ready to join with Terrasen. The country of my friend Celaena Sardothien, who did not forget it, even when she was in the Red Desert; and who did not stop looking north every night that we could see the stars. There was no greater gift I could offer to repay her than saving the kingdom she did not forget. And that was before I got her letter months ago, telling me who she was and that she'd gut me if I didn't assist in her cause. I was on my way with my army already, but . . . then the next letter arrived. Telling me to go to the Gulf of Oro. To meet her here and follow a specific set of instructions."

Aedion snapped his head to Aelin, salt water still gleaming on his tan face from the boat over. "The dispatches from Ilium—"

Aelin waved a lazy hand to Ansel. "Let the woman finish."

Ansel strolled to Aelin and linked her arm through her elbow. She smirked like a fiend. "I'm assuming you lot know how bossy Her Majesty is. But I followed the instructions. I brought the other half of my army when I veered down south, and we hiked through the White Fangs and into Melisande. Its queen assumed we arrived to offer aid. She let us right in the front gates."

Rowan held his breath.

Ansel let out a sharp whistle, and on the nearest ship, clopping and nickering sounded.

And then an Asterion horse emerged from the stables.

The horse was a storm made flesh.

Rowan couldn't remember the last time he'd seen Aelin beam with pure delight as she breathed, "Kasida."

"Do you know," Ansel went on, "that I rather enjoy pillaging? With Melisande's troops spread so thin for Morath, she really had no choice but to yield. Though she was particularly furious to see me claim the horse—made worse when I took her out of her dungeon to reveal that Terrasen's flag now flies alongside my wolf at her own damn house."

"What," Aedion blurted.

Aelin and Ansel faced them, brows high. Dorian staggered forward a step at Ansel's words, and the Queen of the Wastes gave him a look that said she'd like to pillage *him*.

Ansel gestured to the ships around them with a broad sweep of her arm. "Melisande's fleet is now our fleet. And its capital is now ours, too." She jerked her chin at Aelin. "You're welcome."

Manon Blackbeak burst out laughing.

Aedion didn't know who to be more furious with: Aelin, for not telling him about Ansel of Briarcliff *and* the gods-damned army she'd quietly ordered to sack Melisande and seize its fleet, or himself, for not trusting her. For demanding where their allies were, for implying all that he had in those moments before the ilken attack. She'd just taken it.

As Ansel's words sank in to the company still gathered on the main deck, his cousin said quietly, "Melisande meant to assist Morath in cleaving the North and South. I did not take its city for glory or conquest, but I will not allow anything to come between me and defeating Morath. Melisande will now clearly understand the cost of allying with Erawan."

He tried not to bristle. He was her general-prince. Rowan was her consort—or close enough to it. And yet she had not entrusted them with this. He hadn't even contemplated the Wastes as an ally. Perhaps that was why. He would have told her not to bother.

Aedion said to Ansel, "Melisande has likely already sent word to Morath. Its own armies are no doubt rushing back to the capital city. Get your remaining men across the Fangs again. We can lead the armada from here."

Ansel looked to Aelin, who nodded her agreement. The Queen of the Wastes then asked him, "And then march north to Terrasen and cross at the Anascaul passes?"

Aedion gave a single nod of confirmation, already calculating where he'd place her men, who in the Bane he'd give command over them. Without seeing Ansel's men fight . . . Aedion began heading toward the stairs to the quarterdeck, not bothering to wait for permission.

But Aelin halted him with a cleared throat. "Talk to Ansel before she leaves tomorrow morning about where to bring her army once it's whole again."

He merely nodded and continued up the steps, ignoring his father's concerned look as he went. The others eventually split up, and Aedion didn't care where they went, only that he had a few minutes to himself.

He leaned against the rail, peering into the sea lapping against the side of the ship, trying not to notice the men on the surrounding ships sizing up him and his companions.

Some of their whispers hit him from across the water. *The Wolf of the North*; *General Ashryver*. Some began to tell stories—most outright lies, a few close enough to the truth. Aedion let the sound of them bleed into the plunk and hiss of the waves.

Her ever-changing scent hit him, and something in his chest loosened. Loosened a bit further at the sight of her slim golden arms as she braced them on the rail beside his own.

Lysandra glanced over her shoulder to where the witch and Elide—

gods above, *Elide*—had gone to sit by the foremast, talking quietly. Probably recounting their own adventures since parting ways.

The armada wouldn't sail until morning, he'd overheard the captain saying. He doubted it had to do with Aelin waiting to see if the Wing Leader's missing mount would return.

"We shouldn't linger," Aedion said, now scanning the northern horizon. The ilken had come from that direction—and if they had found them so easily, even with an armada now around them . . . "We're carrying two keys and the Lock—or whatever the hell that witch mirror actually is. The tide's with us. We should go."

Lysandra shot him a sharp look. "Go take it up with Aelin."

Aedion studied her from head to toe. "What's chewing on you?"

She'd been distant for the past few days. But now he could practically see that courtesan's mask snap into place as she seemed to will her eyes to brighten, her frowning mouth to soften. "Nothing. I'm just tired." Something about the way she glanced toward the sea rubbed at him.

Aedion said carefully, "We've been battling our way across the continent. Even after ten years of this, it still drains me. Not just physically, but—in my heart."

Lysandra ran a finger down the smooth wood of the railing. "I thought . . . It all seemed a grand adventure. Even when the danger was so horrible, it was still new, and I was no longer caged in dresses and bedrooms. But that day in Skull's Bay, it stopped being any of that. It started being . . . survival. And some of us might not make it." Her mouth wobbled a bit. "I never had friends—not as I do now. And today on that beach, when I saw that fleet and thought it belonged to our enemy . . . For a moment, I wished I'd never met any of you. Because the thought of any of you . . ." She sucked in a breath. "How do you do it? How have you learned to enter a battlefield with your Bane and not fall apart with the terror that not all of you might walk off it?"

Aedion listened to every word, assessed every shaking breath. And he said plainly, "You have no choice but to learn to face it." He wished she didn't need to think of such things, have such weight on her. "The fear of loss . . . it can destroy you as much as the loss itself."

Lysandra at last met his gaze. Those green eyes—the sadness in them hit him like a blow to the gut. It was an effort not to reach for her. But she said, "I think we will both need to remind ourselves of that in the times ahead."

He nodded, sighing through his nose. "And remember to enjoy what time we do have." She'd likely learned that as many times as he had.

Her slender, lovely throat bobbed, and she glanced sidelong at him beneath lowered lashes. "I do enjoy it, you know. This—whatever this is."

His heart ratcheted to a thunderous beat. Aedion debated whether or not to go for subtlety and gave himself the span of three breaths to decide. In the end, he went for his usual method, which had served him well both on and off battlefields: a precise sort of blunt attack, edged with enough outright arrogance to throw his opponents off their guard. "Whatever this is," he said with a half smile, "between *us*?"

Lysandra indeed went on the defensive and showed her hand. "I know my history is . . . unappealing."

"I'm going to stop you right there," Aedion said, daring a step closer. "And I'm going to tell you that there is nothing unappealing about you. *Nothing*. I've been with just as many people. Women, men . . . I've seen and tried it all."

Her brows had risen. Aedion shrugged. "I find pleasure in both, depending on my mood and the person." One of his former lovers still remained one of his closest friends—and most skilled commanders in his Bane. "Attraction is attraction." He steeled his nerve. "And I know enough about it to understand what you and I . . ." Something shuttered in her eyes, and the words slipped from him. Too soon. Too soon for this sort of talk. "We can figure it out. Make no demands of each other beyond honesty." That was really the only thing he cared to request. It was nothing more than he'd ask of a friend.

A small smile played about her lips. "Yes," she breathed. "Let's start there."

He dared another step closer, not caring who watched on the deck or in the rigging or in the armada around them. Color bloomed high on those beautiful cheekbones, and it was an effort not to stroke a finger across them, then his mouth. To taste her skin.

But he'd take his time. Enjoy every moment, as he had told her to do.

Because this would be his last hunt. He had no intention of wasting each glorious moment in one go. Of wasting any of the moments that fate had granted him, and all he wanted to show her.

Every stream and forest and sea in Terrasen. To see Lysandra laugh her way through the autumnal circle dances; to weave ribbons around the maypoles in the spring; and listen, wide-eyed, to ancient tales of war and ghosts before the roaring winter fires in the mountain halls. All of it. He'd show her all of it. And walk onto those battlefields again and again to ensure he could.

So Aedion smiled at Lysandra and brushed her hand with his own. "I'm glad we're in agreement, for once."

CHAPTER 60

Aelin and Ansel clinked bottles of wine over the long, scarred table in the galley and drank deeply.

They were to sail at first light tomorrow. North—back north. To Terrasen.

Aelin braced her forearms on the slick table. "Here's to dramatic entrances."

Lysandra, curled on the bench in ghost leopard form with her head on Aelin's lap, let out a little feline laugh. Ansel blinked in wonder. "So what now?"

"It'd be nice," Aedion grumbled from down the table, where he and Rowan glared at them, "to be included in just *one* of these schemes, Aelin."

"But your faces are so wonderful when I get to reveal them," Aelin crooned.

He and Rowan growled. Oh, she knew they were pissed. So pissed that she hadn't told them about Ansel. But the thought of disappointing them, of failing . . . She'd wanted to do this on her own.

Rowan, apparently, mastered his annoyance enough to ask Ansel, "Were the ilken or Valg not in Melisande?"

"Are you implying my forces weren't good enough to take the city if they had been?" Ansel swigged from her wine, laughter dancing in her eyes. Dorian sat at the table between Fenrys and Gavriel, the three of them wisely keeping quiet. Lorcan and Elide were on the deck—somewhere. "No, Prince," Ansel went on. "I asked the Queen of Melisande about the lack of Morath-bred horrors, and, after some coaxing, she informed me that through whatever wiles and scheming, she managed to keep Erawan's claws from her. And her soldiers."

Aelin straightened a bit, wishing she'd had more wine than the third of a bottle she'd already consumed as Ansel added, "When this war is over, Melisande will not have the excuse of being in thrall to Erawan or the Valg. Everything she and her armies have done, their choice in allying with him, was a human choice." A pointed glance to the darkest part of the galley, where Manon Blackbeak sat alone. "At least Melisande will have the Ironteeth to commiserate with."

Manon's iron teeth flashed in the dim light. Her wyvern hadn't been spotted or heard from since he'd left, apparently. And she and Elide had talked for over an hour on the deck this afternoon.

Aelin decided to do them all a favor and cut in, "I need more men, Ansel. And I do not have the ability to be in so many places at once." They were all watching now.

Ansel set down the bottle. "You want me to raise *another* army for you?"

"I want you to find me the lost Crochan witches."

Manon jerked upright. "What."

Aelin scratched at a mark on the table. "They are in hiding, but they're still out there, if the Ironteeth hunt them. They might have significant numbers. Promise to share the Wastes with them. You control Briarcliff and half the coast. Give them inland and the South."

Manon was prowling over, death in her eyes. "You do not have the right to promise such things." Rowan's and Aedion's hands shot to their swords. But Lysandra opened a sleepy eye, stretched out a paw on the bench, and revealed the needle-sharp claws that now stood between Manon's shins and Aelin.

Aelin said to Manon, "You cannot hold the land, not with the curse. Ansel won it, through blood and loss and her own wits."

"It is *my* home, my people's home—"

"That was the asking price, wasn't it? The Ironteeth get their homeland returned, and Erawan probably promised to break the curse." At Manon's wide eyes, Aelin snorted. "Oh—the Ancients didn't tell you that, did they? Too bad. That's what Ansel's spies picked up." She looked the Wing Leader over. "If you and your people prove to be better than your Matrons, there will be a place for you in that land, too."

Manon just stalked back to her seat and glared at the galley's small brazier as if she could freeze it over.

Ansel murmured, "So touchy, these witches."

Aelin clamped her lips together, but Lysandra let out another breathy cat laugh. Manon's nails clicked against each other from across the room. Lysandra merely answered with her own.

Aelin said to Ansel, "Find the Crochans."

"They're all gone," Manon cut in again. "We've hunted them to near-extinction."

Aelin slowly looked over a shoulder. "What if their queen summoned them?"

"I am no more their queen than you are."

They'd see about that. Aelin laid a hand flat on the table. "Send anything and anyone you find north," she said to Ansel. "Sacking

Melisande's capital on the sly will at least piss off Erawan, but we don't want to be stuck down here when Terrasen is attacked."

"I think Erawan was probably born pissed." Only Ansel, who had once laughed at death as she'd leaped a ravine and convinced Aelin to nearly die doing the same, would mock a Valg king. But Ansel added, "I'll do it. I don't know how effective it'll be, but I have to go north anyway. Though I think Hisli will be heartbroken to say farewell to Kasida once again."

It was no surprise at all that Ansel had managed to hold on to Hisli, the Asterion mare she'd stolen for herself. But Kasida—oh, Kasida was just as beautiful as Aelin remembered, even more so once she'd been led over a gangway onto the ship. Aelin had brushed the mare down when she'd led her into the cramped, wet stables, and bribed the horse to forgive her with an apple.

Ansel slugged from the bottle. "I heard, you know. When you went to Endovier. I was still fighting my way onto the throne, battling Lord Loch's horde with the lords I'd banded together, but . . . even out in the Wastes, we heard when you were sent there."

Aelin picked at the table some more, well aware the others were listening. "It wasn't fun."

Ansel nodded. "Once I'd killed Loch, I had to stay to defend my throne, to make it right again for my people. But I knew if anyone could survive Endovier, it'd be you. I set out last summer. I'd reached the Ruhnn Mountains when I got word you were gone. Taken to the capital by . . ." She glanced at Dorian, stone-faced across the table. "Him. But I couldn't go to Rifthold. It was too far, and I had been gone too long. So I turned around. Went home."

Aelin's words were strangled. "You tried to get me out?"

The fire cast Ansel's hair in ruby and gold. "There was not one hour that I did not think about what I did in the desert. How you fired that arrow after twenty-one minutes. You told me twenty, that you'd shoot even if I wasn't out of range. I was counting; I knew how many it had been. You gave me an extra minute."

Lysandra stretched out, nuzzling Ansel's hand. She idly scratched the shifter.

Aelin said, "You were my mirror. That extra minute was as much for me as it was for you." Aelin clinked her bottle against Ansel's again. "Thank you."

Ansel just said, "Don't thank me yet."

Aelin straightened. The others halted their eating, utensils discarded in their stew.

"The fires along the coast weren't set by Erawan," Ansel said, those red-brown eyes flickering in the lantern light. "We interrogated Melisande's Queen and her lieutenants, but . . . it wasn't an order from Morath."

Aedion's low growl told her they all knew the answer before Ansel replied.

"We got a report that Fae soldiers were spied starting them. Firing from ships."

"Maeve," Gavriel murmured. "But burning isn't her style."

"It's mine," Aelin said. They all looked at her. She let out a humorless laugh.

Ansel just nodded. "She's been setting them, blaming you for it."

"To what end?" Dorian asked, dragging a hand through his blue-black hair.

"To undermine Aelin," Rowan said. "To make her look like a tyrant, not a savior. Like a threat worth banding against, rather than allying with."

Aelin sucked on a tooth. "Maeve plays the game well, I'll give her that."

"So she's reached these shores, then," Aedion said. "But where the hell is she?"

A stone of fear plunked into Aelin's stomach. She couldn't bring herself to say north. To suggest that perhaps Maeve now sailed for undefended Terrasen. A glance at Fenrys and Gavriel revealed them already shaking their heads in silent answer to Rowan's pointed look.

Aelin said, "We leave at first light."

In the dim light of their private cabin an hour later, Rowan drew a line across the map spread in the center of the floor, then a second line beside it, then a third beside that. Three lines, roughly spaced apart, broad swaths of the continent between. Aelin, standing beside him, studied them.

Rowan drew an inward arrow from the leftmost line toward the one in the center, and said quietly so the others in the adjacent rooms or hall couldn't hear, "Ansel and her army hammer from the western mountains." Another arrow in an opposite direction—toward the line on the far right. "Rolfe, the Mycenians, and this armada strike from the eastern coast." An arrow pointing down into the right section of his little drawing, where the two arrows would meet. "The Bane and the other half of Ansel's army sweep down the center, from the Staghorns, to the heart of the continent—all converging on Morath." Those eyes were like green fire. "You've been moving armies into position."

"I need more," she said. "And I need more time."

His brows narrowed. "And what army will you be fighting in?" His mouth twitched up at a corner. "I assume I won't be able to persuade you to stay behind the lines."

"You know better than to even try."

"Where would the fun be, anyway, if I got to win all the glory while you sat on your ass? I'd never let you hear the end of it."

She snorted, and surveyed the other maps they'd spread across the floor of their cabin. Together, they formed a patchwork of their world—not just the continent, but the lands beyond. She stood, towering over it, as if she could spy those armies, both near and far.

Rowan, still kneeling, looked upon the world spread at her feet.

And she realized it indeed was—if she won this war, won the continent back.

Aelin scanned the sprawl of the world, which had once seemed so vast and now, at her feet, seemed so . . . fragile. So small and breakable.

"You could, you know," Rowan said, his tattoo stark in the lantern light. "Take it for yourself. Take it all. Use Maeve's bullshit maneuvers against her. Make good on that promise."

There was no judgment. Only frank calculation and contemplation. "And would you join me if I did? If I turned conqueror?"

"You would unify, not pillage and burn. And yes—to whatever end."

"That's the threat, isn't it?" she mused. "The other kingdoms and territories will spend the rest of their existence wondering if I will one day grow restless in Terrasen. They will do their best to ensure we stay happily within our borders, and find them to be more useful as allies and trade partners than potential conquests. Maeve attacked Eyllwe's coast, posing as me, perhaps to turn those foreign lands against me—to hammer home the point I made with my power at Skull's Bay . . . and use it against us."

He nodded. "But if you could . . . would you?"

For a heartbeat, she could see it—see her face, carved into statues in kingdoms so far away they did not even know Terrasen existed. A living god—Mala's heir and conqueror of the known world. She would bring music and books and culture, wipe out the corruption festering in corners of the earth . . .

She said softly, "Not now."

"But later?"

"Perhaps if being queen bores me . . . I'll think about making myself empress. To give my offspring not one kingdom to inherit, but as many as the stars."

There was no harm in saying it, anyway. In thinking about it, stupid and useless as it was. Even if wondering about the possibilities . . . perhaps it made her no better than Maeve or Erawan.

Rowan jerked his chin toward the nearest map—toward the Wastes. "Why did you forgive Ansel? After what she did to you and the others in the desert?"

Aelin crouched again. "Because she made a bad choice, trying to heal a wound she couldn't ever mend. Trying to avenge the people she loved."

"And you really set all this in motion when we were in Rifthold? When you were fighting in those pits?"

She gave him a roguish wink. "I knew if I gave the name Ansel of Briarcliff, it'd somehow make its way to her that a red-haired young woman was using *her* name to slaughter trained soldiers in the Pits. And that she'd know it was me."

"So the red hair back then—not just for Arobynn."

"Not even close." Aelin frowned at the maps, dissatisfied she hadn't spotted any other armies hiding out around the world.

Rowan dragged a hand through his hair. "Sometimes I wish I knew every thought in that head, each scheme and plot. Then I remember how much it delights me when you reveal it—usually when it's most likely to make my heart stop dead in my chest."

"I knew you were a sadist."

He kissed her mouth once, twice, then the tip of her nose, nipping it with his canines. She hissed and batted him away, and his deep chuckle rumbled against the wooden walls. "That's for not telling me," he said. "*Again.*"

But despite his words, despite everything, he looked so . . . happy. So perfectly content and happy to be there, kneeling among those maps, the lantern down to its last dregs, the world going to hell.

The joyless, cold male she'd first met, the one who had been waiting for an opponent good enough to bring him death . . . He now looked at her with happiness in his face.

She took his hand, gripping it hard. "Rowan."

The spark died from his eyes.

She squeezed his fingers. "Rowan, I need you to do something for me."

Manon lay curled on her side in her narrow bed, unable to sleep.

It was not from the piss-poor sleeping conditions—no, she'd slept in far worse, even considering the shoddily patched hole in the side of the wall.

She stared at that gap in the wall, at the moonlight leaking in on the salty summer breeze.

She would not go find the Crochans. No matter what the Terrasen Queen called her, admitting to her bloodline was different from . . . claiming it. She doubted the Crochans would be willing to serve anyway, given that she'd killed their princess. Her own half sister.

And even if the Crochans did choose to serve her, fight for her . . . Manon put a hand to the thick scar now across her belly. The Ironteeth would not share the Wastes.

But it was that mentality, she supposed as she twisted onto her back, peeling her hair from her sweat-sticky neck, that had sent them all into exile.

She again peered through the gaps in that hole to the sea beyond. Waiting to spot a shadow in the night sky, to hear the boom of mighty wings.

Abraxos should have been here already. She shut out the coiling dread in her stomach.

But instead of wings, footsteps creaked in the hall outside.

A heartbeat later, the door opened on near-silent hinges, then shut again. Locked.

Manon didn't sit up as she said, "What are you doing here."

The moonlight sifted through the king's blue-black hair. "You don't have chains anymore."

She sat up at that, examining where the irons draped down the wall. "Is it more enticing for you if they're on?"

Sapphire eyes seemed to glow in the dark as he leaned against the shut door. "Sometimes it is."

She snorted, but found herself saying, "You never weighed in."

"On what?" he asked, though he knew what she'd meant.

"What I am. Who I am."

"Does my opinion matter to you, witchling?"

Manon stalked toward him, stopping a few feet away, aware of every inch of night between them. "You do not seem outraged that Aelin sacked Melisande without telling anyone, you do not seem to care that I am a Crochan—"

"Do not mistake my silence for lack of feeling. I have good reason to keep my thoughts to myself."

Ice glittered at his fingertips. Manon tracked it. "Will it be you or the queen against Erawan in the end, I wonder."

"Fire against darkness makes for a better story."

"Yes, but so would ripping a demon king to shreds without using your hands."

A half smile. "I can think of better uses for my hands—invisible and flesh."

An invitation and a question. She held his gaze.

"Then finish what you started," Manon breathed.

Dorian's answering smile was soft—edged with that glimmer of cruelty that made her blood heat as if the Fire-Queen herself had breathed flame into it.

She let Dorian back her against the wall. Let him hold her gaze while he tugged the top laces of her white shirt free.

One. By. One.

Let him lean in to brush his mouth against her bare neck, right under her ear.

Manon arched slightly at that caress. At the tongue that flicked against where his lips had been. Then he pulled back. Away.

Even as those phantom hands continued to trail up her hips, over her waist. His mouth parted slightly, body trembling with restraint. Restraint, where most males took and took when she offered it, gorging themselves on her. But Dorian Havilliard said, "The Bloodhound was lying that night. What she said about your Second. I felt her lie—tasted it."

Some tight part in her chest eased. "I don't want to talk about that."

He stepped closer again, and those phantom hands trailed under her breasts. She gritted her teeth. "And what do you want to talk about, Manon?"

She wasn't sure he'd ever said her name before. And the way he'd said it . . .

"I don't want to talk at all," she countered. "And neither do you," she added with a pointed glance.

Again, that dark, edged smile appeared. And when he stepped close once more, his hands replaced those phantom ones.

Tracing her hips, her waist, her breasts. Unhurried, indolent circles that she allowed him to make, simply because no one had ever dared. Each brush of his skin against hers left a wake of fire and ice. She found herself transfixed by it—by each coaxing, luxurious stroke. She did not even consider objecting as Dorian slid off her shirt and surveyed her bare, scar-flecked flesh.

His face turned ravenous as he took in her breasts, the plane of her stomach—the scar slicing across it.

That hunger shifted into something icy and vicious: "You once asked me where I stand on the line between killing to protect and killing for pleasure." His fingers grazed the seam of the scar across her abdomen. "I'll stand on the other side of the line when I find your grandmother."

A chill ran down her body, peaking her breasts. He watched them, then circled a finger around one. Dorian bent, his mouth following the path where that finger had been. Then his tongue. She bit her lip against the groan rising up her throat, her hands sliding into the silken locks of his hair.

His mouth was still around the tip of her breast as he again met her eyes, sapphire framed with ebony lashes, and said, "I want to taste every inch of you."

Manon let go of all pretense of reason as the king lifted his head and claimed her mouth.

And for all his wanting to taste her, as she opened for him, Manon thought the king tasted like the sea, like a winter morning, something so foreign and yet familiar it at last dragged that moan from deep in her.

His fingers slid to her jaw, tipping her face to thoroughly take her mouth, every movement of his tongue a sensuous promise that had her arching into him. Had her meeting him stroke for stroke as he explored and teased until she could hardly think straight.

She had never contemplated what it would be like—to yield control. And not have it be weakness, but a freedom.

Dorian's hands slid down her thighs, as if savoring the muscle there, then around—cupping her backside, grinding her into every hard inch of him. The small noise in her throat was cut off as he hoisted her from the wall in a smooth movement.

Manon wrapped her legs around his waist while he carried her to the bed, his mouth never leaving hers as he devoured and devoured her. As he spread her beneath him. As he freed her pants button by button, then slid them off.

But Dorian pulled back at last, leaving her panting as he surveyed her, utterly bare before him. He caressed a finger along the inside of her thigh. Higher. "I wanted you from the first moment I saw you in Oakwald," he said, his voice low and rough.

Manon reached up to peel off his shirt, white fabric sliding away to reveal tan skin and sculpted muscle. "Yes," was all she told him. She unbuckled his belt, hands shaking. "Yes," she said again, as Dorian brushed a knuckle over her core. He let out an approving growl at what he found.

His clothes joined hers on the floor. Manon let him raise her arms over her head, his magic gently pinning her wrists to the mattress as he touched her, first with those wicked hands. Then with his wicked mouth. And when Manon had to bite his shoulder to muffle her moaning as he brought her over the edge, Dorian Havilliard buried himself deep inside her.

She did not care who she was, who she had been, and what she had once promised to be as he moved. She dragged her hands through his thick hair, over the muscles of his back as it flexed and rippled with each thrust that drove her toward that shimmering edge again. Here, she was nothing but flesh and fire and iron; here, there was only this selfish need of her body, his body.

More. She wanted more—wanted *everything*.

She might have whispered it, might have pleaded for it. Because Darkness save her, Dorian gave it to her. To them both.

He remained atop her when he at last stilled, his lips barely a hairsbreadth above hers—hovering after the brutal kiss he'd given her to contain his roar as release found him.

She was trembling with . . . whatever he'd done to her, her body. He brushed a strand of hair out of her face, his own fingers shaking.

She had not realized how silent the world was—how loud they might have been, especially with so many Fae ears nearby.

He was still atop her, in her. Those sapphire eyes flicked to her mouth, still panting slightly. "This was supposed to take the edge off."

She kept her words low as his clothes slid over, hauled by phantom hands. "And did it?"

He traced her lower lip with his thumb and shuddered as she sucked it into her mouth, flicked it with her tongue. "No. Not even close."

But that was the gray light of dawn creeping into the room, staining the walls silver. He seemed to notice it at the same moment she did. Groaning softly, he pulled himself off her. She tugged on her clothes with trained efficiency, and only when she was lacing up her shirt did Dorian say, "We're not done, you and I."

And it was the purely male *promise* that made her bare her teeth. "Unless you would like to learn precisely what parts of me are made of iron the next time you touch me, I decide those things."

Dorian gave another purely male smile, brows flicking up, and sauntered out the door as silently as he'd arrived. He only seemed to pause on the threshold—as if some word had snagged his interest. But he continued out, the door closing with barely a click. Unruffled, utterly calm.

Manon gaped after him, cursing her blood for heating again, for . . . what she'd allowed him to do.

She wondered what Dorian would say if she told him she had never allowed a male atop her like that. Not once. Wondered what he'd say if she told him she'd wanted to sink her teeth into his neck and find out what he tasted like. Put her mouth on other parts and see what he tasted like there.

Manon dragged her hands through her hair and slumped onto the pillow.

Darkness embrace her.

She sent a silent prayer for Abraxos to return soon. Too much time—she had spent too much damn time among these humans and Fae males. She needed to leave. Elide was safe here—the Queen of Terrasen might be many things, but Manon knew she'd protect Elide.

But, with the Thirteen scattered and likely dead, regardless of what Dorian had claimed, Manon wasn't entirely sure where to go once she left. The world had never seemed quite so vast before.

And so empty.

Even utterly exhausted, Elide barely slept during the long night she and Lorcan swayed in hammocks with the other sailors. The smells, the sounds, the rocking of the sea . . . All of it nagged, none of it left her settled. A finger seemed to keep prodding her awake, as if telling her to be alert, but . . . there was nothing.

Lorcan tossed and turned for hours. As if the same force begged him to wake.

As if he was waiting for something.

His strength had been flagging by the time they'd reached the ship, though he had showed no signs of strain beyond a slight tightening in his mouth. But Elide knew he was near what he'd described as a burnout. Knew, because for hours afterward, the small brace of magic around her ankle kept flickering in and out of place.

After Manon had informed her of the uncertain fates of the Thirteen, Elide had kept mostly out of her companions' way, letting them talk with that red-haired young woman who found them on the beach. So had Lorcan. He'd listened to them debate and plan, his face taut, as if something coiled in him wound itself tighter with every passing moment.

Watching him sleep mere feet away, that harsh face smoothed to softness by slumber, a small part of Elide wondered if she'd somehow brought another danger to the queen. She wondered if the others had noted how often Lorcan's gaze had been fixed on Aelin's back. *Aimed* at her back.

As if sensing her attention, Lorcan opened his eyes. Met her stare without so much as blinking. For a heartbeat, she took in that depthless gaze mere feet away, made ethereal by the silver light before dawn.

He had been willing to offer up his life for her own.

Something softened in that harsh face as his eyes dipped to where her arm dangled out of her hammock, the skin still a bit sore, but . . . miraculously healed. She'd thanked Gavriel twice now, but he'd brushed it aside with a gentle nod and shrug.

A faint smile bloomed on Lorcan's harsh mouth as he reached across the space between them and ran his calloused fingers down her arm. "You choose this?" he murmured so that it was little more than the groaning of the hammock ropes. He brushed a thumb down her palm.

Elide swallowed but let herself take in every line of that face. North—they were going *home* today. "I thought that was obvious," she said with equal quiet, her cheeks heating.

His fingers laced through hers, some emotion she couldn't place flickering like starlight in those black eyes. "We need to talk," he rasped.

It was the shout of the watch that jolted them. The one of pure terror.

Elide nearly flipped out of her hammock, the sailors rushing past. By the time she shoved her hair from her eyes, Lorcan was already gone.

The various decks were packed, and she had to limp onto the stairs to view what had roused them. The other ships were awake and frenzied. With good reason.

Sailing over the western horizon, another armada headed for them.

And Elide knew in her bones it was not one that Aelin had schemed and planned for.

Not as Fenrys breathed, suddenly beside her on the steps. "Maeve."

CHAPTER 61

They had no choice but to meet them. Maeve's armada had the wind and the current, and they would not even reach the shore before they were caught. And outrunning Fae soldiers . . . Not an option.

Rowan and Aedion laid out every course for Aelin. All paths arrived at one destination: confrontation. And she was still so drained, so exhausted, that . . . She knew how this would go.

Maeve had a third more ships. And immortal warriors. With magic.

It took far too little time for those black sails to fill the sky, for them to glean that their enemy's boats were better-made, their soldiers longer-trained. Rowan and the cadre had overseen much of that training—and the details they provided were not heartening.

Maeve sent one ornately carved rowboat to them, bearing a message.

Surrender—or be sent to the bottom of the ocean. Aelin had until dawn tomorrow to decide.

An entire day. So that the fear would fester and spread among their men.

Aelin met with Rowan and Aedion again. The cadre was not summoned by their queen, though Lorcan paced like a caged beast, Elide watching with a face that impressively revealed nothing.

She had no solution. Dorian remained quiet, though he often glanced between her and Manon. As if some puzzle were laid before him. He never said what.

Aedion pushed for attacking—quietly rallying the boats and attacking. But Maeve would see that maneuver coming. And they could strike faster with magic than it'd take for them to fire arrows and harpoons.

Time. That was all she had to play with.

They debated and theorized and planned. Rowan made a decent attempt at trying to suggest she run. She let him talk, only to let him realize in doing so what a stupid idea it was. After last night, he should be well aware she was not leaving him. Not willingly.

So the sun set. And Maeve's armada waited, poised and watching. A lounging panther, ready to strike at first light.

Time. Her only tool—and her downfall. And she had run out of it.

Aelin counted those black sails again and again as night blanketed them.

And had no idea what to do.

It was unacceptable, Rowan had decided, during the long hours they'd debated.

Unacceptable that they had done so much, only to be halted not by Erawan, but Maeve.

She hadn't deigned to make an appearance. But that wasn't her style.

She'd do it at dawn. Accept Aelin's surrender in person, with all eyes watching. And then . . . Rowan didn't know what she'd do then. What Maeve wanted, other than the keys.

Aelin had been so calm. Shock, he'd realized. Aelin had gone into shock. Rowan had seen her rage and kill and laugh and weep, but he had never seen her . . . lost. And he hated himself for it, but he couldn't find a way out. Couldn't find a way for *her* to get out of this.

Aelin was sleeping soundly as Rowan stared at the ceiling above their bed, then slid his gaze over her. He took in the lines of her face, the golden waves of her hair, every moon-white scar and dark swirl of ink. Leaning in, silent as snow in a wood, he kissed her brow.

He would not let it end here, not let this be what broke them.

He knew the house flags that flew beneath Maeve's own crest. Had counted and cataloged them all day, sorting through the catacombs of his memory.

Rowan slid into his clothes and waited until he'd crept into the hall before buckling his sword belt. Still gripping the doorknob, he allowed himself one last look at her.

For a moment, the past snared him—for a moment, he saw her as he'd first spied her on the rooftops of Varese, drunk and battered. He'd been in hawk form, assessing his new charge, and she'd noticed him—broken and reeling, she had still spotted him there. And stuck out her tongue at him.

If someone had told him that the drunken, brawling, bitter woman would become the one thing he could not live without . . . Rowan shut the door.

This was all he could offer her.

Rowan reached the main deck and shifted, little more than a gleam of moonlight as he shielded himself and flapped through the briny night—into the heart of Maeve's fleet.

Rowan's cousin had enough good sense not to try to kill him on sight.

They were close enough in age that Rowan had grown up with him, raised in his uncle's house beside him after his parents had faded. If his uncle ever faded, it would be Enda who took up the mantle as head of their house—a prince of considerable title, property, and arms.

Enda, to his credit, sensed his arrival before Rowan slipped through the flimsy shield on the windows. And Enda remained sitting on the bed, albeit dressed for battle, a hand on his sword.

His cousin looked him over head to toe as Rowan shifted. "Assassin or messenger, Prince?"

"Neither," Rowan said, inclining his head slightly.

Like him, Enda was silver-haired, though his green eyes were speckled with brown that could sometimes swallow the color whole when he was in a rage.

If Rowan had been bred and built for battlefields, Enda was sculpted for intrigue and court machinations. His cousin, while tall and muscled enough, lacked Rowan's breadth of shoulders and solid bulk—though that could also be from the different sorts of training they'd received. Enda knew enough about fighting to warrant being here to lead his father's forces, but their own educations had crossed little after those first decades of youth, when they had run wild together at his family's main estate.

Enda kept his hand on the hilt of his fine sword, utterly calm. "You look . . . different," his cousin said, brows twitching toward each other. "Better."

There had been a time when Enda had been his friend—before Lyria. Before . . . everything. And Rowan might have been inclined to explain who and what was responsible for this change, but he didn't have time. No, time was not his ally this night.

But Rowan said, "You look different as well, Prince."

Enda gave a half smile. "You can thank my mate for that."

Once, it might have sent a pang of agony through him. That Enda spoke of it reminded him that his cousin might not be a battle-honed warrior, but the courtier was as good as any at marking important details—noting Aelin's scent, now forever entwined with his own. So Rowan nodded, smiling a bit himself. "It was Lord Kerrigan's son, wasn't it?"

Indeed, there was another's scent woven through Enda's, the claiming deep and true. "It was." Enda again smiled—now at a ring on his finger. "We were mated and married earlier this summer."

"You mean to tell me you waited a hundred years for him?"

Enda shrugged, his grip on his sword lightening. "When it comes to the right person, Prince, waiting a hundred years is worth it."

He knew. He understood him so damn well that it made his chest crack to think of it.

"Endymion," he said hoarsely. "Enda, I need you to listen."

There were plenty of people who might have called for the guards, but he knew Enda—or had. He was but one of several cousins who'd shoved their noses into his business for years. Tried, Rowan now wondered, not for gossip but . . . to fight to keep some small scrap of him alive. Enda more than any of them.

So Endymion gave him the gift of listening. Rowan tried to keep it concise, tried to keep his hands from trembling. In the end, he supposed his request was simple.

When he finished, Enda studied him, any response hidden behind that court-trained mask of neutrality.

Then Enda said, "I will consider it."

It was the best Rowan could hope for. He said nothing else to his cousin before he shifted again and flapped into the night—toward another banner he had once marched beside.

And ship to ship, Rowan went. The same speech. The same request.

All of them, all his cousins, had the same answer.

I will consider it.

CHAPTER 62

Manon was awake when Dorian stormed into her room an hour before dawn. He ignored her unlaced shirt, the swell of those lush breasts he'd tasted only yesterday, as he said, "Put your clothes on and follow me."

Mercifully, the witch obeyed. Though he had a feeling it was mostly from curiosity.

When he reached Aelin's chamber, he bothered to knock—just in case the queen and Rowan were utilizing their potentially last few hours together. But the queen was already awake and dressed, the prince nowhere to be found. Aelin took one look at Dorian's face. "What is it?"

He didn't tell either woman anything as he led them down into the cargo hold, the upper levels of the ship already astir with battle preparations.

While they'd debated and readied for the past day, he'd contemplated Manon's warning, after she'd made his very blood sing with pleasure. *Unless you would like to learn precisely what parts of me are made of iron the next time you touch me, I decide those things.*

Over and over, he'd considered the way the words had snagged on a sharp corner of memory. He'd lain awake all night while he descended into his still-depleted well of magic. And as the light had begun to shift . . .

Dorian tugged the sheet off the witch mirror carefully held in place against the wall. The Lock—or whatever it was. In the muted reflection, the two queens were frowning at his back.

Manon's iron nails slid out. "I would be careful handling that if I were you."

"The warning is noted and appreciated," he said, meeting those gold eyes in the mirror. She didn't return his smile. Neither did Aelin. He sighed. "I don't think this witch mirror has any power. Or, rather, not a tangible, brute power. I think its power is knowledge."

Aelin's steps were near-silent as she approached. "I was told the Lock would allow me to bind the three keys into the gate. You think this mirror knows how to do that?"

He simply nodded, trying not to be too offended by the skepticism scrunching her face.

Aelin picked at a loose thread on her jacket. "But what does the Lock-mirror-whatever-it-is have to do with the armada breathing down our necks?"

He tried not to roll his eyes. "It has to do with what Deanna said. What if the Lock wasn't just for binding them back into the gate, but a tool for safely controlling the keys?"

Aelin frowned at the mirror. "So I'm going to lug that thing onto the deck and use it to blow apart Maeve's armada with the two keys we have?"

He took a steadying breath, beseeching the gods for patience. "I said I think this mirror's power is knowledge. I think it will *show* you how to wield the keys safely. So you can come back here and wield them without consequence."

A slow blink. "What do you mean, *come back here*?"

Manon answered, now stepping close as she studied the mirror. "It's a traveling mirror."

Dorian nodded. "Think about Deanna's words: '*Flame and iron, together bound, merge into silver to learn what must be found. A mere step is all it shall take.*'" He pointed to the mirror. "Step into the silver—and *learn*."

Manon clicked her tongue. "And I suppose she and I are flame and iron."

Aelin crossed her arms.

Dorian cut the Queen of Terrasen a wry glance. "People other than you *can* solve things, you know."

Aelin glared at him. "We don't have time for what-ifs. Too many things could go wrong."

"You have little magic left," Dorian countered, waving a hand toward the mirror. "You could be in and out of this mirror before dawn. And use what you learn to send Maeve a message in no uncertain terms."

"I can still fight with steel—without the risks and waste of time."

"You can stop this battle before the losses are too great on either side." He added carefully, "We're out of time already, Aelin."

Those turquoise eyes were steady—if not still furious he'd beat her to the riddle—but something flickered in them. "I know," she said. "I was hoping . . ." She shook her head, more at herself. "I ran out of time," she murmured as if it were an answer, and considered the mirror, then Manon. Then blew out a breath. "This wasn't my plan."

"I know," Dorian said with a half smile. "That's why you don't like it."

Manon asked before Aelin could bite off his head, "But where will the mirror lead?"

Aelin clenched her jaw. "Hopefully not Morath." Dorian tensed. Perhaps this plan—

"That symbol belongs to both of us," Manon said, studying the Eye of Elena etched onto it. "And if it takes you to Morath, you're going to need someone who knows the way out."

Steps thudded down the stairs at the back of the hold. Dorian twisted toward them, but Aelin smirked at Manon and approached the mirror. "Then I'll see you on the other side, witch."

Aedion's golden head appeared between the crates. "What the hell are you—"

Aelin's shallow nod seemed all that Manon needed. She placed her hand atop Aelin's.

Golden eyes met Dorian's for a moment, and he opened his mouth to say something to her, the words surging from some barren field in his chest.

But Aelin and Manon pressed their joined hands to the speckled glass.

Aedion's shout of warning rang through the hold as they vanished.

CHAPTER 63

Elide watched the ship rally against the armada looming before them—then descend into utter chaos as Aedion began roaring below.

The news came out moments later. Came out as Prince Rowan Whitethorn landed on the main deck, face haggard, eyes full of nothing but fear as Aedion burst out the door, Dorian on his heels, sporting an already-nasty bruise around his eye. Pacing, seething, Aedion told them of Aelin and Manon walking into the mirror—the Lock—and vanishing. How the King of Adarlan had solved Deanna's riddle and sent them into its silvery realm to buy them a shot at this battle.

They went down into the cargo hold. But no matter how Aedion pushed against the mirror, it did not open to him. No matter how Rowan searched it with his magic, it did not yield where Aelin and Manon had gone. Aedion had spat on the floor, looking inclined to give the king another black eye as Dorian explained there had been little choice. He hadn't seemed sorry about it—until Rowan refused to meet his gaze.

Only when they were gathered on the deck again, the king and shape-shifter off speaking to the captain about the turn of events, did Elide carefully say to Aedion as he paced, "What is done is done. We can't wait for Aelin and Manon to find a way to save us."

Aedion halted, and Elide tried not to cringe at the unrelenting fury as it narrowed on her. "When I want your opinion about how to deal with my missing queen, I'll ask you."

Lorcan snarled at him. But Elide lifted her chin, even as the insult hit something in her chest. "I waited as long as you did to find her again, Aedion. You are not the only one who fears to lose her once more."

Indeed, Rowan Whitethorn now rubbed his face. She suspected it was as much feeling as the Fae Prince would show.

Rowan lowered his hands, the others watching him. Waiting—for his orders.

Even Aedion.

Elide started as realization slapped her. As she searched for proof but found none.

"We continue readying for battle," Rowan said hoarsely. He looked to Lorcan, then Fenrys and Gavriel, and his entire countenance changed, his shoulders pushing back, his eyes turning hard and calculating. "There's not a chance in hell Maeve doesn't know you're here. She'll wield the blood oath when it'll hurt us the most."

Maeve. Some small part of her wished to see the queen who could command Lorcan's relentless focus and affection for so many centuries. And perhaps give Maeve a piece of her mind.

Fenrys put a hand on the hilt of his sword and said with more quiet than Elide had witnessed so far, "I don't know how to play this one."

Indeed, Gavriel seemed at a loss, scanning his tattooed hands as if the answer lay there.

It was Lorcan who said, "If you're spotted fighting on this side, it's over. She'll either kill you both or make you regret it in other ways."

"And what about *you*?" Fenrys challenged.

Lorcan's eyes slid to hers, then back to the males before them. "It was over for me months ago. It's now a matter of waiting to see what she'll do about it."

If she'd kill him. Or drag him back in chains.

Elide's stomach turned, and she avoided the urge to grab his hand, to beg him to run.

"She'll see that we've worked our way around her order to kill you," Gavriel at last said. "If fighting on this side of the line doesn't damn us enough, then that surely will. It likely already has."

"Dawn's still half an hour off, if you two want to try again," Lorcan crooned.

Elide tensed. But it was Fenrys who said, "It's all a ploy." Elide held her breath as he surveyed the Fae males—his companions. "To fracture us when Maeve knows that unified, we could present a considerable threat."

"We'd never turn on her," Gavriel countered.

"No," Fenrys agreed. "But we would offer that strength to another." And he looked at Rowan as he said, "When we got your call for aid this spring—when you asked us to come defend Mistward, we left before Maeve could get wind of it. We ran."

"That's enough," Lorcan growled.

But Fenrys went on, holding Rowan's steady gaze, "When we returned, Maeve whipped us within an inch of our lives. Tied Lorcan to the posts for two days and let Cairn whip him whenever he wished. Lorcan ordered us not to tell you—for whatever reason. But I think Maeve saw what we did together in Mistward and realized how dangerous we could be—to *her*."

Rowan didn't hide the devastation in his eyes as he faced Lorcan—devastation that Elide felt echo in her own heart. Lorcan had endured that . . . and still remained loyal to Maeve. Elide brushed her fingers against his. The motion didn't go unnoticed by the others, but they wisely kept quiet about it. Especially as Lorcan dragged his thumb down the back of her hand in answer.

And Elide wondered if Rowan also understood that Lorcan hadn't ordered their silence for strategy, but perhaps to spare the prince from guilt. From wanting to retaliate against Maeve in a way that would surely harm him.

"Did you know," Rowan said hoarsely to Lorcan, "that she'd punish you before you came to Mistward?"

Lorcan held the prince's stare. "We all knew what the cost would be."

Rowan's throat bobbed, and he took a long breath, his eyes darting toward the stairs, as if Aelin would come prowling out, salvation in hand. But she didn't, and Elide prayed that wherever the queen now was, she was gleaning what they so desperately needed to learn. Rowan said to his companions, "You know how this battle will likely end. Even if our armada teemed with Fae soldiers, we'd still have the odds stacked against us."

The sky began to bleed with pink and purple as the sun stirred beneath the distant waves.

Gavriel only said, "We have had the odds stacked against us before." A glance at Fenrys, who nodded gravely. "We will stay until we are commanded otherwise."

It was to Aedion that Gavriel looked as he said this last piece. There was something in the general's Ashryver eyes that looked almost like gratitude.

Elide sensed Lorcan's attention and found him still watching her as he said to Rowan, "Elide gets to shore, under a guard of whatever men you can spare. My sword is yours only if you do that."

Elide started. But Rowan said, "Done."

Rowan spread them across the fleet, each given command of a few ships. He stationed Fenrys, Lorcan, and Gavriel on ships toward the center and back, farthest away from Maeve's notice. He and Aedion took the front lines, with Dorian and Ansel commanding the line of ships behind his.

Lysandra was already beneath the waves in sea dragon form, ready for his order to do damage to hull and prow and rudder on ships he'd marked for her. He'd bet that while the Fae ships might have shields around them, they wouldn't waste valuable reservoirs of power on shielding below the surface. Lysandra would strike quick and hard—gone before they could realize who and what wrecked them from below.

Dawn broke, clear and bright, staining the sails with gold.

Rowan did not let himself think of Aelin—of wherever she might be.

Minute after minute passed, and still Aelin did not return.

A small oak rowboat slid out from Maeve's fleet and headed for him.

There were only three people on it—none of them Maeve.

He could feel thousands of eyes on either side of that too-narrow band of empty water between their armadas, watching that boat approach. Watching *him*.

A male in Maeve's livery stood with preternatural Fae balance as the oarsmen held the boat steady. "Her Majesty awaits your reply."

Rowan tunneled into his depleted reserve of power, keeping his face bland. "Inform Maeve that Aelin Galathynius is no longer present to give a reply."

A blink from the male was all the shock he'd let show. Maeve's creatures were too well trained, too aware of the punishment for revealing her secrets.

"Princess Aelin Galathynius is ordered to surrender," the male said.

"*Queen* Aelin Galathynius is not on this ship or any other in this fleet.

She is, in fact, not on the shore, or in any nearby lands. So Maeve will find she came a long way for nothing. We will leave your armada in peace, if you will grant us the same courtesy."

The male sneered up at him. "Spoken like cowards who know they're outnumbered. Spoken like a traitor."

Rowan gave the male a small smile. "Let's see what Maeve has to say now."

The male spat into the water. But the ship rowed back into the embrace of the armada.

For a moment, Rowan recalled his last words to Dorian before he'd sent the king to shield his own line of ships.

They were beyond apologies. Aelin would either return or—he didn't let himself consider the alternative. But they could buy her as much time as possible. Try to fight their way out—for her, and the future of this armada.

Dorian's face had revealed the same thoughts as he clasped hands with him and said quietly, "It is not such a hard thing, is it—to die for your friends."

Rowan didn't bother insisting they were going to live through this. The king had been tutored in warfare, even if he hadn't yet practiced it. So Rowan had given him a grim smile and replied, "No, it is not."

The words echoed through him again as that messenger's boat disappeared. And for whatever good it would do, whatever time it would buy them, Rowan reinforced his shields again.

The sun had fully risen over the horizon when Maeve's reply came.

Not a messenger in a longboat.

But a barrage of arrows, so many that they blotted out the light as they arced across the sky.

"*Shield*," Rowan bellowed, not only at the magic-wielders, but also at the armed men who raised their dented and battered shields above them as arrows rained across the line.

The arrows struck, and his magic buckled under their onslaught. Their tips had been wrapped in magic of their own, and Rowan gritted his teeth against it. On other ships, where the shield was stretched thin, some men screamed.

Maeve's armada began crawling toward them.

CHAPTER 64

Aelin had a body that was not a body.

She knew only because in this void, this foggy twilight, Manon had a body. A nearly transparent, wraithlike body, but . . . a form nonetheless.

Manon's teeth and nails glinted in the dim light as she surveyed the swirling gray mists. "What is this place?" The mirror had transported them to . . . wherever this was.

"Your guess is as good as mine, witch."

Had time stopped beyond the mists? Had Maeve held her fire upon learning she was not present—or attacked anyway? Aelin had no doubt Rowan would hold the lines for as long as possible. Had no doubt he and Aedion would lead them. But . . .

Whether the witch mirror was the Lock she'd sought, she'd expected it to have *some* immediate reaction to the two Wyrdkeys she'd snuck into her jacket.

Not . . . this. Not absolutely *nothing*.

Aelin drew Goldryn. In the mist, the sword's ruby flickered—the only color, only light.

Manon said, "We stick close; we only speak when necessary."

Aelin was inclined to agree. There was solid ground beneath them, but the mist hid her feet—hid any inkling that they stood on dirt beyond a faint, crumbling scraping.

"Any guess which way?" Aelin murmured. But they didn't have to decide.

The eddying fog darkened, and Manon and Aelin stepped close together, back to back. Pure night swept around them—blinding them.

Then—a murky, dim light ahead. No, not ahead. Approaching them. Manon's bony shoulder dug into her own as they pressed tighter together, an impenetrable wall.

But the light rippled and expanded, figures within it appearing. Solidifying.

Aelin knew three things as the light and color enveloped them and became tangible:

They were not seen, or heard, or scented by those before them.

And this was the past. A thousand years ago, to be exact.

And that was Elena Galathynius on her knees in a black barren mountain pass, blood dripping from her nose, tears sliding through the dirt crusting her face to splatter on her armor, an obsidian sarcophagus somehow stationed before her.

All across the sarcophagus, Wyrdmarks simmered with pale blue fire. And in the center of it . . . the Eye of Elena, the amulet held within the stone itself, its pale gold unvarnished and gleaming.

Then, as if a phantom breath blew over it, the Eye dimmed, along with the Wyrdmarks.

Elena reached with a trembling hand to twist the Eye, rotating it thrice in the black stone. The Eye clicked and tumbled into Elena's awaiting hand. Sealing the sarcophagus.

Locking it.

"You've had the Lock all along," Manon murmured. "But then the mirror . . ."

"I think," Aelin breathed, "we have been deliberately misled about what we must retrieve."

"Why?" Manon said with equal quiet.

"I suppose we're about to find out."

A memory—that's what this was. But what was so vital that they had been sent to retrieve it when the whole damn world was falling apart around them?

Aelin and Manon stood in silence as the scene unfolded. As the truth, at last the truth, now wove together.

CHAPTER 65

Dawn at the Obsidian Passes

The Lock had crafted the sarcophagus from the mountain itself.

It had taken every ember of its power to bind Erawan within the stone, to seal him inside.

She could feel the Dark King sleeping within. Hear the shrieks of his fell army feasting on human flesh in the valley far below. How long would they continue fighting when word spread that Erawan had fallen?

She wasn't foolish enough to hope her companions had survived the slaughter. Not this long.

On her knees in the sharp black rock, Elena gazed at the obsidian sarcophagus, the symbols carved into it. They initially had been glowing, but had now faded and cooled, settled into place. When she had stolen the Lock from her father all those months ago, she had not known—had not understood—the truth depth of its power. Still did not know why he had forged it. Only that once, just once, could the Lock's power be wielded. And that power . . . oh, that mighty, shattering power . . . it had saved them all.

Gavin, sprawled and bloody behind her, stirred. His face was so mangled she could barely see the handsome, fierce features beneath. His left arm was useless at his side. The price of distracting Erawan while she'd unleashed the Lock's power. But even Gavin had not known what she'd been planning. What she'd stolen and harbored all these months.

She did not regret it. Not when it had spared him from death. Worse.

Gavin took in the sarcophagus, the empty, intricate amulet of the Lock in her palm as it rested on her thigh. He recognized it instantly, having seen it around her father's neck during those initial weeks in Orynth. The blue stone in its center was now drained, dim where it had once flickered with inner fire. Barely a drop of its power left, if that.

"What have you done?" His voice was a broken rasp from screaming during Erawan's ministrations. To buy her time, to save their people—

Elena folded her fingers into a fist around the Lock. "He is sealed. He cannot escape."

"Your father's Lock—"

"It is done," she said, shifting her attention to the dozen ancient, immortal figures now on the other side of the sarcophagus.

Gavin started, hissing at his broken body with the sudden movement.

They had no forms. They were only figments of light and shadow, wind and rain, song and memory. Each individual, and yet a part of one majority, one consciousness.

They were all gazing at the broken Lock in her hands, its stone dull.

Gavin lowered his brow to the blood-soaked rock and averted his eyes.

Elena's very bones quailed in their presence, but she kept her chin high.

"Our sister's bloodline has betrayed us," said one that was of sea and sky and storms.

Elena shook her head, trying to swallow. Failing. "I *saved* us. I stopped Erawan—"

"Fool," said the one of many shifting voices, both animal and human. "Half-breed *fool.* Did you not consider why your father carried it, why he bided his time all these years, gathering his strength? He was to wield it—to seal the three Wyrdkeys back into the gate, and send us *home* before he shut the gate forever. Us, and the Dark King. The Lock was forged for us—*promised* to us. And you *wasted* it."

Elena braced a hand on the earth to keep from swaying. "My father bears the Wyrdkeys?" He had never so much as *hinted* . . . And the Lock . . . she had thought it a mere weapon. A weapon he had *refused* to wield in this bloody war.

They did not answer, their silence confirmation enough.

A small, broken noise came out of her throat. Elena breathed, "I'm sorry."

Their rage rattled her bones, threatened to stop her heart dead in her chest. The one of flame and light and ashes seemed to withhold, seemed to pause in her wrath.

To remember.

She had not seen or spoken to her mother since she had left her body to forge the Lock. Since Rhiannon Crochan had helped Mala cast her very essence into it, the mass of its power contained within the small witch mirror disguised as a blue stone, to be unleashed only once. They had never told Elena why. Never said it was anything more than a weapon that her father would one day desperately need to wield.

The cost: her mother's mortal body, the life she had wanted for herself with Brannon and their children. It had been ten years since then. Ten years, her father had never stopped waiting for Mala to return, hoping he'd see her again. Just once.

I will not remember you, Mala had said to them all before she had given herself to the Lock's forging. And yet there she was. Pausing. As if she remembered.

"Mother," Elena whispered, a broken plea.

Mala Light-Bringer looked away from her.

The one who saw all with wise, calm eyes said, "Unleash him. So we have been betrayed by these earth beasts, let us return the favor. Unleash the Dark King from his coffin."

"*No*," Elena pleaded, rising from her knees. "Please—*please*. Tell me what I must do to atone, but *please* do not unleash him. I beg you."

"He will rise again one day," said the one of darkness and death. "He will awaken. You have wasted *our* Lock on a fool's errand, when you could have solved all, had you only the patience and wits to understand."

"Then let him awaken," Elena begged, her voice breaking. "Let someone else inherit this war—someone better prepared."

"Coward," said the one with a voice of steel and shields and arrows. "Coward to shove the burden to another."

"Please," Elena said. "I will give you anything. *Anything*. But not that."

As one, they looked to Gavin.

No—

But it was her mother who said, "We have waited this long to return home. We may wait a little longer. Watch over this . . . place a little longer."

Not just gods, but beings of a higher, different existence. For whom time was fluid, and bodies were things to be shifted and molded. Who could exist in multiple places, spread themselves wide like nets being thrown. They were as mighty and vast and eternal as a human was to a mayfly.

They had not been born in this world. Perhaps had become trapped here after wandering through a Wyrdgate. And they had struck some bargain with her father, with Mala, to at last send them home, banishing Erawan with them. And she had ruined it.

The one with three faces said, "We will wait. But there must be a price. And a promise."

"Name it," Elena said. If they took Gavin, she'd follow. She was not the heir to her father's throne. It did not matter if she walked out of this mountain pass. She wasn't entirely certain she could bear to see him again, not after her arrogance and pride and self-righteousness. Brannon had begged her to listen, to wait. She had instead stolen the Lock from him and run with Gavin into the night, desperate to save these lands.

The one with three faces studied her. "Mala's bloodline shall bleed again to forge the Lock anew. And *you* will lead them, a lamb to slaughter, to pay the price of this choice *you* made to waste its power here, for this petty battle. *You* will show this future scion how to forge a new Lock with Mala's gifts, how to then use it to wield the keys and send us home. Our original bargain still holds: we will take the Dark King with us. Tear him apart in our own world, where he will be but dust and memory. When we are gone—you will show this scion how to seal the gate behind us, the Lock holding it intact eternally. By yielding every last drop of their life force. As your father was prepared to do when the time was right."

"Please," Elena breathed.

The three-faced one said, "Tell Brannon of the Wildfire what occurred here; tell him the price his bloodline shall one day pay. Tell him to ready for it."

She let the words, the damnation, sink in. "I will," she whispered.

But they were gone. There was only a lingering warmth, as if a beam of sunlight had brushed her cheek.

Gavin lifted his head. "What have you done?" he asked again. "What have you given them?"

"Did you not—not hear it?"

"Only you," he rasped, his face so horribly pale. "No others."

She stared at the sarcophagus before them, its black stone rooted to the earth of the pass. Immovable. They would have to build something around it, to hide it, protect it.

Elena said, "The price will be paid—later."

"Tell me." His swollen, split lips could barely form the words.

Since she had already damned herself, damned her bloodline, she figured there was nothing left to lose in lying. Not this one time, this last time. "Erawan will awaken again—one day. When the time comes, I will help those who must fight him."

His eyes were wary.

"Can you walk?" she asked, extending a hand to help him rise. The rising sun cast the black mountains in gold and red. She had no doubt the valley behind was bathed in the latter.

Gavin released his grip, the fingers still broken, from where it had rested on Damaris's hilt. But he did not take her offered hand.

And he did not tell her what he'd detected while he touched the Sword of Truth, what lies he'd sensed and unraveled.

They never spoke of them again.

Moonrise at the Temple of Sandrian, the Stone Marshes

The Princess of Eyllwe had been wandering the Stone Marshes for weeks, searching for answers to riddles posed a thousand years ago. Answers that might save her doomed kingdom.

Keys and gates and locks—portals and pits and prophecies. That was what the princess murmured to herself in the weeks she'd been stalking through the marshes alone, hunting to keep herself alive, fighting the beasts of teeth and venom when necessary, reading the stars for entertainment.

So when the princess at last reached the temple, when she stood before the stone altar and the chest that was the light twin to the dark one beneath Morath, *she* at last appeared.

"You are Nehemia," she said.

The princess whirled, her hunting leathers stained and damp, the gold tips on her braided hair clinking.

An assessing look with eyes that were too old for barely eighteen; eyes that had stared long into the darkness between the stars and yearned to know its secrets. "And you are Elena."

Elena nodded. "Why have you come?"

The Princess of Eyllwe jerked her elegant chin toward the stone chest. "Am I not called to open it? To learn how to save us, and to pay the price?"

"No," Elena said quietly. "Not you. Not in this way."

A tightening of her lips was the only sign of the princess's displeasure. "Then in what way, Lady, am I required to bleed?"

She had been watching, and waiting, and paying for her choices for so long. Too long.

And now that darkness had fallen . . . now a new sun would rise. *Must* rise.

"It is Mala's bloodline that will pay, not your own."

Her back stiffened. "You have not answered my question."

Elena wished she could hold back the words, keep them locked up. But this was the price, for her kingdom, her people. The price for these people, this kingdom. And others.

"In the North, two branches flow from Mala. One to the Havilliard House, where its prince with my mate's eyes possesses my raw magic—and her brute power. The other branch flows through the Galathynius House, where it bred true: flame and embers and ashes."

"Aelin Galathynius is dead," Nehemia said.

"Not dead." No, she'd ensured that, still paying for what she'd done that wintry night. "Just hiding, forgotten by a world grateful to see such a power extinguished before it matured."

"Where is she? And how does this tie to me, Lady?"

"You are versed in the history, in the players and the stakes. You know the Wyrdmarks and how to wield them. You misread the riddles, thinking it was you who must come here, to this place. This mirror is not the Lock—it is a pool of memory. Forged by myself, my father, and Rhiannon Crochan. Forged so the heir of this burden might understand one day. Know everything before deciding. This encounter, too, shall be held in it. But you were called, so we might meet."

That wise, young face waited.

"Go north, Princess," Elena said. "Go into your enemy's household. Make the contacts, get the invitation, do what you must, but get to your enemy's house. The two bloodlines will converge there. Already, they are on their way."

"Aelin Galathynius is headed to Adarlan?"

"Not Aelin. Not with that name, that crown. Know her by her eyes—turquoise with a core of gold. Know her by the mark on her brow—the bastard's mark, the mark of Brannon. Guide her. Help her. She will need you."

"And the price?"

Elena hated them, then.

Hated the gods who had demanded this. Hated herself. Hated that this was asked, all these bright lights . . .

"You will not see Eyllwe again."

The princess stared at the stars as if they spoke to her, as if the answer were written there. "Will my people survive?" A small, quiet voice.

"I don't know."

"Then I will take the steps for that, too. Unite the rebels while I am in Rifthold, ready the continent for war."

Nehemia lowered her eyes from the stars. Elena wanted to fall to her knees before the young princess, beg her forgiveness. "One of them must be ready—to do what needs to be done," Elena said, if only because it was the sole way to explain, to apologize.

Nehemia swallowed. "Then I shall help in whatever way I can. For Erilea. And my people."

CHAPTER 66

Aedion Ashryver had been trained to kill men and hold a line in battle since he was old enough to lift a sword. Crown Prince Rhoe Galathynius had begun his training personally, holding Aedion to standards that some might have deemed unfair, too unyielding for a boy.

But Rhoe had known, Aedion realized as he stood on the prow of the ship, Ansel of Briarcliff's men armed and ready behind him. Rhoe had known even then that Aedion would serve Aelin, and when foreign armies challenged the might of the Fire-Bringer . . . it might not be mere mortals that he faced.

Rhoe—*Evalin*—had gambled that the immortal army now stretching away before him would one day come to these shores. And they had wanted to ensure that Aedion was ready when it did.

"Shields up," Aedion ordered the men as the second volley of arrows rained from Maeve's armada. The magical cloak around their ships was holding well enough thanks to Dorian Havilliard, and though he was glad for any bloodshed it spared them, after the bullshit the king had pulled with Aelin and Manon, Aedion gritted his teeth at each ripple of color upon impact.

"These are soldiers, the same as you," Aedion went on. "Don't let the pointy ears deceive you. They bleed like the rest of us. And can die from the same wounds, too."

He didn't let himself glance behind—to where his father commanded and shielded another line of ships. Gavriel had kept quiet while Fenrys divulged how to keep a quick-healing Fae warrior down: go for slicing through muscles rather than stabbing wounds. Snap a tendon and you'll halt an immortal long enough to kill.

Easier said than done. The soldiers had gone pale-faced at the thought of it—open combat, blade-to-blade, against Fae warriors. Rightly so.

But Aedion's duty wasn't to remind them of the blunt facts. His duty was to make them willing to die, to make this fight seem utterly necessary. Fear could break a line faster than any enemy charge.

Rhoe—his *real* father—had taught him that. And Aedion had learned it during those years in the North. Learned it fighting knee-deep in mud and gore with the Bane.

He wished they flanked him, not unknown soldiers from the Wastes.

But he would not let his own fear erode his resolve.

Maeve's second volley rose up, up, up, the arrows soaring faster and farther than those from mortal bows. With better aim.

The invisible shield above them rippled with flickers of blue and purple as arrows hissed and slid off it.

Buckling already, because those arrows came tipped with magic.

The soldiers on the deck stirred, shields shifting, their anticipation and rising terror coating Aedion's senses. "Just a bit of rain, boys," he said, grinning widely. "I thought you bastards were used to it out in the Wastes."

Some grumbles—but those metal shields stopped shivering.

Aedion made himself chuckle. Made himself the Wolf of the North, eager to spill blood upon the southern seas. As Rhoe had taught him, as Rhoe had prepared him, long before Terrasen fell to the shadow of Adarlan.

Not again. Never again—and certainly not to Maeve. Certainly not here, with no one to witness it.

Ahead, at the front lines, Rowan's magic flared white in silent signal.

"Arrows at the ready," Aedion ordered.

Bows groaned, arrows pointing skyward.

Another flash.

"*Volley!*" Aedion bellowed.

The world darkened beneath their arrows as they sailed toward Maeve's armada.

A storm of arrows—to distract from the real attack beneath the waves.

The water was dimmer here, the sunlight slim shafts that slid between the fat-bellied boats amassed above the waves.

Other creatures had gathered at the ruckus, flesh-shredders looking for the meals that would surely come when the two armadas at last met.

A flash of light had sent Lysandra diving deep, weaving between the circling scavengers, blending into their masses as best as she could while she launched into a sprint.

She had modified her sea dragon. Given it longer limbs—with prehensile thumbs.

Given her tail more strength, more control.

Her own little project, during the long days of travel. To take one original form and perfect it. To alter what the gods had made to her own liking.

Lysandra reached the first ship Rowan had marked. A careful, precise map of where and how to strike. A snap of her tail had the rudder in pieces.

Their shouts reached her even under the waves, but Lysandra was already flying, soaring for the next marked boat.

She used her claws this time, grabbing the rudder and ripping it clean off. Then bashing a hole in the keel with her clubbed tail. Clubbed, not spiked—no, the spikes had gotten stuck in Skull's Bay. So she'd made her tail into a battering ram.

Arrows fired with better accuracy than the Valg foot soldiers, shooting like those rays of sunshine into the water. She'd prepared for that, too.

They bounced off scales of Spidersilk. Hours spent studying the material grafted onto Abraxos's wings had taught her about it—how to change her own skin into the impenetrable fiber.

Lysandra tore into another rudder, then another. And another.

Fae soldiers were screaming in advance of her. But the harpoons they fired were too heavy, and she was too fast, dove too deep and too swift. Whips of water magic speared for her, trying to ensnare her. She outswam them, too.

The court that could change the world, she told herself over and over, as exhaustion weighed her down, as she kept disabling rudder after rudder, punching holes in those selected Fae ships.

She had made a promise to that court, that future. To Aedion. And to her queen. She would not fail her.

And if gods-damned Maeve wanted to go head-to-head with them, if Maeve thought to strike them when they were weakest . . . Lysandra was going to make the bitch regret it.

Dorian's magic roiled as Maeve's armada went from firing arrows to outright chaos. But he kept his shields intact, patching the spots where arrows had broken through. Already, his power wobbled, too swiftly drained.

Either through some trick of Maeve's or whatever magic coated those arrows.

But Dorian gritted his teeth, leashing his magic to his will, Rowan's bellowed warnings to hold echoing off the water—amplified in the way that Gavriel had used his voice in Skull's Bay.

But even with the chaos of Maeve's armada finding their ships under siege from beneath the water, the lines of it stretched away forever.

Aelin and Manon had not returned.

A Fae male in a raging, lethal panic was a terrifying thing to behold. Two of them were near cataclysmic.

When Aelin and Manon had vanished into that mirror, Dorian suspected it was only Aedion's roaring that had made Rowan snap out of the blood fury he'd descended into. And only the throbbing bruise on Dorian's cheek that made Rowan refrain from giving him a matching one.

Dorian glanced toward the front lines, where the Fae Prince stood at the prow of his ship, his sword and hatchet out, a quiver of arrows and bow strapped across his back, various hunting knives honed razor-sharp. The prince had not snapped out of it at all, he realized.

No, Rowan had already descended to a level of icy wrath that had Dorian's magic trembling, even from the distance now between them.

He could feel it, Rowan's power—feel it as he'd sensed Aelin's surging up.

Rowan had already been deep within his reservoir of power when Aelin and Manon had left. He'd used the last hour, once Aedion had focused that fear and anger on the battle ahead, to plunge even deeper. It now flowed around them like the sea mere feet below.

Dorian had followed suit, falling back on the training the prince had instilled in him. Ice coated his veins, his heart.

Aedion had said only one thing to him before departing for his own section of the armada. The general-prince had looked him over once, his Ashryver eyes lingering on the bruise he'd given him, and said, "Fear is a death sentence. When you're out there, remember that we don't need to survive. Only put enough of a dent in them so that when she comes back . . . she'll wipe out the rest."

When. Not if. But when Aelin found their bodies, or whatever was left of them if the sea didn't claim them . . . she might very well end the world for rage.

Maybe she should. Maybe this world deserved it.

Maybe Manon Blackbeak would help her do it. Maybe they'd rule over the ruins together.

He wished he'd had more time to talk to the witch. To get to know her beyond what his body had already learned.

Because even with the rudders being disabled . . . ships now advanced.

Fae warriors. Born and bred to kill.

Aedion and Rowan sent another volley of arrows aiming for the ships. Shields disintegrated them before they could meet any targets. This would not end well.

His heart thundered, and he swallowed as the ships crept around their foundering brethren, inching toward that demarcation line.

His magic writhed.

He'd have to be careful where to aim. Have to make it count.

He did not trust his power to remain focused if he unleashed it all.

And Rowan had told him not to. Had told him to wait until the armada was truly upon them. Until they crossed that line. Until the Fae Prince gave the order to fire.

For it was fire—and ice—that warred in Dorian now, begging for release.

He kept his chin high as more ships inched toward those disabled at the front, then slipped alongside them.

Dorian knew it would hurt. Knew it would hurt to wreck his magic, and then wreck his body. Knew it would hurt to see his companions go down, one by one.

Still Rowan held the front line, did not let his ships turn to flee.

Closer and closer, those enemy ships speared toward their front lines, hauled by waving limbs of mighty oars. Archers were poised to fire, and sunlight glinted off the burnished armor of the battle-hungry Fae warriors aboard. Ready and rested, primed to slaughter.

There would be no surrender. Maeve would destroy them just to punish Aelin.

He'd failed them—in sending Manon and Aelin away. On that gamble, he'd perhaps failed all of them.

But Rowan Whitethorn had not.

No, as those enemy ships slid into place among their foundering companions, Dorian saw that they each bore the same flag:

A silver banner, with a screaming hawk.

And where Maeve's black flag of a perching owl had once flapped beside it . . . now that black flag lowered.

Now the dark queen's flag vanished entirely, as Fae ships bearing the silver banner of the House of Whitethorn opened fire upon their own armada.

CHAPTER 67

Rowan had told Enda about Aelin.

He had told his cousin about the woman he loved, the queen whose heart burned with wildfire. He had told Enda about Erawan, and the threat of the keys, and Maeve's own desire for them.

And then he had gotten on his knees and begged his cousin to help.

To not open fire on Terrasen's armada.

But on Maeve's.

To not squander this one chance at peace. At halting the darkness before it consumed them all, both from Morath and Maeve. To fight not for the queen who had enslaved him, but the one who had saved him.

I will consider it, Endymion had said.

And so Rowan had gotten off his knees and flown to another cousin's ship. Princess Sellene, his youngest, cunning-eyed cousin, had listened. Had let him beg. And with a small smile, she had said the same thing. *I will consider it*.

So he'd gone, ship to ship. To the cousins he knew might listen.

An act of treason—that was what he had begged them for. Treason and betrayal so great they could never go home. Their lands, their titles, would be seized or destroyed.

And as their unharmed ships sailed into place beside those Lysandra had already disabled, as they opened an assault of arrows and magic upon their unsuspecting forces, Rowan roared at his own fleet, "*Now, now, now!*"

Oars splashed into the waves, men grunting as they rowed like hell for the armada in utter chaos.

Every single one of his cousins had attacked.

Every single one. As if they had all met, all decided to risk ruination together.

Rowan had not possessed an army of his own to give to Aelin. To give to Terrasen.

So he had won an army for her. Through the only things Aelin had claimed were all she wanted from him.

His heart. His loyalty. His friendship.

And Rowan wished his Fireheart were there to see it as the House of Whitethorn slammed into Maeve's fleet, and ice and wind exploded across the waves.

Lorcan didn't believe it.

He didn't believe what he was seeing as a third of Maeve's fleet opened fire upon the stunned majority of her ships.

And he knew—he knew without having it confirmed that the banners flying on those ships would be silver.

However he'd convinced them, whenever he'd convinced them . . .

Whitethorn had done it. For her.

All of it, for Aelin.

Rowan bellowed the order to press their advantage, to break Maeve's armada between them.

Lorcan, a bit dazed, passed on the order to his own ships.

Maeve wouldn't allow it. She'd wipe the Whitethorn line off the map for this.

But there they were, unleashing their ice and wind upon their own ships, accented with arrows and harpoons that speared through wood and soldiers.

Wind whipped at his hair, and he knew Whitethorn was now pushing his magic to the breaking point to haul their own ships into the fray before his cousins lost the advantage of surprise. Fools, all of them.

Fools, and yet . . .

Gavriel's son was bellowing Whitethorn's name. A gods-damned victory cry. Over and over, the men taking up the call.

Then Fenrys's voice lifted. And Gavriel's. And that red-haired queen. The Havilliard king.

Their armada soared for Maeve's, sun and sea and sails all around, blades glinting in the morning brightness. Even the rise and fall of the oars seemed to echo the chant.

On into battle, on into bloodshed, they called the prince's name.

For a heartbeat, Lorcan allowed himself to ponder it—the power of the thing that had compelled Rowan to risk it all. And Lorcan wondered if it would perhaps be the one force that Maeve, that Erawan, would not see coming.

But Maeve—Maeve was in that armada somewhere.

She would retaliate. She would strike back, make them all suffer—

Rowan slammed their armada into Maeve's front lines, unleashing the fury of his ice and wind alongside their arrows.

And where Rowan's power paused, Dorian's magic leaped out.

Not a chance in hell of winning had now become a fool's chance. If Whitethorn and the others could hold their lines, keep themselves steady.

Lorcan found himself scanning for Fenrys and Gavriel across ship and soldier.

And he knew Maeve's answer had come when he spied them, one after the other, go rigid. Spied Fenrys take a running leap and vanish into thin air. The White Wolf of Doranelle instantly appeared at Gavriel's side, men shouting at his appearance out of a pocket of nothing.

But he gripped Gavriel's arm, and then they were both gone again, their faces taut. Only Gavriel managed to look toward Lorcan before they vanished—his eyes wide in warning. Gavriel pointed, then they were nothing but sunlight and spindrift.

Lorcan stared at where Gavriel had managed to point, that bit of defiance that had likely cut deep.

Lorcan's blood went cold.

Maeve was allowing the battle to explode across the water because she had other games afoot. Because she was not on the seas at all.

But on the shore.

Gavriel had pointed to it. Not to the distant beach, but up the shore—westward.

Precisely where he had left Elide hours ago.

And Lorcan did not care about the battle, about what he'd agreed to do for Whitethorn, the promise he'd made the prince.

He had made a promise to her first.

The soldiers weren't stupid enough to try to stop him as Lorcan ordered one of them in charge, and seized a longboat.

Elide couldn't view the battle from where she waited among the sand dunes, the seagrasses hissing around her. But she could hear it, the shouting and the booming.

She tried not to listen to the din of battle, tried to instead beg Anneith to give her friends guidance. To keep Lorcan alive, and Maeve far from him.

But Anneith was sticking close, hovering behind her shoulder.

See, she said, as she always did. *See, see, see.*

There was nothing but sand and grass and water and blue sky. Nothing but the eight guards Lorcan had commanded to stay with her, lounging on the dunes, looking either relieved or put-out to miss the battle raging on the waves around the bend in the coast.

The voice became urgent. *See, see, see.*

Then Anneith vanished entirely. No—*fled*.

Clouds gathered, sweeping from the marshes. Heading toward the sun beginning its ascent.

Elide got to her feet, sliding a bit on the steep dune.

The wind whipped and hissed through the grasses—and warm sand turned gray and muted as those clouds passed over the sun. Blotting it out.

Something was coming.

Something that knew Aelin Galathynius drew strength from sunlight. From Mala.

Elide's mouth dried. If Vernon found her here . . . there would be no escaping him now.

The guards on the dunes behind her stirred, noticing the strange wind, the clouds. Sensing that approaching storm was not of natural origin. Would they stand against the ilken long enough for help to come? Or would Vernon bring more of them this time?

But it was not Vernon who appeared on the beach, as if walking out of a passing breeze.

CHAPTER 68

It was an agony.

An agony, to see Nehemia, young and strong and wise. Speaking to Elena in the marshes, among those same ruins.

And then there was the other agony.

That Elena and Nehemia had known each other. Worked together.

That Elena had laid these plans a thousand years ago.

That Nehemia had gone to Rifthold knowing she'd die.

Knowing she'd need to break Aelin—use her death to *break her*, so she could walk away from the assassin and ascend her throne.

Aelin and Manon were shown another scene. Of a whispered conversation at midnight, deep beneath the glass castle.

A queen and a princess, meeting in secret. As they had for months.

The queen asking the princess to pay that price she'd offered back in the marshes. To arrange for her own death—to set this all in motion. Nehemia had warned Elena that she—that Aelin—would be broken.

Worse, that she would go so far into an abyss of rage and despair that she wouldn't be able to get out. Not as Celaena.

Nehemia had been right.

Aelin was shaking—shaking in her half-invisible body, shaking so badly she thought her skin would ripple off her bones. Manon stepped closer, perhaps the only comfort the witch knew how to offer: solidarity.

They stared into the swirling mist again, where the scenes—the *memories*—had unfolded.

Aelin wasn't sure she could stomach another truth. Another revelation of just how thoroughly Elena had sold her and Dorian to the gods, for the fool's mistake she'd made, not understanding the Lock's true purpose, to seal Erawan in his tomb rather than let Brannon finally end it—and send the gods to wherever they called home, dragging Erawan with them.

Send them home . . . using the keys to open the Wyrdgate. And a new Lock to seal it forever.

Nameless is my price.

Using *her* power, drained to the last drop, *her* life to forge that new Lock. To wield the power of the keys only once—just once, to banish them all, and then seal the gate forever.

Memories flickered by.

Elena and Brannon, screaming at each other in a room Aelin had not seen for ten years—the king's suite in the palace at Orynth. Her suite—or it would have been. A necklace glittered at Elena's throat: the Eye. The first and now-broken Lock, that Elena, now the Queen of Adarlan, seemed to wear as some sort of reminder of her foolishness, her promise to those furious gods.

Her argument with her father raged and raged—until the princess walked out. And Aelin knew Elena had never returned to that shining palace in the North.

Then the reveal of that witch mirror in some nondescript stone chamber, a black-haired beauty with a crown of stars standing before

Elena and Gavin, explaining how the witch mirror worked—how it would contain these memories. Rhiannon Crochan. Manon started at the sight of her, and Aelin glanced between them.

The face . . . it was the same. Manon's face, and Rhiannon Crochan's. The last Crochan Queens—of two separate eras.

Then an image of Brannon alone—head in his hands, weeping before a shrouded body atop a stone altar. A crone's bent shape lay beneath.

Elena, her immortal grace yielded in order to live out a human life span with Gavin. Brannon still looked no older than thirty.

Brannon, the heat of a thousand forges shining on his red-gold hair, his teeth bared in a snarl as he pounded a metal disk on an anvil, the muscles of his back rippling beneath golden skin as he struck and struck and struck.

As he forged the Amulet of Orynth.

As he placed a sliver of black stone within either side, then sealed it, defiance written in every line of his body.

Then wrote the message in Wyrdmarks on the back.

One message.

For her.

For his true heir, should Elena's punishment and promise to the gods hold true. The punishment and promise that had cleaved them. That Brannon could not and would not accept. Not while he had strength left.

Nameless is my price. Written right there—in Wyrdmarks. The one who bore Brannon's mark, the mark of the bastard-born nameless . . . *She* would be the cost to end this.

The message on the back of the Amulet of Orynth was the only warning he could offer, the only apology for what his daughter had done, even as it contained a secret inside so deadly no one must know, no one could ever be told.

But there would be clues. For her. To finish what they'd started.

Brannon built Elena's tomb with his own hands. Carved the messages in there for Aelin, too.

The riddles and the clues. The best he could offer to explain the truth while keeping those keys hidden from the world, from powers who would use them to rule, to destroy.

Then he made Mort, the metal for the door knocker gifted by Rhiannon Crochan, who brushed a hand over the king's cheek before she left the tomb.

Rhiannon was not present when Brannon hid the sliver of black stone beneath the jewel in Elena's crown—the second Wyrdkey.

Or when he set Damaris in its stand, near the second sarcophagus. For the mortal king he hated and had barely tolerated, but he had leashed that loathing for his daughter's sake. Even if Gavin had taken his daughter, the daughter of his soul, away from him.

The final key . . . he went to Mala's temple.

It was where he had wanted to end this all along anyway.

The molten fire around the temple was a song in his blood, a beckoning. A welcoming.

Only those with his gifts—*her* gifts—could get there. Even the priestesses could not reach the island in the heart of the molten river. Only his heir would be able to do that. Or whoever held another key.

So he set the remaining key under a flagstone.

And then he walked into that molten river, into the burning heart of his beloved.

And Brannon, King of Terrasen, Lord of Fire, did not emerge again.

Aelin didn't know why it surprised her to be able to cry in this body. That this body had tears to spill.

But Aelin shed them for Brannon. Who knew what Elena had promised the gods—and had raged against it, the passing of this burden onto one of his descendants.

Brannon had done what he could for her. To soften the blow of that promise, if he could not change its course wholly. To give Aelin a fighting chance.

Nameless is my price.

"I don't understand what this means," Manon said quietly.

Aelin did not have the words to tell her. She had not been able to tell Rowan.

But then Elena appeared, real as they were real, and stared into the fading golden light of Mala's temple as the memory vanished. "I'm sorry," she said to Aelin.

Manon stiffened at Elena's approach, taking a step from Aelin's side.

"It was the only way," Elena offered. That was genuine pain in her eyes. Regret.

"Was it a choice, or just to spare Gavin's precious bloodline, that I was the one who was selected?" The voice that came from Aelin's throat was raw, vicious. "Why spill Havilliard blood, after all, when you could fall back on old habits and choose another to bear the burden?"

Elena flinched. "Dorian was not ready. You were. The choice Nehemia and I made was to ensure that things went according to plan."

"According to plan," Aelin breathed. "According to all your schemes to make me clean up the mess of what *you started with your gods-damned thieving and cowardice*?"

"They wanted me to suffer," Elena said. "And I have. Knowing you must do this, bear this burden . . . It has been a steady, endless shredding of my soul for a thousand years. It was so easy to say yes, to imagine you would be a stranger, someone who would not need to know the truth, only to be in the right place with the right gift, and yet . . . and yet I was wrong. I was so wrong." Elena lifted her hands before her, palms up. "I thought Erawan would rise, and the world would face him. I did not know . . . I did not know darkness would fall. I did not know that your land would suffer. Suffer as I tried to keep mine from suffering. And there were so many voices . . . so many voices even before Adarlan conquered. It was those voices that woke me. The voices of those wishing for an answer, for help." Elena's eyes slid to Manon, then back to hers. "They were from all kingdoms, all races. Human, witch-kind, Fae . . . But they wove a tapestry of dreams, all begging for that one thing . . . A better world.

"Then you were born. And you were an answer to the gathering darkness, with that flame. My father's flame, my mother's might—reborn at last. And you were strong, Aelin. So strong, and so vulnerable. Not to outside threats, but the threat of your own heart, the isolation of your power. But there were those who knew you for what you were, what you could offer. Your parents, their court, your great-uncle . . . and Aedion. Aedion knew you were the Queen Who Was Promised without knowing what it meant, without knowing anything about you, or me, or what I did to spare my own people."

The words hit her like stones. "The Queen Who Was Promised," Aelin said. "But not to the world. To the gods—to the keys."

To pay the price. To be their sacrifice in order to seal the keys in the gate at last.

Deanna's appearance hadn't been only to tell her how to use the mirror, but to remind her that she *belonged* to them. Had a debt owed to them.

Aelin said too quietly, "I didn't survive that night in the Florine River because of pure luck, did I?"

Elena shook her head. "We did not—"

"No," Aelin snapped. "*Show me.*"

Elena's throat bobbed. But then the mists turned dark and colored, and the very air around them became laced with frost.

Breaking branches, ragged breath punctuated with gasping sobs, light footsteps crashing through bramble and brush. A horse's thunderous gait, closing in—

Aelin made herself stand still when that familiar, frozen wood appeared, exactly as she remembered it. As *she* appeared, so small and young, white nightgown torn and muddy, hair wild, eyes bright with terror and grief so profound it had broken her entirely. Frantic to reach the roaring river beyond, the bridge—

There were the posts, and the forest on the other side. Her sanctuary—

Manon swore softly as Aelin Galathynius flung herself through the bridge posts, realized the bridge had been cut . . . and plummeted into the raging, half-frozen river below.

She had forgotten how far that fall was. How violent the black river was, the white rapids illuminated by the icy moon overhead.

The image shifted, and then it was dark, and silent, and they were being tumbled, over and over as the river tossed her in its wrath.

"There was so much death," Elena whispered as they watched Aelin being thrown and twisted and dragged down by the river. The cold was crushing.

"So much death, and so many lights extinguished," Elena said, voice breaking. "You were so small. And you fought . . . you fought so hard."

And there she was, clawing at the water, kicking and thrashing, trying to get to the surface, to the air, and she could feel her lungs begin to seize, feel the pressure building—

Then light flickered from the Amulet of Orynth hanging around her neck, greenish symbols fizzing like bubbles around her.

Elena slid to her knees, watching that amulet glow beneath the water. "They wanted me to take you, right then. You had the Amulet of Orynth, everyone thought you were dead, and the enemy was distracted with the slaughter. I could take you, help you track down the other two keys. I was allowed to help you—to do that much. And once we got the other two, I was to force you to forge the Lock anew. To use every last drop of *you* to make that Lock, summon the gate, put the keys back into it, send them home, and end it all. You had enough power, even then. It'd kill you to do it, but you were likely dead anyway. So they let me form a body, to get you."

Elena took a shuddering breath as a figure plunged into the water. A silver-haired, beautiful woman in an ancient dress. She grabbed Aelin around the waist, hauling her up, up, up.

They hit the surface of the river, and it was dark and loud and wild, and it was all she could do to grab the log Elena shoved her onto, to dig her nails into the soaked wood and cling to it while she was carried downriver, deep into the night.

"I hesitated," Elena breathed. "You clung to that log with all your strength. Everything had been taken from you—*everything*—and yet you still fought. You did not yield. And they told me to hurry, because even then their power to hold me in that solid body was fading. They said to just take you and go, but . . . I hesitated. I waited until you got to that riverbank."

Mud and reeds and trees looming overhead, snow still patching the steep hill of the bank.

Aelin watched herself crawl up that riverbank, inch by painful inch, and she felt the phantom, icy mud beneath her nails, felt her broken, frozen body as it slumped onto the earth and shuddered, over and over.

As lethal cold gripped her while Elena hauled herself onto the bank beside her.

As Elena lunged for her, screaming her name, cold and shock setting in . . .

"I thought the danger would be drowning," Elena whispered. "I didn't realize being out in the cold for so long . . ."

Her lips had gone blue. Aelin watched her own small chest rise, fall, rise . . .

Then stop moving all together.

"You died," Elena whispered. "Right there, you died. You had fought so hard, and I failed you. And in that moment, I didn't care that I'd again failed the gods, or my promise to make it right, or any of it. All I could think . . ." Tears ran down Elena's face. "All I could think was how unfair it was. You had not even lived, you had not even been given a chance . . . And all those people, who had wished and waited for a better world . . . You would not be there to give it to them."

Oh gods.

"Elena," Aelin breathed.

The Queen of Adarlan sobbed into her hands, even as her former self shook Aelin, over and over. Trying to wake her, trying to revive the small body that had given out.

Elena's voice broke. "I could not allow it. I could not endure it. Not for the gods' sake, but—but for your own."

Light flared at Elena's hand, then down her arm, then along her whole body. Fire. She wrapped herself around Aelin, the heat melting the snow around them, drying her ice-crusted hair.

Lips that were blue turned pink. And a chest that had stopped breathing now lifted.

Darkness faded to the gray light of dawn. "And then I defied them."

Elena set her down between the reeds and rose, scanning the river, the world.

"I knew who had an estate near this river, so far away from your home that your parents had tolerated its presence, as long as he was not stupid enough to stir up trouble."

Elena, a mere flicker of light, tugged Arobynn from a deep sleep inside his former residence in Terrasen. As if in a trance, he shoved on his boots, his red hair gleaming in the light of dawn, mounted his horse, and set off into the woods.

So young, her former master. Only a few years older than she was now.

Arobynn's horse paused as if an invisible hand had yanked its bridle, and the assassin scanned the raging river, the trees, as if looking for something he didn't even know was there.

But there was Elena, invisible as sunlight, crouching in the reeds when Arobynn's eyes fell upon the small, dirty figure unconscious on the riverbank. He leaped from his horse with feline grace, slinging off his cloak as he threw himself to his knees in the mud and felt for her breathing.

"I knew what he was, what he'd likely do with you. What training you would receive. But it was better than dead. And if you could survive, if you could grow up strong, if you had the chance to reach adulthood, I thought perhaps you could give those people who had wished and dreamed of a better world . . . at least give them a chance. Help them—before the debt was called in again."

Arobynn's hands hesitated as he noticed the Amulet of Orynth.

He eased the amulet from around her neck and placed it in his pocket. Gently, he scooped her into his arms and carried her up the bank to his waiting horse.

"You were so young," Elena said again. "And more than the dreamers, more than the debt . . . I wanted to give you time. To at least know what it was to live."

Aelin rasped, "What was the price, Elena? What did they do to you for this?"

Elena wrapped her arms around herself as the image faded, Arobynn mounting his horse, Aelin in his arms. Mist swirled again. "When it is done," Elena managed to say, "I go, too. For the time I bought you, when this game is finished, my soul will be melted back into the darkness. I will not see Gavin, or my children, or my friends . . . I will be gone. Forever."

"Did you know that before you—"

"Yes. They told me, over and over. But . . . I couldn't. I couldn't do it."

Aelin slid to her knees before the queen. Took Elena's tearstained face between her hands.

"Nameless is my price," Aelin said, her voice breaking.

Elena nodded. "The mirror was just that—a mirror. A ploy to get you here. So that you could understand everything we did." *Just a bit of metal and glass*, Elena had said when Aelin had summoned her in Skull's Bay. "But now you are here, and have seen. Now you comprehend the cost. To forge the Lock anew, to put the three keys back in the gate . . ."

A mark glowed on Aelin's brow, heating her skin. The bastard mark of Brannon.

The mark of the nameless.

"Mala's blood must be spent—your power must be spent. Every drop, of magic, of blood. You are the cost—to make a new Lock, and seal the keys into the gate. To make the Wyrdgate whole."

Aelin said softly, "I know." She had known for some time now.

Had been preparing for it as best she could. Preparing things for the others.

Aelin said to the queen, "I have two keys. If I can find the third, steal it from Erawan . . . will you come with me? Help me end it once and for all?"

Will you come with me, so I will not be alone?

Elena nodded, but whispered, "I'm sorry."

Aelin lowered her hands from the queen's face. Took a deep, shuddering breath. "Why didn't you tell me—from the start?"

Behind them, she had the vague sense that Manon was quietly assessing.

"You were barely climbing out of slavery," Elena said. "Hardly holding yourself together, trying so hard to pretend that you were still strong and whole. There was only so much I could do to guide you, nudge you along. The mirror was forged and hidden to one day show you all of this. In a way I couldn't tell you—not when I could only manage a few minutes at a time."

"Why did you tell me to go to Wendlyn? Maeve poses as great a threat as Erawan."

Glacier-blue eyes met hers at last. "I know. Maeve has long wished to regain possession of the keys. My father believed it was for something other than conquest. Something darker, worse. I don't know why she only began hunting for them once you arrived. But I sent you to Wendlyn for the healing. And so you would . . . find him. The one who had been waiting so long for you."

Aelin's heart cracked. "Rowan."

Elena nodded. "He was a voice in the void, a secret, silent dreamer. And so were his companions. But the Fae Prince, he was . . ."

Aelin reined in her sob. "I know. I've known for a long time."

"I wanted you to know that joy, too," Elena whispered. "However briefly."

"I did," Aelin managed to say. "Thank you."

Elena covered her face at those words, shuddering. But after a moment, she surveyed Aelin, then Manon, still silent and watching. "The witch mirror's power is fading; it will not hold you here for much longer. Please—let me show you what must be done. How to end it. You won't be able to see me after, but . . . I will be with you. Until the very end, every step of the way, I will be with you."

Manon only put a hand on her sword as Aelin swallowed and said, "Show me, then."

So Elena did. And when she was done, Aelin was silent. Manon was pacing, snarling softly.

But Aelin did not fight it as Elena leaned in to kiss her brow, where that damning mark had been her whole life. A bit of chattel, branded for the slaughterhouse.

Brannon's mark. The mark of the bastard-born . . . the Nameless.

Nameless is my price. To buy them a future, she'd pay it.

She'd done as much as she could to set things in motion to ensure that once she was gone, help would still come. It was the only thing she could give them, her last gift to Terrasen. To those she loved with her heart of wildfire.

Elena stroked her cheek. Then the ancient queen and the mists were gone.

Sunlight flooded them, blinding Aelin and Manon so violently that they hissed and slammed into each other. The brine of the sea, crash of nearby waves, and rustle of seagrasses greeted them. And beyond that, distantly: the clamor and bellowing of all-out war.

They were on the outskirts of the marshes, upon the lip of the sea itself, the battle miles and miles out to sea. They must have traveled within the mists, somehow—

A soft female laugh slithered through the grass. Aelin knew that laugh.

And knew that somehow, perhaps they had not traveled through the mists . . .

But they had been placed here. By whatever forces were at work, whatever gods watching.

To stand in the sandy field before the turquoise sea, dead guards in Briarcliff armor slaughtered upon the nearby dunes, still bleeding out. To stand before Queen Maeve of the Fae.

Elide Lochan on her knees before her—with a Fae warrior's blade at her throat.

CHAPTER 69

Aedion had faced armies, faced death more times than he could count, but this . . .

Even with what Rowan had done . . . the enemy ships still outnumbered them.

The battling between ships had become too dangerous, the magic-wielders too aware of Lysandra to allow her to attack beneath the waves.

She was now fighting viciously beside Aedion in ghost leopard form, taking down whatever Fae warriors tried to board their ship. Whatever soldiers made it through the shredding gauntlet of Rowan's and Dorian's magic.

His father had left. Fenrys and Lorcan, too. He'd last seen his father on the quarterdeck of one of the ships that had been under his command, a sword in each hand, the Lion poised for the kill. And as if sensing Aedion's gaze, a wall of golden light had wrapped around him.

Aedion wasn't stupid enough to demand Gavriel take it away,

not as the shield shrank and shrank, until it covered Aedion like a second skin.

Minutes later, Gavriel was gone—vanished. But that magic shield remained.

That had been the start of the sharp turn they'd taken, going back on the defensive as sheer numbers and immortal-versus-mortal fighting took its toll on their fleet.

He had no doubt Maeve had something to do with it. But that bitch wasn't his problem.

No, his problem was the armada all around him; his problem was the fact that the enemy soldiers he engaged were highly trained and didn't go down easily. His problem was his sword arm ached, his shield was embedded with arrows and dented, and still more of those ships stretched away into the distance.

He did not let himself think about Aelin, about where she was. His Fae instincts pricked at the rumble of Rowan's and Dorian's magic surging up, then snapping into the enemy flank. Ships broke in the wake of that power; warriors drowned beneath the weight of their armor.

Their own ship rocked back from the one they'd been engaging thanks to the flood of power, and Aedion used the reprieve to whirl to Lysandra. Blood from his own wounds and ones he'd inflicted covered him, mixing with the sweat running down his skin. He said to the shifter, "I want you to run."

Lysandra turned a fuzzy head toward him, pale green eyes narrowing slightly. Blood and gore dripped from her maw onto the wood planks.

Aedion held that gaze. "You turn into a bird or a moth or a fish—I don't rutting care—and you go. If we're about to fall, you run. That's an order."

She hissed, as if to say, *You don't give me orders.*

"I technically outrank you," he said, slashing his sword down his shield to clear it of two protruding arrows as they again swung in toward another ship crammed full of well-rested Fae warriors. "So you'll run. Or I'll kick your ass in the Afterworld."

Lysandra stalked up to him. A lesser man might have backed away from a predator that big prowling close. Some of his own soldiers did.

But Aedion held his ground as she rose on her back legs, those huge paws settling on his shoulders, and brought her bloodied feline face up to his. Her wet whiskers twitched.

Lysandra leaned in and nuzzled his cheek, his neck.

Then she trotted back to her place, blood splashing beneath her silent paws.

When she deigned to glance his way, spitting blood onto the deck, Aedion said softly, "The next time, do that in your human form."

Her puffy tail just curled a bit in answer.

But their ship rocked back toward their latest attacker. The temperature plummeted, either from Rowan or Dorian or one of the Whitethorn nobles, Aedion couldn't tell. They'd been lucky that Maeve had brought a fleet whose magic-wielders hailed mostly from Rowan's line.

Aedion braced himself, spreading apart his feet as wind and ice tore into the enemy lines. Fae soldiers, perhaps ones Rowan himself had commanded, screamed. But Rowan and Dorian struck relentlessly.

Line after line, Rowan and Dorian blasted their power into Maeve's fleet.

Yet more ships flooded past them, engaging Aedion and the others. Ansel of Briarcliff held the left flank, and . . . the lines remained steady. Even if Maeve's armada still outnumbered them.

The first Fae soldier who cleared the railing of their ship headed right for Lysandra.

It was the last mistake the male made.

She leaped, dodging past his guard, and closed her jaws around his neck.

Bone crunched and blood sprayed.

Aedion leaped forward to engage the next soldier over the railing, cutting through the grappling hooks that arced and landed true.

Aedion loosed himself into a killing calm, an eye on the shifter, who took down soldier after soldier, his father's gold shield holding strong around her, too.

Death rained upon him.

Aedion did not let himself think about how many were left. How many Rowan and Dorian felled, the ruins of ships sinking around them, blood and flotsam choking the sea.

So Aedion kept killing.

And killing.

And killing.

Dorian's breath burned his throat, his magic was sluggish, a headache pulsed at his temples, but he kept unleashing his power upon the enemy lines while soldiers fought and died around him.

So many. So many trained warriors, a scant few of whom were blessed with magic—and had been wielding it to get past them.

He didn't dare see how the others were faring. All he heard were roars and snarls of wrath, shrieks of dying people, and the crack of wood and the snap of rope. Clouds had formed and gathered above, blocking out the sun.

His magic sang as it froze the life out of ships, out of soldiers, as it bathed in their death. But it still flagged. He'd lost track of how long it had been.

Still, they kept coming. And still, Manon and Aelin did not return.

Rowan held the front line, weapons angled, ready for any soldiers stupid enough to approach. But too many broke past their magic. Too many now steadily overwhelmed them.

As soon as he thought it, Aedion's bark of pain cut across the waves.

There was a roar of rage that echoed it. Was Aedion—

The coppery tang of blood coated Dorian's mouth—the burnout. Another roar, deep and bellowing, cleaved the world. Dorian braced himself, rallying his magic perhaps for the last time.

That roar sounded again as a mighty shape shot down from the heavy clouds.

A wyvern. A wyvern with shimmering wings.

And behind it, descending upon the Fae fleet with wicked delight, flew twelve others.

CHAPTER 70

Lysandra knew that roar.

And then there was Abraxos, plunging from the heavy clouds, twelve other wyverns with riders behind him.

Ironteeth witches.

"*Hold your fire!*" Rowan bellowed from half a dozen ships away, at the archers who had trained their few remaining arrows on the golden-haired witch closest to Abraxos, her pale-blue wyvern shrieking a war cry.

The other witches and their wyverns unleashed hell upon the Fae, smashing through the converging lines, snapping grappling ropes, buying them a moment's reprieve. How they knew who to attack, what side to fight for—

Abraxos and eleven others angled northward in one smooth movement, then plowed into the panicking enemy fleet. The golden-haired rider, however, swept for Lysandra's ship, her sky-blue wyvern gracefully landing on the prow.

The witch was beautiful, a strip of black braided leather across her brow, and she called to none of them in particular, "Where is Manon Blackbeak?"

"Who are you?" Aedion demanded, his voice a rasp. But there was recognition in his eyes, as if remembering that day at Temis's temple—

The witch grinned, revealing white teeth, but iron glinted at her fingertips. "Asterin Blackbeak, at your service." She scanned the embattled ships. "Where is Manon? Abraxos led—"

"It's a long story, but she's here," Aedion shouted over the din. Lysandra crept closer, sizing up the witch, the coven that was now wreaking havoc upon the Fae lines. "You and your Thirteen save our asses, witch," Aedion said, "and I'll tell you anything you damn want."

A wicked grin and an incline of her head. "Then we shall clear the field for you."

Then Asterin and the wyvern soared up, and blasted between the waves, spearing for where the others were fighting.

At Asterin's approach, the wyverns and riders reeled back, rising high into the air, falling into formation. A hammer about to strike.

The Fae knew it. They began throwing up feeble shields, shooting wildly for them, their panic making their aim sloppy. But the wyverns were covered in armor—efficient, beautiful armor.

The Thirteen laughed at their enemy as they slammed into its southern flank.

Lysandra wished she had strength left to shift—one last time. To join them in that glorious destruction.

The Thirteen herded the panicking ships between them, smashed them apart, wielding every weapon in their arsenal—wyverns, blades, iron teeth. What got past them received the brutal mercy of Rowan's and Dorian's magic. And what got past that magic . . .

Lysandra found Aedion's blood-splattered stare. The general-prince smirked in that insolent way of his, sending a thrill wilder than bloodlust through her. "We don't want the witches to make us look bad, do we?"

Lysandra returned his smirk and lunged back into the fray.

Not many more.

Rowan's magic was strained to the breaking point, his panic a dull roaring in the back of his mind, but he kept attacking, kept swinging his blades at any that got past his wind and ice, or Dorian's own blasts of raw, unchecked power. Fenrys, Lorcan, and Gavriel had bolted an hour or lifetimes ago, vanishing to wherever Maeve had no doubt summoned them, but the armada held fast. Whoever Ansel of Briarcliff's men were, they weren't cowed by Fae warriors. And they were no strangers to bloodshed. Neither were Rolfe's men. None of them ran.

The Thirteen continued to wreak havoc on Maeve's panicking fleet. Asterin Blackbeak barked commands high above them, the twelve witches breaking the enemy lines with fierce, clever determination. If this was how one coven fought, then an army of them—

Rowan gritted his teeth as the remaining ships decided to be smarter than their dead companions and began to peel away. If Maeve gave the order to retreat—

Too bad. Too damn bad. He'd send her own ship down to the inky black himself.

He gave Asterin a sharp whistle the next time she passed overhead, rallying her Thirteen again. She whistled back in confirmation. The Thirteen launched after the fleeing armada.

The battle ebbed, red waves laden with debris flowing past on the swift tide.

Rowan gave the order to the captain to hold the lines and deal with any stupidity from Maeve's armada if any ships decided not to turn tail.

His legs trembling, his arms shaking so badly he was afraid that if he let go of his weapons he wouldn't be able to pick them up again, Rowan shifted and soared high.

His cousins had joined the Thirteen in their pursuit of the fleet now trying to run. He avoided the urge to count. But—Rowan flew higher, scanning.

There was one boat missing.

A boat he'd sailed on, worked on, fought on in past wars and journeys.

Maeve's personal battleship, the *Nightingale*, was nowhere to be seen.

Not within the retreating fleet now fending off the Whitethorn royals and the Thirteen.

Not within the sinking hulks of ships now bleeding out in the water.

Rowan's blood chilled. But he dove fast and hard for Aedion and Lysandra's ship, where gore covered the deck so thickly it rippled as he shifted and set down in it.

Aedion was covered in blood, both his own and others'; Lysandra was purging a stomach full of it. Rowan managed to will his legs into maneuvering around fallen Fae. He did not look too closely at their faces.

"Is she back?" Aedion instantly demanded, wincing as he put weight on his thigh. Rowan surveyed his brother's wound. He'd have to heal him soon—as soon as his magic replenished. In a place like this, even Aedion's Fae blood couldn't keep the infection away long.

"I don't know," Rowan said.

"*Find her*," Aedion growled. He broke Rowan's stare only to watch Lysandra shift into her human form—and ran an eye over the injuries that peppered her skin.

Rowan's skin tightened over his bones. He had the feeling that the ground was about to slip from under his feet as Dorian appeared at the rail of the main deck, gaunt-faced and haggard, no doubt having used the last of his magic to propel a longboat over, and panted, "The coast. Aelin is out by the coast where we sent Elide—they all are."

That was miles away. How the hell had they gotten there?

"How do you know?" Lysandra demanded, tying back her hair with bloody fingers.

"Because I can feel something out there," Dorian said. "Flame and shadow and death. Like Lorcan and Aelin and someone else. Someone ancient. Powerful." Rowan braced himself for it, but he still wasn't ready for the pure terror when Dorian added, "And female."

Maeve had found them.

The battle had not been for any sort of victory or conquest.

But a distraction. While Maeve slipped away to get the real prize.

They'd never arrive fast enough. If he flew on his own, his magic already drained to the breaking point, he would be of little help. They stood a better chance, *Aelin* stood a better chance, if they were all there.

Rowan whirled to the horizon behind them—to the wyverns destroying the remnants of the fleet. Rowing would take too long; his magic was gutted. But a wyvern . . . That might do.

CHAPTER 71

The Queen of the Fae was exactly as Aelin remembered. Swirling dark robes, a beautiful pale face beneath onyx hair, red lips set in a faint smile . . . No crown adorned her head, for all who breathed, even the dead who slumbered, would know her for what she was.

Dreams and nightmares given form; the dark face of the moon.

And kneeling before Maeve, a stone-faced sentry holding a blade to her bare throat, Elide trembled. Her guards, all men in Ansel's armor, had likely been killed before they could shout a warning. From the weapons that were only half out of their sheaths, they hadn't even had the chance to fight.

Manon had gone still as death at the sight of Elide, her iron nails sliding free.

Aelin forced a half smile to her mouth, shoved her raw, bleeding heart into a box deep inside her chest. "Not as impressive as Doranelle, if you ask me, but at least a swamp really reflects your true nature, you know?

It'll be a wonderful new home for you. Definitely worth the cost of coming all this way to conquer it."

At the edge of the hill that flowed down to the beach a small party of Fae warriors monitored them. Male and female, all armed, all strangers. A massive, elegant ship idled in the calm bay beyond.

Maeve smiled slightly. "What a joy, to learn that your usual good spirits remain undimmed in such dark days."

"How could they not, when so many of your pretty males are in my company?"

Maeve cocked her head, her heavy curtain of dark hair sliding off a shoulder. And as if in answer, Lorcan appeared at the edge of the dunes, panting, wild-eyed, sword out. His focus—and horror, Aelin realized—on Elide. On the sentry holding the blade against her white neck. Maeve gave a little smile to the warrior, but looked to Manon.

With her attention elsewhere, Lorcan took up a place at Aelin's side—as if they were somehow allies in this, would fight back-to-back. Aelin didn't bother to say anything to him. Not as Maeve said to the witch, "I know your face."

That face remained cold and impassive. "Let the girl go."

A small, breathy laugh. "Ah." Aelin's stomach clenched as that ancient focus shifted to Elide. "Claimed by queen, and witch, and . . . my Second, it seems."

Aelin tensed. She didn't think Lorcan was breathing beside her.

Maeve toyed with a strand of Elide's limp hair. The Lady of Perranth shook. "The girl who Lorcan Salvaterre summoned me to save."

That ripple of Lorcan's power the day Ansel's fleet had closed in . . . She'd known it was a summoning. The same way she'd summoned the Valg to Skull's Bay. She'd refused to immediately explain Ansel's presence, wanting to enjoy the surprise of it, and he had summoned Maeve's armada to take on what he'd believed to be an enemy fleet. To save Elide.

Lorcan just said, "I'm sorry."

Aelin didn't know if it was to her or Elide, whose eyes now widened with outrage. But Aelin said, "You think I didn't know? That I didn't take precautions?"

Lorcan's brows furrowed. Aelin shrugged.

But Maeve went on, "Lady Elide Lochan, daughter of Cal and Marion Lochan. No wonder the witch itches to retrieve you, if her bloodline runs in your veins."

Manon snarled a warning.

Aelin drawled to the Fae Queen, "Well, you didn't drag your ancient carcass all the way here for nothing. So let's get on with it. What do you want for the girl?"

That adder's smile curled Maeve's lips again.

Elide was trembling; every bone, every pore was trembling in terror at the immortal queen standing above her, at the guard's blade at her throat. The rest of the queen's escort remained distant—but it was to the escort that Lorcan kept glancing, his face tight, his own body near-shaking with restrained wrath.

This was the queen to whom he'd given his heart? This cold creature who looked at the world with mirthless eyes? Who had killed those soldiers without a blink of hesitation?

The queen whom Lorcan had summoned for *her*. He'd brought Maeve to save *her*—

Elide's breath turned sharp in her throat. He'd betrayed them. Betrayed *Aelin* for her—

"What should I demand as payment for the girl?" Maeve mused, taking a few steps toward them, graceful as a moonbeam. "Why doesn't my Second tell me? So busy, Lorcan. You've been so, so busy these months."

His voice was hoarse as he lowered his head. "I did it for you, Majesty."

"Then where is my ring? Where are my keys?"

A ring. Elide was willing to bet it was the golden one on her own finger, hidden beneath her other hand as she clenched them before her.

But Lorcan pointed his chin toward Aelin. "She has them. Two keys."

Cold clanged through Elide. "Lorcan." The guard's blade twitched at her throat.

Aelin only leveled a cool stare at Lorcan.

He didn't look at either Elide or Aelin. Didn't so much as acknowledge their existence as he went on, "Aelin has two, and probably has a good inkling where Erawan hides the third."

"Lorcan," Elide pleaded. No—no, he wasn't about to do this, about to betray them again—

"*Be quiet*," he growled at her.

Maeve's gaze again drifted down to Elide. The ancient, eternal darkness in it was smothering. "What familiarity you use when you speak his name, Lady of Perranth. What intimacy."

Aelin's little snort was her only warning sign. "Don't you have better things to do than terrorize humans? Release the girl and let's settle this the fun way."

Flame danced at Aelin's fingertips.

No. Her magic had been emptied, still hovered near burnout.

But Aelin stepped forward, nudging Manon with the side of her body as she passed—forcing the witch to back away. Aelin grinned. "Want to dance, Maeve?"

But Aelin shot a cutting glance over her shoulder at Manon as if to say, *Run. Grab Elide the moment Maeve's guard is down and run.*

Maeve returned Aelin's smile. "I don't think you'd be a suitable dance partner right now. Not when your magic is nearly depleted. Did you think my arrival was merely dependent upon Lorcan's summoning? Who do you think even whispered to Morath you were indeed down here? Of course, the fools didn't realize that when you had drained yourself on their armies, I'd be waiting. You were already exhausted after putting out the fires I had my armada ignite to tire you on Eyllwe's coast. It was a convenience that Lorcan gave your precise location and saved me the energy of tracking you down myself."

A trap. An enormous, wicked trap. To drain Aelin's power over days—weeks. But Aelin lifted a brow. "You brought an entire armada just to start a few fires?"

"I brought an armada to see if you'd rise to the occasion. Which, apparently, Prince Rowan has done."

Hope soared in Elide's chest. But then Maeve said, "The armada was a precaution. Just in case the ilken didn't arrive for you to wholly drain yourself . . . I figured a few hundred ships would make for good kindling until I was ready."

To sacrifice her own fleet—or part of it—to gain one prize . . . This was madness. The queen was utterly insane. "Do something," Elide hissed at Lorcan, at Manon. *"Do something."*

Neither of them responded.

The flame around Aelin's fingers grew to encompass her hand—then her arm as she said to the ancient queen, "All I hear is a lot of chitchat."

Maeve glanced at her escort, and they stepped away. Hauled Elide with them, the blade still at her throat.

Aelin said sharply to Manon, "*Get out of range.*"

The witch fell back, but her eyes were on the guard holding Elide, gobbling down every detail she could.

"You can't possibly hope to win," Maeve said, as if they were about to play cards.

"At least we'll enjoy ourselves until the end," Aelin crooned back, flame now encasing her entirely.

"Oh, I have no interest in killing you," Maeve purred.

Then they exploded.

Flame slammed outward, red and golden—just as a wall of darkness lashed for Aelin.

The impact shook the world.

Even Manon was thrown on her ass.

But Lorcan was already moving.

The guard holding Elide showered her hair with blood as Lorcan slit his throat.

The other two guards behind him died with a hatchet to the face, one after another. Elide surged up, her leg barking in pain, running for Manon on pure, blind instinct, but Lorcan gripped her by the collar of her tunic. "*Stupid fool*," he snapped, and she clawed at him—

"Lorcan, hold the girl," Maeve said quietly, not even looking toward them. "Don't get any stupid ideas about fleeing with her." He went utterly still, his hold tightening.

Maeve and Aelin struck again.

Light and darkness.

Sand shuddered down the dunes, the waves rippled.

Only now—Maeve had only dared attack Aelin now.

Because Aelin at her full strength . . .

Aelin could beat her.

But Aelin, nearly depleted of her power . . .

"Please," Elide begged Lorcan. But he held her firm, slave to the order Maeve had given, one eye on the battling queens, the other on the escorts who weren't foolish enough to approach after witnessing what he'd done to their companions.

"Run," Lorcan said in her ear. "If you wish to live, *run*, Elide. Shove me off—work around her command. Push me, and *run*."

She would not. She'd sooner die than flee like a coward, not when Aelin was going to the mat for all of them, when—

Darkness devoured flame.

And even Manon flinched as Aelin was slammed back.

A paper-thin wall of flame kept that darkness from hitting home. A wall that wavered—

Help. They needed help—

Maeve lashed to the left, and Aelin threw up a hand, fire deflecting.

Aelin didn't see the blow to the right. Elide screamed in warning, but too late.

A whip of black sliced into Aelin.

She went down.

And Elide thought the impact of Aelin Galathynius's knees hitting the sand might have been the most horrible sound she'd ever heard.

Maeve did not waste her advantage.

Darkness poured down, pounding again and again. Aelin deflected, but it got past her.

There was nothing Elide could do as Aelin screamed.

As that dark, ancient power struck her like a hammer over an anvil.

Elide begged Manon, now mere feet away, "Do something."

Manon ignored her, eyes fixed on the battle before them.

Aelin crawled backward, blood sliding from her right nostril. Dripping on her white shirt.

Maeve advanced, the darkness swirling around her like a fell wind.

Aelin tried to rise.

Tried, but her legs had given out. The Queen of Terrasen panted, fire flickering like dying embers around her.

Maeve pointed with a finger.

A black whip, faster than Aelin's fire, lashed out. Wrapped around her throat. Aelin gripped it, thrashing, her teeth bared, flame flaring over and over.

"Why don't you use the keys, Aelin?" Maeve purred. "Surely you'd win that way."

Use them, Elide begged her. *Use them.*

But Aelin did not.

The coil of darkness tightened around Aelin's throat.

Flames sparked and died out.

Then the darkness expanded, encompassing Aelin again and squeezing tight, squeezing until she was screaming, screaming in a way that Elide knew meant unfathomable agony—

A low, vicious snarl rippled from nearby, the only warning as a massive wolf leaped through the seagrasses and shifted. Fenrys.

A heartbeat later, a mountain lion charged over a dune, beheld the scene, and shifted as well. Gavriel.

"Let her go," Fenrys growled at the dark queen, advancing a step. "Let her go *now*."

Maeve turned her head, that darkness still lashing Aelin. "Look who finally arrived. Another set of traitors." She smoothed a wrinkle in her flowing gown. "What a valiant effort you made, Fenrys, delaying your arrival on this beach for as long as you could withstand my summons." She clicked her tongue. "Did you enjoy playing loyal subject while panting after the young Queen of Fire?"

As if in answer, the darkness squeezed in tight—and Aelin screamed again.

"*Stop it*," Fenrys snapped.

"Maeve, please," Gavriel said, exposing his palms to her.

"Maeve?" the queen crooned. "Not Majesty? Has the Lion gone a bit feral? Perhaps too much time with his unchecked, half-breed bastard?"

"Leave him out of this," Gavriel said too softly.

But Maeve let the darkness around Aelin part.

She was curled on her side, bleeding from both nostrils now, more blood dribbling from her panting mouth.

Fenrys lunged for her. A wall of black slammed up between them.

"I don't think so," Maeve crooned.

Aelin gasped for air, eyes glassy with pain. Eyes that slid to Elide's. Aelin's bloody, chapped mouth formed the word again. *Run*.

She would not. Could not.

Aelin's arms shook as she tried to raise herself. And Elide knew there was no magic left.

No fire left in the queen. Not one ember.

And the only way Aelin could face this, accept this, was to go down swinging. Like Marion had.

Aelin's wet, rasping breaths were the only sound above the crashing waves behind them. Even the battle had gone quiet in the distance. Over—or perhaps they were all dead.

Manon still stood there. Still did not move. Elide begged her, "Please. *Please*."

Maeve smiled at the witch. "I have no quarrel with you, Blackbeak. Stay out of this and you are free to go where you wish."

"*Please*," Elide pleaded.

Manon's gold eyes were hard. Cold. She nodded to Maeve. "Agreed."

Something in Elide's chest cleaved open.

But Gavriel said from across their little circle, "Majesty—please. Leave Aelin Galathynius to her own war here. Let us return home."

"Home?" Maeve asked. The black wall between Fenrys and Aelin lowered—but the warrior did not try to cross. He just stared at Aelin, stared at her in that way Elide herself must be looking. He didn't break that stare until Maeve said to Gavriel, "Is Doranelle still your home?"

"Yes, Majesty," Gavriel said calmly. "It is an honor to call it such."

"Honor . . . ," Maeve mused. "Yes, you and honor go hand in hand, don't they? But what of the honor of your vow, Gavriel?"

"I have kept my vow to you."

"Did I or did I not tell you to execute Lorcan on sight?"

"There were . . . circumstances that prevented it from happening. We tried."

"Yet you failed. Am I not supposed to discipline my blood-bonded who fail me?"

Gavriel lowered his head. "Of course—we will accept it. And I will also take on the punishment you intended for Aelin Galathynius."

Aelin lifted her head slightly, glazed eyes going wide. She tried to speak, but the words had been broken from her, her voice blown out from screaming. Elide knew the word the queen mouthed. *No.*

Not for her. Elide wondered if Gavriel's sacrifice was not only for Aelin's sake. But for Aedion's. So the son would not have to bear the pain of his queen being hurt—

"Aelin Galathynius," Maeve mused. "So much talk about Aelin Galathynius. The Queen Who Was Promised. Well, Gavriel"—a vicious smile—"if you're so invested in her court, why don't you join it?"

Fenrys tensed, preparing to lunge in front of the dark power for his friend.

But Maeve said, "I sever the blood oath with you, Gavriel. Without honor, without good faith. You are dismissed from my service and stripped of your title."

"You *bitch*," Fenrys snapped as Gavriel's breathing turned shallow.

"Majesty, please—" Gavriel hissed, clapping a hand over his arm as invisible claws raked two lines down his skin, drawing blood that spilled into the grass. A similar mark appeared on Maeve's arm, her blood spilling.

"It is done," she said simply. "Let the world know you, a male of honor, have none. That you betrayed your queen for another, for a bastard get of yours."

Gavriel stumbled back—then collapsed in the sand, a hand shoved against his chest. Fenrys snarled, his face more lupine than Fae, but Maeve laughed softly. "Oh, you'd like for me to do the same, wouldn't you, Fenrys? But what greater punishment for the one who is a traitor to me in his very soul than to serve me forever?"

Fenrys hissed, his breath coming in ragged gulps, and Elide wondered if he'd leap upon the queen and try to kill her.

But Maeve turned to Aelin and said, "Get up."

Aelin tried. Her body failed her.

Maeve clicked her tongue, and an invisible hand hauled Aelin to her feet. Pain-fogged eyes cleared, then filled with cold rage as Aelin took in the approaching queen.

An assassin, Elide reminded herself. Aelin was an *assassin*, and if Maeve got close enough . . .

But Maeve didn't. And those invisible hands cut the tethers on Aelin's sword belts. Goldryn thunked to the ground. Then daggers slid from their sheaths.

"So many weapons," Maeve contemplated as the invisible hands disarmed Aelin with brutal efficiency. Even blades hidden beneath clothes found their way out—slicing as they went. Blood bloomed beneath Aelin's shirt and pants. Why did she stand there—

Gathering her strength. For one last strike. One last stand.

Let the queen believe her broken. "Why?" Aelin rasped. Buying herself time.

Maeve toed a fallen dagger, the blade edged with Aelin's blood. "Why bother with you at all? Because I can't very well let you sacrifice yourself to forge a new Lock, can I? Not when you already have what I want. And I have known for a very, very long time that you would give me what I seek, Aelin Galathynius, and have taken the steps toward ensuring that."

Aelin breathed, "What?"

Maeve said, "Haven't you figured it out? Why I wanted your mother to bring you to me, why I demanded such things of you this spring?"

None of them dared move.

Maeve snorted, a delicate, feminine sound of triumph. "Brannon stole the keys from me, after I took them from the Valg. They were mine, and he snatched them. And then he mated with that goddess of yours, breeding the fire into the bloodline, ensuring I would think hard before touching his land, his heirs. But all bloodlines fade. And I knew a time would come when Brannon's flames would dim to a flicker, and I'd be poised to strike."

Aelin sagged against the hands that held her up.

"But in my dark power, I saw a glimmer of the future. I saw that Mala's power would surge again. And that you would lead me to the keys. Only you—the one Brannon left clues for, the one who could find all three. And I saw who you were, what you were. I saw who you loved. I saw your mate."

The sea breeze hissing through the grasses was the only sound.

"What a powerhouse you two would be—you and Prince Rowan. And any offspring of that union . . ." A vicious smirk. "You and Rowan could rule this continent if you wished. But your children . . . your children would be powerful enough to rule an empire that could sweep the world."

Aelin closed her eyes. The Fae males were shaking their heads slowly—not believing it.

"I didn't know when *you* would be born, but when Prince Rowan Whitethorn came into this world, when he came of age and was the strongest purebred Fae male in my realm . . . you were still not there. And I knew what I would have to do. To leash you. To break you to my will, to hand over those keys without thought once you were strong and trained enough to acquire them."

Aelin's shoulders shook. Tears slid out past her closed eyes.

"It was so easy to tug on the right psychic thread that day Rowan saw Lyria at the market. To shove him down that other path, to trick those instincts. A slight altering of fate."

"Oh, gods," Fenrys breathed.

Maeve said, "So your mate was given to another. And I let him fall in love, let him get her with child. And then I broke him. No one ever asked how those enemy forces came to pass by his mountain home."

Aelin's knees gave out completely. Only the invisible hands kept her upright as she wept.

"He took the blood oath without question. And I knew that whenever you were born, whenever you'd come of age . . . I'd ensure that your paths crossed, and you'd take one look at each other and I'd have you by the throat. Anything I asked for, you'd give to me. Even the keys. For your mate, you could do no less. You almost did that day in Doranelle."

Slowly, Aelin slid her feet under herself again, the movement so pained that Elide cringed. But Aelin lifted her head, lip curling back from her teeth.

"I will *kill you*," Aelin snarled at the Fae Queen.

"That's what you said to Rowan after you met him, wasn't it?" Maeve's faint smile lingered. "I'd pushed and pushed your mother to bring you to me, so you could meet him, so I could have you at last when Rowan felt the bond, but she refused. And we know how well that turned out for her. And during those ten years afterward, I knew you were alive. Somewhere. But when *you* came to *me* . . . when you and your mate looked at each other with only hate in your eyes . . . I'll admit I did not anticipate it. That I had broken Rowan Whitethorn so thoroughly that he did not recognize his own mate—that you were so broken by your own pain you didn't notice, either. And when the signs appeared, the *carranam* bond washed away any suspicion on his part that you might be his. But not you. How long has it been, Aelin, since you realized he was your mate?"

Aelin said nothing, her eyes churning with rage and grief and despair.

Elide whispered, "Leave her alone." Lorcan's grip on her tightened in warning.

Maeve ignored her. "Well? When did you know?"

"At Temis's temple," Aelin admitted, glancing to Manon. "The moment the arrow went through his shoulder. Months ago."

"And you've hidden it from him, no doubt to save him from any guilt regarding Lyria, any sort of emotional distress . . ." Maeve clicked her tongue. "What a noble little liar you are."

Aelin stared at nothing, her eyes going blank.

"I had planned for him to be here," Maeve said, frowning at the horizon. "Since letting you two go that day in Doranelle was so that you could lead me to the keys again. I even let you think you'd gotten away with it, by freeing him. You had no idea that I *unleashed* you. But if he's not here . . . I'll have to make do."

Aelin stiffened. Fenrys snarled in warning.

Maeve shrugged. "If it's any consolation, Aelin, you would have had a thousand years with Prince Rowan. Longer."

The world slowed, and Elide could hear her own blood roaring in her ears as Maeve said, "My sister Mab's line ran true. The full powers, shifting abilities, and the immortality of the Fae. You're likely about five years away from Settling."

Aelin's face crumpled. This was not a draining of magic and physical strength, but of spirit.

"Perhaps we'll celebrate your Settling together," Maeve mused, "since I certainly have no plans to waste you on that Lock. To waste the keys, when they are meant to be *wielded*, Aelin."

"Maeve, please," Fenrys breathed.

Maeve examined her immaculate nails. "What I find to be truly amusing is that it seems I didn't even need you to be Rowan's mate. Or really need to break him at all. A fascinating experiment in my own powers, if anything. But since I doubt you'll still go willingly, not at least without trying to die on me first, I'll let you have a choice."

Aelin seemed to be bracing herself as Maeve lifted a hand and said, "Cairn."

The males went rigid. Lorcan turned near-feral behind Elide, subtly trying to drag her back, to work around the order he'd been given.

A handsome, brown-haired warrior walked toward them from the cluster of escorts. Handsome, if it weren't for the sadistic cruelty singing in his blue eyes. If it wasn't for the blades at his sides, the whip curled along one hip, the sneering smile. She'd seen that smile before—on Vernon's face. On so many faces at Morath.

"Allow me to introduce the newest member of my cadre, as you like to call them. Cairn, meet Aelin Galathynius."

Cairn stepped up to his queen's side. And the look the male gave Elide's queen made her stomach turn over. *Sadist*—yes, that was the word for him, without him even saying one himself.

"Cairn," Maeve said, "is trained in abilities that you have in common. Of course, you only had a few years to learn the art of torment, but . . . perhaps Cairn can teach you some of the things he's learned in his centuries of practicing."

Fenrys was pale with rage. "Maeve, *I beg you*—"

Darkness slammed into Fenrys, shoving him to his knees, forcing his head to the dirt. "*That is enough*," Maeve hissed.

Maeve was smiling again when she turned back to Aelin. "I said you have a choice. And you do. Either you come willingly with me and get acquainted with Cairn, or . . ."

Those eyes slid to Lorcan. To Elide.

And Elide's heart stopped as Maeve said, "Or I still take you—and bring Elide Lochan with us. I'm certain she and Cairn will get along wonderfully."

CHAPTER 72

Aelin's body hurt.

Everything hurt. Her blood, her breath, her bones.

There was no magic left. Nothing left to save her.

"No," Lorcan said softly.

Just turning her head sparked agony down her spine. But Aelin looked at Elide, at Lorcan forced to hold her, his face white with pure terror as he glanced between Cairn and Maeve and Elide. Manon was doing the same—sizing up the odds, how fast she'd have to be to clear the area.

Good. Good—Manon would get Elide out. The witch had been waiting for Aelin to make a move, not realizing that . . . she had nothing left. There was no power left for a final strike.

And that dark power was still coiled around her bones, so tightly that one move of aggression . . . one move, and her bones would snap.

Maeve said to Lorcan, "No to what, Lorcan? Elide Lochan being taken with us if Aelin decides to put up a fight, or my generous offer to leave Elide be if Her Majesty comes willingly?"

One look at the brown-haired Fae warrior—Cairn—standing at Maeve's side, and Aelin had known what he was. She'd killed enough of them over the years. She'd spent time with Rourke Farran. What he'd do to Elide . . . Lorcan also knew what a male like Cairn would do to a young woman. And if he was sanctioned by Maeve herself . . .

Lorcan said, "She is innocent. Take the queen, and let us go."

Manon even snapped at Maeve, "She belongs to the Ironteeth. If you have no quarrel with me, then you have no quarrel with her. Leave Elide Lochan out of it."

Maeve ignored Manon and drawled to Lorcan, "I command you to stand down. I command you to watch and do nothing. I command you to not move or speak until I say so. The order applies to you as well, Fenrys."

And Lorcan obeyed. So did Fenrys. Their bodies simply stiffened—and then nothing.

Elide twisted to beg Lorcan, "You can stop this, you can fight it—"

Lorcan didn't even look at her.

Aelin knew Elide would fight. Would not understand that Maeve had been playing this game for centuries, and had waited until this moment, until the trap was perfect, to seize her.

Aelin found Maeve smiling at her. She had played, and gambled, and lost.

Maeve nodded as if to say yes.

The unspoken question danced in Aelin's eyes as Elide screamed at Lorcan, at Manon, to help. But the witch knew her orders. Her task.

Maeve read the question in Aelin's face and said, "I will bear the keys in one hand, and Aelin Fire-Bringer in the other."

She'd have to break her first. Kill her or break . . .

Cairn grinned.

The escorts were now hauling something up the beach, from the longboat they'd rowed over from their awaiting ship. Already, the dark sails were unfurling.

Elide faced Maeve, who did not deign to glance her way. "Please, please—"

Aelin simply nodded at the Fae Queen. Her acceptance and surrender.

Maeve bowed her head, triumph dancing on her red lips. "Lorcan, release her."

The warrior's hands slackened at his sides.

And because she had won, Maeve even loosened her power's grip on Aelin's bones. Allowed Aelin to turn to Elide and say, "Go with Manon. She will take care of you."

Elide began crying, shoving away from Lorcan. "I'll go with you, I'll come with you—"

The girl would. The girl would face Cairn, and Maeve . . . But Terrasen would need that sort of courage. If it was to survive, if it was to heal, Terrasen would need Elide Lochan.

"Tell the others," Aelin breathed, trying to find the right words. "Tell the others that I am sorry. Tell Lysandra to remember her promise, and that I will never stop being grateful. Tell Aedion . . . Tell him it is not his fault, and that . . ." Her voice cracked. "I wish he'd been able to take the oath, but Terrasen will look to him now, and the lines must not break."

Elide nodded, tears sliding down her blood-splattered face.

"And tell Rowan . . ."

Aelin's soul splintered as she saw the iron box the escorts now carried between them. An ancient, iron coffin. Big enough for one person. Crafted for her.

"And tell Rowan," Aelin said, fighting her own sob, "that I'm sorry I lied. But tell him it was all borrowed time anyway. Even before today, I knew it was all just borrowed time, but I still wish we'd had more of it." She fought past her trembling mouth. "Tell him he has to fight. He *must* save Terrasen, and remember the vows he made to me. And tell him . . . tell him thank you—for walking that dark path with me back to the light."

They opened the lid of the box, pulling out long, heavy chains within.

One of the escorts handed Maeve an ornate iron mask. She examined it in her hands.

The mask, the chains, the box . . . they had been crafted long before now. Centuries ago. Forged to contain and break Mala's scion.

Aelin glanced at Lorcan, whose dark eyes were fixed on her own.

And gratitude shone there. For sparing the young woman he'd given his heart to, whether he knew it or not.

Elide begged Maeve one last time, "Don't do this."

Aelin knew it would do her no good. So she said to Elide, "I'm glad we met. I'm proud to know you. And I think your mother would have been proud of you, too, Elide."

Maeve lowered the mask and drawled to Aelin, "Rumor claims you will bow to no one, Heir of Fire." That serpentine smile. "Well, now you will bow to me."

She pointed to the sand.

Aelin obeyed.

Her knees barked as she dropped to the ground.

"Lower."

Aelin slid her body until her brow was in the sand. She did not let herself feel it, let her soul feel it.

"Good."

Elide was sobbing, wordlessly begging.

"Take off your shirt."

Aelin hesitated—realizing where this was going.

Why Cairn's belt carried a whip.

"Take off your shirt."

Aelin tugged her shirt out of her pants and slung it over her head, tossing it in the sand beside her. Then she removed the flexible cloth around her breasts.

"Varik, Heiron." Two Fae males came forward.

Aelin didn't fight as they each gripped her by an arm and hauled her up. Spread her arms wide. The sea air kissed her breasts, her navel.

"Ten lashes, Cairn. Let Her Majesty have a taste of what to expect when we reach our destination, if she does not cooperate."

"It would be my pleasure, Lady."

Aelin held Cairn's vicious gaze, willing ice into her veins as he thumbed free his whip. As he raked his eyes over her body and smiled. A canvas for him to paint with blood and pain.

Maeve said, the mask dangling from her fingers, "Why don't you count for us, Aelin?"

Aelin kept her mouth shut.

"Count, or we'll begin again with each stroke you miss. You decide how long this goes on for. Unless you'd rather Elide Lochan receive these strokes."

No. Never.

Never anyone else but her. *Never.*

But as Cairn walked slowly, savoring each step, as he let that whip drag along the ground, her body betrayed her. Began shaking.

She knew the pain. Knew what it'd feel like, what it'd sound like.

Her dreams were still full of it.

No doubt why Maeve had picked a whipping, why she'd done it to Rowan in Doranelle.

Cairn halted. She felt him studying the tattoo on her back. Rowan's loving words, written there in the Old Language.

Cairn snorted. Then she felt him revel in how he'd destroy that tattoo.

"Begin," Maeve said.

Cairn's breath sucked in.

And even bracing herself, even clamping down hard, there was nothing to prepare for the crack, the sting, the pain. She did not let herself cry out, only hissed through her teeth.

A whip wielded by an overseer at Endovier was one thing.

One wielded by a full-blooded Fae male . . .

Blood slid down the back of her pants, her split skin screaming.

But she knew how to pace herself. How to yield to the pain. How to take it.

"What number was that, Aelin?"

She would not. She would *never* count for that rutting *bitch*—

"Start over, Cairn," Maeve said.

A breathy laugh. Then the crack and the pain and Aelin arched, the tendons in her neck near snapping as she panted through clenched teeth. The males holding her gripped her firm enough to bruise.

Maeve and Cairn waited.

Aelin refused to say the word. To start the count. She'd die before she did it.

"Oh gods, oh gods," Elide sobbed.

"Start over," Maeve merely ordered over the girl.

So Cairn did.

Again.

Again.

Again.

They started over nine times before Aelin finally screamed. The blow had been right atop another one, tearing skin down to the bone.

Again.

Again.

Again.

Again.

Cairn was panting. Aelin refused to speak.

"Start over," Maeve repeated.

"Majesty," murmured one of the males holding her. "It might be prudent to postpone until later."

"There's still plenty of skin," Cairn snapped.

But the male said, "Others are approaching—still far off, but approaching."

Rowan.

Aelin whimpered then. Time—she had needed *time*—

Maeve made a small noise of distaste. "We'll continue later. Get her ready."

Aelin could barely lift her head as the males heaved her up. The movement set her body roaring in such pain that darkness swarmed in. But she fought it, gritted her teeth and silently roared back at that agony, that darkness.

A few feet away, Elide slid to her knees as if she'd beg until her body gave out, but Manon caught her. "We're going now," Manon said, tugging her away—inland.

"No," Elide spat, thrashing.

Lorcan's eyes widened, but with Maeve's command, he couldn't move, couldn't do anything as Manon slammed the hilt of Wind-Cleaver into the side of Elide's head.

The girl dropped like a stone. That was all Manon needed to haul her over a shoulder and say to Maeve, "Good luck." Her eyes slid to Aelin's once—only once. Then she looked away.

Maeve ignored the witch as Manon prowled toward the heart of the marshes. Lorcan's body strained.

Strained—like he was fighting that blood oath with everything in him.

Aelin didn't care.

The males half dragged her toward Maeve.

Toward the iron box. And the chains. And the iron mask.

Whorls of fire, little suns, and embers had been shaped into its dark surface. A mockery of the power it was to contain—the power Maeve had needed to ensure was fully drained before she locked her up. The only way she could ever lock her up.

Every inch her feet dragged through the sand was a lifetime; every inch was a heartbeat. Blood soaked her pants. She likely wouldn't be able to heal her wounds within all that iron. Not until Maeve decided to heal them herself.

But Maeve wouldn't let her die. Not with the Wyrdkeys in the balance. Not yet.

Time—she was grateful Elena had given her that stolen time.

Grateful she had met them all, that she had seen some small part of the world, had heard such lovely music, had danced and laughed and known true friendship. Grateful that she had found Rowan.

She was grateful.

So Aelin Galathynius dried her tears.

And did not fight when Maeve strapped that beautiful iron mask over her face.

CHAPTER 73

Manon kept walking.

She didn't dare look back. Didn't dare give that ancient, cold-eyed queen one hint that Aelin did not possess the Wyrdkeys. That Aelin had slipped them both into Manon's pocket when she'd nudged her. Elide would hate her for it—already did hate her for it.

Let that be the cost.

One look from Aelin and she'd known what she had to do.

Get the keys away from Maeve. Get Elide away.

They had forged an iron box to contain the Queen of Terrasen.

Elide stirred, at last coming to, just as they were nearly out of hearing range. She began thrashing, and Manon dumped her behind a dune, gripping the back of her neck so tightly Elide stilled at the iron nails piercing her skin.

"Silence," Manon hissed, and Elide obeyed.

Keeping low, they peered through the grasses. Only a moment—she could spare only a moment to watch, to glean where Maeve was taking the Queen of Terrasen.

Lorcan remained frozen as Maeve had commanded. Gavriel was barely conscious, panting in the grass, as if ripping that blood oath from him had been as grave as any physical wound.

Fenrys—Fenrys's eyes were alive with hatred as he watched Maeve and Cairn. Blood coated Cairn's whip, still dangling at his side as Maeve's soldiers finished strapping that mask over Aelin's face.

Then they clamped irons around her wrists.

Ankles.

Neck.

No one healed her ravaged back, barely more than a bloody slab of meat, as they guided her into the iron box. Made her lie upon her wounds.

And then slid the lid into place. Locked it.

Elide vomited in the grass.

Manon put a hand on the girl's back as the males began carrying the box down the dunes, to the boat, and the ship beyond.

"Fenrys, go," Maeve ordered, pointing to the ship.

Breathing raggedly but unable to refuse the order, Fenrys followed. He glanced once at the white shirt discarded in the sand. It was splattered with blood—spray from the whipping.

Then he was gone, stepping through air and wind and into nothing.

Alone with Lorcan, Maeve said to the warrior, "You have done all this—for me?"

He did not move. Maeve said, "Speak."

Lorcan loosed a shuddering breath and said, "Yes. Yes—it was all for you. All of it."

Elide gripped the seagrass in fistfuls, and Manon half wondered if she'd grow iron nails and shred it apart at the fury in her face. The hate.

Maeve stepped over Aelin's blood-splattered shirt, and brushed her hand over Lorcan's cheek. "I have no use," she crooned, "for self-righteous males who think they know best."

He stiffened. "Majesty—"

"I strip you of the blood oath. I strip you of your assets and your titles and your properties. You, like Gavriel, are released with dishonor and shame. You are exiled from Doranelle for your disobedience, your treachery. Should you step foot inside my borders, you will die."

"Majesty, I beg you—"

"Go beg someone else. I have no use for a warrior I cannot trust. I rescind my kill order. Letting you live with the shame will be far worse for you, I think."

Blood welled at his wrist, then hers. Spilling on the ground.

Lorcan fell to his knees.

"I do not suffer fools gladly," Maeve said, leaving him in the sand, and walked away.

As if she'd dealt him a blow, the twin to Gavriel's, Lorcan couldn't seem to move, to think or breathe. He tried crawling, though. Toward Maeve. The bastard tried crawling.

"We need to go," Manon murmured. The moment Maeve checked to see where those keys were . . . They had to go.

A roar grumbled on the horizon.

Abraxos.

Her heart thundered in her chest, joy sparking, but—

Elide remained in the grass. Watching Lorcan crawl toward the queen now striding across the beach, black gown flowing behind her.

Watching the boat row to the awaiting ship, that iron coffin in its center, Maeve sitting beside it, one hand on the lid. For her sanity, Manon prayed that Aelin wouldn't be awake the entire time she was inside.

And for the sake of their world, Manon prayed the Queen of Terrasen could survive it.

If only so Aelin could then die for them all.

Chapter 74

There was so much blood.

It had spread to where Lorcan was kneeling, gleaming bright as it soaked into the sand.

It covered her shirt, discarded and forgotten beside him. It even speckled the scabbards of her swords and knives, littered around him like bones.

What Maeve had done . . .

What Aelin had done . . .

There was a hole in his chest.

And there was so much blood.

Wings and roaring and he still couldn't look up. Couldn't bring himself to care.

Elide's voice cut across the world, saying to someone, "The ship—the ship just *vanished*; she left without realizing we have the—"

Whoops of joy—female cries of happiness.

Thunderous, swift steps.

Then a hand gripping his hair, yanking back his head as a dagger settled along his throat. As Rowan's face, calm with lethal wrath, appeared in his vision.

"Where is Aelin."

There was pure panic, too—pure panic as Whitethorn saw the blood, the scattered blades, and the shirt.

"Where is Aelin."

What had he done, what had he done—

Pain sliced Lorcan's neck, warm blood dribbled down his throat, his chest.

Rowan hissed, "*Where is my wife?*"

Lorcan swayed where he knelt.

Wife.

Wife.

"Oh, gods," Elide sobbed as she overheard, the words carrying the sound of Lorcan's own fractured heart. "Oh, gods . . ."

And for the first time in centuries, Lorcan wept.

Rowan dug the dagger deeper into Lorcan's neck, even as tears slid down Lorcan's face.

What that woman had done . . .

Aelin had known. That Lorcan had betrayed her and summoned Maeve here. That she had been living on borrowed time.

And she had married Whitethorn . . . so Terrasen could have a king. Perhaps had been spurred into action because she knew Lorcan had already betrayed her, that Maeve was coming . . .

And Lorcan had not helped her.

Whitethorn's wife.

His mate.

Aelin had let them whip and chain her, had gone willingly with Maeve, so Elide didn't enter Cairn's clutches. And it had been just as much a sacrifice for Elide as it had been a gift to him.

She had bowed to Maeve.

For Elide.

"Please," Rowan begged, his voice breaking as that calm fury fractured.

"Maeve took her," Manon said, approaching.

Gavriel rasped from where he knelt nearby, reeling from the severing of his blood oath, "She used the oath to keep us down—keep us from helping. Even Lorcan."

Rowan still didn't remove the knife from Lorcan's throat.

Lorcan had been wrong. He had been so wrong.

And he could not entirely regret it, not if Elide was safe, but . . .

Aelin had refused to count. Cairn had unleashed his full strength on her with that whip, and she had refused to give them the satisfaction of counting.

"Where is the ship," Aedion demanded, then swore at the bloody shirt nearby. He grabbed Goldryn, frantically wiping the blood specks off the scabbard with his jacket.

"It vanished," Elide said again. "It just . . . *vanished*."

Whitethorn stared down at him, agony and despair in those eyes. And Lorcan whispered, "I'm sorry."

Rowan dropped the knife, released the fist gripping Lorcan's hair. Staggered back a step. In the grass nearby, Dorian knelt beside Gavriel, a faint light glowing around them. Healing the wounds in his arms. There was nothing to be done for the soul-wound Maeve had dealt him, dealt Lorcan as well, in severing that oath with such dishonor.

Manon came closer, her witches now flanking her. They all sniffed at the blood. A golden-haired one swore softly.

Manon told them about the Lock.

About Elena. About the cost the gods demanded of her. Demanded of Aelin.

But it was Elide who then took up the thread, leaning against

Lysandra, who was staring at that blood and that shirt as if it were a corpse, telling them what had happened on these dunes. What Aelin had sacrificed.

She told Rowan that he was Aelin's mate. Told him about Lyria.

She told them about the whipping, and the mask, and the box.

When Elide finished, they were silent. And Lorcan only watched as Aedion turned to Lysandra and snarled, "*You knew.*"

Lysandra did not flinch. "She asked me—that day on the boat. To help her. She told me the suspected price to banish Erawan and restore the keys. What I needed to do."

Aedion snarled, "What could *you* possibly . . ."

Lysandra lifted her chin.

Rowan breathed, "Aelin would die to forge the new Lock to seal the keys into the gate—to banish Erawan. But no one would know. No one but us. Not while you wore her skin for the rest of your life."

Aedion dragged a hand through his blood-caked hair. "But any offspring with Rowan wouldn't look anything like—"

Lysandra's face was pleading. "You would fix that, Aedion. With me."

With the golden hair, the Ashryver eyes . . . If that line bred true, the shifter's offspring could pass as royal. Aelin wanted Rowan on the throne—but it would be Aedion secretly siring the heirs.

Aedion flinched as if he'd been struck. "And when were you going to reveal this? Before or after I thought I was taking my gods-damned cousin to bed for whatever reason you concocted?"

Lysandra said softly, "I will not apologize to you. I serve her. And I am willing to spend the rest of my life pretending to be her so that her *sacrifice* isn't in vain—"

"You can go to hell," Aedion snapped. "You can *go to hell, you lying bitch!*"

Lysandra's answering snarl wasn't human.

Rowan just took Goldryn from the general and walked toward the sea, the wind tossing his silver hair.

Lorcan rose to his feet, swaying again. But Elide was there.

And there was nothing of the young woman he'd come to know in her pale, taut face. Nothing of her in the raw voice as Elide said to Lorcan, "I hope you spend the rest of your miserable, immortal life suffering. I hope you spend it alone. I hope you live with regret and guilt in your heart and never find a way to endure it."

Then she was heading for the Thirteen. The golden-haired one held up an arm, and Elide slipped beneath it, entering a sanctuary of wings and claws and teeth.

Lysandra stormed to tend to Gavriel, who had the good sense not to flinch at her still-snarling face, and Lorcan looked to Aedion to find the young general already watching him.

Hatred shone in Aedion's eyes. Pure hatred. "Even before you got the order to stand down, you did nothing to help her. You summoned Maeve here. I will never forget that."

Then he was striding for the beach—to where Rowan knelt in the sand.

Asterin was alive.

The Thirteen were alive. And it was joy in Manon's heart—joy, she realized, as she beheld those smiling faces and smiled back.

She said to Asterin, all of them standing among their wyverns on a dune overlooking the sea, "How?"

Asterin brushed a hand over Elide's hair as the girl wept into her shoulder. "Your grandmother's bitches gave us one hell of a chase, but we managed to gut them. We've spent the past month looking for you. But Abraxos found us and seemed to know where you were, so we followed him." She scratched at some dried blood on her cheek. "And saved your ass, apparently."

Not soon enough, Manon thought, seeing Elide's silent tears, the way the humans and Fae were either standing or arguing or just doing nothing.

Not soon enough to stop this. To save Aelin Galathynius.

"What do we do now?" Sorrel asked from where she leaned against her bull's flank, wrapping up a slice in her forearm.

The Thirteen all looked to Manon, all waited.

She dared to ask, "Did you hear what my grandmother said before . . . everything?"

"The Shadows told us," Asterin said, eyes dancing.

"And?"

"And what?" Sorrel grunted. "So you're half Crochan."

"Crochan *Queen*." And heir to Rhiannon Crochan's likeness. Had the Ancients noted it?

Asterin shrugged. "Five centuries of pure-blooded Ironteeth couldn't bring us home. Maybe you can."

A child not of war . . . but of peace.

"And will you follow me?" Manon asked them quietly. "To do what needs to be done before we can return to the Wastes?"

Aelin Galathynius had not beseeched Elena for another fate. She had only asked for one thing, one request of the ancient queen:

Will you come with me? For the same reason Manon had now asked them.

As one, the Thirteen lifted their fingers to their brows. As one, they lowered them.

Manon looked toward the sea, her throat tight.

"Aelin Galathynius willingly handed over her freedom so an Ironteeth witch could walk free," Manon said. Elide straightened, pulling from Asterin's arms. But Manon continued, "We owe her a life debt. And more than that . . . It is time that we became better than our foremothers. We are all children of this land."

"What are you going to do?" Asterin breathed, her eyes so bright.

Manon looked behind them. To the north.

"I am going to find the Crochans. And I am going to raise an army with them. For Aelin Galathynius. And her people. And for ours."

"They'll never trust us," Sorrel said.

Asterin drawled, "Then we'll have to just be our charming selves."

Some of them smirked; some of them shifted on their feet.

Manon said again to her Thirteen, "Will you follow me?"

And when they all touched their fingers to their brows again, Manon returned the gesture.

Rowan and Aedion were sitting silently on the beach. Gavriel had recovered enough from the shock of the oath's severing that he and Lorcan were now standing atop the bluff, talking quietly; Lysandra was sitting alone, in ghost leopard form, amongst the waving seagrasses; and Dorian was just . . . watching them from the apex of a dune.

What Aelin had done . . . what she'd lied about . . .

Some of the blood on the ground had dried.

If Aelin was gone, if her life would indeed be the cost if she ever got free . . .

"Maeve doesn't have the two keys," Manon said from Dorian's side, having crept up silently. Her coven lingered behind her, Elide ensconced within their ranks. "In case you were concerned."

Lorcan and Gavriel turned toward them. Then Lysandra.

Dorian dared to ask, "Then where are they?"

"I have them," Manon said simply. "Aelin slid them into my pocket."

Oh, Aelin. Aelin. She'd worked Maeve into such a frenzy, made the queen so focused on capturing *her* that she hadn't thought to confirm if Aelin held the keys before she vanished.

She'd been dealt such a wicked, impossible hand—and yet Aelin had made it count. One last time, she'd made it count.

"It's why I couldn't do anything about it," Manon said. "To help her. I had to look uninvolved. Neutral." From where he sat on the beach below,

Aedion had twisted toward them, his keen Fae hearing feeding him every word. Manon said to all of them, "I am sorry. I'm sorry I couldn't help."

She reached into the pocket of her riding leathers and extended the Amulet of Orynth and a sliver of black stone to Dorian. He balked.

"Elena said Mala's bloodline can stop this. It runs in both your houses."

The golden eyes were weary—heavy. He realized what Manon was asking.

Aelin had never planned to see Terrasen again.

She had married Rowan knowing she would have months at best, days at the worst, with him. But she would give Terrasen a legal king. To hold her territory together.

She had made plans for all of them—and none for herself.

"The quest does not end here," Dorian said softly.

Manon shook her head. And he knew she meant more than the keys, than the war, as she said, "No, it does not."

He took the keys from her. They throbbed and flickered, warming his palm. A foreign, horrible presence, and yet . . . all that stood between them and destruction.

No, the quest did not end here. Not even close. Dorian slid the keys into his pocket.

And the road that now sprawled away before him, curving into unknown, awaiting shadow . . . it did not frighten him.

CHAPTER 75

Rowan had married Aelin before dawn barely two days ago.

Aedion and Lysandra had been the only witnesses as they'd awoken the bleary-eyed captain, who married them quickly and quietly and signed a vow of secrecy.

They'd had fifteen minutes in their cabin to consummate that marriage.

Aedion still carried the formal documents; the captain bearing the duplicates.

Rowan had been kneeling on that spit of beach for half an hour now. Silent, wandering the paths of his churning thoughts. Aedion had kept him company, staring blankly at the sea.

Rowan had known.

Part of him had known that Aelin was his mate. And had turned away from that knowledge, again and again, out of respect for Lyria, out of terror for what it'd mean. He'd leapt in front of her at Skull's Bay knowing it, deep down. Knowing mates aware of the bond could not bear to harm each other, and that it might be the only force to compel her to regain control from Deanna. And even when she had proved him right . . . He had turned from that proof, still unready, pushing it from his mind even as he claimed her in every other way.

Aelin had known, though. That he was her mate. And she had not pushed it, or demanded he face it, because she loved him, and he knew she'd rather carve out her own heart than cause him pain or distress.

His Fireheart.

His equal, his friend, his lover. His wife.

His mate.

That gods-damned bitch had put her in an iron box.

She'd whipped his mate so brutally that he'd rarely seen such blood spilled as a result. Then chained her. Then put Aelin in a veritable iron coffin, still bleeding, still hurting.

To contain her. To break her. To torture her.

His Fireheart, locked in the dark.

She'd tried to tell him. Right before the ilken converged.

Tried to tell him she'd vomited her guts up on the ship that day not because she was pregnant but because she'd realized she was going to die. That the cost of sealing the gate, forging a new Lock to do so, was her life. Her immortal life.

Goldryn lying beside him, its ruby dull in the bright sun, Rowan gathered up two fistfuls of sand and let the grains slide out, let the wind carry them toward the sea.

It was all borrowed time anyway.

Aelin did not expect them to come for her.

She, who had come for them, who had found them all. She had arranged for everything to fall into place when she yielded her life. When she gave up a thousand years to save them.

And Rowan knew she believed they'd make the right choice, the wise choice, and remain here. Lead their armies to victory—the armies she'd secured for them, guessing that she wouldn't be there to see it through.

She did not think she'd ever see him again.

He did not accept that.

He would not accept that.

And he would not accept that he had found her, and she had found him, and they had survived such sorrow and pain and despair together, only to be cleaved apart. He would not accept the fate that had been dealt to her, would not accept that her life was the asking price for saving this world. Her life, or Dorian's.

He would not accept it for one heartbeat.

Footsteps thudded on the sand, and he scented Lorcan before he bothered to look. For half a breath, he debated killing the male where he stood.

Rowan knew that today—today he'd win. Something had fractured in Lorcan, and if Rowan attacked now, the other male would die. Lorcan might not even put up much of a fight.

Lorcan's granite-hewn face was hard, but his eyes . . . That was agony in them. And regret.

The others flowed down the dunes, the witch's coven remaining behind, and Aedion rose to his feet.

They all stared at Rowan as he remained kneeling.

The sea rolled away, undulating under the clearing blue sky.

He speared that bond into the world, casting it wide as a net. Flinging it out with his magic, his soul, his cracked heart. Searching for her.

Fight it, he willed her, sending the words down the bond—the mating bond, which perhaps had settled into place that first moment they'd become *carranam*, hidden beneath flame and ice and hope for a better future. *Fight her. I am coming for you. Even if it takes me a thousand years. I will find you, I will find you, I will find you.*

Only salt and wind and water answered him.

Rowan rose to his feet. And slowly turned to face them.

But their attention snagged on the ships now sailing out of the west—from the battle site. His cousins' ships, with what remained of the fleet Ansel of Briarcliff had won for them, and Rolfe's three ships.

But it was not those boats that made him pause.

It was the one that rounded the eastern tip of the land—a longboat. It swept closer on a phantom wind, too fast to be natural.

Rowan braced himself. The boat's shape didn't belong to any of the fleets assembled. But its style nagged at his memory.

From their own fleet, Ansel of Briarcliff and Enda were soaring over the waves in a longboat, aiming for this beach.

But Rowan and the others watched in silence as the foreign boat crested through the surf and slid onto the sand.

Watched the olive-skinned sailors haul it up the beach. A broad-shouldered young man nimbly leaped out, his slightly curling dark hair tossed in the sea breeze.

He did not emit a whiff of fear as he stalked for them—didn't even go for the comforting touch of the fine sword at his side.

"Where is Aelin Galathynius?" the stranger asked a bit breathlessly as he scanned them.

And his accent . . .

"Who are you," Rowan ground out.

But the young man was now close enough that Rowan could see the color of his eyes. Turquoise—with a core of gold.

Aedion breathed as if in a trance, "Galan."

Galan Ashryver, Crown Prince of Wendlyn.

The young man's eyes widened as he took in the warrior-prince. "*Aedion*," he said hoarsely, something like awe and grief in his face. But he blinked it away, self-assured and steady, and again asked, "Where is she?"

None of them answered. Aedion demanded, "What are you doing here?"

Galan's dark brows flicked toward each other. "I thought she would have informed you."

"Informed us of *what*?" Rowan said too quietly.

Galan reached into the pocket of his worn blue tunic, pulling out a crinkled letter that looked like it had been read a hundred times. He silently handed it to Rowan.

Her scent still clung to it as he unfolded the paper, Aedion reading over his shoulder.

Aelin's letter to the Prince of Wendlyn had been short. Brutal. The large letters were sprawled across the page as if her temper had gotten the better of her:

> *TERRASEN REMEMBERS EVALIN ASHRYVER.*
> *DO YOU?*
> *I FOUGHT AT MISTWARD FOR YOUR PEOPLE.*
> *RETURN THE GODS-DAMNED FAVOR.*

And then coordinates—for this spot.

"It only went to me," Galan said softly. "Not to my father. Only to me."

To the armada that Galan controlled—as a blockade runner against Adarlan.

"Rowan," Lysandra murmured in warning. He followed her stare.

Not to where Ansel and Enda now arrived at the edge of their group, giving the Thirteen a wide berth as they lifted their brows at Galan.

But to the small company of white-clad people that appeared on the cresting dunes behind them, splattered in mud and looking like they had trekked across the marshes themselves.

And Rowan knew.

He knew who they were before they even reached the beach.

Ansel of Briarcliff had gone pale at the sight of their layered, flowing clothes. And as the tall male in their center peeled off his hood to reveal a brown-skinned, green-eyed face still handsome with youth, the Queen of the Wastes whispered, "Ilias."

Ilias, son of the Mute Master of the Silent Assassins, gaped at Ansel, his back stiffening. But Rowan stepped toward the man, drawing his attention. Ilias's eyes narrowed in assessment. And he, like Galan, scanned them all, searching for a golden-haired woman who was not there. His eyes returned to Rowan as if he'd marked him as the axis of this group.

In a voice hoarse from disuse, Ilias asked him, "We have come to fulfill our life debt to Celaena Sardothien—to Aelin Galathynius. Where is she?"

"You are the *sessiz suikast*," Dorian said, shaking his head. "The Silent Assassins of the Red Desert."

Ilias nodded. And glanced at Ansel, who still seemed near vomiting, before saying to Rowan, "It seems my friend has called in many debts in addition to ours."

As if the words themselves were a signal, more white-clad figures filled the dunes behind them.

Dozens. Hundreds.

Rowan wondered if every single assassin from that desert Keep had come to honor their debt to the young woman. A lethal legion in themselves.

And Galan . . .

Rowan turned to the Crown Prince of Wendlyn. "How many," he asked. "How many did you bring?"

Galan only smiled a bit and pointed to the eastern horizon.

Where white sails now broke over its rim. Ship after ship after ship, each bearing the cobalt flag of Wendlyn.

"Tell Aelin Galathynius that Wendlyn has never forgotten Evalin Ashryver," Galan said to him, to Aedion. "Or Terrasen."

Aedion fell to his knees in the sand as Wendlyn's armada spread before them.

I promise you that no matter how far I go, no matter the cost, when you call for my aid, I will come, Aelin had told him she'd sworn to Darrow. *I'm going to call in old debts and promises. To raise an army of assassins and thieves and exiles and commoners.*

And she had. She had meant and accomplished every word of it.

Rowan counted the ships that slid over the horizon. Counted the ships in their own armada. Added Rolfe's—and the Mycenians he was rallying in the North.

"Holy gods," Dorian breathed as Wendlyn's armada kept spreading wider and wider.

Tears slid down Aedion's face as he silently sobbed. *Where are our allies, Aelin? Where are our armies?* She had taken the criticism—taken it, because he knew she hadn't wanted to disappoint them if she failed. Rowan put a hand on Aedion's shoulder.

All of it for Terrasen, she had said that day she'd revealed she'd schemed her way into getting Arobynn's fortune. And Rowan knew that every step she had taken, every plan and calculation, every secret and desperate gamble . . .

For Terrasen. For them. For a better world.

Aelin Galathynius had raised an army not just to challenge Morath . . . but to rattle the stars.

She'd known that she would not get to lead it. But she would still hold true to her promise to Darrow: *I promise you on my blood, on my family's name, that I will not turn my back on Terrasen as you have turned your back on me.*

And the last piece of it . . . if Chaol Westfall and Nesryn Faliq could rally forces from the southern continent . . .

Aedion at last looked up at him, eyes wide as he came to the same realization.

A chance. His wife, his mate, had bought them a fool's shot at this war.

And she did not believe that they would come for her.

"Galan?"

Rowan went still as death at the voice that floated over the dunes. At the golden-haired woman who wore the skin of his beloved.

Aedion shot to his feet, about to snarl, when Rowan gripped his arm.

When Lysandra, as Aelin, as she had promised, swept for them, grinning wide.

That smile . . . It punched a hole through his heart. Lysandra had taught herself Aelin's smile, that bit of wickedness and delight, honed with that razor edge of cruelty.

Lysandra's acting, honed in the same hellhole Aelin had learned hers, was flawless as she spoke to Galan. As she spoke to Ilias, embracing him like a long-lost friend, and a relieved ally.

Aedion was trembling beside him. But the world could not know.

Their allies, their enemies, could not know that the immortal fire of Mala had been stolen. Leashed.

Galan said to the one whom he believed to be his cousin, "Where now?"

Lysandra looked to him, then to Aedion, not a sign of regret or guilt or doubt on her face. "We go north. To Terrasen."

Rowan's stomach turned leaden. But Lysandra caught his eye, and said steadily and casually, "Prince—I need you to retrieve something for me before you join us in the North."

Find her, find her, find her, the shifter seemed to beg.

Rowan nodded, at a loss for words. Lysandra took his hand, squeezed it once in thanks, a polite, public farewell between a queen and her consort, and stepped away.

"Come," Lysandra said to Galan and Ilias, motioning them toward where a white-faced Ansel and frowning Enda waited. "We have matters to discuss before we head out."

Then their little company was alone once more.

Aedion's hands clenched and unclenched at his sides as he gazed after the shape-shifter wearing Aelin's skin, leading their allies down the beach. To give them privacy.

An army to take on Morath. To give them a fighting chance . . .

Sand whispered behind him as Lorcan stepped up to his side. "I will go with you. I will help you get her back."

Gavriel rasped, "We'll find her." Aedion at last looked away from Lysandra at that. But he said nothing to his father—had said nothing to him at all since they'd landed on the beach.

Elide took a limping step closer, her voice as raw as Gavriel's. "Together. We'll go together."

Lorcan gave the Lady of Perranth an assessing look that she made a point to ignore. His eyes flickered as he said to Rowan, "Fenrys is with her. He'll know we're coming for her—try to leave tracks if he can."

If Maeve didn't have him on lockdown. But Fenrys had battled the blood oath every day since swearing it. And if he was all that now stood between Cairn and Aelin . . . Rowan didn't let himself think about Cairn. About what Maeve had already had him do, or would do to her before the end. No—Fenrys would fight it. And Aelin would fight it.

Aelin would never stop fighting.

Rowan faced Aedion, and the warrior-prince again peeled his attention away from Lysandra long enough to meet his eyes. Aedion understood the look, and put a hand on the Sword of Orynth's hilt. "I'll go north. With—her. To oversee the armies, make sure it's all in place."

Rowan clasped Aedion's forearm. "The lines have to hold. Buy us whatever time you can, brother."

Aedion gripped his forearm in return, eyes burning bright. Rowan knew how much it killed him. But if the world believed Aelin was returning north, then one of her generals had to be at her side to lead her armies. And since Aedion commanded the loyalty of the Bane . . . "Bring her back, Prince," Aedion said, voice cracking. "Bring her home."

Rowan held his brother's stare and nodded. "We will see you again. All of you."

He did not waste words persuading the warrior-prince to forgive the shifter. He wasn't entirely sure what to even make of Aelin and Lysandra's plan. What *his* role would have been in it.

Dorian stepped forward, but glanced to Manon, who was staring toward the sea as if she could see wherever Maeve had spirited away her ship. Using that cloaking power she'd wielded to hide Fenrys and Gavriel in Skull's Bay—hide her armada from the eyes of Eyllwe. "The witches fly north," Dorian said. "And I will go with them. To see if I can do what needs to be done."

"Stay with us," Rowan offered. "We'll find a way to deal with the keys and the Lock and the gods—all of it."

Dorian shook his head. "If you go after Maeve, the keys should be kept far away. If I can help by doing this, by finding the third . . . I will serve you better that way."

"You'll likely die," Aedion cut in sharply. "We go north to bloodshed and killing fields—you head into dangers far worse than that. Morath will be waiting." Rowan cut him a glare. But his brother was beyond caring. No, Aedion was riding a vicious, vulnerable edge right now—and it wouldn't take much for that edge to turn lethal. Especially when Dorian had played his part in separating Aelin from their group.

Dorian again looked to Manon, who now smiled faintly at him. It was a smile that softened her face, made it come alive. "He won't die if I can help it," the witch said, then surveyed them all. "We journey to find the Crochans—to rally what forces they might have."

A witch army to counter the Ironteeth legions.

Hope—precious, fragile hope—stirred Rowan's blood.

Manon merely jerked her chin in farewell and prowled up the bluff to her coven.

So Rowan nodded to Dorian. But the man bowed his head—not the gesture of a friend to a friend. But of one king to another.

Consort, he wanted to say. He was just her consort.

Even if she'd married him so he could have the legal right to save

Terrasen and rebuild it. To command the armies she'd given everything to gather for them.

"When we are done, I will join you in Terrasen, Aedion," the King of Adarlan promised. "So that when you get back, Rowan—when *both* of you get back—there will be something left to fight for."

Aedion seemed to consider. To weigh the man's words and expression. And then the general-prince stepped forward and embraced the king. It was quick, and hard, and Dorian flinched, but that edge in Aedion's grief-dull eyes had been eased a bit. Silently, Aedion glanced at Damaris, sheathed at Dorian's side. The blade of Adarlan's first and greatest king. Aedion seemed to weigh its presence, who bore it. At last, the general-prince nodded, more to himself than anyone. But Dorian still bowed his head in thanks.

When Aedion had stalked toward the longboats, deliberately stepping around Lysandra-Aelin when she tried to speak to him, Rowan said to the king, "You trust the witches?"

A nod. "They're leaving two wyverns to guard your ship to the edge of the continent. From there, they'll join us again—and you'll set off wherever . . . wherever you need to go."

Maeve could have taken her anywhere, vanished that ship halfway across the world.

Rowan said to Dorian, "Thank you."

"Don't thank me." A half smile. "Thank Manon."

If they all lived through this, if he got Aelin back, he would.

He embraced Dorian, wished the king well, and watched the man climb up the sandbank to the white-haired witch who waited for him.

Lysandra was already giving orders to Galan and Ilias regarding transporting the two hundred Silent Assassins onto Wendlyn's ships, Aedion monitoring with crossed arms. Ansel was deep in conversation with Endymion, who didn't seem to quite know what to do with the red-haired queen with a wolf's smile. Ansel, however, seemed already inclined to raise hell and have a damn good time doing it. Rowan wished he had more than a moment to spare to thank them both—to thank Enda and each one of his cousins.

All was set, all was ready for that desperate push north. As Aelin had planned.

There would be no rest, no waiting. They did not have the time to spare.

The wyverns stirred, flapping their wings. Dorian climbed into the saddle behind Manon and wrapped his arms around her waist. The witch said something that made him smile. Truly smile.

Dorian lifted his hand in farewell, wincing as Abraxos soared into the skies.

Ten other wyverns took to the air behind them.

The grinning, golden-haired witch—Asterin—and a slender, black-haired, green-eyed one named Briar waited atop their mounts for Gavriel, Lorcan, and Elide. To carry them to the ship that would take them hunting across the sea.

Lorcan made to step toward Elide as she approached Asterin's wyvern, but she ignored him. Didn't even look at the male as she took Asterin's hand and was hauled up into the saddle. And though Lorcan hid it well, Rowan caught the glimmer of devastation on those centuries-hardened features.

Gavriel's barked curse as he gripped the golden-haired witch's waist was the only sound of his unease as they flapped into the sky. Only when they were all airborne did Rowan slowly walk up the sandy hill, tying Goldryn's ancient scabbard to his knife belt as he went.

Her blood-splattered shirt was still lying there, just to the side of the pool of her blood soaking the sand. He had no doubt Cairn had purposely left it.

Rowan bent, picking up the shirt, running his thumbs over the soft fabric.

The coven faded into the horizon; his companions reached their ship, and the others were readying to move the army his mate had summoned for them, pushing the longboats into the surf.

Rowan brought the shirt to his face and breathed in her scent. Felt something stir in him—felt the bond flicker.

He let the shirt drop, let the wind carry it far out to sea, far away from this blood-drenched place that reeked of pain.

I will find you.

Rowan shifted and soared high on a fast, wicked wind of his own making, the glimmering sea sprawling to his right, the marshes a green-and-gray tangle to his left. Chaining the wind to him, swiftly catching up with his companions now flying down the coast, he committed her scent to memory, committed that flicker in the bond to memory.

That flicker he could have sworn he felt in answer, like the fluttering heart of an ember.

Unleashing a cry that set the world trembling, Prince Rowan Whitethorn Galathynius, Consort of the Queen of Terrasen, began the hunt to find his wife.

ACKNOWLEDGMENTS

It's always so difficult to sum up my overwhelming gratitude for the people who not only work so tirelessly to make this book a reality, but who also provide me with such unwavering support and friendship. I don't know what I would do without them in my life, and I thank the universe every single day that they're in it.

To my husband, Josh: Even when this world is a forgotten whisper of dust between the stars, I will love you. Thank you for the laughter on the days when I didn't think I could smile, for holding my hand when I needed a reminder that I was loved, and for being my best friend and safe harbor. You are the greatest joy in my life, and even a thousand pages would not be enough to express how much I love you.

To Annie: By now, it would not surprise me at all if you've learned to read. You are the other great joy in my life, and your unconditional love and unfailing sass make a solitary job into something that never feels lonely—not for one moment. I love you, baby pup.

To Tamar Rydzinski: I have been so grateful for your wisdom, badassery, and brilliance from the very first moment you called me all those years ago. But this year especially, I've been even more thankful for your friendship. Thank you for having my back no matter what. I'm so lucky to have you in my corner.

To Cat Onder: Working with you has been such a huge highlight of my career. Thank you from the bottom of my heart for your clever and insightful feedback, for championing my books, and for making this entire process just so *fun*. I'm incredibly proud to have you as an editor and a friend.

To Margaret Miller: Thank you for all of your help and guidance over the years—I've grown so much as a writer because of you, and I'm so grateful for it. To Cassie Homer: Where do I even begin to thank you for all that you do? I truly don't know how I'd manage without your help. You're amazing.

To my unparalleled and marvelous teams at Bloomsbury worldwide and CAA—Cindy Loh, Cristina Gilbert, Jon Cassir, Kathleen Farrar, Nigel Newton, Rebecca McNally, Natalie Hamilton, Sonia Palmisano, Emma Hopkin, Ian Lamb, Emma Bradshaw, Lizzy Mason, Courtney Griffin, Erica Barmash, Emily Ritter, Grace Whooley, Eshani Agrawal, Emily Klopfer, Alice Grigg, Elise Burns, Jenny Collins, Linette Kim, Beth Eller, Kerry Johnson, Kelly de Groot, Ashley Poston, Lucy Mackay-Sim, Melissa Kavonic, Diane Aronson, Donna Mark, John Candell, Nicholas Church, and the entire foreign rights team: I am so blessed to work with such a spectacular group of people, and I can't imagine my books being in better hands. Thank you, thank you, thank you for *everything*.

To my parents: Thank you for the unwavering love, and for owning a truly embarrassing number of copies of all my books. To my in-laws: Thank you for looking after Annie when we're away—and for always being there for us no matter what. To my wonderful family: I love you all.

To Louisse Ang, Sasha Alsberg, Vilma Gonzalez, Alice Fanchiang, Charlie Bowater, Nicola Wilksinson, Damaris Cardinali, Alexa Santiago, Rachel Domingo, Kelly Grabowski, Jessica Reigle, Jamie Miller, Laura Ashforth, Steph Brown, and the Maas Thirteen: Thank you so, so, so much for your kindness, your generosity, and your friendship. I'm honored to know you guys.

And to my readers: Thank you for the letters, the art, the tattoos(!!), the music—thank you for *all* of it. I can't begin to express how much it means to me, or how thankful I am. You make all the hard work worth it.

EXCLUSIVE

Months before Aelin reclaimed her identity as the long-lost Queen of Terrasen, she still called herself Celaena Sardothien—and was trained to wield her rekindled magic by a Fae Prince in a mountain fortress of Wendlyn. . . .

Despite their rough beginning, Aelin and Rowan have finally formed a solid friendship, based on mutual respect, trust, and more than a bit of banter. But just when their bond begins to shift into something neither of them quite anticipates—something far deeper—the fortress of Mistward receives a visit from three Fae nobles. And one of them claims some very, *very* personal ties to Rowan himself.

Read on for an exclusive deleted scene from *Heir of Fire*, in which Aelin gets her first glimpse of the Fae nobility of Doranelle, and a bit more of Rowan's history is revealed to her . . . with fiery consequences.

"What's your favorite food?" Lounging on a boulder like a lizard in the sun, Celaena chucked a nut in the air and caught it in her mouth.

"Whatever keeps me alive at the moment," Rowan said from beside her, forearms braced on his knees as he monitored the foothills and valleys of Wendlyn rippling away below.

She clicked her tongue. "Could you be any more of an animal?"

He slid a glance in her direction, lifting a brow as if to say, *You remember what my other form is, don't you?* When she only scowled, he sighed. "There's a street vendor in Doranelle who sells meat on a stick."

"Meat on a stick," Celaena said as steadily as she could, fighting to keep her lips in a straight line.

"And I suppose yours is some confection or useless bit of sugar."

"Sweets aren't useless. And *yes*. I'd crawl over hot coals for a piece of chocolate hazelnut cake right now." Lies. The last time she'd had it, it had been with Chaol. She wasn't sure she could ever eat it again.

"What good could that possibly be for keeping your body strong?

With your magic, you'd burn through it and be hungry again within half an hour."

She propped herself up on her elbows. "Your priorities are *obscenely* out of order. Not all food is for survival and strength-building. You didn't even *try* one of the chocolates from that town. I guarantee the moment you do, every time I turn my back, you'll be shoveling them down."

The thought of Rowan doing it made her clamp her lips together again. She knew he'd make her start training the moment she started howling, so she quickly asked, "Favorite color?"

"Green."

"I'm surprised you actually know."

He narrowed his eyes, but said, "What's yours?"

"For a while, I made myself believe it was blue. But—it's always been red. You probably know why."

He made an affirmative sound.

Celaena lay down and raised a hand above her, threading a line of fire through her fingers. She plaited it between her knuckles, then snaked it down her palm, until it curled around her wrist, twining and slithering along her skin.

"Good," Rowan said. "Your control is improving."

"Mmhmm." She lifted her other hand, and rings of flame encircled her fingers. She set to work on carving the flames, forging them into individual patterns.

"Try it on me," Rowan said, and she turned her head toward him and frowned deeply. "Do it."

He didn't flinch when she fashioned a crown of flame for him. Right atop his head.

She sat up, kneeling before him, her own jewelry still burning on her hands and wrists, and concentrated as she fashioned the crown into a wreath, each individual leaf a flick of flame, the gold and red and blue bright as any precious stone.

Rowan's silver hair gleamed beneath it.

"Bold move," he said as she continued to add details to his crown. "One that doesn't have much space for error."

"I'm surprised you're not encasing your head with ice."

"I trust you," he said quietly enough that she looked at his face. With the crown of flame, he looked kingly indeed—a warrior-king, as brutal as the lines of his tattoo. "And now one for you," he said, and a delightful chill went down her spine as a crown of ice formed in the space between them, its delicate spikes rising high.

Rowan lifted it between his hands and set it on her head, its weight light, the chill a balm against the heat of her fire.

Celaena smiled at him, and he gave her a tiny lift of his lips in response. But then she remembered—remembered that it was a crown he had made for her. A crown.

Her flames sputtered out as she rose to her feet and strode to the edge of the boulder, wrapping her arms around herself. A moment later, the crown of ice dissolved into mist on the mountain wind.

"We're going to have visitors tonight," Rowan said, approaching her side.

"Should I be concerned?"

"I—need your help."

"Ah. So that's why you let me have an afternoon of peace." He snarled, but she lifted a brow. "Will I finally be meeting your mysterious friends?"

"No. They're Fae nobility, passing through the area. They requested a place to stay for the night, and will arrive around sunset. Emrys is making them dinner, and I am expected to . . . entertain them."

When he just looked at her, she said, "Oh, no. No."

"They will not condescend to dine with the demi-Fae, and—"

"I'm even less acceptable than a demi-Fae!"

"—if I have to play host to them all evening, it will likely end in bloodshed."

She blinked. "Not favorites of yours?"

"They're typical nobility. Not trained warriors. They expect to be treated a certain way."

"So? You're in Maeve's little cabal. And you're a prince to boot. Don't you outrank them?"

"Technically, but there are politics to consider. Especially when they'll be reporting to Maeve."

She groaned. "So what—I'm supposed to play hostess?"

His face was about as miserable as hers. "No. Just—help me deal with them."

Another bit of trust, she realized. "And what am I going to get out of it?"

He clenched his jaw, and she honestly thought he'd say, *I won't kick your ass*, but he sighed. "I'll find you a chocolate hazelnut cake."

"No." When he raised his brows, she threw a wicked smile at him. "You'll just owe me. A favor that I can call in whenever I please."

He sighed, lifting his gaze skyward. "Just look presentable at sundown."

The jingling bells and merry voices reached the fortress long before the party appeared through the ward-stones.

Standing in the small courtyard, Celaena slid a glance to Rowan. "Really? You need my help with these prancing idiots?" But aside from those on watch, the demi-Fae had made themselves scarce.

He glared at her. She'd bathed and dressed in her cleanest tunic, even going so far as to plait her hair into a pleasant coronet. "Keep your voice down," he muttered, giving a pointed glance to her ears.

She rolled her eyes, but didn't say anything else as the party arrived. Their horses were all—gods, those were all Asterion horses. Each worth its weight in gold and then some. She'd once owned one—well, she'd stolen one and kept it—but had sold it to pay off Sam's debts to Arobynn. It had been utterly worth it, but . . . she still missed Kasida. She'd never seen or ridden a finer horse.

There were five in the party now taking in the courtyard and fortress, two of them bored-looking guards whose attention fixed solely on Rowan, and the other three . . . The female in the front was stunning—and undoubtedly the leader.

Beneath her pale blond hair, her face was a concoction of ivory and soft rose, her eyes a vibrant cerulean blue. They flared with delight as they fixed on Rowan.

She didn't so much as spare Celaena a passing glance as she slid gracefully off her white mare. "Rowan!" She advanced, holding out her hands. Her fingers were slender and long—and as flawless as the rest of her.

"Lady Remelle," Rowan said, his massive hands engulfing hers as he took them. His spine was straight as a rod, and though Remelle looked at their joined hands as if expecting him to plant a kiss—gods, the idea of Rowan *kissing* anyone's hand—he dropped her fingers unceremoniously and turned to the other two nobles dismounting.

"Lord Benson," he said to the tall, slender male, who just nodded at him. Benson, Celaena noted, bothered to look at her—his long nose and dark eyes sweeping over her body, then moving on. Dismissed. "Lady Essar," Rowan said to the small, dark-haired Fae female.

Remelle might be the staggering beauty, but Essar had a set of curves that even Celaena found herself envying. Her light brown skin seemed to glow as if lit by an inner light, and her chestnut eyes glinted with genuine kindness as she held out her hands to Rowan and smiled.

He took Essar's fingers a bit more warmly than he had Remelle's—and the blond-haired lady's eyes slightly narrowed. But Remelle recovered swiftly, smiled prettily, and placed a proprietary hand on Rowan's shoulder as she said, "It's been an age, hasn't it? You never come to our parties, and Maeve keeps you all to herself." Rowan's face went blank. Cold. "There was a time," Remelle pouted, "when I got to keep you to myself. Sometimes I miss those days."

Rowan just flicked his eyes to the watching guards, who looked in need of a decent meal—and a break from their companions. "Stables are to the left."

Celaena was too busy glancing from Rowan to Remelle to see if the guards obeyed the prince's order. Lovers.

She didn't know why she'd thought that losing his mate meant he'd been celibate, but—but someone like *Remelle*—

Remembering she existed, Rowan extended an arm in her direction. Celaena honestly debated striding back into the fortress and leaving Rowan at their mercy, but found herself walking to him, closer and closer, until he could have tucked her into his side.

He actually seemed to relax a bit as he said, "This is—Elentiya." She hadn't thought of how he'd introduce her, but she was grateful for the anonymity he offered. "I'm training her at the queen's request. Elentiya, this is Lady Remelle, Lord Benson, and Lady Essar." He began rattling off house names and other nonsense, and Celaena gave a shallow nod that had Benson and Remelle pursing their lips.

Only Essar said hello, a sultry purr that made Celaena wonder why the hell Rowan hadn't taken *her* to his bed instead of the bright, cold smiles of Remelle.

"So you are a half-breed, then," Benson said, his eyes raking over her.

Rowan, to her surprise, bristled—but held in the growl she knew was rumbling in him.

Celaena smiled tightly. "My great-grandmother was Fae. So if that makes me demi-Fae, I don't know."

She caught the look Remelle gave Rowan: a mix of exasperation, as if to say, *Really, Rowan? You brought a half-breed to meet us? How common of you.*

But—Rowan hadn't asked her to appear in her Fae form. No, he'd left her to appear in whatever form she wished. The thought warmed her enough that she stepped a bit closer to him, near enough now to nearly brush his arm with her own. Remelle didn't fail to notice that, either. What sort of visit was this, anyway?

It was Essar who said, "Well, I look forward to hearing about your adventures, Rowan—and how you came to be here, Elentiya. But first, I think I should very much like a bath and something to nibble on." She slid an apologetic look in Celaena's direction. "I'd kill for anything chocolate right now."

Despite herself, Celaena decided that she liked her.

"So, you and Remelle," Celaena said from where she lounged on Rowan's bed, her head propped up by a hand.

At his worktable, sharpening his weapons with a bit too much interest, Rowan snarled.

They'd dumped the nobles at the baths, asked Emrys to bring food to the rooms they'd be taking over while here (there had been three demi-Fae who were more than happy to vacate their large bedrooms if it meant getting out of the path of their visitors). They had an hour until dinner—and though Celaena could have scrounged up a dress . . . she didn't feel like it.

"Remelle was . . . a very, very big mistake," Rowan said, his back to her.

"Seems like she doesn't think so."

He glared over a shoulder. "It was a hundred years ago."

Gods, sometimes she forgot how old he was. "She acts like you cast her aside this winter."

"Remelle just wants whatever she can't have. A condition many immortals suffer from to stave off boredom." He turned, the hunting knife in his hands gleaming in the firelight.

"She was practically clawing at you."

"She can claw all she wants, but I'm not making that mistake again."

"Sounds like you made that mistake a few times."

Rowan leveled a vicious gaze at her. "It was over the course of a season, and then I came to my senses."

"Mmmm."

He stabbed the knife into the table and stalked to the bed until he glowered over her. Celaena lay as she was, brows high and lips pressed together.

"One laugh," he warned. "Just one laugh, and I'm going to dump you in the nearest pond."

She shook with the effort to keep her howl inside.

"Don't. You. Dare," he growled, leaning low enough that his breath warmed her mouth. "If you—"

The door opened, and Rowan froze, a low snarl rumbling in him, so violent that it echoed in her bones. But the threat was just Remelle, who blinked, and said, "Oh!"

It took Celaena a heartbeat to realize what it looked like. She was sprawled on the bed, Rowan braced over her, too close to be casual, but—

"What do you want?" Rowan said, straightening but not stepping away.

Remelle surveyed the room, taking in the details that suggested it was not Rowan's space alone: the brush on the dresser, the undergarments Celaena had left tossed over a chair (oh, how *that* would be interpreted!), the ribbons she used to tie back her hair, the small boots beside Rowan's massive ones, and even the various personal items they kept on their own nightstands.

"I wanted to catch up," Remelle said, looking everywhere but at Celaena, "but it seems you are . . . occupied."

"We'll talk at dinner," Rowan said.

Celaena popped up from the bed. "I have to go help Emrys with the meal, actually." She barely managed to hide her wicked grin. "Why don't you stay, Remelle?"

Rowan could have melted her bones with the look he gave her, but Celaena was already out the door and down the hall, whistling to herself.

Rowan was going to kill her. As soon as they resumed training, he was going to murder her. And then murder her again.

Remelle was still in the doorway, frowning in the direction Aelin had gone. When she turned, a serpentine smile danced on her red lips. "Is this considered part of her training, too?"

"Get out," was all he said.

Remelle clicked her tongue. "Is that how you speak to me these days?"

"I don't know why you bothered to stop here, or what you expect of me—"

"I heard you were here, and thought I'd say hello and spare you the tedious company of half-breeds. I didn't realize you'd taken to them so much."

He knew exactly what it had looked like when she burst in here. Denying it would only lead to a headache, but letting Remelle assume he was sharing a bed with Aelin was equally unacceptable. He couldn't decide how Maeve would interpret it. Unless—

"And who was it that told you I'm here?"

"Maeve, of course. I complained to her that I missed you."

The question was whether or not Remelle was a willing or unknowing spy. Or if Maeve had sent Remelle to see just what manner of relationship Rowan had developed with the princess.

"As your friend, Rowan, I have to say . . . the girl's rather beneath you."

He held in his laugh. Apparently, Maeve hadn't informed her *who*, exactly, he was training. Remelle had been relentless in her pursuit of him a century ago, winning him over with her charm and smiles, but—he didn't really care to think back to that time.

"One," he said, "you're not my friend. Two, it's none of your business."

Her eyes narrowed in a way that made him realize Remelle would make every minute until she left a living hell for the princess—not knowing what manner of predator she was provoking.

So rather than see Remelle's blood splattered on the walls before dawn, he said, "There is a shortage of bedrooms here, and we've had to share quarters as a result." Not quite a lie, but not the entire truth.

Remelle's brows remained high on her moon-white skin. "Well, I suppose that's good news for Benson."

"What."

"He has needs that must be attended to, and finds her attractive enough. Maeve said it was more than fine if she—"

"If Benson lays one finger on her, he's going to find himself without his insides."

Maeve—Maeve had suggested that she was available for—

He clamped down on the blinding rage as Remelle blinked. "Honestly, Rowan, what do you think most of the half-breeds wind up doing in Doranelle?"

He had no answer—no words at all—as soon as she said that.

She shrugged. "Benson will be gentle with—"

"Benson looks twice at her, and he dies. He looks twice at any of the females in this fortress and he dies."

The words were laced with a growl so fierce that they were barely understandable. But Remelle understood.

Did Lorcan know? He was a demi-Fae himself, had proven himself half a millennium ago. Was he aware what went on in their city? It was disgusting—worse than disgusting. The Fae were better than that. But Maeve—

"I'll make sure the warning is conveyed," Remelle purred.

Celaena did indeed go to the kitchen, where she helped Emrys prepare the meal. Luca was there, prattling away, but the chatter stopped mid-sentence.

Essar was standing at the foot of the stairs, smiling faintly.

"Dinner won't be ready for another twenty minutes," Celaena said, wiping her hands on a dishcloth before approaching the lady. Luca was practically gaping at the small beauty, but Essar gave him a polite smile and he immediately found himself interested in whatever he was doing. "I can show you to the dining hall, if you'd like to wait there."

Gods, being polite was . . . strange.

"Oh, no. Benson's in there already, and he . . . I think I'd have more fun in here."

She'd also make Emrys and Luca uncomfortable, if their silence was any indication, but Celaena found herself saying, "It can be chaotic and loud and messy in here—"

"I know how a kitchen operates," Essar said. "Just tell me what work needs to be done, and I'll do it."

Celaena looked to Emrys, who bowed and introduced himself and Luca—who went beet red—and then found herself chopping vegetables beside the lady.

Celaena said to Essar after a minute, "So, you're just . . . traveling around?"

"Maeve gave us a task, which I'm not supposed to talk about, but yes—it involved us traveling for a bit. We're on our way back to Doranelle, though—thank the Bright Lady."

Celaena raised a brow. "Mala?"

Essar lifted a hand, and flames danced on her fingertips. "Not much of a gift, but it kept us warm on the road at least."

Celaena swallowed. She'd never met another fire-wielder. Did Rowan know? "Is it hard—to master the fire?"

Essar shrugged. "I was very young when my training began, and I've had about two centuries to master what little power I have. Aside from a few burns and blisters, I've never really been able to do much harm, or impress anyone, really. Remelle's got the more interesting gift—her magic lends itself toward mastering any language she hears, no matter how briefly. It's why Maeve likes to send her around to places. And Benson's got a knack for becoming invisible whenever he wants to, which . . ." Essar winced.

"Makes him a good listener," Celaena finished. Essar had to be a lousy spy if she was so willing to talk.

Essar brushed back a strand of her silky, dark hair. "You must have impressive gifts, if Prince Rowan is training you."

"I—"

"Those vegetables done?" Emrys asked, and one glance at the male had Celaena sending him her silent thanks. She handed him a bowl of the potatoes, then got to work on the next item. Essar was making neat, perfect slices—too slowly to be useful, but at least she was trying.

Essar said casually, "I can't imagine Rowan is an easy teacher."

"You could say that."

"But they're all like that—Rowan and his companions who serve the queen."

"You know them?"

Essar blushed prettily. "I was involved with Lorcan, their leader, for a time. But—his lifestyle and mine are very different."

"And what is Lorcan like?"

"A demi-Fae, like you."

Was he now? Rowan had failed to mention *that* tidbit. Essar went on, "He has had to prove himself every single day, every hour, since he was born. Even though his power isn't challenged—by anyone other than

Rowan, that is—he . . . Lorcan is not an easy male to be around. Some days, I'm surprised he has friends."

"And Rowan is his friend?"

Essar gave her an amused smile. "In a way. They frighten even us, you know. Especially when they're together. When Rowan and Lorcan are together in a room . . . Let's just say that they sometimes do not leave that room intact by the time they depart. Or the city, for that matter."

"And yet Maeve lets them work together?"

"She would be a fool to let either of them go—which is why she bound them to her with the blood oath. They've leveled cities for her before."

A chill went up Celaena's spine. "Actually leveled cities?"

Essar nodded gravely. "And yet Remelle thinks she can control Rowan—wants to possess him."

Rowan could end Remelle with half a thought, if he was provoked enough. "She's an idiot."

"Indeed. But power is power, and since Remelle can't look past Lorcan's mixed bloodline, Rowan is her only other option."

"Would—would their children also belong to Maeve, the way Rowan does?"

Essar cocked her head. "I don't know. None of his companions have sired offspring, so there's no way of telling what Maeve would do."

Celaena shuddered. "You don't seem to speak as reverently as the others do about her."

"Not all Fae are her willing slaves, you know. And part of—part of why my relationship with Lorcan fell apart was due to that. He is blood-sworn to her, and no matter how I cared for him, I am most certainly *not*. Nor will I ever swear such an oath."

"Why are you telling me this?"

"Because you are training with the most dangerous pure-blooded Fae male in the world, and yet he treats you as an equal. He presented you as his equal." There was an implied question there—*So who are you, really?*—but Celaena couldn't answer.

"I think Rowan just didn't feel like dealing with Remelle alone."

"Probably. But he's also dealt with her on his own plenty. And since Rowan's not one to show off a new companion just to spite an old lover . . ."

"I'm not sure I follow what you're getting at."

"I find it all very interesting."

"I think you're reading a bit into it."

But Essar gave her a soft smile. "I'm sure I am."

Dinner went well for the six seconds it took to walk from the doorway to the large table in the vacant dining hall.

Since the table was so large, they'd set the five places at one end, with Rowan at the head, as his position demanded. The plan had been for Celaena to sit to his left, with Essar beside her, leaving Remelle to take the seat opposite Celaena's, and Benson across from Essar. But Remelle, moving swifter than Celaena had expected, had steered Benson into the seat meant for Celaena, plopped herself next to Rowan, and left Celaena with the choice of sitting beside the white-blond lady or the leering male.

She chose Benson.

Rowan followed the ordeal without comment, his attention pinned on Benson as Celaena took a seat next to the lord. But whether or not Benson noticed the lethal glare in Rowan's eyes—gods, what was *that* about?—the lord revealed nothing. So Celaena had nothing better to do in the silence except take a sip from her wine, and pray that the meal would be over quickly.

The first course—a roast-chicken soup that Remelle and Benson frowned over—came out fast enough. It tasted divine, and Celaena managed all of one delectable spoonful before Remelle said to her, "So you're from Adarlan's empire."

Celaena took a second, slow spoonful of soup. "I am."

"I thought I detected the accent—Adarlan and . . . Terrasen, am I right? They do mangle their words over there so brutally. I doubt even years here will cure you of the boorish accent."

Celaena took another very slow spoonful of soup.

But Essar said, "I find the accent quite charming, actually." Benson grunted his agreement, giving her a too-long look, and Celaena fought the urge to shift her chair down a setting or two. Or to take her spoon and use it to carve out his eyes.

"Well, you had such a provincial upbringing, Essar," Remelle said brightly. "I'm not surprised that you like it."

Essar's round face tightened, but she said nothing. However, when Remelle went to take a delicate sip of her soup, she let out a hiss and nearly dropped her spoon. The liquid was indeed steaming hot—far hotter than any of theirs. Essar gave the female an innocent, questioning look, but Remelle said, "The beastly cook boiled this soup."

Celaena clamped down on a retort. Especially as Rowan's face became a mask of calm. One that usually meant violence was on its way.

That had been his request, hadn't it? To keep him from causing a brawl that would be reported back to Maeve?

So Celaena swallowed her own rage and said to Essar, "You grew up in the countryside?"

Remelle rolled her eyes, but Essar smiled. "My father owns a vineyard in the southeast of our territory. I spent my youth roaming the olive orchards and the cypress groves. But I moved to Doranelle when it was deemed time for me to enter society."

"Alas, Essar has been rather unlucky when it comes to fulfilling her parents' wishes to find a proper husband," Remelle said.

"Husband," Celaena found herself saying. "Not—mate?"

Remelle clicked her tongue. "Of course not. A mate is rare—most Fae don't find them." Celaena couldn't bring herself to look at Rowan, though her heart strained. Remelle waved an idle hand. "So, we marry."

"What if you marry, then you find your mate?"

"Wars have been started for that," Benson finally said, his dark eyes seeming to swallow her whole. "But if that is the case, it is treated very delicately."

"It's a mess, is what he means," Essar clarified. "A male will feel the need to kill any challenger to his mate, even if that challenger is already wed to her. Even if they're in love. For all our refinements, there are still instincts that can't be controlled."

Celaena nodded, finishing off her soup.

Remelle, however, smiled at her. "But as a half-breed, you won't have to worry about such things. Finding a mate is even rarer for those with diluted blood—and none of us would marry you, anyway."

Celaena stared at the female for a long moment, even as she could have sworn she felt the reverberations in the table as Rowan snarled softly.

Remelle refused to break the stare, and Celaena settled in, willing calm to her veins. She could feel Essar's attention, and could almost hear the puzzle pieces snap together in Essar's mind as she recognized the coloring of Celaena's eyes and murmured, "Remelle."

But Remelle looked to Rowan and began saying something in the Old Language, smiling sweetly.

When Rowan didn't respond, Remelle turned to Benson, saying something else, to which the lord replied in the same elegant, lovely language.

Remelle again opened her mouth, but Rowan said with lethal quiet, "Speak the common tongue, Remelle."

Remelle put a hand on her chest in a mockery of an apology. "Sometimes I forget—it's not every day I'm in the company of half-breeds."

Essar swallowed hard, her brown skin going a bit wan as she surveyed Celaena and Remelle. Oh, yes. The lady had figured out that it wasn't some common by-blow seated across from them.

Emrys and Luca entered, clearing the soup away and bringing out the next course—platters of roast meats and vegetables. Emrys loitered by the doorway, and Celaena took one bite of the rabbit, moaned, and turned in her seat to nod her enthusiasm to the ancient cook. He grinned, his face flushing.

Then Remelle said, "Rowan, it must be a trial for you to have to eat this day in and day out." She pushed her meat around on her plate, then set the fork down. Celaena couldn't look back at Emrys—didn't allow herself to glimpse his face.

Rowan said, "I eat better here than I do in Doranelle."

"There's no need to be nice on account of the help," Remelle said. "If they don't learn what we like, whatever will they do in the capital?"

Footsteps scuffed behind them, and Celaena knew Emrys had gone back downstairs.

Celaena said softly, "The next time you insult my friend, I'm going to shove your face into whatever plate is in front of you."

Remelle blinked. "Well, I *never*—"

"Remelle," Essar whispered.

But Remelle put a hand on Rowan's forearm, gripping with such possessiveness that Celaena saw red as the lady hissed at him, "You mean to let her insult me like that? To make threats against a member of the royal household?"

"Get your hand off me," Rowan said too quietly.

But Remelle didn't let go of Rowan as she snapped at Celaena, "You are dismissed from this table. Get out."

Celaena looked at the white hand gripping Rowan. "Take your hand off him."

"I can do as I please, and if you have any sense, you'll vacate this hall before I have you whipped for your—"

Fire erupted, and Remelle's scream echoed off the stones.

Living flame wrapped around the lady, not burning, not singeing, just—encasing. Even the hand on Rowan was aflame, and through the column of gold-and-red fire, Remelle's eyes were wide as she turned to Essar and said, "*Release me.*"

But Essar only looked at Celaena. "It's not my magic."

Rowan went perfectly still as Celaena willed the fire to allow a lick of heat through. Not enough to burn, but enough to make Remelle start sweating. And then Celaena said, "If you ever raise a whip to anyone, I will find you, and I will make sure that these flames burn."

She had to admit: Remelle had no small amount of courage, especially as the woman seethed, "How *dare* you threaten a lady of Doranelle."

Celaena laughed under her breath. "The next time you touch Rowan without his permission, I will burn you into ashes." She turned her head to Benson. "And if you look at me or any female like that again, I will melt your bones before you have a chance to scream."

Benson, wisely, nodded and averted his gaze.

Essar was pale when Celaena pulled back her teeth in a snarl and said to her, "You keep everything you learned here to yourself."

Essar nodded.

Celaena at last faced Rowan, who seemed like he was trying his best not to smirk, though the amusement still danced in his eyes as she said, "I defer judgment to you, Prince."

He studied Remelle, who was barely moving, hardly breathing, then jerked his chin. "Release her and let's eat."

The flames winked out so fast it was as if they'd never existed.

In the silence that fell, Remelle leaned over the arm of her chair and vomited on the floor.

Celaena picked up her fork, took a bite of rabbit, and smiled.

"If I never see them again, it'll be too soon," Celaena said into the darkness of their room.

Rowan let out a low laugh. "I thought you liked Essar."

"I do, but . . . you should have heard her trying to get me to talk in the kitchen."

"About what?"

"About you. About our—relationship. I think you'll go home to a host of unpleasant rumors."

"I think the status of our relationship will be the least of the rumors after tonight."

"Essar said that you—you and Lorcan once decimated a city together."

He hissed. "Ah. Sollemere."

"I've never heard of it."

"That's because it doesn't exist anymore."

She turned over, staring at him in the moonlight that slipped in through the curtains. "You wiped it off the map—literally?"

He pinned her with a long look. "Sollemere was a place so wicked, full of monstrous people who did such unspeakable things, that . . . even Maeve was disgusted by them. She gave them a warning to stop their ways, and said if they . . ." He clenched his jaw. "There are some acts that are unforgivable—and I won't stain this room by mentioning them. But she swore to them that if they continued to do it, she would obliterate them."

"Let me guess: they didn't listen."

"No. We got out as many children as we could with our legion. And when they were safely away, Lorcan and I leveled it to dust."

"You're that powerful."

"You don't seem shocked by it."

"You've told me plenty of harrowing stories. If what these people did was so awful that even you won't repeat it, then I'll say they had it coming."

"So bloodthirsty."

"Is that a problem for you?"

"I find it endearing." She gave him a playful shove, but he caught her hand and held it, his calluses brushing her own. "You could do that, you know. Make an entire city burn."

"I hope I never have to."

"So do I." He threaded his fingers through hers and held them up to examine the scars along the back of her hand, her fingers. "But I'll never forget the look on Remelle's face when you shot fire out of your mouth and eyes."

"I did not."

He laughed, a low, rumbling sound that echoed in her chest. "Part woman, part dragon."

"I didn't spew flames."

"Your eyes were living gold."

Celaena narrowed those same eyes at him. "Are you going to reprimand me?"

He lowered their joined hands to the bed, but didn't let go. "Why should I? She was given fair warning, she ignored it, and you followed through. It follows the Old Ways, and you had every right to show her how serious you were."

She considered it, then after a moment said, "It scared me—how in control I was. How much I meant it. It scared me that I wasn't scared. It scared me that . . ." She made herself look at him. His face was unreadable in the dim light. "It scared me that . . ."

It scared me that I've come to care so much about you that I'd draw that sort of line in the sand. It scared me that I would burn and maim and kill for you, and yet—and yet at the end of the day, you still belong to Maeve, and there is nothing I can do, no amount of burning and maiming and killing, to keep you with me.

He released her hand—only to slide his own against her cheek, the gesture so unexpected that she closed her eyes and leaned into it, hearing the unspoken words in the touch.

I know.

The party departed the next morning, and Rowan didn't bother to bring the princess down to see them off. It was for the best, given that Remelle still appeared jumpy and furious, Benson refused to look at anyone, and even Essar was wide-eyed.

Rowan waited until they were all mounted on their fine horses in the courtyard before he approached. It was to Essar he spoke, grabbing hold of her Asterion mare's bridle. "Let's hope last night was the most eventful of your journey."

Remelle sniffled from her saddle, but said nothing.

Essar, however, looked up at the fortress, as if she could see through moss and stone to the princess sleeping within.

Essar was a beautiful female—soft and inviting and clever—and he'd never understood why Lorcan hadn't tried harder to keep her. She had been good for him. But Lorcan's ruthlessness and cold ambition were his best tools and worst enemies. He had only seen the female for what she offered inside his bedroom.

Essar said, "I do not think any of us will forget last night anytime soon."

Neither would he. When Aelin had engulfed Remelle in flame, he'd been stunned stupid. She hadn't demonstrated skills of that level, hadn't practiced that sort of thing. And if Remelle had tried to fight back, if Remelle had physically hurt him or anyone in that fortress . . . The lady would be ash on the wind right now.

A threat had been made against those Aelin saw as hers. Such things would be dealt with swiftly and brutally. Interesting—so interesting for that side of the princess to have come snarling to the surface.

And she had claimed him.

Essar knew. She'd figured out what kind of magic smoldered in Aelin's veins, and that last night, the Queen of Terrasen had made a claim on him. If Essar told Maeve about it . . .

The others in the party moved out, Remelle stiff-backed, but Rowan remained with Essar.

"Name the price for your silence," Rowan said.

Essar's dark brows rose. "You think I would run to the nearest gossip and tell them Aelin Galathynius is training here?"

"You know what I'm talking about."

Essar's dark eyes narrowed. "I would not run to Maeve, either. Remelle will tell her that the girl threw a tantrum and attacked her without provocation—she'd never admit to any of the truth behind it. Or figure out who she really is. And Benson . . . Leave him to me."

"And your price?"

"There is no price, Prince."

He gripped the bridle harder. "Why?"

Essar studied the disappearing party, then the fortress. "We have known each other for a while now. Through all the centuries, I have never seen you present another female as your equal—as your friend. And I do not think you did it because of who she is." Rowan opened his mouth, but she said, "I would not take that gift away from you, Rowan. Because it is a gift. *She* is a gift—to the world, and to you."

His fingers slackened on the reins, and Essar motioned her mount into a walk.

"She is going to fight for you, Rowan," Essar said, looking over a shoulder. "And you deserve it, after all this time. You deserve to have someone who will burn the earth to ash for you." His heart was pounding wildly, but he kept his face blank, his will ice and steel. "If you see him," Essar added with a sad smile, "tell Lorcan I send my regards."

And then she was gone.

Things fell back into their usual rhythm in the two days that followed, though Rowan couldn't stop thinking about what Essar had said. Because he knew it was true, because . . . because he wanted it to be true.

Aelin said nothing about it, though he'd sometimes catch her frowning at him, as if trying to decipher some puzzle.

He was poring over a report Vaughan had sent him when she walked into his room that night. The smell of chocolate and nuts hit him, and when he twisted in his seat, he discovered her carrying a small, misshapen cake, a sheepish smile on her face.

"It took me hours to make this damn thing, so you'd better say it's good."

She set it in front of him, along with a plate, fork, and knife. The blade she used to slice into the chocolate-frosted lump, cutting a large piece. It was layered with a lighter frosting—some sort of creamy-looking filling between the dark cake.

"Chocolate hazelnut cake?"

She plopped the piece on the plate for him and took his hand to press the fork into it. "You have no idea how hard it was to get the ingredients. Or to find some sort of recipe. I haven't even tasted it yet. Emrys looked like he was going to faint with horror." When Rowan just stared at the cake, she clicked her tongue. "This is the favor you owe me. Just *try* it."

He gave her a long stare that usually sent men running, but she bit her lip and glanced at the cake. It was enough that he adjusted his grip on the fork, picked up a piece, and brought it to his mouth.

While he chewed and swallowed, she was practically hopping from foot to foot and wringing her hands. So he let out a grunt of pleasure, took another bite, then another, until the entire piece was cleaned off his plate.

Then he took another piece. And another. Until his stomach was protesting and all but a sliver was left on the platter.

"I told you it was delicious," she preened, giving him a triumphant smile as he set down his fork. She ruffled his hair, but he caught her wrist, squeezing gently while he rose from his seat and brought his face dangerously close to hers.

He knew every fleck of gold in those remarkable eyes—knew how her very blood tasted. And this near to her, their breath mingling . . . "Now we're even," he said, and stalked out of the room.

He was about three steps down the hall when Aelin's fork scraped against the platter, no doubt scooping up the sliver of cake he'd left. A moment after that, her curse barked off the stones of the fortress, followed by spitting and coughing.

Despite himself, Rowan was smiling when he shouldered open the bathing room door—and quickly cast up the contents of his stomach.